OXFORD WORLD'S CLASSICS

TWENTY YEARS AFTER

ALEXANDRE DUMAS was born at Villers-Cotterêts in 1802, the son of an innkeeper's daughter and of one of Napoleon's most remarkable generals. He moved to Paris in 1823 to make his fortune in the theatre. At 28 he was one of the leading literary figures of his day, a star of the Romantic Revolution, and known for his many mistresses and taste for high living. He threw himself recklessly into the July Revolution of 1830 which he regarded as a great adventure. Quickly wearying of politics, he returned to the theatre and then by the early 1840s was producing vast historical novels at a stupendous rate and in prodigious quantities for the cheap newspapers which paid enormous sums of money to authors who could please the public. His complete works were eventually to fill over 300 volumes and his yarns made him the best-known Frenchman of his age. He earned several fortunes which he gave away, or spent on women and travel, or wasted on grandiose follies like the 'Château de Monte Cristo' which he built to symbolize his success. In 1848 he stood unsuccessfully in the elections for the new Assembly. By 1850 his creditors began to catch up with him and, partly to escape them and partly to find new material for his novels, plays, and travel books, he lived abroad for long periods, travelling through Russia where his fame had preceded him, and Italy where he ran guns in support of Garibaldi's libertarian cause. Without guile and without enemies, he was a man of endless fascination who lived long enough to see his talent desert him. He died of a stroke at Puys, near Dieppe, in 1870.

DAVID COWARD is Senior Fellow and Emeritus Professor of French Literature at the University of Leeds. He is the author of studies of Marivaux, Marguerite Duras, Marcel Pagnol, and Restif de la Bretonne. For Oxford World's Classics, he has edited eight novels by Alexandre Dumas, including the whole of the Musketeer saga, and translated Dumas *fils' La Dame aux Camélias*, two selections of Maupassant short stories, Sade's *Misfortunes of Virtue and Other Early Tales* and Diderot's *Jacques the Fatalist*. Winner of the 1996 Scott-Moncrieff prize for translation, he reviews regularly for the *Times Literary Supplement*.

OXFORD WORLD'S CLASSICS

*For over 100 years Oxford World's Classics have brought
readers closer to the world's great literature. Now with over 700
titles—from the 4,000-year-old myths of Mesopotamia to the
twentieth century's greatest novels—the series makes available
lesser-known as well as celebrated writing.*

*The pocket-sized hardbacks of the early years contained
introductions by Virginia Woolf, T. S. Eliot, Graham Greene,
and other literary figures which enriched the experience of reading.
Today the series is recognized for its fine scholarship and
reliability in texts that span world literature, drama and poetry,
religion, philosophy and politics. Each edition includes perceptive
commentary and essential background information to meet the
changing needs of readers.*

OXFORD WORLD'S CLASSICS

ALEXANDRE DUMAS

Twenty Years After

Edited with an Introduction and Notes by
DAVID COWARD

OXFORD
UNIVERSITY PRESS

OXFORD

UNIVERSITY PRESS

Great Clarendon Street, Oxford OX2 6DP

Oxford University Press is a department of the University of Oxford.
It furthers the University's objective of excellence in research, scholarship,
and education by publishing worldwide in

Oxford New York

Athens Auckland Bangkok Bogotá Buenos Aires Calcutta
Cape Town Chennai Dar es Salaam Delhi Florence Hong Kong Istanbul
Karachi Kuala Lumpur Madrid Melbourne Mexico City Mumbai
Nairobi Paris São Paulo Singapore Taipei Tokyo Toronto Warsaw

with associated companies in Berlin Ibadan

Oxford is a registered trade mark of Oxford University Press
in the UK and in certain other countries

Published in the United States
by Oxford University Press Inc., New York

Editorial material © David Coward 1993

The moral rights of the author have been asserted

Database right Oxford University Press (maker)

First published as a World's Classics paperback 1993
Reissued as an Oxford World's Classics paperback 1998

British Library Cataloguing in Publication Data

Data available

Library of Congress Cataloging in Publication Data

Dumas, Alexandre, 1802–1870.
[Vingt ans après. English]
Twenty years after/Alexandre Dumas:
edited with an introduction by David Coward.
p. cm.
Includes bibliographical references.
1. France—History—Louis XIV, 1643–1715—Fiction.
I. Coward, David. II. Title. III. Title: 20 years after.
PQ2229.V6E5 1993 843'.7–dc20 92–38573

ISBN-13: 978–0–19–283843–8
ISBN-10: 0–19–283843–1

13

Printed in Great Britain by
Clays Ltd, St Ives plc

CONTENTS

Introduction   vii

Select Bibliography   xxi

A Chronology of Alexandre Dumas   xxii

Map   xxvi

TWENTY YEARS AFTER   I

List of Historical Characters   789

Explanatory Notes   803

INTRODUCTION

AT first sight, Alexandre Dumas, grandson of a marquis and son of one of Napoleon's most energetic generals, might seem to have chosen his family wisely. When the monarchy was restored in 1815, a title did not come amiss. With the rise of liberal ideas during the 1820s, the thrusting new Romantic generation revered anyone touched by Napoleonic glory. But Dumas played neither card, and with good reason. His claim to noble blood was slim and his Napoleonic connection clouded. The Marquis Davy de la Pailleterie—it was a courtesy title only—had sold his estate in Normandy in 1760 and emigrated to San Domingo, where he failed as a planter. He returned to France in 1780 with his mulatto son by Marie-Cessette Dumas, a slave. Thomas-Alexandre Dumas enlisted in 1786, rose through the revolutionary ranks, and was a general at 31. But his plain speaking during the Egyptian campaign earned the displeasure of Napoleon, who disowned him in 1799. When Alexandre was born in 1802, the general was ill, destitute, and dependent on his wife who was the daughter of an innkeeper. Thus the Great Dumas started with nothing, not even (or so he claimed) boot-straps to pull himself up with. He honoured his father and mother, but claimed sole responsibility for what he made of his life. During the elections of 1848, when he stood for Parliament as a reformist candidate, a voice in the crowd asked him to be honest: was he not an aristocrat masquerading as a friend of the people? More patient than usual (on other occasions, Dumas was known to pitch hecklers into rivers), he replied: 'When I was a nobody, I could have become somebody by calling myself Marquis de la Pailleterie. But now I am somebody and it is enough that I am known as Alexandre Dumas.'

He spent a happy childhood at Villers-Cotterêts, 50 miles north-east of Paris, ended his schooling by the age of 14, and was set to work as a lawyer's office-boy. He became friendly with Adolphe de Leuven, later director of the Opéra-Comique in Paris, and together they wrote indigestible plays with which

they hoped to storm the capital. In 1823, on the strength more
of his clear handwriting, he said, than of his father's now
dubious connections, he became a very minor secretary in the
employ of the Duc d'Orléans. Dumas loved Paris. He haunted
the theatre and chased girls. In 1824, by Catherine Labay, a
seamstress, he fathered a son ('went into a second edition', as
he later put it) who was to become Alexandre Dumas *fils*,
author of *La Dame aux camélias*.

Dumas wrote poetry, tales, and plays with little success. But
in 1829, he staged *Henri III and his Court*, a controversial
historical melodrama, which captured the Romantic spirit of
revolt against the dull conservatism of the age. Dumas, suddenly catapulted into the front ranks of writers and rebels,
strutted his way through the July Revolution of 1830 which
inaugurated the 'bourgeois' reign of Louis-Philippe. Like many
of his generation, he had hoped to see an end to privilege and
injustice, but as time passed he grew steadily disenchanted with
a regime which replaced Napoleonic—and Byronic—dash and
style with values dictated by money. The vendetta waged by
Edmond Dantès, hero of *The Count of Monte Cristo* (1844–5),
was to express his reservations about capitalism and France's
late-blooming industrial revolution. Yet while he remained
temperamentally committed to the social goals of the Romantics, he was in practice as firm a believer in middle-class energy
as he was in aristocratic superiority. He worked phenomenally
hard, yet based his life-style on society models with the
vulgarity of the *nouveau riche*. He was a happy capitalist with
a social conscience, a paradoxical stance which never troubled
his unbreachable individualism or gave pause to his chronic
optimism.

By 1833, his position had been consolidated by a stream of
sensational plays built around strong situations and highly
charged dialogue. His subject was passion and he milked it
unashamedly with unerring dramatic sense. He enjoyed his
success and spent everything he earned, and more besides, on
women and travel. At 35, recalled the Comtesse Dash in her
Mémoires des autres (1896–7), 'he was a fine figure of a man,
tall and well-made. In those days, it was still the fashion to
wear breeches to certain balls, and Dumas was only too pleased

to show off a pair of well-turned calves. Add to this his striking blue eyes which had the colour of sapphires—and their sparkle too, when his mind was stimulated.' Others saw him as a kind of strong-jawed, bull-necked Mirabeau, and close friends reported that after an evening of dancing or talk—he drank little—he would settle down to write the night away to meet a deadline. Dumas had no strong religious beliefs (except for electoral purposes), but regarded work as sacred. His powers of concentration were extraordinary. He was capable of writing for fourteen hours at a stretch, so losing himself in the world of his imagination that his servants grew accustomed to the whoops of delight and howls of grief which emerged from his study as the completed pages piled up on the floor where he dropped them. He was the least neurotic of writers and was never short of ideas: if he had none of his own he cheerfully stole or borrowed whatever he needed from books and from the writers with whom he frequently collaborated.

By the end of the 1830s, he was turning away from the theatre towards fiction. His motives were mixed. Since 1836, a new generation of cheap newspapers, financed largely by advertising revenue, had begun to offer enormous sums to writers who could meet short deadlines with instalments of high-impact, sensational fiction which, in the hallowed phrase rich in promise first used in France in 1829, were 'to be continued in our next issue'. The stars of the serials were Frédéric Soulié and Eugène Sue, and Dumas, for all his reservations about the capitalist ethic, was determined to join them. But he was never simply a literary mercenary, and now revived an earlier and quite serious ambition to explore the fictional possibilities of history.

The trail had been blazed by Walter Scott who, with Byron, was one of the idols of the French Romantics. History was fashionable. Academic historians such as Guizot and Michelet were avidly read and publishers supplied a buoyant market with new editions of obscure memoirs and private journals. Historical subjects had been exploited by novelists and playwrights of the stature of Vigny and Musset, and Hugo had set *Notre-Dame de Paris* (1831) in the fifteenth century. Dumas, conscious of his defective education, began a haphazard programme of reading in 1831 and the following year published the first of an unremarked series of dramatized 'historical scenes'. But by the end of the decade he had acquired a thorough grounding in the four periods which were to provide the framework for the major cycles of historical novels to come: the political and religious strife of the sixteenth century; the intrigues of the royal courts of the seventeenth; the Regency which opened the eighteenth century and the decades of unrest and revolution which closed it. He published respectable, well-researched histories, such as *Louis XIV and his Century* (1844), but the novelist usually got the better of his genuine fascination with the past, which he tended to see in terms of personalities and simple struggles between good and evil, the whole prettily dressed in the picturesque and sensational detail which he himself found irresistible: betrayals, tortures, prisons, and dramatic reversals of fortune. His readers were both entertained and instructed, and generations of French men and women learned about the greatness of Henri IV or the dastardly dealings of Richelieu and Mazarin through Dumas's highly coloured, racy accounts of their dealings.

In Dumas's handling of the historical novel, it is clear that fiction came first. Scott, he noted in his *Memoirs* (vi. 409), was 'admirable in his picture of manners, dress and personalities' but less successful in 'the depiction of passion'. He found Scott's habit of providing historical background tedious. Near the end of his life, in the *Histoire de mes bêtes* (1868), he gave this advice born of long experience: 'Open with action, rather than with scene-setting; talk about the characters after allowing them to appear, rather than bringing them on only after talking about them.' The novelist should start with a tale to tell, and only then cast about for a period in which to set it. 'History,' he declared grandly, 'is the nail on which I hang my novels.' In reality, he acted on instinct and used whatever came to hand. What prompted him to set pen to paper was a commission, and all was grist to the mill of opportunism and deadlines.

His meeting with Auguste Maquet (1813–88) in 1838 was providential. Maquet, a history teacher with literary ambitions, proved to be an ideal collaborator. Dumas, always a man in a hurry, used him as a kind of 'creative assistant' to test his ideas, develop plots, and undertake 'additional research' in ways which seem closer to Hollywood or the television studios of the late twentieth century than to the staider practices of the nineteenth. Few of Maquet's 'treatments' and 'outlines' have survived, but what remains suggests that his short, rather dry synopses were the record of 'script conferences' which Dumas then enlarged and expanded into hundreds of pages. With Maquet, Dumas hammered out the structure of his epic yarns, but the detailed writing—the suspense, the character, the colour—were his alone.

His contemporaries marvelled (Lamartine's opinion of Dumas was 'an exclamation mark') but some seriously doubted that one man could alone have furnished the stupendous quantities of newsprint to which he put his name. One, the journalist Eugène Mirecourt, alleged in 1845 that Dumas was the master of a 'fiction factory' staffed by ill-paid hacks who turned out dramas and serials to order. Dumas took him to court and won his case. He made no secret of his debts to Maquet and others—'I have collaborators the way Napoleon had generals'—but insisted that he always rewarded and openly acknowledged their contribution. He shared the billing for plays when he could, and if his name appeared on the title-pages of his novels it was usually because publishers were prepared to pay more for manuscripts signed by 'Alexandre Dumas' alone, a fact of life accepted by those who had stimulated his imagination or helped with the historical background. Indeed, though there were occasional misunderstandings, none of his collaborators impeached Dumas's honesty. In 1852, Maquet finally abandoned Dumas who, with his relaxed attitude to money, regularly failed to pay him what they had agreed, and resumed his own literary career. But none of the magic had rubbed off on him. The Great Dumas went on his unstoppable way. Maquet sank without trace.

Maquet served Dumas well and their collaboration spanned the 1840s, when Dumas published his finest work and became king of the newspaper serial. But the Musketeer saga began with Dumas. In 1841, he borrowed—and never returned—from Marseilles public library the first volume of the apocryphal

Mémoires de M. d'Artagnan (1700) by Courtilz de Sandras (1644–1712). Courtilz, soldier, adventurer, and minor novelist, claimed to have acquired a bundle of authentic 'fragments' which he had merely 'arranged', giving them 'the sequence which they lacked'. Fragments there may have been and Courtilz may indeed have known the author of them—Charles de Batz-Castelmore, *sieur* d'Artagnan, who was born at Lupiac (Gers) in about 1615, fifth son of a recently ennobled merchant, Bertrand de Batz, and of Françoise de Montesquiou. The tradition of Gascon loyalty to the King, begun during the reign of Henri IV, remained strong and Charles de Batz travelled to Paris where he enlisted in the King's Guards in 1635. He took part in the Flanders and Roussillon campaigns of the early 1640s and in 1643 travelled to England where, according to Courtilz, he fought with Charles I against Essex at Newbury. The following year he was made a Musketeer and, when the Musketeers were disbanded in 1646, became a 'gentilhomme de Mazarin' whom he was to serve loyally. Indeed, after the civil wars known as the Fronde began in 1648, he became one of the cardinal's most trusted agents, 'Mazarin's creature', it was said. He may have been sent to London with confidential messages for Cromwell, for Mazarin's correspondence reveals that he was certainly used as a trusted diplomatic courier. He was wounded at the battle of Stenay in 1654 and, still with Mazarin's protection, became Captain of the King's Guards the following year. When the Musketeers were re-formed in 1657 under nominal control of a largely absentee nephew of Mazarin, d'Artagnan was named as his deputy and assumed effective command. He married in 1659 but separated from his wife, who bore him two sons, in 1665. By then, he had acquired important friends and had carried out important missions: it was he who arrested Fouquet, Louis XIV's disgraced finance minister, in 1661. Madame de Sévigné recalled that 'he stayed up all night' to watch the comet of 1664 and remembered him as 'loyal to the King and to the prisoners he guarded'. In 1667, he was appointed Captain-Lieutenant of Musketeers, fought in Flanders, became acting Governor of Lille in 1672, and was killed at Maastricht in 1673. Charles de Batz was no flashing blade but, if his few surviving letters are anything to go by, a

rather dull, literal-minded career soldier who followed the
rule-book and furthered his ambition with a generous measure
of sly patience.

Courtilz made him much more attractive. His d'Artagnan is
an adventurer, a gambler, always ready for a fight, eternally
susceptible to a pretty face, who picks his way carefully, not
to say cynically, through a maze of political intrigue and
personal dangers. Like the characters of Defoe whom he at
times resembles, he learns to trust no one and works alone. He
is not without comrades, however, like the wily and self-interested Besmaux, or the three Gascon brothers, also Musketeers,
named Athos, Porthos, and Aramis, who figure in an early
chapter but subsequently play no significant role in events. Yet,
like Besmaux (c. 1613–97), who became Governor of the Bastille in 1658, they were real enough. Armand de Sillègue
d'Athos d'Autevielle was a Gascon who hailed from the Oloron
valley, east of Pau. He was born in about 1615, became a
Musketeer in 1640, and died in December 1643. Isaac de
Portau was born in Pau in 1617, entered the King's Guards in
about 1640, became a Musketeer in 1643, and then disappears
from sight. Henri d'Aramitz, a nephew of the Comte de
Tréville who commanded the Musketeers, entered his uncle's
company in 1640 and married in 1654. Courtilz may have
encountered them in one of his 'fragments', but saw no future
for them in his tale. Dumas, who was not aware even of these
sparse details, seems to have been intrigued by their names and
on each hung a character: Athos, the laconic aristocrat with a
mysterious past, more Romantic hero than seventeenth-century
Musketeer; Porthos, the gentle giant with an appetite matched
only by his strength; and the infinitely more complex Aramis,
a man of intellect and ambition, secret in his dealings and the
least likeable of the companions.

Dumas began *The Three Musketeers* (1844) by rewriting
Courtilz in exactly the same way as he expanded Maquet's
drafts. Once his characters were well established, he cast about
for a suitable framework for their talents. A brief reference in
the *Memoirs* of La Rochefoucauld to a set of diamond studs
said to have been given by the Queen to the Duke of Buckingham in 1626 was turned into a dozen sensational chapters

which also spawned the perfect foil for their honourable dealing
and good-hearted chivalry: a viperish woman, more dangerous
than a nest of Borgias. For though the doughty quartet pit
their wits against Richelieu, their real enemy is Milady de
Winter, the embodiment of evil, and their battle to the death
overshadows the larger events—the siege of La Rochelle and
the murder of Buckingham in 1628—against which it is played
out with epic, even Shakespearian, grandeur. There may be
more breadth than depth in Dumas, but his instinct for a good
story and the unflagging pace at which he told it kept readers
on the edge of their seats and eager to buy the next issue of
Le Siècle in which his Musketeers first appeared. The paper's
circulation rose dramatically and its editor asked Dumas for
more. The fact that he was then in the middle of half a dozen
other long novels, not least the equally enthralling *Count of
Monte Cristo*, did not prevent him from signing a contract
immediately. *Twenty Years After* was serialized in 1845 and
began appearing in volume form even before Dumas had
written the ending. Paris could not get enough of the Musketeers and, in Belgium, unscrupulous publishers brought out
pirated editions of both titles which were immediately translated and made Dumas's name famous throughout the world.
In October 1845, sharing the billing with Maquet, he staged a
play based on the 'English' episode of *Twenty Years After*
which concentrated on the real dramatic centre of the novel:
Mordaunt's obsessive attempt to avenge the death of his
mother, Milady. Subsequently, Dumas completed the saga with
an immensely long final instalment, *Le Vicomte de Bragelonne*
(1847–50), set in 1660–1, which tells how, with the help of
d'Artagnan and company, the English monarchy was restored
and Louis XIV finally assumed absolute power. It is better
known in English in its three parts: *The Vicomte de Bragelonne*,
Louise de La Vallière, and *The Man in the Iron Mask*.

The five instalments cover more than forty years and run to
a million and a quarter words of high adventure set into the
weave of history. Dumas's tactic, which was quite simple,
consisted of giving characters of his own invention secret roles
in leading events. Buckingham was not murdered by the puritan fanatic John Felton, as the textbooks say, but by a Felton

goaded to action by the sexual wiles of Milady. The enigma
of the Man in the Iron Mask is resolved when the prisoner,
the King's harshly treated twin, is substituted for the selfish,
autocratic Louis XIV and rules, more justly, in his place: thus
Dumas's champions save the French from the exactions of a
tyrant and give France a glorious monarch. Dumas's alternative
history, which is far more exciting than the real thing, is not
for the purist. Even his admirers are required at times to
stretch a point when they observe how his cuckoo eggs hatch
out. From a passing reference to Botany Bay more than a
century before Captain Cook set foot there, to his habit of
dividing all historical figures into Heroes with a zest for life,
and Villains fit only for treasons, stratagems, and spoils, Dumas
rewrote history as it ought to have been.

Twenty Years After is a case in point. The tale is anchored
in five distinct historical events over a period of fifteen months:
the opposition to Mazarin of January 1648; the escape of
Beaufort on Whit Sunday; the civil unrest in the capital in
August; the execution of Charles I on 30 January 1649; and
the close of the first Fronde in April. Dumas focuses on each
in turn, establishing the historical framework from authentic
contemporary sources, but squeezing drama, adventure, and
humour into convenient gaps in the historical record: Beaufort's flight from Vincennes was a minor episode but far too
thrilling to omit. Background becomes foreground, invented
characters upstage historical figures, and chronology is cast to
the winds. When the novel opens, it is January and Mazarin
gives d'Artagnan a matter of days to join forces with his former
comrades; before the week is up, Beaufort has escaped and it
is Whitsun. With only a perfunctory nod to the changing
seasons, Dumas's eternal present turns into August and then,
with an effortless skip, the story moves to England, where it
is suddenly January again. If Dumas's characters inhabit the
margins of history, they also exist outside historical time.

Nor is Dumas's reading of history at all clear. By setting the
events of the Fronde against the fate of Charles of England,
he establishes a parallel and appears to issue an awful but rather
confusing warning about the fate of political regimes. The civil
wars in France and England both contested the principle of

absolute royal power, still a live issue in Dumas's France. But whereas Cromwell stood on the rights of Parliament, the *frondeurs* had no programme but their own corporate and personal interests. Neither the discontented Princes of the Blood, nor their aristocratic hangers-on, nor the *parlementaires* who led the revolt were unduly concerned with the public good or the future of the French monarchy as an institution. Yet Dumas gives the impression that here were champions of freedom, and that the English regicides were no more than anarchists 'seized with a sort of madness which will be only removed by blood'. The opposite was true: the English Rebellion was a far more progressive step on the road to modern representative systems of government than the Fronde. If Dumas, the democrat and enemy of privilege, backs the wrong political horses, he gives an equally lopsided view of their riders, who sport only two colours. Against the sinister Cromwell is entered the nobility of Charles's kingly heart. Against the wily Mazarin and the French Queen's party runs 'goodman' Broussel, the people's choice. In the Red stable are the Roundheads, Cromwell, and Mazarin—ambitious, contemptible, career politicians to a man. In the Blue stable, life's Cavaliers, Charles I, Beaufort, and Condé, form an honourable company bound by the valour and chivalry which are the mark of truly noble souls. In other words, Dumas presents the Fronde and the English rebellion in the most romantic light, not as political struggles but as clashes of individual wills and styles.

Of course, as a serious historian, he subscribed to a more orthodox viewpoint: the Fronde was the necessary purging of the aristocratic threat to the monarchy, and Richelieu and Mazarin were the essential architects of the greatness of the reign of Louis XIV. But as a novelist, he followed not his head but his own political instincts, which were a curious mix of snobbery and liberalism. He despised the populace (fickle and savage), sneered at the middle classes (grasping and ridiculous), and scorned aristocrats (fatuous and arrogant). Yet at the same time he regarded the people and their rights as sacred, defended middle-class energy and the 'career open to talents' as defined by the Revolution of 1789, and had an unshakeable admiration for aristocratic superiority. Dumas was a meritocrat who never lost his nostalgia for the sporting side of feudalism. Out of these contradictions within himself he drew the tensions which at first divide the Musketeers and then unite them in common cause.

Dumas was too interested in his heroes to take the easy way to a sequel. A lesser novelist would simply have allowed d'Artagnan to assemble his old comrades and then have launched them on a fresh round of thrilling adventures. But Dumas goes out of his way to deepen the differences between his heroes. Approached by any appeal to his vanity, Porthos is as biddable as ever. But Athos has matured into a country squire who despises politics and remains unshakeably attached to a lofty ideal of kingship and aristocratic selflessness. Aramis, lover of the troublesome *frondeuse*, Madame de Longueville, and a career prelate with hopes of a bishopric, keeps his own counsel while pursuing dark and secret goals. D'Artagnan is the talented, slightly embittered outsider whose wit and courage have gone unrecognized in the ranks. It is not the civil wars that divide them, but the twenty years which have passed since they were young and carefree together. But if the old spirit is dimmed by time, the flame still burns. Brought to the brink, they refuse to fight each other in the name of the brotherhood which once united them. Friendship transcends personal differences just as monarchy is greater than monarchs, and right is always on the side of the just. But their rediscovered alliance remains fragile until it is revitalized by Mordaunt.

Twenty Years After has many structural similarities with *The Three Musketeers*. The court intrigues are repeated and there is another English interlude. More crucially, the roles of Richelieu, Anne, and Madame de Chevreuse are mirrored by Mazarin, Charles I, and Madame de Longueville. Yet the most blatant, but also the most effective, duplication is the appearance of the Son of Milady. Dumas takes care to make Mordaunt human and at first Athos's lingering guilt over the judgement and execution of Milady seems all too reasonable. Mordaunt hates Lord de Winter who rejected him, Charles I who deprived him of his inheritance, and the faceless men who butchered his mother. Hatred, he says, has made him 'corrupt, wicked and implacable'. But hating is one thing, murder another, and Mordaunt's appetite for revenge, unlike that of Monte Cristo who remains a moral man, turns him into malevolence on legs, a ghoul of reptilian intelligence: 'serpent' is the word all the Musketeers have for him. Kingly majesty, nobility, and friendship may be immortal, but so is transcendental, unkillable evil, which lived in Milady and now resurfaces in her deadly offspring.

Mordaunt is the common enemy who restores the bonds of friendship, but he is also given other roles to play. When, at the start of Chapter LXVI, it becomes clear that Charles cannot be rescued—even the Musketeers must bow to history— Dumas's tale threatens to lose its pace and tension. But the drama is rekindled by Mordaunt who relaunches the plot which suddenly moves into a higher narrative gear. The events which lead up to his death, by the hand not of Athos but of Destiny, are not merely a replay of the execution of Milady but a re-enactment of the eternal battle between the forces of good and evil. Justice, divine as well as human, is done and a blow is struck in defence of the human spirit. God and nature conspire and Dumas's Musketeers regain all their lustre as the invincible champions of right.

The twenty chapters which follow may not maintain the epic note but they do provide a conclusion, not in historical terms since the Fronde was to continue for a further four years, but in terms of values. The Musketeers continue to follow their separate paths, but do not cease to be comrades. D'Artagnan's 'great diplomatic feat' in out-thinking Mazarin and Anne and imposing Musketeer ideals on a mad world is a tribute to his wit and energy. But it is no less a celebration of friendship which survives the test of time, overcomes pure evil and restores a divided France to sanity. The Musketeers may no longer be in the first flush of youth, nor do they now see the world with the same eyes. But they know—and Dumas ensures that we do too—that they will always answer the call.

The whole Musketeer saga is an unashamed festival of masculine clubbability. Here are the sense of team camaraderie, the thirst for adventure, and the heady wine of victory which are the stuff of all good yarning. And yet Dumas is much greater than a teller of tall tales or an industrial wholesaler of suspense and excitement. D'Artagnan, Athos, Porthos, and Aramis and their cry of 'All for one and one for all!' are known the world over, even to those who have never read any of their exploits. Dumas's characters exist outside his books as they exist outside historical time and have become common, universal property. That this is so may be explained to some extent in literary terms—Dumas's considerable narrative skills and sense of drama, the power of his psychological insights, and so on—but that comes nowhere near being the whole story. Ultimately, the answer is more mysterious. Dumas had an instinctive feel for the human grandeur which from Homer onwards has raised icons, set standards of conduct, and inspired mere mortals with ideals greater than themselves. He had the extraordinary ability to tap into the collective psyche and create modern heroes to rival those of antiquity. Dumas was a maker of a peculiarly joyous myth, a bringer of comfort. His Musketeers are permanently on our side, and our side, of course, stands for right, fair-play and plain-dealing. This is not escapism but an affirmation of the most civilized of values.

When the din of battle dies, Aramis resumes his affair with Madame de Longueville in Normandy, Athos returns to Bragelonne, and Porthos to his estates. D'Artagnan, now a captain of Musketeers with his eye on a marshal's baton, rejoins his unit: he still has his way to make. He takes a larger apartment on the first floor in the rue Tiquetonne as befits his newly acquired status. But he refuses to relinquish his old room on the fifth: 'one never knows what may happen'. But of course we do. When the challenge comes—and it surely will—the Musketeers will again rise gloriously to meet it. That is what they are for. They are oxygen to the wilting spirit.

SELECT BIBLIOGRAPHY

Twenty Years After was serialized in *Le Siècle* between 21 January and 2 August 1845. The first French edition was published the same year (Paris, Baudry, 10 vols.) in five instalments of two volumes each between March and September. The standard French text is the richly annotated Pléiade edition (Paris, 1962; reprinted 1987), prepared by Gilbert Sigaux, which contains both *Les Trois Mousquetaires* and *Vingt ans après*. Separate translations, based on hastily produced pirated editions printed in Belgium, appeared in London and Baltimore in 1846. A version of the authorized French text, by William Robson, was issued in London by Routledge in 1856. Robson's classic version served as the basis of most subsequent 'new' translations and survives substantially in the present edition. Readers wishing to follow the complex printing history of Dumas's voluminous writings in both French and English may usefully consult two works of reference by Douglas Munro: *Dumas: A Bibliography of Works Published in French, 1825–1900* (New York and London, 1981), and *Alexandre Dumas père: A Bibliography of Works Translated into English to* 1910 (New York and London, 1978).

Courtilz de Sandras's *Mémoires de M. d'Artagnan* (1700) has been edited by Gilbert Sigaux (Paris, 1965), and the English translation by Ralph Nevill (London, 1899) still makes lively reading. The most detailed account of the historical Musketeer, Charles de Batz Castelmore, is Charles Samaran's *D'Artagnan* (Paris, 1912).

Dumas's autobiography (*Mes mémoires (1852–1855)* (ed. Pierre Josserand, Gallimard, 1954–68, 5 vols.; English translation, London, 1907–9) is an entertaining but highly romanticized account of his life to 1832. The best French biographies are those of Henri Clouard, *Alexandre Dumas* (Paris, 1955); André Maurois, *Les Trois Dumas* (Paris, 1957; English translation, London, 1958); and Claude Schopp, *Dumas, le génie de la vie* (Paris, 1985; trans., New York and Toronto, 1988). Isabelle Jan, *Dumas romancier* (Paris, 1973) offers the fullest study of the novels.

Among the many books in English devoted to Dumas, very readable introductions are provided by Ruthven Todd, *The Laughing Mulatto* (London, 1940), A. Craig Bell, *Alexandre Dumas* (London, 1950), and Richard Stowe, *Dumas* (Boston, 1976). Michael Ross's *Alexandre Dumas* (Newton Abbot, 1981) gives a sympathetic account of Dumas's life. The most balanced and comprehensive guide, however, is F. W. J. Hemmings's excellent *The King of Romance* (London, 1979).

A CHRONOLOGY OF
ALEXANDRE DUMAS

1762   25 March: Birth at Saint-Domingo of Thomas-Alexandre, son of the French-born Marquis Davy de la Pailleterie and Marie-Cessette Dumas. After returning to France in 1780, he enlists in 1786 and rises rapidly through the ranks during the Revolution.

1802   24 July: Birth at Villers-Cotterêts of Alexandre Dumas, second child of General Dumas and Marie-Louise-Elizabeth Labouret, an innkeeper's daughter.

1806   26 February: Death of General Dumas. Alexandre is brought up in straitened circumstances by his mother. He attends local schools and has a happy childhood.

1819   Dumas, now a lawyer's office-boy, falls in love with Adèle Dalvin who rejects him. Meets Adolphe de Leuven, with whom he collaborates in writing unsuccessful plays.

1822   Visits Leuven in Paris, meets Talma, the leading actor of the day, and resolves to become a playwright.

1823   Moves to Paris. Enters the service of the Duc d'Orléans. Falls in love with a seamstress, Catherine Labay.

1824   27 July: Birth of Alexandre Dumas *fils*, author of *La Dame aux Camélias*.

1825   22 September: Dumas's first performed play, written in collaboration with Leuven and Rousseau, makes no impact.

1826   Publication of a collection of short stories, Dumas's first solo composition, which sells four copies.

1827   A company of English actors, which includes Kean, Kemble, and Mrs Smithson, performs Shakespeare in English to enthusiastic Paris audiences: Dumas is deeply impressed. Liaison with Mélanie Waldor.

1828-9 Dumas enters Parisian literary circles through Charles Nodier.

1829   11 February: First of about 50 performances of *Henri III and his Court* which makes Dumas famous and thrusts him into the front ranks of the Romantic revolution in literature. Dumas meets Victor Hugo. He consolidates his reputation as a dramatist with *Antony* (1831), *La Tour de Nesle* (1832), and *Kean* (1836), which are all landmarks in the history of Romantic drama.

1830   May: Start of an affair with the actress Belle Krelsamer. Active in the July Revolution: Dumas single-handedly captures a gunpowder magazine at Soissons and is sent by Lafayette to promote the National Guard in the Vendée (Aug.).

1831   5 March: Birth of Marie, his daughter by Belle Krelsamer. 17 March: Dumas acknowledges Alexandre, his son by Catherine Labay.

1832   6 February: Start of his affair with the actress Ida Ferrier. 15 April: Dumas succumbs to the cholera which kills 20,000 Parisians. 29 May: First performance of *La Tour de Nesle*: Gaillardet accuses Dumas of plagiarism. July: Suspected of republican sympathies, Dumas leaves Paris for Switzerland. After the spectacular failure of his next play, he begins to take a systematic interest in the literary possibilities of French history.

1833   Serialization of a book of impressions of Switzerland, the first of his travelogues.

1834–5 October: Dumas travels in the Midi. From the Riviera, he embarks on the first of many journeys to Italy.

1836   31 August: Dumas returns triumphantly to the theatre with *Kean*.

1838   Death of Dumas's mother. Travels along the Rhine with Gérard de Nerval who introduces him to Auguste Maquet in December.

1840   1 February: Dumas marries Ida Ferrier, travels to Italy, and publishes *Le Capitaine Pamphile*, the best of his children's books.

1840–2 Dividing his time between Paris and Italy, Dumas increasingly abandons the theatre for the novel.

1842   June: Publication of *Le Chevalier d'Harmental*, the first of many romances written in association with Maquet.

1844   March–July: Serialization of *The Three Musketeers* in Le Siècle. August: First episode of *The Count of Monte Cristo* published in *Le Journal des débats*.

15 October: Amicable separation from Ida Ferrier. Publication of *Louis XIV and his Century*.

1845   21 January–2 August: serialization of the second d'Artagnan story, *Twenty Years After*, in *Le Siècle*.

February: He wins his libel suit against the journalist Jacquot, author of *A Fiction Factory: The Firm of Alexandre Dumas and Company*, in which he was accused of publishing other men's work under his own name.

27 October: First performance of *Les Mousquetaires*, an adaptation of *Twenty Years After*. Beginning at 6.30 p.m., it lasts until 1 a.m.

1846   Final break with Ida Ferrier. Brief liaison with Lola Montès. November–January: Travels with his son to Spain and North Africa.

1847   30 January: Loses a lawsuit brought by newspaper proprietors for failure to deliver copy for which he had accepted large advances.

11 February: Questions are asked in the National Assembly about Dumas's appropriation of the Navy vessel, *Le Véloce*, during his visit to North Africa.

20 February: Opening of the 'Théâtre historique'.

7 March: Completion of the 'Château de Monte Cristo' at Marly-le-Roi.

20 October–12 January 1850: Serialization of the final Musketeer adventure, *The Vicomte de Bragelonne*, in *Le Siècle*.

1848   Dumas stands unsuccessfully as a parliamentary candidate and votes for Louis-Napoleon in the December elections.

1849   17 February: First performance at the 'Théâtre historique' of *La Jeunesse des Mousquetaires*, based on *The Three Musketeers*.

1850   20 March: The 'Théâtre historique' is declared bankrupt. The 'Château de Monte Cristo' is sold off for 30,000 francs.

1851   Michel Lévy begins to bring out the first volumes of Dumas's complete works which will eventually fill 301 volumes.

7 December: Dumas flees to Belgium to avoid his creditors.

1852   Publication of the first volumes of *My Memoirs*. Dumas declared bankrupt with debts of 100,000 francs.

1853   November: Returns to Paris and founds a periodical, *Le Mousquetaire* (last issue 7 February 1857) for which he writes most of the copy himself.

1857   23 April: Founds a literary weekly, *Le Monte Cristo*, which, with one break, survives until 1862.

1858   15 June: Dumas leaves for a tour of Russia and returns in March 1859.

1859   11 March: Death of Ida Ferrier. Beginning of a liaison with Emilie Cordier which lasts until 1864.

1860   Meets Garibaldi at Turin and just misses the taking of Sicily (June). Returns to Marseilles where he buys guns for the Italian cause and is in Naples just after the city falls in September. Garibaldi stands, by proxy, as godfather to Dumas's daughter by Emilie Cordier.
        11 October: Founds *L'Indipendente*, a literary and political periodical published half in French and half in Italian.

1863   The works of Dumas are placed on the Index by the Catholic Church.

1864   April: Dumas returns to Paris.

1865   Further travels through Italy, Germany, and Austria.

1867   Publishes *The Prussian Terror*, a novel intended to warn France against the coming Prussian threat. Begins a last liaison, with Adah Menken, an American actress (d. 1868).

1869   10 March: Dumas's last play, *The Whites and the Blues*.

1870   5 December: Dumas dies at Puys, near Dieppe, after a stroke in September.

1872   Dumas's remains transferred to Villers-Cotterêts.

1883   Unveiling of a statue to Dumas by Gustave Doré in the Place Malesherbes.

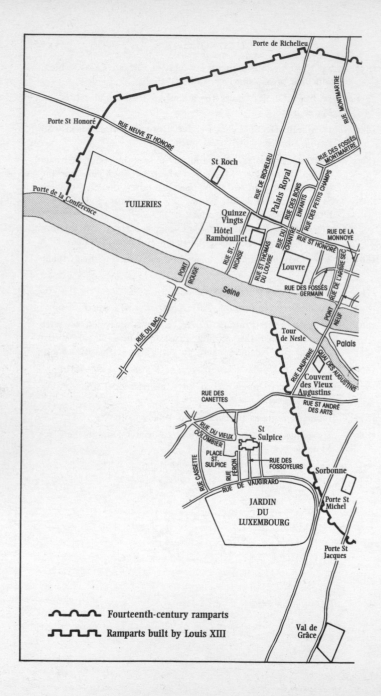

Porte de Richelieu

Porte St Honoré

RUE NEUVE ST HONORÉ

St Roch

RUE DE RICHELIEU

RUE DES FOSSÉS MONTMARTRE

RUE MONTMARTRE

Porte de la Conférence

TUILERIES

Quinze Vingts

Hôtel Rambouillet

Palais Royal

RUE DES BONS ENFANTS

RUE DES PETITS CHAMPS

RUE DU CHANTRE

RUE ST HONORÉ

RUE DE LA MONNOYE

RUE ST NICAISE

RUE ST THOMAS DU LOUVRE

Louvre

RUE DE L'ARBRE SEC

PONT ROUGE

Seine

RUE DES FOSSÉS GERMAIN

RUE DU BAC

Tour de Nesle

PONT NEUF

Palais

RUE DAUPHINE

QUAI DES AUGUSTINS

Couvent des Vieux Augustins

RUE DES CANETTES

RUE ST ANDRÉ DES ARTS

RUE DU VIEUX COLOMBIER

St Sulpice

RUE CASSETTE

PLACE ST. SULPICE

RUE FÉRON

RUE DES FOSSOYEURS

Sorbonne

RUE DE VAUGIRARD

JARDIN DU LUXEMBOURG

Porte St Michel

Porte St Jacques

⌒⌒⌒⌒ Fourteenth-century ramparts

⊓⊓⊓⊓ Ramparts built by Louis XIII

Val de Grâce

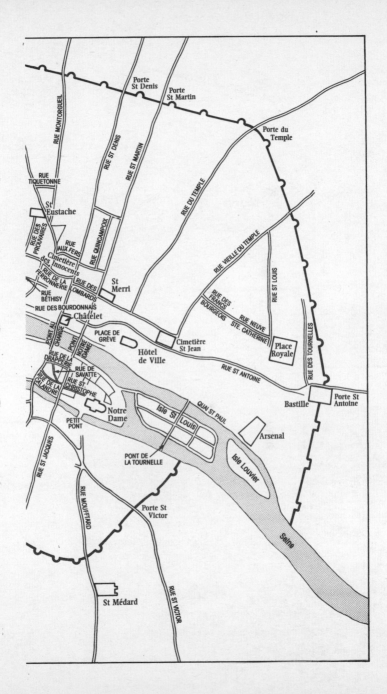

TWENTY YEARS AFTER

CONTENTS

I.	THE PHANTOM OF RICHELIEU	7
II.	A NIGHT-ROUND	17
III.	TWO OLD ENEMIES	25
IV.	ANNE OF AUSTRIA AT THE AGE OF FORTY-SIX	40
V.	THE GASCON AND THE ITALIAN	51
VI.	D'ARTAGNAN AT FORTY YEARS OF AGE	56
VII.	D'ARTAGNAN IS AT A LOSS, BUT ONE OF OUR OLD ACQUAINTANCES COMES TO HIS AID	63
VIII.	OF THE DIFFERENT INFLUENCES WHICH HALF A PISTOLE CAN HAVE ON A BEADLE AND A CHOIR BOY	72
IX.	HOW D'ARTAGNAN, LOOKING FOR ARAMIS FAR AWAY, PERCEIVED HIM ON THE CRUPPER BEHIND PLANCHET	79
X.	THE ABBÉ D'HERBLAY	87
XI.	THE TWO GASPARDS	95
XII.	M. PORTHOS DU VALLON DE BRACIEUX DE PIERREFONDS	105
XIII.	HOW D'ARTAGNAN PERCEIVED IN FINDING PORTHOS THAT RICHES DO NOT MAKE HAPPINESS	110
XIV.	IN WHICH IS SHOWN THAT IF PORTHOS WAS DISCONTENTED WITH HIS LOT, MOUSQUETON WAS SATISFIED WITH HIS	119
XV.	TWO ANGELS' HEADS	126
XVI.	THE CHÂTEAU DE BRAGELONNE	134
XVII.	ATHOS'S DIPLOMACY	142
XVIII.	MONSIEUR DE BEAUFORT	152
XIX.	HOW THE DUC DE BEAUFORT AMUSED HIMSELF IN THE PRISON AT VINCENNES	158
XX.	GRIMAUD ON DUTY	168
XXI.	WHAT THE PIES MADE BY FATHER MARTEAU'S SUCCESSOR CONTAINED	179

CONTENTS

XXII. AN ADVENTURE OF MARIE MICHON   190

XXIII. THE ABBÉ SCARRON   202

XXIV. ST DENIS   218

XXV. ONE OF M. DE BEAUFORT'S FORTY MEANS OF ESCAPE   226

XXVI. D'ARTAGNAN'S TIMELY ARRIVAL   236

XXVII. THE KING'S HIGHWAY   245

XXVIII. THE MEETING   252

XXIX. FOUR OLD FRIENDS PREPARING FOR A CONFERENCE   260

XXX. THE PLACE ROYALE   268

XXXI. THE OISE FERRY-BOAT   273

XXXII. SKIRMISH   282

XXXIII. THE MONK   288

XXXIV. THE ABSOLUTION   298

XXXV. GRIMAUD SPEAKS   303

XXXVI. THE EVE OF BATTLE   309

XXXVII. A DINNER AS OF YORE   320

XXXVIII. THE LETTER FROM CHARLES I   329

XXXIX. CROMWELL'S LETTER   334

XL. MAZARIN AND QUEEN HENRIETTA   341

XLI. HOW THE UNFORTUNATE SOMETIMES MISTAKE CHANCE FOR PROVIDENCE   346

XLII. THE UNCLE AND THE NEPHEW   354

XLIII. PATERNITY   358

XLIV. AGAIN A QUEEN WHO ASKS AID   366

XLV. IN WHICH IT IS PROVED THAT THE FIRST MOVE IS ALWAYS A GOOD ONE   377

XLVI. THE TE DEUM FOR THE VICTORY OF LENS   384

XLVII. THE MENDICANT OF ST EUSTACHE   402

XLVIII. THE TOWER OF ST JACQUES LA BOUCHERIE   412

XLIX. THE RIOT   418

L. THE RIOT BECOMES A REVOLT   425

LI. MISFORTUNE IS A HELP TO MEMORY   437

LII. THE INTERVIEW   443

LIII. THE FLIGHT   450

LIV. MONSIEUR THE COADJUTOR'S COACH   461

CONTENTS

LV. HOW D'ARTAGNAN GAINED TWO HUN-
DRED AND NINETEEN LOUIS, AND
PORTHOS
TWO HUNDRED AND FIFTEEN LOUIS,
BY SELLING STRAW   474

LVI. NEWS FROM ARAMIS   483

LVII. L'ÉCOSSAIS, PARJURE A SA FOI, POUR
UN DENIER VENDIT SON ROI   493

LVIII. THE AVENGER   502

LIX. OLIVER CROMWELL   510

LX. THE GENTLEMEN   515

LXI. THE LORD OUR SAVIOUR   520

LXII. IN WHICH IS PROVED THAT IN THE
MOST TRYING CIRCUMSTANCES BRAVE
MEN NEVER LOSE THEIR COURAGE,
NOR HUNGRY ONES THEIR APPETITE   527

LXIII. HEALTH TO THE FALLEN MAJESTY   535

LXIV. D'ARTAGNAN FINDS A PLAN   543

LXV. THE PARTY AT LANSQUENET   554

LXVI. LONDON   560

LXVII. THE TRIAL   567

LXVIII. WHITEHALL   576

LXIX. THE WORKMEN   585

LXX. REMEMBER   592

LXXI. THE MAN IN THE MASK   599

LXXII. CROMWELL'S HOUSE   608

LXXIII. THE CONVERSATION   615

LXXIV. THE 'LIGHTNING' FELUCCA   624

LXXV. THE PORT WINE   634

LXXVI. THE PORT WINE (concluded)   643

LXXVII. FATALITY   648

LXXVIII. IN WHICH IS TOLD HOW MOUSQUE-
TON, AFTER HAVING MISSED BEING
ROASTED, ESCAPED BEING EATEN   655

LXXIX. THE RETURN   663

LXXX. THE AMBASSADORS   671

LXXXI. THE THREE LIEUTENANTS OF THE
GENERALISSIMO   678

LXXXII. THE COMBAT AT CHARENTON   692

LXXXIII. JOURNEY TO PICARDY 702

LXXXIV. THE GRATITUDE OF ANNE OF AUS-
TRIA 710

LXXXV. THE ROYALTY OF M. DE MAZARIN 715

LXXXVI. PRECAUTIONS 719

LXXXVII. STRENGTH OF MIND AND STRENGTH
OF ARM 725

LXXXVIII. STRENGTH OF MIND AND STRENGTH
OF ARM (*concluded*) 728

LXXXIX. STRENGTH OF ARM AND STRENGTH
OF MIND 734

XC. STRENGTH OF ARM AND STRENGTH OF
MIND (*concluded*) 736

XCI. M. MAZARIN'S OUBLIETTES 743

XCII. CONFERENCES 747

XCIII. IN WHICH ONE BEGINS TO BELIEVE
THAT PORTHOS WILL AT LAST BE
MADE A BARON, AND D'ARTAGNAN A
CAPTAIN 753

XCIV. HOW GREATER PROGRESS IS MADE
WITH A PEN AND A THREAT THAN
BY THE SWORD AND DEVOTEDNESS 761

XCV. HOW GREATER PROGRESS IS MADE
WITH A PEN AND A THREAT THAN BY
THE SWORD AND DEVOTEDNESS
(*concluded*) 769

XCVI. WHERE IT IS SHOWN THAT IT IS
SOMETIMES MORE DIFFICULT FOR
KINGS TO RETURN TO THEIR CAPI-
TAL THAN TO LEAVE IT 775

XCVII. WHERE IT IS SHOWN THAT IT IS SOME-
TIMES MORE DIFFICULT FOR KINGS
TO RETURN TO THEIR CAPITAL THAN
TO LEAVE IT (*concluded*) 781

CONCLUSION 786

THE PHANTOM OF RICHELIEU

IN a room of the Palais-Cardinal* which we already know, near a table with silver gilt corners, loaded with papers and books, a man was sitting, his head resting in his hands.

Behind him was a vast fireplace, red with fire, whose blazing brands were crumbling upon large gilded fire-dogs. The light from this fire illumined from behind the magnificent dress of this dreamer, as the light from a candelabra filled with candles illumined it in front.

To see this red gown and these rich laces, to see this forehead pale and bent down in meditation, to see the solitude of this cabinet, the silence of the antechambers, the measured step of the guards upon the landing, one could well believe that the ghost of Cardinal Richelieu was still in his chamber.

Alas, it was in fact only the shadow of the great man. France, enfeebled, the authority of the king disregarded, the great nobles again strong and turbulent, the enemy once more on this side of the frontiers, everything bore testimony that Richelieu was no longer there.

But that which showed still more than all else that the red gown was not that of the old cardinal was this isolation, which seemed, as we have said, rather that of a phantom than of a living person; it was these corridors void of courtiers, these courtyards full of guards; it was the mocking expressions which came up from the streets and penetrated the windows of this chamber shaken by the breath of a whole city leagued against the minister;* it was, in fine, the distant sound, continually renewed, of fire-arms, discharged happily without aim or effect, and only to show the Guards, the Swiss, the Musketeers,* and the soldiers who surrounded the Palais-Royal—for the Palais-Cardinal itself had changed its name—that the people also had arms.

This phantom of Richelieu was Mazarin. Now, Mazarin was alone, and felt himself to be weak.

'Foreigner!' murmured he, 'Italian! This is their great epithet launched at me. With this word they assassinated, hanged, and destroyed Concini; and if I let them do it, they would assassinate, hang, and destroy me like him, although I have never done them other harm than to squeeze them a little. Simpletons! They do not perceive that their enemy is not this Italian who speaks French badly, but rather those who have the talent to say to them fine words in a very pure Parisian accent.

'Yes, yes,' continued the minister, with his subtle smile which this time seemed strange on his pale lips—'yes, your mutterings tell me the lot of favourites is precarious; but if you know that, you ought also to know that I am not an ordinary favourite. The Earl of Essex* had a splendid ring enriched with diamonds that his royal mistress gave him; as for me, I have only a plain ring with initials and a date, but this ring has been blessed in the chapel of the Palais-Royal.[1] So they will not ruin me as they would like to. They do not perceive that with their eternal cry of "Down with Mazarin", I make them at one time cry, "Long live Beaufort", at another, "Long live the prince", and at another, "Long live the parliament".* Very well. Beaufort is at Vincennes.* The prince will go to rejoin him one day or another, and the parliament——'
Here the smile of the cardinal changed to an expression of hate of which his mild face seemed incapable. 'Well, the parliament——We will see what we will do with the parliament. We have Orléans and Montargis.* Oh, I will take time for this! But those who have commenced by crying "Down with Mazarin" will finish by crying "Down with all those people", each one in his turn. Richelieu, whom they hated when he was living, and of whom they are always talking since he is dead, was lower down than I—for he was dismissed several times, and oftener still feared to be so. The queen will never dismiss *me*; and if I am forced to yield to the people, she will yield with me. If I fly, she will fly; and we will see then what the rebels will do without their queen and without their king. Oh, if only I were not a foreigner! if I were only French! if I were only well born!' And he relapsed into his reverie.

---

[1] It is known that Mazarin, having taken none of the orders that forbid marriage, had espoused Anne of Austria. See the Memoirs of Laporte and those of the Princesse Palatine.*

In fact, the position was difficult; and the day which had just closed had complicated it still more. Mazarin, always spurred on by his sordid avarice, was crushing the people with taxes; and the people, to whom nothing was left but the soul, as was said by the Advocate-General Talon, and still more because one cannot sell one's soul at auction—the people whom they tried to make patient by the noise of the victories achieved, and who found that laurels were not meat with which they could be fed'—the people for a long time had not ceased to murmur.

But this was not all—for when it is only the people who grumble, separated as they are by the middle class and the nobility, the court does not hear them. But Mazarin had had the imprudence to embroil himself with the magistrates. He had sold twelve warrants* for members of the Council of State; and as these officials paid very dearly for their posts, and the addition of these twelve new associates would lower its value, the old officials had united, sworn upon the Gospels not to suffer this increase and to resist all the persecutions of the court, promising one another that in case one of them by this rebellion should lose his post the rest would contribute to re-imburse him its value.

Now see what had resulted from both these sources. The seventh of January,* seven or eight hundred shopkeepers of Paris were assembled and mutinous on account of a new tax about to be imposed upon the proprietors of houses, and they had deputed ten of their number to confer with the Duc d'Orléans, who according to his old habit was seeking popularity. The Duc d'Orléans had received them, and they had declared that they were determined not to pay this new tax, even if forced to defend themselves with the armed hand against the king's officials who might come to collect it.

The Duc d'Orléans had listened to them with great complaisance, had given them hope of some diminution, had promised to speak of it to the queen, and had dismissed them with the ordinary phrase of princes, 'It shall be seen to.'

' Madame de Motteville.*

On their side, on the ninth, the members of the Council of State sought an audience with the cardinal, and one of them, who spoke for all the others, had addressed him with so much firmness and spirit that the cardinal had been astonished; he also sent them away, saying, like the Duc d'Orléans, that it should be seen to.

Then in order to *see to it* the Council was assembled, and they sent to find the Superintendent of Finances, d'Émery.

This d'Émery was much detested by the people: first, because he was Superintendent of Finances, and every Superintendent of Finances ought to be detested; and finally, because he somewhat deserved to be so. He was the son of a banker of Lyons who called himself Particelli, and who, having changed his name after his bankruptcy, assumed that of d'Émery, which did not prevent the Advocate-General, Omer Talon, from always calling him Particelle, following the custom of the times of gallicizing foreign names. Cardinal Richelieu, who recognized in him great financial ability, had presented him to King Louis XIII. under the name of d'Émery, and wishing to appoint him Intendant of Finances, praised him highly.

'Admirable!' replied the king, 'and I am pleased that you talk to me of M. d'Émery for this office, which requires an honest man. They told me that you were pressing the appointment of that rascal of a Particelli, and I was afraid that you might persuade me to take him.'

'Sire,' answered the cardinal, 'let your Majesty be reassured; the Particelli of whom you speak has been hanged.'

'Ah, so much the better!' cried the king. 'It is not, then, in vain that I am called "Louis the Just".'

And he signed the appointment of M. d'Émery. It was this same d'Émery who had become Superintendent of Finances.

They had sent for him on the part of the minister, and he arrived pale and thoroughly frightened, saying that his son had barely escaped assassination* that very day in the square of the Palais. The crowd met him and reproached him for the luxury of his wife, who had a suite of rooms with red velvet hangings and fringes of gold. She was the daughter of Nicholas le Camus, secretary in 1617, who came to Paris with twenty livres, and who, while reserving to himself forty thousand livres of income, had just divided nine millions among his children.

The son of d'Émery had just escaped being strangled, one of the rioters having proposed to squeeze him until he gave up all the gold he had swallowed. The Council decided nothing that day, the superintendent being too much occupied with this event to have his head clear. The following day the first president, Matthew Molé—whose courage in all these affairs, said Cardinal Retz, equalled that of the Duc de Beaufort and of the Prince de Condé, two men who were esteemed the bravest in France—the following day the first president, we say, had been attacked in his turn. The people threatened to hold him responsible for the evil measures which threatened them; but the first president replied with his habitual calmness, without emotion or surprise, that if the disturbers of the peace did not obey the king's will he should erect gibbets in the squares to hang at once the most mutinous of them, to which they answered that they asked nothing better than to see gibbets erected, and that they would serve for hanging the bad judges who purchased the favour of the court at the cost of the misery of the people.

This was not all: the eleventh, the queen, going to Mass at Notre-Dame, which she did regularly every Saturday, was followed by more than two hundred women crying and demanding justice. They had not, indeed, any bad intention, wishing only to fall upon their knees before her to try and excite her compassion; but the guards prevented it, and the queen, haughty and disdainful, passed on without listening to their complaints.

In the afternoon the Council met again, and it was there decided that the authority of the king should be maintained; consequently parliament was convoked for the following day, the twelfth.

This day, during the evening of which we commence this new story, the king, then ten years of age, and who had just had the smallpox, under the pretext of rendering thanks at Notre-Dame for his recovery, called out his Guards, the Swiss, and the Musketeers, and placed them in *echelons* around the Palais-Royal, upon the quays and upon the Pont Neuf; and after hearing Mass he proceeded to the parliament house, where, upon a Bed of Justice* then improvised, he not only confirmed his former edicts, but issued five or six new ones; each one, said Cardinal de Retz, more ruinous than the other.* So much so that the first president, who, as we have seen, during the preceding days supported the court, had raised his voice boldly against this method of leading the king to the Palais to surprise and force the liberty of suffrage.

But those especially who resisted strongly these new taxes were the president, Blancmesnil, and the councillor Broussel. These edicts issued, the king returned to the Palais-Royal. A vast multitude of people lined his route; but although they knew that he came from the parliament they were ignorant whether he had gone there to render justice to the people or to oppress them still further, and not a single joyful shout was heard during his passage to felicitate him on his return to health. Every countenance was gloomy and anxious; some even were menacing.

Notwithstanding his return, the troops remained in the square; it was feared that a riot might break out when the result of the sitting of parliament should be known—and in fact, hardly had the rumour spread through the streets that instead of lightening the taxes, the king had increased them, than groups were formed and a great clamour resounded with cries of 'Down with Mazarin!' 'Long live Broussel!' 'Long live Blancmesnil!' for the people knew that Broussel and Blancmesnil had spoken in their favour, and though their eloquence was wasted, they retained no less good-will towards them.

It was desired to disperse the groups and to silence these cries; and as happens in such cases, the groups increased in size, and the cries redoubled. Orders had just been given to the royal Guard and to the Swiss Guards, not only to stand firm, but to send out patrols to the streets of St Denis and St Martin,* where these groups appeared more numerous and more excited, when the provost of the merchants* was announced at the Palais-Royal. He was introduced immediately; he came to say that if these hostile demonstrations did not cease instantly, in two hours the whole of Paris would be in arms.

They were deliberating what should be done, when Comminges, lieutenant of the Guards, returned, his uniform torn and his face bleeding.

On seeing him appear, the queen uttered a cry of surprise, and demanded of him what had happened.

It had happened that at the sight of the Guards, as the provost of the merchants had foreseen, the mob had become exasperated. They had taken possession of the bells and sounded the tocsin. Comminges stood firm, and arrested a man who appeared one of their ringleaders, and to make an example, ordered that he should be hanged at the cross of Du Trahoir.* The soldiers dragged him along to execute the order. But in the market-place they were attacked with stones and halberds; the prisoner profited of this moment to escape, gained the Rue des Lombards, and took refuge in a house whose doors were immediately broken open. This violence was useless; they were not able to find the culprit. Comminges left a picket in the street, and with the rest of his detachment returned to the Palais-Royal to report to the queen what had taken place.

During the whole route, he was pursued by cries and by threats; several of his men were wounded by pikes and halberds, and he himself was struck by a stone cutting open the eyebrow.

The recital of Comminges supported the opinion of the provost of the merchants, that the government was not in condition to make head against a serious revolt. The cardinal caused it to be circulated among the people that troops had been stationed on the quays and on the Pont Neuf only on account of the ceremonial, and that they would soon withdraw. In fact, about four o'clock they were all concentrated near the Palais-Royal; a detachment was placed at the Barrière des Sergents, another at the Quinze-Vingts, and a third at the hill St Roch.* The courtyards and the basements were filled with Swiss and musketeers, and they awaited the result.

Such then was the state of affairs when we introduced our readers into the cabinet of Cardinal Mazarin—formerly that of Cardinal Richelieu. We have seen in what state of mind he listened to the murmurs of the people which reached even to him, and to the echo of the fire-arms which resounded in his chamber.

Suddenly he raised his head, the brow slightly contracted like that of a man who has taken a resolution, fixed his eyes upon an enormous clock about to strike ten, and taking up a silver gilt whistle lying on the table within reach of his hand, he blew it twice.

A door hidden by the tapestry opened noiselessly, and a man dressed in black advanced silently and remained standing behind the armchair.

'Bernouin,' said the cardinal, not even turning around, for having whistled twice he knew that this must be his *valet de chambre*, 'what musketeers are in the palace?'

'The Black Musketeers, my Lord.'

'What company?'

'Tréville's company.'

'Is there some officer of this company in the ante-chamber?'

'Lieutenant d'Artagnan.'

'A good officer, I believe?'

'Yes, my Lord.'

'Give me the uniform of a musketeer, and help me to dress.'

The *valet de chambre* went out as silently as he entered, and returned an instant afterwards, bearing the costume demanded. The cardinal, silent and thoughtful, began to take off the ceremonial dress which he had assumed to attend the sitting of parliament, and to attire himself in the military coat, which he wore with a certain ease, owing to his former campaigns in Italy. When he was completely dressed, he said, 'Bring me M. d'Artagnan.'

And the *valet de chambre* went out this time by the main door, but always equally silent and mute. One might have said it was a shadow.

Left alone, the cardinal, with a certain satisfaction, surveyed himself in a mirror. Still young—for he was scarcely forty-six years of age—he was of an elegant figure, and a little under the middle height; his complexion was high-coloured and handsome; his glance full of fire; his nose large, but well proportioned; his forehead broad and majestic; his chestnut-coloured hair was a little curly, his beard darker than his hair and always well dressed with the curling-iron, which lent him an additional charm.

Next he put on his belt, looked with complacency at his hands, which were very handsome and of which he took the greatest care, then, throwing aside the large buckskin gloves which he had already taken as part of the uniform, he put on plain silk gloves.

At this moment the door opened.

'M. d'Artagnan,' said the *valet de chambre*.

An officer entered.

He was a man of thirty-nine or forty years of age, of small but well-shaped figure, thin, the eye bright and animated, the beard black and the hair turning grey, as happens always when one has found life too gay or too sad, and especially when one is dark-complexioned.

D'Artagnan advanced four steps into the cabinet, which he remembered having entered once in the time of Cardinal Richelieu, and seeing no one there but a musketeer of his company, he fixed his eyes upon this musketeer, under whose dress at the first glance he recognized the cardinal. He remained standing, in a respectful but dignified attitude, as became a man of rank who in his life had often been in the society of the highest nobles.

The cardinal fixed upon him his eye more subtle than penetrating, examined him with attention, then after a few seconds of silence, 'You are M. d'Artagnan?' said he.

'I am he, my Lord,' said the officer.

The cardinal looked a moment longer at this intellectual head and this countenance whose excessive mobility had been subdued by years and experience in life; but d'Artagnan sustained the examination like one who had formerly been examined by eyes far more piercing than those now turned upon him.

'Sir,' said the cardinal, 'you are to come with me, or rather I am going with you.'

'At your orders, my Lord,' responded d'Artagnan.

'I wish to visit, personally, the posts surrounding the Palais-Royal; do you think there is any danger?'

'Any danger, my Lord!' demanded d'Artagnan, with a look of surprise; 'and what danger?'

'They say the people are actually in insurrection.'

'The uniform of the king's Musketeers is much respected, my Lord; and if it were not, I would engage, with three of my men, to put to flight a hundred of these clowns.'

'Yet you saw what happened to Comminges?'

'M. de Comminges belongs to the Guards and not to the Musketeers,' replied d'Artagnan.

'Which means,' said the cardinal, smiling, 'that the Musketeers are better soldiers than the Guards?'*

'Every one prefers his own uniform, my Lord.'

'Except me, Monsieur,' replied Mazarin, smiling, 'since you see that I have left off my own to put on yours.'

'*Peste*, my Lord!' said d'Artagnan, 'that is modesty. As for me, I declare that if I had the uniform of your Eminence, I would content myself with it, and would engage, at need, never to wear any other.'

'Yes; but for going out this evening, perhaps it would not have been very safe. Bernouin, my hat.'

The *valet de chambre* returned, bringing a military hat with a broad brim. The cardinal donned it with an easy air, and turning towards d'Artagnan, 'You have horses saddled in the stables, haven't you?'

'Yes, my Lord.'

'Well, then, let us set out.'

'How many men does my Lord wish?'

'You say that with four men you will engage to put to flight a hundred clowns; as we may meet two hundred of them, take eight.'

'As my Lord wishes.'

'I will follow you, or rather,' said the cardinal, 'no, this way; light us, Bernouin.'

The valet took a candle; the cardinal took a small key from his bureau, and opening the door of a secret staircase found himself in a moment in the court of the Palais-Royal.

A NIGHT-ROUND

TEN minutes after, the little troop went out through the street of Les Bon Enfants,* behind the theatre that Cardinal Richelieu had built in which to play 'Mirame', and in which Cardinal Mazarin, more fond of music than of literature, had just caused to be given the first operas that had ever been produced in France.

The city presented all the appearances of extreme agitation; numerous groups circulated in the streets, and whatever d'Artagnan had said of them, stopped their course to see the soldiers pass with an air of threatening mockery that indicated that the citizens had for the moment laid aside their usual quiet for more warlike intentions. From time to time sounds came from the direction of the markets. Musket-shots were heard cracking from the direction of the Rue St Denis, and sometimes suddenly, without any reason, some bell began to ring, set in motion by the popular caprice.

D'Artagnan pursued his way with the unconcern of a man upon whom such follies make no impression. Where a group occupied the middle of the street, he pressed his horse through it without saying, 'Look out'; and as if those composing it, rebellious or not, knew with what kind of man they had to do, they opened a way and allowed the patrol to pass. The cardinal envied this composure, which he ascribed to familiarity with danger; but he conceived none the less for the officer under whose orders he was for the moment placed that kind of consideration that prudence itself accords to cool courage.

On approaching an outpost of the Barrière des Sergents, a sentinel cried out, 'Who's there?' d'Artagnan replied, and having asked the countersign of the cardinal, advanced at the order. The countersign was *Louis and Rocroy*.

These signs of recognition interchanged, d'Artagnan asked if it was not M. de Comminges who commanded the outpost.

The sentinel then pointed out to him an officer who was conversing on foot, his hand resting upon the neck of the horse of his interlocutor. It was he whom d'Artagnan sought.

'Here is M. de Comminges,' said d'Artagnan, returning to the cardinal.

The cardinal turned his horse towards them, while d'Artagnan withdrew, out of respect; but, from the manner in which the officer on foot and the one mounted took off their hats, he saw that they recognized his Eminence.

'Bravo, Guitaut,' said the cardinal to the mounted officer; 'I see that despite your sixty-four years you are always the same, active and devoted. What are you saying to this young man?'

'My Lord,' replied Guitaut, 'I was saying that we live at a singular epoch, and that today resembles much one of those days of the League* which I heard so much talked about in my youth. Do you know that there was question, in the Rue St Denis and the Rue St Martin, of nothing less than throwing up barricades?'

'And what was Comminges's response, then, my dear Guitaut?'

'My Lord,' said Comminges, 'I answered that to make a League, there was wanting to them one thing which seemed to me quite essential—a Duc de Guise; besides, one does not do the same thing twice.'

'No, but they will make a Fronde, as they say,' replied Guitaut.

'And what is a Fronde?' demanded Mazarin.

'My Lord, it is the name they give to their party.'

'And whence comes this name?'

'It appears that some days ago the councillor Bachaumont said at the Palais that all the rioters resemble those scholars who sling stones in the moats of Paris,* who disperse at the approach of the civil officer, to assemble again when he has passed. Then they have picked up the word at the rebound, as the beggars at Brussels have done; they call themselves "Frondeurs." Today and yesterday everything was "à la Fronde"— bread, hats, gloves, muffs, fans; but hold, listen——'

At this moment a window opened; a man appeared at the window and began to sing:

> A breeze from the Fronde
> Blew to-day;
> I think that it blows
> Against Mazarin.*

'Insolent wretch!' muttered Guitaut.

'My Lord,' said Comminges, whose wound had put him in bad humour, and who sought nothing better than revenge, and to return blow for blow, 'shall I send a ball at that jester to teach him not to sing so much out of tune another time?' And he laid his hand upon the holsters of his uncle's saddle.*

'Certainly not, certainly not,' exclaimed Mazarin. '*Diavolo!** my dear friend, you are going to spoil everything. Things are going on marvellously well, on the contrary! I know your Frenchmen as if I had made them from the first to the last. They sing; they will pay. During the League of which Guitaut was speaking just now, they only chanted Mass; so everything went badly. Come, Guitaut, come, and let us see if they keep as good watch at the Quinze-Vingts as at the Barrière des Sergents.'

And saluting Comminges with his hand, he rejoined d'Artagnan, who resumed the head of his little troop, followed immediately by Guitaut and the cardinal, who were followed in their turn by the rest of the escort.

'Just so,' muttered Comminges, looking at him as he rode away; 'I forgot that provided they pay, that is all *he* wants.'

The party passed through the Rue St Honoré, meeting continually large groups, in which they were discussing the edicts of that day. They pitied the young king, who was ruining his people in this way without being aware of it; they threw the whole blame on Mazarin; they talked of addresses to the Duc d'Orléans and the Prince de Condé; they praised highly Blancmesnil and Broussel. D'Artagnan passed through the midst of these groups as unconcernedly as if he and his horse were of iron. Mazarin and Guitaut conversed in undertones; the musketeers, who finally had recognized the cardinal, followed in silence. On arriving at the Rue St Thomas du Louvre,* where was the post of Quinze-Vingts, Guitaut called a sub-officer, who came to report.

'Well?' demanded Guitaut.

'Ah, Captain,' said the officer, 'all is quiet in this quarter, if I did not think that something is going on in yonder house,' pointing to a magnificent residence situated on the spot since occupied by the Vaudeville.*

'In that hotel? But that is the Hôtel Rambouillet,'* cried Guitaut.

'I don't know whether it is the Hôtel Rambouillet, but I do know that I observed a great number of suspicious-looking people go in there.'

'Nonsense!' exclaimed Guitaut, with a burst of laughter, 'those are poets.'

'Come, Guitaut,' said Mazarin, 'be good enough not to speak so irreverently of these gentlemen; you do not know that I was a poet also in my youth, and wrote verses in the style of Benserade.'*

'You, my Lord?'

'Yes, I. Shall I repeat some of them?'

'As you please, my Lord! I don't understand Italian.'

'Yes, but you understand French, my brave Guitaut,' replied Mazarin, laying his hand amicably upon his shoulder; 'and whatever order is given you in that language, you will execute?'

'Certainly, my Lord, as I have always done, provided that it comes from the queen.'

'Yes, ah, yes!' said Mazarin, biting his lips; 'I know your entire devotion to her Majesty.'

'I have been a captain in her Guards for twenty years.'

'Let us go on, M. d'Artagnan,' said the cardinal, 'everything is quiet in this quarter.'

D'Artagnan took the head of his detachment without a word, and with the passive obedience which marks the character of an old soldier. He led the way towards the hill of St Roch, where was the third post, passing through the Rue Richelieu and the Rue Villedot. It was the most isolated, for it almost touched the ramparts, and the city was thinly inhabited in this quarter.

'Who is in command here?' asked the cardinal.

'Villequier,' replied Guitaut.

'*Diavolo!* Speak to him yourself; we are on bad terms since you had the order to arrest the Duc de Beaufort. He claimed that the honour belonged to him as captain of the king's Guards.'

'I know it well, and have told him a hundred times that he was wrong; since the king could not give him this order, as he was then scarcely four years old.'

'Yes, but I could have given it for him, Guitaut; and I preferred you.'

Guitaut, without replying, rode forward and desired the sentinel to call M. de Villequier, who forthwith appeared.

'Ah! it is you, Guitaut,' said the officer, in that tone of ill-humour habitual to him; 'what the devil are you doing here?

'I come to ask you if there is anything new in this quarter.'

'What do you expect? People cry out, "Long live the king! down with Mazarin!" that's nothing new; we've been used to those cries for some time.'

'And you play chorus,' replied Guitaut, laughing.

'Faith, I've sometimes a great desire to do it! I think they are right, Guitaut. I would willingly give five years of my pay—which they don't pay me, by the way—to make the king five years older.'

'Truly! and what would happen if the king were five years older?'

'It would happen that the moment the king comes of age he will issue his orders himself, and that it is pleasanter to obey the grandson of Henry IV than the son of Pietro Mazarini.* S'death! I would die willingly for the king; but if I was killed on account of Mazarin, as your nephew was near being today, there is no Paradise, however well placed I might be there, which would ever console me for it.'

'Very well, M. de Villequier,' here Mazarin interposed, 'be assured that I shall bear in mind your devotion to the king.' Then turning to his escort, 'Come, gentlemen, everything is well; let us return.'

'Hold,' exclaimed Villequier, 'Mazarin was there! so much the better. I have been wanting for a long time to tell him to his face what I think of him. You have given me the opportunity, Guitaut, and I thank you for it, although your intentions towards me may not have been of the best.' And turning upon his heel, he re-entered the guard-house whistling an air of the

Fronde, while Mazarin returned to the Palais-Royal in a thoughtful mood. What he had successively heard from Comminges, Guitaut, and Villequier confirmed him in the conviction that in case of grave events there would be no one for him but the queen; and yet the queen had so often abandoned her friends that her support appeared sometimes to the minister, despite the precautions he had taken, very uncertain and very precarious.

During the whole of this nocturnal ride—during nearly an hour—the cardinal, while studying the characters of Comminges, Guitaut, and Villequier, had closely examined one man. This man, who remained unmoved when menaced by the mob, not a muscle of whose face had changed at the pleasantries of Mazarin nor at those directed against him—this man seemed to the cardinal a being apart, and well fitted for the events then occurring; and especially for those which were on the eve of taking place.

Besides, the name of d'Artagnan was not entirely unknown to him; and although Mazarin had not arrived in France until 1634 or 1635—that is, seven or eight years after the events we have related in a preceding story[1]—it seemed to the cardinal that he had heard this name mentioned as that of a man who in an adventure he could not at that moment recall had distinguished himself as a model of courage, address, and devotion.

This idea so impressed him that he resolved to seek information without delay; but it was not to d'Artagnan himself that he should address these enquiries. In the few words the lieutenant of Musketeers had spoken the cardinal had recognized his Gascon origin. Now, the Italians and the Gascons know each other too well and are too much alike to place much reliance upon what they say of themselves. So on arriving at the walls of the garden of the Palais-Royal, the cardinal knocked at a little door situated very near where today is the Café de Foy,* and after thanking d'Artagnan, and requesting him to wait in the court of the Palais-Royal, made a sign to Guitaut to follow him. Both dismounted, gave the reins of their horses to the lackey who opened the door, and disappeared in the garden.

[1] In *The Three Musketeers.**

'My dear Guitaut,' said the cardinal, leaning upon the arm of the old captain of the Guards, 'you told me just now that you have been twenty years in the queen's service.'

'Yes, that is true,' returned Guitaut.

'Now, my dear Guitaut,' continued the cardinal, 'I have remarked that in addition to your courage, which is incontestable, and your fidelity, which is proof against everything, you have an admirable memory.'

'You have remarked that, my Lord?' said the captain of the Guards; 'the deuce! so much the worse for me.'

'How is that?'

'Without doubt one of the first qualities of a courtier is to know how to forget.'

'But you are not a courtier, Guitaut, you are a brave soldier— one of those captains, of whom a few remain, of the times of Henry IV, but of whom soon unfortunately none will be left.'

'*Peste*, my Lord! have you brought me here with you to draw my horoscope?'

'No,' said Mazarin, laughing, 'I brought you here to ask whether you noticed our lieutenant of Musketeers.'

'M. d'Artagnan?'

'Yes.'

'I had no need to notice him, my Lord; he is an old acquaintance.'

'What kind of a man is he, then?'

'Eh!' said Guitaut, surprised at the question; 'he is a Gascon.'

'Yes, I know that; but I wished to ask if he is a man in whom one can put confidence.'

'Tréville holds him in the highest esteem; and Tréville, as you know, is one of the queen's greatest friends.'

'I wished to know whether he was a man who had been proved.'

'If you mean as a brave soldier, I believe I can answer yes. At the siege of Rochelle, at Suze, at Perpignan,* I have heard it said that he did more than his duty.'

'But you know, Guitaut, we poor ministers often want men of other qualities besides courage; we need men of adroitness. Was not M. d'Artagnan, in the time of the cardinal, engaged in some intrigue from which according to public report he extricated himself very skilfully?'

'My Lord, as to this matter,' said Guitaut, who perceived that the cardinal wished to make him talk, 'I am forced to say to your Eminence that I only know what public report has also told you. I never meddle with intrigues; and if I have occasionally become a confidant in the intrigues of others; as the secret is not mine, my Lord, you will approve of my keeping it for those who have confided it to me.'

Mazarin shook his head.

'Ah!' he said, 'some ministers are very fortunate, and find out all they wish to know.'

'My Lord,' replied Guitaut, 'such ministers do not weigh all men in the same scales; they get their information as to warlike matters from military men, as to intrigues from intriguers. Apply to some intriguer of the period of which you speak, and you will draw from him all you wish to know, by paying for it, be it well understood.'

'Eh, *pardieu!*' replied Mazarin, with a grimace he always made when the question of money was touched upon in the way used by Guitaut, 'we will pay—if there is no means of doing otherwise.'

'Is it seriously that my Lord asks me to name a man who has been engaged in all the intrigues of that period?'

'*Per Baccho!*' replied Mazarin, who began to grow impatient, 'it is an hour since I have asked any other question, iron-headed as you are.'

'There is one man for whom I can answer, if he will speak out.'

'That is my affair.'

'Ah, my Lord! it is not always easy to make people talk about matters of which they do not wish to speak.'

'Bah! with patience one succeeds. Well! this man; it is——'

'It is the Comte de Rochefort.'*

'The Comte de Rochefort!'

'Unfortunately, he has disappeared these four or five years, and I do not know what has become of him.'

'But *I* know, Guitaut,' said Mazarin.

'Then why did your Eminence complain just now of knowing nothing?'

'And,' said Mazarin, 'you think that Rochefort——'

'He was a tool of the cardinal, my Lord; but I warn you, it will cost you dearly. The cardinal was prodigal with his creatures.'

'Yes, yes, Guitaut,' said Mazarin, 'Richelieu was a great man, but he had that defect. Thanks, Guitaut, I shall profit by your advice this very evening.'

And as at this moment they arrived at the court of the Palais-Royal, the cardinal saluted Guitaut with his hand, and approached an officer who was promenading up and down. It was d'Artagnan, awaiting the return of the cardinal, as he had been ordered.

'Come, M. d'Artagnan,' said Mazarin, in his sweetest tone, 'I have an order to give you.'

D'Artagnan bowed, followed the cardinal up the secret stair-case, and a moment afterwards found himself in the cabinet whence he had set out. The cardinal seated himself before his desk, and took a sheet of paper upon which he wrote several lines. D'Artagnan, erect, imperturbable, waited without impatience and without curiosity. He had become a military automaton, acting, or rather obeying, at the touch of a spring.

The cardinal folded the letter, and put his seal upon it.

'M. d'Artagnan,' he said, 'you will carry this despatch to the Bastille* and bring back the person to whom it refers; you will take a carriage, an escort, and you must guard carefully the prisoner.'

D'Artagnan took the letter, carried his hand to his hat, pivoted upon his heels like a drill sergeant, went out, and a moment after was heard commanding briefly in his monotonous tone, 'Four men for escort, a carriage, my horse.'

Five minutes afterwards, the wheels of the carriage and the sound of horses' hoofs were heard upon the pavement of the court.

III

TWO OLD ENEMIES

D'ARTAGNAN arrived at the Bastille as it was striking half-past eight. His visit was announced to the governor, who, learning that he came from the minister with an order, went to receive him at the outside steps. The governor of the Bastille was then

M. du Tremblay, brother of the famous capuchin, Joseph—that dreaded favourite of Richelieu who was called his Grey Eminence.

While the Marshal de Bassompierre* was in the Bastille, where he remained twelve whole years, his companions, in their dreams of liberty, said to one another, 'As for me, I shall go out of prison at such a time,' and another at such and such a time, but Bassompierre used to say: 'And I, gentlemen, shall leave only when M. du Tremblay leaves,' meaning that at the death of the cardinal, Tremblay would certainly lose his position at the Bastille, and Bassompierre would regain his own at court.

His prediction came near being fulfilled, but in another way than Bassompierre had thought; for on the death of the cardinal, contrary to all expectation, everything went on as before— M. du Tremblay was not removed, and Bassompierre was not released.

M. du Tremblay was still governor of the Bastille when d'Artagnan presented himself to execute the minister's order; he received him with extreme politeness, and as he was about sitting down to the table, he invited d'Artagnan to join him.

'I should do so with the greatest pleasure,' was the reply; 'but if I am not mistaken, there is upon the envelope of the letter the words, "In great haste".'

'You are right,' said Tremblay. 'Holloa, Major! Let them bring down Number two hundred and fifty-six.'

On entering the Bastille one ceased to be a man, and became only a number. D'Artagnan shuddered at the rattling of the keys; so he remained in the saddle without wishing to dismount, looking at the great bars, the strong windows, and the immense walls, which he had never seen except from the other side of the moat, and which had caused him a great terror some twenty years before. A bell sounded.

'I must leave you,' said Tremblay to him. 'They call me to sign the release of the prisoner. I shall hope to see you again, M. d'Artagnan.'

'May the devil annihilate me if I return thy wish!' muttered d'Artagnan, accompanying the imprecation with the most gracious smile. 'I am already ill from stopping five minutes in the courtyard. Come, come! I see that I should prefer to die upon straw, which will probably happen to me, than to amass a fortune of ten thousand livres* of income by being governor of the Bastille.'

He had scarcely finished this soliloquy when the prisoner appeared. On seeing him, d'Artagnan made a movement of surprise which he checked immediately. The prisoner entered the carriage without appearing to have recognized d'Artagnan.

'Gentlemen,' said d'Artagnan to the four musketeers, 'I am directed to exercise the greatest watchfulness in regard to the prisoner, and since there are no locks to the carriage doors, I shall sit beside him. M. de Lillebonne, have the goodness to lead my horse by the bridle.'

'Willingly, Lieutenant,' replied the person addressed.

D'Artagnan dismounted, gave the bridle of his horse to the musketeer, entered the carriage, and placing himself at the side of the prisoner, said in a voice in which it was impossible to detect the least emotion, 'To the Palais-Royal, and at a trot.'

Immediately the carriage started, and d'Artagnan, profiting by the obscurity of the archway under which they were passing, threw himself upon the neck of the prisoner. 'Rochefort!' he exclaimed, 'you! it is really you! I am not mistaken!'

'D'Artagnan!' cried Rochefort, in his turn astonished.

'Ah, my poor friend!' continued d'Artagnan. 'Not having seen you for four or five years, I believed you to be dead.'

'Faith,' said Rochefort, 'there is no great difference, I think, between a dead man and one buried. Now, I am buried, or very nearly.'

'And for what crime are you in the Bastille?'

'Do you wish me to tell you the truth?'

'Yes.'

'Well, then, I know nothing about it.'

'Have you any distrust of me, Rochefort?'

'No, on the honour of a gentleman; for it is impossible that I am imprisoned for the charge alleged.'

'What charge?'

'As night-robber.'

'You, night-robber! Rochefort, you are jesting?'

'I understand. This demands explanation, does it not?'

'I should think so.'

'Well, here is what happened: One evening after a debauch at Reinard's,* near the Tuileries, with the Duc d'Harcourt, Fontrailles, Rieux and others, the Duc d'Harcourt proposed going to pull cloaks* on the Pont Neuf. It is, you know, an amusement that the Duc d'Orléans had made very much the fashion.'

'Were you insane, Rochefort? At your age?'

'No, I was tipsy; and nevertheless, as the amusement seemed to me indifferent, I proposed to the Chevalier de Rieux to be spectators instead of actors, and in order to see the scene from the first row of boxes to mount upon the bronze horse. No sooner said than done. Thanks to the spurs which served us for stirrups, we were in a moment perched upon its rump. We were grandly placed, and saw everything charmingly. Already four or five cloaks had been carried off with a dexterity unsurpassed and without those losing them daring to say a word, when some imbecile less patient than the others thought fit to cry "Guard! guard!" and drew towards us a patrol of archers. D'Harcourt, Fontrailles, and the others take flight; Rieux wishes to do the same; I hold him back, saying that they will not come to dislodge us where we are. He does not listen, puts his foot on the spur to descend; the spur breaks; he falls, fractures a leg, and instead of keeping silent, begins to cry out like a man being hanged. I wish to jump down in my turn, but it is too late, and I leap into the arms of the archers, who conduct me to the Châtelet,* where I sleep soundly, quite sure that in the morning I shall come out. The day passes; the next day passes; eight days pass. I write to the cardinal. The same day they come to find me, and conduct me to the Bastille. It is five years that I have been there. Do you believe that it can be for committing the sacrilege of mounting *en croupe* behind Henry IV?'

'No, you are right, my dear Rochefort; it cannot be that. But you are going to learn, probably, the reason why.'

'Ah, yes—for I have forgotten to ask you where you are taking me.'

'To the cardinal.'

'What does he want of me?'

'I know nothing about it, since I was ignorant even that it was you whom I was to bring.'

'Impossible. You, a favourite.'

'A favourite, I!' exclaimed d'Artagnan. 'Ah, my poor count, I am more the cadet of Gascony than when I saw you at Meung,* you know, some twenty-two years ago! Alas!' And a great sigh finished his phrase.

'Nevertheless, you come with an order?'

'Because by chance I happened to be in the ante-chamber, and the cardinal called for me as he would for another; but I am still lieutenant of Musketeers,* and if I count aright it is nearly twenty-one years that I have been so.'

'In fine, no misfortune has befallen you, that is much.'

'And what misfortune do you think could happen to me? As says a certain Latin verse, which I have forgotten, or rather poorly learned—

> The lightning does not strike the valleys.

And I am a valley, my dear Rochefort, and one of the lowest kind.'

'Then Mazarin is still Mazarin?'

'More than ever, my friend; they say that he is married to the queen.'

'Married?'

'If not her husband, he is certainly her lover.'

'To resist Buckingham and yield to a Mazarin!'

'Such are women!' replied d'Artagnan, philosophically.

'Women, true, but not queens.'

'Egad! in these affairs queens are women twice over.'

'And M. de Beaufort, is he still in prison?'

'Yes; why?'

'Ah! because, being well disposed towards me, he would have been able to extricate me from this affair.'

'You are probably nearer being free than he; so it is you who will extricate him.'

'Then, the war——'

'We are going to have it.'

'With Spain?'

'No, with Paris.'

'What do you mean?'

'Do you hear those musket-shots?'

'Yes; well, then?'

'Well, it is the citizens knocking the ball about before the game begins.'

'Do you really think one could do anything with these *bourgeois?*'

'Certainly they are promising; and if they had a leader to unite all these groups——'

'How unfortunate not to be free!'

'Eh, *mon Dieu!* don't be downcast. Since Mazarin has sent for you it is because he wants you; and if he wants you, well, I congratulate you. It is many years since any one has wanted me; so you see where I am.'

'Complain, then, I advise you.'

'Listen, Rochefort, a compact——'

'What is it?'

'You know we are good friends?'

'Egad! I bear the marks of our friendship—three cuts of your sword!'*

'Very well, if you are restored to favour, don't forget me.'

'On the honour of Rochefort, but on condition of a return.'

'It's agreed; there's my hand.'

'Therefore, the first occasion that you find to speak of me——'

'I speak in your favour; and you?'

'I do the same.'

'*A propos*, and your friends, must I speak of them also?'

'What friends?'

'Athos, Porthos and Aramis. Have you forgotten them?'

'Almost.'

'What's become of them?'

'I know nothing about it.'

'Truly?'

'Ah, *mon Dieu*, yes! We separated, as you know; they are alive, and that's all I can tell you. From time to time I hear of them indirectly. But in what part of the world they are, devil take me if I know at all. No, on my honour, I have no other friend than you, Rochefort.'

'And the illustrious—what's the name of that young man whom I made sergeant in the regiment of Piedmont?'

'Planchet?'*

'Yes, and the illustrious Planchet; what's become of him?'

'He has married a confectioner's shop in the Rue des Lombards, for he was a youth always fond of sweet things; so he is a citizen of Paris, and in all probability engaged in the insurrection at this moment. You will see that this queer fellow will be alderman before I shall be captain.'

'Come, my dear d'Artagnan, have a little courage! It is when one is lowest on the wheel of fortune that the wheel turns and elevates us. This evening your lot is going, perhaps, to change.'

'Amen!' exclaimed d'Artagnan, stopping the carriage.

'What are you doing?' demanded Rochefort.

'We have arrived, and I don't wish that they should see me come out of your carriage. We are not acquainted.'

'You are right. Adieu.'

'Remember your promise.'

And d'Artagnan re-mounted his horse and took the head of the escort. Five minutes afterwards they entered the courtyard of the Palais-Royal. D'Artagnan conducted the prisoner by the great staircase and through the ante-chamber and corridor. Arrived at the door of Mazarin's cabinet, he was about to have himself announced when Rochefort laid his hand upon his shoulder.

'D'Artagnan,' said Rochefort, 'do you wish me to confess to you one thing I was thinking about during our whole drive on seeing the groups of citizens who met us, and who regarded you and your four men with angry looks?'

'Speak?' answered d'Artagnan.

'It is that I had only to cry "Help!" to cause you and your escort to be cut to pieces, and then I should have been free.'

'Why didn't you do it?' asked d'Artagnan.

'Come, then!' returned Rochefort, 'our sworn friendship! Ah! if it had been another than you who brought me I don't say——'

D'Artagnan nodded.

'Can it be that Rochefort has become better than I?' said he to himself, and he caused himself to be announced to the minister.

'Let M. de Rochefort come in,' said the impatient voice of Mazarin, as soon as he heard the two names pronounced, 'and beg M. d'Artagnan to wait; I have not yet finished with him.'

These words rendered d'Artagnan radiant. As he had said, it was a long time since anyone had had need of him, and this persistence of Mazarin in respect to him seemed a happy augury.

As to Rochefort, these words only put him thoroughly upon his guard. He entered the apartment, and found Mazarin sitting at the table dressed in his ordinary garb—that of a monsignor, which was nearly that of the abbé's of that day, excepting that he wore stockings and cloak of a violet colour. The doors closed. Rochefort looked at Mazarin furtively, and surprised a glance of the minister meeting his own.

The minister was always the same—his hair well arranged, curled, and perfumed, and thanks to his nicety of dress, he looked less than his age. As to Rochefort, it was different. The five years passed in prison had much aged this worthy friend of M. de Richelieu; his dark locks had become entirely white, and the bronzed colours of his complexion had given place to a pallor which seemed to indicate debility. On seeing him, Mazarin shook his head slightly, as much as to say, 'This is a man who does not appear to me any longer good for much.'

After a somewhat long silence, but which seemed an age to Rochefort, Mazarin drew from a bundle of papers an open letter, and showing it to the count, said—

'I have found there a letter in which you sue for liberty, M. de Rochefort. You are, then, in prison?'

Rochefort trembled at this question. 'But,' said he, 'I thought your Eminence knew it better than any one.'

'I? oh, no! There is still in the Bastille a crowd of prisoners who have been there from the time of M. de Richelieu whose names even I do not know.'

'Oh, but in my case it is different, my Lord! and you knew mine, since it was upon the order of your Eminence that I was transferred from the Châtelet to the Bastille.'

'You think so?'

'I am certain of it.'

'Ah, yes! I think I remember it. Did you not once refuse to undertake a journey to Brussels for the queen?'*

'Ah, ah!' said Rochefort, 'this, then, is the true reason? I have been seeking for it five years. Simpleton that I am I had not found it.'

'But I do not say that it was the cause of your arrest; I merely ask you this question: Did you not refuse to go to Brussels for the queen, while you had consented to go there for the service of the late cardinal?'

'It is exactly because I had been there for the service of the late cardinal that I could not return there for that of the queen. I had been at Brussels at a fearful moment. It was the time of the conspiracy of Chalais.* I had been there to intercept the correspondence between Chalais and the archduke, and already at that time, when recognized, I barely escaped being torn to pieces. How could I return there? I should injure the queen instead of serving her.'

'Well, you understand how the best intentions are misconstrued, my dear M. de Rochefort. The queen saw in your refusal only a refusal pure and simple; she had also much to complain of you under the late cardinal—her Majesty the queen——'

Rochefort smiled contemptuously. 'It is precisely because I had served faithfully the Cardinal Richelieu against the queen, that, he being dead, you ought to comprehend, my Lord, that I would serve you faithfully against all the world.'

'I, M. de Rochefort,' said Mazarin, 'I am not like M. de Richelieu, who aimed at the whole power; I am only a minister who wants no servants, being myself but a servant of the queen. Now, the queen is very sensitive; she knew of your refusal; she took it for a declaration of war, and knowing you to be a man of superior talent and therefore dangerous, my dear M. de Rochefort, she ordered me to make sure of you. That is the reason for your being shut up in the Bastille.'

'Well, my Lord, it seems to me,' said Rochefort, 'that it is by an error that I find myself at the Bastille——'

'Yes, yes,' replied Mazarin, 'all that can be arranged. You are the man to comprehend certain affairs; and once understood, to act with energy.'

'Such was the opinion of Cardinal Richelieu; and my admiration for that great man increases, since you are kind enough to say that it is also your opinion.'

'It is true,' returned Mazarin, 'the cardinal was a great politician, and therein lay his vast superiority over me. I am a man entirely simple and without subterfuge; that's my disadvantage. I am of a frankness wholly French.'

Rochefort compressed his lips to prevent a smile.

'I come now to the point. I have need of good friends, of faithful servants. When I say *I* need, I mean the queen needs them. I do nothing except by her commands; pray understand that—not like M. le Cardinal Richelieu who did everything according to his own caprice. So I shall never be a great man like him, but in exchange I am a simple soul, M. de Rochefort, and hope to prove it to you.'

Rochefort knew well that silky voice, in which from time to time could be heard a slight lisp, resembling the hissing of a viper.

'I am ready to believe you, my Lord,' said he, 'although for my part I have had few proofs of this simplicity of which your Eminence speaks. Do not forget, my Lord,' continued Rochefort, seeing the movement the minister tried to repress—'do not forget that I have been five years in the Bastille, and that nothing gives one falser ideas than looking at things through the bars of a prison.'

'Ah, M. de Rochefort, I have already told you that I had nothing to do with your imprisonment. The queen—the pettishness of a woman and of a princess. But that passes away as suddenly as it comes, and is forgotten.'

'I can conceive, my Lord, that she has forgotten it,—she who has passed five years at the Palais-Royal in the midst of fêtes and courtiers; but I who have passed them in the Bastille——'

'Ah, *mon Dieu!* my dear M. de Rochefort! Do you think the Palais-Royal is the abode of gaiety? No. We have had our great annoyances there, I assure you. But let us speak no longer of all that. As for me, I play an open hand, as I always do. Come, are you on our side, M. de Rochefort?'

'You should understand, my Lord, that I can desire nothing better, but I am entirely ignorant of the state of affairs. At the

Bastille one talks politics only with soldiers and gaolers, and you have no idea, my Lord, how little that sort of people knows of passing events. I am of M. de Bassompierre's party. Is he still one of the seventeen lords?'*

'He is dead, sir, and it is a great loss. He was devoted to the queen, and men of loyalty are rare.'

'Zounds, I think so,' said Rochefort, 'and when you find them you send them to the Bastille.'

'But if that is so,' said Mazarin, 'what proves devotion?'

'Deeds,' said Rochefort.

'Ah, yes! deeds,' returned the minister, reflecting, 'but where to find these men of deeds?'

Rochefort shook his head. 'They are never wanting, my Lord, only you don't know how to seek for them.'

'I don't know how to seek for them! what do you mean, my dear M. de Rochefort? Come, instruct me. You should have learned much in your intimacy with the late cardinal. Ah! he was a great man.'

'Will my Lord be angry if I read him a lesson?'

'I, never! you know you may say anything to me. I try to be beloved and not to be feared.'

'Well, my Lord, there is a proverb written on the wall of my cell with the point of a nail.'

'And what is the proverb?' asked Mazarin.

'Here it is, my Lord: "Like master——" '

'I know it; "like valet".'

'No; "like servant". It is a little change that those devoted characters of whom I was speaking just now introduced for their private satisfaction.'

'Well! what does the proverb mean?'

'It means that M. de Richelieu was able to find trusty servants—dozens and dozens of them.'

'He!—the mark for every poniard! he who passed his life in warding off the blows forever aimed at him!'

'But he *did* ward them off, and yet they were rudely given. For if he had active enemies, he had true friends.'

'Ah,' cried Mazarin, 'that is all that I ask.'

'I have known persons,' continued Rochefort, who thought the moment arrived to keep his word with d'Artagnan—'I have

known persons, who by their address have a hundred times put
at fault the penetration of the cardinal, by their valour defeated
his guards and his spies; persons, who without money, without
support, without credit, preserved to a crowned head its crown,
and made the cardinal beg for mercy.'

'But these persons of whom you speak,' said Mazarin, smiling
to himself because Rochefort reached the point to which he
wished to lead him, 'these persons were not devoted to the
cardinal, since they fought against him.'

'No, for they had been better recompensed; but they had the
misfortune to be devoted to this same queen for whom just
now you were asking servants.'

'But how could you know all these things.'

'I know them because these persons were my enemies at that
time, because they fought against me, because I did them all
the harm I could, because they returned it of their best, because
one of them with whom I was more particularly engaged gave
me a sword-cut, some seven years ago—the third from the same
hand, the close of an old account.'

'Ah,' said Mazarin, with an admirable simplicity, 'if I only
knew such men!'

'Eh, my Lord, you have had one of them at your very door
for more than six years, and during six years you have judged
him good for nothing.'*

'Who is it?'

'M. d'Artagnan.'

'That Gascon!' cried Mazarin, with an air of surprise perfectly counterfeited.

'That Gascon saved a queen, and made M. de Richelieu
confess that in point of ability, address, and political skill he
was himself only a scholar.'

'In very truth?'

'It is as I have the honour to tell it to your Excellence.'

'Relate to me how it happened, then, my dear M. de
Rochefort.'

'It is quite difficult, my Lord,' said he, smiling.

'He will relate it to me himself, then.'

'I doubt it, my Lord.'

'And why so?'

'Because the secret is not his own; because, as I have told you, the secret concerns a great queen.'

'And he was alone in accomplishing such an enterprise as this?'

'No, my Lord, he had three friends, three brave men who aided him; such brave men as you were seeking just now.'

'And these four men were united, you say?'

'As if these four men had been but one, as if their four hearts had pulsated in one breast. So what have they not accomplished, those four!'

'My dear M. de Rochefort, truly you pique my curiosity to a point I cannot describe. Can you not narrate to me this story?'

'No; but I can tell you a tale—a veritable fairy tale, I answer for it, my Lord.'

'Oh, tell it to me, M. de Rochefort; I am fond of tales.'

'You really wish it, my Lord?' said Rochefort, attempting to discover a motive in that cunning and crafty face.

'Yes.'

'Well, listen, then. Once upon a time there lived a queen—a powerful queen, the queen of one of the greatest kingdoms of the world—whom a great minister wished much to injure, though he had before loved her too well. (Do not try, my Lord; you cannot guess who it is. All this happened long before you came into the kingdom where this queen reigned.) Now, there came to the court an ambassador so brave, so magnificent, so elegant, that every woman lost her heart to him; and the queen herself, in remembrance doubtless of the manner in which he had treated affairs of State, had the indiscretion to give him certain personal ornaments so rare that they could not be replaced.

'As these ornaments were a gift of the king, the minister persuaded him to request the queen to wear them at an approaching ball. It is useless to tell you, my Lord, that the minister knew with certainty that these ornaments went with the ambassador; and the ambassador was then far away across the seas. The great queen was lost!—lost like the lowest of her subjects—for she was falling from the height of all her grandeur.'

'Truly!'

'Well, my Lord, four men resolved to save her. These four men were not princes, they were not dukes, neither were they men of influence—they were not even rich men. They were four soldiers having great hearts, strong arms, and free swords. They set out. The minister knew of their departure, and had posted people upon the road to prevent their arrival at their destination. Three of them were disabled by numerous assailants; one of them alone arrived at the port, killing or wounding those who wished to stop him, crossed the sea, and brought back the set of ornaments to the great queen, who was able to wear them upon her shoulder on the day designated, and this nearly ruined the minister. What do you say of this deed, my Lord?'*

'It is splendid!' said Mazarin, musing.

'Well, I know of ten similar ones.'

Mazarin did not speak; he was reflecting. Five or six minutes passed.

'You have nothing further to ask of me, my Lord?' said Rochefort.

'Yes; and M. d'Artagnan was one of these four men, you say?'

'It was he who led the enterprise.'

'And the others, who were they?'

'My Lord, permit me to leave it for M. d'Artagnan to name them to you. They were his friends, not mine; he only would have some influence over them, and I do not even know them under their true names.'*

'You distrust me, M. de Rochefort. Well, I wish to be frank to the end: I want him, and you and all.'

'Begin with me, my Lord, since you have sent to bring me, and I am here; then you can speak of the others. You will not be surprised at my curiosity; when one has been five years in prison, one is not sorry to know where one is to be sent.'

'You, my dear M. de Rochefort, shall have the post of confidence; you shall go to Vincennes, where M. de Beaufort is prisoner. You will guard him well for me. Well! What is the matter with you?'

'The matter is that you propose to me a thing impossible,' said Rochefort, shaking his head with a disappointed air.

'How, an impossible thing! And why is this thing impossible?'

'Because M. de Beaufort is one of my friends, or rather I am one of his. Have you forgotten, my Lord, that it was he who was responsible for me to the queen?'

'M. de Beaufort, since then, has been the enemy of the State.'

'Yes, my Lord, it is possible; but as I am neither king nor queen nor minister, he is not my enemy, and I cannot accept the post you offer me.'

'That is what you call devotion? I congratulate you upon it. Your devotion does not carry you too far, M. de Rochefort.'

'And then, my Lord,' returned Rochefort, 'you will understand that to come out of the Bastille to enter at Vincennes is only a change of prisons.'

'Say at once that you are of the party of M. de Beaufort, and this will be more frank on your part.'

'My Lord, I have been so long shut up that I am only of one party—the party of the open air. Employ me in any other matter; send me on a mission, occupy me actively, but on the highways, if possible.'

'My dear M. de Rochefort,' said Mazarin, with his bantering air, 'your zeal carries you away; you think yourself still a young man, because your heart is yet young, but your strength fails you. Believe me, then, what you want now is rest. Holloa, some one!'

'You decide, then, nothing about me, my Lord?'

'On the contrary, I have decided.'

Bernouin entered.

'Call an officer,' said he; 'and remain near me,' he added in a low tone.

The officer came in. Mazarin wrote a few words which he gave to him; then bowing, 'Adieu, M. de Rochefort,' said he.

Rochefort bent low.

'I see, my Lord, that I am to be taken back to the Bastille.'

'You are sagacious.'

'I return there, my Lord; but I repeat it, you are wrong not to know how to employ me.'

'You, the friend of my enemies!'

'What do you wish? It was only necessary to make me the enemy of your enemies.'

'Do you think that it is only you who can serve me, M. de Rochefort? Believe me, I shall find others who will be worth as much.'

'I wish you may, my Lord.'

'Very well, you can go! *A propos*, it is useless for you to write me again, M. de Rochefort; your letters would be wasted.'

'I have pulled the chestnuts out of the fire,' muttered Rochefort, on retiring; 'and if d'Artagnan is not content with me when I relate to him presently the panegyrics I have bestowed upon him he will be difficult to please. But where the devil are they taking me?'

In fact, they re-conducted Rochefort by the little staircase, instead of through the antechamber where d'Artagnan was waiting. In the courtyard he found the carriage and his escort of four men, but he looked around in vain for his friend.

'Ah, ah!' said Rochefort to himself; 'this changes things, indeed! and if there are still as large crowds in the streets— well, we will try to prove to Mazarin that we are still good for some other business, thank God, than to guard a prisoner.'

And he jumped into the carriage as lightly as if he was a man of only five and twenty.

IV

ANNE OF AUSTRIA AT THE AGE OF FORTY-SIX

LEFT alone with Bernouin, Mazarin remained a moment thoughtful. He had learned much, and yet he did not know enough. Mazarin was a cheat at cards. That detail Brienne has preserved for us; he called that using his opportunities. He resolved not to commence the game with d'Artagnan until he knew well all his adversary's cards.

'My Lord orders nothing?' asked Bernouin.

'Yes, indeed,' replied Mazarin; 'light me, I am going to the queen.'

Bernouin took a candlestick and led the way. There was a secret passage which connected the apartments and cabinet of Mazarin with the apartments of the queen. It was through this corridor that the cardinal passed to visit, at any hour, Anne of Austria.[1]

On arriving in the bedchamber where this passage ended, Bernouin met Madame Beauvais. Madame Beauvais and Bernouin were the confidants of these superannuated amours; and Madame Beauvais undertook to announce the cardinal to Anne of Austria, who was in her oratory with the young king, Louis XIV.

Anne of Austria, seated in a great armchair, her elbow resting upon a table, and her head supported by her hand, was regarding the royal child, who, lying upon the carpet, was turning the leaves of a great book full of battle pictures. Anne of Austria was a queen who knew well how to weary herself with dignity. She remained sometimes whole hours retired in her chamber or her oratory without reading or praying. The book with which the king played was a Quintus Curtius enriched by engravings representing the feats of arms of Alexander.*

Madame Beauvais appeared at the door of the oratory and announced the Cardinal Mazarin. The child raised himself upon one knee, frowned, and looking at his mother, 'Why then,' said he, 'does he enter thus without asking for an audience?'

Anne coloured slightly.

'It is important,' replied she, 'that a prime minister, in these unsettled times, should come to render account at any hour of all that is happening, to the queen, without exciting the curiosity or remarks of the whole court.'

'But it seems to me that M. de Richelieu did not enter in this manner,' returned the persistent child.

'How can you recollect what M. de Richelieu did? You could not know it; you were too young.'

'I do not recollect it; I have asked, and they have told me about it.'

[1] This passage is still to be seen in the Palais-Royal (Memoirs of the Princesse Palatine).

'And who has told you that?' replied Anne of Austria, with a movement of anger poorly disguised.

'I know that I ought never to name the persons who answer my questions,' responded the child, 'or I should learn nothing more.'

At this moment Mazarin entered; the king arose, took his book, closed it, and carried it to the table, near which he continued standing in order to compel Mazarin to remain standing also.

Mazarin watched with his keen eyes all this scene, and seemed to ask an explanation of what had preceded it. He bent respectfully before the queen, and made a low inclination to the king, who replied by a slight bend of the head; but a look from his mother reproved him for this expression of the dislike which from his infancy Louis XIV had entertained towards the cardinal, and he received with a smile upon his lips the homage of the minister. Anne of Austria sought to divine from the countenance of Mazarin the cause of this unexpected visit, the cardinal usually not coming to her apartments until every one had retired. The minister gave a slight nod; then addressing Madame Beauvais, 'It is time that the king should retire to rest,' said she; 'call Laporte.'

Already, before this, the queen had several times told the young Louis that he must retire; but each time the child had coaxingly begged leave to remain. This time he made no remark; he only compressed his lips, and grew pale. An instant afterwards Laporte entered. The child went directly to him without embracing his mother.

'Well, Louis,' said Anne, 'why do you not embrace me?'

'I thought you were angry with me, Madame; you send me away.'

'I do not send you away; you have just had the smallpox,* and are still weak, and I fear that sitting up late may fatigue you.'

'You did not have the same fear when you made me go today to the Palais to pass those odious decrees which have caused so much murmuring among the people.'

'Sire,' interposed Laporte, to change the subject, 'to whom does your Majesty wish me to give the candle-stick?'

'To any one you please, Laporte,' replied the child, 'provided,' added he, in a loud voice, 'that it is not Mancini.'

Mancini was a nephew of the cardinal, whom Mazarin had placed near the person of the king as child of honour, and upon whom Louis XIV turned a portion of the hatred he felt for his minister.

And the king went out without embracing his mother and without bowing to the cardinal.

'Well and good!' said Mazarin; 'I am glad to see that his Majesty is being brought up with a horror of dissimulation.'

'Why so?' asked the queen, a little timidly.

'It seems to me that the *sortie* of the king does not require any commentary; besides, his Majesty does not give himself the trouble to conceal the little affection he bears me, which does not prevent me, however, from being entirely devoted to his service, as well as to that of your Majesty.'

'I ask pardon of you for him, Cardinal,' said the queen, 'he is a child, who cannot yet know all the obligations he is under to you.'

The cardinal smiled.

'But,' continued the queen, 'you have come, doubtless, for some important object; what is it, then?'

Mazarin seated, or rather threw himself, into a large chair with a melancholy air.

'It is,' said he, 'that in all probability we shall soon be forced to separate, unless you carry your devotion to me so far as to follow me into Italy.'

'And why so?' demanded the queen.

'Because, as is said in the opera of "Thisbé" '* replied Mazarin, ' "The whole world conspires to divide our loves." '

'You jest, sir!' said the queen, attempting to resume something of her former dignity.

'Alas, no, Madame!' rejoined Mazarin; 'I do not jest the least in the world. I should much rather weep, I pray you to believe it; and there is reason for it, for mark well that I have said: "The whole world conspires to divide our loves." Now, as you are part of the whole world, I wish to say that you also desert me.'

'Cardinal!'

'Eh! *mon Dieu*, did I not see you the other day smile very agreeably on the Duc d'Orléans, or rather at what he was saying to you?'

'And what was he saying?'

'He said to you, Madame, "It is your Mazarin who is the stumbling-block; dismiss him, and everything will go well."'

'What do you wish me to do?'

'Oh, Madame, you are the queen, it seems to me!'

'Fine royalty! at the mercy of every scribbler of the Palais-Royal, or of every lordling in the kingdom.'

'Nevertheless you have the power to banish from your presence those who displease you.'

'That is to say those who displease *you*,' returned the queen. 'Me?'

'Yes, indeed. Who sent away Madame de Chevreuse, who during twelve years had been persecuted under the other reign?'

'An intriguing woman who wished to continue against me the cabals begun against M. de Richelieu!'

'Who dismissed Madame de Hautefort—that friend so perfect that she had refused the good graces of the king in order to remain in mine?'

'A prude who told you every night as she undressed you that it was to lose your soul only to love a priest; as if one were a priest because one happens to be a cardinal!'

'Who caused M. de Beaufort to be arrested?'

'A blunderhead who was talking of nothing less than assassinating me!'

'You see, Cardinal,' returned the queen, 'that your enemies are mine.'

'That is not enough, Madame, it is further necessary that your friends should be mine also.'

'My friends, sir!' The queen shook her head. 'Alas! I have no longer any.'

'How is it that you have no longer friends in prosperity, when you had many in adversity?'

'Because in prosperity I have forgotten those friends, sir; because I have done like the queen, Marie de Médicis, who on her return from her first exile neglected all those who suffered for her, and who, proscribed a second time, died at Cologne, abandoned by the whole world and even by her son, because every one neglected her in their turn.'

'Well, let us see!' said Mazarin, 'is there not time to repair the evil? Recall to mind your friends, your oldest ones.'

'What do you mean to say, sir?'

'Nothing else than what I say: recall them to mind.'

'Alas! I look in vain around me. I have no influence over any one. Monsieur,* as always, is led by his favourite: yesterday it was Choisy; today it is La Rivière; tomorrow it will be another. Monsieur the Prince is led by the Coadjutor, who is led by Madame de Guéménée.'

'Therefore, Madame, I do not tell you to look among your friends of today, but among those of former times.'

'Among my friends of former times?' said the queen.

'Yes, among your friends of former times, among those who aided you to contend with M. le Duc de Richelieu, and even vanquish him.'

'What does he wish to learn?' murmured the queen, looking at the cardinal anxiously.

'Yes,' continued he, 'in certain circumstances, with the powerful and shrewd mind which characterizes your Majesty, you have known how, thanks to the aid of your friends, to repel the attacks of that adversary.'

'I!' said the queen. 'I have suffered, that is all.'

'Yes,' said Mazarin, 'as women suffer, in avenging themselves. Come, let us come to the fact! Do you know M. de Rochefort?'

'M. de Rochefort was not one of my friends,' said the queen; 'but on the contrary one of my most bitter enemies; one of the most faithful servants of Monsieur the Cardinal. I thought you knew that.'

'I know it so well,' responded Mazarin, 'that we have put him in the Bastille.'

'Has he come out?' demanded the queen.

'No; reassure yourself; he is there still. I have only spoken of him to call to mind another person. Do you know M. d'Artagnan?' continued Mazarin, looking the queen in the face.

Anne of Austria received the blow full in her heart.

'Could the Gascon have been indiscreet?' she murmured; then aloud, 'd'Artagnan!' added she. 'Wait a moment; yes, certainly that name is familiar to me. D'Artagnan, a musketeer who was in love with one of my women—* poor little creature! she was poisoned on my account.'

'And that is all?' said Mazarin.

The queen regarded the cardinal with surprise.

'But, sir,' said she, 'it seems that you are making me undergo an interrogation?'

'In which,' said Mazarin, with his constant smile and soft voice, 'you answer only according to your own fancy.'

'Explain clearly your desires, sir, and I will reply in the same manner,' said the queen, beginning to show impatience.

'Well, Madame,' said Mazarin, bowing, 'I desire that you share with me your friends, as I have shared with you the little of industry and talent which Heaven has bestowed upon me. Circumstances are serious, and it is going to be necessary to act with energy.'

'Again!' said the queen. 'I thought that we had finished with M. de Beaufort.'

'Yes; you have seen only the torrent which strove to overturn everything, and you have paid no attention to the stagnant water. There is, however, in France, a proverb about the water that stagnates.'*

'Finish,' said the queen.

'Well!' continued Mazarin, 'every day I suffer affronts from your princes and titled servants—all automata who do not see that I hold the string that moves them, and who under my patient gravity have not divined the laugh of the irritated man who has sworn to himself to become one day their master. We have caused the arrest of M. de Beaufort, it is true; but he is the least dangerous of them. There is still Monsieur the Prince——'

'The conqueror of Rocroy! Do you think of him?'

'Yes, Madame, and very often; but *patienza*, as we Italians say. Then after M. de Condé, there is the Duc d'Orléans.'

'What are you saying? The first prince of the blood, the uncle of the king!'

'No! not the first prince of the blood, not the uncle of the king, but the cowardly conspirator, who during the other reign, impelled by his capricious and whimsical character, gnawed by miserable idleness, devoured by a dull ambition, jealous of every one who surpassed him in loyalty and courage, irritated at being nothing, thanks to his nullity, made himself the echo of every bad report, made himself the soul of all the cabals, gave the signal of forward to all those brave men who had the folly to believe in the honour of a man of royal blood, and who disowned them when they mounted the scaffold! No, not the first prince of the blood, not the uncle of the king, I repeat it, but the assassin of Chalais, of Montmorency and of Cinq-Mars,* who attempts today to play the same game, and thinks he shall succeed because he has changed adversaries, and instead of having opposed to him a man who threatens, there is only a man who smiles. But he is mistaken; he has lost in losing M. de Richelieu, and it is not my interest to leave near the queen this leaven of discord with which the late cardinal for twenty years caused the anger of the king to boil.'

Anne blushed, and buried her face in her hands.

'I do not wish to humiliate your Majesty,' continued Mazarin, returning to a calmer tone, but at the same time with unusual firmness. 'I wish that the queen should be respected, and that her minister should be respected, since in the eyes of all I am only that. Your Majesty knows that I am not, as many people say, a "dancing puppet" come from Italy. It is necessary that every one should know it like your Majesty.'

'Well, then, what must I do?' said Anne of Austria, bowed down under this domineering voice.

'You must seek in your memory the names of those faithful and devoted men who crossed the sea despite M. de Richelieu, leaving traces of their blood all along their route, to bring back to your Majesty certain jewels given to M. de Buckingham.'

Anne arose, majestic and incensed, as if moved by a steel spring, and regarding the cardinal with that haughtiness and dignity which rendered her so powerful in the days of her youth.

'You insult me, sir!' said she.

'I wish, in fine,' continued Mazarin, finishing the thought which the movement of the queen had interrupted,—'I wish you to do today for your husband what you did formerly for your lover.'

'Again that calumny!' cried the queen. 'I thought it killed and completely stifled, for you had spared me till now; but lo! you speak of it to me in your turn. So much the better, for it will be a question this time between us; and the whole shall be finished, do you understand that?'

'But, Madame,' said Mazarin, astonished at this return of courage, 'I do not ask that you should tell me all.'

'And I—I wish to tell you all,' responded Anne of Austria. 'Listen, then. I wish to tell you that there were at this time four devoted hearts, four loyal souls, four faithful swords who saved more than my life, sir, who saved my honour.'

'Ah, you avow it,' said Mazarin.

'Is it only the guilty whose honour may be at stake, sir, and cannot one dishonour another, a woman especially, by appearances? Yes, appearances were against me, and I was about to be dishonoured, but nevertheless, I swear it to you, I was not guilty. I swear it——'

The queen sought for some sacred object upon which she could swear; and drawing from a closet concealed by the tapestry a small coffer of rosewood, inlaid with silver, and laying it on the altar—'I swear it,' said she, 'on these sacred relics, that I loved M. de Buckingham, but M. de Buckingham was not my lover!'

'And what are these relics on which you make this oath, Madame?' said Mazarin, smiling; 'for I forewarn you, in my character of Roman I am incredulous. There are relics and relics.'

The queen detached a small golden key from her neck, and presented it to the cardinal.

'Open it, sir,' said she, 'and look for yourself.'

Mazarin, astonished, took the key, and opened the coffer, in which he found only a dagger, corroded with rust, and two letters, one of which was spotted with blood.

'What is that?' demanded Mazarin.

'What is that, sir?' said Anne of Austria, with a queenly gesture, and stretching out over the open coffer an arm still beautiful despite the lapse of years. 'I am going to tell you.

Those two letters are the only ones that I ever wrote to him. This dagger is the one with which Felton* stabbed him. Read these letters, sir, and you will see if I have told a falsehood.'

Notwithstanding this permission, Mazarin, by a natural sentiment, instead of reading the letters, took the dagger which the dying Buckingham had torn from his wound, and sent by Laporte to the queen. Its, blade was wholly corroded, for the blood had become rust; then, after a momentary examination, during which the queen grew as white as the altar-cloth on which she was leaning, he replaced it in the coffer with an involuntary shudder.

'It is well, Madame,' said he; 'I trust to your oath.'

'No, no, read,' said the queen, frowning—'read; I wish it, I order it, so that, as I am resolved, everything shall be finished this time, and we shall never recur again to this subject. Do you think,' added she, with a ghastly smile, 'that I shall be inclined to re-open this coffer at each one of your future accusations?'

Mazarin, dominated by this energy, obeyed almost mechanically, and read the two letters. One was that in which the queen asked the return of the ornaments—the one borne by d'Artagnan, and which arrived in time. The other was the one Laporte had given the duke, in which the queen warned him that he was about to be assassinated, and which had arrived too late.

'It is well, Madame,' said Mazarin; 'there is nothing to reply to that.'

'If, sir,' said the queen, closing the coffer, and resting her hand upon it—'if there is anything to say, it is that I have always been ungrateful to those men who saved me, and who had done all they could do to save him also; it is that I gave nothing to that brave d'Artagnan of whom you were speaking just now, but my hand to kiss and this diamond.'

The queen extended her beautiful hand towards the cardinal, and showed him a fine stone which sparkled on her finger. 'He sold it, as it appears,' continued she, 'in a moment of need; he sold it to save me a second time, for it was to send a messenger to the duke, and warn him that he was to be assassinated.'

'D'Artagnan knew it, then?'

'He knew all. How did he do it? I am ignorant; but in fine, he sold it to M. d'Essart,* on whose finger I saw it, and from whom I repurchased it. But this diamond belongs to him, sir; return it to him on my part, and since you have the honour to have near you such a man, try to make him useful.'

'Thanks, Madame!' said Mazarin, 'I will profit by the counsel.'

'And now,' said the queen, her voice broken by emotion, 'have you any other question to ask me?'

'Nothing, Madame,' responded the cardinal, with his most caressing voice, 'except to beg you to pardon me my unjust suspicions; but I love you so much that it is not strange that I should be jealous—even of the past.'

A smile of indefinable expression crossed the lips of the queen. 'Well, then, sir,' said she, 'if you have no further question to ask, leave me; you ought to understand that after such a scene I have need to be alone.'

Mazarin bent low. 'I retire, Madame,' said he; 'do you permit me to return?'

'Yes, but tomorrow; all that time will not be too much in which to compose myself.'

The cardinal took the queen's hand, raised it with an air of gallantry to his lips, and then retired.

Scarcely had he gone out than the queen passed into the apartment of her son, and asked Laporte if the king had retired. Laporte pointed with his hand to the child, who was asleep. Anne of Austria ascended the steps of the bed, approached her lips to the ruffled forehead of her son, and left there a gentle kiss; then she retired as silently as she came, merely saying to the *valet de chambre*:

'Try, then, my dear Laporte, that the king may be more courteous to Monsieur the Cardinal, to whom both he and I are under such great obligations.'

V

MEANWHILE, the cardinal had returned to his cabinet, at the door of which Bernouin was watching, of whom he asked if anything had occurred, and if any news from outside had arrived. Upon his negative reply, he made a sign to him to withdraw. Left alone, he opened the door of the corridor, then that of the antechamber; d'Artagnan, fatigued, was sleeping on a cushioned bench.

'M. d'Artagnan!' said he, with a gentle voice. D'Artagnan did not move.

'M. d'Artagnan!' said he, louder.

D'Artagnan continued to sleep. The cardinal approached him, and touched his shoulder with the end of a finger. This time d'Artagnan started, awoke, and on awaking, stood erect like a soldier under arms. 'Here I am,' said he; 'who calls me?'

'I,' said Mazarin, with his most smiling countenance.

'I ask pardon of your Eminence,' said d'Artagnan; 'but I was so fatigued——'

'Do not ask my pardon, sir,' said Mazarin, 'for you were fatigued in my service.'

D'Artagnan admired the gracious look of the minister. 'Bless me!' said he, between his teeth, 'is the proverb true which says that good luck comes while sleeping?'*

'Follow me, sir,' said Mazarin.

'Come, come!' murmured d'Artagnan, 'Rochefort has kept his word; only, by what way, in the devil's name, has he gone out?' And he looked even into the smallest recess of the cabinet, but there was no Rochefort there.

'M. d'Artagnan,' said Mazarin, seating himself at his ease in his armchair, 'you have always seemed to me to be a brave and honest man.'

'Possibly,' thought d'Artagnan; 'but he has taken a long time to tell me!'—which did not prevent his bowing to the very ground in reply to the compliment.

'Well,' continued Mazarin, 'the moment has arrived to profit by your talents and your valour.'

The eyes of the officer shot forth a flash of joy which was immediately extinguished, for he did not yet know Mazarin's intentions. 'Order, my Lord,' said he. 'I am ready to obey your Eminence.'

'M. d'Artagnan,' continued Mazarin, 'you performed in the last reign certain exploits——'

'Your Eminence is too good to remember——It is true that I fought with tolerable success.'

'I do not speak of your warlike exploits,' said Mazarin; 'for although they have made some noise, they have been surpassed by your other deeds.'

D'Artagnan appeared surprised.

'Well,' said Mazarin, 'you do not answer.'

'I am waiting that my Lord may tell me of what exploits he wishes to speak.'

'I speak of the adventure——*Hé!* You know well that of which I wish to speak.'

'Alas, no, my Lord!' responded d'Artagnan, all surprise.

'You are discreet. So much the better. I wish to speak of that adventure of the queen's, of those ornaments, of that journey you made with three of your friends.'

'*Hé, hé!*' thought the Gascon. 'Is this a snare? Let us hold firm.' And he assumed an air of astonishment that Mondori or Bellerose,* the two best comedians of that day, would have envied him.

'Very well,' said Mazarin, laughing. 'Bravo! They told me that you were the man I wanted. Let us see, what will you do for me?'

'Everything that your Eminence shall order me to do,' said d'Artagnan.

'You will do for me what you have done formerly for a queen?'

'Decidedly,' thought d'Artagnan, 'he wishes to make me speak. Let us see him arrive at it. He is not more cunning than Richelieu. What the devil——For a queen, my Lord! I don't comprehend.'

'You don't comprehend that I have need of you and your three friends?'

'Of what friends, my Lord?'

'Of your three friends of former days.'

'In former days,' responded d'Artagnan, 'I had not three friends; I had fifty. At twenty, one calls everyone his friend.'

'Well, well, Sir officer!' said Mazarin, 'discretion is a fine thing; but today you might regret having been too discreet.'

'My Lord, Pythagoras* made his disciples keep silent for five years, to teach them to hold their tongues.'

'And you have kept silent twenty years, sir. That is fifteen years more than a Pythagorean philosopher, which seems to me reasonable. Speak, then, now, for the queen herself releases you from your promise?'

'The queen!' said d'Artagnan, with an astonishment which this time was not feigned.

'Yes, the queen. And for proof that I speak in her name, she told me to show you this diamond, which she pretends you know, and which she has repurchased of M. d'Essart.' And Mazarin extended his hand towards the officer, who sighed as he recognized the ring given to him by the queen on the night of the ball at the Hôtel de Ville.*

'It is true,' said d'Artagnan. 'I remember that diamond, which has belonged to the queen.'

'You see, then, that I speak to you in her name. Answer me, then, without playing comedy any longer. I have already told you, and I repeat it, your fortune is concerned in it.'

'My faith, my Lord, I have great need to make my fortune, your Eminence has forgotten me so long!'

'It only needs a week to repair that. Let us see, you are here—you—but where are your friends?'

'I do not know at all, my Lord.'

'How, you do not know at all?'

'No; it is a long time since we separated, for all three have left the service.'

'But where will you find them?'

'Wherever they may be. That concerns me.'

'Well, your conditions?'

'Money, my Lord—as much as our enterprises shall demand. I recall too well how much we have been hindered by the want of money, and without that diamond, which I was obliged to sell, we should have been stopped on our way.'

'Devil! Money, and much!' said Mazarin. 'How you go on, Sir officer! Are you aware that there is no money in the coffers of the king?'

'Do, then, as I did, my Lord—sell the crown diamonds. Trust me, do not try to cheapen things; great affairs are badly done with small means.'

'Well,' said Mazarin, 'we will see how to satisfy you.'

'Richelieu,' thought d'Artagnan, 'would already have given me five hundred pistoles in advance.'

'You will be, then, at my service?'

'Yes, if my friends wish it.'

'But, on their refusal, I could count upon you?'

'I have never been good for anything alone,' said d'Artagnan, shaking his head.

'Go, then, and find them.'

'What shall I say to make them decide to serve your Eminence?'

'You know them better than I do. You will promise them according to their characters.'

'What shall I promise?'

'Let them serve me as they served the queen and my gratitude shall be brilliant.'

'What are we to do?'

'Everything; since it appears that you know how to do everything.'

'My Lord, when one has confidence in people, and wishes that they have confidence in us, one instructs them better than does your Eminence.'

'When the time for action comes, make your mind easy,' continued Mazarin, 'you shall have my whole intention.'

'And until then?'

'Wait, and seek for your friends.'

'My Lord, perhaps they are not at Paris; that is probable, even. It will be necessary to travel. I am only a very poor lieutenant of Musketeers, and journeys are dear.'

'My intention,' said Mazarin, 'is that you should not appear with a great train; my projects require mystery, and would suffer from too great an equipage.'

'Still, my Lord, can I travel with my pay when that is three months in arrears with me? And I cannot travel with my economies, considering that during the twenty-two years I have been in the service I have economized only debts.'

Mazarin remained an instant thoughtful, as if combating strongly with himself; then going to a closet closed with a triple lock, he drew out a bag, and weighed it two or three times in his hand before giving it to d'Artagnan.

'Take this,' said he, with a sigh; 'this is for the journey.'

'If these are Spanish doubloons, or even golden crowns,' thought d'Artagnan, 'we can yet work together.'

He saluted the cardinal, and plunged the bag into his large pocket.

'Well, then, it is all settled,' replied the cardinal; 'you are going to travel——'

'Yes, my Lord.'

'Write me every day, giving news of your negotiation.'

'I will not fail to do so, my Lord.'

'Very well. *A propos*, the names of your friends?'

'The names of my friends?' repeated d'Artagnan, with a residue of uneasiness.

'Yes; while you will search on your side, I will inform myself on mine, and perhaps I shall learn something.'

'M. le Comte de la Fère, otherwise called Athos; M. du Vallon, otherwise called Porthos; and M. le Chevalier d'Herblay, today the Abbé d'Herblay, otherwise called Aramis.'*

The cardinal smiled.

'Younger sons,' said he, 'who joined the Musketeers under false names so as not to compromise their family names. Long rapiers, but light purses; we know that class.'

'If God wills that these rapiers pass into the service of your Eminence,' said d'Artagnan, 'I dare express a wish that it shall be in its turn the purse of my Lord which becomes light, and theirs which becomes heavy; for with these three men and me your Eminence shall move all France, and even all Europe, if that suits him.'

'These Gascons,' said Mazarin, laughing, 'almost equal the Italians in bravado.'

'In every case,' said d'Artagnan, with a smile like the cardinal's, 'they more than equal them in the thrust.'

And he went out after asking for his military leave, which was at once granted and signed by Mazarin himself.

Scarcely outside, he drew near a lantern in the courtyard, and hastily looked into the bag.

'Silver crowns!' said he, with disdain; 'I suspected it. Ah, Mazarin, Mazarin! thou hast not confidence in me. So much the worse! that will bring thee misfortune!'

Meanwhile, the cardinal was rubbing his hands.

'A hundred pistoles!' murmured he, 'a hundred pistoles! For a hundred pistoles I have discovered a secret for which M. de Richelieu would have paid twenty thousand crowns. Without reckoning this diamond'—casting loving eyes upon the ring he had kept, instead of giving it to d'Artagnan—'without reckoning this diamond, which is worth at least ten thousand livres.'

The cardinal returned to his room, all radiant from this evening in which he had made so fine a profit, placed the ring in a casket filled with brilliants of every sort—for the cardinal was fond of precious stones—and called Bernouin to undress him, without further attention to the noises which continued to come by puffs against the windows, and to the musket-shots which resounded through Paris, although it was past eleven o'clock of the evening.

Meanwhile, d'Artagnan was making his way towards the Rue Tiquetonne,* where he dwelt at the Hôtel de la Chevrette. Let us say in a few words how d'Artagnan had been led to choose this dwelling.

VI

D'ARTAGNAN AT FORTY YEARS OF AGE

ALAS! since the epoch when, in our romance of 'The Three Musketeers,' we left d'Artagnan at No. 12, Rue des Fossoyeurs,* many events had happened and many years had passed.

D'Artagnan had not failed his opportunities, but opportunities had failed to d'Artagnan. While his friends surrounded him, d'Artagnan remained in his youth and his poetry. His was one of those delicate and ingenious natures which easily assimilates to itself the qualities of others. Athos imparted to him of his greatness of soul, Porthos of his enthusiasm, Aramis of his elegance. If d'Artagnan had continued to live with these three men, he would have become a superior man. Athos left him first to retire to that little estate he had inherited near Blois.* Porthos, the second, to marry the procurator's widow; and lastly, Aramis, the third, to take orders and make himself an abbé. From this moment, d'Artagnan, who seemed to have blended his future with that of his three friends, found himself isolated and weak, without courage to pursue a career in which he felt that he could become distinguished only on the condition that each of his friends should cede to him, if one may say so, a part of the electric fluid which he had received from heaven.

So that, although become lieutenant of Musketeers, d'Artagnan found himself only more isolated. He was not of sufficiently high birth, like Athos, for the great houses to open before him; he had not enough vanity, like Porthos, to pretend that he mixed in high society; he was not sufficiently well-born, like Aramis, to maintain himself in his native elegance, drawing his elegance from himself. For some time the charming remembrance of Madame Bonacieux* had imprinted upon the spirit of the young lieutenant a certain poetic tinge; but like that of all worldly things, this perishable memory was little by little effaced. Garrison life is fatal even to aristocratic organizations. Of the two opposite natures which composed the individuality of d'Artagnan, his material nature had little by little assumed the control, and slowly, without perceiving it himself, d'Artagnan, always in garrison, always in camp, always on horseback, had become (I know not how that was called at that time) what we call in our days a 'complete trooper'. It was not that d'Artagnan had lost any of his primitive shrewdness; no. On the contrary, perhaps that shrewdness was increased, or at least seemed doubly remarkable under an appearance a little coarse; but this shrewdness he had applied to the little and not to the great affairs of life—to his material well-being, to well-being as soldiers understand it; that is, to securing good lodging, good table, and a good hostess. And d'Artagnan had found all that for six years in the Rue Tiquetonne, at the sign of the Chevrette.

At the time of his first residence in this hotel, the mistress of the house, a handsome and florid Flemish woman of twenty-five years of age, was singularly smitten with him; and after some attentions much interfered with by an inconvenient husband, to whom a dozen times d'Artagnan had made a pretence of running his sword through his body, this husband had disappeared one fine morning, deserting his post forever, after having sold furtively several puncheons of wine, and taken with him some silver and jewels. He was believed to be dead; his wife especially, who flattered herself with the agreeable idea of being a widow, maintained boldly that he was dead. At last, after three years of a *liaison* that d'Artagnan had taken care not to break, finding each year his lodging and his mistress more agreeable—for one did credit to the other—his mistress had the exorbitant pretension to become a wife, and proposed to d'Artagnan to marry her.

'Ah, fie!' responded d'Artagnan. 'Bigamy, my dear! Come, you don't think of it!'

'But he is dead, I am sure of it.'

'He was a very contrary dog, and one who would return to have us hanged.'

'Well! if he return you will kill him; you are so brave and so adroit!'

'*Peste*, my dear! another mode of being hung.'

'So you reject my demand?'

'How! yes, most obstinately.'

The handsome landlady was in despair. She would willingly have made M. d'Artagnan not only her husband but also her God, he was so fine a man and so fierce a soldier.

Towards the fourth year of this liaison came the expedition of Franche Comté.* D'Artagnan was ordered to join it, and prepared to set out. There were great griefs, tears without end, solemn promises to remain faithful—all on the part of the hostess, be it well understood. D'Artagnan was too much *grand seigneur* to promise anything; so he promised only to do what he could to add to the glory of his name.

In this respect we know the courage of d'Artagnan; he paid admirably with his person, and charging at the head of his company, he received through his breast a ball which stretched him at length upon the field of battle. He was seen to fall from his horse, was not seen to arise; he was believed to be dead; and all those who had hope of succeeding to his grade said at hazard that he was so. One easily believes what one desires. Now, in the army, from the division-generals who desire the death of the commander-in-chief to the soldiers who desire the death of the corporals, every one desires the death of some one. But d'Artagnan was not the man to permit himself to be slain like that. After having remained senseless during the heat of the day on the field of battle, the coolness of the night restored his senses. He reached a village, knocked at the door of its finest house, was received as the French are always and everywhere when they are wounded; he was cared for, pampered, cured; and in better health than ever, he one fine day resumed the road to France, once in France the route to Paris, and once in Paris the direction to the Rue Tiquetonne. But d'Artagnan found his chamber occupied by a man's portmanteau, complete except the sword, installed against the wall.

'He must have returned,' said he, 'so much the worse and so much the better!'

Of course d'Artagnan was thinking of the husband. He sought information; a new waiter, a new servant-girl. The mistress had gone for a promenade.

'Alone?' demanded d'Artagnan.

'With Monsieur.'

'Monsieur is then returned?'

'Without doubt,' replied the servant-girl, naïvely.

'If I had any money,' said d'Artagnan to himself, 'I would go away; but I haven't any. I must remain and follow the advice of my hostess in thwarting the conjugal projects of this importunate ghost.'

He finished this monologue, which proves that on great occasions nothing is more natural than the monologue, when the servant-girl, who was watching at the door, cried out suddenly—

'Ah, here is Madame, who returns with Monsieur.'

D'Artagnan looked down the street and saw in the distance, at the corner of the Rue Montmartre, the hostess returning upon the arm of a gigantic Swiss, who twisted himself about in walking with airs which agreeably recalled Porthos to the memory of his old friend.

'That is Monsieur?' said d'Artagnan to himself; 'Oh, oh! he has grown very tall it seems to me.'

And he seated himself in the salon in a place in full view. The hostess, on entering, perceived d'Artagnan at once, and uttered a little cry. At this little cry, d'Artagnan, judging himself recognized, arose, ran to her, and embraced her tenderly.

The Swiss looked with a stupefied air at the hostess, who was quite pale.

'Ah, it is you, sir! What do you wish of me?' asked she, in the greatest trouble.

'Monsieur is your cousin? Monsieur is your brother?' said d'Artagnan, without any embarrassment in the role he was playing; and without waiting her reply, he threw himself into the arms of the Swiss, who suffered his embrace with a great coldness.

'Who is this man?' demanded he.

The hostess replied only with some chokings.

'Who is this Swiss?' demanded d'Artagnan.

'Monsieur is going to marry me,' replied the hostess, between her spasms.

'Your husband is then dead at last?'

'How does that concern you?' responded the Swiss.

'It concerns me much,' replied d'Artagnan, 'considering that you cannot marry Madame without my consent, and that——'

'And that?' demanded the Swiss.

'And that—I do not give it,' said the musketeer.

The Swiss became as purple as a peony. He wore his fine uniform laced with gold; d'Artagnan was enveloped in a grey cloak. The Swiss was six feet tall; d'Artagnan was little more than five.* The Swiss thought himself at home; d'Artagnan seemed to him an intruder.

'Will you go out from here?' demanded the Swiss, stamping his foot violently, like a man who begins to grow seriously angry.

'I? not at all,' said d'Artagnan.

'But it is only to bring him with the strong hand,' said a waiter, who could not comprehend how this little man should dispute possession with one so large.

'As for thee,' said d'Artagnan, whose anger began to rise, seizing the waiter by the ear, 'thou art going to commence by remaining in this place; and do not stir, or I will tear off what I have hold of. As to you, illustrious descendant of William Tell,* you are going to make a bundle of your clothes now in my chamber, and which annoy me, and go out quickly and find another inn.'

The Swiss began to laugh noisily.

'I go out, and why?'

'Ah, it is well!' said d'Artagnan. 'I see that you understand French, then come and take a turn with me and I will explain to you the rest!'

The hostess, who knew d'Artagnan was a fine swordsman, began to weep and tear her hair.

D'Artagnan turned round towards the handsome weeper.

'Send him away, then, Madame,' said he.

'Pah,' replied the Swiss, to whom a certain time was necessary to grasp the proposition made to him by d'Artagnan— 'pah, who are you, then, to propose to me to take a turn with you?'

'I am lieutenant in the Musketeers of his Majesty,' said d'Artagnan, 'and consequently your superior in everything; only as this is not a question of grade here, but of a ticket of lodgment, you know the custom. Come and seek yours; the first to return here will take his chamber.'

D'Artagnan led away the Swiss, despite the lamentations of the hostess, who in the main felt her heart inclining towards her old love, but who would not have been sorry to give a lesson to this proud musketeer, who had committed the affront of rejecting her hand.

The two adversaries went directly to the moats at Montmartre;* it was growing dark when they arrived there. D'Artagnan politely begged the Swiss to yield to him the chamber, and not to return; he refused with a sign of his head, and drew his sword.

'Then you will lie here,' said d'Artagnan; 'it is a miserable lodging, but it is not my fault, and it is you who will have wished it.' At these words he drew his blade in his turn, and crossed swords with his adversary. He had to do with a strong wrist, but his suppleness was superior to every force. The rapier of the German could never find the musketeer's. The Swiss received two cuts before perceiving it, on account of the cold; nevertheless, suddenly the loss of his blood and the weakness it caused him constrained him to seat himself.

'There,' said d'Artagnan, 'what did I predict to you? There you are well advanced, obstinate fellow that you are! Happily you will only be laid up for a fortnight. Remain there; and I am going to send your clothes to you by the waiter. *Au revoir. A propos*, you can get rooms in the Rue Montorgueil, at the Playful Cat;* one is grandly fed there, if there is still the same hostess. Adieu.'

And thereupon he returned gaily to his lodging, despatched his possessions to the Swiss, whom the waiter found sitting in the same place where d'Artagnan had left him, entirely dismayed still at the coolness of his adversary. The waiter, the hostess, and the whole house had for d'Artagnan the consideration that one would have for Hercules if he should return on earth to recommence his twelve labours. But when he was alone with the hostess, 'Now, fair Madeleine,' said he, 'you know the distance between a Swiss and a gentleman! As to you, you have conducted yourself like a low tavern-keeper. So much the worse for you—for by this conduct you lose my esteem and my patronage. I drove out the Swiss to humiliate you; but I shall lodge here no longer. I do not take quarters where I despise people. Holloa, waiter! let them carry my valise to the Muid d'Amour, Rue des Bourdonnais. Adieu, Madame.'

D'Artagnan, in saying these words, was, as happened, at the same time majestic and tender. The hostess threw herself at his feet, demanded his pardon, and held him by a gentle violence. What can we say more? The spit was turning, the stove puffing, the fair Madeleine weeping. D'Artagnan perceived hunger, cold, and love returning to him all together. He pardoned; and having pardoned, he remained.

This was how d'Artagnan was lodged in the Rue Tiquetonne, at the Hôtel de la Chevrette.

VII

D'ARTAGNAN IS AT A LOSS, BUT ONE OF OUR OLD ACQUAINTANCES COMES TO HIS AID

D'ARTAGNAN was returning then in a thoughtful mood, finding a lively pleasure in carrying the bag of Cardinal Mazarin, and thinking of that fine diamond, once his own, and which for an instant he had seen sparkling on the finger of the first minister.

'Should that diamond ever fall again into my hands,' he was saying, 'I should turn it at once into money, I should purchase certain properties around my father's château*—a pretty residence, but which has for all its dependencies only a garden scarcely as large as the Cimetière des Innocents*—and there I would await in my majesty, until some rich heiress, attracted by my good looks, came to espouse me. Then I would have three sons;* I would make of the first a great nobleman like Athos; of the second a handsome soldier like Porthos; and of the third a pretty abbé like Aramis. My faith! that would be infinitely better than the life I am leading; but unfortunately M. de Mazarin is a contemptible fellow who will not dispossess himself of his diamond in my favour.'

What would d'Artagnan have said if he had known that the diamond had been entrusted by the queen to Mazarin to be given back to him?

On entering the Rue Tiquetonne, he saw that a great disturbance was going on there; there was a considerable mob all around his lodging.

'Oh,' said he, 'there is a fire at the Hôtel de la Chevrette, or Madeleine's husband has certainly returned.'

It was neither the one nor the other. The mob was next door. He heard loud cries; he saw the reflection of *flambeaux*, and saw some military uniforms.

He enquired what was going on.

He was told that a citizen, with twenty of his friends, had attacked a carriage escorted by the cardinal's Guards; but that the latter, being reinforced, had put the citizens to flight. The head of the riotous party had taken refuge in the house next to the inn, and it was being searched.

In his youthful days d'Artagnan would have hastened where he saw uniforms, and have lent aid to the soldiers against the citizens; but these hot-headed deeds were laid aside. Besides, he had in his pocket the cardinal's hundred pistoles, and he did not wish to risk losing them in a mob. He entered the hotel without further questions. Formerly d'Artagnan always wished to know everything; now he always knew enough.

He found fair Madeleine, who did not expect him, thinking, as d'Artagnan had told her, he would pass the night at the Louvre.* She gave him, therefore, a hearty welcome at this unexpected return, which this time was the more pleasing to her from her fear at what was going on in the street, and from having no Swiss to protect her.

She wished, then, to open the conversation with him, and to tell him what had happened; but d'Artagnan told her to send up supper to his room, and to add to it a bottle of old Burgundy.

Fair Madeleine was taught to obey in military fashion; that is, at a sign. This time d'Artagnan had deigned to speak; he was obeyed, therefore, with double expedition.

D'Artagnan took his key and candle, and went up to his room. He was satisfied, so as not to hurt the letting of rooms, with a room on the fourth floor. The respect we have for the truth compels us even to say that the room was immediately below the gutter and the roof.

There was his tent of Achilles. D'Artagnan used to shut himself up in this room when he wished by his absence to punish fair Madeleine.

His first care was to lock up his bag in an old desk which had a new lock; then, as a moment after, his supper was ready, his bottle of wine brought, he dismissed the waiter, shut the door, and sat down to table.

It was not to reflect, as one might perhaps suppose; but d'Artagnan thought that a number of things could only be well done by doing each in its turn. He was hungry; he supped, and then went to bed. D'Artagnan no longer belonged to those people who think that night brings counsel. At night d'Artagnan used to sleep. But in the morning, on the contrary, quite fresh, quite circumspect, he found the best inspirations. For a long time he had had no occasion to think in the morning, but he had always slept at night.

At daybreak he awoke, jumped out of bed with a resolution quite military, and walked about the room reflecting.

'In 1643,'* said he, 'nearly six months before the death of the late cardinal, I received a letter from Athos. Where was that? Let us see——Ah! at the siege of Besançon, I remember. I was in the trenches. What did he tell me? That he was living on a small estate; but where? I had read to there when a blast of wind carried off my letter. Formerly I should have looked for it, although the wind might have carried it to a spot greatly exposed. But youth is a great defect—when one is no longer young. I allowed my letter to carry the address of Athos to the Spaniards, who had no use for it, and should have sent it back to me. There is no occasion to think any longer of Athos. Let us see—Porthos.

'I received a letter from him; he invited me to a grand shooting over his lands, for September, 1646. Unhappily, as at that·time I was at Béarn, because of my father's death, the letter followed me there; I had gone when it arrived. But it was sent after me, and got to Montmédy some days after I had left the city. At last I got it in April, but as it was April, 1647, and as the invitation was for September, 1646, I could not avail myself of it. Let me try and find this letter; it must be with my title-deeds.'

D'Artagnan opened an old cash-box which lay in a corner of the room, full of parchments relative to d'Artagnan's estate, which for two hundred years had entirely gone from his family, and he uttered a cry of joy; he had just recognized the bold writing of Porthos, and below, some lines in a scrawl traced by the plain hand of his worthy spouse.

D'Artagnan did not amuse himself by reading the letter again; he knew what it contained. He reached the address. This was at the Château du Vallon.

Porthos had forgotten every other detail. In his vanity, he thought that everybody ought to know the château to which his name was attached.

'Devil take the vain fellow!' said d'Artagnan; 'always the same. I was going to begin with him, seeing he ought not to have need of money, who has inherited eight hundred thousand livres of M. Coquenard.* Ah! it is the best who fails me. Athos will have become an idiot from drink. As for Aramis, he ought to be deep in his acts of devotion.'

D'Artagnan once more threw his eyes upon Porthos's letter. There was a postscript which contained this phrase—

'I am writing, by the same courier, to our worthy friend Aramis at his convent.'

'At his convent! yes, but what convent? There are two hundred in Paris and three thousand in France. And then perhaps on entering a convent he has changed his name the third time. Ah! if I was learned in theology, and only could remember the subject of his theses* which he discussed so well at Crèvecoeur with the curate of Montdidier and the superior of the Jesuits, I should see what doctrine he preferred, and I should deduce from that to what saint he would devote himself.

'What if I go to the cardinal and ask of him a safe-conduct to enter into all the existing convents, even into those of the nuns! That would be a good idea, and perhaps I should find him there as Achilles. Yes, but that is to confess my weakness at the very commencement, and at the first step I am lost in the opinion of the cardinal. The great are grateful only when one does the impossible. "If it had been possible, they tell us, I should have done it myself." And the great are right. But let us wait a little and see. I received a letter also from him, the dear friend, in which he asked of me also a small service that I rendered him. Ah, yes; but where have I put this letter now?'

D'Artagnan reflected a moment, and then went to the clothes-pegs where his old clothes were hung; he there looked for his doublet of the year 1648, and as he was an orderly fellow, he found it hanging on its nail. He felt in the pocket, and drew thence a paper; it was truly the letter of Aramis. It said—

M. D'ARTAGNAN—You must know that I have had a quarrel with a certain gentleman, who has named a meeting for this evening, Place Royale;* as I am a churchman, and as the affair might do me injury if any other than a trusty friend like yourself took part in it, I write to ask that you will act as my second.

You will enter by the Rue Neuve St Catherine; under the second lamp on the right you will find your adversary. I shall be with mine under the third.

Ever yours,
ARAMIS

This time there were not even adieux. D'Artagnan tried to recall his recollections; he had gone to the rendezvous, there met the adversary indicated, whose name he had never known, and had given him a good swordcut in the arm; then he drew near to Aramis, who had already finished his affair.

'It is finished,' Aramis had said. 'I think I have killed the impudent fellow. But, my dear friend, if you should need me, you know that I am entirely yours.'

Upon which Aramis had given him his hand, and had disappeared under the piazza.

He did not, therefore, know any more where Aramis was than where Athos and Porthos were; and the matter began to be somewhat embarrassing, when he fancied he heard a pane of glass being smashed in his room. He at once thought of his bag in the desk. He was not mistaken; as he entered by the door, a man entered by the window.

'Ah, wretch!' cried d'Artagnan, taking the man to be a thief, and unsheathing his sword.

'Monsieur,' cried the man, 'in Heaven's name put back your sword into the sheath, and do not kill me before hearing me! I am not a thief, far from it! I am an honest citizen, having a house of my own. My name is——Eh! but I am not deceived, you are M. d'Artagnan!'

'And you Planchet!' cried the lieutenant.

'At your service, Monsieur,' said Planchet, 'in the height of delight, if I were still capable of it.'

'Perhaps,' said d'Artagnan; 'but what the devil are you doing, running on the roofs at seven in the morning in the month of January?'

'Monsieur,' said Planchet, 'you must know. But in fact, you perhaps ought not to know.'

'Come now, what?' said d'Artagnan. 'But first put a towel before the window-pane and draw the blinds.'

Planchet obeyed; then, when he had finished, 'Well?' said d'Artagnan.

'Monsieur before everything,' said the prudent Planchet, 'how are you with M. de Rochefort?'

'Oh, wonderfully well. What then? Rochefort—but you know well enough that now he is one of my best friends.'

'Ah, so much the better.'

'But what has this way of entering my room to do with Rochefort?'

'Ah, that is it, Monsieur. It is necessary to tell you first of all that M. de Rochefort is——'

Planchet hesitated.

'Don't I know very well?' said d'Artagnan; 'he is in the Bastille.'

'That is to say that he was there!' replied Planchet.

'What do you mean, he was there?' cried d'Artagnan. 'Has he had the good fortune to escape?'

'Ah, Monsieur,' said Planchet, in his turn, 'if you call that good fortune, all is well. I must tell you then that it seems they sent M. de Rochefort yesterday back to the Bastille.'

'Eh! I know that well enough, since it was I who went to fetch him.'

'But it was not you who reconducted him thither, fortunately for him; for if I had recognized you in the escort, believe me, Monsieur, I have too much respect for you——'

'Finish then, animal! Let us hear how it happened.'

'Well, thus: in the middle of Rue de la Ferronnerie,* as M. de Rochefort's coach was passing a group of people, and the escort were roughly treating them, some murmurs arose. The prisoner thought it a good opportunity; he called out his name, and cried for help. I was there, and recognized the name as that of him who made me sergeant in the regiment of Piedmont. I said aloud it was a prisoner—a friend of the Duc de Beaufort. A row arose; the horses were stopped, and the escort overthrown. During this I opened the coach-door; M. de

Rochefort sprang out, and was lost in the crowd. Unfortunately a patrol passed, took the part of the escort, and charged at us. I beat a retreat in the direction of the Rue Tiquetonne, and took refuge in the next house to this; they searched it, but in vain. I found on the fifth floor a compassionate person who hid me under two mattresses. I remained in my hiding-place or about, until daylight, and as in the evening they might perhaps make a fresh search, I ventured on the roof, seeking an entrance first of all, then a way out by some house or other which might not be guarded. That is my story; and upon my honour, Monsieur, I should be in despair if it should be disagreeable to you.'

'Not at all,' said d'Artagnan. 'On the contrary, I am, upon my word, very glad that Rochefort is at liberty. But know this for certain, that if you fall into the hands of the king's officers, you will be hanged without mercy.'

'Ah, yes, I know it,' said Planchet. 'It is that, indeed, which distresses me, and that is why I am so glad to have fallen in with you—for if you have a mind to hide me, no one can do it more effectually.'

'Yes,' said d'Artagnan, 'I don't ask anything better, although I risk neither more nor less than my rank should it be known that I have sheltered a rebel.'

'Ah, Monsieur, you know well enough that I would risk my life for you.'

'You might even add that you have risked it, Planchet. I forget those things only that I ought to forget; and as to this, I wish to keep it in mind. Sit down, then, and eat in peace, for I see you look at the remains of my supper with a most expressive glance.'

'Yes, Monsieur, for my neighbour's cupboard was very poorly supplied; and I have eaten since mid-day yesterday only some bread and jam. Although I do not despise sweet things in their proper time and place, I found my supper a little too light.'

'Poor fellow!' said d'Artagnan. 'Well, we shall see. Refresh yourself.'

'Ah, Monsieur, you have twice saved my life!' said Planchet; and he sat down, and commenced eating as in the fine days of the Rue des Fossoyeurs.

D'Artagnan kept walking up and down. He was thinking of all the profit he might secure from Planchet in his present circumstances. During this time Planchet was doing his best to make up for lost time. At last he heaved the sigh of satisfaction of one famished, which indicates that after having received a first and substantial instalment he is going to make a short halt.

'Come,' said d'Artagnan, who thought the time had arrived to commence his questioning, 'let us go on in an orderly manner. Do you know where Athos is?'

'No, Monsieur,' answered Planchet.

'The deuce! Do you know where Porthos is?'

'Not at all.'

'Botheration! And Aramis?'

'No more.'

'Confound it!'

'But,' said Planchet, with a sly look, 'I know where Bazin* is.'

'What? You know where Bazin is?'

'Yes, Monsieur.'

'And where is he?'

'At Notre-Dame.'

'And what is he doing at Notre-Dame?'

'He is beadle.'

'Bazin beadle at Notre-Dame! Are you quite sure?'

'Perfectly sure. I have seen him; I have spoken to him.'

'He ought to know where his master is.'

'Doubtless.'

D'Artagnan reflected; then he took his cloak and sword, and prepared to go out.

'Monsieur,' said Planchet, with a pitiful air, 'are you abandoning me in this way? Think that I have no hope but in you.'

'But they will not come and look for you here,' said d'Artagnan.'

'After all, if any come here,' said the cautious Planchet, 'remember that in the eyes of the people of the house, who did not see me come in, I am a thief.'

'That is true,' said d'Artagnan. 'Let us see, do you know any *patois*?'

'Something better than that, Monsieur,' said Planchet. 'I speak Flemish.'

'Where the devil did you learn that?'

'In Artois, where I was in the wars for two years. Listen: Goeden morgen, mynheer! ith ben begeeray te weeten the ge sond hects omstand.'

'What does that mean?'

'Good morning, sir! I am anxious to learn the state of your health.'

'He calls that a language! However, no matter,' said d'Artagnan, 'that happens wonderfully well.'

D'Artagnan went to the door, called a servant, and ordered him to tell the fair Madeleine to come up.

'What are you doing, Monsieur?' said Planchet; 'you are going to confide our secret to a woman!'

'Be quiet; this one will not whisper a word.'

At that moment the hostess came in. She had hastened up with smiling look, expecting to find d'Artagnan alone; but on seeing Planchet she stepped back, much astonished.

'My dear hostess,' said d'Artagnan, 'allow me to introduce your brother, who has come from Flanders, and whom I am taking into my service for a few days.'

'My brother!' said the hostess, more and more astonished.

'Say how do you do to your sister, M. Peter.'

'Wilkom, zuster!' said Planchet.

'Goeden day, broer!' replied the astonished hostess.

'That is it,' said d'Artagnan. 'Monsieur is your brother, whom you do not know, perhaps, but whom I know; he has come from Amsterdam. You dress him up while I am away; on my return, in an hour's time, you present him to me, and on your recommendation, although he does not speak a word of French, as I can refuse you nothing, I will take him into my service. You understand?'

'I can guess what you want, and that is all I require,' said Madeleine.

'You are a precious woman, my dear hostess, and I leave it to you.' Upon which, making a sign of understanding to Planchet, he went out to go to Notre-Dame.

VIII

OF THE DIFFERENT INFLUENCES WHICH HALF A PISTOLE
CAN HAVE ON A BEADLE AND A CHOIR BOY

D'ARTAGNAN crossed the Pont Neuf while congratulating himself on having come across Planchet; for though seeming to render him a service, it was d'Artagnan in reality who was receiving one from Planchet. Nothing could at that moment be more agreeable to him than to possess a brave, intelligent servant. It is true that Planchet could not, in all probability, continue long in his service; but when resuming his social position in the Rue des Lombards, Planchet would continue indebted to d'Artagnan, who had in concealing him saved his life or nearly so; and the latter was not sorry to have some connections among the citizens just at the time when they were preparing war against the court. It was a correspondent in the enemy's camp, and for a man as shrewd as d'Artagnan the smallest things could lead to great ones.

It was then in this frame of mind, tolerably satisfied with fortune and himself, that d'Artagnan reached Notre-Dame. He mounted the steps, entered the church, and addressing a sacristan who was sweeping a chapel, asked him if he knew M. Bazin.

'M. Bazin the beadle?' said the sacristan.

'The very same.'

'That is he who is assisting at Mass, over there in the Chapel of the Virgin.'

D'Artagnan trembled with joy; it seemed to him that whatever Planchet had told him, he should never find Bazin, but now that he had the clew,* he felt sure of reaching the other end of the thread.

He went and knelt in front of the chapel so as not to lose sight of his man. It was fortunately Low Mass, which would soon be finished. D'Artagnan, who had forgotten his prayers, and had neglected to take a prayer-book, used the leisure in examining Bazin.

Bazin wore his official dress with as much dignity as happiness. It could be seen that he had reached, or lacked little of

reaching, the apogee of his ambition, and that the *baleine*,*
ornamented with silver, which he held in his hand, appeared
to him as honourable as the commander's *bâton*, which Condé
threw, or did not throw, into the enemy's lines at the battle
of Fribourg. His physique had undergone a change, so to speak,
perfectly analogous to his dress. His whole body was grown
round, and as if canonized. As to his face, the salient parts
seemed to have become wiped out. He had the same nose, but
the cheeks, while growing larger, had drawn a part of it to
each of them; the chin disappeared under the throat; something
which was not fat but a swelling had shut in his eyes; as to
the forehead, the hair, cut squarely and saintly, covered it to
the three wrinkles over the eyebrows. Let us hasten to say that
Bazin's forehead had never had, even when most uncovered,
more than an inch and a half of height.

The priest finished Mass at the same time as d'Artagnan his
examination; he pronounced the sacramental words and withdrew after giving, to the great astonishment of d'Artagnan, his
benediction, which every one received on his knees. But d'Artagnan's astonishment ceased when in the celebrant he recognized the Coadjutor himself; that is to say, the famous Jean
François de Gondy, who at this time, foreseeing the part he
was going to play, began by his almsgivings to make himself
very popular.

D'Artagnan went down on his knees like the rest, received
his share of the benediction, and made the sign of the cross;
but just when Bazin was passing in his turn, his eyes raised to
heaven, and walking humbly last, d'Artagnan held him by the
bottom of his robe. Bazin cast down his eyes, and made a
backward movement as if he had seen a serpent.

'M. d'Artagnan!' he cried. '*Vade retro, Satanas!*'

'I say, my dear Bazin,' said the officer, laughing, 'is this how
you receive an old friend?'

'Monsieur,' replied Bazin, 'the Christian's true friends are
those who help on his salvation, not those who turn him aside
from it.'

'I do not understand you, Bazin,' said d'Artagnan; 'and I
do not see in what I can be a stumbling-block to your salvation.'

'You forget, Monsieur,' replied Bazin, 'that you were near destroying forever that of my poor master, and that if he had held to you, he would have been damned while remaining a musketeer, when his vocation drew him so earnestly towards the Church.'

'My dear Bazin,' replied d'Artagnan, 'you ought to see, by the place where you are meeting me, that I am much changed in all things. Age brings reason; and as I do not doubt that your master is in the way of working out his salvation, I am come to learn of you where he is, that he may help me by his counsels to work out mine.'

'Say, rather, to take him back with you into the world. Happily,' added Bazin, 'I do not know where he is, for as we are in a sacred place, I should not dare to tell a lie.'

'What!' cried d'Artagnan, at the height of disappointment. 'You do not know where Aramis is?'

'First of all,' said Bazin, 'Aramis was his name of perdition. In Aramis one finds Simara,* which is the name of a demon; and happily for him, he has given up this name forever.'

'Then,' said d'Artagnan, determined to be patient to the end, 'it is not Aramis at all for whom I am looking, but the Abbé d'Herblay. Come, my dear Bazin, tell me where he is.'

'Did you not hear my answer, M. d'Artagnan, that I do not know?'

'Yes, no doubt; but to that I reply that it is impossible.'

'It is the truth, for all that, Monsieur—the simple truth, the truth of the good God.'

D'Artagnan saw clearly that he could draw nothing from Bazin. It was clear that Bazin was lying; but he did so with such ardour and firmness that one could easily guess that he would not retract.

'Very well, Bazin,' said d'Artagnan, 'since you do not know where your master resides, let us say no more about it. Let us part good friends, and take this half-pistole to drink my health.'

'I do not drink, Monsieur,' said Bazin, while majestically pushing away the officer's hand; 'it will do for the laity.'

'Incorruptible!' muttered d'Artagnan. 'I am playing for misfortune.'

And while d'Artagnan, distracted by his reflections, had let go Bazin's robe, the latter took the occasion to beat a hasty retreat towards the sacristy, in which he did not deem himself safe until he had fastened the door behind him.

D'Artagnan stood motionless, thoughtful, with eyes fixed on the door which had put a barrier between him and Bazin, when he felt himself lightly touched on the shoulder.

He turned round, and was going to make an exclamation of surprise, when he who had touched him put his finger to his lips as a sign of silence.

'You here, my dear Rochefort!' said he, in a subdued voice.

'*Chut!*'* said Rochefort. 'Did you know I was free?'

'I learned it at first hand.'

'And by whom?'

'By Planchet.'

'What, by Planchet?'

'Certainly! It is he who saved you.'

'Planchet! Really, I thought I recognized him. This shows, my dear friend, that a good deed is never lost.'

'And what are you come to do here?'

'I come to thank God for my happy deliverance,' said Rochefort.

'And then what next? for I presume that is not all.'

'And then to take orders of the Coadjutor, to see if we shall not be able in some degree to enrage Mazarin.'

'Silly fellow! you are going to get yourself thrust into the Bastille again!'

'Oh, as to that, I shall be on my guard, I answer you! The open air is so good! So,' continued Rochefort, while taking in a full breath, 'I am going to take a turn in the country, to make a tour in the provinces.'

'Bless me,' said d'Artagnan, 'and so am I.'

'And without indiscretion on my part, may I ask you where you are going?'

'To search for my friends.'

'What friends?'

'Those of whom you asked some news yesterday.'

'Athos, Porthos, and Aramis? You are looking for them?'

'Yes.'

'Upon honour!'

'What is there so astonishing in that?'

'Nothing. It is funny! And for whom are you looking for them?'

'You do not suspect, even?'

'Yes, indeed I do.'

'Unfortunately, I do not know where they are.'

'And you have no means of learning news of them? Wait a week, and I will give you some tidings of them.'

'A week—too long; I must before three days have found them.'

'Three days! That's short,' said Rochefort; 'and France is large.'

'Never mind, you know the word *must*; with that word one does many things.'

'And when do you begin the search?'

'I am on it.'

'Good success!'

'And you, prosperous journey!'

'Perhaps we shall meet on the road.'

'It is not probable.'

'Who knows? Chance is capricious.'

'Adieu.'

'*Au revoir.* By the by, if Mazarin speaks to you about me, tell him that I have enjoined you to let him know that he will see before long if I am, as he says, too old for action.'

And Rochefort went off with one of those diabolical smiles which had formerly made d'Artagnan shudder so often; but d'Artagnan looked at him this time without pain, and smiled in his turn with an expression of melancholy that this recollection alone, perhaps, could give to his countenance.

'Go, demon,' said he, 'and do what you please, it is nothing to me; there is no second Constance in the world!'

On turning round, d'Artagnan saw Bazin, who, after having taken off his ecclesiastical dress, was talking with the sacristan to whom d'Artagnan had talked on entering the church. Bazin seemed very animated, and made with his fat little arms a number of movements. d'Artagnan guessed that in all probability he was enjoining him to use the greatest caution in respect to himself.

D'Artagnan took advantage of their being preoccupied to slip out of the cathedral, and go and hide at the corner of the Rue des Canettes.* Bazin was unable to leave without being seen from the spot where d'Artagnan was hiding.

Five minutes after, d'Artagnan being at his post, Bazin appeared on the steps; he looked all around to be assured that he was not observed. But he was unable to perceive our officer, whose head alone passed the corner of a house fifty paces distant. Satisfied by his survey, he ventured into the Rue Notre-Dame. D'Artagnan darted from his hiding-place, and was in time to see him turn around by the Rue la Juiveric, and enter a house of decent appearance in the Rue de la Calandre; so our officer did not at all doubt that the worthy beadle lodged in that house.

D'Artagnan was disinclined to go and make enquiries at it. The concierge, if there was one, would have already been apprised; and if there was not one, to whom should he address himself?

He entered a small public-house which formed the corner of the Rue St Eloi and the Rue de la Calandre, and asked for some hippocras.* This drink required a good half-hour to be prepared; he had the whole time for watching Bazin without awakening suspicion.

He caught sight in the establishment of a small sharp fellow from twelve to fifteen years of age, whom he thought he remembered having seen twenty minutes before in a chorister's dress. He questioned him, and as the apprenticed sub-deacon had no interest in dissimulating, d'Artagnan learned that he exercised from six to nine in the morning the profession of chorister, and from nine till midnight that of waiter in the public.

While talking to the boy, a horse was brought to the door of Bazin's house. The horse was ready saddled and bridled. A moment after, Bazin came down.

'Bless me,' said the boy, 'there is our beadle, who is about starting.'

'And where is he going in that style?' asked d'Artagnan.

'I am bothered if I know.'

'Half a pistole,' said d'Artagnan, 'if you can find out.'

'For me,' said the boy, whose eyes lighted up with joy, 'if I can tell where Bazin goes? It is not difficult. Are you laughing at me?'

'No, on the word of an officer! There is the half-pistole,' and he showed him the corrupting coin, but without yet giving it to him.

'I am going to ask him.'

'That is exactly the way of knowing nothing,' said d'Artagnan; 'wait till he is gone, and then, after that, ask questions and find out. That is your lookout; the half-pistole is there,' and he put it back into his pocket.

'I understand,' said the boy, with that sly grin which belongs only to the gamin of Paris; 'well, we'll wait.'

They had not long to wait. Five minutes after, Bazin set out at a gentle trot, quickening his horse's pace by blows of an umbrella. Bazin had always had the habit of carrying an umbrella by way of whip.

Scarcely had he turned the corner of the Rue de la Juiverie before the boy darted forth like a bloodhound on the track.

D'Artagnan took his place again at the table where he sat down on entering, perfectly sure that before ten minutes he should know what he wished to know. In fact, before that time had elapsed the boy returned.

'Well?' asked d'Artagnan.

'Well,' said the boy, 'I know it all.'

'And where has he gone?'

'The half-pistole is still for me?'

'Certainly! answer.'

'I ask to see it. Lend it to me, that I may see it is not counterfeit.'

'There it is.'

'Master,' then said the boy, 'Monsieur wants some change.'

The master was at the counter; he gave the change, and took the half-pistole. The boy put the change into his pocket.

'And now, where is he gone?' said d'Artagnan, who had seen him practising this little dodge, while laughing.

'He has gone to Noisy.'*

'How do you know that?'

'Ah, he doesn't lack slyness. I recognized the horse as the butcher's, who lets it now and then to M. Bazin. Now, I thought the butcher would not let his horse without knowing where he is going, though I do not believe M. Bazin capable of over-riding a horse.'

'And he has told you that M. Bazin——'

'Was going to Noisy. Besides, it seems that is his custom. He goes there two or three times a week.'

'And do you know Noisy?'

'I believe so. My nurse lives there.'

'Is there a convent at Noisy?'

'Yes, and a fine one! a convent of Jesuits.'

'Good,' said d'Artagnan, 'there is no longer a doubt!'

'Then are you satisfied?'

'Yes. What is your name?'

'Friquet. Say, then, Monsieur officer,' said the boy, 'are there more half-pistoles to earn?'

'Perhaps,' said d'Artagnan.

D'Artagnan took his tablets, and wrote down the boy's name and the address of the public-house. He then paid for the hippocras, which he had not touched, and took the road back to the Rue Tiquetonne.

IX

HOW D'ARTAGNAN, LOOKING FOR ARAMIS FAR AWAY, PERCEIVED HIM ON THE CRUPPER BEHIND PLANCHET

ON entering, d'Artagnan saw a man seated by the fire; it was Planchet, but so metamorphosed, thanks to the old clothes which Madeleine's husband had left behind, that even d'Artagnan could scarcely recognize him. Madeleine introduced him in sight of all the waiters. Planchet addressed the officer in a fine Flemish phrase, to which the officer replied in some words which were of no language, and the bargain was made. Madeleine's brother entered d'Artagnan's service.

D'Artagnan's scheme was perfectly arranged; he did not wish to reach Noisy in the daytime, for fear of being recognized.

He had therefore some time before him, Noisy being only three or four leagues from Paris, on the road to Meaux.

He began with a substantial breakfast, which forms a bad opening for brainwork, but an excellent provision when bodily work is required; then he changed his dress, fearing that his musketeer's cloak might lead to suspicion; then he took the strongest of his three swords, which he only wore on grand occasions; then, about two o'clock, he had two horses saddled, and followed by Planchet, left by the Barrière de la Villette.* A most active search continued to be made in the next house to find Planchet.

When a league and a half from Paris, d'Artagnan, seeing that in his impatience he had still left too soon, pulled up to give his horses a breathing time. The inn was full of ill-looking men, who looked as if on the point of making some nocturnal expedition. A man enveloped in a cloak appeared at the door, but seeing a stranger, he made a sign with his hand, and two drinkers went out to converse with him.

As for d'Artagnan, he carelessly approached the landlady, praised the wine, which was horrible stuff from Montreuil,* put some questions to her about Noisy, and learned that there were in that village only two houses of good size—one belonging to the Archbishop of Paris,* and in which at this time his niece, the Duchesse de Longueville, was staying; the other was a Jesuit convent, and which, according to custom, was the property of these worthy fathers. One could not make a mistake.

At four d'Artagnan started off at a footpace, for he wished to reach there close upon night. Now, when one goes riding at a walk on a winter's day in raw weather, through country without anything eventful, one has at least nothing better to do than, according to La Fontaine,* what the hare does in its form—to muse. D'Artagnan, then, was musing, and so was Planchet. Only, as we shall see, their musings were different.

One of the hostess's words had given a particular direction to d'Artagnan's thoughts, and that was the name of Madame de Longueville.

The fact is, she possessed all that led one to think. She was one of the greatest ladies of the kingdom, as well as one of the most beautiful women of the court. Married to the old Duc de Longueville, whom she did not love, she had first passed for being mistress of Coligny, who had been killed in a duel on the Place Royale by the Duc de Guise on her account; then they had talked of a friendship a little too tender that she had for Prince de Condé, her brother, and which had scandalized the timorous souls of the court; then, finally, they said again, a real and deep hatred had followed this friendship, and the duchess at this time had a political liaison with Prince de Marcillac*—eldest son of the old Duc de la Rochefoucauld, whom she was in the way of making an enemy to the Duc de Condé, her brother.

D'Artagnan thought of all these things. He thought how when he was at the Louvre he had often seen pass before him, radiant and dazzling, the beautiful Madame de Longueville; he thought of Aramis, too, who without being higher placed than himself had formerly been Madame de Chevreuse's lover,* who was at the other court what Madame de Longueville was at this. And he asked why there were people in the world who obtained all they wished for—some in the way of ambition, others in that of love—while there were others who from chance, bad fortune, or natural hindrances implanted in them, stopped halfway to all their hopes.

He was forced to confess that in spite of his intelligence and cleverness he belonged, and would probably belong, to this latter class, when Planchet drew near him and said:

'I bet, Monsieur, that you are thinking of the same thing as I.'

'I doubt it, Planchet,' said d'Artagnan, smiling; 'but of what were you thinking?'

'Of those ill-looking fellows, Monsieur, who were drinking at the inn where we halted.'

'Always cautious, Planchet.'

'Monsieur, it is by instinct.'

'Well, let us see; what does your instinct say in such circumstances?'

'Monsieur, my instinct tells me that those fellows were met at that inn for a bad purpose; and I was thinking over what my instinct told me in the darkest corner of the stable, when a man enveloped in a cloak entered, followed by two others.'

'Ah!' ejaculated d'Artagnan. Planchet's story corresponded with his preceding observations. 'Well?'

'One of the men said, "He must certainly be at Noisy, or reach there this evening, for I recognized his servant." "You are sure?" said the man in the cloak. "Yes, Prince." '

'Prince!' interrupted d'Artagnan.

'Yes; Prince. But listen further. "If he is there, let us see decidedly what must be done!" said the other drinker. "What ought to be done?" said the prince. "Yes, he is not a man to let himself be taken like that; he will use his sword." "Ah, well, we must do as he does, and yet try to take him alive. Have you any cords to fasten him, and a gag?" "We have all that." "Observe that he will in all probability be disguised as a cavalier." "Oh, yes, yes, Monseigneur; it's all right." "Besides, I shall be there, and I will direct you." "You engage that justice——" "I will answer for everything," said the prince. "That is good. We shall do our best." And upon that they left the stable.'

'Well,' said d'Artagnan, 'how does that concern us? It is one of those enterprises made daily.'

'Are you sure that it is not directed against ourselves?'

'Against ourselves! and why?'

'Hang it! recall their words! "I recognized his servant," said one of them; and this might well concern me.'

'What next?'

' "He ought to be at Noisy, or reach there this evening," said the other; and that might have reference to you.'

'Afterwards?'

'Afterwards the prince said, "Observe that he will in all probability be disguised as a cavalier;" which seems to me to leave no doubt in the matter, since you are dressed as a cavalier, and not as an officer of Musketeers. Well, what do you say to that?'

'Alas, my dear Planchet!' said d'Artagnan, heaving a sigh. 'I maintain that I am, unfortunately, no longer living at the time when princes wished to have me assassinated. Ah, that was a fine time! Do not bother yourself. These people do not want anything with us.'

'Monsieur is sure?'

'I answer for it.'

'It is well, then. Let us say no more about it.' And Planchet followed d'Artagnan with the sublime confidence he had had always in his master, and which fifteen years of separation had not at all changed.

At the end of a league Planchet rode up to d'Artagnan. 'Monsieur,' said he.

'Well,' said the latter.

'Stop, Monsieur; look this way,' said Planchet. 'Does it not seem to you that you can see some shadows passing in the dark? Listen! I think I hear horses' steps.'

'Impossible,' said d'Artagnan. 'The ground is softened by the rains. However, as you say, I fancy I see something.' And he stopped to look and listen. 'If we do not hear the horses' steps, at least we hear their whinnying. Stop!' And in fact the neighing of a horse caught d'Artagnan's ear. 'They are our men who are in the field,' said he; 'but that is nothing to us. Let us go on.' And they resumed their way.

Half an hour after, they reached the first houses in Noisy. It might have been half-past eight or nine o'clock. According to village habits, everybody had gone to bed, and not a light was seen in the village.

D'Artagnan and Planchet continued their course. To the right and left of their road was cut out in the sombre grey of the sky the still darker outlines of the house-roofs. From time to time, a dog, awaking, barked behind some door, or a frightened cat precipitately left the middle of the road to take refuge in a pile of faggots, where its eyes sparkled like carbuncles. These were the only living beings which seemed to dwell in the village.

Nearly in the middle of the town, commanding the principal square, arose a dark mass, isolated by two lanes, and on the front of which two enormous lime trees extended their bare branches. D'Artagnan examined the building with attention.

'That,' said he to Planchet, 'must be the archbishop's château, the abode of Madame de Longueville. But where is the convent?'

'The convent,' said Planchet, 'is at the end of the village. I know it.'

'Well,' said d'Artagnan, 'gallop there, while I tighten the girth of my horse, and return and tell me if there is any lighted window at the Jesuits' house.'

Planchet obeyed, and was soon lost in the darkness, while d'Artagnan got down and re-adjusted his horse's girth.

At the end of five minutes Planchet returned. 'Monsieur,' said he, 'there is one window only with a light on the side which looks towards the fields.'

'H'm,' said d'Artagnan, 'if I were a Frondeur, I could knock here, and be sure of having a good lodging; if I were a monk, I could knock down there, and be sure of a good supper; while, on the contrary, it is possible that between château and convent, we may lie on the bare ground, dying of hunger and thirst.'

'Yes,' added Planchet, 'like the famous ass of Buridan.* In the meanwhile, would you wish me to knock?'

'*Chut!*' said d'Artagnan. 'The only window lighted up has just become dark.'

'Do you hear, Monsieur?' said Planchet.

'I do indeed. What noise is it?'

It was like the sound of an approaching storm. At the same moment two troops of cavaliers, each of ten men, passed forth from each of the two lanes which ran along by the house, and stopping all exit, surrounded d'Artagnan and Planchet.

'Bless me!' said d'Artagnan, drawing his sword and sheltering himself behind his horse, while Planchet executed the same manœuvre, 'have you thought rightly? And can it be us that they really want?'

'That is he! we have him!' said the horsemen, dashing at d'Artagnan with drawn swords.

'Do not miss him,' said a high voice.

'No, Monseigneur; rest assured.'

D'Artagnan thought the moment was come for him to join in the conversation. 'Holloa, gentlemen!' said he, with his Gascon accent. 'What do you want? What do you ask?'

'You will soon know,' growled the horsemen in chorus.

'Stop, stop!' cried he whom they called Monseigneur. 'Stop, as you value your heads! That is not his voice!'*

'Come, gentlemen,' said d'Artagnan, 'do people become mad by accident at Noisy? Only take care, for I forewarn you that the first who comes within the length of my sword—and my sword is long—I will rip open.'

The chief approached.

'What are you doing, then?' said a haughty voice, as if accustomed to command.

'And you yourself?' said d'Artagnan.

'Be polite, or your hide will be tanned in fine fashion—for though we may wish to remain nameless, yet we want the respect due to our rank.'

'You do not wish your name known because you are directing an ambush; but I, a peaceful traveller with my servant, have not the same reason for concealing my name.'

'That's enough! What is your name?'

'I tell you my name that you may know where to find me, Monsieur, Monseigneur, or my prince, as it may please you to be styled,' said our Gascon, who did not wish to have the appearance of yielding to a threat. 'Do you know M. d'Artagnan?'

'Lieutenant in the king's Musketeers?' said the voice.

'The same.'

'Oh, yes; certainly.'

'Well,' continued the Gascon, 'you ought to have heard that he has a tough wrist and a keen blade.'

'You are M. d'Artagnan?'

'I am.'

'Then you come here to defend *him*?'

'*Him*? And who is he?'

'He for whom we are searching.'

'It seems,' continued d'Artagnan, 'that while thinking I am at Noisy, I have landed in the kingdom of enigmas.'

'Come, answer,' said the same haughty voice. 'Are you waiting for him under these windows? Did you come to Noisy to defend him?'

'I am expecting no one,' said d'Artagnan, who began to grow impatient; 'I don't intend to defend any one but myself, but this I will do vigorously, I forewarn you.'

'Very well,' said the voice, 'go from here, and leave the place.'

'Go from here?' said d'Artagnan, whose projects were upset by this order; 'it is not easy, seeing that I am falling from fatigue, and my horse also—unless you feel disposed to offer me supper and a bed in the neighbourhood.'

'Knave!'

'Eh, Monsieur!' said d'Artagnan; 'mind your words, I beg you, for if you say that a second time, might you be marquis, duke, prince, or king,* I will run you through. Do you hear?'

'Come,' said the chief, 'we cannot be mistaken here; it is clearly a Gascon who speaks, and consequently not he whom we want. Our throw has failed for this night. Retire! We shall meet again, M. d'Artagnan,' added the chief, raising his voice.

'Yes, but never with the same advantages,' said the Gascon, in raillery; 'for when you meet me again, perhaps you will be alone and it will be in the daytime.'

'Very good, very good,' said the voice. 'Proceed, Messieurs.' And the troop, grumbling and growling, disappeared in the darkness, and took the road to Paris.

D'Artagnan and Planchet remained a little longer on the defensive; but the sounds continuing to grow less, they sheathed their swords.

'You see plainly, you fool,' said d'Artagnan, quietly, to Planchet, 'that it was not I whom they wanted.'

'But who, then?' asked Planchet.

'I know nothing about it, and little it concerns me. What concerns me is how to get into the Jesuits' convent. So, to horse, and let us go and knock there. At all events they will not eat us;' and d'Artagnan got into the saddle.

Planchet was going to do the same, when an unexpected weight fell on the hindquarters of his horse, causing him to flinch.

'Hi, Monsieur!' cried Planchet. 'I have a man on the crupper.'

D'Artagnan turned round, and actually saw two human forms on Planchet's horse.

'It is then the Devil who is pursuing us!' cried he, drawing his sword and preparing to charge the new-comer.

'No, my dear d'Artagnan,' said the latter; 'it is not the Devil. It is I; it is Aramis. At the gallop, Planchet, and at the end of the village turn to the left.'

And Planchet, carrying Aramis behind him, went off at a gallop, followed by d'Artagnan, who began to think he was dreaming some fantastic and incoherent dream.

X

THE ABBÉ D'HERBLAY

AT the end of the village Planchet turned to the left, and stopped under the lighted window. Aramis jumped down, and clapped his hands three times. The window was at once opened, and a rope ladder came down.

'My dear friend,' said Aramis, 'if you will go up, I shall be delighted to receive you.'

'Oh! ah!' said d'Artagnan. 'Is that the way to enter with you?'

'After nine at night, it is. *Pardieu!*' said Aramis; 'the rule of the convent is most severe.'

'Pardon, my dear friend,' said d'Artagnan. 'It seems to me that you said "*Pardieu*." '

'You think so,' said Aramis, laughing; 'it is possible. You can't imagine, my dear fellow, how in these cursed convents one learns bad habits, and what wicked ways have all these people of the Church with whom I am forced to live. But you do not go up?'

'Pass before me! I follow you.'

'As the deceased cardinal said to the late king, "To show you the way, Sire;" ' and Aramis briskly went up the ladder, and in a moment he had reached the window.

D'Artagnan followed, but more carefully. This sort of way was evidently less familiar to him than to his friend.

'Pardon,' said Aramis, remarking his awkwardness. 'If I had known previously of your visit, I would have had the gardener's ladder brought; but for myself this does very well.'

'Monsieur,' said Planchet, when he saw d'Artagnan nearly at the top; 'that suits M. Aramis and yourself also. It would, at a stretch, do for me; but the two horses cannot mount the ladder.'

'Lead them into that shed, my friend,' said Aramis, pointing out to Planchet a sort of erection on the open ground. 'You will there find straw and oats for them.'

'But for myself?' said Planchet.

'Return under this window; clap your hands thrice, and we will pass you down some food. Don't be alarmed, *morbleu!* we don't die of hunger here. Be off;' and Aramis, pulling up the rope ladder, closed the window.

D'Artagnan examined the room. He had never seen a room at the same time more warlike and more elegant. At each corner were trophies of arms, presenting to eye and to hand swords of all kinds, and four large paintings represented, in military costume, Cardinal Lorraine, Cardinal Richelieu, Cardinal Lavalette, and the Archbishop of Bordeaux.* It is true that in addition there was nothing to indicate the abode of an abbé; the hangings were damask, the carpets came from Alençon,* and the bed especially seemed more fit for an elegant lady, with its lace hangings and its counterpane, than for a man who had taken a vow to gain heaven by abstinence and hardship.

'You are looking at my den,' said Aramis. 'Ah, my dear friend, excuse me. What would you? I am lodged like a Chartreux. But whom are you looking for so sharply?'

'For him who dropped the ladder. I don't see any one, and yet the ladder could not drop of itself.'

'No; it is Bazin.'

'Ah, ah!' said d'Artagnan.

'But,' continued Aramis, 'Bazin is a well-trained fellow, who, seeing I did not return alone, has discreetly retired. Sit down, and let us talk;' and Aramis pushed an armchair towards d'Artagnan, in which the latter reclined at his ease.

'First of all, you will have some supper with me, won't you?' asked Aramis.

'Yes, if you really mean it,' said d'Artagnan; 'and with real pleasure, I assure you. The journey has given me a devilishly good appetite.'

'Ah, my poor friend,' said Aramis, 'you will get meagre fare; you were not expected.'

'Am I threatened with the omelet of Crèvecoeur* and the *théobromes* in question? Was it not thus that you formerly called spinach?'

'I hope that with God's help and Bazin's we shall find something better in the pantry of the worthy Jesuit fathers. Bazin, my friend, come here.'

The door opened and Bazin appeared; but on seeing d'Artagnan he uttered an exclamation like a cry of despair.

'My dear Bazin,' said d'Artagnan, 'I am very glad to see with what admirable coolness you tell lies, even in a church.'

'Monsieur,' said Bazin, 'I have learned from the worthy Jesuit fathers that one may lie if it be with a good purpose.'

'Very good. Bazin, d'Artagnan is dying of hunger, and so am I; serve up your best supper, and especially bring some good wine.'

Bazin bowed to signify obedience, sighed deeply, and went out.

'Now we are alone, my dear Aramis,' said d'Artagnan, while casting his eyes from the room to its owner, and finishing his examination, begun at the furniture, at the dress of the latter, 'tell me, where the devil did you come from when you dropped behind Planchet?'

'Oh, *corbleu!*' said Aramis, 'from heaven, of course.'

'From heaven!' replied d'Artagnan, shaking his head. 'You have no more the appearance of returning thence than of going there.'

'My dear fellow,' said Aramis, with an air of affectation which d'Artagnan had never seen in him at the time when he was a musketeer, 'if I did not come from heaven, I at least came from Paradise, and they are not much unlike.'

'Then the learned have settled it,' replied d'Artagnan. 'Up to the present nothing positive was known of its position. Some placed it on Mount Ararat; others between the Tigris and the Euphrates. It seems that they sought for it afar off while it was close by. Paradise is at Noisy-le-Sec, on the site of the Archbishop of Paris's château. One leaves it, not by the door, but by the window; one comes down, not by the marble steps of a peristyle, but by the branches of a lime tree, and the angel with the flaming sword who guards it has to me the air of having changed his celestial name of Gabriel to the more terrestrial one of the Prince de Marcillac.'

Aramis burst into laughter.

'You were always a jolly companion, my dear fellow,' said he, 'and your lively Gascon humour has not left you. Yes, there is something in what you tell me; only at least don't believe that I am in love with Madame de Longueville.'

'Hang it! I shall take care of that!' said d'Artagnan. 'After having been so long the lover of Madame de Chevreuse, you could not have transferred your heart to her mortal enemy.'

'Yes, that is true,' said Aramis, with an indifferent air. 'Yes, that poor duchess! I did love her formerly, and to do her justice, she has been very useful to us; but what could I do? She had to leave France. A rough antagonist was that cardinal,' continued Aramis, throwing a glance at the old minister's portrait. 'He had ordered her confinement in the Château de Loches.* He would have sliced off her head, upon my faith, as he did that of Chalais, of Montmorency and of Cinq-Mars; but she escaped, disguised as a man, with her maid, that poor Kitty.* There even happened to her, as I have heard it said, a strange adventure in I know not what village, with I know not what curate of whom she asked hospitality, and who having only one chamber, and taking her for a cavalier offered to share it with her. She wore a man's dress in a wonderful fashion, that dear Marie. I know only one woman who wears it as well. They have composed this couplet upon her—

Laboissière, dis-moi,——

You know it?'

'No; sing it, my dear fellow.'

And Aramis, assuming the most cavalier-like manner:

'Laboissière, dis-moi,
Suis-je pas bien en homme?'
"Vous chevauchez, ma foi,
Mieux que tant que nous sommes."

Elle est
Parmi les hallebardes
Au régiment des gardes
Comme un cadet.'*[1]

[1] 'Tell me, Laboissière,   She is among the halberdiers
Do I not look well in a man's dress?'   In the regiment of guards
    "Upon my word, you sit astride   Like a military cadet.'
Better than we do ourselves."

'Bravo!' said d'Artagnan. 'You always sang marvellously well, and I see that the Mass has not spoiled your voice.'

'My dear fellow,' said Aramis, 'you understand that when a musketeer, I mounted guard as rarely as possible; now I am an abbé, I say as few Masses as I can. But let us return to the poor duchess.'

'Which? The Duchesse de Chevreuse or the Duchesse de Longueville?'

'My dear fellow, I have told you there is nothing between me and the Duchesse de Longueville—a few coquetries, perhaps, and that's all. I was speaking of the Duchesse de Chevreuse. Have you seen her since her return from Brussels, after the death of the king?'

'Yes, certainly; and she was still very beautiful.'

'Yes,' said Aramis; 'I have seen her, too, and gave her good advice, by which she did not profit. I took great pains to tell her that Mazarin was the queen's lover. She would not believe it, saying she knew Anne of Austria, and that she was too proud to love such a fop. Then the duchess entered the Duc de Beaufort's cabal, and the fop has arrested Monsieur the Duke, and exiled Madame de Chevreuse.'

'You know she has got permission to come back?'*

'Yes; and also that she is back. She is sure to be doing some piece of folly.'

'Oh, but this time perhaps she will follow your advice.'

'Oh, this time,' said Aramis, 'I have not seen her. She is much changed.'

'That is not your case, my dear Aramis, for you are always the same. You have still your beautiful black hair, elegant figure, and lady's hands, which are admirable ones for a churchman.'

'Yes,' said Aramis; 'it is true I take much care of myself. Do you know that I am getting old? I shall soon be thirty-seven.'

'Listen, my dear fellow,' said d'Artagnan, smiling; 'since we have met again, let us agree on one thing—the age which we shall be for the future.'

'What for?' said Aramis.

'Yes,' replied d'Artagnan; 'formerly I was your junior by two or three years, and if I don't make a mistake I am a good forty years.'

'Really!' said Aramis. 'Then it is I who am in error, for you have always been, my dear fellow, a capital mathematician. I should be then forty-three,* according to your account. *Diable, diable,* my dear fellow! Don't go and tell it at the Hôtel de Rambouillet! That would injure me.'

'Don't be alarmed,' said d'Artagnan. 'I don't go there.'

'But,' cried Aramis, 'what is that animal of a Bazin about, I wonder? Bazin! Make haste, will you! We are going mad with hunger and thirst!'

Bazin, who entered at that moment, raised to heaven his hands, each holding a bottle.

'At last,' said Aramis, 'are we ready? Come!'

'Yes, Monsieur, this very moment,' said Bazin; 'but I have not had time to bring up all the——'

'Because you think you always have your beadle's costume on your shoulders,' interrupted Aramis, 'and pass all your time in reading your breviary. But I forewarn you that if by dint of polishing the things in the chapels you forget how to clean my sword, I will make a great fire of all your holy images and roast you in it.'

Bazin, scandalized, made the sign of the cross with a bottle which he was holding. As for d'Artagnan, more surprised than ever at the tone and manners of the Abbé d'Herblay, which contrasted so strongly with those of the musketeer Aramis, he stood with open eyes before his friend.

Bazin briskly covered the table with a damask cloth, and on it laid so many things, gilt, perfumed, and dainty, that d'Artagnan stood amazed at it all.

'But were you expecting someone?' asked the officer.

'Oh,' said Aramis, 'I have always one at all events; then, I knew that you were looking for me.'

'From whom?'

'Why, from M. Bazin, who has taken you for the Devil, and who hurried off here to forewarn me of the danger which threatened my soul if I met again such bad company as an officer of Musketeers.'

'Oh, Monsieur,' said Bazin, with his hands joined, and in a supplicating manner.

'Come, none of your hypocrisies! you know I do not like them. You would do much better to open the window, and let down a loaf, a fowl, and a bottle of wine to your friend Planchet, who for the last hour has been killing himself by clapping his hands.

In fact, Planchet, after having given the straw and oats to his horses, had returned beneath the window, and had several times repeated the pre-arranged signal.

Bazin obeyed, attached to the end of a cord the three objects mentioned, and let them down to Planchet, who, asking nothing more, retired immediately under the shed.

'Now let us have supper,' said Aramis.

The two friends sat down to table, and Aramis began to cut up fowls, partridges, and ham with complete gastronomic skill.

'I say,' said d'Artagnan, 'how you feed yourself!'

'Yes, pretty well. I have for fast-days a dispensation from Rome which Monsieur the Coadjutor procured on account of my health; then I have taken for cook the ex-cook of Lafollone,* you know, the old friend of the cardinal—that famous gourmand who said for his only prayer after his dinner, "Lord, grant me the power to well digest what I have so well eaten." '

'Which did not prevent his dying of indigestion,' said d'Artagnan, laughing.

'What do you wish?' returned Aramis, with a resigned air. 'One cannot escape his destiny.'

'But I beg pardon, my dear fellow; I have a question that I want to put to you,' resumed d'Artagnan.

'Well, then, put it; you know well enough that between ourselves there cannot be any want of discretion.'

'You are then become rich?'

'Oh, no! I make twelve thousand francs per annum, without reckoning a small benefice of a thousand crowns which Monsieur the Prince made me accept.'

'And with what do you make these twelve thousand francs?' said d'Artagnan; 'with your poems?'*

'No; I have given up poetry, except to compose now and then a drinking-song, some fine sonnet, or innocent epigram. I write sermons, my friend.'

'What! sermons?'

'Oh, but wonderful sermons, do you see! So it seems, at least.'

'Which you preach?'

'No, which I sell.'

'To whom?'

'To those of my brethren who aim at being grand orators.'

'Ah, really! And you have not yourself been attracted by this desire for fame?'

'Yes, yes, my dear fellow; but nature has taken it away. When I am in the pulpit, and by chance a pretty woman looks at me, I look at her; if she smiles, I smile too. Then I beat about the bush; in place of speaking of the torments of hell, I speak about the joys of paradise. This once happened to me in the church of St Louis au Marais.* A gentleman laughed in my face; I stopped to tell him he was a fool. The people went out to gather stones; but during that time I had so well changed the minds of the audience that it was he whom they stoned. The next day he came to my house, thinking he had an affair of honour with an abbé like abbés in general.'

'And what was the result of the visit?' said d'Artagnan, holding his sides with laughter.

'Why, we named a meeting for the following evening on the Place Royale, and by the bye, you know something of that.'

'Was it then that rude fellow against whom I acted as your second?' asked d'Artagnan.

'Precisely so. You saw how I arranged the matter.'

'Did he die?'

'I know nothing of that. But at all events I gave him absolution *in articulo mortis*. It is enough to kill the body without killing the soul.'

Bazin made a sign of desperation, which meant that while he might approve this moral, yet he strongly disapproved of the mode in which it was taught.

'Bazin, my friend, you do not observe that I can see you in this glass, and that once for all I interdict you from any sign of approbation or disapprobation. You are going to do me the pleasure to serve us some Spanish wine, and retire. Besides, my friend d'Artagnan has some secrets to tell me. Is it not so, d'Artagnan?'

D'Artagnan gave a nod of assent, and Bazin retired, after having placed some Spanish wine on the table.

The two friends, now alone, remained silent a moment, looking at each other. Aramis seemed awaiting digestion to commence; d'Artagnan was preparing his exordium. Each of them, when the other was not looking, risked a sly look.

Aramis broke the silence.

XI

THE TWO GASPARDS

'WHAT are you musing on, d'Artagnan,' said he, 'and what thought makes you smile?'

'I am thinking, my dear fellow, that when you were a musketeer you were forever becoming the abbé, and now you are an abbé you appear to me to have a strong leaning to the musketeers.'*

'That is true,' said Aramis, laughing. 'Man is a strange creature, made up of contrasts. Since I have been an abbé I dream only of battles.'

'That is seen in your furnishing; you have there rapiers of all forms, and for the most difficult tastes. Do you still fence well?'

'I! I fence as you used to formerly, even better perhaps. I do nothing else all day.'

'And with whom?'

'With an excellent instructor in fence whom we have here.'

'What, here?'

'Yes, here in this convent. There is something of everything in a convent of Jesuits.'

'Then you would have killed M. de Marcillac if he had come to attack you alone, instead of leading twenty men?'

'Decidedly,' said Aramis; 'and even at the head of his twenty, if I had been able to draw without being recognized.'

'Heaven pardon me!' said d'Artagnan to himself, 'I think he has become more of a Gascon than I am;' then aloud, 'Well, my dear Aramis, you ask me why I was seeking for you.'

'No, I did not ask you,' said Aramis, with his usual shrewdness; 'but I was waiting for you to tell me.'

'Well, then, it was to offer you simply a means of killing M. de Marcillac, if that will give you any pleasure, prince as he is.'

'Bless me,' said Aramis, 'that is a good idea.'

'Which I invite you to profit from, my dear friend. Let us see! with your abbey of a thousand crowns, and the twelve thousand francs you make by selling sermons, are you well off? Answer freely.'

'I! I am as poor as Job, and I believe you would not find in my pockets and coffers a hundred pistoles.'

'A hundred pistoles!' said d'Artagnan, in a low vice; 'he calls that being as poor as Job! If I had them always before me I should regard myself as rich as Croesus.' Then quite aloud, 'Are you ambitious?' he added.

'As Enceladus.'*

'Well, my friend, I bring the means of being rich, powerful, and free to do what you like.'

A shade passed across the countenance of Aramis as rapidly as that which floats across the corn in August; but rapid as it was, d'Artagnan saw it.

'Speak,' said Aramis.

'One question first. You engage in politics?'

A light shone in the eyes of Aramis as rapidly as the shade passed over his face, but not so rapidly that d'Artagnan did not notice it.

'No,' said Aramis.

'Then all propositions will be pleasing to you, since you have not for the moment other master than God,' said d'Artagnan, laughing.

'It is possible.'

'Have you, my dear Aramis, sometimes dreamed of those happy days of youth which we passed laughing, drinking, or fighting?'

'Ah, yes, indeed! and I have more than once regretted them. That was a happy time—*delectabile tempus!*'

'Well, my dear friend, those jolly days can return. I have received a commission to go in search of my companions, and

I have desired to begin with you, who were the soul of our fellowship.'

Aramis here bowed, more from politeness than from affection.

'To introduce me again to politics!' said he, with a feeble voice, and throwing himself back in his chair. 'Ah, dear d'Artagnan, see how I live, regularly and comfortably. We have experienced the ingratitude of the great, you know well enough.'

'That is true,' said d'Artagnan; 'but perhaps the great are repentant of their ingratitude.'

'Then,' said Aramis, 'that would alter the case. Come; to every sin pardon. Besides, you are right on one point; it is that if inclination should take us to mix in political affairs, the moment, I believe, has come.'

'How do you know that, who are not mixed up in politics?'

'Why, without being personally occupied with it, I live in a world where they are occupied with it. While cultivating poetry, while making love, I am connected with M. Sarazin, and he is with M. de Conti, and with M. Voiture, and he with the Coadjutor; so that the political world is not entirely unknown to me.'

'I suspected it,' said d'Artagnan.

'Besides, dear friend, do not take all that I am going to say for the word of a cenobite, simply repeating what he has heard,' replied Aramis. 'I have heard that at this time Cardinal Mazarin is very uneasy at the way in which matters are going. It seems his orders do not get all that respect which those of our old bugbear, the deceased cardinal, had—for whatever may be said, we all agree he was a great man.'

'I will not contradict you there, my dear Aramis; he it was who made me lieutenant.'*

'My early opinion was entirely in the cardinal's favour. I said to myself, a minister is never liked, but with the genius which is allowed to be his, he will finally triumph over his enemies, and make himself feared, which according to my belief is worth more than to be loved.'

D'Artagnan made a sign with his head which meant that he approved entirely this doubtful maxim.

'That, then,' continued Aramis, 'was my former opinion; but as I am very ignorant in this sort of matters, and as the humility of which I make profession obliges me not to trust to my own judgement, I make enquiries. But, my dear friend——'

Aramis made a pause.

'Well, what?' asked d'Artagnan.

'Well,' resumed Aramis, 'I must mortify my pride; I must confess I was deceived.'

'Really?'

'Yes, I am told as I was telling you—and this is what many persons quite differing in taste and ambition have expressed—that M. de Mazarin is by no means a man of genius, as I thought.'

'Bah!' said d'Artagnan.

'No; a man of nought, who has been a servant of Cardinal Bentivoglio, who has pushed himself by intrigue—a *parvenu*, without name, who will in France go the road of a partisan. He will heap up wealth, waste the king's revenues, will pay to himself all the pensions that the late Cardinal Richelieu paid to every one; but he will never govern by the law of the strongest, the grandest, the most honourable. He seems to be, not a gentleman in manners or in heart, this minister, but a sort of buffoon, pantaloon. Do you know him? I do not.'

'Well!' said d'Artagnan, 'there is some truth in what you have told me.'

'Ah, well! you increase my pride, my dear fellow, if I have been able, thanks to a certain vulgar penetration which belongs to me, to agree with a man like you, living at the court.'

'But you have spoken of him personally only, and not of his party and resources.'

'That is true. He has the queen on his side.'

'That is something, it seems to me.'

'But not the king.'

'A mere child.'

'A child who will be of age in four years' time.'*

'This is the present time.'

'Yes, this is not the future. And even in the present he has in his favour neither parliament nor people, that is, money; neither the nobility nor the princes, that is, the sword.'

D'Artagnan rubbed his ear. He was forced to confess to himself that these remarks were not only comprehensive, but just.

'See, my friend, if I am still endowed with my usual penetration. Perhaps I am wrong in speaking to you so ingenuously, for you seem to lean towards Mazarin.'

'I?' cried d'Artagnan; 'not the least in the world!'

'You were talking of a commission.'

'Did I mention that? Then I was wrong. I say to myself, as you say, affairs are becoming confused. Well, let us throw the feather into the air; let us go the side where the wind carries it, and resume our life of adventures. We were four valiant knights, four hearts closely united. Let us unite afresh, not our hearts which have never been separated, but our fortunes and our courage. The opportunity is favourable for winning something better than a diamond.'

'You are right, d'Artagnan; you always were so,' continued Aramis. 'And the proof is that I have had the same idea; only to me, who have not your strong and fruitful imagination, it has been suggested. Everyone today has need of auxiliaries. Something has transpired of our famous prowess of former days. Propositions have been made to me, and I will tell you frankly that the Coadjutor has spoken to me about it.'

'M. de Conti, the cardinal's enemy!' cried d'Artagnan.

'No, the king's friend,' said Aramis—'the king's friend; do you understand? Yes, the question should be of serving the king—that which is the duty of a gentleman.'

'But the king is with M. de Mazarin, my dear fellow.'

'In fact, not in will; in appearance, but not in heart. And that is exactly the snare which the king's enemies lay for the poor child.'

'Oh! ah! but that is simply civil war that you are proposing to me, my dear Aramis.'

'War for the king.'

'But the king will be at the head of the army where Mazarin will be.'

'But he will be in his heart in the army which M. de Beaufort will command.'

'Beaufort? He is in Vincennes.'

'Did I say Beaufort?' said Aramis. 'Perhaps another—Monsieur the Prince.'

'But the latter is setting out for the army. He is quite for the cardinal.'

'Oh,' said Aramis, 'they are having disputes together at this very time. But besides, if not the prince, M. de Conti——'

'But M. de Conti is going to be made a cardinal.'

'Are there not very warlike cardinals?' said Aramis. 'Look; around you are four cardinals who at the head of armies did as well as M. de Guébriant or M. de Gassion.'

'But a humpbacked general!'*

'Under his cuirass they will not see his hump. Besides, remember that Alexander limped, and Hannibal was one-eyed.'

'Do you see very great advantages in this party?' asked d'Artagnan.

'I see in it the protection of powerful princes.'

'With the proscription of the government.'

'Annulled by parliaments and outbreaks.'

'All that may possibly happen, as you say, if they succeed in separating the king from his mother.'

'They will succeed in that, perhaps.'

'Never!' cried d'Artagnan, regaining his own convictions this time. 'I appeal to you, Aramis, who know Anne of Austria as well as I do. Do you think she will ever be able to forget that her son is her security—the pledge of her consideration, fortune, and life? She would have to go over with him, and abandon Mazarin; but you know better than any one, she has strong reasons for never abandoning him.'

'Perhaps you are right,' said Aramis, reflecting; 'therefore I will not bind myself.'

'To them,' said d'Artagnan; 'but to me?'

'To no one. I am a priest; what have I to do with politics? I do not read my breviary; I have a little connection of witty abbés and charming women. The more public affairs are troubled, the less noise my escapades will make; all goes on wonderfully without mixing up in them, and decidedly, my friend, I shall not do so.'

'Well, my dear fellow,' said d'Artagnan, 'your philosophy has won me over, word of honour, and I do not know what sting

of ambition has pricked me. I have bread and cheese; I can, at
the death of poor M. de Tréville, who is old, become captain.
That is a very pretty marshal's *bâton* for a cadet of Gascony,
and I feel that I am re-attached to the charms of modest, daily
bread. Instead, then, of seeking adventures, well! I will accept
the invitations of Porthos—shoot over his lands. You know he
has some?'

'Of course I do. Ten leagues of forest, marsh, and valley.
He is lord of the mountain and the plain; and he is contesting
for his feudal rights with the Bishop of Noyon.'*

'Good,' thought d'Artagnan; 'that is what I wanted to know.
Porthos is in Picardy.' Then aloud, 'And he has resumed his
old name of Vallon?'

'To which he has added that of Bracieux—a property which
was a barony.'

'So that we shall see Porthos a baron.'

'I don't doubt it. The baroness Porthos especially is admirable.'

The two friends burst into a laugh.

'You do not wish to belong to Mazarin's party?'

'Nor you to the prince's?'

'No. Do not let us then go over to any one; let us keep
friends, and be neither Cardinalists nor Frondeurs.'

'Yes,' said Aramis, 'let us be musketeers.'

'Even with the little collar of the abbé.'

'Above all with the little collar,' said Aramis, 'it is that which
makes the charm of it.'

'Adieu, then,' said d'Artagnan.

'I will not detain you, my dear fellow,' said Aramis, 'seeing
I do not know where to lodge you, and I cannot with decency
offer you half the shed with Planchet.'

'Besides, I am scarcely three leagues from Paris; the horses
have rested, and in less than an hour I shall be back to Paris.'
And d'Artagnan poured out a last glass of wine.

'To our good old days!' said he.

'Yes,' replied Aramis, 'unfortunately it is a time gone by,—
fugit irreparabile tempus.'*

'Bah!' said d'Artagnan 'it will perhaps return. In any case,
if you want me—Hôtel de la Chevrette, Rue Tiquetonne.'

'And I at the Jesuits' convent—from six in the morning till
eight in the evening, by the door; from eight at night till six,
by the window.'

'Adieu, my dear fellow.'

'Oh, I cannot leave you so; let me conduct you back.' And
he took his sword and cloak.

'He wants to make sure that I am going,' said d'Artagnan to
himself.

Aramis whistled for Bazin, but he was sleeping in the
antechamber on the remains of his supper; Aramis was compelled to give him a shake by the ear to awake him.

'Come, come, Monsieur sleeper, the ladder; quick!'

'But,' said Bazin, gaping enough to dislocate his jaw, 'it is
still against the window—the ladder.'

'The other—the gardener's. Did you not see that d'Artagnan
had difficulty in getting up, and he will have more in getting
down.'

D'Artagnan was about assuring Aramis that he could get
down very well, when an idea struck him; it was to be silent.
A moment after, a strong and solid wooden ladder was placed
against the window.

'Come now!' said d'Artagnan, 'that's what may be called a
means of communication. A woman could go up a ladder like
that.'

A piercing look from Aramis seemed to aim at reaching his
friend's thought to the very bottom of his heart; but d'Artagnan
bore the look with an air of admirable *naïveté*. Besides, at that
moment he put his foot on the first step of the ladder, and
was descending.

He was soon on the ground. As for Bazin, he stopped at the
window.

'Stop there,' said Aramis, 'I shall soon be back.'

The two walked towards the shed; at their approach Planchet
came out, holding the two horses by the bridles.

'Well and good!' said Aramis, 'there is an active and vigilant
servitor. He is not like that lazy Bazin, who is no longer good
for anything since he is a man of the Church.'

'Follow us, Planchet; we are going, while talking, to the end
of the village.' In fact, the two friends traversed the whole

village talking of indifferent things. Then at the last houses, 'Well, then, dear friend,' said Aramis, 'follow up your career, fortune smiles on you; do not let her escape you. Remember that she is a courtesan, and treat her accordingly; as for me, I shall continue in my humble condition and in idleness. Adieu.'

'So it is quite decided,' said d'Artagnan; 'what I have offered does not please you.'

'It would please me much, on the contrary,' said Aramis, 'if I were like other men; but, as I said, I am made up of contrasts—what I hate today I shall adore tomorrow, and vice versa. You see clearly that I cannot pledge myself as you can, for example, who have fixed ideas.'

'You are lying, slyboots,' said d'Artagnan to himself. 'On the contrary, you are the only one who knows how to choose an end and reach it secretly.'

'Farewell, then, my dear fellow,' continued Aramis; 'thanks for your kind intentions, and especially for the pleasing recollections that your presence has awakened in me.'

They embraced. Planchet was already mounted. d'Artagnan got into his saddle in turn; then they shook hands once more. The horsemen spurred their horses, and moved off in the direction of Paris.

Aramis remained standing still in the middle of the road till he lost sight of them.

But at the end of two hundred paces d'Artagnan stopped short, jumped down, threw the horse's bridle on Planchet's arm, took his pistols from the holsters, and put them in his belt.

'What is the matter, then, Monsieur?' said Planchet, quite frightened.

'The matter is, that however sly he may be,' said d'Artagnan, 'it shall not be said that I am his dupe. Stop here! only turn round and wait for me.'

At these words d'Artagnan rushed off to the other side of the ditch bordering the route, and crossed the level ground in such a manner as to turn the village.

He had noticed that between the house where Madame de Longueville lived and the Jesuits' convent was a wide space only shut in by a hedge. Perhaps an hour before he would have had trouble to find this hedge, but the moon had just risen, and although from time to time it was covered with clouds, one could see, even during the obscuration, clearly enough to find one's way. D'Artagnan reached the hedge and hid behind it. While passing before the house where the scene took place which we related, he had observed the same window lighted up afresh, and he was convinced that Aramis had not gone home, and that when he did go it would not be alone.

He in fact soon heard approaching steps, and voices speaking in a low tone. The steps ceased at the beginning of the hedge. D'Artagnan put one knee on the ground, seeking the greatest thickness of the hedge to hide himself there. Then two men appeared, to the great astonishment of d'Artagnan; but that soon ceased when he heard a soft and harmonious voice. One of the two was a woman disguised as a cavalier.

'Be reassured, my dear René,' said the voice; 'the same thing will not be renewed. I have discovered a sort of vault under the street, and we have only to raise one of the flagstones before the door to open a way out for you.'

'Oh!' said the other voice, which d'Artagnan recognized as that of Aramis. 'I swear to you, Princess, that if our good name did not depend on all these precautions, and that if my life only were at stake——'

'Yes, yes; I know you are as brave and adventurous as any one; but you belong not to me only, but to all our party. Be careful, then.'

'I obey always, Madame, when one commands me with so gentle a voice.'

He tenderly kissed her hand:

'Ah!' cried the cavalier with the gentle voice.

'What?' asked Aramis.

'But do you not see that the wind has carried off my hat?' And Aramis darted after the fugitive hat. D'Artagnan profited by this circumstance to seek a thinner place in the hedge which would permit his eye to penetrate freely to the problematic cavalier. At that moment the moon, as inquisitive perhaps as the officer, came from behind a cloud, and d'Artagnan recognized the fine blue eyes, the golden hair, and the noble head of the Duchesse de Longueville.

Aramis returned, laughing, one hat on his head and the other in his hand, and the two then took their way towards the Jesuits' convent.

'Good!' said d'Artagnan, rising and brushing his knee. 'Now I have got it; you are a Frondeur, and lover of Madame de Longueville.'

XII

M. PORTHOS DU VALLON DE BRACIEUX DE PIERREFONDS

THANKS to the information gained from Aramis, d'Artagnan, who already knew that Porthos, from his family name,* was called Vallon, had learned that from his lands he was called Bracieux, and that on account of this estate he had gone to law with the Bishop of Noyon. It was, therefore, in the neighbourhood of Noyon that this estate would have to be sought, that is to say, on the borders of the Île de France and Picardy. His itinerary was promptly planned; he would go to Dammartin, where two roads branched off—one which went to Soissons, the other to Compiègne; there he would enquire about the estate of Bracieux, and according to the answer would follow right on or take to the left.

Planchet, who was not yet quite reassured about his hiding-place, declared he would follow d'Artagnan to the end of the world. Only he begged his old master to set out in the evening, the dusk presenting more security.

D'Artagnan proposed to him then to notify his wife to assure her at least of his safety; but Planchet answered with much sagacity that it was certain that his wife would not die of anxiety in not knowing where he was, while knowing the incontinence of tongue with which she was afflicted, he, Planchet, would die of inquietude if she did know where he was.

These reasons appeared so good to d'Artagnan that he did not insist any longer. Therefore, towards eight in the evening, at the time when the fog began to thicken in the streets, he set out from the Hôtel de la Chevrette, and followed by Planchet, left the capital by Porte St Denis. At midnight the two travellers reached Dammartin. It was too late to obtain any information. The host of the Cygne de la Croix had gone to bed. D'Artagnan put it off till the next day.

In the morning he called the host. He was one of those sly Normans who said neither yes nor no, and who always thought they compromised themselves by giving a straightforward answer; only having thought that he understood that he ought to go straight on, d'Artagnan resumed his journey with this doubtful information. At nine in the morning he was at Nanteuil; there he stopped for breakfast.

This time the host was a frank Picardian, who, recognizing Planchet as a fellow-countryman, made no difficulty about giving the desired information. The Bracieux estate was a few leagues from Villers-Cotterêts.

D'Artagnan knew this place from having accompanied the court there two or three times—for at that time it was a royal residence. He took his way thither, and dismounted at his usual hotel, the Golden Dauphin. There he gained most satisfactory intelligence. He learned that the Bracieux estate was situated four leagues from that town, but that Porthos was not to be found there. Porthos had certainly had a misunderstanding with the Bishop of Noyon about the estate of Pierrefonds,* which bounded his own; but at last, tired out by the judicial contentions of which he understood nothing, he had bought Pierrefonds, so that he added this new name to his old ones. He was now, therefore, named M. du Vallon de Bracieux de Pierrefonds, and lived on his new property. In default of other title, Porthos was evidently looking forward to that of Marquis de Carabas.

There was need to wait till next day, for the horses had done ten leagues in the course of the day, and were done up. They could have taken others, it is true; but there was a great forest to pass through, and Planchet, we recollect, did not like forests in the night. There was one thing more, that Planchet did not like setting out while fasting; so on getting up d'Artagnan found his breakfast quite ready. There was no reason to complain of such an attention. So d'Artagnan sat down to table; it may be taken for granted that Planchet, while resuming his old duties, resumed also his former humility, and felt no more shame in eating d'Artagnan's leavings than had Mesdames de Motteville and de Fargis those of Anne of Austria.

It was not, therefore, till about eight that they started. There was no chance of going astray; they must follow the road which led from Villers-Cotterêts to Compiègne, and on coming out of the woods take to the right. It was a fine spring morning. The birds were singing in the tall trees; the bountiful rays of the sun crossed the forest glades, and looked like curtains of gilded gauze; in other parts, the light scarcely penetrated the thick vault of leaves, and the old oaks, among which the nimble squirrels at the sight of the travellers hurriedly took shelter, were immersed in shade. There arose a perfume from plants, flowers, and leaves, which rejoiced the heart. D'Artagnan, wearied with the poisonous air of Paris, said to himself that when one bore the names of three estates strung together into a single title, one ought to be very happy in such a paradise; then shaking his head, he said, 'If I were Porthos, and d'Artagnan came to propose to me what I am going to propose to him, I know very well what I should answer d'Artagnan.'

As for Planchet, he was thinking of nothing; he was digesting.

At the verge of the wood d'Artagnan perceived the road indicated, and at the end of the road the towers of an immense feudal château. 'Oh, oh!' murmured he. 'I believe that this château belongs to the ancient branch of the Orléans family. Could Porthos have been in treaty for it with the Duc de Longueville?'

'I say, Monsieur, here are well kept lands. If they belong to M. Porthos, I compliment him on them.'

'Hang it!' said d'Artagnan. 'Don't go and call him Porthos, nor even Vallon; but either Bracieux or Pierrefonds. You will make me fail in my mission.'

As he approached the château which had first attracted his notice, d'Artagnan could see it was not there his friend could live. The towers, although solid as if built but yesterday, were open and as if emptied out. One might have said that some giant had cut them by blows of his axe.

On reaching the end of the road d'Artagnan found it commanded a magnificent valley at the bottom of which a charming little lake was sleeping at the foot of some houses scattered here and there, humble-looking, and roofed some with tiles and some with thatch, which seemed to recognize as their feudal lord a pretty château built towards the beginning of Henry IV's reign, which was surmounted by some seigniorial weather-cocks. This time d'Artagnan felt sure that the house of Porthos was before him.

The road led direct to this charming château, which was to its ancestor, the château of the mountain, what a fop of the côterie of M. le Duc d'Enghien* was to a chevalier in armour of the time of Charles VII. D'Artagnan put his horse to the trot, and followed the road. At the end of ten minutes he came to the end of an avenue, planted regularly with fine poplars, and which abutted on an iron gate, the heads and the transverse bands of which were gilded. In this avenue was a sort of lord, dressed in green and gilded like the gate, who was mounted on a fat stallion. On his right and left were two grooms covered with gold lace. A good number of peasants collected together were paying him very respectful homage.

'Ah,' said d'Artagnan to himself, 'is that the Lord du Vallon de Bracieux de Pierrefonds? Why, bless me! how he has shrivelled up since he has lost the name of Porthos!'

'That can't be he,' said Planchet, answering what d'Artagnan had said to himself. 'M. Porthos was nearly six feet high, and that man is hardly five.'

'Yet,' said d'Artagnan, 'they bow very low to that gentleman.' At these words he hastened towards him. As they drew nearer he seemed to recognize the features of this personage.

'Good gracious, Monsieur!' said Planchet, who on his part thought he knew the stranger. 'Can it be possible that it is he?'

At this exclamation the man on horseback turned round gently and with a very noble air, and the two travellers could see sparkling in all their brilliancy the great eyes, the bright red moon face, and the smile so eloquent of Mousqueton.

It was in fact he, fat as bacon, heavy from good health, swollen with good living, who, on recognizing d'Artagnan, quite the reverse of that hypocrite Bazin slipped off his horse,

and approached the officer hat in hand; so that the homage of
the assembly performed a quarter-turn towards this new sun
which was eclipsing the old one.

'M. d'Artagnan! M. d'Artagnan!' repeated Mousqueton, in
his enormous cheeks, all sweating with joy—'M. d'Artagnan!
Oh, what joy for Monseigneur my master du Vallon de Bracieux de Pierrefonds!'

'My good Mousqueton! Is, then, your master here?'

'You are on his lands.'

'But how pleasant it is to see you! How fat! how flourishing!'
continued d'Artagnan, unwearied in detailing the changes
which good fortune had brought to the formerly famished one.

'Ah, yes, thank God, Monsieur!' said Mousqueton. 'I am
very well.'

'But don't you say anything to your friend Planchet?'

'My friend Planchet! Can it possibly be you?' cried Mousqueton, with open arms, and eyes filled with tears.

'Myself,' said Planchet, ever discreet. 'But I wanted to see
if you were not grown proud.'

'Grown proud with an old friend! Never, Planchet! You have
not thought that, or you do not know Mousqueton.'

'That's right!' said Planchet, dismounting and extending his
arms to Mousqueton. 'You are not like that beast of a Bazin,
who left me for two hours in a shed without even seeming to
recognize me.'

And Planchet and Mousqueton embraced with an effusion
which much touched the lookers-on, and which made them
believe that Planchet was some disguised lord, so thoroughly
they appreciated at its highest value the position of Mousqueton.

'And now, Monsieur,' said Mousqueton, when he was set
free from Planchet's embrace, who had in vain tried to join his
hands behind the back of his friend, 'let me leave you—for I
do not wish my master to learn the news of your arrival from
any other than myself. He would not pardon me for letting
anyone precede me.'

'The dear friend,' said d'Artagnan, taking care not to give
to Porthos either his own or his new name, 'has not, then,
forgotten me?'

'Forgotten! he!' cried Mousqueton, 'that is to say, Monsieur, that not a day passes that we do not expect to learn that you have been gazetted as marshal, either in M. de Gassion's place, or that of M. de Bassompierre.'

D'Artagnan allowed a melancholy smile to escape his lips— one of those which had survived in the depth of his heart the disenchantment of his young years.

'And you, rustics,' continued Mousqueton, 'stay near M. le Comte d'Artagnan, and pay him great honour while I go to inform my Lord of his arrival.'

And again mounting his robust horse, aided by two worthy souls, while Planchet, more brisk, got up alone upon his, Mousqueton took a little gallop along the turf of the avenue, which gave evidence more in favour of the back than of the quadruped's legs.

'Ah, now! this is a fellow of a promising look!' said d'Artagnan; 'no mystery, no cloak, no trickery here; he laughs heartily, cries with joy. I sée faces an ell broad; in truth it seems that nature is *en fête*, that the trees, in place of leaves and flowers, are covered with little green and rose-coloured ribbons.'

'And I,' said Planchet—'I seem to scent from here the delightful odour of roast meats. Ah, Monsieur, what a cook ought M. de Pierrefonds to have, who at the time when still called M. Porthos loved to eat so much and so well.'

'Halt!' said d'Artagnan; 'you make me afraid. If the reality corresponds to the appearance, I am lost. Such a happy man will never leave his happiness, and I am going to be foiled in his case as I have been in that of Aramis.'

XIII

HOW D'ARTAGNAN PERCEIVED IN FINDING PORTHOS THAT RICHES DO NOT MAKE HAPPINESS

D'ARTAGNAN entered the iron gate and found himself in front of the château; he was just alighting when a sort of giant appeared on the front steps. Let us do this act of justice to d'Artagnan, to say that apart from every feeling of egotism, his heart beat with joy at the sight of this tall, martial figure which recalled to him a brave and good man.

He ran towards Porthos and threw himself into his arms; all the domestics, ranged in a circle at a respectful distance, looked on with an humble curiosity. Mousqueton, in the front rank, wiped his eyes; the poor fellow had not ceased weeping from joy since he had recognized d'Artagnan and Planchet. Porthos seized his friend by the arm.

'Ah! what joy to see you again, dear d'Artagnan,' cried he, with a voice which had turned from baritone to bass; 'you have not forgotten me, then?'

'Forgotten you! ah, dear Vallon, does one forget the finest days of one's youth and one's devoted friends and the perils faced together? but that is the same thing as saying that in seeing you there is not a moment of our old friendship which does not present itself to my thoughts.'

'Yes, yes,' said Porthos, trying to give his moustache again that coquettish turn which it had lost in solitude,—'yes, we did some fine things in our time, and gave that poor cardinal some thread to twine.'

And he heaved a sigh. D'Artagnan looked at him.

'Anyhow,' continued Porthos, in a languishing tone, 'be welcome, dear friend; you will help me recover my joy. To-morrow we will course the hare on the level, or the roebuck in my woods, which are very fine. I have four hounds which are reckoned the swiftest in the district, and a pack which has not its equal for twenty leagues round.'

And Porthos sighed again.

'Oh, oh!' thought d'Artagnan. 'Is my jolly fellow less happy than he looks?' Then aloud, 'But before all,' said he, 'you will present me to Madame du Vallon—for I recall a certain letter of pressing invitation which you wrote me, and at the foot of which she kindly added a few lines.

Third sigh from Porthos.

'I lost Madame du Vallon two years ago,' said he, 'and you see me still mourning for her. That is why I have left my Château du Vallon near Corbeil,* to come and live on my Bracieux estate—a change which has led me to buy this one. Poor Madame du Vallon,' continued Porthos, making a grimace of regret; 'she was not a woman of a very equal character, but she had finished, however, by accustoming herself to my ways and by accepting my little wishes.'

'So you are rich and free?' said d'Artagnan.

'Alas!' said Porthos; 'I am a widower with a rent-roll of forty thousand francs. Come, let us get breakfast; what say you?'

'I wish it by all means,' said d'Artagnan; 'the morning air has given me an appetite.'

'Yes,' said Porthos, 'my air is excellent.'

They entered the château. There was gilding from top to bottom; the cornices were gilt, the mouldings were gilt, the woodwork of the chairs was gilt. A table fully laid was ready.

'You see,' said Porthos, 'this is my usual style.'

'Hang it!' said d'Artagnan, 'I compliment you on it. The king has not the like.'

'Yes,' said Porthos, 'I have heard it said that he is badly fed by M. de Mazarin. Taste this cutlet, my dear d'Artagnan; it is from one of my own sheep.'

'You have some very tender mutton,' said d'Artagnan, 'and I congratulate you.'

'Yes, my meadows afford excellent pasture.'

'Give me a little more.'

'No; take some of this hare which I killed yesterday in one of my warrens.'

'What a flavour!' said d'Artagnan. 'Why, you feed them only on wild thyme, then—your hares?'

'And what do you think of my wine?' said Porthos. 'It is pretty good, is it not?'

'It is delicious.'

'Yet it is the wine of the district.'

'Really!'

'Yes; a little slope towards the south, over there on my mountain. It produces twenty hogsheads.'

'Why, that is a real vintage!'

Porthos sighed the fifth time. D'Artagnan had counted them.

'Ah! but,' said he, inquisitive to probe the problem, 'one would say, my dear friend, that something distresses you. Is it your health——'

'Excellent, my dear fellow; better than ever. I could slay an ox with a blow from my fist.'

'Perhaps family troubles.'

'Thank goodness, I have no one but myself in the world.'

'But then what is it that makes you sigh?'

'My dear fellow,' said Porthos, 'I will be frank with you; I am not happy.'

'You not happy, Porthos? With a château, fields, hills, woods, with a rent-roll of forty thousand francs, you are not happy?'

'My dear friend, I have all that, it is true; but I am alone in the midst of it all.'

'Ah, I understand! you are surrounded by country fellows whom you cannot see without stooping to them.'

Porthos turned slightly pale, and emptied an enormous glass of his small vintage.

'No, no,' said he; 'on the contrary, fancy to yourself that they are all country squires, who have all some title or other, and profess to go back to Pharamond, to Charlemagne, or at the very least to Hugh Capet.* At the beginning, I was the last comer, and consequently had to make the first advances, which I did; but you know, my dear fellow, Madame du Vallon——'

Porthos while saying these words seemed to swallow with difficulty.

'——Madame du Vallon,' he resumed, 'was of doubtful family; she had married before me (I believe, d'Artagnan, that I tell you nothing new) a lawyer. They found that distasteful. They said it was disgusting. You understand—it was an expression to make one kill thirty thousand men. I have killed two; that has made the rest hold their tongues, but has not made me their friend. So that I have no society; I live alone. I am sick of it; I am eaten up with trouble.'

D'Artagnan smiled; he saw the weak place in the armour, and he prepared the stroke.

'But at last,' said he, 'you are quite by yourself; and your wife cannot hurt you now.'

'Yes; but you understand, not being of the historic nobility like the Coucys who are satisfied with being squires, and the Rohans* who do not desire to be dukes, all these folks, who are all either viscounts or counts, have the precedence over me in church, in ceremonies, everywhere, and I can say nothing. Ah! if I were only——'

'Baron, eh?' said d'Artagnan, finishing his friend's sentence.

'Ah!' cried Porthos, whose features lighted up, 'if I were a baron.'

'Good!' thought d'Artagnan; 'I shall succeed here.' Then aloud, 'Well, dear friend, the very title you wish for is what I am come to bring you today.'

Porthos took a bound which shook the room; two or three bottles rolled off, and were broken. Mousqueton ran in at the noise.

'Does Monsieur call me?' asked he.

Porthos made a sign for him to collect the pieces of glass.

'I see with pleasure,' said d'Artagnan, 'that you have still that capital fellow.'

'He is my steward,' said Porthos; then raising his voice, 'he has made money, the droll fellow, one sees that, but,' continued he, in a lower tone, 'he is attached to me, and would not leave me for anything in the world.'

'And he calls him Monseigneur,' thought d'Artagnan.

'You can go, Mouston.'

'You call him Mouston?* Ah, yes!—an abbreviation. Mousqueton is too long to pronounce.'

'Yes,' said Porthos, 'and then that savours of the quartermaster a league off. But we were talking of business when he came in.'

'Yes,' said d'Artagnan; 'yet let us put it off for a bit, your people might suspect something; perhaps there are spies about. You divine, Porthos, that we have to do with serious things.'

'Well,' said Porthos, 'to assist digestion, let us take a walk in my park.'

'Willingly.'

And as both had sufficiently breakfasted, they took a turn round a magnificent garden. Avenues of chestnuts and limes enclosed a space of thirty acres at least; at the end of each quincunx,* well filled with shrubs, the rabbits could be seen disappearing into the acorn crops, and gambolling among the tall plants.

'In truth,' said d'Artagnan, 'the park corresponds with all the rest; and if the fish in your lakes are as numerous as the rabbits in your warrens, you are a lucky fellow, my dear Porthos, however little you have kept the love of the chase and acquired that of fishing.'

'My friend,' said Porthos, 'I leave the fishing to Mousqueton—it is a vulgar pleasure; but sometimes when full of *ennui* I sit on one of the marble seats, call for my gun and my favourite dog Gredinet, and shoot rabbits.'

'Oh! that is very diverting.'

'Yes,' replied Porthos, with a sigh, 'it is; very.'

D'Artagnan had given up counting sighs.

'Then,' added Porthos, 'Gredinet goes and picks them up, and carries them himself to the cook; he is trained to do that.'

'Ah, the charming little animal!' said d'Artagnan.

'But let us leave Gredinet, whom you may have if you wish him, for I am growing tired of the subject; and let us return to business.'

'Willingly,' said d'Artagnan; 'only I tell you first, dear friend, that you may not say I have taken you unawares, you must change your mode of life.'

'How so?'

'Put on your armour, gird on your sword, meet adventures, leave, as in past days, a little of one's flesh on the road, you know—the old style, in short.'

'The devil I must!' said Porthos.

'Yes, I see you have been spoiled, dear friend; you are too corpulent, and your wrist has no longer that elasticity of which the cardinal's Guards have had so many proofs.'

'Ah! my wrist is still strong, I swear,' said Porthos, showing a hand like a shoulder of mutton.

'So much the better.'

'We must make war, then?'

'Ah, *mon Dieu!* yes.'

'And against whom?'

'Have you kept up your politics, my friend?'

'I? Not the least bit.'

'Then are you for Mazarin, or for the princes?'

'I am for no one.'

'That means you are for us. So much the better, Porthos. It is a good position to accomplish your object. Well, dear fellow, I will tell you that I am come on the part of the cardinal.'

This produced some effect on Porthos, as if it was still 1640, and the matter in question came from the true cardinal.

'Oh!' said he, 'what does his Eminence want?'

'He wants to have you in his service.'

'And who spoke to him about me?'

'Rochefort. You remember him?'

'Yes, rather! He who gave us so much annoyance in the past, who has made us take so many journeys, to whom you gave three sword-cuts, which he well deserved, moreover.'

'But you know he has become our friend?' said d'Artagnan.

'No, I did not. Ah! he shows no spite.'

'You are wrong, Porthos,' said d'Artagnan, in his turn. 'It is I who have none.'

Porthos did not quite understand; but one remembers that comprehension was by no means his *forte*.

'You say, then,' continued he, 'that it is Comte de Rochefort who has spoken of me to the cardinal?'

'Yes; and then the queen.'

'What? The queen?'

'To inspire confidence in us she has herself given the cardinal the famous diamond, you know, which I sold to M. d'Essart, and which—I know not how—fell into her hands again.'

'But it seems to me,' said Porthos, with his great good sense, 'that she would have done better to give it back to you.'

'That is my opinion also,' said d'Artagnan. 'What can I do? Kings and queens have sometimes singular caprices. After all, as it is they who have riches and honours, who give away money and titles, one is devoted to them.'

'Yes, one is devoted to them,' said Porthos. 'Then you are so at this time?'

'To king, queen, and cardinal; and I have also answered for you.'

'And you say that you have made certain conditions on my behalf?'

'Splendid ones, my dear fellow, splendid! First of all you have money, have you not? Forty thousand francs of rent, you have told me.'

Porthos felt rather distrustful.

'Ah, my friend!' said he, 'one has never too much money. Madame du Vallon has left a disputed inheritance. I am not a great accountant, so that I live a little from day to day.'

'He is afraid that I have come to borrow some money,' thought d'Artagnan. 'Ah, my friend!' said he, aloud, 'so much the better if you are rather hard pushed.'

'How, so much the better?' said Porthos.

'Yes; for his Eminence will give what you desire—lands, money, or titles.'

'Ah! ah! ah!' said Porthos, opening wide his eyes at the last word.

'Under the other cardinal,' continued d'Artagnan, 'we did not know how to utilize our fortune, although we had the opportunity. It is of no consequence to you who have forty thousand francs of rent, and who seem the happiest man on earth.'

Porthos sighed.

'Anyhow,' continued d'Artagnan, 'in spite of your rent-roll, and perhaps because of it, it seems to me that a little coronet would suit your carriage well. Eh?'

'Well, yes,' said Porthos.

'Well, then, dear friend, win it; it is at the end of your sword. We shall not injure each other. Your object is a title; mine is money. I want to build up Artagnan, which my ancestors,* impoverished by the Crusades, have suffered to fall into ruins since that time, and to buy some thirty acres of land around it. That is all I want. I shall retire there, and then I shall die happy.'

'And I,' said Porthos, 'want to be a baron.'

'You shall be.'

'And have you not thought of our other friends?' asked Porthos.

'Certainly. I have seen Aramis.'

'And what does he want—to be a bishop?'

'Aramis,' said d'Artagnan, who did not wish to disenchant Porthos, 'just fancy, has become a monk and Jesuit, and lives like a bear. He has given up everything, and thinks only of his own salvation. My offers could not make him decide.'

'So much the worse,' said Porthos; 'he had some spirit. And Athos?'

'I have not seen him yet, but I shall go and see him on leaving you. Do you know where I shall find him?'

'Near Blois, on a little estate that he has come into from some relative.'

'And what is the name of it?'

'Bragelonne.* Do you understand, my dear fellow—Athos who was noble as an emperor, and who inherits an estate which has the title of County? What will he do with all those counties—County de la Fère,* County de Bragelonne?'

'With that to have no children,' said d'Artagnan.

'Ah!' said Porthos, 'I have heard it said that he has adopted a young man much like him in the face.'

'Athos, our Athos, who was as virtuous as Scipio!* Have you seen him again?'

'No.'

'Ah, well! I shall go tomorrow to carry him news of you. I am afraid, between ourselves, that his liking for wine has made him look old and wasted.'

'Yes,' said Porthos; 'it is true he used to drink a good deal.'

'Then he was the oldest of us all,' said d'Artagnan.

'Only a few years; for his serious look aged him considerably.'

'Yes, that is true. Then if we have Athos, it will be so much the better; if not, well, we must go without. We two are worth twelve.'

'Yes,' said Porthos, smiling at the remembrance of their old exploits; 'but we four would have equalled twenty-four, even supposing that the work shall be as hard as you seem to imply.'

'Hard for recruits, yes; but for us, no.'

'Will it be long?'

'Well, it may last three or four years.'

'Will there be much fighting?'

'I hope so.'

'So much the better, after all—so much the better,' cried Porthos; 'you have no idea, my dear fellow, how my bones crack since I have been here. Sometimes on Sundays, coming from Mass, I go for a ride in the fields and on my neighbours' lands to meet some nice little quarrel, for I feel I need it; but no, nothing. Whether it is that they respect me, or that they fear me, which is more probable, they let me beat down the grass with my dogs, ride over them all, and I return more wearied than ever, and that is all. At least tell me, cannot one fight more easily in Paris?'

'As to that, my dear fellow, it is lovely; no more edicts, no more guards of the cardinal, no more of Jussac* and other spies. Goodness me! why, under a lantern, in an inn, everywhere, Are you a Frondeur?—one draws, and all is said. M. de Guise has killed M. de Coligny openly in the Place Royale, and nothing has been done.'

'Ah, that is the thing now,' said Porthos.

'And then before long,' continued d'Artagnan, 'we shall have pitched battles, cannonades, conflagrations; that will be very amusing.'

'Then I decide.'

'I have your word, then?'

'Yes, I give it to you. I shall cut and thrust for Mazarin. But——'

'But?'

'But he will make me a baron?'

'Eh, yes,' said d'Artagnan; 'that is arranged in advance. I have told you, and repeat it, I answer for your barony.'

On that promise Porthos, who had never doubted his friend's word, took the road back with him to the château.

XIV

IN WHICH IS SHOWN THAT IF PORTHOS WAS DISCONTENTED WITH HIS LOT, MOUSQUETON WAS SATISFIED WITH HIS

WHILE returning towards the château, and while Porthos was indulging in his dreams of a barony, d'Artagnan was reflecting on the misery of our poor human nature, always discontented with what it has, always wanting what it has not. In Porthos's place d'Artagnan would have felt himself to be the happiest man on earth, and to make Porthos happy he wanted—what? Five letters to prefix to his many names, and a little coronet to be painted on the panels of his carriage.

'I shall, then, pass my whole life,' said d'Artagnan to himself, 'looking to my right and left without ever seeing the face of a man thoroughly happy?'

He was making this philosophical reflection when Providence seemed desirous to negative it utterly. Just as Porthos left him to give some orders to his cook, he saw Mousqueton approaching. The face of the jolly fellow, except a slight trouble which like a summer's cloud threw a gauze rather than a veil over his countenance, seemed that of a man completely happy.

'I was looking for him. Here he is,' said d'Artagnan to himself; 'but, alas! the poor fellow does not know why I have come.'

Mousqueton kept at a distance. D'Artagnan seated himself on a bench, and made a sign for him to approach.

'Monsieur,' said Mousqueton, availing himself of the permission, 'I have a favour to ask you.'

'Speak, my friend,' said d'Artagnan.

'I do not dare to do so. I am afraid you must think that prosperity has ruined me.'

'You are then happy, my friend?' said d'Artagnan.

'As happy as it is possible to be; and nevertheless you can render me still happier.'

'Well, speak, and if the matter depends on me it is done.'

'Oh, Monsieur, it depends only on you.'

'I am waiting.'

'Monsieur, the favour I wish to ask is that you call me no more Mousqueton, but Mouston. Since I have had the honour of being Monseigneur's steward, I have assumed this latter name, which makes my inferiors respect me—you know, Monsieur, how much subordination is necessary to a crowd of servants.'

D'Artagnan smiled; Porthos was extending his names, Mousqueton was abbreviating his.

'Well, yes, my dear Mouston,' said d'Artagnan, 'don't disturb yourself; I shall not forget your request. And if it will give you pleasure I will not even *tutoyer* you any more.'

'Oh,' cried Mousqueton, blushing from joy, 'if you would do me such an honour I should be grateful all my life for it; but perhaps it is too much to ask?'

'Alas,' said d'Artagnan to himself, 'it is very little in exchange for the unexpected tribulations that I bring to this poor devil, who has so well received me.'

'Does Monsieur stay long with us?' said Mousqueton, whose face, restored to its old serenity, bloomed out like a peony.

'I shall set out again tomorrow, my friend,' said d'Artagnan.

'Ah, Monsieur, it was only to give us cause for regret that you came.'

'I am afraid it was,' said d'Artagnan, in so low a tone that Mousqueton, who was retiring while making a bow, could not hear him.

A pang of remorse crossed d'Artagnan, although his heart was much hardened. He did not regret engaging Porthos in a course where life and fortune would be compromised, for Porthos was voluntarily risking it all for the title of baron; but Mousqueton, who desired nothing more than to be called Mouston, it seemed cruel to bear him away from this delightful life in the granary of abundance. This idea was preoccupying him when Porthos re-appeared.

'Come to table!' said Porthos.

'What, to table?' said d'Artagnan. 'What is the time, then?'

'Why, past one.'

'Your home is a paradise, Porthos; one forgets time here. I follow you, but I am not hungry.'

'Come; if you cannot always eat, you can always drink. This is one of poor Athos's maxims, the soundness of which I have recognized since I have been alone.'

D'Artagnan, whom his natural Gascon temperament always made sober enough, did not appear so convinced as his friend of the truth of Athos's maxim; nevertheless, he did his best to keep abreast of his friend.

Yet while looking at Porthos eating and drinking at his best, the thought of Mousqueton returned to d'Artagnan's mind, and this with so much more force, because Mousqueton, without himself waiting at table, which would have been beneath his position, appeared from time to time at the door and betrayed his gratitude to d'Artagnan by the age and vintage of the wines which he sent in.

So when at dessert, on a sign from d'Artagnan, Porthos dismissed the servants, and the two friends found themselves alone, 'Porthos,' said d'Artagnan, 'who will accompany you in your campaigns?'

'Who but Mouston?' he naturally replied.

This was a blow for d'Artagnan; he saw already the benevolent smile of the steward change into a look of grief.

'Yet,' replied d'Artagnan, 'he is no longer in his early youth, my dear fellow; he has besides grown very fat, and perhaps has lost the habitude of active service.'

'I know it,' said Porthos. 'But I am accustomed to him, and besides, he would not wish to leave me, he loves me too much.'

'Oh, blind self-love!' thought d'Artagnan.

'Besides, in your own case,' asked Porthos, 'have you not always at your service that good, brave, and intelligent—what is his name?'

'Planchet. Yes, I found him again, but he is no longer my servant.'

'What is he, then?'

'Well, with his sixteen hundred livres, you know, which he gained at the siege of Rochelle by carrying the letter* to Lord de Winter, he has started a little shop in the Rue des Lombards, and is a confectioner.'

'Ah, he is confectioner in the Rue des Lombards! but how is it he is attending you?'

'He has been at some pranks,' said d'Artagnan, 'and he fears being disturbed;' and the musketeer related to his friend how he had fallen in again with Planchet.

'Well, now,' said Porthos at that, 'who would have thought it possible that Planchet would one day save Rochefort, and that you should conceal him for that!'

'I should not have thought it. But how to help it? Events change men.'

'Nothing more true,' said Porthos; 'but that which does not change, or which changes for the better, is wine. Taste this; it is a Spanish vintage which our friend Athos highly values. It is sherry.'

At this moment, the steward came to consult his master respecting next day's menu, and also about the projected shooting-party.

'Tell me, Mouston, whether my arms are in good order?'

D'Artagnan began to keep time on the table to hide his embarrassment.

'Your arms, Monseigneur,' asked Mouston, 'what arms?'

'Why! my arms for fighting.'

'Well, yes, Monseigneur. At least I think so.'

'Make sure of it, and if they need it, have them cleaned. Which is my best roadster?'

'Vulcan.'

'And for work?'

'Bayard.'

'Which horse do you prefer?'

'I prefer Rustaud, Monseigneur; she is a fine animal, to which I am thoroughly accustomed.'

'She has endurance, hasn't she?'

'Normand crossed with Mecklembourg; that breed will go day and night.'

'You will feed up these three; you will see that my arms are cleaned; also pistols for yourself and a hunting-knife.'

'Are we going to travel, then, Monseigneur,' said Mousqueton, looking ill at ease.

D'Artagnan, who had till now only given some uncertain beats, beat a march.

'Better than that, Mouston,' replied Porthos.

'We are going on an expedition, Monsieur?' said the steward, whose roses began to change into lilies.

'We are re-entering the service, Mouston,' replied Porthos, trying to make his moustache assume the military curl which it had lost.

These words were scarcely spoken before Mousqueton was so agitated that his fat marbly cheeks quite shook; he regarded d'Artagnan with an indescribable air of tender reproach that the officer could not bear without feeling himself moved; then he staggered, and with a choked voice, 'Service! in the king's armies?' said he.

'Yes and no. We are going campaigning again, seeking adventures—living the former life, in short.'

This last word fell on Mousqueton like a thunderbolt. It was that *former* so terrible that made the *now* so sweet.

'Oh! *mon Dieu*, what is it that I hear?' said Mousqueton, with a look still more supplicating than the first, in the direction of d'Artagnan.

'What would you have, my poor Mouston?' said d'Artagnan; 'fatality——'

Despite the precaution d'Artagnan had taken not to *tutoyer* him, and to give to his name the length he desired, Mousqueton none the less received the blow, and it was so terrible that he went out entirely upset, forgetting even to shut the door.

'The good Mousqueton will feel no more joy,' said Porthos, in the tone which Don Quixote might have assumed to encourage Sancho to saddle his ass for a last campaign.

The two friends now left to themselves began to talk of the future, and to build a thousand castles in the air. Mousqueton's good wine caused d'Artagnan to see a dazzling perspective of double and single pistoles, and Porthos the blue ribbon and ducal mantle. The fact is they were asleep at the table when someone came to ask them to go to bed.

However, on the morrow Mousqueton was a little reassured by d'Artagnan, who told him that probably the fighting would be always in the heart of Paris within reach of the Château du Vallon, of Bracieux and of Pierrefonds.

'But it seems to me that formerly——' said Mousqueton, timidly.

'Oh!' said d'Artagnan, 'they don't make war as they used to. Nowadays there are diplomatic matters—ask Planchet.'

Mousqueton went to seek information from his old friend, who confirmed what d'Artagnan had said. 'Only,' added he, 'in this war the prisoners run the risk of being hung.'

'*Peste!*' said Mousqueton, 'I think I prefer the siege of Rochelle.'

As for Porthos, after having had a buck killed by his guest, having taken him from his woods to the mountain, from that to his ponds, after having shown him his leverets, his pack of hounds, Gredinet—in short, all he possessed—and made three more of the most sumptuous repasts, he asked for definite instructions from d'Artagnan, who was obliged to resume his journey.

'Here they are, dear friend!' said the ambassador; 'I shall require eight or nine days for my journey to Blois and return to Paris. Set out, then, in a week's time with your equipment. Go to the Hôtel de la Chevrette, Rue Tiquetonne, and await my return.'

'That is settled,' said Porthos.

'I am going on a hopeless errand to Athos,' said d'Artagnan. 'But though I believe he has become disabled, one must follow the usual course with one's friends.'

'If I were to go with you,' said Porthos, 'it would divert me perhaps.'

'That is possible,' said d'Artagnan, 'and me too; but you would not then have the time for making your preparations.'

'That's true,' said Porthos. 'Go then, and keep up your courage. As for me, I am full of ardour.'

'Wonderful!' said d'Artagnan.

And they separated on the limits of Pierrefonds, to the extremity of which Porthos wished to conduct his friend.

'At least,' said d'Artagnan, taking the road to Villers-Cotterêts, 'I shall not be alone. That fellow Porthos has still wonderful strength. If Athos comes, well! there will be three to laugh at Aramis—the little monk with his adventures.'

At Villers-Cotterêts he wrote to the cardinal:—

MONSEIGNEUR—I have already found one to present to your Eminence, and he is worth twenty men. I am setting out for Blois, as the Comte de la Fère dwells in the Château de Bragelonne in the vicinity of that city.

Upon that he took the route for Blois, talking to Planchet, who was a great source of entertainment during that long journey.

XV

TWO ANGELS' HEADS

A LONG journey was the matter in hand; but d'Artagnan felt no anxiety on that point. He knew that his horses had been well baited* from the plentiful stable-racks of the Lord de Bracieux. He therefore started off with confidence on the four or five days' march which he had to make, accompanied by the faithful Planchet.

As we said, they were travelling side by side and talking together to while away the time. D'Artagnan had little by little laid aside the master, and Planchet had quite left the character of servant. He was a shrewd fellow, who, since his extemporized civic life had often regretted the free quarters of the high-road as well as the brilliant conversation and company of gentlemen, and conscious of some personal valour, was distressed at being worn down by perpetual contact with people of low ideas.

He rose therefore to the rank of confidant with him whom he still called his master. D'Artagnan for long years had not opened his heart. It happened that these two men on coming together agreed admirably. Besides, Planchet was not by any means a vulgar companion in adventures. He was a man of good sense; without seeking danger, he did not retreat from hard knocks, as d'Artagnan had on several occasions observed. In short, he had been a soldier, and arms were ennobling; and then, more than that, if Planchet had need of him, Planchet was none the less useful to him. It was then almost on the footing of two good friends that they reached the Blois country.

While going on, d'Artagnan said, shaking his head and returning to the idea which unceasingly possessed him, 'I know well enough that my present journey is useless and absurd; but I owe this proceeding to my old friend—a man who had in him the stuff of the noblest and most generous of all men.'

'Oh, M. Athos was a bold gentleman!' said Planchet.

'Was he not?' replied d'Artagnan.

'Sowing money as the sky sends down hail,' continued Planchet, taking his sword in his hand with a kingly air. 'You remember his duel with the English on the clos Des Carmes?* Ah! how handsome and magnificent M. Athos was that day when he said to his adversary, "You have required me to tell you my name, Monsieur; so much the worse for you, for I shall be obliged to kill you." These were his very words. And that look when he struck his adversary, as he had said, who fell without saying, Oh! Ah, Monsieur, I repeat it!—he was a bold gentleman.'

'Yes,' said d'Artagnan, 'all that is as true as the Gospel; but he will have lost all those qualities from one single fault.'

'I remember,' said Planchet, 'he loved drink; or rather he used to drink. But he did not drink like the rest. His eyes said nothing when he put the glass to his lips. In truth, never was silence so speaking. As to me, I seemed to hear him murmur, "Enter, liquor, and drive away my griefs." And how he broke the foot of a glass or the neck of a bottle! He alone could do it.'

'Well, now,' said d'Artagnan, 'see the sad sight that awaits us! This proud-looking, noble gentleman, this fine cavalier, so brilliant under arms that one was always astonished that he held a simple sword in his hand instead of the *bâton* of command, will be transformed into a bent old man with red nose and weeping eyes. We are going to find him on some grass-plot whence he will look at us with dull eye, and perhaps will not recognize us. God is my witness, Planchet,' continued d'Artagnan, 'that I would fly from this sad spectacle if I was not bound to prove my respect to this illustrious shade of the glorious Comte de la Fère, whom we have so much loved.'

Planchet nodded, but said nothing. It could be easily seen that he shared his master's fears.

'And then,' continued d'Artagnan, 'this decrepitude, for Athos is old now; poverty, perhaps, for he will have neglected the little property he had; and the dirty Grimaud,* more mute than ever and more a drunkard than his master—there, Planchet, all that rends my heart.'

'It seems to me that I am there, and that I see him stammering and staggering,' said Planchet, in a pitiful tone.

'My only fear, I avow,' continued d'Artagnan, 'is lest Athos should accept my proposals in a moment of warlike inebriation. That would be a great calamity for Porthos and me, and above all a real embarrassment; but during his first orgy we shall leave him, that's all. On coming to himself, he will understand.'

'In any case, Monsieur,' said Planchet, 'we shall not be long without enlightenment, for I think these high walls which are red from the setting sun are the walls of Blois.'

'It is probable,' replied d'Artagnan; 'and those pointed and carved bell-turrets which we see there to the left in the wood resemble what I have heard said of Chambord.'*

'Shall we go into the city?' asked Planchet.

'Certainly, to get information.'

'Monsieur, I beg you then to taste some cream of which I have heard much, and which ought to be eaten on the spot.'

'All right! we will try some,' said d'Artagnan.

At that moment one of those lumbering wagons drawn by oxen, which carry the wood cut in the forests of the country as far as the ports of the Loire, passed out of a path full of ruts into the road which the travellers were following. A man accompanied it, carrying a long goad, armed with a nail, with which he was pricking on his slow team.

'Hi, friend!' cried Planchet, to the driver.

'What can I do for you, Messieurs?' said the peasant, with that purity of language* peculiar to the people of that country, and which would shame the purest citizens of the Place de la Sorbonne and the Rue de l'Université.

'We are looking for M. le Comte de la Fère's house,' said d'Artagnan. 'Do you know this name among those of the noblemen of the neighbourhood?'

The peasant took off his hat on hearing this name, and replied, 'Messieurs, this wood that I am carting is his. I have cut it in his forest, and am taking it to the château.'

D'Artagnan did not wish to question this man. It was repugnant to him to hear another say what he had himself said to Planchet.

'The château!' he said to himself. 'The château! Ah, I see! Athos is not patient. He has obliged his peasants, like Porthos, to call him Monseigneur, and to call his hovel a château. He had a heavy hand, this dear Athos, especially when he had been drinking.'

The oxen advanced slowly. D'Artagnan and Planchet walked behind the wagon. This pace made them impatient.

'This, then, is the road,' asked d'Artagnan of the driver; 'and can we follow it without fear of losing ourselves?'

'Oh, yes, Monsieur,' said the man, 'and you can take it in place of tiring yourselves by accompanying such slow beasts. In half a league you will see a château on the right; you cannot see it from here on account of a curtain of poplars which hides it. This is not Bragelonne, but La Vallière;* at three gun-shots thence, a large white house, slate roof, built on an eminence, shaded by enormous sycamores—that is the château of M. le Comte de la Fère.'

'And this half-league, is it long?' asked d'Artagnan, 'for there are leagues and leagues in our fine country of France.'

'Ten minutes of riding, Monsieur, for the fine legs of your horse.'

D'Artagnan thanked the driver, and pushed on at once, then trembled in spite of himself at the thought of seeing this singular man again, who had shown such affection for him, and had contributed so much by advice and example to his education as a gentleman. He little by little slackened his horse's pace, and continued to advance with drooping head as if musing.

Planchet also had found in this meeting, and in the bearing of this peasant matter for grave reflection. Never, in Normandy, nor in Franche Comté, nor in Artois, nor in Picardy—places in which he had principally lived—had he met among the villagers that easy address, that polished air, that refined language. He was tempted to believe that he had met some gentleman, Frondeur like himself, who from political causes had been forced like him to disguise himself.

Soon at the bend of the road, the Château de la Vallière, as the ox-driver had told them, came into sight; then about a quarter of a league farther on, the white house, encircled by sycamores, was seen in the centre of a clump of massive trees which spring had powdered white like snow, with blossoms.

At the view, d'Artagnan, who ordinarily was little subject to emotion, felt a strange trouble penetrate to the bottom of his heart, so powerful are the souvenirs of youth during the whole course of life. Planchet, who had not the same causes for such feelings, nonplussed at seeing his master so agitated, looked alternately at d'Artagnan and the house.

The musketeer made some steps in advance, and found himself before a gate, wrought with the taste which distinguishes the castings of that period.

There could be seen through the gate a kitchen-garden kept with care, a tolerably spacious courtyard, in which several horses led by grooms in different liveries were walking about, and a carriage drawn by two horses of the district.

'We have made a mistake, or that man has deceived us,' said d'Artagnan; 'it cannot be that Athos lives there. *Mon Dieu!* can he be dead, and the property belong to someone of his name? Get down, Planchet, and make enquiry; I confess I have not the courage.'

Planchet dismounted.

'You can add,' said d'Artagnan, 'that a gentleman in passing desires the honour of calling on M. le Comte de la Fère, and if you are satisfied with the information, well! then give him my name.'

Planchet, leading his horse by the bridle, approached the gate, rang the bell, and immediately a servant with white hair and erect figure despite his age, presented himself and received Planchet.

'Does M. le Comte de la Fère live here?' asked Planchet.

'Yes, Monsieur,' replied the servant, who was not in livery.

'A nobleman retired from the service?'

'The very same.'

'And who has a servant named Grimaud?' said Planchet, who with his habitual prudence did not think it possible to obtain too much information.

'M. Grimaud is absent just at present,' said the servant, beginning to look at Planchet from head to foot, not being much used to such questionings.

'Then,' cried Planchet, radiant, 'I see well enough that it is the same count for whom we are looking. Be good enough to open the gate, and announce to Monsieur the Count that my master, an old friend of his, wishes to see him.'

'Would you not prefer saying so yourself, rather?' said the servant, opening the gate. 'But where is your master?'

'He is following me.'

The servant opened the gate and preceded Planchet, who made a sign to his master, and d'Artagnan entered the court-yard with beating heart.

While Planchet was on the doorsteps he heard, coming from within, a voice which said, 'Well, where is this gentleman, and why do they not bring him here?'

This voice, which reached d'Artagnan, awoke in his heart a thousand feelings and souvenirs which he had forgotten. He jumped off his horse, while Planchet, with a smile on his face, advanced towards the master of the house.

'Why, I know that fellow,' said Athos, appearing on the doorstep.

'Oh, yes, Monsieur the Count, I am Planchet, you know.' But the honest servant could say no more, so much had the unexpected sight of the gentleman surprised him.

'What, Planchet!' cried Athos. 'Is then M. d'Artagnan here?'

'Here am I, friend; here am I, dear Athos,' said d'Artagnan, stammering and almost falling.

At these words a visible emotion showed itself in its turn on the fine face and calm features of Athos. He took two rapid steps towards d'Artagnan, gazing earnestly on him, and pressed him tenderly in his arms. D'Artagnan, relieved of his trouble, pressed him in his turn with a cordiality which shone in the tears in his eyes.

Athos took him then by the hand, which he held in his, and led him to the drawing-room, where several persons were assembled. Every one rose.

'I present to you,' said Athos, 'M. le Chevalier d'Artagnan, lieutenant in his Majesty's Musketeers—a devoted friend, and one of the bravest and most amiable gentlemen I have ever known.'

D'Artagnan, according to custom, received the compliments of those present, returned them to the best of his ability, took a place in the circle, and while the conversation, for a moment interrupted, became once more general, he began to examine Athos.

Strange thing! Athos had hardly aged at all. His fine eyes, freed from the circle of bistre which watchings and orgies produce, seemed larger and more liquid than ever; his face slightly elongated, had gained in majesty what it had lost of feverish agitation; his hand, always wonderfully fine and nervous in spite of the softness of the skin, was resplendent in lace cuffs like certain hands by Titian and Van Dyck. He was slighter than formerly; his shoulders showed uncommon strength; his long black hair, sparsely sprinkled with a few grey hairs, fell elegantly over his shoulders, and waved naturally; his voice was as fresh as if he were only about twenty-five; and his fine teeth, which he had kept white and sound, gave an inexpressible charm to his smile.

However, the count's guests, who saw by the almost imperceptible coldness of the conversation that the two friends burned with the desire of being by themselves, began to prepare, with all the politeness of former times, for their departure—that grave affair of people of the great world, when there were people of the great world. But at that moment there was heard a great noise of dogs barking in the courtyard, and several persons said together, 'Ah! that's Raoul returned.'

Athos, at the name of Raoul, looked at d'Artagnan, and seemed to notice the curiosity which at this name appeared on his face. But d'Artagnan comprehended nothing as yet; he had not yet recovered from his bewilderment. It was then almost mechanically that he turned when a fine young man of fifteen, dressed simply but in perfect taste, entered the room, gracefully raising his hat, ornamented with long red feathers.

Nevertheless this new personage, entirely unlooked for, impressed him. A whole world of new ideas presented themselves to his mind, explaining to him through all the sources of his intelligence the change in Athos which until then had appeared to him inexplicable.

A singular resemblance between the gentleman and the youth explained the mystery of this renewed life. He waited, looking and listening.

'You have returned, then, Raoul?' said the count.

'Yes, Monsieur,' he replied respectfully; 'and I have performed the commission which you gave me.'

'But what is the matter, Raoul?' said Athos, with solicitude. 'You are pale and agitated.'

'An accident has just happened to our neighbour.'

'To Mademoiselle de la Vallière?'* said Athos, quickly.

'What, then?' asked several voices.

'She was walking in the enclosure with her *bonne*, Marcelline, where the woodmen were squaring their trees. When passing on horseback I perceived her and stopped. She had perceived me in her turn, and wishing to leap down from a pile of wood, fell, and has, I think, dislocated her ankle.'

'Oh, *mon Dieu!*' said Athos. 'And has her mother, Madame de Saint-Rémy,* been told of it?'

'No, Monsieur; she is at Blois with Madame the Duchesse d'Orléans. I am afraid that the first applications were unskilfully used, and I come to you, Monsieur, to ask your counsel.'

'Send quickly to Blois, Raoul! Or rather, take your horse, and go there yourself.'

Raoul bowed.

'But where is Louise?' said the count.

'I have brought her here, Monsieur, and left her with Charlot's wife, who meanwhile has bathed her foot in cold water.'

Upon this explanation, which had given a reason for rising, Athos's guests took leave, except the old Duc de Barbé* who, acting familiarly in virtue of a friendship of twenty years with the house of La Vallière, went to see Louise, who was weeping, and who, on seeing Raoul, wiped her handsome eyes and immediately smiled. The duke then proposed to take her in his carriage to Blois.

'You are right, Monsieur,' said Athos; 'she will be sooner with her mother. As for you, Raoul, I fear you have acted thoughtlessly, and that it is your fault.'

'Oh, no, no, Monsieur, I swear it to you!' cried the little girl; while the young man grew pale at the idea that he was perhaps the cause of this accident.

'Oh, Monsieur, I assure you!' murmured Raoul.

'You will none the less go to Blois,' added the count, kindly, 'and make your excuses and mine to Madame de Saint-Rémy, and then return.'

The colour returned to the cheeks of the youth. He took the little girl up in his arms, smiling in spite of her pain, as she rested her pretty head upon his shoulder, and put her gently into the carriage; then leaping on his horse with the elegance and agility of a practised horseman, after having saluted Athos and d'Artagnan he went off rapidly, keeping near the door of the carriage, towards the interior of which his eyes were constantly directed.

XVI

THE CHÂTEAU DE BRAGELONNE

D'ARTAGNAN had remained during this scene with wild look and open mouth. He had found matters so different from his expectations that he was in a state of great astonishment.

Athos took him by the arm, and led him into the garden.

'While they are preparing supper,' said he, smiling, 'you will not be sorry, will you, my friend, to have this mystery cleared up somewhat which makes you ponder so?'

'It is true, Monsieur the Count,' said d'Artagnan, who felt himself little by little influenced by that immense superiority of nobility which he had always felt in Athos.

Athos looked at him with his sweet smile.

'First of all,' said he, 'my dear d'Artagnan, there is no Monsieur the Count here at all. If I styled you chevalier, it was to present you to my guests so as to make them know who you were; but for you, d'Artagnan, I am, I hope, always Athos—your companion, your friend. Do you give preference for ceremoniousness because you love me less?'

'Oh, God, keep me from that!' said the Gascon, with one of those loyal bursts of youth which occur so rarely in mature age.

'Then, as a commencement, let us be frank. All here astonishes you?'

'Deeply.'

'But what astonishes you most,' said Athos, smiling, 'is
myself. Confess it!'

'I do.'

'I am still young, am I not, in spite of my forty-nine years?
I am still the same?'

'On the contrary,' said d'Artagnan, quite ready to go beyond
the recommendation of frankness which Athos had professed,
'you are no longer so at all.'

'Ah, I understand!' said Athos, with a slight blush; 'all tends
to an end, d'Artagnan—folly like everything else.'

'Then, a change has taken place in your fortune, it seems to
me. You are capitally housed. I suppose this house is yours?'

'Yes. This is the small property, you know, my friend, which
I told you that I inherited when I left the army.'

'You have a park, horses, and carriages?'

Athos smiled.

'The park has twenty acres,' said he, 'out of which is taken
our kitchen-garden and outhouses. I have two horses, not
counting my groom's cob. My hunting equipage is reduced to
four setters, two greyhounds, and a pointer. Still, all this
extravagance in having a pack,' added Athos, smiling, 'is not
for myself.'

'Yes, I understand; it is for young Raoul.' And d'Artagnan
regarded Athos with an involuntary smile.

'You have guessed rightly, my friend.'

'And this youth is your adopted son—your relative, perhaps?
Ah, how changed you are, my dear Athos!'

'This young man,' answered Athos, calmly, 'is an orphan
whom his mother left at the house of a poor country curate. I
have brought him up.'

'He ought to be much attached to you?'

'I think he loves me as much as if I were his own father.'

'Thoroughly grateful, especially?'

'Oh, as to gratitude,' said Athos, 'that is mutual. I owe him
as much as he owes me. I do not tell him, but I can you,
d'Artagnan—I am still his debtor.'

'How so?' said the astonished soldier.

'Ah, yes! It is he who has brought about the change you see in me. I was wasting away like a poor isolated tree which is losing its hold in the ground; it was only a strong attachment which could make me take root once more in life. A mistress? I was too old. Some friends? I had you no longer. Well, this child has helped me to recover all that I had lost. I have lived not for myself, but for him. Instruction is good for a child; but example is worth more. This I have given him. The vices I had I have corrected. The virtues that I had not I have feigned to have. So I do not think I deceive myself, d'Artagnan, in thinking that Raoul will be as perfect a gentleman as it is given to our impoverished age still to furnish.'

D'Artagnan looked at Athos with increasing admiration. They were walking in a fresh, shady avenue, through which penetrated obliquely some rays of the setting sun. One of these golden rays lighted up Athos's countenance, and his eyes seemed to give back the mild, calm evening light which they received. The idea of Milady just then presented itself to d'Artagnan's mind.

'And are you happy?' he said to his friend.

Athos's penetrating eye pierced to the bottom of d'Artagnan's heart, and seemed to read his thought there.

'As happy as one is permitted to be on earth. But finish your thought, d'Artagnan, for you have not told me the whole of it.'

'You are a terrible fellow, Athos; and one can hide nothing from you. Well, yes, I should like to ask you if you have not sometimes unexpected emotions of dread approaching to——'

'To remorse?' continued Athos. 'I will finish your thought, my friend. Yes and no. I have not, because that woman, I believe, merited the punishment she has undergone; because, too, if we had allowed her to live, she would without doubt have continued her work of destruction. But that does not mean, friend, that I am convinced that we had the right to do what we did. Perhaps all bloodshed demands expiation. She has paid hers; perhaps it is our turn to furnish ours.'

'I have sometimes thought as you do, Athos,' said d'Artagnan.

'This woman had a son?'*

'Yes.'

'Have you ever heard him spoken of?'

'Never.'

'He must be about twenty-three,' said Athos; 'I often think of that young man, d'Artagnan.'

'It is strange. I had forgotten him.'

Athos gave a melancholy smile.

'And Lord de Winter, have you any news of him?'

'I know he was in great favour with King Charles I.'

'He has followed his fortune, which is bad at present. Stay, d'Artagnan,' continued Athos; 'that brings us back to what I was saying just now. He has shed the blood of Strafford; blood demands blood. And the queen?'

'What queen?'

'Madame Henrietta of England, Henry IV's daughter.'

'She is at the Louvre, as you know.'

'Yes, where she is in great want; is it not so? During the severe cold of this winter, her daughter, who is ill, was obliged, so they tell me, to keep in bed. Can you understand that?' said Athos, shrugging his shoulders. 'Henry IV's daughter shivering from cold for want of a faggot! Why did she not ask any of us instead of Mazarin? She would have wanted for nothing.'

'Do you know her, then?'

'No; but my mother saw her when a child. Have I ever told you that my mother was once maid of honour* to Marie de Médicis?'

'Never. You did not speak of those things, Athos.'

'Oh, yes, I did, you know it,' replied Athos; 'but still there is need for the occasion to occur.'

'Porthos would not wait so patiently,' said d'Artagnan, with a smile.

'Each to his nature, my dear d'Artagnan. Porthos has, in spite of a little vanity, some excellent qualities. Have you seen him lately?'

'I left him five days ago.'

And then he related, with the force of his Gascon humour, all the splendour of Porthos and his Château de Pierrefonds;

and while riddling his friend, he launched two or three arrows in the direction of that excellent M. Mouston.

'I am astonished,' replied Athos, smiling with that gaiety which recalled their former jolly days, 'that we formed by mere hazard a society of men still so closely bound to one another in spite of twenty years of separation. Friendship throws out very deep roots into sincere hearts, d'Artagnan. Believe me, it is only worthless people who deny that there is any friendship, because they do not comprehend it. And Aramis?'

'I have seen him also,' said d'Artagnan, 'but he seemed cold.'

'Ah! you have seen Aramis,' replied Athos, looking at d'Artagnan with his scrutinizing eye. 'Why, it is a real pilgrimage, dear friend, that you are making to the Temple of Friendship, as the poets would say.'

'Well, yes,' said d'Artagnan, embarrassed.

'Aramis, you know,' continued Athos, 'is naturally cold; then he is always entangled in intrigues with women.'

'I believe there is at this time a very intricate one.'

Athos did not answer.

'He is not curious,' thought d'Artagnan.

Not only Athos did not reply, but he sought to change the conversation.

'You see we have in about an hour's walk made the tour, so to speak, of my domains.'

'All is charming, and especially smacks of the gentlemanly,' replied d'Artagnan.

At that moment they heard the step of a horse.

'It is Raoul come back,' said Athos; 'we shall have news of the poor little girl.'

In fact, the young man appeared at the gate, and entered the courtyard all covered with dust; then dismounting, he came to salute the count and d'Artagnan.

'This is the Chevalier d'Artagnan, of whom you have often heard me speak, Raoul,' said Athos, putting his hand on d'Artagnan's shoulder.

'Monsieur,' said the young man, making a deep bow, 'the count has mentioned your name in my presence as an example of an intrepid and generous gentleman.'

This little compliment did not fail to move d'Artagnan, who felt his heart gently stirred.

'My young friend, all these eulogiums passed on me really belong to Monsieur the Count; for he has educated me in every respect, and it is not his fault if his pupil has so badly profited from the instruction. I am pleased with your manner, Raoul, and your politeness has touched me.'

Athos was more delighted than can be expressed; he looked gratefully at d'Artagnan, then cast on Raoul one of those rare smiles of which young people are so proud when they secure them.

'Now,' said d'Artagnan to himself, whom this mute play of the countenance had not escaped—'now I am certain of it.'

'Well,' said Athos, 'I hope that the accident has not had bad results.'

'They know nothing yet, Monsieur, and the doctor has been able to say nothing on account of the swelling; he fears, however, that some nerve may be injured.'

'And you have not remained later with Madame de Saint-Rémy?'

'I was afraid of not returning in season for your dinner, Monsieur,' said Raoul, 'and consequently of making you wait.'

At this moment a little boy, half-peasant, half-servant, came to say that supper was ready.

Athos led his guest into a very plain dining-room; but on one side the windows opened on the garden, and on the other on a conservatory in which some lovely flowers were growing.

D'Artagnan cast his eyes on the dinner-service. The plate was very fine; one saw that it was the old family plate. On the sideboard was a superb silver ewer; d'Artagnan stopped to look at it.

'Ah, that is a splendid piece of art,' said he.

'Yes,' replied Athos; 'it is a *chef-d'œuvre* of a great Florentine artist named Benvenuto Cellini.'*

'And the battle it represents?'

'Is that of Marignan.* It is the moment when one of my ancestors gives his sword to Francis I, who has just broken his own. It was on that occasion that Enguerrand de la Fère, my ancestor, was made Knight of St Michael. Besides, the king, fifteen years later—for he had not forgotten that he had fought for three hours with his friend Enguerrand's sword without its breaking—made him a present of that ewer, and of a sword which you have perhaps seen formerly in my possession, which is also a fine piece of goldsmith's work. Those were the days of giants,' said Athos. 'We are dwarfs, in these times, by the side of those men. Let us be seated, d'Artagnan, and get supper. Now call Charlot,' said Athos to the small servant, who had just served the soup.

The boy went out, and a moment after, the man-servant to whom the travellers spoke on arriving entered.

'Charlot,' said Athos to him, 'I particularly desire you to take care of Planchet, M. d'Artagnan's servant, as long as he stays. He likes good wine; you have the cellar key. He also does not dislike a good bed. Look after that also, I beg of you.'

Charlot bowed and went out.

'Charlot is also a fine fellow,' said the count. 'For eighteen years has he been in my service.'

'You think of everything,' said d'Artagnan, 'and I thank you on Planchet's behalf, my dear Athos.'

The young man opened his eyes wide at this name, and looked to see if it were really the count to whom d'Artagnan spoke.

'That name seems odd to you, does it not, Raoul?' said Athos, smiling. 'It was an assumed name at the time that M. d'Artagnan, two brave friends, and myself did warlike feats at Rochelle under the deceased cardinal and M. de Bassompierre, who has died since. Each time I hear it used by my friend my heart feels joyful.'

'That name was celebrated,' said d'Artagnan, 'and it had one day the honours of a triumph.'

'What do you mean, Monsieur?' asked Raoul, with childish curiosity.

'Really I know nothing about it,' said Athos.

'You have forgotten the Bastion St Gervais,* Athos, and that napkin which three bullets transformed into a flag. I have a better memory than you, and I am going to relate it to you, young man;' and he told Raoul all the history of the bastion, as Athos had recounted that of his ancestor.

On hearing this, the youth imagined he saw laid before him a feat of arms like those related by Tasso or Ariosto, which belong to the fascinating times of chivalry.*

'But what has not been told you, Raoul,' replied Athos in his turn, 'is that this gentleman is one of the best swordsmen of our time; muscles of iron, wrist of steel, sure glance, burning look—that is what he offers to his adversary. He was eighteen,* three years older than you, Raoul, when I saw him in action for the first time, and against experienced men.'

'And M. d'Artagnan was victor?' said the youth, whose eyes shone during this conversation, and seemed to ask for details.

'I killed one, I think,' said d'Artagnan, looking at Athos enquiringly. 'As for the other, I disarmed or wounded him, I forget which.'

'Oh, yes; you wounded him. Oh, you were a rough athlete.'

'Ah, I have not yet lost very much,' replied d'Artagnan, with his little Gascon laugh full of self-satisfaction; 'and recently, also——'

A look from Athos made him silent.

'I wish you to know, Raoul,' replied Athos, 'who think yourself a fine swordsman, and whose vanity will one day suffer a cruel undeceiving, how dangerous the man is who unites coolness with alertness, for I shall never be able to offer you a more striking example. Tomorrow ask M. d'Artagnan, if he is not too tired, to be good enough to give you a lesson.'

'Nonsense, my dear Athos; you are a good master, above all with respect to the very qualities which you boast of in me. Why, it was today Planchet was mentioning the famous duel in the clos Des Carmes with Lord de Winter and his companions. Ah, young man,' continued d'Artagnan, 'there ought to be here somewhere a sword that I have often called the first in the kingdom.'

'Oh! I have spoiled my hand with this boy,' said Athos.

'There are hands which never spoil, my dear Athos,' said d'Artagnan, 'but which spoil those of others.'

The youth would have liked to prolong this conversation the whole night, but Athos observed that their guest must be very tired, and want rest. D'Artagnan politely denied, but Athos insisted. Raoul showed the way to the room; and as Athos feared he would detain D'Artagnan by obtaining more stories of the past, he himself went shortly after to look for him, and closed this pleasant evening by a very friendly shake of the hand, wishing the musketeer a good night.

XVII

ATHOS'S DIPLOMACY

D'ARTAGNAN had gone to bed not so much to sleep as to be alone and think over all he had seen and heard that evening. As he had a good disposition, and had had from the first an instinctive liking for Athos which had ripened into a sincere friendship, he was delighted to find a man sparkling with intelligence in place of a boorish drunkard whom he expected to see sleeping himself sober on some dunghill. He accepted without too much resisting that constant superiority of Athos over him; and in place of feeling the jealousy and disappointment which would have annoyed a less generous nature, he felt, after all, only a sincere and loyal joy which led him to entertain the most favourable hopes respecting his negotiations.

Yet it seemed to him that he did not find Athos quite sincere and explicit on all points. Who was this youth whom he said had been adopted by him, and who bore such a strong likeness to him? What was this return to the life of the world, and that exaggerated sobriety which he had remarked at table? One thing also insignificant in appearance, this absence of Grimaud, from whom Athos formerly could not be separated, and whose name had not been mentioned in spite of references made to it—all this disquieted d'Artagnan. He did not any longer possess his friend's confidence, or Athos was bound by some invisible chain; or perhaps, he thought, Athos had been fore-warned of his (d'Artagnan's) visit.

He could not help thinking of Rochefort, and of what he had told him in Notre-Dame. Could Rochefort have seen Athos before him?

D'Artagnan had no time to lose in long studies; he was therefore resolved to get an explanation on the morrow. The smallness of Athos's fortune, so cleverly disguised, evinced the desire to shine, and betrayed the remains of an ambition easy to awaken. Athos's vigour of mind and clearness of ideas made him a man more prompt than another to be moved. He would enter into the minister's plans with all the more ardour because his natural activity would be doubled by a dose of necessity.

These thoughts kept d'Artagnan awake in spite of his fatigue; he drew up plans of attack, and although he knew that Athos was a rough adversary, he fixed on the next day after breakfast as the time of action.

Yet he said to himself also, on the other hand, that on so new ground there was need to advance with caution, to study for several days Athos's friends, to follow his new habits of life and find the reason for them, to try and extract from the artless young man, either in exercising in arms or in coursing, that intermediate information which he needed to connect the Athos of former times with the Athos of the present; and that should be easy, for the preceptor ought to have impressed himself upon the heart and spirit of his pupil. But d'Artagnan, who was himself possessed of much finesse, saw at once what chances he would give in case any indiscretion or awkwardness on his part exposed his plans to the practised eye of Athos.

Then it must be said that d'Artagnan, though quite ready to employ artifice against the finesse of Aramis or the vanity of Porthos, was ashamed to shuffle with Athos, the frank man, the loyal heart.

'Ah! why is not Grimaud the silent here?' said d'Artagnan. 'There are so many things which I should have understood from him; Grimaud had such an eloquent silence!'

However, all the noises in the house died away successively: d'Artagnan had heard the doors and shutters closed; then the dogs outside, after having for some time answered the one to the other, had become silent in their turn; at last, a nightingale lost in a mass of trees had for some time poured out his harmonious scales in the middle of the night, and had gone to sleep. In the château there was no sound heard except that of an even and monotonous step underneath his chamber; he supposed it was the chamber of Athos.

'He walks and reflects,' thought d'Artagnan; 'but of what? That it is impossible to know. One could guess the rest, but not that.'

At last Athos went to bed. The silence which reigned throughout the house united with his fatigue overcame d'Artagnan; his eyes closed, and almost immediately he fell asleep.

D'Artagnan was not a great sleeper. Scarcely had dawn gilded his curtains than he jumped out of bed and opened the windows. He thought he saw then through the blind someone moving about the courtyard, while trying to avoid making any noise. According to his habit of letting nothing pass within reach without learning what it was, d'Artagnan looked attentively without making a noise, and recognized the garnet-coloured coat and brown locks of Raoul.

The young fellow—for it was he—opened the stable-door, took out the bay horse which he had ridden the evening before, saddled it himself with as much promptness and skill as the most accomplished groom, then passed along the path at the right of the kitchen-garden, opened a little side-door, and then d'Artagnan saw him pass like an arrow, bending under the hanging branches of maples and acacias.

D'Artagnan had noticed in the evening that the path was in the direction of Blois.

'Eh, eh!' said the Gascon, 'here is a gay spark who does not seem to share Athos's dislike to the fair sex. He is not going shooting, for he has neither arms nor dogs; he is not bearing a message, for he conceals himself. From whom does he hide? Is it from me or from his father? (For I am sure that the count is his father.) *Parbleu!* as to that, I will know it, for I will speak of it plainly to Athos.'

The day advanced. All the sounds that d'Artagnan had heard successively cease at night now arose one after the other—the bird in the branches, the dog in the stable, the sheep in the fields; the boats on the Loire even seemed alive, moving away along the stream. D'Artagnan stayed thus at the window so as to wake no one; then, when he had heard the doors and shutters of the château being opened, he gave a last turn to his hair, a last curl to his moustache, brushed, from habit, his hat with the sleeve of his doublet, and went downstairs. He had scarcely left the last step of the front-door flight than he saw Athos bent towards the ground, and in the attitude of a man who is looking for a crown in the sand.

'Good-day, my dear host,' said d'Artagnan.

'Good-day, dear friend; have you had a good night?'

'Excellent, Athos! like your bed, your supper of yesterday evening which ought to have brought me sleep, and your reception of me when you saw me again. But what are you looking at there so attentively? Have you perchance become an amateur of tulips?'

'My dear friend, there is no need to make fun of me on that account. In the country tastes change, and we learn to like all the beautiful things which God produces from the bosom of the earth, and which we neglect in the towns. I was looking simply at some lilies which I have planted near this reservoir, and which have been crushed this morning. These gardeners are most awkward fellows. While leading off the horse used for drawing water, they have let it walk on this bed.'

D'Artagnan smiled.

'Ah!' said he, 'do you believe it?' and he led his friend along the avenue, where a good number of footprints similar to that which had crushed the lily were seen.

'Here are more of them, it seems to me; here, Athos,' said he, with indifference.

'Yes, certainly; as well as some which are quite recent.'

'Quite recent,' repeated d'Artagnan.

'Who has then gone out this way this morning?' asked Athos, with some anxiety. 'Has a horse escaped from the stable?'

'It is not probable,' said d'Artagnan, 'for the footprints are quite equal and regular.'

'Where is Raoul?' cried Athos, 'and how is it I have not seen him?'

'*Chut!*' said d'Artagnan, putting his finger to his mouth with a smile.

'What has happened, then?' asked Athos.

D'Artagnan related what he had seen, while he scanned his host's countenance.

'Ah! I guess it all now,' said Athos, with a slight shrug of the shoulders; 'the poor boy has gone to Blois.'

'What to do?'

'Why, to obtain news of the little La Vallière.'

'Do you think so?' said d'Artagnan, incredulous.

'I am sure of it,' replied Athos. 'Have you not noticed that Raoul is in love?'

'Good! but with whom—this child of seven years?'*

'My dear fellow, at Raoul's age the heart is so full that it must bestow itself on something, real or imaginary. Ah, well! his love is half of each.'

'Are you joking? What! this little girl?'

'Have you not looked at her? She is the prettiest little creature in the world; hair of a silver blond, blue eyes already rebellious and languishing at the same time.'

'But what do you say to this passion?'

'I say nothing; I laugh and make fun of Raoul. But these first needs of the heart are so imperious, these outpourings of amorous melancholy in young people are at once so sweet and so bitter, that they have often all the real marks of the passion. I remember that at the age of Raoul I had become amorous of a Greek statue that the good King Henry IV had given to my father, and that I thought I should become insane with grief when they told me that the story of Pygmalion* was only a fable.'

'It is want of occupation. You do not employ Raoul enough, and he finds occupation for himself.'

'Nothing else. So I have thought of sending him away.'

'And you would act rightly.'

'Without doubt; but it would break his heart, and he will suffer as much as for a veritable love. For three or four years, and at that time he himself was quite a child, he used to deck himself out, and admire this little idol, whom he will end by adoring if he stays here. These children dream together all the day, and talk of a thousand serious things like true lovers of twenty years. In short, this has made the parents of the little La Vallière smile; but I think they are beginning to feel serious about it.'

'Child's play! but Raoul must be taken away. Send him soon from here, or you will never make a man of him.'

'I think,' said Athos, 'that I shall send him to Paris.'

'Ah!' said d'Artagnan, and he thought the moment had come for opening fire. 'If you wish,' said he, 'we can make a career for the young fellow.'

'Ah!' said Athos, in his turn.

'In fact, I want to consult you on something which has come into my mind.'

'Go on.'

'Do you believe the time to be come for taking service?'

'But are you not always in the service, d'Artagnan?'

'I mean active service. Has not the life of former days anything to tempt you? And if some real advantages await you, would you not be glad to begin it again with me and our friend Porthos?'

'You are then making me a proposition?' said Athos.

'Clear and frank.'

'To enter on active service?'

'Yes.'

'For and against whom?' asked Athos, suddenly, as he looked with clear and kindly eye on the Gascon.

'Ah, the deuce! you are pressing.'

'And above all, precise. Listen now, d'Artagnan. There is but one person, or rather but one cause, to which a man like myself might be useful—that of the king.'

'Precisely so,' said the musketeer.

'Yes, but let us understand,' replied Athos, seriously; 'if by the king's cause you mean that of M. de Mazarin, we cease to understand each other.'

'I did not speak precisely,' answered the Gascon, embarrassed.

'Now, d'Artagnan,' said Athos, 'don't let us finesse. Your hesitation, your shifts, tell me on whose authority you come. No one does, in fact, like to confess this openly, and when recruiting for it the head is lowered, and the voice is embarrassed.'

'Ah, my dear Athos!' said d'Artagnan.

'And you know well enough that I do not speak of yourself, who are the pearl of brave men, but of that cunning, intriguing Italian; of that mean fellow who tries to put on his head a crown which he has stolen under a pillow; of that puppy who calls his party that of the king, and who bethought himself of putting the princes of the blood into prison, not daring to kill them, as did the great cardinal; of a skinflint who weighs his golden crowns and keeps the clipped ones from fear that although he cheats he may lose them at his next day's game—of a fool, in short, who ill-treats the queen, as we are assured, and who goes hence in three months to make civil war on us to protect his pensions. Is that the master you propose to me, d'Artagnan? Goodness gracious!'

'You are more sensitive than formerly, excuse me,' said d'Artagnan; 'and years have warmed your blood instead of cooling it. Who told you, then, that this was my master, and that I wish to impose him on you?—Hang it!' the Gascon had thought, 'I must not deliver up my secrets to one so ill-disposed.'

'But, dear friend,' replied Athos, 'what then are your propositions?'

'There is nothing more simple: you live on your own lands, and it seems that you are happy in your gilded mediocrity; Porthos has an income of perhaps fifty or sixty thousand livres; Aramis has always fifteen duchesses who wrangle over the ecclesiastic as they used to respecting the musketeer—he is still a sort of spoiled child; but I, what am I doing in the world? I have worn my cuirass and cloak for the last twenty years, tethered to this inadequate rank, without advancing, retreating, living. In a word, I am dead. Well, then, when it is a question with me how to awake a bit, you all come and tell me, "He is a mean fellow, a fool, a bad master!" Eh, well! I am of your opinion, but find me a better, or give me an income.'

Athos reflected for three seconds, and comprehended d'Artagnan's device, who, having advanced too fast at first, now broke off short to hide his game. Athos saw clearly enough that the proposals d'Artagnan had just made were genuine, and would have been gradually developed if he had lent an ear.

'Good!' said he to himself. 'D'Artagnan is for Mazarin.'

From this moment he exercised extreme prudence. On his side d'Artagnan played more closely than ever.

'But you have an idea, however,' continued Athos.

'Certainly. I wished to take the advice of you all as to the means of doing something, for without one another we shall continue incomplete.'

'That is true. You were speaking to me of Porthos. Have you determined him to seek after fortune? But he has it.'

'Without doubt. But man is so created that he always wants something.'

'And what does Porthos want?'

'To be made a baron.'

'Ah, yes! I forgot,' said Athos, laughing.

'Ah, yes!' thought d'Artagnan. 'Where did he learn that? Does he correspond with Aramis? Ah! if I knew that I should know all.'

The conversation stopped there, for Raoul entered at that moment. Athos wished to scold him without severity, but the youth was so troubled that he had not the courage, and interrupted himself to ask him what was the matter.

'Is your little neighbour worse?' said d'Artagnan.

'Ah, Monsieur!' replied Raoul, almost choked with grief, 'her fall was serious; and though without apparent deformity, the doctor thinks that she will be lame all her life.'*

'Ah, that would be terrible!' said Athos.

D'Artagnan had a pleasantry on his lips; but seeing the part that Athos took in this misfortune, he refrained from uttering it.

'Ah, Monsieur! what distresses me above all,' said Raoul, 'is that I was the cause of it.'

'How you, Raoul?' asked Athos.

'Without a doubt it was to run to me that she leaped from the top of the wood heap.'

'There only remains one resource, my dear Raoul, and that is to espouse her in expiation,' said d'Artagnan.

'Ah, Monsieur!' said Raoul, 'you sport with a real grief; that is too bad!'

And Raoul, who wanted to be alone to weep, returned to his room, from which he came out only at the hour of breakfast.

The harmony of the two friends had not been broken in the least by the morning's skirmish, so they breakfasted with the best appetite, looking from time to time at Raoul, who, with moist eyes and heavy heart, scarcely ate anything.

At the end of the meal two letters came which Athos read with extreme attention, without being able to keep himself from starting several times. D'Artagnan, who saw him read these letters from the other side of the table, and whose glance was penetrating, swore that he recognized beyond a doubt Aramis's little handwriting. As for the other, it was in a woman's hand, long and intricate.

'Come,' said d'Artagnan to Raoul, seeing that Athos wished to be alone, 'let us take a turn in the fencing-room; that will divert you.'

The youth looked at Athos, who replied by a sign of acquiescence. They both went into the room, where foils, masks, gloves, plastrons, and all the accessories for fencing were hung up.

'Well?' said Athos, coming in about a quarter of an hour after.

'He has already your style, my dear Athos,' said d'Artagnan; 'and if he had your coolness I should have only compliments to make him.'

As to the young man, he was a little shamefaced. For one or two times that he had touched d'Artagnan, either on the arm or the thigh, the latter had buttoned him twenty times full in the body.

At that moment Charlot came in, bringing a letter of great importance for d'Artagnan which a messenger had just left.

It was now Athos's turn to look askance.

D'Artagnan read the letter without any apparent emotion, and having read it, with a slight toss of the head, 'See, my friend,' said he, 'what the service is; and you have, in faith, good reason for not wishing to rejoin it. M. de Tréville is ill, and in fact the company cannot do without me, so that my leave of absence is lost.'

'You return to Paris?' said Athos, briskly.

'Eh! indeed, yes,' said d'Artagnan; 'but are not you coming too?'

Athos slightly blushed, and replied, 'If I were going there I should be very happy to see you.'

'Holloa, Planchet!' cried d'Artagnan from the door, 'we start in ten minutes; give the horses some oats.' Then turning to Athos, 'It seems to me that something is wanting here, and I am truly vexed to leave you without having seen good Grimaud.'

'Grimaud!' said Athos. 'I was astonished also that you did not ask any news of him. I have lent him to one of my friends.'

'Who will understand his signs?'

'I hope so.'

The two friends cordially embraced. D'Artagnan pressed Raoul's hand, made Athos promise to visit him if he came to Paris, to write to him if he did not, and mounted his horse. Planchet, always punctual, was already in saddle.

'Do you not come with me?' said he, smiling at Raoul; 'I pass by Blois.'

Raoul turned towards Athos, who restrained him by an almost imperceptible sign.

'No, Monsieur,' responded the young man; 'I remain with Monsieur the Count.'

'Adieu to both, my good friends,' said d'Artagnan, pressing their hands for the last time, 'and may God preserve you! as we used to say to one another every time we separated in the time of the deceased cardinal.'

Athos waved his hand to him, Raoul bowed, and d'Artagnan and Planchet set off.

The count followed them with his eyes, his hand resting on the youth's shoulder, whose height almost equalled his own; but as soon as they disappeared behind the wall, 'Raoul,' said the count, 'we start this evening for Paris.'

'What!' said the youth, turning pale.

'You can go and present my adieux and yours to Madame de Saint-Rémy. I shall expect you here at seven.'

The young man bowed with a mixed expression of grief and gratitude, and withdrew to go and saddle his horse.

As for d'Artagnan, when scarcely out of sight he had taken the letter from his pocket and read it again:

Return immediately to Paris.

J. M.

'The letter is brief,' murmured d'Artagnan, 'and if there had been no postscript I should not perhaps have understood it, but fortunately there is one;' and he read this precious postscript, which made him pass over the brevity of the letter.

P.S. Call on the king's treasurer at Blois; tell him your name, and show him this letter; you will receive two hundred pistoles.

'Decidedly,' said d'Artagnan, 'I like this prose, and the cardinal writes better than I thought. Now then, Planchet, let us pay a visit to the king's treasurer, and then push on.'

'Towards Paris, Monsieur?'

'Towards Paris.'

And they both set off at the best pace of their horses.

XVIII

MONSIEUR DE BEAUFORT

THIS is what had taken place, and these are the reasons which necessitated d'Artagnan's return to Paris.

One evening when Mazarin, according to his custom, went to visit the queen after every one had retired, and on passing near the guard-room, the door of which opened on to the antechambers, heard loud talking there, he had desired to learn what was the subject of the soldiers' conversation; so he approached on tiptoe, according to his custom, pushed open the door, and put his head through the opening.

A discussion was going on among the guards.

'And I tell you,' said one of them, 'that if Coysel* has foretold that, the thing is as sure as if it had happened I don't know it, but I have heard it said that he is not only an astrologer, but a magician also.'

'Nonsense! if he is a friend of yours, take care; you do him a poor service.'

'Why so?'

'Because they could commence a prosecution against him.'

'Stuff! sorcerers are not burned nowadays.'

'No? It seems to me not so long ago since the late cardinal

caused Urbain Grandier to be burned. I know something of that; I was guard at the stake, and I saw him roasted.'

'My good fellow, Urbain Grandier was not a sorcerer, but a learned man, which is quite another thing. He did not foretell the future. He knew the past, which is sometimes much worse.'

Mazarin nodded by way of assent; but desiring to know the prediction about which the dispute was, he remained.

'I do not say,' rejoined the guard, 'that Coysel is not a sorcerer; but I say that if he made known his prediction beforehand, that is the way to prevent its accomplishment.'

'Why?'

'No doubt about it. If we were fighting one against the other, and I said to you, "I am going to give you a straight thrust, or a thrust *en seconde*," you would parry it, naturally. Well, if Coysel said loud enough for the cardinal to hear, "Before such a day, such a prisoner will escape," it is very clear that the cardinal will use such precautions that the prisoner will not escape.'

'Eh!' said another, who seemed asleep, lying on a bench, but who in spite of his apparent sleep did not lose a word of the conversation, 'bless me, do you think men can escape their destiny? If it is written above that the Duc de Beaufort must escape, he will, and all the cardinal's precautions will avail nothing.'

Mazarin started. He was an Italian—that means superstitious; he stepped forward into the midst of the guards, who on seeing him ceased their conversation.

'What were you saying, Messieurs?' said he, with his soft manner. 'That M. de Beaufort had escaped, was that it?'

'Oh, no, Monseigneur,' said the incredulous soldier. 'For the moment he is in custody. They only said that he is sure to escape.'

'Who said that?'

'Come, repeat your story, Saint-Laurent,' said the guard, turning towards the narrator.

'Monseigneur,' said the guard, 'I was simply telling these gentlemen what I have heard of the prediction of a man named Coysel, who pretends that, however well guarded M. de Beaufort is, he will escape before Whitsuntide.'

'And is this Coysel a dreamer, a fool?' rejoined the cardinal, smiling.

'No, no,' said the guard, firm in his credulity; 'he has foretold many things that have happened: as, for example, that the queen would have a son; that M. de Coligny would be killed in the duel with the Duc de Guise; then, lastly, that the Coadjutor would be made a cardinal.* Well, the queen has not only one son, but another, two years after; and M. de Coligny has been slain.'

'Yes,' said Mazarin; 'but the Coadjutor is not yet a cardinal.'

'No, Monseigneur; but he will be.'

Mazarin made a grimace which meant—he does not yet wear the cardinal's hat. Then he added, 'So then your opinion, my friend, is that M. de Beaufort will escape.'

'It is indeed so, Monseigneur,' said the soldier, 'if your Eminence were to offer me at this moment the office of M. de Chavigny,* the governorship of Vincennes, I would not accept it. After Whitsuntide it would be another matter entirely.'

There is nothing more convincing than a firm conviction; it has an influence over even the incredulous, and far from being incredulous, Mazarin was superstitious. He withdrew, therefore, very thoughtful.

'The niggard!' said the guard who was leaning against the wall, 'he makes pretence of not believing in your magician, Saint-Laurent, so as not to give you anything; but he will no sooner return to his cabinet than he will make his profit out of your prediction.'

The fact is, Mazarin, instead of going towards the queen's rooms, returned to his cabinet, and calling Bernouin, gave him the order that very early the next morning they should send and fetch the officer who had charge of M. de Beaufort, and that they should call the cardinal as soon as he arrived.

Without knowing it, the guard had touched the cardinal's sorest place. During the five years that M. de Beaufort had been in prison, not a day passed that Mazarin did not think he would make his escape. One could not keep prisoner all his life a grandson of Henry IV, especially as he was scarcely thirty.* But if he did escape, what hatred he would have against him who had taken him, rich, brave, glorious, loved by women, feared by men, from all the pleasures of life to merely exist in a prison. Meanwhile Mazarin redoubled his vigilance towards him. But he was like the miser in the fable,* who could only sleep near his hoard. Many times he started at night from his sleep, dreaming that M. de Beaufort had been carried off. Then he informed himself about him, and each time he had the pain to hear that the prisoner played, drank, sang marvellously; but that in playing, drinking, singing, he interrupted himself constantly to swear that Mazarin should pay dearly for all the pleasure he forced him to take at Vincennes.

This thought had very much preoccupied the minister during his sleep, so when at seven in the morning Bernouin entered his room to awake him, his first words were, 'Eh, what is the matter? Is M. de Beaufort escaped from Vincennes?'

'I believe not, Monseigneur,' said Bernouin, whose official calm never belied itself; 'but anyhow, you will obtain information—for the officer, La Ramée, is here awaiting your Eminence's orders.'

'Bid him come in,' said Mazarin, arranging his pillows so as to receive him while sitting up in bed.

The officer entered. He was a tall, stout man, fat-cheeked and good-looking. He had a calm look which caused Mazarin much disquietude.

'This droll fellow has to me the appearance of a fool!' murmured he.

The officer remained standing and silent at the door.

'Come near, Monsieur,' said Mazarin.

He obeyed.

'Do you know what they are saying here?' continued the cardinal.

'No, your Eminence.'

'Well, they say that M. de Beaufort is going to escape from Vincennes, if he has not already done so.'

The officer's face expressed the profoundest astonishment. He opened wide his little eyes and large mouth to take in the joke which his Eminence did the honour of making before him; then, not being able to keep a serious countenance at such a supposition, he burst out laughing, but in such a manner that his great limbs were shaken by this hilarity as by a violent fever.

Mazarin was delighted at this disrespectful unreservedness, though he still preserved a grave look.

When La Ramée had had his laugh and wiped his eyes, he thought it time to begin speaking and to excuse his inopportune gaiety.

'To escape, Monseigneur!' said he—'to escape! Surely your Eminence does not, then, know where M. de Beaufort is?'

'Yes, indeed, Monsieur; I know he is in the prison of Vincennes.'

'Yes, Monseigneur; in a cell whose walls are seven feet thick, with windows whose cross-bars are as thick as my arm.'

'Monsieur,' said Mazarin, 'with patience any wall may be cut through, and with a watch-spring a bar can be severed.'

'But Monseigneur does not know, then, that eight guards are near him—four in the antechamber, and four in the cell—and that these guards never leave him.'

'But he goes out of his cell—he plays at mall and tennis.'*

'Monseigneur, these amusements are allowed the prisoners. Yet, if your Eminence wish it, he can be deprived of them.'

'Oh, no,' said Mazarin, who feared that if he did so, and his prisoner came out of prison, he would be all the more exasperated against him. 'Only I ask with whom he plays?'

'Monseigneur, with the officer of the guard, or with me, or sometimes with the other prisoners.'

'But does he not approach the wall while playing?'

'Monseigneur, your Eminence does not know the walls. They are sixty feet high; and I doubt whether M. de Beaufort is already so tired of his life as to risk breaking his neck by leaping down.'

'Hum!' said the cardinal, who began to feel reassured. 'You say, then, my dear M. la Ramée——'

'That unless M. de Beaufort finds a way of becoming a little bird, I answer for him.'

'Take care, you are too fast,' replied Mazarin; 'M. de Beaufort said to the guards who took him to Vincennes that he had often thought of being imprisoned, and in that case he had found forty ways of escaping.'

'My Lord, if among those forty ways there had been one good one,' answered La Ramée, 'he would have been outside long before this.'

'Come, come, not so stupid as I thought him,' muttered Mazarin.

'Besides, Monseigneur forgets that M. de Chavigny is governor of Vincennes,' continued La Ramée, 'and that he is not one of M. de Beaufort's friends.'

'Yes, but M. de Chavigny is away.'

'When he is, I am there.'

'But when you yourself are absent?'

'Oh, in that case I have in my place a fellow who hopes to become his Majesty's officer, and who, I will answer to you for it, keeps good guard. I have only one reproach to make against him, that of being too severe.'

'And who is this Cerberus?' said the cardinal.

'A certain M. Grimaud.'

'And what was he doing before coming to you at Vincennes?'

'He was in the country, so the one told me who recommended him. He did something wrong, and I believe he would not be sorry to escape punishment by wearing the king's uniform.'

'And who recommended the man to you?'

'M. le Duc de Grammont's steward.'

'Then, in your opinion, he can be relied on?'

'As myself, Monseigneur.'

'He is not a chatterer?'

'Goodness, no, Monseigneur! I thought for some time he was dumb; he spoke and answered only by signs. It seems that his former master thus trained him.'

'Well, tell him, my dear M. la Ramée,' resumed the cardinal, 'that if he keeps good and faithful guard his escapades in the country shall be overlooked, he shall put on a uniform which will win him respect, and there will be some pistoles in the pockets to drink the king's health.'

Mazarin was great in promises, quite the opposite of good M. Grimaud, who spoke little and did much, as La Ramée boasted of him.

The cardinal put a crowd of questions to La Ramée about the prisoner—how he was fed, lodged, and bedded—to which

La Ramée replied so satisfactorily that Mazarin dismissed him, nearly reassured.

Then, as it was nine o'clock, the cardinal got up, perfumed himself, dressed, and went to the queen's apartments to acquaint her with the reasons which had detained him. The queen, who feared M. de Beaufort no less than did the cardinal himself, and who was nearly as superstitious as he, made him repeat word for word all La Ramée's promises and all the praises which he had given to his second. Then, when the cardinal had finished, 'Alas, Monsieur!' said she, in a low voice, 'it is a pity we have not a Grimaud close to every prince.'

'Patience!' said Mazarin, with his Italian smile, 'that will happen perhaps some day. But meanwhile——'

'Well! but meanwhile?'

'I intend to use the best precautions.' And upon that he had written to d'Artagnan to hurry his return.

XIX

HOW THE DUC DE BEAUFORT AMUSED HIMSELF IN THE
PRISON AT VINCENNES

THE prisoner who caused Monsieur the Cardinal so much fear, and whose means of escape troubled the peace of the whole court, did not in the least suspect the fright that was felt on his account at the Palais-Royal.

He found himself so securely guarded that he saw the uselessness of any attempts. His whole revenge consisted in hurling at Mazarin a number of imprecations and insults. He had tried to make some verses, but had soon given up the attempt. The fact is, M. de Beaufort had not only not received from Heaven the gift of versifying, but could only express himself in prose with the greatest difficulty. So Blot, the song-writer of the period, said of him:

> In a fight he shines, he thunders!
> With reason do they fear him;

But from the way he reasons,
One would take him for a goose.

Gaston in making a speech,
Shows less embarrassment;
Why has not Beaufort a tongue?
Why has not Gaston an arm?

This being stated, we comprehend that the prisoner should be limited to insults and imprecations.

The Duc de Beaufort was grandson of Henry IV and Gabrielle d'Estrées, as good, brave, haughty, and above all, as Gascon as his ancestor, but much less educated. After having for some time been—at the death of Louis XIII—the favourite, the confidant, in short, the first at court, he had one day been obliged to give place to Mazarin, and had found himself the second. The next day, as he had had the bad taste to get angry at this change of position and the imprudence to speak of it, the queen (be it well understood that *the queen* means Mazarin) had ordered his arrest, and he was taken to Vincennes by that same Guitaut whom we introduced at the beginning of this story, and whom we shall have occasion to bring in again. Not only were they thus freed from his person and his pretensions, but still more no one reckoned farther upon him, popular prince as he was; and for five years he had occupied a room by no means royal-looking in the prison of Vincennes.

This space of time, which would have ripened the ideas of any other than M. de Beaufort, had passed over his head without effecting any change. Other men would have reflected that if he had not affected to set the cardinal at defiance, to despise the princes, and to march alone without other followers, as the Cardinal Retz said, than some melancholy individuals who had the air of dreamers, he might have had five years ago either his liberty or obtained supporters. Probably these considerations did not even enter the duke's mind, so that his long captivity only on the contrary strengthened him more in his mutiny, and every day the cardinal received news of him which could not be more disagreeable to his Eminence.

After having failed in poetry, M. de Beaufort had tried painting. He drew the cardinal's likeness in chalk; and as his talent, very moderate in this art also, did not enable him to reach a great resemblance, he wrote below it so as to leave no doubt of its original, 'Ritratto dell' illustrissimo facchino Mazarini'.* M. de Chavigny, apprised of this, made a visit to the duke, and begged him to find some other pastime, or at the least to make portraits without inscriptions. The next day the room was full of inscriptions and portraits. M. de Beaufort, like all prisoners, resembled children very much in taking delight in things prohibited.

M. de Chavigny was informed of this increase of likenesses in profile. M. de Beaufort, not quite confident in his rendering of the full face, had made his room into a real exhibition. This time the governor said nothing; but one day when M. de Beaufort was playing at tennis, he had the drawings all sponged out and the room painted in distemper.

M. de Beaufort thanked M. de Chavigny for having had the goodness to give him back his drawing-spaces afresh; and this time he divided his room into compartments, and devoted each to some incident in the cardinal's life.

The first was intended to represent the illustrious puppy Mazarini receiving a sound thrashing from Bentivoglio, whose servant he had been.* The second, Mazarini playing the part of Ignatius Loyola in the tragedy of that name. The third represented him stealing the portfolio of the prime minister from M. de Chavigny, who thought he would have it. Then the fourth showed him refusing sheets to Laporte, Louis XIV's *valet de chambre*, and saying that it was quite often enough for a king of France to change them every three months. These were grand compositions, which certainly went beyond the talent of the prisoner; so he contented himself with tracing the frames and adding the inscriptions. But the drawings and inscriptions were quite enough to awaken M. de Chavigny's feelings, who forewarned M. de Beaufort that if he would not give up his proposed drawings, all materials for doing them should be taken away.

M. de Beaufort responded that since they deprived him of the chance of making a reputation in arms, he wished to make one in painting; and if he could not be a Bayard or a Trivulce,* he wished to become a Michael Angelo or a Raphael.

One day when he was taking exercise in the yard, they removed his fire, then his wood and the cinders, so that on returning he could not find the smallest object from which he could make a crayon pencil.

M. de Beaufort swore, stormed, and yelled, said they wished to kill him by means of damp and cold, as had died Puylaurens, the Marshal Ornano, and the Grand-Prior of Vendôme, to which M. de Chavigny replied that he had only to give his word of honour to leave off drawing, or promise not to make any historic sketches, and they would give him all that was needful for a fire. M. de Beaufort would not give his word, and so he had no fire for the rest of the winter.

Moreover, during one of the prisoner's absences they scraped out the inscriptions, and the room was left blank and bare without the least trace of fresco.

M. de Beaufort then bought from one of his keepers a dog called Pistache, no objection being made to the prisoner's having a dog. M. de Beaufort remained sometimes whole hours shut up with the dog. They had no doubt that during these hours the prisoner was occupying himself with the education of Pistache, but they were ignorant in what path he was directing it. One day, Pistache being considered enough trained, M. de Beaufort invited Chavigny and the turnkeys of Vincennes to a grand representation in his room. This was lighted up with as many candles as M. de Beaufort could procure. The exercises began.

The prisoner, with a piece of plaster off the wall, had drawn a long white line across the room to represent a cord. Pistache, at the command of his master, put himself on the line, stood up on his hind-legs, and holding a stick used for beating clothes between his fore-paws, he began to follow the line with the contortions which a rope-dancer makes. Then having passed over two or three times forward and back the length of the line he gave up the stick to M. de Beaufort and recommenced the same evolutions without balancing.

The intelligent creature was loaded with applause. They passed to the second part of the spectacle. The first thing to do was to tell the hour. M. de Chavigny showed his watch to Pistache. It was half-past six. Pistache raised and lowered his paw six times, and at the seventh he kept it up. It was impossible to be clearer; a solar quadrant could not have answered better. As everyone knows, the sun-dial has the disadvantage of telling the hour only while the sun shines.

Then, next, the question was to say before all the company who was the best jailer of all the prisons in France. The dog made three turns round, and then went in the most respectful manner and lay down at the feet of M. de Chavigny, who professed to find this a great bit of fun, and laughed. When he had finished laughing he bit his lips and began to frown.

At last M. de Beaufort proposed to Pistache to solve this difficult question; namely, Who was the greatest robber in the known world? Pistache this time went round the room, but did not stop at any one, and on going to the door he began to scratch and cry.

'You see, Messieurs,' said the prince, 'this interesting animal, not finding here what I ask, goes to look for it outside. But rest easy, you shall not be deprived of his answer for all that. Pistache, my friend, come here.'

The dog obeyed. 'Is the greatest thief in the world the king's secretary, M. le Camus,* who came to Paris with twenty livres, and now possesses ten millions?'

The dog moved its head, as meaning No.

'Is it then,' continued the prince, 'M. le Surintendant d'Emery, who gave his son on his marriage three hundred thousand francs of income and a mansion to which the Tuileries and the Louvre are but hovels?'

The dog gave the sign for No.

'It is not, then, he,' rejoined the prince. 'Let us see; let us seek carefully. Might it, perchance, be l'illustrissimo facchino Mazarini di Piscina, eh?'

The dog made the sign of Yes by raising and lowering the head eight or ten times in succession.

'Messieurs, you see it,' said M. de Beaufort to the assistants, who this time did not dare even to smile—'l'illustrissimo facchino Mazarini di Piscina is the greatest robber in the known world; Pistache says so. Let us pass to another exercise.

'Messieurs,' continued the duke, taking the opportunity of the deep silence to produce the third part of the programme, 'you remember that M. le Duc de Guise had taught all the dogs of Paris to jump for Mademoiselle de Pons, whom he had proclaimed the belle of belles; well, that is nothing—for these animals obeyed mechanically, not knowing how to make any dissidence [he meant difference]* between those for whom they should jump, and those for whom they should not. Pistache will show you that he is far above his fellow-dogs. M. de Chavigny, please lend me your stick.' He did so. Beaufort placed it horizontally at the height of a foot.

'Pistache, my friend, do me the pleasure to jump for Madame de Montbazon.'

They all began to laugh; they knew that when Beaufort was arrested he was the declared lover of Madame de Montbazon.

Pistache made no difficulty, but leaped readily over the stick.

'But,' said M. de Chavigny, 'it seems to me that Pistache does exactly what his fellows did when they jumped for Mademoiselle de Pons.'

'Wait,' said the prince. 'Pistache, jump for the queen;' and he raised the stick six inches.

The dog leaped respectfully over the stick.

'Pistache, my friend,' continued the duke, raising the cane six inches, 'jump for the king.'

The dog took his spring, and despite its height, leaped lightly over it.

'And now, attention!' said the duke, lowering the stick almost level with the ground. 'Pistache, my friend, jump for l'illustrissimo facchino Mazarini di Piscina.'

The dog turned his back to the stick.

'Eh! what is that?' said he, while describing a half-circle from the animal's tail to his head, and presenting again the stick. 'Jump, now, M. Pistache.'

But the dog, as at the first time, made a half-turn and presented his back to the stick.

M. de Beaufort made the same evolution and repeated the same words; but this time the dog's patience was at an end. He angrily seized the stick, snatched it from the prince's hands, and broke it between his teeth.

Beaufort took the two pieces from the dog's mouth, and with great seriousness returned them to M. de Chavigny, making him many excuses, and saying that the entertainment was over, but that if he wished in three months to assist at another session, Pistache would have learned some new tricks.

Three days after, Pistache was found poisoned. They sought for the culprit, but, as may be supposed, he remained unknown. M. de Beaufort had a tomb erected to his memory, with this epitaph: 'Here lies Pistache, one of the most intelligent dogs that ever lived.'

There was nothing to be said against this eulogium. But then the duke said aloud that the drug had been tried on the dog which they meant to use for him; and one day after dinner, he went to bed crying that he had the colic, and that it was Mazarin who had caused him to be poisoned.

This new trick came to the cardinal's ears, and made him full of fear. The prison of Vincennes was considered very unhealthy. Madame de Rambouillet had said that the cell in which Puy-laurens, Marshal Ornano, and the Grand-Prior of Vendôme died was worth its weight of arsenic,* and the saying grew celebrated. He ordered, therefore, that the prisoner should eat nothing unless it had been tasted. It was then that the officer La Ramée was placed with him, with the title of taster.

However, M. de Chavigny had not pardoned the duke's impertinences, which the innocent Pistache had already expiated. Chavigny was a creature of the late cardinal; it was said he was his son. He ought to have known a little of tyranny. He began to seek quarrels with the duke. He took from him the steel knives and silver forks which he had used up to this time, and gave him silver knives and wooden forks. Beaufort complained. M. de Chavigny replied that, having just learned that the cardinal had told Madame de Vendôme that her son was in prison at Vincennes for life, he feared that at this terrible news his prisoner might make an attempt at suicide. A fortnight afterwards, M. de Beaufort found two rows of trees as large as the little finger set out on the road which led to the tennis-court. He asked what they were, and they answered him that they were to give him shade some day. Finally, one morning the gardener came to him, and under the pretext of pleasing him, told him that they were going to plant some asparagus. Now, as everyone knows, asparagus,* which now takes four years to come to maturity, took five then, when gardening had not reached such perfection. This civility put Beaufort in a fury.

Then he thought it was time to resort to one of his forty means, and he tried first of all the simplest—that of corrupting La Ramée; but as he had bought his post of officer for fifteen hundred crowns, he kept to his duty. So instead of entering into the prisoner's views, he at once warned M. de Chavigny, who immediately put eight men into the very room of the prince, doubled the sentinels, and tripled the posts. From this moment, the prince walked like the kings of the theatre, with four men before him and four behind, without reckoning those who followed in the rear.

M. de Beaufort laughed a good deal at this severity at first. He repeated as often as possible, 'It is very amusing; it diversifies me [he meant, 'it diverts me'; but he did not always say what he meant, as is well known].' Then he used to add, 'Besides, when I may wish to escape from the honours which you do me I still have thirty-nine other means.' But this distraction became at last wearisome. Through blustering, M. de Beaufort held good for six months; but at the end of that time, seeing always eight men sitting down when he sat, rising when he arose, stopping when he stopped, he began to frown and to count the days.

These new severities brought out a recrudescence of hate against Mazarin. The prince used to swear from morning till evening, speaking of nothing but a mince of Mazarin's ears; it was to make him tremble. The cardinal, who knew all that took place at Vincennes, pulled his *beretta* on right over his ears.

One day M. de Beaufort assembled his guardians, and despite his difficulty of elocution, become proverbial, he made to them this speech, which it is true was prepared in advance:

'Messieurs—Will you permit, then, a grandson of the good King Henry IV. to be loaded with outrages and *ignobilies* [he meant to say *ignominies*]? *Ventre-saint-gris!* as my grandfather used to say. I have almost reigned in Paris—do you know it? I have had in guard the whole of a day the king and Monsieur. The queen flattered me then, and called me the most honest man in the kingdom. Messieurs citizens, now put me outside.

I will go to the Louvre; I will twist Mazarin's neck. You shall be my body-guard. I will make all of you officers with good pensions. *Ventre-saint-gris!* forward, march!'

But pathetic as it was, the eloquence of the grandson of Henry IV had not touched these stony hearts. Not one moved. Seeing which, M. de Beaufort told them that they were all blackguards, and made of them cruel enemies.

Sometimes when M. de Chavigny came to see him, which he did not fail to do two or three times a week, the duke used the occasion to threaten him.

'What would you do, Monsieur,' he said to him, 'if one fine day you saw an army of Parisians appear, all covered with armour, and bristling with muskets, coming to set me free?'

'Monseigneur,' replied M. de Chavigny, making a low bow, 'I have on the ramparts twenty pieces of artillery, and in my casemates thirty thousand shots to fire. I would cannonade them to the best of my power.'

'Yes, but when you had fired off your thirty thousand shots they would take the prison; and that done, I should be compelled to let them hang you, for which I should be sorry, certainly.' And in his turn the prince bowed to M. de Chavigny with great politeness.

'But, Monseigneur,' resumed M. de Chavigny, 'when the first man should pass the doorstep of the postern gate, or put his foot on my ramparts, I should be compelled, to my very great regret, to kill you with my own hands, since you were placed under my special care, and I am responsible for you, dead or alive.' And he bowed again to his Highness.

'Yes,' continued the duke; 'but as most certainly those brave fellows would not come here until after having hanged M. Giulio Mazarini, you would be careful about laying your hand upon me, and would let me live, for fear of being tied to four horses* by the Parisians—a far more disagreeable thing even than being hanged—come, now.'

These pleasantries sour-sweet were continued perhaps for ten minutes or a quarter of an hour or more, but they always ended thus:

M. de Chavigny, turning towards the door, cried, 'Holloa, La Ramée!'

La Ramée entered.

'La Ramée,' continued Chavigny, 'I recommend to your particular care M. de Beaufort; treat him with all the respect due to his name and rank, and to this end don't let him be out of sight for a moment.' Then he retired, saluting M. de Beaufort with an ironical politeness which rendered the duke blue with passion.

La Ramée had then become the compulsory boarder of the prince, his continual guardian, the shadow of his body; but it must be said that the company of La Ramée, a jolly companion, a free liver, a confirmed toper, a good tennis-player, devilish good fellow at the bottom, and having only one fault in M. de Beaufort's eyes—that of being incorruptible—had become rather a distraction than a fatigue to the prince.

Unfortunately, it was not always the same as regards La Ramée; and although he felt a certain honour in being shut up with a prisoner of such great importance, the pleasure of living in the society of Henry IV's grandson did not compensate for that which he used to get from time to time in visiting his family. One can be an excellent officer of the king and at the same time a good father and a good husband. Now M. la Ramée adored his wife and children, whom he could just catch a glimpse of from the top of the wall, when for his consolation they used to take a walk on the other side of the moats; decidedly that was too little for him, and La Ramée felt that his joyous humour, which he had considered as the cause of his good health, without calculating that, on the contrary, it was probably only the result, would not last a long time with such a life. This conviction only became stronger in his mind, when little by little the relations between M. de Beaufort and the governor became more and more strained, and they ceased entirely to see each other. La Ramée felt the responsibility weigh more heavily upon himself, and as justly, for the reasons which we have explained, he sought some relief. He accepted very warmly the offer which the steward of Marshal de Grammont had made him, to give him a helper; he had at once spoken of it to M. de Chavigny, who had replied that he made no objection if the person pleased him.

We regard it as quite useless to give our readers a description either of Grimaud's body or mind. They must remember this admirable personage with sufficient clearness, to whom no other change had happened except that of being twenty years older—a gain which made him only more taciturn, although, since the change which had come upon him, Athos had given him full permission to speak.

But at this period twelve or fifteen years had already elapsed since Grimaud had kept silent, and a habit so long continued became a second nature.

XX

GRIMAUD ON DUTY

GRIMAUD therefore came to the Vincennes prison with these favourable accessories. The governor piqued himself on possessing an infallible eye, which would make one believe that he was truly the son of the Cardinal Richelieu, who also had had this constant pretension; he therefore attentively scrutinized the candidate, and conjectured that his contracted eyebrows, his thin lips, his hooked nose, his projecting cheekbones, were unfailing marks of character. He spoke only a dozen words to him; Grimaud replied in four.

'Here is an accomplished fellow, that is my judgement of him,' said M. de Chavigny. 'Go and make yourself acceptable to M. la Ramée, then you will satisfy me.'

Grimaud turned on his heels and went away to undergo the more rigorous inspection of La Ramée. What made it more difficult was that M. de Chavigny knew he could trust La Ramée, who, in his turn, wanted to be able to trust Grimaud.

Grimaud had the very qualities which could charm an officer who needs a subordinate; so, after a thousand questions which obtained only very curt replies, La Ramée, fascinated by this sobriety of words, rubbed his hands, and enrolled Grimaud.

'The orders?' asked Grimaud.

'Here they are: Never allow the prisoner to be by himself; take away every pointed or cutting instrument; prevent him from making any sign to people outside, or from talking too long with his guards.'

'Is that all?' asked Grimaud.

'All for the present,' replied La Ramée. 'Fresh circumstances, should any occur, will bring fresh orders.'

'Good,' said Grimaud, and he entered the room of the Duc de Beaufort.

The latter was in the act of combing his beard, which he was allowing to grow as well as his hair, to serve as a trick on Mazarin, by showing his wretchedness and making a parade of his sad looks. But as some days ago he thought he recognized from the top of the prison the beautiful Madame de Montbazon inside a carriage, the remembrance of whom was always dear, and he did not wish to appear to her as he did to Mazarin, he had therefore, in the hope of seeing her again, asked for a leaden comb, which had been granted him. He had asked for a leaden one because, like all fair people, his beard was somewhat red; he dyed it by combing it.

Grimaud, on entrance, saw the comb, which the prince had just put down on the table; he took it up very respectfully. The duke looked at this strange figure with astonishment. The figure put the comb into his pocket.

'Holloa! hi! what are you about?' cried the duke. 'And who is this old fool?'

Grimaud said nothing, but made a second salute.

'Are you dumb?' cried the duke.

Grimaud made a sign meaning No.

'Who are you, then? Answer, I command you,' said the duke.

'Keeper,' replied Grimaud.

'Keeper!' cried the duke; 'well, this gallows-bird is a fine addition to my collection. Holloa, La Ramée! someone!'

La Ramée came running in; unfortunately for the prince, he was going, trusting in Grimaud, to Paris. He was already in the courtyard, and returned very cross.

'What is it, Prince?' he asked.

'Who is this knave who has pocketed my comb?' asked the duke.

'He is one of your guards, Monseigneur, a well-deserving fellow, and whom you will appreciate as much as M. de Chavigny and I do, I am quite sure.'

'Why, then, does he take my comb?'

'Tell me,' said La Ramée, 'why you took Monseigneur's comb.'

Grimaud took the comb from his pocket, and passing his finger along it, pointed out the large teeth, simply saying the one word, 'Pointed.'

'That is true,' said La Ramée.

'What does the animal say?' asked the duke.

'That every pointed instrument is forbidden you by the king.'

'Oh! ah!' said the duke. 'Are you a fool, La Ramée? Why, it was you yourself who gave it to me.'

'And I did very wrong, Monseigneur—for by giving it to you I have been disobedient to my orders.'

The duke looked furiously at Grimaud, who had returned the comb to La Ramée.

'I see that this rogue will displease me enormously,' muttered the prince.

In fact, there is no intermediate feeling in a prison. Since both men and things are either friends or enemies, one loves or hates sometimes with reason, but much more often by instinct. Now, for this very simple reason that Grimaud had at first sight pleased M. de Chavigny and La Ramée, he must—his good qualities in the eyes of the governor and of the officer becoming defects in the eyes of the prisoner—at once displease M. de Beaufort.

Yet Grimaud did not wish on the very first day to insult the prisoner directly to his face; he required, not a sudden repugnance, but a thoroughly tenacious hatred. He withdrew, therefore, to give place to the four guards, who coming from dinner could resume their service near the prince.

On his part, the prince had to finish a new trick on which he relied a good deal. He had asked for some lobsters for his next day's dinner, and counted on passing the day in making a little gallows in the middle of his room, to hang the finest of them. The red colour which the cooking gave it could leave no doubt as to its meaning; and so he would have the pleasure of hanging the cardinal in effigy, in the hope that he might be hanged in reality; without anyone being able to reproach him for hanging anything but a lobster.

The day was employed in making preparations for the execution. Prisoners grow very childish; and M. de Beaufort was of a character to become so more than anyone else. He took his exercise as usual, broke off two or three small branches intended to play a part in the rehearsal, and having searched, found a bit of broken glass—a find which seemed to give him the greatest pleasure. On coming in, he unravelled his handkerchief. None of these details escaped the keen eye of Grimaud.

Next morning the gallows was ready, and that he might be able to set it up in the middle of the room, Beaufort tapered off one of the ends with his broken glass.

La Ramée looked at him as he was making it, with all the curiosity of a father who thinks that he is finding out a new toy for his children, and the four guards with that air of idleness which formed then, as now, the principal trait in the soldier's physiognomy.

Grimaud entered when the prince had just laid down his piece of glass, although he had not finished sharpening the foot of the gallows. But he had interrupted himself to attach the thread to its opposite extremity. He cast a look at Grimaud which showed some of last evening's bad humour; but as he was already much pleased at the result which his new invention could not fail to have, he paid no further attention. Only when he had finished making a sailor's knot at one end of his cord, and a slip-knot at the other, when he had cast a look on the dish of lobsters, and had selected the finest of them, he turned round to look for his bit of glass. It had disappeared.

'Who has taken my bit of glass?' asked the prince, frowning.

Grimaud made a sign that he had.

'Why? You again? Why have you taken it?'

'Yes,' asked La Ramée, 'why have you taken his Highness's bit of glass?'

Grimaud, who held the piece of glass in his hand, touched the edge with his finger, and said, 'Cutting.'

'That is true, Monseigneur,' said La Ramée. 'Hang it, what an acquisition this fellow is!'

'M. Grimaud,' said the prince, 'in your own interest I conjure you to keep out of the reach of my hand.'

Grimaud bowed, and retired to the end of the room.

'*Chut, chut*, Monseigneur,' said La Ramée; 'give me your little gallows, and I will sharpen it with my knife.'

'You?' said the duke, laughing.

'Yes, I will; don't you want it done?'

'Certainly. Well, in truth,' said the duke, 'that will be more droll. Take it, my dear La Ramée.'

La Ramée, who had not understood the prince's exclamation, sharpened the end of the gallows very properly.

'There,' said the duke; 'now make me a little hole in the ground while I fetch the culprit.'

La Ramée went down on his knee, and made a hole.

Meanwhile, the prince suspended his lobster to the thread. Then he set up the gallows in the middle of the room, bursting out into laughter.

La Ramée also laughed heartily, without knowing exactly at what he was laughing, and the guards acted as chorus.

Grimaud only did not laugh. He approached La Ramée, and pointing to the lobster which was spinning round at the end of the cord, 'Cardinal,' said he.

'Hanged by his Highness the Duc de Beaufort,' rejoined the prince, laughing louder than ever, 'and by M. James Chrysostom la Ramée, the king's officer.'

La Ramée uttered a cry of terror, and rushed towards the gallows, which he tore up into bits, and threw the pieces out of the window. He was going to do the same to the lobster, he had so lost his temper, when Grimaud took it from his hands.

'Good to eat,' said he, and put it into his pocket.

This time the duke had taken such pleasure in the scene that he almost pardoned the part that Grimaud had played in it. But as in the course of the day he thought on the motive his guardian showed, and that this was really bad, he felt his hatred against him sensibly increase.

But the story of the lobster had not less, to the great despair of La Ramée, caused an immense sensation within the prison, and even outside. M. de Chavigny, who at the bottom of his heart strongly detested the cardinal, took care to tell the story to two or three well-meaning friends, who soon spread it about.

That caused M. de Beaufort to pass two or three pleasant days.

In the meantime the duke had noticed among his guards a man of a very good figure, and he coaxed him all the more because Grimaud displeased him at every moment. Now, one morning he had taken this man aside, and he was speaking to him for a little time tête-à-tête. Grimaud came in, saw what was passing, and approaching the guard and the prince in a respectful manner, took the guard by the arm.

'What do you mean?' asked the duke, roughly.

Grimaud led the guard four paces, and showed him the door.

'Go,' said he.

The guard obeyed.

'Oh,' cried the prince, 'you are unbearable. I will chastise you.'

Grimaud made a respectful salute.

'Monsieur spy, I will break your bones!' cried out the exasperated prince.

Grimaud, with a bow, drew back.

'Monsieur spy,' continued the duke, 'I will strangle you with my own hands.'

Grimaud bowed again, still drawing back.

'And that not later than this very instant;' and he stretched his nervously twitching hands towards Grimaud, who was satisfied with pushing the guard before him and closing the door behind.

At the same moment he felt the prince's two hands drop on his shoulders like two iron nails; he was satisfied, instead of calling or defending himself, with lifting his forefinger gently to his lips, and pronouncing in a low voice, at the same time smiling, the word, '*Chut!*'

A gesture, a smile, and a word, together, was a thing so rare on Grimaud's part that his Highness stopped short in a complete state of stupefaction.

Grimaud used this moment to draw out from his doublet a charming little letter with aristocratic seal, the first perfume of which had not been quite lost from being so long in Grimaud's clothes; and he gave it to the duke without a word.

The duke, astonished more and more, released Grimaud, took the billet, and recognizing the handwriting, 'From Madame de Montbazon!' he exclaimed.

Grimaud signified Yes by a nod.

The duke rapidly tore off the envelope, passed his hands over his eyes, so much was he dazzled, and read what follows:

My DEAR DUKE—You can rely thoroughly on the good fellow who will transmit you this note, for he is the servant of a gentleman who is on our side and who has proved his fidelity by twenty years of service. He has consented to enter the service of your officer, and to shut himself up with you at Vincennes to prepare for and aid your flight, about which we are engaged.

The moment of your deliverance draws near. Have patience and courage in believing that in spite of your long absence all your friends have retained the sentiments which they avowed for you.

Your wholly and for ever affectionate
MARIE DE MONTBAZON

P.S. I sign my name at full length, for I should be too vain to think that after five years of absence you would recognize my initials.

The duke remained for a moment stunned. What he had been seeking for five years without being able to find it—that is to say, a servant, a help, a friend—fell all of a sudden from heaven just when he expected it the least. He looked at Grimaud with astonishment, and returned to his letter, which he read again from end to end.

'Oh, dear Marie!' he murmured, on finishing. 'It was indeed she whom I saw at the back of her carriage! How, she still thinks of me after five years of separation! *Morbleu!* There's a constancy that one only sees in Astraea!'* Then turning to Grimaud, 'And you, my brave fellow,' added he, 'you agree then to help us?'

Grimaud signified Yes.

'And you have come here for that purpose?'

Grimaud repeated the same sign.

'And I wanted to strangle you!' cried the duke.

Grimaud smiled.

'But wait,' said the duke, and he fumbled in his pocket. 'Wait,' continued he; 'they shall not say that such devotion for a grandson of Henry IV shall remain unrewarded.'

The duke's movement showed the best intention in the world. But one of the precautions they took at Vincennes was not to allow any money to the prisoners.

Upon which Grimaud, seeing the duke's disappointment, took from his pocket a purse full of gold and gave it to him.

'That's what you are looking for,' said he.

The duke opened the purse, and wanted to empty it into Grimaud's hands, but the latter shook his head.

'Thanks, Monseigneur,' added he, withdrawing; 'I am paid.'

The duke was surprised afresh. He stretched out his hand, which Grimaud kissed respectfully. The fine manners of Athos had left their mark upon Grimaud.

'And now,' asked the duke, 'what are we going to do?'

'It is eleven in the morning,' resumed Grimaud. 'At two let Monseigneur ask to make up a tennis party with La Ramée, and knock two or three balls over the ramparts.'

'Well; and after?'

'After—Monseigneur is to go near the walls and call out to a man who works in the moat to throw them back.'

'I understand,' said the duke.

Grimaud's face seemed to express a lively satisfaction; the little use which he had made of the habit of speaking made conversation difficult for him. He made a movement to retire.

'So,' said the duke, 'you will not then accept anything?'

'I should like Monseigneur to make me one promise.'

'What is it? Speak!'

'That when we have escaped, I shall pass first, always and everywhere; for if you are caught, Monseigneur, the greatest risk you run is to be returned to prison, while if I am caught, the least I can expect is to be hanged.'

'That is too true,' said the duke, 'and, on the word of a gentleman, it shall be done as you ask.'

'Now,' said Grimaud, 'I have one thing more to ask; it is that you continue to do me the honour of detesting me as hitherto.'

'I will try,' said the duke.

There was a knock at the door.

The duke put his letter and purse into his pocket, and threw himself on his bed. This was known as his resource in moments of weariness. Grimaud went to open the door; there stood La Ramée, who had returned from the cardinal's, where the scene passed which we have related.

La Ramée threw a scrutinizing glance about him, and seeing as before the same marks of antipathy between prisoner and guardian, he smiled from inward satisfaction. Then turning to Grimaud, 'Well, my friend,' said he to him—'well. You have just been spoken of in a good place, and you will, I hope, soon have news by no means disagreeable to you.'

Grimaud bowed in a way which he tried to make gracious, and withdrew, as his custom was when his superior came in.

'Well, Monseigneur!' said La Ramée, with his coarse laugh, 'are you still sulky with that poor fellow?'

'Ah, it is you, La Ramée,' said the duke; 'it was indeed time for you to come. I have thrown myself on the bed, and turned my face away to prevent me from keeping my promise of strangling that rascal Grimaud.'

'I doubt, however,' said La Ramée, making a witty allusion to the dumbness of his subordinate, 'whether he has said anything disagreeable to your Highness.'

'I well believe it! An Eastern mute! I swear, La Ramée, that I was in haste to see you again.'

'Monseigneur is too good,' said La Ramée, flattered by the compliment.

'Yes,' continued the duke; 'in fact, I feel more than usually unskilful today, which it will please you to see.'

'We will make up a tennis party, then,' said La Ramée, mechanically.

'If you wish to do so.'

'I am at your command.'

'That is to say, my dear La Ramée,' said the duke, 'that you are a charming fellow, and I should like to stay at Vincennes for ever, to pass my life with you.'

'Monsieur,' said La Ramée, 'I think it will not depend on the cardinal if your desire is not carried out.'

'How so? Have you seen him recently?'

'He sent for me this morning.'

'Truly! To speak to you about me?'

'Of what do you suppose he would speak to me. In truth, Monseigneur, you are his nightmare.'

The duke smiled bitterly.

'Ah,' said he, 'if you would accept my offers, La Ramée!'

'Now, Monseigneur, you are going to talk again about that, but you must see that you are not reasonable.'

'La Ramée, I have already told you, and I repeat it again, that you would make your fortune.'

'With what? You will no sooner be out of prison than your property will be confiscated.'

'I shall no sooner be out of prison than I shall be master of Paris.'

'*Chut*, now! Well—but am I to listen to things like this? A fine conversation to be having with a king's officer! I see well enough, Monseigneur, that we must get a second Grimaud.'

'Well, then, let us say no more about it. So, then, the cardinal has been talking to you about me? La Ramée, you ought some day, when he sends for you, to let me wear your clothes; I would go, I would strangle him, and, on my word of honour, if it was made a condition, I would return again to my prison.'

'Monseigneur, I see well that I must call Grimaud.'

'I was wrong; and what did the *cuistre* say to you?'

'I excuse the word, Monseigneur,' said La Ramée with a cunning air, 'because it rhymes with *ministre*. What did he tell me? To look sharply after you.'

'And why so?' asked the duke, distressed.

'Because an astrologer has predicted that you would escape.'

'Ah, an astrologer has predicted that?' said the duke, trembling in spite of himself.

'Oh, good gracious, yes! they only imagine things, on my word of honour, just to torment quiet folks, those wretches of magicians.'

'And what have you replied to his most illustrious Eminence?'

'That if the astrologer in question made almanacs, I should not advise him to purchase one.'

'Why?'

'Because, for you to escape, you must become a chaffinch or a wren.'

'And you are too nearly right, unfortunately. Let us play a game of tennis, La Ramée.'

'Monseigneur, I beg pardon of your Highness, but I must ask you to give me half an hour.'

'Why so?'

'Because M. Mazarin is more haughty than you are, although of not quite such high birth, and he has forgotten to invite me to breakfast.'

'Eh, do you wish me to let you breakfast here?'

'Oh, no, Monseigneur. I must tell you that the pastry-cook who used to live in front of the prison, whom they called Father Marteau,* sold his business to one from Paris to whom the doctors have recommended country air.'

'Well, what has that to do with me?'

'Stop a moment, Monseigneur. So that this confounded pastry-cook has in his shop a lot of things which make one's mouth water.'

'Gourmand!'

'Oh, no, Monseigneur,' continued La Ramée, 'one is not a gourmand because one is nice in one's eating. It is man's nature to seek perfection in pastry as in other things. Now, this beggar of a pastry-cook, when he saw me stop before his stall, came to me and said, "M. la Ramée, I need to have the custom of the prisoners. I have purchased my predecessor's business because he assured me that he supplied the prison. Yet, upon honour, during the week I have been here M. de Chavigny has not allowed a single tartlet to be bought."

' "But," I said to him, "probably M. de Chavigny fears that your pastry is not good."

' "My pastry not good! Come, I wish you to be judge of it, and that this very instant."

' "I cannot," I answered him; "I must really return to the prison."

' "Well, since you seem in a hurry, come back in half an hour. Have you breakfasted?"

' "No, indeed."

' "Well, here is a pie awaiting you, with a bottle of old Burgundy." And you understand, Monseigneur, as I am fasting,

I should like, with your Highness's permission—' and La Ramée bowed.

'Go, then, animal,' said the duke; 'but mind, I give you only half an hour.'

'Can I promise your custom to Father Marteau's successor, Monseigneur?'

'Yes, provided he does not put mushrooms into his pies. You know,' added the prince, 'that the mushrooms of Vincennes forest are fatal to my family.'

La Ramée left without understanding the allusion, and five minutes after the officer of the guard came in really to carry out the cardinal's orders not to let the prisoner go out of sight.

But during those five minutes the duke had had time to read again Madame de Montbazon's note, which showed him that his friends had not forgotten him and were engaged in helping his escape. In what manner? He as yet did not know, but he resolved to make Grimaud speak, notwithstanding his dumbness, which indeed only gave the duke the greater confidence in him, explaining as it did his conduct, and showing clearly why he had invented all the little persecutions which he had employed towards the duke, which was simply to remove from his guardians all idea of a secret understanding between them. This trick gave the duke a high opinion of Grimaud's understanding, in whom he resolved to put entire trust.

XXI

WHAT THE PIES MADE BY FATHER MARTEAU'S SUCCESSOR CONTAINED

HALF an hour after, La Ramée came back light and gay, like a man who has eaten as well as drunk well. He had found the pastry excellent, and the wine delicious.

The weather was fine, and permitted the projected game. Tennis as played at Vincennes was in the open air; nothing was therefore more easy for the duke than to do as Grimaud had recommended—to send some balls into the moat.

Yet, until two o'clock struck, the duke was not too awk-ward—for two was the hour named. Up to that hour he lost the matches made, which permitted him to become angry, and to do what one does in that case—make mistake after mistake.

So when two struck, the balls began to fly in the direction of the moat, to the great delight of La Ramée, who marked fifteen at each outside stroke which the prince made. They increased so quickly that soon they fell short of balls. La Ramée suggested sending some one to pick them up in the moat. But the duke very judiciously observed that it was so much time lost, and approaching the rampart, which at that place was at the least fifty feet high, he saw a man who was working in one of the thousand little gardens which the peasants cultivated on the opposite side of the moat.

'Hi, friend!' cried the duke.

The man raised his head, and the duke was almost on the point of uttering a cry of surprise. This man, this peasant, this gardener, was Rochefort, whom the prince thought in the Bastille.

'Well, what is the matter up there?' asked the man.

'Be so kind as to throw back our balls,' said the duke.

The gardener nodded, and began to throw the balls, which La Ramée and the guards picked up. One of them fell at the duke's feet, and as it was clearly intended for him, he put it into his pocket. Then, having signified his thanks to the gardener, he returned to the game.

But clearly it was the duke's off day. The balls continued to fly off, and two or three went into the moat; but as the gardener was no longer there to throw them back, and they were lost, the duke said he did not wish to continue play. La Ramée was delighted with having so completely beaten a prince of the blood.

The prince came in and went to bed; he did this nearly the whole day since they had taken away his books. La Ramée took the prince's clothes, under the pretence that they were dusty, and that he was to have them brushed, but really to make sure that the prince should not stir. La Ramée was a man of precautions. Happily the prince had had time to hide the ball under his bolster.

As soon as the door was closed, the duke tore off the covering of the ball with his teeth, for he was allowed no cutting instrument; he ate with knives of pliant silver blades, which could not cut. Under the envelope was a letter, which contained these lines:

MONSEIGNEUR—Your friends are watching, and the hour of your deliverance is drawing near. Ask, the day after tomorrow, to eat a pie made by the new pastry-cook who has bought the good-will of the shop, and who is no other than Noirmont,* your steward. Only open the pie when you are alone. I hope you will be pleased with what is in it.

The ever devoted servant of your Highness, in the Bastille and elsewhere,

COMTE DE ROCHEFORT

P.S.—Your Highness can rely on Grimaud in everything. He is a very intelligent fellow, who is thoroughly devoted to us.

The Duc de Beaufort, to whom they had granted a fire since he had given up painting, burned the letter as he had, with many regrets, Madame de Montbazon's; and he was going to do the same with the ball, when he thought it might be useful in sending a reply to Rochefort.

He was well guarded, for at the movement he made La Ramée entered.

'Has Monseigneur need of anything?' said he.

'I was cold,' replied the duke, 'and I stirred the fire to make it throw out more heat. You know, my dear fellow, that the rooms in Vincennes prison are famous for their coolness. They could preserve ice in them, and gather saltpetre. Those in which Puylaurens, Marshal Ornano, and my uncle the Grand-Prior died are worth in this respect, as Madame de Rambouillet said, their weight in arsenic;' and the duke lay down again, hiding the ball under the bolster.

La Ramée smiled slightly. He was a fine fellow, who had taken a great liking for his prisoner, and would have been sorry for any misfortune to happen to him. Now, the successive misfortunes which happened to the three personages the duke named were incontestable.

'Monseigneur,' he said to him, 'you should not give yourself up to such thoughts. Thoughts like these kill, and not saltpetre.'

'Eh!' said the duke, 'you are delightful. If I could, like you, go and eat pastry and drink Burgundy at the shop of the successor of Father Marteau, that would divert me.'

'The fact is, Monseigneur,' said La Ramée, 'that that new pastry-cook's pies and wine are famous.'

'In any case,' replied the duke, 'his cellar and kitchen have no difficulty in excelling those of M. de Chavigny.'

'Well, Monseigneur,' said La Ramée, falling into the trap, 'who prevents you from tasting? I have promised your custom.'

'You are right,' said the duke; 'and if I must stay here for life, as M. de Mazarin has had the goodness to give me to understand, I must create an amusement for my old age. I must become a gourmand.'

'Monseigneur,' said La Ramée, 'take a piece of good advice: don't wait till you are old for that.'

'Good!' said the Duc de Beaufort aside; 'every man ought to have, in order to lose his body and his soul, received from the celestial munificence one of the seven capital sins, when he has not received two. It appears that the one of M. la Ramée is gluttony. So be it, we will profit by it.' Then aloud, 'Ah, well, my dear La Ramée,' he added, 'is the day after tomorrow a festival?'

'Yes, Monseigneur, it is Whitsunday.'*

'Will you give me a lesson on that day?'

'In what?'

'Gormandizing.'

'Willingly, Monseigneur.'

'But a lesson together. We will let the guards dine at M. de Chavigny's canteen, and we will have a supper here, of which I leave the arrangement to you.'

'H'm!' said La Ramée.

The offer was tempting, but La Ramée was an old stager who knew all the traps which a prisoner can set. M. de Beaufort had, he said, prepared forty ways of escape. Did not this meal hide some trick? He reflected a moment, but the result was that he thought he would order the eatables and wine, and that consequently no powder could be mixed in the former and no liquid in the latter. As to making him tipsy, the duke could not have such a wish; and he began to laugh at the thought. Then an idea came which settled everything.

The duke had followed this inward monologue of La Ramée with a somewhat unquiet eye, so far as his countenance betrayed him; but at last the officer's face brightened.

'Well,' asked the duke, 'is it settled?'

'Yes, Monseigneur, on one condition.'

'What?'

'That Grimaud waits at table.'

Nothing could serve the prince's purpose better. However, he was able to put on a very plain touch of ill-humour.

'To the devil with your Grimaud!' cried he. 'He will spoil the feast.'

'I will order him to keep behind your Highness, and as he does not whisper a word, your Highness will neither see nor hear him, and with a little good-will can imagine that he is a hundred leagues away.'

'My dear fellow,' said the duke, 'do you know what I see clearer than ever in that? You distrust me.'

'Monseigneur, the day after tomorrow is Whitsuntide.'

'Well, what has that to do with me? Are you afraid that the Holy Ghost will descend under the form of a tongue of fire to open for me the doors of my prison?'

'Why, that confounded magician has foretold that Whitsuntide will not pass by without your Highness escaping from Vincennes.'

'You believe, then, in magicians, you old fool?'

'I?' said La Ramée. 'I don't care a snap for it;' and he snapped his fingers. 'But it is M. Giulio who does; being an Italian, he is superstitious.'

The duke shrugged his shoulders.

'Well, let it be so,' said he, with an acquiescence well assumed. 'I accept Grimaud, for without that the matter will not be settled at all; but I don't want any one else. You will order the supper as you like. The only dish which I ask is one of those pies of which you have spoken. You will command it for me that the pastry-cook may surpass himself. You will promise Father Marteau's successor my custom, not only as long as I remain in prison, but even for the time when I shall be out of it.'

'You keep believing that you will get out!' said La Ramée.

'Yes, indeed,' replied the prince, 'should it not be till Mazarin's death. I am fifteen years younger than he. It is true,' added he, smiling, 'that in here one lives faster, or one dies sooner, which comes to the same thing.'

'Monseigneur,' said La Ramée, 'I am going to order the supper.'

'And you believe you will be able to make something out of your pupil?'

'Well, I hope so, Monseigneur.'

'If enough time is allowed,' muttered the duke.

'What did Monseigneur say?' asked La Ramée.

'Monseigneur said that you should not spare the cardinal's purse, who has desired to take the burden of our board and lodging.'

La Ramée stopped at the door.

'Whom would Monseigneur like me to send to him?'

'Whom you please, except Grimaud.'

'The officer of the guard, then?'

'With his chess?'

'Yes.'

And La Ramée went out.

Five minutes after, the officer entered, and the Duc de Beaufort seemed deeply immersed in the sublime combinations of chess.

What a singular thing is thought, and what revolutions a sign, a word, a hope, effect in it! The duke had already been five years in prison, and a look back on them made them seem, slowly as they had passed, not so long as the two days which still separated him from the time fixed for his escape.

Then there was one thing especially which harassed his mind—in what way this escape could be effected. He had been led to hope for this result, but the details which the mysterious pie was to contain had been kept from him. What friends expected him? He had then still some friends after five years of imprisonment! In this respect he was a highly privileged prince.

He forgot that besides his friends a woman retained recollections of him; it is true that she had not perhaps been scrupulously faithful, but she had not forgotten him, and that was enough.

There was more than enough to preoccupy the duke's mind; so he was checkmated as he had been beaten at tennis. M. de Beaufort made blunder after blunder, and the officer beat him in the evening as he had been beaten in the morning by La Ramée.

But his defeats had gained him an advantage—they brought the prince nearer to eight in the evening; then night would come, and with it sleep.

The duke thought so at least; but sleep is a very capricious goddess, and it is precisely when she is invoked that she delays coming. The duke waited for her till midnight, turning over on his mattress as Saint Lawrence did on his gridiron.* At last he went to sleep.

But with the day he awoke. He had had some strange dreams: he thought he had wings; he had then quite naturally wished to fly, and at first his wings had kept him up, but on reaching a certain height, this new support had failed suddenly, his wings broke, and he seemed to roll in bottomless abysses; he woke up covered with perspiration, and bruised as if he had really made an aërial fall.

Then he went to sleep to wander in a labyrinth of dreams, each one more foolish than the last. Hardly were his eyes closed than his mind, directed to a single end—his escape—began to try this evasion. Then it was another thing; they had found a subterranean passage which would conduct him out of Vincennes. He had entered this passage, and Grimaud marched before him with a lantern in his hand; but little by little the passage grew narrower, and nevertheless the duke continued always his way. At last it grew so narrow that the fugitive tried in vain to go farther. The sides of the wall drew nearer and pressed him between them; he made unheard-of efforts to advance, but the thing was impossible. And nevertheless he saw in the distance Grimaud with his lantern, who continued to go on. He wished to call him that he might aid him to draw himself from this defile which was suffocating him; but it was impossible to pronounce a word. Then at the other extremity— at that from which he had come—he heard the steps of those who pursued him; these steps drew nearer constantly; he was discovered; he had no longer hope of flight. The wall seemed to be in league with his enemies, and to press upon him the more as he had more need to fly. At last he heard the voice of La Ramée; he perceived him. La Ramée extended his hand, and put it upon his shoulder, bursting into laughter; he was recaptured and conducted into that low and vaulted room, where had died the Marshal Ornano, Puylaurens, and his uncle. Their three tombs were there rising from the ground, and a fourth grave was open awaiting only one dead body.

So when he awoke, the duke made as many efforts to keep awake as he had made to go to sleep; and when La Ramée came in, he found him so pale and worn out that he asked if he were ill.

'In fact,' said one of the guards who had slept in the room, and who had not been able to sleep from a toothache which the damp air had given him, 'Monseigneur has had a very disturbed night, and two or three times in his dreams has called for help.'

'What is the matter, Monseigneur?' asked La Ramée.

'Why, it is you, you fool,' said the duke, 'who, with all the silly trash about escape, turned my brain yesterday, made me dream that I was escaping, and that in doing so I broke my neck.'

La Ramée burst into laughter.

'You see, Monseigneur,' said he, 'it is a warning from heaven; so I hope Monseigneur will never commit such folly except in his dreams.'

'And you are right, my dear La Ramée,' said the duke, wiping off the perspiration which was still running down his face; 'although wide awake, I do not wish to dream of anything else but eating and drinking.'

'*Chut!*' said La Ramée, and he sent away the guards, one after another, under some pretext or other.

'Well?' asked the duke, when they were alone.

'Well,' said La Ramée, 'your supper is ordered.'

'Ah!' said the prince; 'and what is it made up of? Tell us, Monsieur Majordomo.'

'Monseigneur has promised to leave it to me.'

'And will there be a pie?'

'I believe so, like a tower.'

'Made by Father Marteau's successor? And you told him it was for me?'

'Yes, and he said he would do his best to please your Highness.'

'That's right!' said the duke, rubbing his hands.

'Hang it, Monseigneur,' said La Ramée, 'how you nibble at gormandizing! I have never, during five years, seen you looking so pleased as now.'

The duke saw that he had by no means kept the proper mastery of himself, but at this moment, as if he had been listening at the door, and had seen that some diversion to La Ramée's ideas was urgently needed, Grimaud entered, and made a sign to La Ramée that he had something to tell him.

La Ramée approached Grimaud, who spoke to him in a low tone.

The duke recovered himself during this time.

'I have already forbidden this man,' said he, 'to come here without my permission.'

'Monseigneur,' said La Ramée, 'you will pardon him, for it was I who sent for him.'

'And why have you, since you know it displeases me?'

'Monseigneur remembers what has been agreed upon,' said La Ramée, 'and that he must wait on us at this grand supper.'

'But I had forgotten M. Grimaud.'

'Monseigneur knows that there will be no supper without him.'

'Go on then; act your own pleasure.'

'Come near, my good fellow,' said La Ramée, 'and listen to what I am going to say.'

Grimaud approached with a scowling look.

La Ramée continued, 'Monseigneur does me the honour to invite me to supper with him tomorrow.'

Grimaud made a sign which meant that he did not see how that concerned him.

'Indeed, indeed,' said La Ramée, 'it does concern you, for you will have the honour of waiting, without reckoning also that if there shall be anything left in the dishes and bottles, it shall be for you.'

Grimaud thanked him with a bow.

'And now, Monseigneur,' said La Ramée, 'I must ask pardon of your Highness, but it seems that M. de Chavigny will be absent for a few days, and before he goes he wishes to leave me some orders.'

The duke tried to exchange looks with Grimaud, but his eye was unchanged.

'Be off,' said the duke to La Ramée, 'and come back as soon as possible.'

'Does Monseigneur then want to take his revenge for yesterday's tennis?'

Grimaud made an almost imperceptible nod of his head.

'Yes,' said the duke; 'but take care, my dear La Ramée—the days pass and are not alike, so that today I have made up my mind to beat you soundly.'

La Ramée went out. Grimaud followed him with his eyes without the least movement of his body; then, when he saw the door closed, he took quickly out of his pocket a pencil and a square piece of paper.

'Write, Monseigneur,' said he to the duke.

'And what must I write?'

Grimaud made a sign with his finger and dictated, 'All is ready for tomorrow evening; be on the lookout from seven to nine; have two horses saddled quite ready. We shall descend by the first window of the gallery.'

'What then?' said the duke.

'What then, Monseigneur!' repeated Grimaud, astonished. 'Then sign.'

'And is that all?'

'What do you want more, Monseigneur?' replied Grimaud, who was for the utmost brevity.

The duke signed.

'Now,' said Grimaud, 'has Monseigneur lost the ball?'

'What ball?'

'The one that held the letter.'

'No, I thought it might be useful to us. Here it is,' and the duke took the ball from under his pillow and gave it to Grimaud.

Grimaud smiled as pleasantly as it was possible for him.

'Well, Monseigneur,' said Grimaud, 'I will sew up the paper in the ball, and you when playing at tennis will send it into the moat.'

'But perhaps it will be lost?'

'All right, Monseigneur; there will be someone there to pick it up.'

'A gardener?' said the duke.

Grimaud signified Yes.

'The same as yesterday?'

Grimaud repeated his sign.

'The Comte de Rochefort, then. But come,' said the duke, 'at least give me some details as to the way in which we are to escape.'

'That is forbidden me,' said Grimaud, 'before the actual time of carrying it out.'

'Who are they who are waiting for me on the other side of the moat?'

'I know nothing about it, Monseigneur.'

'But at least tell me what this famous pie will contain, if you do not wish that I should become insane.'

'Monseigneur,' said Grimaud, 'it will contain two poniards, a knotted cord, and a choke-pear.'[1]

'Well, I understand.'

'Monseigneur sees that there will be enough for every one.'

'We shall use the poniards and the cord,' said the duke.

'And we shall make La Ramée eat the pear,' replied Grimaud.

'My dear Grimaud,' said the duke, 'you do not often speak, but when you do—it is only just to say so—your words are gold.'

---

[1] The *poire d'angoisse* was an improved gag; it was in the shape of a pear, was stuffed into the mouth, and by means of a spring expanded in such a way as to stretch the jaws to their utmost extent.

XXII

AN ADVENTURE OF MARIE MICHON

ABOUT the same time when these projects of escape were in train between the Duc de Beaufort and Grimaud, two men on horseback, followed at a few paces off by a servant, entered Paris by the Rue du Faubourg St Marcel.* These two men were the Comte de la Fère and the Vicomte de Bragelonne.

It was the first time that the young man had come to Paris, and Athos had not shown great partiality for his old friend (the capital) by showing it to the youth from that side. Truly the last village of Touraine was more pleasing to the sight than Paris seen from the part which lies towards Blois. One must say, therefore, to the shame of this too much praised city, that it produced a poor effect on the young man.

Athos preserved his usual indifferent and serene look.

On reaching St Médard, Athos, who served as guide to his travelling companion in this labyrinth, took the Rue des Postes, then L'Estrapade, then Des Fossés St Michel, then Vaugirard. On reaching the Rue Férou the travellers turned down it. When halfway down, Athos raised his eyes, and with a smile pointed out a private house to the young man.

'Stop, Raoul,' said he. 'That is a house where I passed seven of the sweetest and most painful years of my life.'*

The young man smiled in his turn, and saluted the house. Raoul's profound respect for his guardian showed itself in all his actions.

As for Athos, as we have said, Raoul was not only for him the centre, but except for his old memories of his regiment, the sole object of his affections, and one understands in what a tender and deep way the heart of Athos could love in this case.

The two travellers stopped in the Rue du Vieux-Colombier,* at the sign of the Green Fox. Athos had known the inn for a long time, and had visited it with his friends a hundred times; but during twenty years there had been many changes in it, beginning with its landlords.

The travellers handed over their horses to the groom, and as they were high-bred horses, they desired the greatest care to be shown them,—that they should be given only straw and oats, and that their breasts and legs should be bathed with lukewarm wine. They had done twenty leagues that day. Then, having first looked after their horses, as all good cavaliers should do, Athos and Raoul next asked for two rooms.

'You must go and dress, Raoul,' said Athos; 'I want to introduce you to someone.'

'Today, Monsieur?' asked the young man.

'In half an hour.'

Perhaps, being more easily tired than Athos, who seemed made of iron, Raoul would have preferred a bath in that river, the Seine, of which he had heard so much talk, but which seemed inferior to the Loire, and then his bed; but the Comte de la Fère had spoken, and he had but to obey.

'By the by, Raoul,' said Athos, 'I want you to look your best.'

'I hope, Monsieur,' said he, smiling, 'that it is not a question of marriage. You know my engagement with Louise.'

Athos now smiled.

'No, don't be frightened,' said he, 'although it is a lady to whom I am going to present you.'

'A lady?' asked Raoul.

'Yes; and I hope, too, that you will like her.'

The young man looked at the count with some uneasiness; but at a smile from Athos he was quickly reassured.

'And how old is she?' asked the Vicomte de Bragelonne.

'My dear Raoul, learn once for all,' said Athos, 'that is a question which is never asked. When you can read her age upon the face of a woman, it is useless to ask it; when you can no longer do so, it is indiscreet.'

'Is she beautiful?'

'Sixteen years ago she was considered not only the most beautiful, but also the most gracious lady in France.'

This reply completely reassured the viscount, for Athos could have no design respecting himself and a lady who was the most beautiful in France a year before he was born.

He withdrew to his room, and with that coquetry which goes so well with youth, he applied himself to follow the instructions of Athos to make himself look as well as possible. Now this was an easy thing to do with what nature had done for him. When he came back, Athos received him with that fatherly smile with which he had received d'Artagnan, but which bore the impress of a deeper tenderness for Raoul.

Athos cast a look at his feet, hands, and hair—those three indications of good birth. His black hair was carefully parted as it was worn at that period, and fell into ringlets surrounding his face; greyish buckskin gloves, which harmonized with his hat, set off a fine, elegant hand; while his boots, of the same colour as hat and gloves, covered a foot which seemed that of a child of ten.

'Well,' muttered he, 'if she is not proud of him, she is hard to please.'

It was three in the afternoon—the suitable hour for making visits. The travellers went by the Rue de Grenelle, took the Rue des Rosiers, entered into the Rue St Dominique, and stopped before a magnificent mansion facing the Jacobins, over which were the arms of the Luynes.*

'This is it,' said Athos.

He entered with that firm and assured step which showed the Swiss* that he had the right of so doing. He ascended the steps, and speaking to a footman dressed in a fine livery, asked if Madame la Duchesse de Chevreuse* was at home, and if she would receive M. le Comte de la Fère.

A moment after, the footman returned, with the message that although the duchess did not know the Comte de la Fère, would he kindly come in?

Athos followed the footman through a long file of apartments, but at last they stopped before a closed door. They had arrived at a drawing-room. Athos made a sign to the viscount to stay where he was. The footman opened the door and announced M. le Comte de la Fère.

Madame de Chevreuse, of whom we so often spoke in our history of 'The Three Musketeers', without having had occasion to bring her on the stage, passed still for a very beautiful woman. In fact, though at this time she was already forty-four or five, she seemed scarcely more than thirty-eight or nine. She still retained her beautiful fair hair, her large, quick, intelligent eyes, which intrigue had so often opened and love so often shut, her nymph-like figure, which made her, looking at her from behind, seem to be still the young girl who leaped with Anne of Austria the moat of the Tuileries—a feat which deprived the crown of France in 1683* of an heir. In other respects she continued the same giddy creature who has set upon her amours such a seal of originality that they have almost become an illustration for her family.

She was in a little boudoir, the window of which opened upon the garden. It was hung—after the fashion which Madame de Rambouillet had introduced when building her house—with a sort of blue damask covered with red flowers and foliage of gold. It showed much coquetry in a woman of Madame de Chevreuse's age to be in such a boudoir, and especially as she was at that moment reclining on a long chair, her head resting against the tapestry. She had an open book in her hand, and had a cushion to support the arm which held the book. At the announcement of Athos by the footman she raised herself a little, and advanced her head, out of curiosity. Athos entered.

He was dressed in violet velvet with suitable trimmings; his aigulets were of burnished silver, his cloak had no gold embroidery, and a simple violet feather enveloped his black hat. He had on boots of black leather, and at his leather girdle hung that sword with a magnificent hilt which Porthos had so often admired, but which Athos had never consented to lend him. Some splendid lace formed the turned-down collar of his shirt; some lace hung also over the tops of his boots.

Under a name utterly unknown to Madame de Chevreuse, there was such an air of a gentleman of high position that she half rose, and graciously made a sign for him to take a seat near her. Athos bowed and obeyed. The footman was going to withdraw, when Athos indicated a wish for him to stay.

'Madame,' said he to the duchess, 'I have had the boldness to present myself to you without being known to you; I have been so far successful, since you have condescended to receive me. I now wish to ask half an hour's conversation.'

'I grant it you, Monsieur,' replied the duchess, with her most gracious smile.

'But that is not all, Madame. Oh, I am very ambitious, I know. I ask a tête-à-tête conversation, which I strongly desire may not be interrupted.'

'I am at home to no one,' said the duchess to the footman. 'You may go.'

The footman went out.

There was a short silence, during which these two personages, recognizing high birth at first sight, examined each other without embarrassment on either side. The duchess was the first to break silence.

'Well, Monsieur,' said she, smiling, 'do you not see that I am waiting with impatience?'

'And I, Madame,' replied Athos, 'I am looking with admiration.'

'Monsieur,' said Madame de Chevreuse, 'you must excuse me, for I am anxious to know whom I am addressing. You are a courtier, it is clear, and yet I have never seen you at court. Perhaps you are just from the Bastille?'

'No, Madame,' replied Athos, smiling; 'I am perhaps on the way which leads thither.'

'Ah! in that case, tell me quickly who you are, and depart,' replied the duchess, in that sportive tone which had such a charm in her; 'for I am already quite enough compromised in that direction without becoming more so.'

'Who I am? Madame, you have been told my name—Comte de la Fère. You have never known that name. Formerly I had another, which you knew perhaps, but which you have certainly forgotten.'

'Tell it to me, Monsieur.'

'Formerly,' said the count, 'I was called Athos.'

Madame de Chevreuse opened her eyes wide with astonishment. It was clear, as the count had told her, that this name was not entirely effaced from her memory, although it was mixed up with old remembrances.

'Athos?' said she; 'stop now!' and she put her two hands to her forehead, as if to force the multiplicity of ideas within to fix themselves for a moment, to let her see clearly their brilliant and variegated crowd.

'Would you like me to help you, Madame?' said Athos, with a smile.

'Well, yes,' said the duchess, already tired with her search; 'you will do me a kindness.'

'This Athos was conjoined with three young musketeers, whose names were d'Artagnan, Porthos, and——' Athos stopped.

'And Aramis,' said the duchess, quickly.

'And Aramis, that is it,' resumed Athos. 'You have not then quite forgotten this name?'

'No,' said she—'no; poor Aramis, he was a charming person—elegant, discreet, and made lovely verses. I think he has turned out ill,' added she.

'Very ill indeed; he has become an abbé.'

'Ah! what a misfortune!' said Madame de Chevreuse, playing negligently with her fan. 'Monsieur, I truly thank you.'

'For what, Madame?'

'For having recalled this souvenir—one of the most pleasing of my younger days.'

'Will you permit me then, Madame, to recall a second?'

'Which is connected with the former?'

'Yes, and no.'

'My faith,' said Madame de Chevreuse, 'speak on; with a man like you I risk everything.'

Athos bowed.

'Aramis was intimately acquainted with a young needlewoman of Tours.'

'A young needlewoman of Tours?' said Madame de Chevreuse.

'Yes; a cousin of his, whose name was Marie Michon.'

'Ah! I know her,' exclaimed the duchess; 'it was she to whom he wrote* from the siege of Rochelle to prevent a plot which was hatched against that unfortunate Buckingham.'

'Exactly,' said Athos; 'will you allow me to speak of her?'

Madame de Chevreuse looked at Athos.

'Yes,' she said; 'provided you do not speak too much evil.'

'I should be ungrateful,' said Athos; 'and I look upon ingratitude not as a defect or crime, but as a sin, which is much worse.'

'You ungrateful towards Marie Michon, Monsieur? But how could that possibly be? You never knew her personally.'

'Ah, Madame, who knows?' replied Athos. 'There is a popular proverb that it is only the mountains that never meet one another, and popular proverbs are sometimes strangely correct.'

'Oh, go on, Monsieur,' said Madame de Chevreuse, briskly, 'you cannot form an idea how this conversation amuses me.'

'You encourage me,' said Athos, 'to pursue the story. This cousin of Aramis, this young needlewoman, in spite of her humble condition, had very well-to-do connections; she called the finest court ladies her friends, and the queen, haughty as she is in her double quality of Austrian and Spaniard, called her sister.'

'Alas!' said the duchess, with a light sigh, and a little movement of the eyebrows which belonged to her only, 'things have much changed since then.'

'And the queen was right,' continued Athos; 'for Marie was very devoted to her, even to the extent of acting as intermediary with her brother, the King of Spain.'

'A thing which,' replied the duchess, 'is imputed to her now as a great crime.'

'So much so,' continued Athos, 'that the cardinal, the real cardinal, resolved one fine morning to have poor Marie Michon arrested and taken to the Château de Loches.* Happily the matter could not be done so secretly but that it transpired. The event was foreseen; although Marie Michon was menaced with danger, the queen caused a prayer-book bound in velvet to reach her.'

'That is so, Monsieur. You are well informed.'

'One morning the green book came, brought by Prince de Marcillac.* There was no time to lose. Fortunately Marie Michon and a servant whom she had, named Kitty, wore men's clothes capitally. The prince obtained for Marie Michon a cavalier's dress, and for Kitty a groom's, put them on two excellent horses, and the two fugitives rapidly left Tours, going towards Spain, trembling at the least sound, following out-of-the-way roads because they did not dare to take the highways, and asking hospitality when they did not find any inn.'

'Why, in fact, that is it exactly!' cried Madame de Chevreuse, clapping her hands. 'It is really curious.' She stopped.

'Need I follow the two fugitives to the end of their journey? No, Madame; we will accompany them only as far as a little village of Limousin, situated between Tulle and Angoulême, called Roche-l'Abeille.'*

Madame de Chevreuse made an exclamation of surprise, and looked at Athos with an expression of astonishment which made him smile.

'Wait, Madame,' continued Athos; 'for what remains for me to tell you is still more strange than what I have said.'

'Monsieur,' she said, 'I take you for a sorcerer. I am listening to all; but in fact——Never mind; go on.'

'This time the journey had been long and fatiguing. It was cold,—the 11th of October.* The village had neither inn nor château; the peasants' houses were mean and dirty. Marie Michon was a very aristocratic person; like the queen her sister, she was used to delicate scents and fine linen. She resolved, therefore, to ask hospitality at the vicarage.' Athos made a pause.

'Oh, go on,' said the duchess. 'I have told you that I am carefully listening.'

'The travellers knocked at the door. It was late. The priest, who had gone to bed, called out to them to come in. They did so, for the door was unfastened. A lamp was burning in the priest's room. Marie Michon, who made a most charming cavalier, pushed open the door, put in her head, and begged hospitality. "Willingly, my young cavalier," said the priest, "if you can be satisfied with the remains of my supper and the half of my room." The travellers consulted a moment. The priest heard them burst out laughing; then the master, or rather the mistress, replied, "Thank you, Monsieur the Curate; I accept." "Then get your supper, and make as little noise as you can, for I have been about all day, and should not be sorry to sleep tonight." '

Madame de Chevreuse evidently passed from surprise to astonishment, and from that to stupefaction. Her face, while looking at Athos, had taken an expression impossible to picture. Evidently she would have liked to speak, and yet she was silent, for fear of losing one of her interlocutor's words.

'What then?' said she.

'What then?' said Athos. 'Ah! here is the most difficult part.'

'Tell me, tell me! You must tell me all. Besides, it does not concern me; it is the affair of Mademoiselle Marie Michon.'

'Ah, that is true!' said Athos. 'Well, then, Marie Michon took supper with her servant, and then she entered the room where her host was resting, while Kitty took up her position in an armchair in the room where they had supped.'

'In fact, Monsieur,' said the duchess, 'unless you are the Devil himself, I don't know how you can be acquainted with all these details.'

'Marie Michon was a charming creature—one of those fanciful beings through whose mind the strangest ideas pass. Now, on reflecting that her host was a priest, it came into her mind what a pleasant souvenir it would be in her old age to have damned an abbé.'

'Count,' said the duchess, 'on my word of honour you quite frighten me.'

'Alas,' replied Athos, 'the poor abbé was not a Saint Ambrose;* and I repeat it, Marie Michon was an adorable creature.'

'Tell me at once how you know all these details, or I will send for a monk from the convent of the old Augustinians* to exorcize you.'

Athos began to laugh.

'Nothing more easy, Madame. A cavalier, who was himself charged with an important mission, had, an hour before, come and asked hospitality of the curate, and that at the very moment when the latter left for the night, not only his house but the village, to see a dying person. It was then of the abbé's guest, and not of the abbé himself, that Marie Michon had asked hospitality.'

'And this cavalier, this gentleman, arrived before her?'

'It was I, the Comte de la Fère,' said Athos, rising and bowing to the Duchesse de Chevreuse.

The duchess remained for a moment quite stupefied, then suddenly bursting into laughter, 'Ah, my goodness!' said she, 'it is very comical; and this foolish act of Marie Michon has turned out better than she expected. Sit down, dear count, and resume your story.'

'Now I must accuse myself, Madame. I have already told you I was on a pressing mission. At daybreak I left the room without noise, leaving my charming companion asleep. In the first room, also asleep, in the armchair, was the maid, one in all respects worthy of her mistress. Her pretty figure struck me, and I, on coming closer, recognized that little Kitty whom our friend Aramis had placed in his cousin's service. It was thus I learned that the charming traveller was——'

'Marie Michon!' said the duchess, quickly.

'Marie Michon,' rejoined Athos. 'Then I left the house, went to the stable, found my horse saddled, and my servant ready. We set off.'

'And you have never passed by that village since?' asked Madame de Chevreuse.

'One year after, Madame.'

'Well?'

'Well, I wanted to see the curate again. I found him much concerned with an event which passed his comprehension. He had, a week before, received in a small cradle a dear little boy three months old, with a purse of gold and a note containing only these words: "Oct. 11, 1633." '

'That was the date of this strange adventure,' rejoined Madame de Chevreuse.

'Yes; but he understood nothing further than that he had passed that night with a dying person, for Marie Michon had herself left the vicarage before his return.'

'You know, Monsieur, that Marie Michon, when she returned to France in 1643, made enquiries at once about this child—for being a fugitive, she could not keep it, but on her return to Paris she wished him brought up near her.'

'And what did the abbé say to her?' asked Athos, in his turn.

'That a nobleman whom he did not know had desired to take charge of him, had made himself responsible for his future, and had taken him away with him.'

'That is the truth.'

'Ah, I understand, then. This nobleman was you—the child's father!'

'*Chut!* don't speak so loud, Madame; he is there.'

'He is there!' cried the duchess, rising quickly; 'he is there—my son, Marie Michon's son! Well, I want to see him at once.'

'Mind, Madame, that he knows neither his father nor his mother,' interposed Athos.

'You have kept the secret, and you bring him to me in this way, hoping you will make me very happy. Oh, thank you, Monsieur!' exclaimed Madame de Chevreuse, seizing his hand, which she raised to her lips, 'thanks. You have a noble heart.'

'I bring him to you,' said Athos, withdrawing his hand, 'that you may also do something for him, Madame. Up to the present I have watched over his education, and made of him, I hope, an accomplished gentleman; but the time has come when I am obliged to resume the errant and perilous life of a party man. Tomorrow I join in a perilous affair in which I may be killed; in that case there will be no one but yourself to advance him in the world in which he is called to take a place.'

'Oh, don't be concerned as to that,' said the duchess. 'Unhappily, I have little influence at this time, but what I have is his; as regards future and title——'

'About these do not be concerned, Madame; I have entailed to him the Bragelonne estate which I inherited, and this gives him the title of viscount and ten thousand livres of rent.'

'Upon my soul, Monsieur,' said the duchess, 'you are a true gentleman. But I long to see our young viscount. Where is he?'

'There in the drawing-room. I will call him if you wish it.' Athos made a movement towards the door. Madame de Chevreuse stopped him.

'Is he handsome?' asked she.

Athos smiled.

'He resembles his mother,' said he.

At the same time he opened the door, and motioned to the young man, who appeared at the doorway.

Madame de Chevreuse could not refrain from a joyful exclamation on seeing so fine a cavalier, who surpassed all the hopes that her pride had entertained.

'Viscount, come near,' said Athos. 'Madame the Duchess allows you to kiss her hand.'

The young man drew near with his charming smile, and with uncovered head knelt down and kissed her hand.

'Monsieur the Count,' said he, turning towards Athos, 'have you not tenderly treated my bashfulness in telling me that Madame is the Duchesse de Chevreuse, and not rather the queen?'

'No, Viscount,' said the duchess, taking his hand, and making him sit by her side, while she looked at him with eyes sparkling with pleasure—'no, unhappily I am not the queen, or I would this very moment do for you what you deserve; but never mind, such as I am,' added she, scarcely restraining herself from kissing him, 'let us see, what career do you desire to follow?'

Athos, standing, looked at both with an expression of unspeakable happiness.

'Well, Madame, it seems to me there is but one career open to a gentleman—that of arms. The count has educated me, I believe, with that intention, and he gave me to expect that he would present me here to some one who might introduce me to Monsieur the Prince.'

'Yes, I understand; it is quite right for a young soldier like you to serve under such a general; but stop—I am personally not friendly with him, because of my mother-in-law Madame de Montbazon's disputes with Madame de Longueville. But by the Prince de Marcillac—eh! stop now! Count, that's it! He is an old friend of mine. He will recommend our young friend to Madame de Longueville, who will give him a letter of introduction to her brother, the prince.'

'Ah, well! that suits capitally,' said the count; 'only I should venture to recommend to you the greatest despatch. I have reasons for desiring that he should not be with us in Paris tomorrow evening.'

'Do you wish it known that you are interested in him, Monsieur the Count?'

'It would perhaps be better for his future that it should not be known that he ever knew me.'

'Oh, Monsieur!' exclaimed the young man.

'You know, Bragelonne,' said the count, 'that I do nothing without some reason.'

'Yes, Monsieur,' replied the young man, 'I know that you have the highest wisdom, and I will obey you as I always have done.'

'Well, Count, leave it to me,' said the duchess; 'I will send for the Prince de Marcillac, who is fortunately in Paris just now, and I will not leave him till the matter is settled.'

'Very good; a thousand thanks. I have several matters to attend to this evening, and on my return, about six, I shall expect the viscount at the hotel.'

'What are you doing this evening?'

'We are going to the Abbé Scarron's, for whom I have a letter, and where I expect to meet one of my friends.'

'Very well,' said the duchess; 'I shall be going there myself presently. Don't leave that drawing-room until you have seen me.'

Athos bowed and prepared to go.

'Well, Monsieur the Count,' said the duchess, laughing, 'do old friends leave one another so ceremoniously?'

'Ah!' murmured Athos, kissing her hand, 'if I had known sooner that Marie Michon was such a charming creature!' and he withdrew with a sigh.

XXIII

THE ABBÉ SCARRON

THERE were in the Rue des Tournelles* some rooms which all sedan-bearers and men-servants of Paris knew, and yet they did not belong to a great lord or rich financier. No eating, no playing, and certainly no dancing took place there. Yet it was the rendezvous of the fashionable world, and all Paris visited there. It was the home of little Scarron.

Plenty of laughter was there at this clever abbé's; plenty of news was retailed there; this was so quickly criticized, dissected, and transformed, either into stories or epigrams, that everyone desired to pass an hour with the little Scarron to hear what he said, and to report it elsewhere. Many burned to insert their word also; and if it was funny they were welcome.

The little Abbé Scarron, who, by the by, was one because he enjoyed an abbacy, had been formerly one of the most coquettish prebendaries of his city, Le Mans. Now, one day of the carnival he had wished to amuse beyond measure this city of which he was the soul. He made his valet rub him over with honey; then, having opened a feather bed, he rolled himself in it, so that he became the most grotesque bird possible. He then began paying visits to his friends in this strange costume. First he was followed with astonishment, then with crics; he was then insulted by the street porters; the children threw stones at him; at last he had to take flight to escape the projectiles. As soon as he began to run, everybody pursued him; pressed on, hunted on all sides, Scarron had no other means of escaping than by throwing himself into the river. He could swim like a fish, but the water was frozen. Scarron was in a perspiration; the cold seized him, and on reaching the other bank he was paralysed.

All known means were tried to give him back the use of his limbs; he had suffered so much from medical treatment that he packed off the doctors, declaring that he much preferred his disease. Then he came to Paris, where his reputation of being a very clever man was established. There he invented a chair for his own use; and when one day in this chair he made a visit to the queen, Anne of Austria, she, charmed with his wit, asked him if he desired any title.

'Yes, your Majesty, there is one for which I have a great ambition,' Scarron answered.

'What is that?' asked the queen.

'That of being your patient.'

And Scarron had been entitled 'The Queen's Patient,' with a pension of fifteen hundred francs.

From this time, having no longer any solicitude respecting the future, Scarron had led a joyous life, living on his pension.

One day, however, an emissary from the cardinal had given him to understand that he did wrong to receive Monsieur the Coadjutor.

'And why so?' asked Scarron; 'is he not a man of good birth?'

'Most certainly.'

'Amiable?'

'Incontestably.'

'Clever?'

'He has unfortunately too much cleverness.'

'Well, then,' replied Scarron, 'why do you wish me no longer to see such a man?'

'Because he thinks ill——'

'Really! and of whom?'

'Of the cardinal.'

'What!' said Scarron, 'I continue seeing M. Gilles Despréaux, who thinks ill of me, and do you suppose that I must not see Monsieur the Coadjutor because he thinks ill of another? Impossible!'

The conversation ended there, and Scarron, through the spirit of contrariety, had seen M. de Gondy oftener than ever.

Now, on the morning of the day to which we have come, and which was the day of receiving his pension for three months, Scarron, according to custom, had sent his servant with a receipt to draw the amount at the Pay-Office of Pensions; but the answer was, 'the State has no more money for M. l'Abbé Scarron.'

When the servant brought this reply to Scarron, M. le Duc de Longueville was with him, who offered to give him double the pension which Mazarin had stopped; but the sharp fellow was not disposed to accept it. He took such measures that at four in the afternoon the whole city knew of the cardinal's refusal. It was Thursday, too, the abbé's reception day; visitors came in crowds, and Mazarin was censured in a strong fashion by the whole city.

Athos met in the Rue St Honoré two gentlemen whom he did not know, on horseback like himself, followed by a servant, as he was, and going the same way. One of them, taking off his hat, said to him:

'Do you really believe, Monsieur, that this wretch of a Mazarin has stopped poor Scarron's pension?'

'It is absurd,' said Athos in his turn, saluting the two cavaliers.

'It is clear that you are an upright man,' said the one who had spoken to Athos, 'and this Mazarin is a real plague.'

'Alas, Monsieur,' replied Athos, 'take care to whom you say so;' and they separated with much politeness.

'This happens capitally for our going there this evening,' said Athos to the viscount. 'We shall make our compliments to this poor fellow.'

'But who is M. Scarron, who puts all Paris into a flutter? Is he some disgraced minister?' asked Raoul.

'Oh, no, Viscount,' replied Athos; 'he is simply a little gentleman of great talents who has fallen into disgrace with the cardinal for having made some verses about him.'

'Do gentlemen make verses?'* asked Raoul, naïvely. 'I thought it was beneath them.'

'Yes,' replied Athos, laughing, 'when they make bad ones; but when they are good, that increases their fame. See M. de Rotrou. Yet I think that it is better not to make them.'

'And then this M. Scarron is a poet?'

'Yes, you know this beforehand, Viscount. Mind how you behave at his house; speak only by looks, or rather listen. You will see me talking a good deal with one of my friends, the Abbé d'Herblay, of whom you have often heard me speak.'

'I remember, Monsieur.'

'Approach us sometimes as though to speak to us, but do not speak or listen either. This will serve to prevent intruders from disturbing us.'

'Very well, Monsieur, I will obey you in every respect.'

Athos made two visits in Paris. Then at seven they went towards the Rue des Tournelles. It was blocked by porters, horses, and servants on foot. Athos made a passage through, and entered. The first person whom he saw on entering was Aramis. Installed in a large wheeled armchair with a canopy of tapestry over it was a slight figure, young-looking, of smiling countenance, but sometimes growing pale, without the eyes ceasing however to express a lively, clever, or graceful sentiment. This was the Abbé Scarron, always laughing, joking, complimenting, suffering, and rubbing himself with a little stick.

Around this kind of movable tent was a crowd of ladies and gentlemen. The room was very suitably and conveniently furnished. Fine curtains of brocaded silk, whose colours had once been brilliant but were at this time somewhat faded, fell from the large windows. The tapestry was simple, but of good taste. Two very polite and attentive footmen did the waiting with special ease.

On perceiving Athos, Aramis came to him, took him by the hand, and presented him to Scarron, who showed equal pleasure and respect for the new guest, and made a clever compliment to the viscount. Raoul felt quite abashed, for he had not been prepared for such imposing cleverness. Still, he bowed with much grace. Athos next received the compliments of several noblemen to whom Aramis presented him. Then the slight commotion of his entrance died away, and the conversation became general.

At the end of a few minutes, which Raoul employed in obtaining a topographical knowledge of the assembly, the door opened and a servant announced Mademoiselle Paulet.*

Athos touched the viscount's shoulder.

'Look at that lady, Raoul,' said he, 'for she is an historic personage. It was to her house that Henry IV was going when he was assassinated.'

Raoul started. For several days past some curtain had been continually raised, making known to him some historic incident. This lady, still young and beautiful, had known and spoken to Henry IV.

Everyone pressed towards the newcomer, for she was always quite in the fashion. She had a slim and graceful figure, with a profusion of golden hair such as Raphael loved, and Titian has given to all his Magdalenes. This fawn-coloured hair, or perhaps also the supremacy she had acquired over other women, had obtained for her the name of the Lioness.

Our beautiful women of today who aspire to this fashionable title should know that it comes to them, not from England, as they think perhaps, but from their beautiful and witty compatriot, Mademoiselle Paulet.

Mademoiselle Paulet went direct to Scarron in the midst of the murmurs which arose from all sides on her arrival.

'So, my dear abbé,' said she, in a quiet tone, 'I see you a poor man. We have learned that this afternoon at Madame de Rambouillet's. It was M. de Grasse who told us.'

'Yes; but the State is rich now,' said Scarron. 'We must learn to make sacrifices for our country.'

'Monsieur the Cardinal is going to buy for himself fifteen hundred livres' worth more of pomade and perfume every year,' said a Frondeur, whom Athos recognized as the gentleman whom he met in the Rue St Honoré.

'But what will the Muse say,' replied Aramis, in honeyed tones—'the Muse, who needs a golden mediocrity? For, in short:

> Si Virgilie puer aut tolerabile desit
> Hospitium, caderent omnes a crinibus hydri.*

'Good!' said Scarron, giving his hand to Mademoiselle Paulet; 'but if I have my hydra no longer, my Lioness remains.'

All Scarron's expressions seemed in exquisite taste. That is the privilege of persecution.

Mademoiselle Paulet went and took her usual place; but before sitting down she directed with all her dignity a queenly look upon the whole assembly, and her eyes rested on Raoul.

Athos smiled.

'You have been observed by Mademoiselle Paulet, Viscount; go and greet her. Declare yourself to be only a frank provincial, but do not think of speaking to her about Henry IV.'

The viscount, blushing, approached the Lioness, and soon made one of the group of gentlemen surrounding her chair.

Two separate groups were already formed,—that surrounding M. Ménage, and the other about Mademoiselle Paulet. Scarron went from the one to the other, manœuvring his wheeled chair in the midst of all with as much skill as an experienced pilot would use with a ship in the midst of a sea studded with rocks.

'When shall we talk?' said Athos to Aramis.

'Presently,' replied the latter. 'There is not enough company yet, and we should be remarked.'

At this moment the door opened, and the servant announced Monsieur the Coadjutor. At this name everyone turned round, for it was a name which was already beginning to be very famous.

Athos did as the rest. He knew the Abbé de Gondy* only by name. He saw a little dark man entering, badly made, short-sighted, awkward with his hands at everything except at drawing sword and pistol, who first of all knocked against a table which he nearly upset, but having withal something haughty and imperious in his face.

Scarron also turned round and came before him in his chair. Mademoiselle Paulet greeted him by a wave of the hand.

'Eh, well!' said the Coadjutor, when he saw Scarron, which was only when he was almost upon him, 'I see you then in disgrace, abbé?'

That was the essential expression. It had been used a hundred times in the evening, and Scarron was at his hundredth witticism on the same subject; so he was nearly falling short, but a desperate effort saved him.

'M. le Cardinal Mazarin has been good enough to think of me,' said he.

'Wonderful!' exclaimed Ménage.

'But how are you going to continue to receive us?' continued the Coadjutor. 'If your revenues decline, I shall be obliged to nominate you to a canonry in Notre-Dame.'

'Oh, no,' said Scarron, 'I should compromise you too much.'

'Then you have resources of which we know nothing?'

'I shall borrow from the queen.'

'But her Majesty has nothing of her own,' said Aramis. 'Does she not live under the regime of the community?'*

The Coadjutor turned round, and smiled on Aramis, making him a sign of amity.

'Pardon, my dear abbé,' he said to him, 'you are behind time, and I must make you a present.'

'Of what?' said Aramis.

'Of a hatband.'

All turned towards the Coadjutor, who took out of his pocket a silk band of a singular shape.

'Ah,' said Scarron, 'that is a sling.'

'Precisely!' said the Coadjutor. 'Everything is made sling-fashion. Mademoiselle Paulet, I have a fan for you in the same style. I will tell you the name of my glover, d'Herblay; he makes gloves similarly. And for you, Scarron, my baker, with unlimited credit; he makes loaves *à la Fronde* which are excellent.'

Aramis took the band, and fastened it round his hat. At that moment the door opened, and the servant announced in a loud voice:

'Madame la Duchesse de Chevreuse!'

At that name everybody got up. Scarron directed his arm-chair towards the door. Raoul blushed. Athos made a sign to Aramis, who went and hid himself in the recess of a window.

In the midst of the respectful greetings which met her at her entrance, the duchess was visibly looking for someone or something. At last she noticed Raoul, and her eyes became sparkling. She saw Athos, and became thoughtful; she caught sight of Aramis in the window, and made a slight movement of surprise behind her fan.

'By the by,' said she, as if to drive away the ideas which filled her mind in spite of herself, 'how is poor Voiture? Do you know, Scarron?'

'What, is M. de Voiture ill?' asked the nobleman who had spoken to Athos in the Rue St Honoré; 'and what is the matter with him, then?'

'He has been playing without taking care to let his servant take a change of shirts,' said the Coadjutor; 'so that he has caught a cold, and is near his death.'

'Where is he?'

'Oh, at my house. Imagine then that poor Voiture had made a solemn vow to play no more. At the end of three days he could no longer keep it, and came to the archbishop's palace that I might relieve him of his vow. Unfortunately, at this moment I was engaged in very serious matters with the good counsellor, Broussel, at the farther end of my apartment, when Voiture perceived the Marquis de Luynes seated at a table waiting for a player. The marquis calls him, invites him to join him; Voiture replies that he cannot play, as I had not released him from his vow. Luynes engages in my name, and takes the sin to his account. Voiture sits down, loses four hundred crowns, takes cold in going out, and goes to bed not to get up again.'

'Is he then so bad as all that?' asked Aramis, half-hidden behind the window-curtain.

'Alas!' replied M. Ménage, 'he is very bad; and perhaps this great man is soon about to leave us, *deseret orbem*.'*

'Nonsense!' said Mademoiselle Paulet, with bitterness. 'He going to die! he has no nurse! He is surrounded by sultanas like a Turkish sultan. Madame de Saintot is with him, and gives him broth, La Renaudot* warms his sheets, and every one is doing something, even up to our friend la Marquise de Rambouillet, who sends him light drinks.'

'You do not love him, my dear Parthénie,' said Scarron, laughing.

'Oh, what an injustice, my dear Patient! I hate him so little that I would with pleasure have some Masses said for the repose of his soul.'

'You are not named the Lioness for nothing, my dear,' said Madame de Chevreuse; 'and you bite sharply.'

'You are unkind to a great poet, it seems to me, Madame,' Raoul ventured to say.

'He a great poet? Come, it is quite clear, Viscount, that you are fresh from the country, as you told me just now, and that you have never seen him. He a great poet? Why, he is scarcely five feet high.'*

'Bravo!' said a tall, spare, dark man, with a long moustache and an enormous rapier. 'Bravo, fair Paulet! it is quite time to send this little Voiture to his own place. I assert boldly that I am a connoisseur of poetry, and that I have always found his very hateful.'

'Who is that captain, Monsieur,' asked Raoul of Athos.

'M. de Scudéry.'*

'The author of "Clelia" and of "Cyrus the Great"?'

'Which he wrote in conjunction with his sister, who is at this moment talking with a charming person over there near M. Scarron.'

Raoul turned round and saw two persons who had just come in—the one delicate, sad, with beautiful dark hair, with velvety eyes like beautiful heart's-ease violets, under which glitters a gold calyx; the other lady, seeming to hold the former under her guardianship, was cold-looking, spare, and sallow—a thorough duenna or devotee.

Raoul determined not to leave without having spoken to the beautiful young lady with the velvety eyes, who, by a strange freak of fancy, although there was not the least resemblance, reminded him of his poor little Louise, whom he had left suffering at the Château de la Vallière, and whom in the midst of all these people he had forgotten for an instant.

During this time Aramis had approached the Coadjutor, who with a smiling look had whispered some words into his ear. Aramis, in spite of his mastery over himself, could not help making a slight movement.

'Laugh now,' said M. de Retz to him; 'they are looking at us;' and he went away to talk to Madame de Chevreuse, who was surrounded by a large circle.

Aramis assumed a laugh to mislead the curiosity of any listeners, and seeing that Athos was now gone into the window-recess, where he had been some time, he went to him in a straightforward manner, after having spoken a few words to those whom he passed. As soon as they met they commenced a very animated conversation. Raoul then drew near them, as Athos had previously requested him.

'It is a *rondeau* by M. de Voiture which Monsieur the Abbé is reciting to me,' said Athos, in a high voice, 'and I find it most excellent.'

Raoul remained near them for a few moments; he then went and joined the group around Madame de Chevreuse, to which also Mademoiselle Paulet and Mademoiselle de Scudéry drew near from different directions.

'Well,' said the Coadjutor, 'I am not altogether of the opinion of M. de Scudéry; on the contrary, I consider that M. de Voiture is a poet, and a genuine one also. He is completely wanting in political ideas.'

'So then?' asked Athos.

'Tomorrow,' said Aramis, hastily.

'At what hour?'

'At six.'

'Where to be?'

'At St Mandé.'*

'Who told you so?'

'Comte de Rochefort.'

Someone drew near.

'So philosophical ideas are utterly wanting in poor Voiture. I place myself on the side of Monsieur the Coadjutor—a genuine poet.'

'Yes, certainly, in poesy he is wonderful,' said Ménage, 'and yet posterity, while admiring him, will reproach him for one thing—for having introduced too great a license in poetical composition; he has killed poesy without knowing it.'

'Killed—that is the word,' said Scudéry.

'But what a masterpiece his letters are!' said Madame de Chevreuse.

'Oh, under that head,' said Mademoiselle de Scudéry, 'he is quite a celebrity.'

'That is true,' replied Mademoiselle Paulet, 'but so long only as he is jesting; for in serious letter-writing he is pitiable, and if he does not say things crudely, for all that he says them badly.'

'But you will at least agree that in jocularity he is inimitable.'

'Yes, certainly,' replied Scudéry, twisting his moustache. 'I find only that his comic writing is forced, and his jests too familiar. See his "Letter from the Carp to the Pike".'*

'Without considering,' resumed Ménage, 'that his best inspirations came to him from the Rambouillets. See his "Zelide and Alcidalea".'*

'As for me,' said Aramis, drawing near the circle, and bowing to Madame de Chevreuse, who replied by a gracious smile, 'I shall accuse him of having been too free with the great. He has often failed in respect towards Madame the Princess, Marshal d'Albret, M. de Schomberg, and the queen herself.'

'What, to the queen?' asked Scudéry, advancing his right leg as if to be on guard. 'Bless me! I never knew that. And how has he failed in respect to her Majesty?'

'Don't you know his piece, "I was thinking"?'

'No,' said a chorus of voices.

'In truth, I think the queen has made it known but to a few; but I have it from a reliable source.'

'And you know it?'

'I could remember it, I think.'

'Do so, do so!' said all of them.

'This was the occasion when it was made,' said Aramis. 'M. de Voiture was in the queen's carriage, who was taking a drive with him in private in the forest of Fontainebleau. He put on the appearance of deep thought so that the queen might ask him what he was thinking about. This did not fail to happen. "What are you thinking about?" asked her Majesty. Voiture smiled, assumed a thoughtful air for a few seconds to give the idea that he was improvising, and then he repeated:*

> 'Je pensais que la destinée
> Après tant d'injustes malheurs,
> Vous a justement couronnée
> De gloire, d'éclat, et d'honneurs;
> Mais que vous étiez plus heureuse
> Lorsque vous étiez autrefois
> Je ne dirai pas amoureuse!
> La rime le veut toutefois.'[1]

Scudéry, Ménage, and Mademoiselle Paulet shrugged their shoulders.

'Wait, wait,' said Aramis; 'there are three strophes.'

'Oh, say three couplets,' said Mademoiselle de Scudéry; 'it is at the least a song.'

> 'Je pensais que ce pauvre Amour,
> Qui toujours vous prêta ses armes,
> Est banni loin de votre cour,
> Sans ses traits, son arc, et ses charmes;
> Et de quoi puis-je profiter,
> En pensant près de vous, Marie,
> Si vous pouvez si maltraiter,
> Ceux qui vous ont si bien servie?'[2]

---

[1] I was thinking that destiny,
After so many unjust ills,
Has justly crowned you
With glory, splendour, and honours;
But that you were more happy
When you lived in former days—
I will not say more amorous,
Although the rhyme requires it.

[2] I was thinking that this poor Love,
Who always lent to you his arms,
Is banished far from your court,
Without his shafts, his bow, his charms;
And in what way can I profit
In being near to you, Marie,
If you can so ill-use
Those who have served you so well?

'Oh, as to that last trait,' said Madame de Chevreuse, 'I do not know if it is poetically just, but I ask forgiveness for it as the truth; and in this Madame de Hautefort and Madame de Sennecey will join with me if it be necessary, without counting M. de Beaufort.'

'Go on, go on,' said Scarron; 'that concerns me no more; ever since the morning I have been no longer her Patient.'

'And the last couplet, if you please?' said Mademoiselle de Scudéry.

'This is it,' said Aramis. 'This has the advantage of employing proper names, so that there is no possibility of making a mistake:

> 'Je pensais—nous autres poëtes,
> Nous pensons extravagamment—
> Ce que, dans l'humeur où vous êtes,
> Vous feriez si dans ce moment
> Vous avisiez en cette place
> Venir le duc de Buckingham,
> Et lequel serait en disgrâce
> Du duc ou du père Vincent.'[1]

At this last strophe an exclamation arose on the impertinence of Voiture.

'Still,' said the young lady with velvety eyes, in a mild voice, 'I am unfortunate enough to find these verses quite charming.'

It was also Raoul's opinion, and he approached Scarron, and said to him with a blush:

'M. Scarron, do me the honour, I beg you, to tell me who that young lady is who holds an opinion opposed to that of the whole assembly.'

> [1] I was thinking—we who are poets,
> We think very fanciful things,—
> What, in your present humour
> You would do, if at this instant
> You were to perceive into this place
> The Duke of Buckingham coming,
> And who would be in disgrace,—
> The duke or Father Vincent.

(Father Vincent was the queen's confessor.)

'Ah, ah, my young viscount,' said Scarron, 'I believe you want to propose to her an alliance offensive and defensive.'

Raoul blushed again.

'I confess,' said he, 'that I think those verses very pretty.'

'And so they are,' said Scarron; 'but, *chut!* between poets one does not speak of these things.'

'But,' said Raoul, 'I have not the honour of being a poet, and I ask you——'

'That's true; who is that young lady, did you not ask? That is the beautiful Indian.'

'Pray pardon me, Monsieur,' said Raoul, blushing, 'but I am no wiser than before. Alas! I am a provincial.'

'Which means you do not understand the wild talk which trickles here from every mouth. So much the better, young man; so much the better. Don't try to understand it. It would be a waste of time; and even when you do, one must hope that they will no longer speak it.'

'Then you pardon me, Monsieur,' said Raoul; 'and you will condescend to tell me who is that person whom you call the beautiful Indian?'

'Yes, certainly. She is one of the most charming persons living—Mademoiselle Françoise d'Aubigné.'

'Does she belong to the family of the famous Agrippa*—the friend of King Henry IV?'

'She is his granddaughter. She comes from Martinique; that is why I call her the beautiful Indian.'*

Raoul opened his eyes wide, and they met the eyes of the young lady, who smiled.

They went on talking of Voiture.

'Monsieur,' said Mademoiselle d'Aubigné, addressing Scarron as if to join in the conversation which he was holding with the young viscount, 'do you not admire the friends of poor Voiture? But listen now how they pluck him while in the very act of. praising him. One denies him the possession of good sense; another of originality, another of comic force, another of independence, another—eh! indeed, what then will they leave to this celebrity?'

Scarron and Raoul also began to laugh. The beautiful Indian herself, astonished at the effect she had produced, cast down her eyes, and resumed her natural look.

'There is a witty person,' said Raoul.

Athos from the recess of the window surveyed the whole scene with a smile of disdain on his face.

'Call M. le Comte de la Fère to me,' said Madame de Chevreuse to the Coadjutor. 'I want to speak to him.'

'And I,' said the Coadjutor—'I want it to be thought that I do not speak to him. I admire him, for I know his former adventures—some of them at least; but I did not count on greeting him till the morning of the day after tomorrow.'

'And why at that particular time?' said Madame de Chevreuse.

'You shall know that tomorrow evening,' said the Coadjutor, laughing.

'In truth, my dear Gondy,' said the duchess, 'you speak like the Apocalypse. M. d'Herblay,' added she, returning to Aramis, 'will you yet once more this evening be my servant?'

'Indeed, yes. This evening, tomorrow, always command me.'

'Well, go and fetch the Comte de la Fère. I want to speak to him.'

Aramis went to Athos, and brought him back with him.

'Monsieur the Count,' said the duchess, giving him a letter, 'this is what I promised you. Our *protégé* will be well received.'

'Madame,' said Athos, 'it is very pleasant to be indebted to you for anything.'

'You are not indebted to me in this respect, for I owe to you my having known him,' replied the sharp woman, with a smile which recalled Marie Michon to Aramis and Athos.

Upon that she rose and called for her carriage. Mademoiselle Paulet had already gone, and Mademoiselle de Scudéry was going.

'Viscount,' said Athos, addressing Raoul, 'follow Madame la Duchesse de Chevreuse; beg her to do you the favour of taking your hand to descend, and in descending, thank her.'

The beautiful Indian approached Scarron to take leave.

'Are you going already?' said he.

'I am one of the last to go, as you see. If you have any news of M. de Voiture and it is especially good, do me the favour to let me know tomorrow.'

'Oh, now,' said Scarron, 'he may die.'

'How so?' said the young lady.

'Without doubt, his panegyric is bestowed.'

So they separated, the young lady turning round to look at the poor paralytic with deep interest, the poor paralytic following her with his eyes and with love.

By degrees the groups broke up. Scarron pretended not to see that some of his guests had been talking mysteriously, that letters had come for several, and that his soirée seemed to have had a mysterious object which strayed aside from literature, of which, however, there had been much outward parade. But what mattered it to Scarron? They might plot at his house as they liked; since the morning, as he had said, he was no longer the queen's Patient.

As for Raoul, he had accompanied the duchess to her carriage, in which she had taken her seat after giving him her hand to kiss; then, by one of those fancies which made her so admired and yet so dangerous, she had seized him suddenly and kissed him on the forehead, saying:

'Viscount, may my good wishes and this kiss bring you happiness!' Then she had dismissed him and ordered the coachman to stop at the Hôtel de Luynes. The carriage started; Madame de Chevreuse made a last sign to the young man through the door, and Raoul ascended again, in amazement.

Athos understood what had passed, and smiled.

'Come, Viscount,' said he, 'it is time to go; you set out tomorrow for the army under Monsieur the Prince. Sleep well during your last night of citizen life.'

'I shall be a soldier then,' said the young man. 'Oh! thanks to you from my heart!'

'Adieu, Count,' said Abbé d'Herblay; 'I am returning to my convent.'

'Adieu, abbé,' said the Coadjutor; 'I preach tomorrow, and have twenty texts to consult this evening.'

'Adieu, gentlemen,' said the count; 'I am going to sleep for twenty-four hours at a stretch, I am so tired out.'

Scarron followed them with a side look across the doorway of the room.

'Not one of them will do what he has said,' muttered he, with his ape-like smile; 'but let them go, the brave gentlemen!

Who knows that they are not working to get my pension restored! They can move their arms; it is a good deal. Alas! I have only a tongue, but I try to show that that is something. Holloa, Chauperrois! it is eleven. Come and roll me towards my bed. In truth, that demoiselle d'Aubigné is very charming.'

Upon this the poor paralytic disappeared in his bedroom, the door of which closed behind him; and the lights were put out one after another in the drawing-room of the Rue des Tournelles.

XXIV

ST DENIS

THE day began to break when Athos rose and dressed; it was easy to see from his paleness (greater than usual) and the traces that want of sleep left in his countenance, that he had passed a sleepless night. Contrary to the habitude of this man, so firm and decided, there was in his appearance this morning something of inertness and irresolution.

The reason was that he was preparing for Raoul's departure, and that he was trying to gain time. First of all he furbished a sword which he took from its perfumed leather sheath, examined carefully the belt, and looked to see if the blade held firmly in the hilt.

Then he put into a trunk intended for the young man a bag full of louis, called Olivain, the groom who had come with him from Blois, and ordered him to see that all things needful for a young gentleman going on a campaign should be put into it. At last, after having spent nearly an hour in all these matters, he opened the door leading into the viscount's room, and entered it gently.

The sun, already beaming, shone into the room through a window with large panes, the curtains of which Raoul, who had returned late, had neglected to close. He was still sleeping, with his head gracefully resting on his arm. His long dark hair covered his beautiful forehead, which was damp with that moisture which like pearls rolls down the cheeks of the wearied child.

Athos drew near, and in an attitude full of tender melancholy he for a good while gazed at the young man with the smiling mouth, with his eyelids half closed, whose dreams ought to have been sweet and his slumber light, so much of solicitude and affection his protecting angel exhibited in his silent watch. Little by little Athos allowed himself to be allured into the delights of reverie in the presence of this rich and pure youthfulness. His youth re-appeared, bringing with it all those sweet souvenirs which are rather perfumes than thoughts. Between that past and the present there was an abyss. But imagination has the angel's or lightning's wing; it clears seas in which we should certainly have been shipwrecked; it removes the darkness in which our illusions were lost, the precipice where our happiness was engulfed. He fancied that all the first part of his life had been shattered by a woman; he thought with dread what influence love might have upon a constitution as fine and vigorous as Raoul's. In recalling all that he had suffered, he foresaw all that Raoul might suffer, and the expression of the tender and deep pity which arose in his heart expressed itself in the tear which dropped upon the sleeper.

At this moment Raoul awoke without any sadness or shadow of the fatigues which characterize certain constitutions which are as delicate as any bird's. His eyes rested on Athos, and he clearly understood all that was passing in the heart of this man, who awaited his waking like a lover that of his beloved, for his look in its turn took the expression of an infinite love.

'You are there, Monsieur,' said he, with respect.

'Yes, Raoul, I am here,' said the count.

'And you did not awake me!'

'I wanted to let you have a few moments of this sound sleep, my friend. You must have been fatigued with yesterday's journey, which was prolonged so far into the night.'

'Oh, Monsieur, how good you are!' said Raoul.

Athos smiled.

'How are you?' said he.

'Oh, perfectly well, Monsieur, and thoroughly rested.'

'You are still growing,' continued Athos, with a fatherly interest so charming in the mature man for the young one, 'and your fatigues are doubly felt at your age.'

'Oh, Monsieur, I beg your pardon,' said Raoul, ashamed of so much care; 'but in a moment I shall be dressed.'

Athos called Olivain, and at the end of ten minutes, with the punctuality which Athos had impressed on his pupil, the young man was ready.

'Now,' said Raoul to the servant, 'look after my baggage.'

'Your baggage is ready for you, Raoul,' said Athos. 'I have myself seen the portmanteau packed, and that you have all that is requisite; and it ought already, as well as the portmanteau of the servant, to be placed on the horses if they have followed the orders I have given.'

'All has been done according to the wish of Monsieur the Count,' said Olivain, 'and the horses are waiting.'

'And I,' exclaimed Raoul, 'have been sleeping while you, Monsieur, have had the goodness to be engaged in all these details. You are loading me with favours.'

'So you love me a little? I hope so at least,' said Athos, much moved.

'Oh, Monsieur,' said Raoul, who, in order not to show his emotion, in a burst of tenderness tried hard to repress it, 'God is witness that I love and venerate you.'

'See that you have forgotten nothing,' said Athos, pretending to look all around him to hide his emotion.

'Nothing,' said Raoul.

The lackey approached Athos with a certain hesitation, and said in a low tone, 'Monsieur the Viscount has no sword, for Monsieur the Count made me take away last night the one he took off.'

'Very well,' said Athos; 'that concerns me.'

Raoul did not appear to notice this conversation. He descended, looking at the count at each instant to see if the moment for his adieux had arrived; but Athos was unmoved.

On reaching the hall-steps Raoul saw three horses.

'Oh, Monsieur,' exclaimed he, joyously, 'you are going with me, then?'

'I wish to go a short distance with you,' said Athos.

Pleasure sparkled in Raoul's eyes, and he mounted his horse lightly.

Athos slowly mounted his, after saying something in a low tone to the servant, who, instead of following at once, returned to the rooms. Raoul, delighted at having the count's company, did not see or pretended he did not notice this.

The two gentlemen crossed Pont Neuf, went along the quays, or rather, what was then called Pepin's Watering-Place,* and passed by the walls of the Grand Châtelet. They then entered the Rue St Denis, where they were rejoined by the servant.

They journeyed in silence. Raoul felt that the time of separation was drawing near. The count had the evening before given different directions respecting matters which concerned Raoul in the course of the day's journey. Besides, his looks increased in tenderness, and the few words he let fall were full of affection. From time to time a reflection or piece of advice was spoken; and his words showed his great solicitude. After having passed the Porte St Denis, and when the two had reached the height of the Récollets,* Athos cast a look on the horse Raoul was riding.

'Take care of it, Raoul,' he said to him. 'You must not forget that, for to do so is a great fault in a horseman. See, your horse is already tired, and is foaming, while mine is fresh as if just out of the stable. You will harden his mouth by tightening the rein too much; and pay attention to it, or you will not be able to make him manœuvre with the necessary promptness. A horseman's safety depends often on the prompt obedience of his horse. In a few days you will ride, not in a riding-school, but on a battlefield.' Then all at once, so as not to give a sad importance to this remark, 'Look, now, Raoul,' continued Athos, 'this is a fine level country for shooting partridges.'

The young man profited by the lesson, and especially admired the delicacy with which it was given.

'I have noticed also,' said Athos, 'that in firing a pistol you extend the arm too much. This tension makes one lose the accuracy of his aim; so that out of twelve shots you might miss the mark three times.'

'You would hit the twelve times, Monsieur,' said Raoul, smiling.

'Because I bend my arm and rest my elbow on the other hand. Do you clearly understand this?'

'Yes, Monsieur; I have tried this when alone, and found it quite successful.'

'So in fencing,' resumed Athos, 'you charge your adversary too much. It is a defect of your time of life, I know very well. But the movement of the body while charging turns the sword from the direct line; and if you had as opponent a cool-headed man, he would stop you at the first stroke by a simple extrication, or even by a direct stroke.'

'Yes, Monsieur, as you have very often done; but it is not everyone who has your address and courage.'

'What a fresh breeze is blowing!' resumed Athos. 'It has quite a touch of winter.* By the by, when you are under fire, as you will be,—for your young general loves powder—remember not to fire first. He who does rarely hits his man—for he fires with a fear of being disarmed before an enemy armed. Then when he fires, make your horse rear; this manœuvre has several times saved my life.'

'I will do this, if only out of gratitude.'

'Eh,' said Athos, 'are not those poachers who are being seized over there? Yes, undoubtedly——Then again—an important thing, Raoul—if you are wounded in a charge, if you fall from your horse, and if you have any strength, take yourself out of the line your regiment has followed; otherwise it may be brought back, and you would be trodden under the feet of the horses. And also, should you be wounded, write to me at once, or get some one to do so; we understand wounds,' added Athos, smiling.

'Thank you, Monsieur,' replied the young man, quite moved.

'Ah, we have reached St Denis,'* said Athos.

In fact they at that moment reached the gate of the town, guarded by two sentinels. The one said to the other:

'There is another young gentleman who seems to be going to join the army.'

Athos turned round; all that concerned Raoul, even indirectly, took an interest in his eyes.

'How do you tell that?' asked he.

'By his look, Monsieur,' said the sentinel. 'Besides, he is of the right age. He is the second today.'

'Has a young man like me already passed today?' asked Raoul.

'Yes, faith; of high bearing and with a fine equipage. He had the air of some son of a noble house.'

'He may be my travelling companion, Monsieur,' resumed Raoul, moving forward; 'but alas, he will not cause me to forget the one I am losing.'

'I do not think you will overtake him, Raoul, for I have to say something to you here which will give time for this gentleman to get in advance of you.'

'As it may please you, Monsieur.'

While thus conversing they passed along the streets, at that time full of people on account of the festival, and they came in front of the old church, in which early Mass was being said.

'Let us dismount, Raoul,' said Athos. 'Olivain, mind the horses, and give me the sword.'

Athos took the sword from the servant, and the count and Raoul entered the church. Athos offered the holy water to Raoul. There is in some fathers' hearts a portion of that anticipatory love which a lover has for his beloved. The young man touched the hand of Athos, bowed, and crossed himself.

Athos said a word to one of the vergers, who bowed, and moved towards the crypt.

'Come, Raoul,' said Athos, 'let us follow this man.'

The verger opened the gate of the royal tombs, and stayed on the first step while Athos and Raoul descended the steps.

The darkness was partially lessened by a silver lamp on the last step, just under which rested, enveloped in a large velvet mantle embroidered with gold *fleurs-de-lis*, a catafalque supported by carved oak horses.

The young man, prepared for this position by his own heart being full of sadness, by the majesty of the church he had passed through, had descended with slow, solemn pace, and stood upright with uncovered head before the mortal remains of the last king, who would go to rejoin his ancestors only when his successor should come to rejoin him,* and who seemed to say to human pride, so ready at times to elevate itself when on the throne, 'Dust of the earth, I await thee.'

There was a moment of silence. Then Athos raised his hand, and pointing to the tomb: 'This is the sepulchre,' said he, 'of a man who was weak and without grandeur, but whose reign was, nothwithstanding, full of important events. Above this king* watches another man's spirit, as this lamp watches over this tomb, and lights it up. The latter was a real king, Raoul; the other only a phantom into which he put a soul. And yet so powerful is the monarchy among us, that he has not ever the honour of a tomb at the feet of him for the glory of whom he wore out his life—for that man, if he made this king an insignificant one, has made the kingdom great. And there are two things enclosed in the Louvre Palace—the king who dies, and the royalty which does not. That reign has ended, Raoul; that minister so renowned, feared and hated by his master, has gone to the tomb, drawing after him the king whom he did not wish to leave alone for fear he should destroy his work—for a king only builds up when he has God, or the spirit of God, near him. Yet then everyone thought the cardinal's death a deliverance, and I, blind like my contemporaries, sometimes opposed the designs of the great man who held France's destiny in his hands, and who, just as he opened or closed them, held her in check or gave her the impress of his choice. If he did not crush me and my friends in his terrible anger, it was without doubt that I should be able to say to you today: Raoul, learn ever to separate the king and the principle of royalty. The king is but man; royalty is the spirit of God. When you are in doubt as to which you should serve, forsake the material appearance for the invisible principle, for this is everything. Only God has wished to render this principle palpable by incarnating it in a man. Raoul, it seems to me that I see your future as through a cloud. It will be better than ours. We have had a minister without a king; you, on the contrary, will have a king without a minister. You will be able then to serve, love, and honour the king. If he prove a tyrant—for power in its giddiness often becomes tyranny—serve, love, and honour the royalty; that is the infallible principle. That is to say, the spirit of God on the earth; that is, that celestial spark which makes this dust so great and so holy that we, gentlemen of high condition indeed, are as unimportant before this body extended on the last step of this staircase as this body itself is before the throne of the Supreme Being.'

'I shall worship God, Monsieur,' said Raoul; 'I shall honour royalty, I shall serve the king; and I shall endeavour, even if I die in the cause, to be for king, royalty, and God. Have I understood you?'

Athos smiled. 'You have a noble nature,' said he; 'here is your sword.'

Raoul knelt down.

'My father has worn it—a loyal gentleman. So have I; and I have done honour to it sometimes when the hilt was in my hand and its scabbard was at my side. If your hand is still too weak to wield it, Raoul, so much the better; you will have more time to learn to draw it only when it is a duty to do so.'

'Monsieur,' said Raoul, receiving the sword from the count's hand, 'I owe you everything; yet this sword is the most precious present you have made me. I will wear it, I swear to you, as a grateful man;' and he lifted it up, and kissed the hilt with reverence.

'That is well,' said Athos. 'Rise, Viscount, and let us embrace.'

Raoul rose, and threw himself eagerly into the arms of Athos.

'Adieu,' murmured the count, who felt his heart breaking— 'adieu, and think of me.'

'Oh, always,' exclaimed the young man. 'Oh, I swear it, Monsieur; and if misfortune happens to me, your name will be the last name I shall pronounce, your memory my last thought.'

Athos mounted the steps quickly to hide his emotion, gave a gold piece to the verger, bowed towards the altar, and strode towards the porch, at the foot of which Olivain was waiting with the two horses.

'Olivain,'—pointing to Raoul's sword-belt—'tighten the buckle of the sword, for it is a little low. Right. Now, you are to accompany Monsieur the Viscount until Grimaud meets you; then you will return. You understand, Raoul? Grimaud is an old servant, full of courage and foresight; he will go with you. Now to horse, that I may see you set off.' Raoul obeyed.

'Adieu, Raoul, my dear boy,' said the count.

'Adieu, Monsieur, my dearly loved guardian,' said Raoul.

Athos made a sign with his hand, for he could not trust himself to speak.

Raoul started with uncovered head. Athos remained motionless, watching until he disappeared at the turning of a street; then the count gave the horse's bridle to a peasant, slowly re-entered the church, went and knelt down in an obscure corner, and prayed.

XXV

ONE OF M. DE BEAUFORT'S FORTY MEANS OF ESCAPE

THE time passed alike for prisoner and for those engaged in effecting his escape, only it passed more slowly. Just the opposite of other men who ardently form a perilous resolution, and who grow cool as the time of execution draws near, the Duc de Beaufort, whose boiling courage had become a proverb, seemed to drive the time before him, and summoned the hour of action by his ardent desires. There was in his escape, besides the projects which he was entertaining for the future—projects, one must confess, still very vague and uncertain—a commencement of revenge which gave him satisfaction. First of all, his escape would be an awkward matter for M. de Chavigny, whom he hated for his petty persecutions; then, still more serious for the cardinal, whom he execrated for the treatment that he had received. The reader will notice that the proper ratio was preserved between the sentiments M. de Beaufort had vowed towards the governor and the minister,—towards the subordinate and his master.

Then Beaufort, who knew so well the interior of the Palais-Royal and the relations existing between the queen and the cardinal, was picturing to himself in his prison all that dramatic movement which would take place when this report resounded from the cabinet of the minister to the apartments of Anne of Austria, 'M. de Beaufort has escaped.' In saying all this to himself, he kept smiling softly, believing himself already outside, breathing the air of plains and forests, pressing firmly his horse's sides, and crying loudly, 'I am free!'

It is true that in coming to himself he was still between four walls, saw ten paces from him La Ramée, who was twiddling his thumbs, and in the anteroom were his guards laughing or drinking. The only thing which gave him any satisfaction in this odious tableau, so great is the instability of the human mind, was the frowning face of Grimaud whom he had first hated, but who afterwards was his sole hope. Grimaud was like an Antinous* to him.

It is useless to say that all this was the mere play of the prisoner's feverish imagination. Grimaud was always the same. Thus he had kept the confidence of his superior, La Ramée, who now trusted in him more than in himself; for, as we have said, La Ramée felt at the bottom of his heart a certain weakness for M. de Beaufort.

So the good La Ramée was making quite an entertainment of this little supper alone with his prisoner. La Ramée had but one fault—he was a gourmand; he loved good pastry and excellent wine. Now, the successor to Father Marteau had promised him a pheasant pasty instead of fowl, and Chambertin instead of Mâcon. All this, increased by the presence of this excellent prince who was really so good, who invented such droll tricks against M. de Chavigny and Mazarin, made this Whitsuntide just at hand one of the four great feasts in the year for La Ramée. He therefore awaited six in the evening with as much impatience as the duke did.

Since the morning he had been engaged on its details, and trusting to himself only, he paid a visit in person to Marteau's successor. The latter had surpassed himself. He showed La Ramée a real monster of a pie, decorated on the top with M. de Beaufort's arms; it was still empty, but near it were a pheasant and two partridges, interlarded so finely that they each looked like a pin-cushion. La Ramée's mouth watered, and he returned to the duke's room rubbing his hands. To heighten the pleasure, M. de Chavigny, trusting La Ramée, had gone for a short journey that very morning, so that La Ramée became sub-governor of the prison. As for Grimaud, he seemed more scowling than ever. M. de Beaufort had played a game of tennis with La Ramée; a sign from Grimaud had made him understand that he must give attention to everything.

Grimaud went on in front, and marked out the road which they were to follow in the evening. Tennis was played in what was called the enclosure of the small courtyard of the prison. It was a part little guarded, where sentinels were placed at the time when Beaufort was playing; still, from the great height of the wall this precaution seemed superfluous.

There were three gates to open before reaching this close. Each was opened by a different key. On reaching the close, Grimaud went and seated himself mechanically near a loop-hole, with his legs hanging outside the wall. It was clear that at this point the rope ladder should be fastened.

The whole of these movements, understood by the duke, were, as one may see, unintelligible to La Ramée.

The game began. This time M. de Beaufort was in the vein, and one might have said he sent the balls just where he wished them to go. La Ramée was utterly beaten.

Four of the duke's guards had followed to pick up the balls. At the end of the game, M. de Beaufort, while rallying La Ramée on his want of skill, offered the guards two louis to go and drink his health with their four comrades.

The guards asked La Ramée's leave, who granted it, but for the evening only. Till then La Ramée was engaged in important matters; he ordered, as he had his rounds to make, that the prisoner should not be lost sight of.

M. de Beaufort might have arranged everything himself, with less convenience, in all probability, than was done for him by his guardian.

At last six o'clock struck; although seven was the hour for sitting down to table, yet the dinner was ready and served up. On a sideboard was the colossal pie, which seemed cooked to perfection, so far as one could judge by the golden colour of the crust. The rest of the dinner was to come.

Every one was impatient—the guards to go and drink, La Ramée to sit down to dinner, and M. de Beaufort to escape. Grimaud alone was immovable. One might have thought that Athos had educated him with an eye to this great occasion.

There were moments when, on looking at him, the duke asked himself if he were not dreaming, and if this figure of marble was actually at his service and would be alert at the right moment.

La Ramée sent away the guards to drink the health of the
prince; then, when they were gone, he closed the doors, put
the keys into his pockets, and pointed to the table in a manner
which meant, When Monseigneur shall please.

The prince looked at Grimaud, and the latter at the clock.
It was scarcely a quarter past six, the escape was fixed for
seven; there were three-quarters of an hour to wait.

The prince, in order to gain a quarter of an hour, pretended
to be interested in his book, and asked to finish the chapter.
La Ramée approached, looked over his shoulder at the book
which had the effect of preventing the prince from sitting down
to table when dinner was ready.

It was the 'Commentaries of Caesar,' which he himself,
contrary to Chavigny's orders, had procured for him three days
ago.

La Ramée was quite determined no longer to disobey the
prison rules. While waiting, he uncorked the bottles and went
to sniff the pie. At the half-hour the duke rose and gravely
said:

'Decidedly, Caesar was the greatest man of ancient times.'

'You think so, Monseigneur?' said La Ramée.

'Yes.'

'Well, but I prefer Hannibal,' replied La Ramée.

'Why so?' asked the duke.

'Because he has left no Commentaries,' said La Ramée, with
a coarse smile.

The duke understood the allusion, and sat down, making a
sign to La Ramée to sit in front of him. The officer did not
require to be told twice.

There is no figure so expressive as that of a real gourmand
before a good table; so on receiving his plate of soup from
Grimaud, La Ramée's face beamed with perfect contentment.
The duke looked at him with a smile.

'By Jove, La Ramée,' exclaimed he, 'do you know that if any
one told me that at this moment there was in France a happier
fellow than you, I would not believe him.'

'And you would be right, upon honour, Monseigneur,' said
La Ramée. 'As for me, I confess that when I am hungry I do
not know a more cheering sight than a well-spread table; and

if you add that he who does the honours of the table is Henry the Great's grandson, then you will plainly see, Monseigneur, that the honour one receives doubles the pleasure which one enjoys.'

The prince bowed, and an almost imperceptible smile appeared on Grimaud's face, who stood behind La Ramée.

'My dear La Ramée,' said the duke, 'in truth, there is no one like you for turning a compliment.'

'No, Monseigneur,' said La Ramée, in his fulness of soul; 'no, in truth, I say what I think; there is no compliment in what I said to you then.'

'Then you are attached to me?' asked the prince.

'That is to say,' replied La Ramée, 'I should not get over it if your Highness went out of Vincennes.'

'A droll manner of showing your affliction' (the prince meant affection).

'But, Monseigneur,' said La Ramée, 'what would you do outside? Some foolish act which would embroil you with the court, and would get you sent to the Bastille instead of being here. M. de Chavigny is not amiable, I admit,' continued La Ramée, sipping a glass of Madeira, 'but M. du Tremblay is much worse.'

'That might happen,' said the duke, who was amused at the turn which the conversation was taking, and who from time to time looked at the clock, the hand of which was moving with terrible slowness.

'What would you expect from the brother of a Capuchin friar brought up in Cardinal Richelieu's school? Ah, Monseigneur, believe me, it is a great happiness that the queen, who has always wished you well, had the idea of sending you here, where you can walk about, play at tennis, have a good table and good air.'

'In fact,' said the duke, 'to hear you talk, La Ramée, I must be very ungrateful to have had the thought even of trying to escape.'

'Oh, Monseigneur, it is the height of ingratitude; but your royal Highness has never seriously thought of it.'

'In fact,' replied the duke, 'and I ought to avow it to you—it is perhaps a foolish thought, I don't say it is not—but from time to time I still think of it.'

'Always by one of your forty means, Monseigneur?'

'Well, yes,' said the duke.

'Monseigneur,' said La Ramée, 'since you are so affable, tell me one of those forty ways invented by your Highness.'

'Willingly,' said the duke. 'Grimaud, give me the pie.'

'I am listening,' said La Ramée, leaning back in his chair, raising his glass, and half closing his eye to see the sun through the ruby wine in it.

The duke cast a look at the clock. Ten minutes still to seven.

Grimaud placed the pie before the prince, who took his silver-bladed knife to raise the top; but La Ramée, who feared some misfortune might occur to this delicate dish, passed his knife with steel blade to the prince.

'Thanks, La Ramée,' said the duke, taking the knife.

'Well, Monseigneur,' said the officer, 'now this famous way?'

'Need I tell you,' replied the duke, 'that it is the one that I had resolved to employ—the one upon which I counted the most? Well,' he continued, holding the pie with one hand and describing a circle with the knife in the other, 'I hoped first to have as guardian a brave fellow like you, La Ramée.'

'Well,' said La Ramée, 'so you have, Monseigneur. Then?'

'I am happy that it is so.'

La Ramée bowed.

'I was saying,' continued the prince, 'if I once had near me a good fellow like La Ramée, I should try to have recommended to him by some friend of mine a man who would be faithful to me, and with whom I might concert means for my escape.'

'Go on, go on,' said La Ramée; 'not badly conceived.'

'Is it not?' replied the duke. 'For example, the servant of some gentleman, himself an enemy to Mazarin, as every gentleman ought to be.'

'*Chut*, Monseigneur!' said La Ramée, 'don't let us talk politics.'

'When I had such a man, who was clever, and could inspire confidence in my guardian, the latter would trust him, and then I should get news from without.'

'Well, yes,' said La Ramée; 'but how so?'

'Oh, nothing more easy,' said the duke; 'by playing at tennis, for instance.'

'By playing at tennis?' asked La Ramée, beginning to lend the greatest attention to the duke's recital.

'Yes; listen. I send a ball into the moat. A man is there to pick it up; the ball has a letter in it. Instead of sending that one back which I asked for from the top of the wall, he sends me another which also contains a letter. Thus we have exchanged ideas, and no one has observed it.'

'The devil!' said La Ramée, scratching his ear; 'you do right to tell me that, Monseigneur. I shall look after these pickers-up of balls.'

The duke smiled.

'But,' continued La Ramée, 'all that is nothing more than a means of corresponding.'

'That is a good deal, it seems to me.'

'It is not much.'

'I beg your pardon. For example, I say to my friends, "Be on such a day and at such an hour on the other side of the moat, with two horses ready." '

'What next?' said La Ramée, with some disquiet. 'At any rate these horses have no wings to reach the walls and come for you.'

'Hey!' said the prince, negligently; 'there is no need for that, but only that I should have a means of descending.'

'What means?'

'A rope ladder.'

'Yes; but,' said La Ramée, trying to laugh, 'a rope ladder is not sent like a letter in a tennis-ball.'

'No; but in something else.'

'In something else? In what?'

'In a pie, for example.'

'In a pie?' said La Ramée.

'Yes; suppose,' resumed the duke, 'for example, that my steward Noirmont has treated for the stock of Father Marteau's shop.'

'Well?' asked La Ramée, with a shudder.

'Well, La Ramée, who is a gourmand, sees Noirmont's pies, finds they have a better look than those of his predecessors, and offers to let me taste them. I accept on the condition that he partakes with me. To be more at his ease he dismisses his guards, and keeps Grimaud only to wait on us. Grimaud is the man given to me by a friend, ready to second me in everything. The time of escape is fixed at seven. Well, at a few minutes to seven——'

'At a few minutes to seven?' replied La Ramée, down whose face the perspiration began to roll.

'At a few minutes to seven,' said the duke, suiting the action to the word, 'I raise the crust of the pie. I find in it two poniards, a rope ladder, and a gag. I hold one of these poniards to La Ramée's heart and say to him, "My friend, I am truly distressed, but if you make any movement or utter a cry, you are a dead man." '

As we have said, in pronouncing these last words the duke had joined the action to the words.

The duke was actually close to La Ramée, and resting the dagger's point on his chest with a look which could allow no doubt that he would do as he had said.

During this time Grimaud, who had not spoken, took the second poniard, the rope ladder, and the gag from the pie. La Ramée saw these objects with increasing terror.

'Oh, Monseigneur,' he cried, turning on the duke a stupefied look, which at any other moment would have made the prince burst into laughter, 'you will not have the heart to kill me?'

'Not if you do not prevent my escape.'

'But, Monseigneur, if I let you flee I am a ruined man.'

'I will reimburse the value of your office.'

'And you are quite determined to leave the prison?'

'Most decidedly.'

'All that I could say to you would not make you change your resolution?'

'This evening I wish to be free.'

'But if I defend myself, or cry out for help?'

'Upon my honour, I kill you.'

At that moment the clock struck seven.

'Seven o'clock,' said Grimaud, who had not said a word till now.

'Seven,' said the duke. 'You see I am behind time.'

La Ramée made a movement as if to acquit his conscience. The duke frowned, and the officer felt the point of the poniard, which, after having penetrated his clothes, was ready to pierce his breast.

'That is enough, Monseigneur. I won't move.'

'We must be quick,' said the duke.

'Monseigneur, one last favour!'

'What? Speak! Look sharp!'

'Bind me fast.'

'Why bind you?'

'That they may not believe I am an accomplice.'

'The hands,' said Grimaud.

'Not in front; behind me.'

'But what with?' said the duke.

'Your belt, Monseigneur.'

The duke undid his belt and gave it to Grimaud, who bound his hands so as to satisfy La Ramée.

'The feet,' said Grimaud.

La Ramée stretched out his legs. Grimaud took a table-napkin, tore it in strips, and tied him.

'Now my sword,' said La Ramée. 'Fasten the guard of it to me.'

The duke tore off one of the tapes of his small-clothes, and did as the officer asked.

'Now,' said the poor La Ramée, 'the gag—I demand it. Without that, they would institute a process against me because I had not cried out. Push it in, Monseigneur; push it in.'

Grimaud made ready to fulfil the desire of the officer, who made a movement in sign that he had something to say.

'Speak,' said the duke.

'Now, Monseigneur,' said La Ramée, 'do not forget, if I meet with misfortune on your account, that I have a wife and four children.'

'Very well. Gag him, Grimaud.'

In a second La Ramée was gagged and placed on the ground; two or three chairs were upset to give the appearance of a struggle. Grimaud took all the keys from the officer's pockets, opened first the door of the room in which they were, double-locked it when they were out of it, then they quickly went along the passage which led to the small enclosure. The three gates were opened and closed one after another with a rapidity which did credit to Grimaud's dexterity. At last they reached the tennis-court. It was quite clear of sentinels, and there was no one at the windows.

The duke ran to the wall, and saw on the other side of the moat three cavaliers with two led horses. The duke exchanged signs with them. It was well for him that they were there. Meanwhile Grimaud was fastening the cord for descending. It was not a rope ladder, but a roll of silk with a stick to be put between the legs, and unwinding by the weight of the person who was seated astride.

'Go!' said the duke.

'First, Monseigneur?' asked Grimaud.

'Of course,' said the duke. 'If they retake me, I risk prison only; but if they take you, you will be hanged.'

'True,' said Grimaud. And he at once, sitting astride on the stick, began the perilous descent. The duke followed him with his eyes with involuntary terror. Grimaud had already accomplished three-quarters of the descent when suddenly the rope broke. He fell, precipitated into the moat.

The duke uttered a cry; but Grimaud uttered not even a groan, and yet he must have been sadly hurt, for he remained stretched on the place where he fell. At once one of the men who were waiting slipped into the ditch, fastened the end of a cord under Grimaud's shoulders, and the other two drew Grimaud to them.

'Come down, Monseigneur,' said the man who was in the ditch. 'There are only fifteen feet of fall, and the turf is soft.'

The duke was already at work. His task was the more difficult because he had not the stick to hold him. He had to descend by strength of wrist, and that from a height of fifty feet. But the duke was agile, vigorous, and full of sang-froid. In less than five minutes he was at the end of the cord, and was only fifteen feet from the ground; he let go his support, and fell on his feet without receiving any hurt.

He at once began to climb the slope of the moat, at the top of which he found Rochefort. The other two gentlemen were not known to him. Grimaud, who had fainted, was fastened to a horse.

'Gentlemen,' said the prince, 'I will thank you later on; but now there is not a moment to lose. Off, then! Who loves me, follows me!' And he sprang on his horse, set off at a hard gallop, breathing freely, and shouting with an expression of joy impossible to describe. 'Free! free! free!'*

XXVI

D'ARTAGNAN'S TIMELY ARRIVAL

D'ARTAGNAN drew out at Blois the sum of money that Mazarin, in his desire to have him near him, had decided to give him for his future services.

The journey from Blois to Paris usually took four days. D'Artagnan reached St Denis's gate about four in the afternoon of the third day; formerly he would have taken but two. We have already seen that Athos, who set out three hours after him, arrived twenty-four hours before him. Planchet could no longer make forced marches, and d'Artagnan reproached him for his slowness.

'Forty leagues in three days, Monsieur! I think that's pretty good for a seller of almonds.'

'Have you really become a shopkeeper, Planchet, and do you seriously think, now that we have met again, of vegetating in a shop?'

'Ah,' replied Planchet, 'you only in fact were made for an active life. Look at M. Athos; who would say he was such a seeker of adventures as we have known him? He now lives like a gentleman farmer, as a country squire. Come, Monsieur, a tranquil existence is the one thing desirable.'

'You hypocrite,' said d'Artagnan, 'one can see well enough that you are drawing close to Paris, and that there is a rope and a scaffold awaiting you!'

And in fact, as they reached that point of their conversation, the two travellers also reached the gate of the city. Planchet pulled down his hat, thinking that he would pass through streets where he was well known. D'Artagnan curled his moustache while remembering that Porthos ought to be awaiting him in the Rue Tiquetonne. He was thinking how he should make him forget his manor of Bracieux and the Homeric kitchens of Pierrefonds.

On turning the corner of the Rue Montmartre, he saw, at one of the windows of the Hôtel de la Chevrette, Porthos dressed in a splendid close-fitting coat, sky-blue in colour, all embroidered with silver, and gaping as though he would dislocate his jaw, so that the passers-by contemplated with a certain respectful admiration such a fine rich gentleman, who seemed so wearied with his riches and grandeur.

Scarcely had d'Artagnan and Planchet turned the corner than Porthos recognized them.

'Ah, d'Artagnan!' he cried, 'thank goodness, it is you!'

'Ah! how do you do, my dear friend?' replied d'Artagnan.

A little crowd of idlers soon formed round the horses, which the grooms were holding by the bridle, and the cavaliers, who were thus talking mere chit-chat; but a frown from d'Artagnan, and two or three decided gestures of Planchet, soon understood, scattered the crowd, who had begun to be the more compact as they were ignorant why they had assembled. Porthos had already come down to the entrance of the hotel.

'Ah, my dear friend!' said he, 'my horses are badly off here.'

'Indeed!' said d'Artagnan; 'I am distressed about them.'

'And I too was uncomfortable,' said Porthos; 'and had it not been for the hostess,' continued he, rocking from side to side on his legs, from a feeling of self-satisfaction, 'who is tolerably pretty, and understands a joke, I should have looked for lodging somewhere else.'

The fair Madeleine, who had come near during this colloquy, made a step backwards, and became pale as death on hearing Porthos's words, for she thought that the scene with the Swiss might be played over again; but to her great surprise d'Artagnan did not frown, and instead of becoming angry, he said laughingly to Porthos:

'Oh, yes, I understand, dear friend; the air of the Rue Tiquetonne is not so good as that of the Pierrefonds valley; but all right, I am going to take you where it is better.'

'When so?'

'Soon, I hope, upon honour.'

'Ah! so much the better.'

To this exclamation of Porthos succeeded a low and deep groan, which came from the angle of a door. D'Artagnan, who had just dismounted, saw designed in relief on the wall the enormous stomach of Mousqueton, whose saddened mouth gave vent to low complaints.

'And you also, my poor M. Mouston, are out of place in this wretched hotel, isn't it so?' asked d'Artagnan, with that tone of raillery which could be either compassion or mockery.

'He finds the cookery detestable,' responded Porthos.

'Very well, but,' said d'Artagnan, 'why doesn't he do it himself as at Chantilly?'*

'Ah, Monsieur! I have no longer here as down there the ponds of Monsieur the Prince in which to catch those fine carp, and the forests of his Highness in which to snare fine partridges. As to the cellar, I have visited it in detail, and truly it is a small affair.'

'M. Mouston,' said d'Artagnan, 'truly I would sympathize with you, if I had not for the moment something much more pressing to do.'

Then, taking Porthos aside:

'My dear Vallon,' he continued, 'I see you are already dressed, and that is fortunate, for I am going to take you directly to the cardinal's.'

'Nonsense! are you?' said Porthos, opening his eyes with wonder.

'Yes, my friend.'

'A presentation?'

'Does that frighten you?'

'No, but it upsets me.'

'Oh, be at ease; you have not to do with the other cardinal, and this one will not confound you with his majesty.'

'I am indifferent to that; you understand, d'Artagnan, the court——'

'Ah, my friend! there is no longer any court.'

'The queen!'

'I was about saying there is no queen now. The queen?—do not be disquieted, we shall not see her.'

'And you say we are going at once to the Palais-Royal?'

'At once. Only, not to cause any delay, I will borrow one of your horses.'

'With pleasure. They are all four at your service.'

'Oh, I have only need of one for the present.'

'Shall we not take our valets with us?'

'Let us take Mousqueton; there is no harm in it. As for Planchet, he has reasons for not going to court.'

'Why so?'

'Alas! he is out of favour with his Eminence.'

'Mouston,' said Porthos, 'saddle Vulcan and Bayard.'

'And shall I take Rustaud?'

'No, take a showy horse—Phœbus or Superb; we are going on a ceremonious visit.'

'Ah!' said Mousqueton, drawing in his breath, 'it is then only a question of making a visit.'

'Oh, yes; nothing else. Only, to be ready, put the pistols in the holsters; you will find mine charged by my saddle.'

Mousqueton gave a sigh; he could scarcely understand such visits of ceremony as required going armed to the teeth.

'In fact,' said Porthos, looking complacently at his old lackey as he withdrew, 'you are right, d'Artagnan, Mouston will do. He makes a fine appearance.'

D'Artagnan smiled.

'And you,' said Porthos, 'are you not going to change your dress?'

'No; I go as I am.'

'But you are all covered with perspiration and dust, and your boots are very dirty.'

'All this will bear witness to my haste to show myself at the cardinal's orders.'

Mousqueton returned just then with the three horses. D'Artagnan sprang into the saddle as if he had taken rest for a week.

'Oh,' said he to Planchet, 'my long sword.'

'I,' said Porthos, showing a little parade sword with gilt guard—'I have my court sword.'

'Take your rapier, my friend.'

'And why?'

'I don't know; but take it always, believe me.'

'My rapier, Mouston,' said Porthos.

'But that is an implement of war, Monsieur,' said Mousqueton. 'Are we going on a campaign? If so, tell me at once, and
I will take my measures accordingly.'

'With us, Mouston, you know,' replied d'Artagnan, 'precautions are always proper. Either your memory is not good, or
you have forgotten that we are not in the habit of passing our
nights at balls and serenades.'

'Alas! it is true,' said Mousqueton, arming himself cap-a-
pie;* 'but I had forgotten it.'

They set off at a pretty rapid pace, and got to the cardinal's
palace about a quarter past seven. There was a crowd in the
streets, for it was Whitsunday, and they looked at these two
cavaliers with surprise—one looking fresh as from a bandbox,
and the other as dusty as if just from the field of battle.

Mousqueton also attracted the notice of the idlers, and as
the romance of 'Don Quixote'* was then in its popularity, some
said it was Sancho, who after having lost one master had found
two.

On reaching the antechamber, d'Artagnan found himself among acquaintances. It was his company of the Musketeers, then on guard. He called the usher and showed the
cardinal's letter, which ordered his return without the loss of
a moment. The usher bowed, and entered the cardinal's apartment.

D'Artagnan turned towards Porthos, and thought that he
seemed agitated and trembled a little. He smiled, and whispering in his ear, said:

'Courage, my good friend! believe me, the eye of the eagle
is closed, and we have to do only with a vulture. Hold yourself
stiffly as you did on the day of the St Gervais bastion, and do
not bow too low to this Italian; that would give him a poor
idea of you.'

'Very well,' replied Porthos.

The usher came back.

'Enter, gentlemen,' said he; 'his Eminence awaits you.'

In fact, Mazarin was seated in his cabinet, labouring to erase
as many names as possible from the lists of pensions and
livings. He saw by a side look the entrance of d'Artagnan and
Porthos, and although his eyes sparkled with joy at the

announcement of the usher, he did not seem to be in the least moved.

'Ah, it is you, Monsieur the Lieutenant,' said he; 'you have been expeditious. Quite right; you are welcome.'

'Thanks, Monseigneur. I am at the orders of your Eminence, and also M. du Vallon, one of my old friends—he who hid his nobility under the name of Porthos.'

Porthos bowed.

'A splendid cavalier,' said Mazarin.

Porthos turned his head right and left, and moved his shoulders with much dignity.

'The best sword in the kingdom, Monseigneur,' said d'Artagnan; 'and many know it who do not say so—and cannot say so.'

Porthos bowed to d'Artagnan.

Mazarin had almost as great a liking for fine soldiers as Frederick of Prussia* had later on. He admired the sinewy hands, the broad shoulders, and the steady eye of Porthos. He seemed to have before him the saviour of his ministry and the kingdom, shaped in flesh and bone. That recalled to his mind the fact that the old society of the musketeers consisted of four persons.

'And your other two friends?' asked Mazarin.

Porthos was about to speak, thinking it his turn to put in a word. D'Artagnan gave him a look.

'Our other friends are prevented at present, but they will rejoin us later on.'

Mazarin gave a slight cough.

'And Monsieur, freer than they are, will voluntarily take service?' asked Mazarin.

'Yes, Monseigneur; and that from pure devotedness, for M. de Bracieux is rich.'

'Rich?' said Mazarin, in whom this one word could always inspire great consideration.

'An income of fifty thousand livres,' said Porthos. It was the first word that he had said.

'From pure devotedness, then,' resumed Mazarin, with his cunning smile.

'Monseigneur does not perhaps believe in such a thing?' asked d'Artagnan.

'And you, Monsieur the Gascon?' said Mazarin, resting his two elbows on his desk and his chin in his hands.

'I,' said d'Artagnan, 'believe in devotedness as in a baptismal name, for instance, which should be naturally followed by a surname. Man is by disposition more or less devoted, it is true; but there must be always some object at the end of it.'

'And what, for example, would your friend desire at the end of his devotedness?'

'Well, Monseigneur, my friend has three fine estates—that of Vallon at Corbeil, that of Bracieux in the Soissonais, and that of Pierrefonds in Valois; now, Monseigneur, he would wish that one of his three estates should be created a barony.'

'Only that?' said Mazarin, his eyes sparkling with joy when he saw he could recompense Porthos's devotion without undoing his purse—'only that? the thing can be managed.'

'I shall be a baron?' said Porthos, taking a step forward.

'I told you so,' replied d'Artagnan, stopping him with his hand, 'and Monseigneur repeats it.'

'And you, M. d'Artagnan, what do you wish?'

'Monseigneur,' said d'Artagnan, 'it will be twenty years next September since M. le Cardinal Richelieu made me lieutenant.'*

'Yes, and you would wish Cardinal Mazarin to make you a captain.'

D'Artagnan bowed.

'Well, that is not at all impossible. We shall see, gentlemen, we shall see. Now, M. du Vallon,' said Mazarin, 'what service do you prefer—in the city, or in the country?'

Porthos opened his mouth to reply.

'Monseigneur,' said d'Artagnan, 'M. du Vallon is like myself. He prefers extraordinary service; that is, enterprises which are regarded as foolish and impossible.'

This gasconade by no means displeased Mazarin, who began to reflect.

'Yet I must confess that I have sent for you to give you a settled post. I have certain disquietudes—eh! what is that?' said Mazarin.

Indeed, a great noise was heard in the antechamber, and almost at the same time the door of the room was opened. A man covered with dust came suddenly in, crying out, 'Monsieur the Cardinal! where is he?'

Mazarin thought that they wanted to assassinate him, and retreated by pushing back his armchair. D'Artagnan and Porthos made a movement which placed them between the newcomer and the cardinal.

'Eh, Monsieur! said Mazarin, 'what is the matter, I pray, which makes you come here as if it were a market?'

'Monseigneur,' said the officer to whom this reproach was spoken, 'two words; I would wish to speak to you quickly and in private. I am M. de Poins, officer of the guard in Vincennes prison.'

The officer was so pale that Mazarin, certain that he brought some important news, asked d'Artagnan and Porthos to give place to the messenger. They went to a corner of the room.

'Speak quickly!' said Mazarin, 'what is it, then?'

'Monseigneur, M. de Beaufort has just made his escape from Vincennes.'

Mazarin uttered a cry, and became as pale as the messenger; he fell into his armchair quite astounded.

'Escaped?' said he. 'M. de Beaufort escaped?'

'Monseigneur, I saw him escape from the top of the terrace.'

'And you did not fire down at him?'

'He was out of range.'

'But what was M. de Chavigny doing then?'

'He was absent.'

'But La Ramée?'

'They found him garrotted in the prisoner's room, a gag in his mouth, and a poniard close to him.'

'But that man whom he took as helper?'

'He was an accomplice of the duke, and has escaped with him.'

Mazarin gave a groan.

'Monseigneur,' said d'Artagnan, approaching the cardinal.

'What?' said Mazarin.

'It seems to me that your Eminence is losing precious time.'

'How so?'

'If your Eminence ordered a pursuit, perhaps he might even yet be overtaken. France is large, and the nearest frontier is at sixty leagues' distance.'

'And who would pursue him?' exclaimed Mazarin.

'I, by Jove!'

'And you would arrest him?'

'Why not?'

'And you would arrest him, the Duc de Beaufort, armed, in the open country?'

'If Monseigneur ordered me to arrest the Devil, I would seize him by the horns and bring him to you.'

'So would I,' said Porthos.

'You too?' said Mazarin, looking with astonishment at the two men. 'But the duke would not surrender without a sanguinary combat.'

'Well,' said d'Artagnan, whose eyes began to flash, 'battle! it is a long time since we have fought, is it not, Porthos?'

'Battle!' said Porthos.

'And you believe you could take him?'

'Yes, if we are better mounted than he.'

'Then collect what guards there are here, and set off.'

'You order it, Monseigneur?'

'I sign it,' said Mazarin, taking a paper and writing some lines.

'Add, Monseigneur, that we can take any horses we meet with on the road.'

'Yes, yes,' said Mazarin; 'king's service! Take and be off!'

'Right, Monseigneur.'

'M. du Vallon, your barony is on the crupper of the duke's horse; the only thing is to seize him. As for you, my dear d'Artagnan, I do not promise you anything, but if you bring him back, alive or dead, you may ask for what you please.'

'To horse, Porthos!' said d'Artagnan, taking his friend's hand.

'Here I am,' replied Porthos, with his sublime coolness.

And they went down the grand staircase, taking with them the guards whom they met on the way, crying, 'To horse! to horse!' Ten men joined them.

D'Artagnan mounted Vulcan, and Porthos Bayard, while Mousqueton got astride Phoebus.

'Follow me!' cried d'Artagnan.

'*En route*,' said Porthos.

They drove their spurs into the flanks of their noble steeds, who dashed along the Rue St Honoré like a wild tempest.

'I say, Monsieur the Baron, I promised you some exercise; you see I have kept my word.'

'Yes, Captain,' replied Porthos.

They turned round. Mousqueton, sweating more than his horse, was at the regular distance in the rear. Behind him galloped the ten guards. The citizens, wondering, came out on the thresholds of their doors, and the frightened dogs followed, barking at the cavaliers. At the corner by the cemetery of St John,* d'Artagnan overturned a man, but this was too small an event to stop men in such a hurry. The galloping troop continued its way as if the horses had wings. Alas! there are no small events in this world, and we shall see that this nearly caused the downfall of the monarchy.

XXVII

THE KING'S HIGHWAY

THEY dashed along thus the whole length of the faubourg St Antoine towards Vincennes. They were soon out of the city, soon in the forest, and then in sight of the village. The horses seemed to become more and more excited at each step, and their nostrils began to redden like blazing furnaces. D'Artagnan, using his spurs freely, was quite two feet* in advance of Porthos. Mousqueton followed two lengths off, the guards at different distances according to the goodness of their horses.

From rising ground d'Artagnan saw a group of persons standing on the other side of the moat, fronting that part of the prison which overlooks St Maur.* He was sure the prisoner had escaped from that side, and that there he must obtain information. In five minutes he had reached that point, where the guards successively rejoined him.

The group of people were fully occupied; they were looking at the cord still hanging to the loop-hole, and broken off about twenty feet from the ground. Their eyes measured the height, and they exchanged many conjectures. On the top of the rampart were sentinels with a scared look going to and fro. A guard of soldiers, commanded by a sergeant, kept the people off the place where the duke had taken horse.

D'Artagnan spurred directly to the sergeant.

'Officer,' said the sergeant, 'you must not stop here.'

'That order is not for me,' said d'Artagnan. 'Have they pursued the fugitives?'

'Yes, officer; but unfortunately they are well mounted.'

'And how many are there?'

'Four all right, and a fifth carried off wounded.'

'Four!' said d'Artagnan, looking at Porthos. 'Do you hear, Baron? Only four of them!'

A glad smile lighted up Porthos's face.

'And how far in advance are they?'

'Two hours and a quarter, officer.'

'That's nothing; we are well mounted, are we not, Porthos?' Porthos sighed; he was thinking what awaited his poor horses.

'Very well,' said d'Artagnan; 'in what direction are they gone?'

'As to that, officer, I must not say.'

D'Artagnan drew a paper from his pocket.

'Order from the king,' said he.

'Speak to the governor, then.'

'And where is he?'

'In the country.'

Rage showed itself in d'Artagnan's face. He frowned; he was red to his temples.

'You rascal,' said he to the sergeant, 'I believe you are laughing at me. Listen!'

He unfolded the paper, presented it with one hand to the sergeant, and with the other took out a pistol and cocked it.

'Order from the king, I tell you. Read and reply, or I blow out your brains. Which road have they taken?'

The sergeant saw that d'Artagnan was in earnest.

'The road towards Vendômois,'* he replied.

'By what gate did they go out?'

'St Maur gate.'

'If you are deceiving me, you rogue, you shall be hanged tomorrow.'

'And if you catch up with them you will not return to have me hanged,' muttered the sergeant.

D'Artagnan shrugged his shoulders, made a sign to his escort, and spurred on.

'This way, this way!' cried d'Artagnan, directing his course towards the gate of the park indicated.

But now that the duke had escaped, the concierge had thought it proper to double-lock the gate. He had to be obliged to open it as the sergeant had been forced, and that caused a loss of ten minutes more. This last obstacle cleared, the troop resumed their course with the same speed. But the horses could not all keep up with the same ardour. Three came to a stand after an hour's running; one fell. D'Artagnan, who did not turn his head, did not observe it. Porthos told it to him in his quiet way.

'If only we two come up with them,' said d'Artagnan, 'it is all that is necessary, since there are only four of them.'

'That is true,' said Porthos, and he put spurs to his horse.

At the end of two hours the horses had gone twelve leagues without a halt; their legs began to tremble, and the foam sprinkled the doublets of the cavaliers, while the sweat penetrated their clothing.

'Let us rest a moment to let these poor creatures breathe,' said Porthos.

'On the contrary, let us kill them,' said d'Artagnan, 'and overtake the fugitives. I see fresh traces; they have passed here not more than a quarter of an hour ago.' In fact, the road was ploughed by horses' feet.

They saw these traces by the lingering rays of the sun. They set out afresh, but after two leagues Mousqueton's horse came down.

'Good!' said Porthos, 'there is Phoebus ruined!'

'The cardinal will pay you a thousand pistoles for him.'

'Oh,' said Porthos, 'I am above that.'

'Let us go on again at a gallop.'

'Yes, if we can.'

In fact, d'Artagnan's horse refused to go any farther; a last stroke of the spur, instead of making it go, caused it to fall.

'Ah, the deuce! There is Vulcan come to grief!'

'*Mordieu!*' cried d'Artagnan, tearing his hair, 'I am brought to a stand! Give me your horse, Porthos. Eh! but what the devil are you doing?'

'Ah, I am falling!' said Porthos, 'or rather it is Bayard.'

D'Artagnan wished to raise the horse, while Porthos drew himself out from his stirrups as well as he could, but he perceived that blood was pouring out from the animal's nostrils. 'And that makes three!' said he; 'now all is finished!'

At that moment they heard a neigh.

'*Chut!*' said d'Artagnan.

'What is the matter?'

'I can hear a horse.'

'It is one of our companions who has caught up with us.'

'No,' said d'Artagnan; 'it is in front.'

'Then that's another matter,' said Porthos, and he listened in the direction referred to by d'Artagnan.

'Monsieur,' said Mousqueton, who, after having left his horse on the road, had just come up to them on foot, 'Phoebus has been unable——'

'Silence!' said Porthos.

In fact, at that moment a second neigh was heard, brought by the night breeze.

'It is only five hundred paces from here, in front of us,' said d'Artagnan.

'In fact, Monsieur,' said Mousqueton, 'at that distance there is a hunting-lodge.'

'Mousqueton, your pistols.'

'I have them, Monsieur.'

'Take yours, Porthos.'

'I am holding them.'

'Well,' said d'Artagnan, seizing his, 'now you understand, Porthos.'

'Not too well.'

'We are riding on the king's service.'

'Well?'

'For the king's service we require these horses.'

'That's it,' said Porthos.

'Not a word. To work!'

All three advanced in the dark as silent as ghosts. At a turn in the road they saw a light shining among the trees.

'There's the house,' said d'Artagnan, in a whisper. 'Do as I do, Porthos.'

They glided from tree to tree, and got within twenty paces of the house without being seen. From there they saw, by means of a lantern hung up in a shed, four good-looking horses. A man was grooming them. Near them were the saddles and bridles. D'Artagnan drew near quickly, making a sign to his two companions to keep a few steps behind.

'I buy these horses,' said he to the groom.

The latter turned round astonished, but said nothing.

'Didn't you understand, stupid?' said d'Artagnan.

'Well enough,' said the latter.

'Why didn't you answer?'

'Because they are not for sale.'

'Then I take them,' said d'Artagnan, and he laid hold of the one within reach.

His two companions appeared just then, and did the same.

'But, Messieurs,' cried the lackey, 'they have just done a journey of six leagues, and it is scarcely a half-hour since they were unsaddled.'

'A half-hour of rest is enough,' said d'Artagnan, 'and they will only be better in wind.'

The groom called for help. A sort of steward came out just at the moment when d'Artagnan and his companions were saddling the horses. The steward talked very big.

'My dear friend,' d'Artagnan said, 'if you say another word I will blow out your brains;' and he showed him the barrel of his pistol, which he put immediately under his arm to continue his work.

'But, Monsieur,' said the steward, 'do you know that these horses belong to M. de Montbazon?'

'So much the better; they ought to be good ones.'

'Monsieur,' said the steward, retreating step by step in his endeavour to gain the door, 'I forewarn you that I am going to call my people.'

'And I mine,' said d'Artagnan. 'I am lieutenant in the king's Musketeers; I have ten troopers following me, and—stop, you can hear them galloping. We shall soon see them.'

They heard nothing, but the steward was afraid to listen.

'Are you ready, Porthos?' said d'Artagnan.

'I have finished.'

'And you, Mouston?'

'I too.'

'Then mount and set off.'

All three sprang into their saddles.

'Help!' said the steward; 'help! servants and guns!'

'Off!' said d'Artagnan; 'we shall get musket-shots for that;' and the three set off like the wind.

'Help!' bellowed the steward, while the groom ran towards the neighbouring building.

'Take care not to kill your horses!' cried d'Artagnan, bursting into laughter.

'Fire!' responded the steward.

A gleam like that of a lightning flash lighted up the road, then a bang; and the three travellers heard the balls whiz by, which were lost in the air.

'They shoot like lackeys,' said Porthos. 'They fired better than that in the time of M. de Richelieu. Do you recollect the route of Crèvecœur, Mousqueton?'

'Ah! Monsieur, my right buttock yet pains me.'

'Are you sure we are on the scent, d'Artagnan?' asked Porthos.

'Why, didn't you understand, then?'

'What?'

'That these horses are M. de Montbazon's.'

'Well?'

'Well, M. de Montbazon is the husband of Madame de Montbazon, and she is M. de Beaufort's mistress.'

'Ah! I see now,' said Porthos. 'She has placed the relays.'

'Exactly.'

'And we are chasing the duke with the horses he has just left behind?'

'My dear Porthos, you really possess a superior understanding,' said d'Artagnan, with a half-serious, half-jesting manner.

'Pooh, take me as I am.'

They went on for an hour; the horses were white with foam, and the blood dripped from them.

'Hi! what's that I saw then?' said d'Artagnan.

'You are very fortunate if you see anything on such a night,' said Porthos.

'Sparks.'

'So did I,' said Mousqueton; 'I saw them.'

'Ah, ah! have we caught up with them?'

'Good! a dead horse,' said d'Artagnan, bringing back his horse from a bolt he had just made; 'it seems that they also are at the end of their breath.'

'It seems we hear the sound of a troop of horsemen,' said Porthos, leaning over the horse's mane.

'Impossible.'

'They are many in number.'

'Then that's another matter.'

'Another horse,' said Porthos.

'Dead?'

'No, dying.'

'Saddled or unsaddled?'

'Saddled.'

'It is they, then.'

'Courage! we have them.'

'But if they are many in number,' said Mousqueton, 'it is not we who will take them, but they who will capture us.'

'Bah!' said d'Artagnan; 'they will believe us to be stronger than they because we are in pursuit; then they will be afraid, and separate.'

'That's certain,' said Porthos.

'Ah, do you see?' exclaimed d'Artagnan.

'Yes, more sparks; I saw them too this time,' said Porthos.

'Forward, forward!' said d'Artagnan, in a rough voice, 'and in five minutes we shall have fun;' and they were off again.

The horses, furious from pain and emulation, flew along the dark road, in the midst of which they began to perceive a more compact and darker mass than the rest of the horizon.

XXVIII

THE MEETING

They went on for ten minutes in this way. Suddenly two black patches detached themselves from the mass, advanced, grew larger, and as they grew larger, took the form of two cavaliers.

'Oh, oh!' said d'Artagnan, 'they are coming towards us.'

'So much the worse for those who come,' said Porthos.

'Who goes there?' said a hoarse voice.

The three horsemen in pursuit did not stop nor answer; they heard only the clatter of swords being drawn, and the click of pistols being cocked, by the two black phantoms.

'Bridle in mouth!' said d'Artagnan.

Porthos understood, and d'Artagnan and he each took a pistol in the left hand and cocked it.

'Who goes there?' someone called again. 'Not a step more, or you are dead!'

'Bah!' replied Porthos, almost choked by the dust, and chewing his bridle as his horse was champing his bit,—'bah! we have seen many others.'

At these words the two shadows barred the road, and one could see the glitter of the barrels of their lowered pistols.

'Back!' cried d'Artagnan, 'or you are the dead men.'

Two shots replied to this threat, but the two assailants came on with such rapidity that they were at the same moment upon their adversaries. A third pistol-shot was heard, fired by d'Artagnan, and an enemy fell. As for Porthos, he struck his enemy with such force that though his sword was turned aside, he sent him rolling ten paces from his horse.

'Finish, Mousqueton!' said Porthos, and he dashed forward to his friend's side, who had already resumed the pursuit.

'Well?' said Porthos.

'I shattered his head,' said d'Artagnan, 'and you?'

'I overthrew him only—but, hold—'

A carbine-shot was heard; it was Mousqueton, who in passing executed the order of his master.

'Come, come!' said d'Artagnan; 'that goes well, and we have the first trick!'

'Ah, ah!' said Porthos, 'here are some other players.'

Two other cavaliers appeared, detached from the principal group, and rapidly advanced to bar the route afresh. This time d'Artagnan did not even wait to be spoken to.

'Give way!' he cried first; 'give way!'

'What do you want?' said the voice.

'The duke,' bawled out Porthos and d'Artagnan at once.

A burst of laughter was the response, but it ended in a groan; d'Artagnan had pierced the laugher through with his sword. At the same time two reports seemed to be one shot—Porthos and his adversary had fired at each other.

D'Artagnan turned, and saw Porthos near him.

'Bravo! Porthos,' said he, 'you have killed him, it seems to me.'

'I think that I have only wounded the horse,' said Porthos.

'What do you wish, dear friend? One does not hit the centre every time, and there is no ground for complaint if one comes within the circle. *Hé! parbleu!* what's the matter with my horse?'

'Your horse seems to be distressed,' said Porthos, pulling up.

In fact, d'Artagnan's horse stumbled and fell on his knees; then the death-rattle was heard, and he lay dead. He had received in his chest the ball of d'Artagnan's first adversary.

D'Artagnan uttered a terrible oath.

'Does Monsieur wish for a horse?' said Mousqueton.

'*Pardieu!* do I wish for one!' cried d'Artagnan.

'Here is one,' said Mousqueton.

'How the devil come you to have two led horses?'

'Their masters are dead; I thought they might be useful, and took them.'

During this time Porthos had reloaded.

'Look out!' said d'Artagnan; 'here are two more.'

'Oh, yes, indeed! they will keep on till tomorrow,' said Porthos.

In fact, two other horsemen rapidly advanced.

'Eh, Monsieur!' said Mousqueton, 'the one whom you overturned has got up.'

'Why have you not treated him as you did the other?'

'I was holding the horses, Monsieur.'

A shot was heard; Mousqueton uttered a cry.

'Ah, Monsieur!' cried he, 'in the other! just in the other! This shot will be the match for the one on the route to Amiens.'*

Porthos turned round like a lion, and rushed upon the dismounted cavalier, who tried to draw his sword; but before he was able, Porthos had struck him such a terrible blow on the head that he fell like an ox under the butcher's axe.

Mousqueton, with a groan, threw himself down upon his horse's withers, the wound he had received preventing him from sitting up in the saddle.

When d'Artagnan saw the horsemen, he had stopped and reloaded; his fresh horse had, besides, a carbine at the saddle-bow.

'I am ready,' said Porthos; 'shall we wait, or charge them?'

'Let us charge them.'

'Let us charge,' said Porthos.

They drove their spurs into their horses' sides. The cavaliers were only about twenty paces off.

'For the king!' cried d'Artagnan; 'let us pass.'

'The king has no business here,' replied a deep, wiry voice which seemed to come from a thick cloud, for the cavalier was enveloped in a whirlwind of dust.

'Well, we shall see if the king does not go everywhere,' replied d'Artagnan.

'See!' said the same voice.

There were two shots almost at the same moment—one fired by d'Artagnan, the other by Porthos's opponent. D'Artagnan's ball carried away his enemy's hat; the ball of Porthos's adversary hit his horse in the neck, which at once dropped with a groan.

'For the last time, where are you going?' said the same voice.

'To the devil!' replied d'Artagnan.

'Good! you will soon get there.'

D'Artagnan saw the barrel of a musket levelled at him. He had no time to fumble in his holsters, but he thought of a counsel which Athos had formerly given him: he made his horse rear. The ball struck the animal full in the stomach;

d'Artagnan felt his horse failing under him, and with his marvellous agility he threw himself on one side.

'Why, now,' said the same wiry and mocking voice, 'this is a butchery of horses, and not a combat of men that we are carrying on. To the sword, Monsieur! to the sword!' and he leaped off his horse.

'Be it then to the sword,' said d'Artagnan; 'that suits me.'

In two bounds d'Artagnan was facing his adversary, whose sword he felt on his. D'Artagnan, with his usual skill, had used his favourite guard—his sword in *tierce*.*⁻

During this time Porthos, holding a pistol in each hand, knelt behind his horse, which was kicking in convulsions of agony. However, the fight had begun between d'Artagnan and his adversary. The former had attacked him roughly, as was his custom; but this time he met with a play of wrist which made him reflect. Twice recalled in *quarte*, d'Artagnan made a step back; his adversary did not stir. D'Artagnan advanced and engaged afresh in tierce. Several strokes passed on both sides without result, the sparks flying in clusters from their swords. At last d'Artagnan thought it time to use his favourite feint; he executed it with the rapidity of lightning, and brought down the stroke with a force which he thought invincible. The stroke was parried.

'*Mordioux*,' he cried with a strong Gascon accent.

At this exclamation his adversary sprang back, and bending down his uncovered head by an effort, just made out through the gloom d'Artagnan's face. As for d'Artagnan, fearing a feint, he kept on the defensive.

'Take care,' said Porthos to his adversary, 'I have still my two pistols loaded.'

'Greater reason then for you to fire first,' replied the latter.

Porthos fired; a flash lighted up the scene of the fight. At this gleam the two combatants uttered a cry.

'Athos!' said d'Artagnan.

'D'Artagnan!' said Athos.

Athos raised his sword; d'Artagnan lowered his.

'Aramis,' cried Athos, 'don't fire.'

'Ah, ah! it is you, Aramis?' said Porthos, and he threw down his pistol.

Aramis put his back into the holster, and sheathed his sword.

'My son,' said Athos, extending his hand to d'Artagnan. It was the name that he gave him formerly in his moments of affection.

'Athos,' said d'Artagnan, wringing his hands, 'so you are defending him? And I have sworn to take him dead or alive! Ah, I am dishonoured.'

'Slay me,' said Athos, uncovering his chest, 'if your honour needs my death.'

'Oh, what a misfortune!' cried d'Artagnan. 'There is only one man in the world who could stop me, and fatality puts this man in my way! Ah, what shall I tell the cardinal?'

'You will tell him, Monsieur,' replied a voice which ruled the battlefield, 'that he has sent against me the only two men who could beat four, who could fight without disadvantage against Comte de la Fère and Chevalier d'Herblay, and yield only to fifty men.'

'The prince!' said Athos and Aramis together, bringing the Duc de Beaufort into view, while d'Artagnan and Porthos took a step backwards.

'Fifty cavaliers!' muttered d'Artagnan and Porthos.

'Look around you, Messieurs, if you doubt it,' said the duke.

D'Artagnan and Porthos looked around them; they were in fact entirely surrounded by a troop of horsemen.

'By the din of your fighting,' said the duke, 'I thought there were twenty men, and I have returned with all my escort, tired of flight, and wishing to do a little sword practice in my turn; but there are only two of you.'

'Yes, Monseigneur,' said Athos, 'but, you have said it, two who are worth twenty.'

'Come, Messieurs, your swords,' said the duke.

'Our swords!' said d'Artagnan, raising his head and coming to himself—'our swords, never!'

'Never!' said Porthos.

Some of the men made a movement.

'A moment, Monseigneur,' said Athos; 'two words.' And he approached the prince, who bent towards him, and to whom he whispered a few words.

'As you please, Count,' said the prince, 'I am too much indebted to you to refuse your first request. Extend your ranks, gentlemen,' said he to his escort. 'MM. d'Artagnan and du Vallon, you are free.'

The order was at once obeyed; and d'Artagnan and Porthos found themselves the centre of a large circle.

'Now, d'Herblay,' said Athos, 'dismount and come here.'

Aramis did so, and approached Porthos, while Athos came near to d'Artagnan. The four then were reunited.

'Friends,' said Athos, 'do you regret still not having shed our blood?'

'No,' said d'Artagnan; 'I regret that we should be opposed to one another, who have been always so united. Ah! we shall succeed in nothing any more.'

'Oh, yes, all is finished!' said Porthos.

'Well, then, be of our party,' said Aramis.

'Silence, d'Herblay!' said Athos, 'don't make such propositions to them. If they are of Mazarin's party, it is from conscientious motives, as we were impelled in the same way to the side of the princes.'

'Meanwhile, we are enemies,' said Porthos; 'by Jove, who would have thought it?'

D'Artagnan said nothing, but uttered a sigh.

'Gentlemen,' said Athos, who took their hands in his, 'this is a grave matter, and my heart suffers as if you had pierced it through and through. Yes, we are separated—that is the great, the sad truth; but we have not yet declared open hostility. Perhaps we can come to an understanding, and for that a conference is indispensable.'

'For my part I beseech it,' said Aramis.

'I accept,' said d'Artagnan, haughtily.

Porthos nodded by way of assent.

'Let us then name a rendezvous,' continued Athos, 'within the reach of all of us, and in a last interview let us regulate definitely our reciprocal position and the conduct we ought to observe the one side towards the other.'

'Good,' said the three others.

'You are then of my opinion?' asked Athos.

'Entirely.'

'Well, what place?'

'Does the Place Royale suit you all?' asked d'Artagnan.

'At Paris?'

'Yes.'

Athos and Aramis looked at each other; Aramis made an affirmative sign with his head.

'Let it be the Place Royale!' said Athos.

'And when?'

'Tomorrow evening, if you all agree.'

'Shall you be returned?'

'Yes.'

'At what hour?'

'At ten at night. Does that hour suit?'

'Very well indeed.'

'Then,' said Athos, 'peace or war will be settled; but our honour, friends, will at least be safe.'

'Alas!' muttered d'Artagnan, 'our honour as soldiers is lost.'

'D'Artagnan,' said Athos, gravely, 'I swear that you do me wrong to think of this, when I only think of one thing—that we have crossed swords one against the other. Yes,' continued he, shaking his head sadly—'yes, you have said it; misfortune is upon us. Come, Aramis.'

'Let us return, Porthos, and carry our shame to the cardinal,' said d'Artagnan.

'And tell him especially,' exclaimed a voice which d'Artagnan recognized as Rochefort's, 'that I am not too old to be a man of action.'

'Can I be of any use to you, Messieurs?' said the prince.

'Bear witness, Monseigneur, that we have done what lay in our power.'

'Don't be distressed about that, it shall be done. Adieu, Messieurs. In a little time we shall see one another, I hope, under the walls of Paris, and even in Paris perhaps, and then you will be able to take your revenge.'

At these words the duke waved his hand, put his horse to a gallop, and followed by his escort, was soon out of sight.

D'Artagnan and Porthos were left alone on the high-road with a man holding two horses. They thought it was Mousqueton, and approached him.

'Whom do I see?' cried d'Artagnan; 'why it's you, Grimaud.'

'Grimaud!' said Porthos.

Grimaud showed that they had not made a mistake.

'Who gives us these horses?' asked Porthos.

'M. le Comte de la Fère.'

'Athos, Athos!' murmured d'Artagnan, 'you think of every-thing; you are a true gentleman.'

'Just in time!' said Porthos. 'I was afraid I should be obliged to do the march on foot;' and he mounted. D'Artagnan had already done so.

'Where are you going, Grimaud?' asked d'Artagnan. 'Are you leaving your master?'

'Yes,' said Grimaud; 'I am going to accompany the Vicomte de Bragelonne to the army of Flanders.'

They went a short distance in silence on the return to Paris, when suddenly they heard some groans which seemed to come from a ditch.

'What is that?' asked d'Artagnan.

'That,' said Porthos, 'is Mousqueton.'

'Eh, yes, Monsieur, it is I,' while a sort of shadow was getting up on to the road.

Porthos ran to his servant, to whom he was really attached.

'Are you seriously wounded, my dear Mouston?' said he.

'Mouston!' said Grimaud, opening his eyes, surprised.

'No, Monsieur; but in a troublesome manner.'

'Then you cannot ride on horseback?'

'Ah, Monsieur, what do you propose to me?'

'Can you go on foot?'

'I will try to go as far as the first house.'

'What are we to do?' said d'Artagnan. 'We must nevertheless return to Paris.'

'I will take charge of Mousqueton,' said Grimaud.

'Thanks, good Grimaud!' said Porthos.

Grimaud dismounted, and went to give his arm to his old friend, who received him with tears in his eyes, though Gri-maud could not positively know whether the tears came from the pleasure of seeing him again or from the pain caused by his wound.

D'Artagnan and Porthos then continued in silence their return to Paris.

Three hours after they were passed by a sort of courier all covered with dust; he had been sent by the duke with a letter to the cardinal, in which, as the prince had promised, he bore witness to the deeds of Porthos and d'Artagnan, announced his own liberty, and that he was going to wage mortal war with him.

The cardinal read it two or three times, then folding it up, and putting it into his pocket, 'What comforts me,' said he, 'since d'Artagnan has failed, is that while pursuing the duke he has crushed Broussel. This Gascon is decidedly a valuable fellow, whose mistakes even serve me.'

The cardinal alluded to the man whom d'Artagnan had knocked down at the corner of St John's cemetery, and who was no other than Councillor Broussel.

XXIX

FOUR OLD FRIENDS PREPARING FOR A CONFERENCE

'WELL,' said Porthos, seated in the courtyard of the Hôtel de la Chevrette, to d'Artagnan, who with sullen face was returning from the Palais-Cardinal—'well, he has received you badly, d'Artagnan?'

'Upon my honour, yes; he is certainly an ugly beast! What are you taking now, Porthos?'

'Why, you see I am soaking a biscuit in a glass of Spanish wine. Do the same.'

'You are right. Gimblou, a glass.'

The waiter apostrophized by this sweet name brought the glass, and d'Artagnan sat down by his friend.

'How did you get on?'

'Oh, you understand, there are not two ways of telling the affair. I entered; he looked up at me. I shrugged my shoulders, and said, "Ah, Monseigneur, we have not been the stronger."

' "Yes, I know all that," replied the cardinal; "but tell me the details."

'You see, Porthos, I could not do so without naming my friends, and that was to ruin them.'

'Alas, yes,' said Porthos.

' "Monseigneur," I said, "there were fifty of them against two."

' "Yes; but that did not prevent some pistol-shots from being exchanged," he replied.

' "The fact is that on one side or the other there were a few charges of powder burned."

' "And the swords saw the day?" he added.

' "That is to say, the night, Monseigneur," I replied.

' "Ah, so!" continued the cardinal; "I believed you to be Gascon, my dear fellow."

' "I am only Gascon when I succeed, Monseigneur." The reply pleased him, for he began to laugh.

' "That teaches me," he said, "to give better horses to my guards; for if they had been able to keep up with you, you might have kept your word, and brought him to me dead or alive." '

'Come, now; but that does not seem badly said,' replied Porthos.

'Hey! but it was the manner in which it was spoken. It is wonderful,' interposed d'Artagnan, 'how these biscuits hold the wine; they are like sponges. Gimblou, another bottle.'

The bottle was brought with a promptitude which showed the degree of consideration enjoyed by d'Artagnan in the establishment. He continued:

'I was about retiring when he called me back.

' "You have had three horses killed?" he asked me. "How much were they worth?" '

'Now,' said Porthos, 'that was a pretty good move, it seems to me.'

' "A thousand pistoles," I replied.'

'A thousand pistoles!' said Porthos; 'oh, oh! that's a good deal. If he understands horses, he should have hesitated.'

'Upon honour, he had a good desire to do so, the coward,— for he gave a terrible start, and looked at me. I looked at him also; then he understood, and putting his hand into a drawer, he took out notes on the Lyons bank.'

'For a thousand pistoles?'

'For a thousand pistoles! the exact amount, the stingy fellow, not one more.'

'And you have them with you?'

'Here they are.'

'Upon honour, I think that is acting generously,' said Porthos.

'Generously! towards those who have not only risked their lives, but have done him a great service!'

'A great service! what?' asked Porthos.

'Well, it seems that I have crushed a councillor of parliament.'

'What, that little dark man whom you upset near the cemetery?'

'Exactly, my dear fellow. He embarrassed the cardinal. Unfortunately I did not crush him flat. It seems he will recover, and then embarrass him again.'

'There!' said Porthos, 'and I turned my horse aside when he would have struck him squarely! that will be for another time.'

'He should have paid me for the councillor, the pedant!'

'*Dame!*' said Porthos, 'if he was not entirely crushed——'

'Ah, M. de Richelieu would have said, "Five hundred crowns for the councillor." However, we will not talk any more about it. How much did your horses cost you, Porthos?'

'Ah, if Mousqueton were here, he would tell you to the very farthing.'

'Never mind; say within ten crowns or so.'

'Well, Vulcan and Bayard cost me each nearly two hundred pistoles; and in putting Phoebus at a hundred and fifty I think we should be near the mark.'

'Then there remain four hundred and fifty pistoles,' said d'Artagnan, satisfied.

'Yes,' said Porthos; 'but there is the harness.'

'Say a hundred pistoles for the three,' said d'Artagnan. 'There are three hundred and fifty pistoles left.'

Porthos nodded assent.

'Let us give fifty pistoles to the hostess for our expenses,' said d'Artagnan, 'and divide the remaining three hundred. It is a paltry matter,' muttered d'Artagnan, putting up his bills.

'Yes!' said Porthos, 'of course it is. But say then?'

'What?'

'Hasn't he in any fashion spoken of me?'

'Ah, yes,' exclaimed d'Artagnan, who feared to discourage his friend by telling him the cardinal had not breathed a word about him. 'He said—I am trying to recall the exact words—"As for your friend, tell him he may sleep on his two ears." '

'Good,' said Porthos; 'that means as clear as the day that he fully intends making me a baron.'

The neighbouring church clock struck nine just then. D'Artagnan started.

'Ah, it is true,' said Porthos, 'nine has struck; and at ten we have to meet at the Place Royale.'

'Ah, stay, Porthos, be silent!' cried d'Artagnan, impatiently; 'do not recall that. That is what has made me so sullen since yesterday. I shall not go.'

'And why?' asked Porthos.

'Because it is to me a sad matter to see those men again who caused the failure of our enterprise.'

'Nevertheless,' replied Porthos, 'neither the one nor the other had the advantage. I had still a loaded pistol, and you were facing each other, sword in hand.'

'Yes,' said d'Artagnan; 'but if this rendezvous conceals something——'

'Oh!' said Porthos, 'you surely do not believe it, d'Artagnan!'

It is true. D'Artagnan did not believe Athos capable of employing a ruse, but he sought a pretext for not going to this meeting.

'We must go,' said the lord of Bracieux, 'or they would believe we were afraid of them. Come, my friend, we have boldly faced fifty enemies on the king's highway; we surely can face two friends on the Place Royale.'

'Yes, yes,' said d'Artagnan, 'I know it; but they have taken the prince's side without telling us beforehand. Athos and Aramis have played a game with me which alarms me. We found out the truth yesterday. What is the good of going to learn something else today?'

'Do you really mistrust them?' said Porthos.

'Aramis, yes; since he has become an abbé. You cannot picture to yourself, my dear fellow, what he has become. He sees us on the road which should lead up to a bishopric, and he would not perhaps be sorry to push us aside.'

'Ah! as for Aramis, that's another thing,' said Porthos; 'and that would not astonish me.'

'M. de Beaufort may try and have us captured in his turn.'

'Rubbish! since he had us in his power and let us go. Besides, let us be on our guard; let us take our arms and Planchet with his carbine.'

'Planchet is a Frondeur,' said d'Artagnan.

'To the devil with civil wars!' said Porthos; 'one can neither trust one's friends nor one's servants. Ah, if poor Mousqueton were here! There's one who will never leave me.'

'Yes, so long as you are rich. Ah, my friend, it is not civil wars which disunite us; it is that we are all twenty years older. The loyal outbursts of youth have gone, and given place to the din of interests, the breath of ambition, and the counsels of egotism. Yes, you are right; let us go, then, but well armed. If we don't go, they will say that we are afraid. Holloa! Planchet,' said d'Artagnan.

Planchet appeared.

'Saddle the horses, and take your carbine.'

'But, Monsieur, whom are we going to encounter today?'

'No one,' said d'Artagnan; 'it is a simple measure of precaution, in case we should be attacked.'

'Do you know, Monsieur, that they have tried to kill the good Councillor Broussel—the father of the people?'

'Ah! really?' said d'Artagnan.

'Yes, but he has been well revenged; for the people carried him in their arms to his house. Ever since yesterday his house has not been free of visitors. The Coadjutor, M. de Longueville, and the Prince de Conti have visited him. Madame de Chevreuse and Madame de Vendôme left their names at his house, and when he shall be willing——'

'Ah, yes! when he is willing.'

Planchet began to hum—

'A breeze from the Fronde
Blew today;

I think that it blows
Against Mazarin.'

'It no longer astonishes me,' said d'Artagnan, in a whisper
to Porthos, 'that Mazarin would have much preferred to have
me altogether crush his councillor.'

'You understand then, Monsieur,' replied Planchet, 'that if
it was for some enterprise like that which they plotted against
M. Broussel that you asked me to take my carbine——'

'No, be easy; but from whom do you have all these details?'

'Oh, from a good source, Monsieur; from Friquet.'

'From Friquet?' said d'Artagnan; 'I know that name.'

'It is the son of M. Broussel's servant, a fellow who, I can
answer for it, in a street row would not give his share to the
dogs.'

'Is he not choir-boy at Notre-Dame?'

'Yes, he is; Bazin is his patron.'

'Ah! ah! I know,' said d'Artagnan. 'And waiter in the little
tavern of the Rue de la Calandre?'

'Exactly.'

'What will you do with this brat?' said Porthos.

'Hey!' said d'Artagnan, 'he has already given me good
information, and on occasion he could give me more.'

'To you who just failed in crushing his master?'

'And who will tell him of it?'

'That's true.'

At this very time Athos and Aramis were entering Paris by
the Faubourg St Antoine. They had rested on the road, and
were hastening so as not to fail of being at the rendezvous.
Bazin alone followed them. Grimaud, we recollect, had remained to take care of Mousqueton, and was directly to join
the Vicomte de Bragelonne.

'Now,' said Athos, 'we must go into some inn to put on
citizens' dress, leave our pistols and rapiers, and disarm our
servants.'

'Oh, by no means, dear count; in this you will allow me not
only to differ from your opinion, but even to try and bring
you to mine.'

'And why so?'

'Because we are going to a rendezvous of a warlike kind.'

'What do you mean, Aramis?'

'That the Place Royale is the sequel to the scene on the road to Vendômois, and nothing else.'

'What! our friends——'

'Have become our most dangerous enemies, Athos. Believe me, we must distrust them, and especially you.'

'Oh! my dear d'Herblay!'

'How do you know that d'Artagnan has not thrown his defeat upon our shoulders, and has not apprised the cardinal; and how do you know that the cardinal will not profit by this rendezvous to cause us to be seized?'

'What? Do you think, Aramis, that d'Artagnan and Porthos would lend their hands to such an infamous deed?'

'Between friends, you are right, it would be such; but between enemies it would be a ruse.'

Athos crossed his arms, and let his head droop on his chest.

'What do you expect, Athos?' said Aramis. 'Men are so constituted, and are not always twenty years old. We have cruelly wounded, as you well know, d'Artagnan's self-esteem. He has been vanquished. Did you not hear his despair on the road. As for Porthos, his barony perhaps depended on the success of this affair. Well! he has met us on his road, and will not be baron this time. Who knows that this famous barony does not hang upon our interview of this evening? Let us take precautions, Athos.'

'But if they come without arms—what shame for us, Aramis!'

'Oh, be easy, my dear fellow, I engage that it will not be so. Besides, we have an excuse; we come from a journey, and we are rebels!'

'An excuse for us! It is necessary to foresee the case in which we shall have need of an excuse with d'Artagnan and with Porthos! Oh, Aramis, upon my soul you make me feel very unhappy! You are disenchanting a heart not quite dead to friendship. I would almost prefer, I swear to you, that my heart should be plucked from my breast. You may go there as you please, Aramis; I shall go unarmed.'

'By no means, for I will not let you go so. Not only a man, nor only Athos, nor even the Comte de la Fère, is it whom

you are injuring by this weakness, but a whole party to which
you belong, and which reckons upon you.'

'Let it be, then, as you say,' Athos replied sadly, and they
continued their journey in silence.

Scarcely had they reached by the Rue Pas de la Mule* the
gates of the solitary Place than they saw under the arcade at
the entrance of the Rue St Catharine three horsemen. In front
rode d'Artagnan and Porthos, at a walking pace, enveloped in
their cloaks, which their swords lifted up. Behind them came
Planchet, with his musket at his side.

Athos and Aramis dismounted on perceiving d'Artagnan and
Porthos. The latter did so also. D'Artagnan observed that the
three horses, instead of being held by Bazin, were fastened to
the rings of the arcades. He ordered Planchet to do as Bazin
did. Then the pairs approached, followed by the grooms, and
politely bowed.

'Where shall we have our talk, Messieurs?' said Athos, who
saw several persons stop and look at them, as if the matter
were one of those famous duels still living in the memory
of the Parisians, and especially of those living on the Place
Royale.

'The gate is shut,' said Aramis; 'but if these gentlemen like
the fresh air under the trees, and an inviolable solitude, I can
get the key at the Hôtel de Rohan,* and we shall be all right.'

D'Artagnan turned his eyes into the obscurity of the Place,
and Porthos thrust his head between two bars to test the
darkness.

'If you prefer another place, Messieurs,' said Athos, with his
noble and persuasive voice, 'choose for yourselves.'

'This place, if M. d'Herblay can get the key, will be, I
believe, the best possible.'

Aramis went off immediately, warning Athos not to remain
thus alone within reach of d'Artagnan and of Porthos; but he
to whom he gave this counsel only smiled disdainfully, and
made a step towards his old friends, who both remained in
their places.

Aramis went and knocked at the Hôtel de Rohan. A man
soon appeared with a key, who said, 'You swear it, Monsieur?'

'Take it,' said Aramis, giving him a louis.

'Ah, you do not wish to swear, my gentleman!' said the concierge, shaking his head.

'I can swear to nothing. I assure you only that at this moment these gentlemen are our friends.'

'Yes, certainly,' said Athos, d'Artagnan, and Porthos, coldly.

D'Artagnan overheard the colloquy, and understood it.

'You see?' said he to Porthos.

'What is it that I see?'

'That he has not wished to swear.'

'To swear what?'

'This man wished that Aramis should swear to him that we were not going into the Place Royale to fight.'

'And Aramis was not willing to swear?'

'No.'

'Attention, then.'

Athos did not lose sight of the two talkers.

Aramis opened the gate, and stepped back to permit d'Artagnan and Porthos to enter. While entering, d'Artagnan caught the hilt of his sword in the gate, and was obliged to push aside his cloak. In doing so he exposed the glittering butt-end of his pistols, on which the moon's rays were reflected.

'Do you see?' said Aramis, touching Athos's shoulder, and pointing to the weapons d'Artagnan had at his belt.

'Alas, yes!' said Athos, with a deep sigh.

Aramis entered last, and closed the gate. The two servants stayed outside, but as if they also felt mutual distrust, they kept apart.

XXX

THE PLACE ROYALE

THEY walked on silently to the centre of the Place; but as at that moment the moon came from behind a cloud, and as they thought that at this exposed part they could easily be seen, they reached the lime trees, where the shade was thicker.

Some seats were at different points. The four stopped before one of them. Athos asked d'Artagnan and Porthos to be seated.

Athos and Aramis remained standing before them. After a moment's silence, in which they felt embarrassed to know how to begin their explanation—

'Messieurs,' said Athos, 'a proof of the strength of our old friendship lies in our very presence at this rendezvous; not one is absent, not one has any reproaches to make to himself.'

'Listen, Monsieur the Count,' said d'Artagnan; 'instead of making us compliments which perhaps none of us deserve, let us explain matters like right-minded men.'

'I ask nothing better,' replied Athos; 'I am frank. Speak with all frankness. Have you anything to reproach the Abbé d'Herblay or myself with?'

'Yes,' said d'Artagnan; 'when I visited you at the Château de Bragelonne, I made you some propositions which you clearly understood, and instead of replying to me as to an old friend, you replied as to a child, and our friendship, of which you boast, was not broken yesterday by crossing swords, but by your dissimulation.'

'D'Artagnan!' said Athos, in a tone of mild reproach.

'You have asked me to be frank, and I am so; you ask what I think, and I tell you. And now I have the same reproach for you, M. l'Abbé d'Herblay. I did the same in your case, and you took advantage of me.'

'Really, Monsieur, you are very odd,' said Aramis. 'You came to me to make certain propositions, but did you make them to me? No; you simply sounded me, that is all. And what did I say? That Mazarin is a vulgar pedant, and that I would not serve him. That was all. Did I tell you I would not serve another? On the contrary I gave you to understand, it seems to me, that I was for the princes. We have even, if I am not mistaken, jested very agreeably on the very probable case that you should receive from the cardinal the mission of arresting me. Are you a party man? Yes, without doubt. Well, why should not we also be party men? You have your secret as we have ours. We have not interchanged them. So much the better. That proves that we know how to keep our secrets.'

'I do not reproach you at all, Monsieur,' said d'Artagnan; 'it is only because the Comte de la Fère has spoken of friendship that I examine your conduct.'

'And what do you find in it?' asked Aramis, haughtily.

The blood immediately mounted to d'Artagnan's cheeks; he rose and replied, 'I find it truly befitting a pupil of the Jesuits.'

On seeing d'Artagnan get up, Porthos got up too. The four men found themselves facing one another in a threatening manner.

At d'Artagnan's reply Aramis made a movement as if to put his hand to his sword. Athos stopped him.

'D'Artagnan,' said he, 'you come here this evening quite furious over our adventure of yesterday. I believe you to be large-hearted enough to permit a twenty years' friendship to overcome the wounded self-love of a quarter of an hour. Come now, tell me this. Do you believe really that you have anything to reproach me with? If I am in fault, d'Artagnan, I will confess it.'

Athos's serious, tuneful voice had still its old influence on d'Artagnan, while that of Aramis, which became sharp and scolding in his moments of bad humour, irritated him. So he said to Athos—

'I believe, Monsieur, that you had a disclosure to make to me at your château, and that Monsieur,' referring to Aramis, 'had one to make also in his convent. I had not then engaged in an adventure where you needed to bar my way; yet, because I have been discreet, there is no need quite to take me for a fool. If I had wished to dive into the difference between people whom M. d'Herblay receives by a rope ladder and those received by wooden steps, I should have forced him to talk with me.'

'With what are you intermeddling?' cried Aramis, pale with anger at the suspicion which entered his mind that he had been seen by d'Artagnan with Madame de Longueville.

'I intermeddle with what concerns me, and I know how to appear not to have seen what does not concern me; but I hate hypocrites, and in that class I put musketeers who play abbés, and vice versa, and,' added he, turning to Porthos, 'this gentleman is of my own opinion.'

Porthos, who had not yet spoken, only answered by a word and a gesture. He said Yes, and took his sword in his hand.

Aramis made a bound backwards and drew his. D'Artagnan bent forwards, ready to attack or defend.

Then Athos stretched out his hand with a movement of lofty command which belonged to him specially, gently took both sword and sheath together, broke both into two parts over his knee, and threw the pieces away. Then turning towards Aramis, 'Aramis,' said he, 'break your sword.' Aramis hesitated. 'You must,' said Athos; then in a lower and sweeter voice, 'I wish it done.'

Aramis, paler than ever, but subdued by this expressed wish, broke the blade, then crossed his arms, and waited, trembling with rage. This movement made d'Artagnan and Porthos step back. D'Artagnan did not draw; Porthos replaced his sword in its sheath.

'Never,' said Athos, slowly raising his right hand towards heaven—'never, I swear before God, who sees and hears us in the solemnity of this night, shall my sword touch yours; never shall my eye have for you a look of anger; never shall my heart have a pulsation of hatred. We have lived together, hated and loved together, have spilt our blood, and perhaps, I will add also, there is between us a tie more powerful than that of friendship—the compact of crime; for we four have condemned, judged, and executed a human being* whom we had not perhaps the right of sending out of the world, although she seemed to belong to hell rather than this world. D'Artagnan, I have always loved you as my son. Porthos, we have slept ten years side by side; Aramis is your brother as he is mine—for Aramis has loved you as I love you still, as I shall love you always. What can Cardinal Mazarin be for us who have forced both the hand and heart of a man like Richelieu? What is such and such a prince for us, who have established the crown upon the head of a queen? D'Artagnan, I ask your pardon for having yesterday crossed swords with you; Aramis does the same as regards Porthos. And now, hate me if you please, but I swear that in spite of hate I shall have nothing but friendship for you. Now repeat my words, Aramis; and then, if they wish it, and you wish it, let us leave our old friends for ever.'

There was a moment of solemn silence which was broken by Aramis.

'I swear,' said he, with calm brow and loyal look, but with a voice still trembling with emotion, 'that I have no longer any hate against those who were my friends. I regret having touched your sword, Porthos; I swear, in short, not only that mine shall not be directed against your breast, but also that in my most secret thoughts there shall not in the future be any appearance of hostile feelings towards you. Come, Athos.'

Athos was on the point of retiring.

'Oh, no, don't go away,' cried d'Artagnan, carried away by an irresistible impulse which revealed the heat of his blood, and the natural integrity of his soul; 'I have an oath to take. I swear that I would shed even the last drop of my blood and give the last fragment of my flesh to keep the esteem of a man like you, Athos, and the friendship of a man like you, Aramis,' and he threw himself into Athos's arms.

'My son!' said Athos, pressing him to his heart.

'And I,' said Porthos, 'I have no need to swear, but I am choking. If it were necessary for me to fight against you, I believe I should allow myself to be pierced through, for I have loved no one but you in the world;' and honest Porthos began to shed tears, while throwing himself into the arms of Aramis.

'My friends,' said Athos, 'this is what I was hoping; this is what I expected from two hearts like yours. Yes, I have said it and I repeat it, our destinies are irrevocably united, although we follow a different route. I respect your opinion, d'Artagnan; I respect your conviction, Porthos. But although we are fighting for opposite sides, let us keep friends; ministers, princes, kings will pass by like a torrent, civil war like a flame, but we—shall we remain? I feel the presentiment of it.'

'Yes,' said Aramis; 'Cardinalists or Frondeurs, what does it matter? Let us again find our good seconds for duels, our devoted friends in grave affairs, our joyous companions in pleasure!'

'And every time,' said Athos, 'that we meet in the fray, at this one word, Place Royale, let us pass our swords into our left hands and stretch out the right even if it be in the midst of carnage.'

'You speak admirably,' said Porthos.

'You are the greatest of men,' said d'Artagnan; 'and as for us, you surpass us by ten arm's lengths.'

Athos smiled with unspeakable joy.

'It is then concluded,' said he. 'Come, Messieurs, your hands. Are you in any degree Christians?'

'*Pardieu!*' said d'Artagnan.

'We will be so on this occasion, to remain faithful to our oath,' said Aramis.

'Ah! I am ready to swear by whatever you wish,' said Porthos, 'even by Mahomet! The devil take me if I have ever been so happy as at this moment.' And the good Porthos wiped his eyes, still moist.

'Has one of you a cross?' asked Athos.

'Porthos and d'Artagnan looked, while shaking their heads, like men caught in a destitute condition. Aramis smiled, and took from his breast a diamond cross, suspended from his neck by a string of beads.

'Here is one,' said he.

'Well,' resumed Athos, 'let us swear on this cross to be united in spite of any obstacle, and always; and may this oath bind not only us, but even our descendants! Does this oath suit you?'

'Yes,' said they, all with one voice.

'Ah, traitor!' said d'Artagnan, in a whisper to Aramis, 'you have made us swear on the crucifix of a lady Frondeur.'

XXXI

THE OISE FERRY-BOAT

WE hope the reader has not quite forgotten the young traveller whom we left on the route to Flanders.

Raoul, on losing sight of his protector, whom he had left following him with his eyes in front of the royal church, had spurred his horse in order to drown his sad thoughts, as well as to hide from Olivain the emotion which changed his looks.

An hour of rapid riding soon however dissipated all those dark shadows which had saddened the fruitful imagination of the young man. The strange pleasure of being free—a pleasure which has its sweetness, even for those who have never suffered from dependence—gilded both heaven and earth for him, and especially that distant bright horizon of life termed the future.

However, he saw, after some attempts at conversation with Olivain, that long days thus passed would be very dull; and the recollection of the count's conversation, so sweet and interesting, recurred to him as he passed through cities, valuable information about which Athos, the wisest and most amusing of guides, would have imparted to him.

Another remembrance saddened Raoul; they reached Louvres,* where he saw behind a curtain of poplars a small château which so strongly recalled that of La Vallière that he stopped to look at it for nearly ten minutes, and resumed his journey without even answering Olivain, who respectfully asked the reason for this delay. The aspect of external objects is a mysterious conductor which corresponds to the fibres of the memory, and leads to their revelation, sometimes in spite of ourselves. When once this thread is touched, like that of Ariadne,* it leads into a labyrinth of thoughts where we go astray while following this shadow of the past which is termed recollection. Now, the view of this château had transferred Raoul fifty leagues away, and had carried back his life from the time when he had taken leave of little Louise to the moment when he saw her first; and each clump of oak, every weathercock of which he caught a glimpse on the slate roofs, reminded him that instead of returning towards the friends of his childhood, he was going further off, and that perhaps he had left them for ever.

With swelling heart and heavy head, he ordered Olivain to lead the horses to a little inn which he saw on the route, about half a musket-shot from the place they had reached. He himself took up a position at a table under a fine group of chestnuts in flower, about which multitudes of bees were murmuring; and he told Olivain to procure paper and ink for him from the landlord of the inn.

Olivain obeyed, while Raoul sat down with his elbow on the table, his looks vaguely dwelling on the charming landscape of green fields and clusters of trees, while he shook from his hair the blossoms which kept falling like snow.

Raoul had been there scarcely ten minutes when he saw come within the circle of vision a rubicund figure, which, with a table-napkin round his body, another on his arm, and a white cap on his head, drew near, holding paper, ink and pen.

'Ah! ah!' said the apparition, 'it is clear that all gentlemen have similar thoughts, for only a quarter of an hour ago, a young nobleman, well mounted, good-looking, and about your own age, stopped before this clump of trees, had table and chairs brought, and then dined with an old gentleman who appeared to be his tutor upon a pâté of which they have not left a morsel, and a bottle of old Mâcon wine of which they did not leave a drop; but happily we have some of the same wine and some similar pâtés, and if Monsieur wishes to give his orders——'

'No, friend,' said Raoul, smiling, 'I thank you, but I need for the time only the things I have asked for; only I should be very happy if the ink is black and the pen good. On these conditions, I will pay for the pen the price of a bottle of wine, and for the ink the price of the pastry.'

'Well, Monsieur,' said the host, 'I will give the wine and pastry to your servant, so you will get pen and ink into the bargain.'

'Do as you wish,' said Raoul, who was beginning his acquaintance with that particular class of society, which when there were robbers on the highways, was associated with them, and since there are none, has advantageously replaced them.

The host, quieted by the payment, put down the paper, ink, and pen. By chance the pen was passable, and Raoul began to write.

The host stayed by him, and looked with a sort of involuntary admiration at this charming face, so grave and so sweet at the same time. Beauty always has been and always will be a sovereign.

'He is not like the guest who was here a little while ago,' said the host to Olivain, who came to Raoul to see if he wanted anything; 'and your young master has no appetite.'

'Monsieur had appetite enough three days ago, but what would you have? He lost it day before yesterday.' Olivain and the host walked towards the inn. Olivain, according to the custom of servants satisfied with their station, was telling the innkeeper all he thought it proper to tell respecting the young gentleman.

In the mean time Raoul was writing.

MONSIEUR—After travelling four hours, I stop to write to you, for I miss you every moment, and am ready to turn my head as if to reply when you speak to me. I was so bewildered by our separation, and so affected with grief by it, that I could but feebly express all the tenderness and gratitude which I feel for you. You will excuse me, Monsieur, for you are so noble-hearted that you have understood all that is passing in my heart. Write to me, I beg of you, for your counsels are a part of my existence. And then, if I may venture to say so, I feel distressed; for it seemed to me that you were preparing for some perilous expedition, about which I did not dare to ask you, since you told me nothing about it. I have then, as you see, great desire to receive news from you. Since you are no longer near me I am every moment afraid of going wrong. You used powerfully to sustain me, Monsieur, and today, I confess, I feel very lonely.

Will you be kind enough, Monsieur, if you receive news from Blois, to send me a few words about my little friend Mademoiselle de la Vallière, whose health, you know, at the time of our departure, gave some anxiety? You see, Monsieur and dear protector, that recollections of the time that I have passed with you are still precious and indispensable. I hope that you will sometimes think of me, and if you miss me at certain times, and feel some regret at my absence, I shall be filled with joy in thinking that you have felt by experience my affection for you, and that I have led you to understand this while I have had the happiness of living with you.

Having finished the letter, Raoul felt more at ease; he looked to see that Olivain and the host were not observing him, and then imprinted a kiss upon that paper—a mute and touching caress which Athos's heart was able to imagine when he opened the letter.

During this time, Olivain drank his bottle of wine and ate his pastry; the horses also were refreshed. Raoul made a sign to the host to approach, threw a crown upon the table, re-mounted his horse, and at Senlis* put the letter in the post.

The rest that the horsemen and their horses had had, enabled them to resume their journey without stopping. At Verberie, Raoul desired Olivain to get some information about that young gentleman who was ahead of them; he had been seen going by less than three-quarters of an hour ago, but he was well mounted, as the innkeeper had told him, and was going at a good pace.

'Let us try to overtake this gentleman,' said Raoul to Olivain; 'he is also going to join the army, and will be agreeable company for us.'

It was four o'clock in the afternoon when Raoul reached Compiègne. He made a hearty dinner, and got fresh news of the young gentleman ahead of them; he had stopped also at the Bell and Bottle Hotel, which was the best in Compiègne, and had continued his journey, saying he intended sleeping at Noyon.

'Let us sleep at Noyon,' said Raoul.

'Monsieur,' Olivain respectfully replied, 'allow me to observe that we have already tired the horses a good deal this morning. It will be better, I think, to sleep here and set out early tomorrow morning. Eighteen leagues are enough for the first stage.'

'M. le Comte de la Fère wishes me to hasten,' said Raoul, 'so as to join Monsieur the Prince on the morning of the fourth day; let us push on, then, as far as Noyon. It will be a stage like those we have made going from Blois to Paris. We shall reach there by eight. The horses will have the night for rest, and tomorrow at five we will resume our march.'

Olivain did not dare oppose this determination; but he followed, muttering to himself, 'Go on, go on; throw away your fire the first day. Tomorrow, instead of twenty leagues, you will do but ten, the next day only five, and in three days you will be laid up. All the young people are regular bragga- docios.'

One can see that Olivain had not been trained in the school of the Planchets and Grimauds. Raoul did in fact feel fatigued; but he wanted to try his strength, and brought up on the principles of Athos, sure of having heard him speak a thousand times of stages of twenty-five leagues, he did not wish to stop short of his model. D'Artagnan, that man of iron, who seemed built up of nerve and muscle, had filled him with admiration.

He kept urging on his horse more and more, in spite of Olivain's remarks; and following a charming little road which led to a ferry, and which took off a league from the distance, so he had been assured, when he reached the top of a hill he saw the river before him. A small body of horsemen were on the bank ready to cross. Raoul did not at all doubt that this was the gentleman and his escort. He uttered a cry of appeal, but he was too distant to be heard, so Raoul put his horse into a gallop, although it was very tired; but an undulation of the ground soon hid the travellers from his sight, and when he reached a fresh height the boat had left the bank and was going across to the other side.

Raoul, seeing that he could not reach it in time to cross with the other travellers, awaited Olivain. At that moment a cry was heard which seemed to come from the river. Raoul turned in the direction of the sound, and covering his eyes with his hands to keep off the dazzling light of the setting sun, 'Olivain,' he cried, 'what do I see down there?'

A second cry was heard, more piercing than the former.

'Ha, Monsieur!' said Olivain; 'the rope of the ferry has broken, and the boat is drifting. But what do I see struggling in the water?'

'Ah, doubtless,' said Raoul, fixing his looks upon a point of the river which the rays of the sun illumined brightly. 'A horse, a cavalier!'

'They are sinking!' cried Olivain.

That was true; and Raoul now felt sure that an accident had happened, and that a man was drowning. He put spurs to his horse, and the animal, seeing that room was given him, leaped over a sort of rail which surrounded the place of embarkation, and fell into the river, causing waves of foam to uprise.

'What,' cried Olivain, 'are you going to do? Good gracious!'

Raoul guided his horse towards the one in danger. It was in fact an exercise with which he was familiar. Brought up on the banks of the Loire, he had been, so to speak, cradled on its waves. A hundred times he had crossed it on horseback, and a thousand times swimming. Athos, foreseeing the time when the viscount would become a soldier, had accustomed him to such attempts.

'Oh, heavens!' continued Olivain, in despair, 'what would Monsieur the Count say if he saw you?'

'Monsieur the Count would have done as I am doing,' answered Raoul, pressing his horse vigorously.

'But I!' cried Olivain, pale and agitated on the bank, 'how shall I cross?'

'Jump, coward!' cried Raoul, still swimming.

Raoul, addressing the traveller, who was struggling, twenty paces off, said, 'Courage, Monsieur! help is coming to you.'

Olivain advanced, fell back, made his horse rear, turned him round, and at last, goaded by shame, plunged in as Raoul had done, but saying, 'I am dead; we are lost!'

In the meanwhile the ferry-boat was rapidly going down stream, driven by the current, and those in it could be heard calling out.

A man with grey hair had jumped from the boat into the stream, and was swimming vigorously towards the drowning person; but he made little progress, for he had to swim against the stream.

Raoul kept on, and was visibly gaining ground; but the horse and rider, whom he did not lose sight of, were rapidly sinking. The horse had only his nostrils above the water, and the cavalier, who had in struggling dropped the reins, was extending his arms and dropping his head. A minute more, and all would have been over.

'Keep up,' said Raoul; 'keep up!'

'Too late, too late!' said the young man.

The water passed over his head and drowned his voice. Raoul got off his horse, leaving him to look after his own safety, and in three or four strokes was near the man. He immediately seized the horse's curb, and raised his head out of the water; the animal then breathed more freely, and as if he understood that someone had come to his aid, he redoubled his efforts. Raoul at the same time seized one of the young man's hands, and placed it on the horse's mane, which the youth laid hold of with the tenacity of a drowning man. Sure that the cavalier would not let go, Raoul turned his attention to the horse, which he guided towards the other shore, encouraging him with his voice to strike out. Suddenly the animal reached shallow water, and got a foothold.

'Saved!' cried the grey-haired man, as he himself reached the shore.

'Saved!' mechanically uttered the young man, while letting go the mane, and letting himself slip off the horse into Raoul's arms. The latter was only some ten paces from the shore; he carried the now senseless stranger there, put him down on the grass, loosened his collar, and unbuttoned the fastenings of his doublet. A minute after the grey-haired man was near him.

Olivain had managed to reach land also, after making the sign of the cross many times; and the people in the boat directed their course to the shore as best they could with the aid of a pole which was by chance in the boat. By degrees, thanks to Raoul and the old gentleman, life returned into the face of the nearly drowned man, who opened his eyes first wildly, but soon fixed them on him who had saved him.

'Ah, Monsieur,' he exclaimed, 'it is you for whom I am looking. But for you I should be dead, thrice dead.'

'But you are coming to, and we shall get off with only a ducking,' said Raoul.

'Ah, Monsieur, what gratitude is due to you!' said the grey-haired man.

'Ah, is that you, my good D'Arminges? I caused you a great fright, did I not? but it's your own fault. You were my preceptor; why did you not teach me to swim better?'

'Ah, Monsieur the Count!' said the old man, 'if any misfortune had happened to you, I should never have dared to present myself before the marshal.'

'But how did the accident happen?' asked Raoul.

'In the simplest manner possible,' replied he addressed as count. 'We had scarcely crossed a third of the river when the rope of the ferry-boat broke. At the cries and movements of the boatmen, my horse took fright and leaped into the water. I am a bad swimmer, and did not dare to throw myself into the water. Instead of helping the horse's endeavours, I paralysed them, and was in the way of drowning myself bravely, when you reached me just in time for my rescue. So, Monsieur, henceforth we are friends for ever.'

'Monsieur,' said Raoul, bowing, 'I am your servant entirely, I assure you.'

'My name is the Comte de Guiche;* my father is Maréchal de Grammont. And now that you know who I am, do me the honour of telling me who you are.'

'I am Vicomte de Bragelonne,' said Raoul, blushing because he was unable to name his father, as the count had done.

'Viscount, your face, goodness, and courage draw me towards you. Let us embrace. I ask your friendship.'

'Monsieur,' said Raoul, while granting his request, 'I love you already with my whole heart; treat me therefore as a devoted friend.'

'Where are you now going, Viscount?' asked Comte de Guiche.

'To the prince's army, Count.'

'And so am I,' exclaimed the young man, in a transport of joy. 'So much the better; we shall be under our first fire together.'

'That is well, love each other,' said the preceptor. 'Both are young; you have doubtless the same star, and you should meet.'

The two young men smiled with the confidence of youth.

'And now,' said the count's preceptor, 'you must change your clothes; your servants ought by this time to have reached the inn. Linen and wine are being made warm. Come.'

The young men made no objection to the proposal, so they at once remounted, each observing and admiring the other. They were indeed two elegant cavaliers, with figures slim and graceful, two noble faces with open foreheads, looks pleasant and proud, and smiles loyal and intelligent. Guiche might have been about eighteen, but he was scarcely taller than Raoul, who was only fifteen.

They stretched their hands out as by a spontaneous impulse, and urging on their horses, made their way side by side for the hotel, the one feeling the life to be pleasant which he had nearly lost, and the other thanking God for having let him live long enough to perform an act which would be gratifying to his protector.

As for Olivain, he was the only one whom the action of his young master did not quite satisfy. He twisted the sleeves of his coat, while thinking that a halt at Compiègne might have not only prevented the accident from which he had just escaped, but also the inflammation of the chest and rheumatism which might be the result of it.

XXXII

SKIRMISH

THE stay at Noyon was short; all enjoyed a good rest there. Raoul had ordered them to call him if Grimaud came; but he did not come. The horses doubtless appreciated, on their part, the eight hours' absolute rest and the abundant litter furnished them. The Comte de Guiche was called at five by Raoul, who came to wish him good-morning. They hastily breakfasted, and by six they had done two leagues.

The young count's conversation was very interesting to Raoul. So Raoul listened much, and the young count did the talking.

Brought up in Paris, where Raoul had been but once, and at court, which Raoul had never seen, the count's fooleries as a page, two duels which he had managed to have in spite of edicts and preceptor, were things which engaged Raoul's curiosity. Raoul had been only to M. Scarron's house. He named the persons whom he had seen there. Guiche knew everybody; he made jokes about everyone. Raoul was fearful lest Guiche should make a jest about Madame de Chevreuse, for whom he himself felt a real, deep sympathy; but whether instinctively or from affection for her, the count spoke most highly of her. This increased Raoul's friendship for him.

Then came the matter of gallantries and flirtations. Under this head also Bragelonne had much more to hear than to tell. He therefore listened, and seemed to see clearly enough through three or four adventures that, like himself, the count was keeping a secret hid deep in his heart. The intrigues of the court were, as we said, well known to him. Raoul had heard

the Comte de la Fère talk much of it, only it had changed
greatly since Athos frequented it. Guiche's narrative was therefore new to his travelling companion. The young, witty, scan-
dal-mongering count passed everyone in review. He told of the
former amours of Madame de Longueville with Coligny, and
the duel of the latter on the Place Royale, which caused his
death, and which Madame de Longueville witnessed through
the window-blinds; of her fresh intrigues with Prince de
Marcillac, who they said was so jealous of her as to wish
everybody to be killed, even the Abbé d'Herblay, her confessor;
of the amours of the Prince of Wales with Mademoiselle, who
later on was styled the Great Mademoiselle,* so celebrated
afterwards for her secret marriage with Lauzun. The queen
herself was not spared, and the Cardinal Mazarin had his share
also.

The day's journey passed like an hour. The count's preceptor—a jovial fellow, a man of the world, wise to the very teeth,
as his pupil expressed it—often recalled to Raoul the deep
learning and the clever, biting raillery of Athos; but as regards
grace, delicacy, and nobility of appearance no one was to be
compared to the Comte de la Fère.

The horses, having been more carefully treated than the
evening before, pulled up about four at Arras. They were
approaching the scene of the war;* and it was determined to
stay in that city until next day, as some parties of Spaniards
were taking advantage of the night to make expeditions even
in the environs of Arras. The French army held ground from
Pont à Marc to Valenciennes, covering Douai. They said
Monsieur the Prince was at Béthune. The army of the enemy
extended from Cassel to Courtray; and as there was no sort of
pillaging or violence that it did not commit, the poor people
on the frontier left their isolated habitations, and came for
refuge to the fortified cities, which furnished them protection.
Arras was encumbered with fugitives.

They were talking of an expected battle which might prove
decisive, the prince having only manœuvred up to that time,
while awaiting reinforcements which had at last just arrived.
The young men thought themselves fortunate to arrive so
opportunely. They supped together, and slept in the same

room. They were just at the age when speedy friendships are formed. It seemed to them as if they had known each other from childhood, and that it would be impossible ever again to be separated.

The evening was employed in talking of the war. The servants polished their arms. The young men loaded their pistols in readiness for a skirmish, and they awoke feeling disappointed, both having dreamed that they arrived too late to take part in the battle.

In the morning the report spread that the Prince de Condé had evacuated Béthune to retire upon Carvin, leaving a garrison, however, in that city; but as the news was not quite certain, the young men decided on continuing their journey towards Béthune, prepared on the way to bear off to the right, and march to Carvin.

The Comte de Guiche's preceptor knew the country perfectly. He therefore proposed to take a cross-road which kept midway between the road to Lens and that to Béthune. At Ablain they made enquiries. Directions were left for Grimaud. They began their journey about seven in the morning.

Guiche, who was young and hot-brained, said to Raoul, 'There are six of us, three masters and three servants. The latter are well armed, and yours seems stubborn enough.'

'I have never seen him at work,' replied Raoul. 'But he is a Breton, that is promising.'

'Oh, yes,' replied Guiche; 'and I am sure he could fire a musket if needful. I have two reliable men who were in the wars with my father; so we are six combatants. If we find a small party of the enemy equal or even superior in number to us, we should be the ones to commence the attack, should we not?'

'By all means,' replied the viscount.

'Holloa, young fellows!' said the preceptor, joining in the conversation. 'Bless my soul! what are you going to do? Do you forget that my orders are to conduct you safe and sound to the prince? Once in the army, kill away at your good pleasure; but till then I warn you, in my character of general I order a retreat, and turn my back on the first soldier that I see.'

The young men glanced at each other and smiled. The country was tolerably wooded; and from time to time they met small parties of peasants withdrawing, driving their cattle before them, conveying in wagons or carrying in their arms their most valuable property.

They reached Ablain without accident. There they learned that the prince had actually left Béthune, and lay between Cambrin and La Venthie. They heard also, when leaving the route for Grimaud, of a cross-road which led them in half an hour to the bank of a little stream which runs into the Lys.

The country was beautiful, intersected by valleys of emerald green. From time to time they passed small woods which the paths they were following traversed. In each of these, fearing an ambuscade, the preceptor put the count's two servants in front to form the vanguard. The preceptor and the two young men were the main body, and Olivain, carbine on knee and eye on the watch, protected the rear. They thus were passing through a tolerably thick wood; at a hundred paces from this wood, M. d'Arminges had taken his usual precautions, and sent forward the count's two lackeys. The servants had just disappeared under the trees; the young men and the preceptor, laughing and talking, were following at about a hundred paces. Olivain was about an equal distance in the rear, when suddenly five or six musket-shots were heard. The preceptor called a halt, and the young men pulled up their horses. At the same moment they saw the two servants returning at a gallop. The two young men, anxious to learn the cause of the firing, pricked on towards them. The preceptor followed.

'Have you been stopped?' asked the two young men.

'No,' they replied; 'it is even probable that we were not seen. The musket-shots sounded in front of us, and we have returned to ask orders.'

'My advice is,' said M. d'Arminges, 'to beat a retreat. This wood may hide an ambuscade.'

'Have you then seen nothing?' the count asked the servants.

'I thought I saw,' said one of them, 'some horsemen dressed in yellow, who were stealing along the bed of the stream.'

'That is it,' said the preceptor. 'We have got among a party of Spaniards. Back, gentlemen, back!'

The young men looked at each other; and at that instant they heard a pistol-shot and then some cries for help. Then seeing that each was determined not to retire, and as the preceptor had already turned his horse round, they both pressed on, Raoul crying out, 'Come on, Olivain and Guiche; come on, Urbain and Planchet!' And before the preceptor had recovered from his surprise, they had already disappeared in the forest. At the same time that they spurred their horses, the two young men had taken their pistols in their hands. Five minutes after, they reached the spot whence the noise seemed to come. Then they slackened speed, advancing carefully.

'*Chut!*' said Guiche; 'some horsemen.'

'Yes, three on horse, and three dismounted.'

'What are they doing? Do you see?'

'Yes, they seem to be searching a man who is wounded or dead.'

'It is some wretched assassination,' said Guiche.

'They are soldiers, nevertheless,' replied Bragelonne.

'Yes, but partisans; that is, robbers of the highway.'

'Let us give it to them,' said they both.

'Messieurs!' exclaimed the poor preceptor, 'in Heaven's name ——' But the young men did not listen at all. They set off in emulation of each other, and the preceptor's cries had no other result than to give warning to the Spaniards.

Immediately the three mounted partisans sprang forward to meet the young men, while the three others finished plundering the two travellers—for on approaching, the two young men perceived two bodies lying on the ground, instead of one.

At ten paces Guiche was the first to fire, and missed his man; the Spaniard who came up to Raoul fired, and Raoul felt a pain in his left arm like the stroke of a whip. At four paces he fired, and the Spaniard, struck in the breast, threw up his arms and fell back on the horse, which turned and bolted.

At that moment Raoul saw as through a cloud the barrel of a musket directed at him. Athos's advice came to mind; by a movement like lightning he made his horse rear. The shot was fired. The horse shied, missed his footing, and fell with Raoul's leg under him.

The Spaniard sprang forward, seizing his musket by the barrel in order to break Raoul's head with the butt-end. Unfortunately, from Raoul's position he was neither able to draw sword nor pistol; he saw the butt-end moving above his head, and in spite of himself, he was about closing his eyes, when with a bound Guiche came to the rescue, and put his pistol to the Spaniard's throat.

'Surrender!' he said to him; 'or you are a dead man.'

The soldier dropped his musket, and gave in at once.

Guiche called one of his servants, gave him the prisoner in charge with orders to blow out his brains if he made a movement to escape, leaped off his horse, and came up to Raoul.

'Upon my word,' said Raoul, laughing, although his pallor showed the emotion natural to a first encounter, 'you pay your debts quickly. But for you,' added he, repeating the count's words, 'I should be dead, thrice dead.'

'My enemy, in taking flight,' said Guiche, 'left me every facility for coming to your aid; but are you badly wounded, for I see you all covered with blood?'

'I think,' said Raoul, 'I have something like a scratch on the arm. Help me to get from under my horse, and nothing will, I hope, prevent us from continuing our journey.'

M. d'Arminges and Olivain were on foot trying to raise the horse, which was struggling in death agony. Raoul succeeded in getting his foot from the stirrup and disengaging his leg. In an instant he was up.

'Anything broken?' said Guiche.

'Upon honour, no; thank Heaven! But what has become of the unfortunate people whom these wretches were assassinating?'

'We came too late; they are killed, and the booty is carried off.'

'Let us go and see whether they are quite dead, or if we can give any help,' said Raoul. 'Olivain, we have become possessed of two horses; but I have lost mine. Take the better of the two for yourself and give me yours.'

And they approached the spot where the victims were lying.

XXXIII

THE MONK

Two men lay there; one of them motionless, lying on his face, pierced by three shots—he was quite dead. The other had been placed against a tree by the two servants; his eyes were raised to heaven, his hands clasped together, and he was praying earnestly. He had received a ball which had broken his thigh.

The young men went up first of all to the dead man, and looked at him with astonishment.

'It is a priest,' said Bragelonne; 'he wears the tonsure. Oh, the wretches, to raise their hands against God's ministers!'

'Come here, Monsieur,' said Urbain—an old soldier who had gone through all the campaigns with the cardinal duke*—'come here. Nothing can be done with the other, while perhaps we can save this one.'

The wounded man smiled sadly.

'Save me? no,' said he; 'but help me to die—yes.'

'Are you a priest?' asked Raoul.

'No, Monsieur.'

'Your unfortunate companion seems to me to belong to the Church,' replied Raoul.

'He is the curate of Béthune. He was conveying to a safe place the sacred vessels of his church and the treasure of the chapter—for the prince abandoned our city yesterday, and perhaps the Spaniard will be there tomorrow. Now, as they knew that hostile parties were traversing the country, and the mission was perilous, no one dared to accompany him, and then I offered myself.'

'And these wretches have attacked you? These wretches have fired upon a priest?'

'Messieurs,' said the wounded man, looking around him, 'I am suffering much, and yet I should like to be carried to some house.'

'Where you might be attended to?' said Guiche.

'No; but where I might confess.'

'But perhaps,' said Raoul, 'you are not wounded so danger-ously as you think.'

'Monsieur,' said the wounded man, 'believe me, there is no time to lose. The ball has broken the thigh-bone, and pene-trated to the intestines.'

'Are you a doctor?' asked Guiche.

'No,' said the dying man; 'but I know something of wounds, and mine is mortal. Try to remove me to a place where I can find a priest, or take the trouble to bring one to me here, and God will recompense you for this holy act. It is my soul I want to save; my body is lost.'

'Since you die while doing a good action, that is impossible! and God will help you.'

'Messieurs, for Heaven's sake,' said the wounded man, sum-moning up all his strength as if to rise, 'don't lose time in useless talk! Help me to gain the nearest village, or bring to me here the first monk or priest you may meet with. But perhaps no one will dare to come, and I shall die without absolution. Oh!' added the wounded man, with an expression of terror which made the young men shudder, 'you will not permit that, will you? It would be too terrible!'

'Monsieur, be calm,' said Guiche. 'I swear to you that you are going to have the consolation you ask; tell me only where there is a house where we can ask help, or a village where we can go for a priest.'

'Thanks; and may God reward you! There is an inn half a league from here following this road, and scarcely a league beyond the inn you will come to the village of Greney. Go and find the curate. If he is not in, go to the convent of the Augustinians, which is the last house on the right, and bring any one who has received from our holy Church the power of absolution *in articulo mortis*.'

'M. d'Arminges,' said Guiche, 'stay by this unfortunate man, and take care that he is removed as gently as possible. Make a litter of branches; put all our cloaks on it. Two of our servants will carry it, while the third will hold himself ready to take the place of the tired bearer. We are going to find a priest.'

'Go, Count,' said the preceptor; 'but for Heaven's sake do not expose yourself!'

'Don't be alarmed. Besides, we are saved for the day. You know the saying, *Non bis in idem.*'*

'Keep up your courage, Monsieur!' said Raoul to the wounded man; 'we are going to do what you desired.'

'May God bless you, Messieurs!' answered the dying man, with an accent of gratitude impossible to describe.

The young men set off at a gallop in the direction indicated, while the preceptor attended to the making of the litter.

In about ten minutes they came to the inn. Raoul, without dismounting, called the host, and told him they were bringing to him a wounded man, and begged him in the mean while to get all things prepared for dressing his wound—a bed, bandages, some lint—desiring him if he knew of a doctor in the neighbourhood to send for him at once, and offering to pay the messenger.

The host, who saw two young lords richly dressed, promised to do all they asked, and our cavaliers therefore set off afresh, and went at a brisk pace towards Greney.

They had gone more than a league, and could see the first houses of the village, whose roofs of red tiles presented a strong contrast to the green trees which surrounded them, when they perceived, coming towards them, mounted on a mule, a poor monk, who from his large hat and robe of grey wool they took for an Augustinian friar. This time chance seemed to send them what they were looking for.

The monk drew near. He was about twenty-two or twenty-three, but older in appearance from his ascetic practices. He was pale, not of that dead paleness which is beautiful, but of a bilious yellow; his short hair, which reached scarcely lower than the circle traced on his forehead by his hat, was light, and his eyes, of a clear blue, seemed devoid of life.

'Monsieur,' said Raoul, with his usual politeness, 'are you an ecclesiastic?'

'Why do you ask me that?' said the stranger, with an almost rude impassiveness.

'To know it,' said Guiche, haughtily.

The stranger touched his mule with his heel, and went on. Guiche leaped before him, and stopped his progress.

'Answer, Monsieur!' said he; 'we have asked you in a polite manner, and every question deserves a reply.'

'I am free, I suppose, to tell or not to tell who I am to the first persons who take the liberty of questioning me.'

Guiche had great difficulty in restraining the strong desire he felt to break the monk's bones.

'First of all,' said he, trying to restrain himself, 'we are not persons to be treated with impertinence; my friend is the Vicomte de Bragelonne, and I am the Comte de Guiche. It is not from mere caprice we asked you the question, for a man who is wounded and dying desires the aid of the Church. If you are a priest, I summon you, in the name of humanity, to follow me to aid this man; if you are not, that alters the case. I forewarn you, in the name of that courtesy which you appear so completely to ignore, that I shall punish you for your insolence.'

The monk's paleness turned into lividness, and he smiled in such a strange manner that Raoul, who kept his eyes on him, felt this smile oppress his heart as if it were an insult.

'It is some Spanish or Flemish spy,' said he, putting his hand upon his pistol. A menacing look like a flash replied to Raoul.

'Well, Monsieur,' said Guiche, 'will you answer me?'

'I am a priest, Messieurs,' said the young man; and his face resumed its usual impassiveness.

'Then, Father,' said Raoul, letting his pistol drop again into the holster, and impressing upon his words a respectful accent which did not come from his heart, 'then if you are a priest, you will have, as my friend has told you, an opportunity of exercising your calling. An unfortunate fellow who is wounded begs the help of a minister of God; our people are waiting on him.'

'I will go,' said the monk; and he touched the mule with his heel.

'If you do not go there, Monsieur,' said Guiche, 'remember that we have horses capable of overtaking your mule, and sufficient influence to cause you to be seized wherever you are; and then, I swear it to you, your trial will be soon finished. A tree and a cord can be found anywhere.'

The eye of the monk flashed anew, but that was all. He repeated his phrase—'I will go there;' and he set out.

'Let us follow him,' said Guiche, 'that will be the surest way.'

'I was going to propose it to you,' said Bragelonne; and the two young men turned round, regulating their pace by that of the monk, whom they thus followed within pistol-shot.

At the end of five minutes the monk turned round to make sure whether he were followed or not.

'Do you see?' said Raoul. 'We have done right to follow him.'

'What a horrible-looking fellow he is!' said the count.

'Horrible,' replied Raoul. 'In expression above all; that yellowish hair, those leaden eyes, those lips which disappear at the least word he utters.'

'Yes, yes,' said Guiche, who had been less struck than Raoul with all these details, because Raoul was examining while Guiche was talking—'yes, a strange face; but these monks are subjected to such degrading practices! The fasts make them pale; the strictness of discipline makes them hypocrites; and it is by force of weeping for the good things of life which they have lost, and which we enjoy, that their eyes grow dull.'

'However,' said Raoul, 'the poor man will have a priest; but really, the penitent has the look of possessing a better conscience than his confessor. I must confess I have been used to seeing better-looking priests.'

'Ah,' said Guiche, 'don't you understand? This is one of the begging friars who travel about till a living drops from heaven. They are mostly foreigners: Scotch, Irish, Danes. I have sometimes had pointed out to me such as this one.'

'As ugly?'

'No; but reasonably hideous, nevertheless.'

'What a misfortune for this poor wounded man to die in the hands of such a monk!'

'Bah!' said Guiche; 'absolution comes not from him who gives it, but from God. Yet I would rather die impenitent than have to do with such a confessor. You agree with me, don't you, Viscount? And I see you caress the pommel of your pistol as if you had some intention of breaking his head.'

'Yes, Count; and what will surprise you, I have felt an indefinable horror at the look of this man. Have you ever disturbed a serpent when going along?'

'Never.'

'Well, that has happened to me in our forests about Blois. I well remember the first which I ever saw, with its dull eye and curved body, shaking its head and brandishing its tongue; I stopped, fixed, pale, and as if fascinated, till M. le Comte de la Fère——'

'Your father?' asked Guiche.

'No; my guardian,' replied Raoul, blushing.

'Very well.'

'Till the count said to me, "Come, Bragelonne, draw." Then only I ran at the reptile, and cut it in two just when it raised itself on its tail, and hissing, prepared to attack me. Well, I swear to you, I felt the same sensation at the sight of this man when he said, "Why do you ask me that?" and looked at me.'

'Then you reproach yourself for not having cut him in two as you did the serpent?'

'Faith, yes! almost,' said Raoul.

Just then they came in sight of the little inn, and saw coming towards it the wounded man's party, led by M. d'Arminges. Two men carried the dying man; the third led the horses. The young men spurred forward.

'There's the wounded man,' said Guiche, when passing by the friar; 'be good enough to hasten a little, Sir monk.'

As to Raoul, he separated himself from the monk the whole width of the road, and passed him, turning aside his head with disgust. Thus, the young men preceded the confessor instead of following him.

They went up to the wounded man, and announced the good news. The latter raised himself up to look in the direction indicated, saw the monk hastening on, and fell back on his litter, his face lit up with joy.

'Now,' said the young man, 'we have done all we can for you, and as we are in haste to join the prince's army, we must resume our journey; you will excuse us, will you not, Monsieur? They say there is going to be a battle, and we would not wish to arrive the next day.'

'Go, my young lords,' said the wounded man; 'and may you both be blessed for your piety! You have in fact, and as you have said, done for me all that you could do. I can only say to you once more: "May God preserve you, you and those who are dear to you!" '

'Monsieur,' said Guiche to his preceptor, 'we are going on; you will rejoin us on the way to Cambrin.'

The host was at his door, and had prepared everything—bed, bandages, and lint—and a groom had gone to find a physician at Lens, the nearest city.

'Well,' said the host, 'it shall be done as you desire; but do you not stop, Monsieur, to dress your wound?' continued he, addressing Bragelonne.

'Oh, my wound is nothing,' said the viscount; 'and it will be time for me to occupy myself with it at the next halt—only have the goodness, if you see a horseman pass who enquires of you concerning a young man riding a chestnut horse, and followed by a servant, to tell him you have seen me, but that I have resumed my journey, and expect to dine at Mazingarbe, and sleep at Cambrin. That horseman is my servant.'

'Would it not be better, and for greater security,' replied the landlord, 'that I should ask his name and tell him yours?'

'There is no harm in an increase of precaution,' said Raoul; 'my name is Vicomte de Bragelonne, and his Grimaud.'

At this moment the wounded man arrived from one side, and the monk from the other. The two young men stepped aside to allow the litter to pass; on his side the monk dismounted from his mule, and ordered that it should be taken to the stables without unsaddling it.

'Sir monk,' said Guiche, 'confess well this honest man, and do not trouble yourself as to your expense or that of your mule; it is all paid.'

'Thanks, Monsieur!' said the monk, with one of those smiles which had made Bragelonne shiver.

'Come, Count,' said Raoul, who seemed instinctively to be unable to bear the presence of the Augustinian—'come, I feel myself ill here.'

'Thanks, still once more, my fine young lords,' said the wounded man, 'and do not forget me in your prayers.'

'Rest tranquil,' said Guiche, spurring his horse to rejoin Bragelonne, now in advance.

At that moment, the litter, borne by the two servants, was entering the house. The landlord and his wife were standing on the stairs. The wounded man seemed to suffer terrible pain; and yet his chief concern was to know if the monk was following.

At the sight of this pale and blood-stained man, the wife seized her husband's arm.

'Well, what's the matter?' said the latter. 'Do you feel ill?'

'No; but look!' said the wife, pointing to the wounded man. 'Do you not recognize him?'

'That man? wait now——'

'Ah, I see you recognize him,' said the wife, 'for you are turning pale.'

'Indeed,' exclaimed the landlord. 'Ill luck to our house! It is the former public executioner of Béthune.'*

'The executioner of Béthune!' muttered the monk, starting, and showing on his face the feelings of repugnance which the penitent produced in him. M. d'Arminges, who stood at the door, observed his hesitation.

'Sir monk,' said he, 'whether he is or has been an executioner, he is none the less a man. Render him the last service he demands from you, and your work will be only the more meritorious.'

The monk answered nothing, but he continued silently his way towards the chamber, where the two servants had already placed the dying man on a bed.

On seeing the man of God approach the bedside of the wounded man, the two servants went out, closing the door on the monk and the dying man. D'Arminges and Olivain awaited them; they all mounted, and set off at a trot, following the road at the extremity of which Raoul and his companion had already disappeared. Just as the preceptor and his escort disappeared, a fresh traveller stopped before the inn.

'What does Monsieur want?' said the landlord, still pale and trembling from the discovery he had just made.

The traveller imitated a man drinking, and dismounting, pointed to his horse, and signified that he wished it to be groomed.

'Ah, devil!' said the host to himself, 'it seems that this one is mute.'

'And where would you like to drink?'

'Here,' said the traveller, pointing to a table.

'I made a mistake,' said the host; 'he is not quite dumb;' and he bowed, and went to fetch a bottle of wine and some biscuits, which he placed before his taciturn guest.

'Does Monsieur wish anything else?'

'Yes, indeed,' said the traveller.

'What does Monsieur wish?'

'To know if you have seen a young gentleman, about fifteen years of age, on a chestnut horse, and followed by a servant, pass this way.'

'Vicomte de Bragelonne?' said the host.

'Precisely.'

'Then your name is Grimaud?'

The traveller nodded assent.

'Well, then! your master was here a quarter of an hour ago. He will dine at Mazingarbe, and sleep at Cambrin.'

'How far to Mazingarbe?'

'Two leagues and a half.'

'Thanks.'

Grimaud, sure of overtaking his master before the end of the day, seemed more at ease, wiped his forehead, and poured out a glass of wine, which he drank in silence. He had just put the glass on the table, and was going to fill it again, when a terrible cry came from the room where the monk and dying man were. Grimaud jumped up at once.

'What is that?' said he. 'Where does that cry come from?'

'From the wounded man's room,' said the landlord.

'What wounded man?' asked Grimaud.

'The former executioner of Béthune, who has just been assassinated by some Spanish partisans, and who is now confessing to an Augustinian friar. He seems to be suffering a good deal.'

'The former executioner of Béthune?' muttered Grimaud, bringing him back to his recollection—'a man from fifty-five to sixty years of age, tall, muscular, swarthy, with black hair and beard?'

'That is he, except that his beard is grey and his hair has become white. Do you know him?' asked the host.

'I saw him once,' said Grimaud, whose countenance grew severe at the picture which his memory recalled.

The host's wife had run to them, trembling all over.

'Did you hear?' said she to her husband.

'Yes,' replied the host, looking with uneasiness towards the door. At this moment a cry less strong than the first, but followed by a prolonged groan, was heard. The three persons looked at one another, shuddering.

'We must see what it is,' said Grimaud.

'One would say it was the cry of a man being killed,' muttered the host.

'Jesus!' said his wife, crossing herself.

If Grimaud spoke little, as has been seen, he could act with vigour. He rushed towards the door, and shook it vigorously, but it was fastened inside by a bolt.

'Open the door!' cried the host. 'Sir monk, open at once!'

No one replied.

'Open, or I will break down the door,' then said Grimaud. Still silence.

Grimaud looked about him, and caught sight of a crow-bar which by chance lay in a corner. He snatched it up, and before the host could prevent him, he had forced open the door.

The room was saturated with blood, which ran through the mattresses. The wounded man did not speak, and was at the point of death. The monk had disappeared.

'The monk?' cried the host. 'Where is he?'

Grimaud rushed to a window which looked upon a courtyard.

'He has escaped that way,' cried he.

'Do you think so?' said the scared host. 'Boy, see if the monk's mule is in the stable.'

'No mule there!' said the boy.

Grimaud frowned. The host clasped his hands together, and looked round with disgust. As for his wife, she did not dare enter the room, but stood frightened at the door.

Grimaud came close up to the wounded man, looking at his coarse, strongly marked features, which recalled such a terrible recollection.

At last, after a moment of sad and mute contemplation, 'There is no longer any doubt,' said he; 'it is really he.'

'Is he still alive?' asked the host.

Grimaud, without answering, opened the wounded man's waistcoat to feel his heart, while the host approached; but all of a sudden they both drew back, the host uttering a cry of terror, Grimaud turning pale.

The blade of a poniard was thrust up to the hilt into the left side of the executioner's breast.

'Run and fetch help,' said Grimaud; 'I will stay by him.'

The host left the room thoroughly frightened; as for his wife, she had fled at the cry uttered by her husband.

XXXIV

THE ABSOLUTION

THIS is what had happened. We have seen that it was not of his own will, but on the contrary much against it, that the monk attended on the wounded man so strangely recommended to him. He would perhaps have endeavoured to flee had he seen the possibility of it; but the threats of the two gentlemen, their suite staying behind after having doubtless received their instructions, and in short the intention which filled the monk's mind of playing out to the end his part of confessor without showing too much ill-will, prevented him. So when once in the room he drew near to the wounded man's bedside.

The executioner examined the face of the one who should be his consoler with that sharp look peculiar to those dying, who consequently have no time to lose; he showed his surprise, and said, 'You are very young, Father?'

'Those who wear my dress are of no age,' the monk replied drily.

'Pray speak to me more mildly, Father; I want a friend in my last moments.'

'Are you suffering much?'

'Yes, but in soul more than in body.'

'We shall save your soul,' said the young man; 'but are you really the executioner of Béthune, as people say?'

'I have been, but am that no longer,' said the wounded man, for he feared that this name might deprive him of the last aid that he begged for; 'fifteen years ago I gave up the office. I am still present at executions, but do not strike the blow myself!'

'You feel great horror at your condition?'

The executioner gave a deep sigh.

'So long as I executed only in the name of law and justice,' said he, 'I was able to sleep peaceably, sheltered as I was under justice and law; but since that terrible night when I acted as the instrument of private revenge, and raised the sword with hatred over one of God's creatures—since then——'

The executioner stopped, shaking his head with a look of despair.

'Speak on,' said the monk, as he sat at the foot of the bed, and began to take an interest in the narrative begun so strangely.

'Ah!' cried the dying man, with an outburst of grief long restrained, and which at last gave itself vent, 'I have, nevertheless, tried to check remorse by twenty years of good works. I have laid aside the ferocity natural to those who shed blood. I have many times exposed my life to save those in peril; and I have preserved the lives of many by way of exchange for those I have taken away. That is not all: I have distributed the wealth acquired in the exercise of my office among the poor; I am an assiduous attendant at church. All have pardoned me, some even have shown affection for me; but I believe God has not pardoned me, for the recollection of that execution has unceasingly followed me, and every night the spectre of that woman seems to stand before me.'

'A woman! Was it a woman whom you assassinated?'

'You too!' exclaimed the executioner; 'you use this word which resounds in my ears! I then assassinated her, not executed her! I am then an assassin, and not a lover of justice.' And he closed his eyes, uttering deep groans.

The monk feared he would die before adding any more, for he quickly replied, 'Go on, I don't know anything; when you have finished your tale, God and I will decide.'

'Oh, Father!' continued the executioner, with his eyes still closed, as if he feared on opening them to see some frightful object, 'it is especially at night, and when crossing a river, that this terror, which I cannot overcome, increases. My hand seems then to grow heavy as if my cutlass was weighing it down; the water looks like blood, and all the sounds of Nature—the rustling of the trees, the murmur of the wind, the rippling of the water—unite to form a weeping, despairing, terrible voice which cries out to me, "Make way for the justice of God."'

'Delirious,' muttered the monk, shaking his head.

The executioner opened his eyes, tried to turn towards the young man, and seized his arm.

'Delirious,' he repeated, 'do you say? Oh, no; for it was evening. I threw the body into the river, with the words which my remorse spoke to me; those were the words which I in my pride uttered. After having been the instrument of human justice, I believed I had become that of God's justice.'

'But, come, how was it done? Speak,' said the monk.

'One evening, a man came for me, and showed me an order; I followed him. Four other lords awaited me. They took me away masked. I always reserved the right of resisting if the duty required of me seemed unjust. We went on for five or six leagues, gloomy, silent, scarcely exchanging a word; at last, through the window of a little cottage they pointed out a woman leaning on a table, and said to me, "That is she whom you must execute."'

'Horrible!' said the monk. 'And did you obey?'

'Father, this woman was a monster. She had poisoned, they said, her second husband, tried to assassinate her brother-in-law, who was one of these men; she had just poisoned a young woman who was her rival; and before leaving England, she had, they said, caused the king's favourite to be stabbed.'

'Buckingham?'

'Yes, that was he.'

'Was this woman English, then?'

'No; she was French, but had been married in England.' The monk turned pale, wiped his forehead, and went and bolted the door. The executioner thought he was leaving him, and fell back with a groan on the bed.

'No, no, here I am,' said the monk, returning quickly to him; 'go on. Who were these men?'

'One was a foreigner—an Englishman, I believe. The other four were French, and wore the dress of musketeers.'

'Their names?' asked the monk.

'I did not know them. Only the four other nobles called the Englishman my Lord.'

'And was this woman beautiful?'

'Young and beautiful! Oh, yes, very beautiful. I see her still, when on her knees at my feet she prayed with her head thrown back. I could never understand since how I could strike one so beautiful and so pale.'

The monk seemed agitated by a strange feeling. All his limbs shook; it was evident that he wished to ask a question, but did not dare.

At length, after a strong effort of self-control, 'The name of this woman?' said he.

'I don't know it. As I told you, she was married twice, so it seemed. Once in France, and then in England.'

'And she was young, say you?'

'Twenty-five years.'

'Beautiful?'

'Wonderfully.'

'A blonde?'

'Yes.'

'Long hair, had she not, which fell over her shoulders?'

'Yes.'

'Eyes of wonderful expression?'

'When she pleased. Oh, yes, that was so.'

'A voice of strange softness?'

'How do you know that?'

The executioner raised himself on his elbows, and fixed an affrighted look on the monk, who became livid.

'And you killed her! You served as the tool of those cowards who did not dare to do it themselves! You had no pity for her youth, her beauty, her weakness! You killed this woman?'

'Alas, Father! this woman under this heavenly exterior concealed an infernal spirit; and when I saw her and recalled all the ill she had done to myself——'

'To you? and what had she done to you? Tell now.'

'She had led astray and destroyed my brother, who was a priest. She had escaped with him from her convent.'

'With your brother?'

'Yes; he had been her first lover. She was the cause of his death. Oh, Father, don't look so at me! Am I guilty? You will not pardon me, then?'

The monk composed his features.

'Well, well; I will pardon you if you tell all.'

'Oh!' cried the executioner; 'all! all!'

'Then answer, if she seduced your brother—you said that she seduced him, did you not?'

'Yes.'

'If she caused his death—you have said that she caused his death?'

'Yes,' repeated the executioner.

'Then you must know her name as a young girl!'

'Oh, God, I am dying! Give me absolution, Father—absolution!'

'Tell her name, and I will give it to you.'

'Her name was—pity me!' and he fell back on the bed, shuddering, and like a man about to die.

'Her name!' repeated the monk, bending over him as if to drag from him the name which he was unwilling to say—'her name! Speak, or no absolution!'

The dying man seemed to gather up all his strength.

The monk's eyes sparkled.

'Anne de Breuil,'* whispered the dying man.

'Anne de Breuil!' cried the monk, sitting upright and raising his hands to heaven—'Anne de Breuil! You used that name, did you not?'

'Yes, yes, that's her name. And now absolve me, for I am dying.'

'I absolve you?' cried the priest, with a laugh which made the dying man's hair stand on end—'I absolve you? I am not a priest.'

'You are not a priest? What then are you?'

'I am going to tell you in my turn, wretch!'

'Ah, Lord! *Mon Dieu!*'

'I am John Francis de Winter!'

'I don't know you!' cried the executioner.

'Wait, you will know me presently. I am John Francis de Winter,' he repeated, 'and that woman——'

'Well! that woman?'

'Was my mother!'

The executioner uttered that piercing cry which was heard first.

'Oh, pardon, pardon!' he muttered; 'if not in God's name at least in your own; if not as a priest, at least as her son.'

'Pardon you!' exclaimed the pretended monk; 'God will perhaps do so, but I never will!'

'For pity's sake!' said the executioner, stretching out his arms towards him.

'No pity for him who had no pity! die impenitent, die in despair, die, and go to hell!'

And drawing a poniard from his robe and striking it into the executioner's breast, 'Take that,' said he; 'that's my absolution.'

It was then that the second cry was heard, weaker than the first, which had been followed by a prolonged groan.

The executioner, who had lifted himself up, fell back on his bed. As for the monk, without drawing the poniard from the wound, he ran to the window, opened it, leaped on a flower-bed, slipped into the stable, took his mule, escaped by a back-door, hurried to the nearest covert, threw off his monk's garments, took from his valise a complete cavalier's dress, put it on, gained on foot the first posting-house, took a horse, and went at full speed towards Paris.

XXXV

GRIMAUD SPEAKS

GRIMAUD remained alone by the executioner. The host had gone to get medical help; his wife was praying. In a few moments the wounded man again opened his eyes.

'Help me!' he muttered. 'Oh God! shall I not find a friend in the world to help me to live or to die?' and he with difficulty put his hand to his breast. He touched the handle of the poniard.

'Ah!' said he, like a man who recalls something. And he let his hand fall down by his side.

'Keep up your courage,' said Grimaud; 'they have gone for help.'

'Who are you?' asked the wounded man, fixing his eyes with a wild stare on Grimaud.

'An old acquaintance.'

'You?'

The wounded man tried to recall the features of the one who thus spoke to him. 'Under what circumstances did we meet?' he asked.

'Twenty years ago, one night; my master had taken you from Béthune, and led you to Armentières.'

'I recollect you well,' said the executioner; 'you were one of the four servants.'

'That is it.'

'Where have you come from?'

'I am on a journey. I stopped at this inn to rest my horse. They were telling me that the executioner of Béthune was here wounded when you uttered those two cries. At the first we ran to the door; at the second we forced it open.'

'And the monk? Have you seen the monk?'

'What monk?'

'The monk shut up in the room with me.'

'No; he is here no longer. He seems to have escaped by the window. It was he who struck you the blow?'

'Yes.'

Grimaud moved towards the door.

'What are you going to do?'

'Pursue him.'

'Don't do it.'

'And why not?'

'He has only taken his revenge; he has done right. Now I hope that God will pardon me, for there is expiation for my crime.'

'Explain yourself,' said Grimaud.

'That woman whom your masters and you made me put to death——'

'Milady?'

'Yes, Milady; it is true that you called her so——'

'What is there in common between Milady and the monk?'

'She was his mother.'

Grimaud staggered, and looked at the dying man as if stupefied.

'His mother?' he repeated.

'Yes, his mother.'

'But he knows the secret, then?'

'I took him for a monk, and revealed it to him in confession.'

'Unfortunate!' cried Grimaud, whose hair became moistened with perspiration at the mere idea of the consequences which such a revelation might have; 'you have not named any one, I hope?'

'No; for the reason that I knew none of their names, except his mother's maiden name. And by this he recognized her; but he knows that his uncle was among the judges——' and he fell back exhausted. Grimaud wished to give him aid, and brought his hand near the handle of the poniard.

'Don't touch me,' said the executioner; 'if you draw out the poniard I shall die.'

Grimaud stopped with extended hand, then suddenly striking his forehead with his fist, 'Ah! but if this man ever learns who the others are, my master is lost also.'

'Quick, quick!' cried the executioner; 'forewarn him if he is still living; forewarn his friends. My death will not be the end of this terrible adventure.'

'Where was he going?'

'Towards Paris.'

'Who stopped him?'

'Two young gentlemen who were going to join the army, and one of whom—for I heard his name pronounced by his comrade—is called Vicomte de Bragelonne.'

'And that was the young man who brought this monk to you?'

'Yes.'

Grimaud raised his eyes to heaven.

'It was the will of God, then!' said he.

'Without doubt,' said the wounded man.

'And yet this woman deserved her fate. Is not that your opinion?' said Grimaud.

'At the point of death,' said the other, 'the crimes of others seem very small compared with one's own——' and he fell back exhausted, and closed his eyes.

Grimaud was in a strait between the pity which prevented him from leaving this man without help and the fear which bade him at that instant set out to convey this discovery to the Comte de la Fère, when he heard a sound in the passage, and saw the host, who was returning with the surgeon whom he had at last found. Several inquisitive people were following out of curiosity; the report of the strange event was becoming spread about.

The surgeon drew near to the dying man, who had fainted.

'We must first draw the blade from his chest,' said he, giving a very significant nod of the head.

Grimaud remembered the remark which the wounded man had just made, and turned away his eyes. The surgeon removed the coat, tore open the shirt, and so bared the chest. He took the poniard by the hilt; as he pulled it out, the wounded man opened his eyes with a frightful stare. When the blade was entirely drawn out of the wound, a reddish froth appeared on the lips of the wounded man; then at the moment he breathed, a flow of blood leaped from the orifice of the wound. The dying man fixed his eyes on Grimaud with a singular expression, and immediately expired.

Then Grimaud picked up the poniard covered with blood, which was lying in the room and horrifying every one, asked the host to follow him, paid the bill with a generosity worthy of his master, and got on his horse.

He had thought first of returning directly to Paris; but he remembered the uneasiness which his prolonged absence would cause Raoul. He remembered that Raoul was only two leagues from this place, that in a quarter of an hour he could reach him, and that the going, explanation, and return would not take an hour. He set off at a gallop, and ten minutes after he dismounted at the Crowned Mule—the only inn at Mazingarbe.

At the first words he exchanged with the host, he acquired the certainty that he had overtaken him whom he was seeking.

Raoul was at dinner with the Comte de Guiche and his preceptor; but the melancholy adventure of the morning left a sadness in their faces which all the gaiety of M. d'Arminges, more of a philosopher than they by his greater familiarity with this sort of spectacles, could not succeed in removing.

All of a sudden the door opened, and Grimaud appeared pale, dusty, and still covered with some of the wounded man's blood.

'Grimaud, good Grimaud!' exclaimed Raoul; 'I see you at last. Excuse me, Messieurs; he is not a servant, but a friend.' And rising and hurrying towards him, 'How is Monsieur the Count?' said he. 'Have you seen him since we started? Tell me—but I have also many things to tell you. Well, for the last three days we have met with many adventures—but what is the matter? How pale you are! Blood, too! Why!'

'Indeed there is some blood on him,' said the count, rising. 'Are you wounded, my friend?'

'No, Monsieur; it is not my blood.'

'But whose is it?' asked Raoul.

'It is the blood of the unfortunate man whom you left at the inn, and who died in my arms.'

'In your arms!—that man! But do you know who he was?'

'Yes,' said Grimaud.

'But he was the former executioner at Béthune.'

'I know it.'

'And you know him?'

'I know him.'

'And he is dead?'

'Yes.' The two young men looked at each other.

'What of that, Messieurs?' said d'Arminges; 'it is the universal law, and from it not even an executioner is free. I thought badly of the wound when I saw it, and you know it was his opinion too, since he asked for the monk.'

At the word *monk* Grimaud turned pale.

'Come to the table,' said d'Arminges, who like all men of that period, and especially of his age, do not interpose sentiment between two courses.

'Yes, Monsieur, you are right,' said Raoul. 'Come, Grimaud, give your orders, be served; and when you are rested, we will have a talk.'

'No, Monsieur,' said Grimaud. 'I cannot stop a moment; I must return to Paris.'

'What, return to Paris! You are mistaken; it is Olivain. You are to stay.'

'On the contrary, Olivain must remain, and I must go. I have come expressly to tell you this.'

'What does this change mean?'

'I cannot tell you.'

'Explain yourself.'

'I cannot explain.'

'Come, now, what does this joke mean?'

'Monsieur the Viscount knows that I never joke.'

'Yes; but I know also that M. le Comte de la Fère told me you were to remain, and Olivain to return. I shall follow the count's instructions.'

'Not under the present circumstances, Monsieur.'

'Will you disobey me, by any chance?'

'Yes, Monsieur, for it is necessary.'

'So you persist?'

'So I set out; be at ease, Monsieur the Viscount;' and Grimaud bowed, and turned towards the door to go out. Raoul, angry and uneasy at the same time, ran after him, and held him by the arm.

'Grimaud!' he exclaimed, 'stop, I want you to!'

'Then,' said Grimaud, 'in that case, you wish me to let Monsieur the Count be killed.'

'Grimaud, my friend, don't go away thus; don't leave me in such anxiety. Speak, for Heaven's sake!' And Raoul, staggering, fell upon a chair.

'I can tell you one thing only, Monsieur—for the secret you ask of me does not belong to me. You have met with a monk, have you not?'

'Yes.'

The two young men looked at each other affrightedly.

'You conducted him to the wounded man?'

'Yes.

'Did you have time to see him?'

'Yes.'

'And would you be able to recognize him if you ever met him?'

'Oh, yes, I swear I could,' said Raoul.

'And so could I,' said Guiche.

'Well, if you ever meet him,' said Grimaud, 'wherever it may be—on the highway, in the street, in a church—put your foot upon him, and kill him without pity, as you would strike a serpent. Don't leave him till he is dead; the lives of five men will be in jeopardy so long as he lives.'

Without adding another word, Grimaud took advantage of the terror and astonishment which he had caused his hearers, to rush out of the room.

'Well, Count,' said Raoul, turning round towards Guiche, 'did not I tell you truly that that monk affected me like a reptile?'

Two minutes after they heard a horse's gallop. It was Grimaud, *en route* for Paris. He raised his hat to the viscount, who had gone to the window, and soon disappeared at a turn in the road.

While travelling, Grimaud remembered two things; first, that at that pace his horse could not carry him ten leagues; second, that he had no money. But Grimaud's inventive faculties had been quickened by his habit of silence. At the first posting-house he sold his horse, and with the proceeds travelled with post-horses.

XXXVI

THE EVE OF BATTLE

RAOUL was interrupted in very sombre reflections by the host, who unceremoniously entered the room, crying out, 'The Spaniards! the Spaniards!'

This cry was serious enough to remove, from its importance, all preoccupation. The young men asked for information, and learned that the enemy was in fact advancing* by Houdin and Béthune.

While M. d'Arminges gave orders to bring the horses, the young men went upstairs; and from the highest windows of the house saw, in fact, appearing in the direction of Marsin and Lens, a considerable corps of infantry and cavalry. This time it was no longer a straggling party, but quite an army. There was nothing better to do than follow the wise instructions of M. d'Arminges, and beat a retreat.

The young men came quickly down. M. d'Arminges was already mounted. Olivain was holding the two horses of the young men. The Comte de Guiche's servants carefully guarded the Spanish prisoner, placed on a nag which had been bought for the purpose. For increase of precaution, his hands were tied.

The little troop went at a trot towards Cambrin, where they hoped to find the prince; but he had gone in the evening and had retired to La Bassée, some false intelligence having come that the enemy would be passing the Lys* at Estaire.

The fact is, that, deceived by this intelligence, the prince had withdrawn his troops from Béthune, had concentrated all his forces between Vieille Chapelle and La Venthie, and having just returned from a reconnaissance along the whole line with Maréchal de Grammont, had sat down to table, questioning the officers who were seated near him about the information he had requested each of them to procure; but no one had any certain news to tell. The enemy's forces had disappeared during the last forty-eight hours, and seemed to have vanished.

Now, an army is never so near, and consequently so threatening, as when it has quite been lost sight of. The prince was therefore sullen and anxious, contrary to his habit, when an officer on duty entered, and informed the marshal that someone wanted to speak to him. The Duc de Grammont asked, by a look, the prince's permission, and went out. The prince followed him with his eyes, and kept looking towards the door, no one daring to speak for fear of disturbing his thoughts.

Suddenly a sound was heard. The prince rose quickly, extending his hand in the direction whence it came. He knew it well. It was the firing of cannon. Everyone else rose too. At that moment the door opened.

'Monseigneur,' said the marshal, looking pleased, 'will your Highness permit my son, the Comte de Guiche, and his travelling companion, the Vicomte de Bragelonne, to come and give you news of the enemy whom we are in search of, and whom they have found?'

'Why, indeed,' said the prince, briskly; 'will I permit? Let them come in by all means.'

The marshal led the young men forward, who found themselves in the prince's presence.

'Speak, Messieurs,' said the prince, bowing to them, 'Speak first; then we will exchange the usual compliments. The most important matter for us just now is to know where the enemy is, and what he is doing.'

It naturally fell to the Comte de Guiche to speak. He was not only the older, but he had already been presented to the prince by his father. He had known the prince for a long time. Raoul now saw him for the first time. The count therefore told the prince what he had seen from the inn at Mazingarbe. Meanwhile, Raoul was scanning this young general, already so famous for the battles of Rocroy, Fribourg, and Nordlingen.*

Louis de Bourbon, Prince de Condé, who, since the death of Henri de Bourbon, his father, was called, by abbreviation and according to the custom of the time, Monsieur the Prince, was a young man of about twenty-six years of age, with eagle look—'*agl occhi grifani*',* as Dante writes—with curved nose, long hair flowing in curls; of moderate size, but well made; having all the qualities of a great warrior—that is to say, quick glance, ready decision, and fabulous courage. But this did not prevent him from being at the same time a man of fashion and wit to such an extent that besides the revolution he effected in warfare by the new ideas which he embodied in it, he made a complete change at Paris among the young courtiers, of whom he was the natural chief, and who, in opposition to the fashionable leaders of the older court, of which Bassompierre, Bellegarde, and the Duc d'Angoulême had been the models, were styled coxcombs.

At the first words of the Comte de Guiche, and from the direction whence the cannon fire proceeded, the prince had comprehended it all. The enemy intended to cross the Lys at St Venant, and march upon Lens, doubtless intending to take that city, and cut off the French army from France. The cannonading which was heard, whose booming prevailed from time to time over the other, proceeded from cannon of large calibre replying to the Spanish and Lorraine artillery.

But what was the amount of the force? Was it merely a corps intended to make a diversion, or the entire army? That was the prince's last question, to which Guiche was unable to give an answer. Now, as that was the most important, so was it that also to which the prince would have desired an exact, positive reply. Raoul had by that time overcome the very natural feeling of timidity, which he felt in spite of himself, of thrusting himself into the prince's notice.

'Will Monseigneur permit me to say a few words on this matter, which will perhaps remove the difficulty?' said Raoul.

The prince turned round, and seemed in a single look to read the young man thoroughly. He smiled to see a mere boy of scarcely fifteen.

'Certainly, Monsieur, speak,' said he, softening his usually abrupt and emphasized voice, as if he were now speaking to a woman.

'Monseigneur,' replied Raoul, blushing, 'could interrogate the Spanish prisoner.'

'You have taken a Spaniard prisoner?'

'Yes, Monseigneur.'

'Ah, that's true!' said Guiche. 'I had forgotten him.'

'That is quite natural, for it was you who took him, Count,' said Raoul, smiling.

The old marshal turned towards the viscount, grateful for this praise bestowed on his son; while the prince exclaimed, 'The young man is right; let the prisoner be brought in.'

Meanwhile the prince took Guiche aside, and asked him how he had taken this prisoner, and who this young man was.

'Monsieur,' said the prince, going towards Raoul, 'I know you have a letter from my sister, Madame de Longueville; but I see you have preferred to recommend yourself to me by giving good advice.'

'Monseigneur,' said Raoul, blushing, 'I did not wish to interrupt your Highness in your important conversation with Monsieur the Count. Here is the letter.'

'That is right,' said the prince; 'you can give it to me later on. Here is the prisoner; let us think of the more pressing matter.'

In fact, the prisoner was just led in. He was one of those *condottieri* of whom some still existed at that time—men who sold their lives to any who would buy them, and who were grown old in roguery and pillage. He had not spoken a word since he had been taken; so that those who had captured him did not themselves know of what nation he was.

The prince gave him a look of unutterable distrust.

'To what nation do you belong?' he asked.

The prisoner replied in some foreign language.

'Ah, he seems to be a Spaniard! Do you speak Spanish, Grammont?'

'Upon my word, Monseigneur, very little.'

'And I not at all,' said the prince, laughing. 'Messieurs,' he added, turning round towards those who surrounded him, 'does any one of you speak Spanish, who can act as interpreter?'

'I, Monseigneur,' said Raoul.

'Ah! You speak Spanish?'

'Enough, I think, to execute your Highness's orders on this occasion.'

All this time the prisoner remained impassive, and as if he did not in the least understand what was going on.

'Monseigneur wants to know of what nation you are,' said the young man, in the purest Castilian.

'Ich bin ein Deutcher,' replied the prisoner.

'What the devil does he say?' asked the prince; 'and what new gibberish is that?'

'He says he is a German, Monseigneur,' replied Raoul; 'yet I doubt it—for his accent is bad, and his pronunciation is defective.'

'You speak German as well?' asked the prince.

'Yes, Monseigneur.'

'Enough to question him in that language?'

'Yes, Monseigneur.'

'Question him, then.'

Raoul began, but facts supported his opinion. The prisoner did not, or pretended he did not, understand what Raoul said to him, nor could Raoul make out his medley of Flemish and Alsatian. However, in the midst of all the efforts of the prisoner to escape a formal interrogatory, Raoul had recognized the man's natural accent.

'You are not a Spaniard,' he said, 'nor a German; you are an Italian.'

The prisoner started, and bit his lips.

'Ah, then, I understand it thoroughly,' said the prince; 'and since he is an Italian, I can continue the examination. Thanks, Viscount,' he added, laughing, 'I shall call you from this moment my interpreter.'

But the prisoner was no more disposed to answer in Italian than in any other language; what he wished was to elude the questioning. So he knew nothing, neither the number of the army, nor the names of the commanders, nor the direction of the movements.

'Very well,' said the prince, who quite understood the reasons for this ignorance; 'this man has been taken while pillaging and assassinating. He might have purchased his life by speaking; but as he does not mean to, take him off and shoot him.'

The prisoner turned pale; the two soldiers who had led him in each took him by an arm, and led him towards the door, while the prince, turning towards Maréchal de Grammont, seemed to have already forgotten the order which he had given.

When he reached the threshold, the prisoner stopped. 'One moment,' said he, in French; 'I am ready to speak, Monseigneur.'

'Ah, ah!' said the prince, 'I knew well enough that it would end thus. I have a first-rate secret for loosening tongues. Young men, profit by it, as you may require it when you yourselves are in command.'

'But on the condition,' continued the prisoner, 'that your Highness will swear not to take my life.'

'Upon the honour of a gentleman,' said the prince.

'In that case, put your questions, Monseigneur.'

'Where did the army cross the Lys?'

'Between St Venant and Aire.'

'By whom is it commanded?'

'By Comte de Fuonsaldagna, General Beck, and the archduke in person.'

'How many men in it?'

'Eighteen thousand, and thirty-six pieces of cannon.'*

'And it is marching?'

'On Lens.'

'Do you see, Messieurs?' said the prince, turning round with a triumphant air towards the marshal and the other officers.

'Yes, Monseigneur,' said the marshal; 'you have divined all that the human mind possibly could.'

'Recall Le Plessis, Bellièvre, Villequier, and d'Erlac,' said the prince, 'and all the troops which are on this side of the Lys. Let them hold themselves ready to march to-night. Tomorrow probably we shall attack the enemy.'

'But, Monseigneur,' said the Maréchal de Grammont, 'remember that in uniting all we have of disposable force, we shall hardly reach the number of thirteen thousand men.'

'Monsieur the Marshal,' said the prince, with that admirable look which belonged only to him, 'it is with small armies that one gains great battles.' Then turning towards the prisoner, 'Let him be removed, and kept carefully within sight. His life depends on the information he has given us. If true, he will be set free; if false, he will be shot.'

They removed the prisoner.

'Comte de Guiche,' replied the prince, 'it is a long time since you have seen your father; stay with him. Monsieur,' continued he, speaking to Raoul, 'if not too fatigued, follow me.'

'To the end of the world, Monseigneur,' cried Raoul, showing for this young general, who seemed to him so worthy of his renown, an unexpected enthusiasm.

The prince smiled. He despised flatterers, but highly valued enthusiasts.

'Well, Monsieur,' said he, 'you are a good adviser; we have just proved that. Tomorrow we shall see how you behave in action.'

'And I, Monseigneur,' said the marshal—'what shall I do?'

'Remain to receive the troops. Either I shall return to seek them myself, or I shall send you a messenger that you may lead them to me. Twenty guards well mounted is all that I have need of for my escort.'

'That is very few,' said the marshal.

'It is enough,' said the prince. 'Have you a good horse, M. de Bragelonne?'

'Mine was killed this morning, Monseigneur, and I am riding my servant's for the present.'

'Ask and choose for yourself the one that will suit you best in my stables. No mock modesty; take the one you think the best. You will need it this evening perhaps, but certainly tomorrow.'

Raoul did not want the words repeated. He knew that with superiors, and especially if they are princes, the highest politeness is to obey without delay or arguing. He went to the stables, chose a dun-coloured Andalusian horse, saddled it himself—for Athos had recommended him in time of danger not to entrust these important concerns to any one—and then rejoined the prince, who was by that time on horseback.

'Now, Monsieur,' said he to Raoul, 'will you give me the letter of which you are the bearer?'

Raoul handed the letter to the prince.

'Keep near me, Monsieur.'

The prince used both spurs, threw the bridle on the pommel of the saddle, as he was in the habit of doing when he wanted to have both hands at liberty, opened Madame de Longueville's letter, and set off at a gallop on the route to Lens, accompanied by Raoul, and followed by his escort of twenty guards, while the aides-de-camp, who had to recall the troops, started off at full gallop in different directions. The prince read while going along.

'Monsieur,' said he, after a moment or two, 'they speak of you in the best terms. I have only one thing to inform you of; namely, after the little I have seen and heard, I have a still higher opinion of you than they have expressed.' Raoul bowed.

In the mean time, at each step which the small troop took nearer Lens, the boom of the cannon sounded much closer. The attention of the prince was drawn towards the sound with the fixedness of a bird of prey. One might have said that he had the power of piercing the barrier of trees which stretched before him and bounded the horizon.

From time to time the nostrils of the prince dilated, as if he was in haste to inhale the odour of the powder, and he breathed hard like his horse.

At last the cannon was heard so near that it was evident that the battlefield was not more, at least, than a league off. In fact, at a turn in the road, they saw the little village of Aunay.

The peasants were in great confusion; the report of the cruelties of the Spaniards had spread, and frightened every one. The women had already fled towards Vitry; some men alone remained. On seeing the prince, they ran towards him. One of them recognized him.

'Ah, Monseigneur,' said he; 'have you come to drive away these beggarly Spaniards and all the pillagers of Lorraine?'

'Yes,' said the prince, 'if you are willing to act as guide.'

'Willingly, Monseigneur; where does your Highness wish me to guide you?'

'To some elevated spot whence I can spy out Lens and its environs.'

'I am your man in this case, Monseigneur.'

'I can trust in you? You are a good Frenchman?'

'I am an old soldier of Rocroy, Monseigneur.'

'Here,' said the prince, giving him his purse, 'this is for Rocroy. Now, do you want a horse, or do you prefer going on foot?'

'On foot, Monseigneur; I have always served in the infantry. Besides, I count on helping your Highness to pass along roads where one is obliged to go on foot.'

'Go on, then,' said the prince, 'and don't let us lose any time.'

The peasant set off, running before the prince's horse; then, a few yards from the village, he took a by-road which was lost in the bottom of a small, pretty valley. For half a league they thus marched under the cover of trees; the firing sounded so near that one would have said each report would precede the hissing of the ball. At last they came to a path which left the road to reach the mountainside. The peasant took the path, inviting the prince to follow. The latter dismounted, ordered one of his aides-de-camp and Raoul to do the same, and the rest to await orders; then keeping on the alert, he began to climb the path.

At the end of ten minutes they reached the ruins of an old château that crowned the summit of a hill from which was a wide prospect. Scarcely a quarter of a league distant appeared Lens, hard pressed, and before it the whole army of the enemy.

At a single glance the prince took in the whole extent of country from Lens to Vimy. In a moment the whole plan of the battle which was to save France the next day from a second invasion unfolded itself in his mind. He took a pencil, tore out a page from his writing-tablets, and wrote:

MY DEAR MARSHAL—In an hour Lens will be in the enemy's hands. Come to me; bring with you the whole army. I shall be at Vendin to show the position it is to take up. Tomorrow we shall have retaken Lens, and beaten the enemy.

Then, turning to Raoul, 'Go, Monsieur,' said he, 'at a gallop, and deliver this letter to M. de Grammont.'

Raoul bowed, took the letter, descended the hill rapidly, jumped upon his horse and rode off at a gallop, and in a quarter of an hour had reached the marshal. One part of the troops had already arrived; the rest were expected every moment.

The Maréchal de Grammont put himself at the head of all the disposable infantry and cavalry, and took the road to Vendin, leaving the Duc de Châtillon to wait, and bring up the rest.

All the artillery was ready to start at the instant, and began its march.

It was seven in the evening when the marshal reached the rendezvous. The prince was awaiting him there. As he had foreseen, Lens fell into the enemy's hands almost immediately after Raoul's departure. The cessation of the cannonade had announced it also.

They awaited night. As the darkness increased, the troops ordered up by the prince successively arrived. Orders had been given not to beat a drum nor sound a trumpet.

At nine night was quite come. Yet some last rays of twilight still lighted up the plain. The army marched in silence, the

prince heading the column. On the other side of Aunay the
army came in sight of Lens; some houses were in flames, and
a dull noise, which indicated the agony of a town taken by
assault, reached the ears of the soldiers.

The prince arranged the positions: the marshal was to hold
the extreme left, and to rest on Méricourt; the Duc de Châtillon commanded the centre; finally, the prince, on the right
wing, rested in front of Aunay. Tomorrow's order of battle was
to be the same as that of the positions taken the evening before.
All on awaking would be on the ground where they would
manœuvre.

The movement was executed in the profoundest silence, and
with the greatest precision. At half-past ten the prince visited
the positions, and gave the orders for the next day.

Three things were enjoined above all upon the chiefs, who
were to see to it that the soldiers observed them scrupulously.
The first, that the different corps should look at one another
in the march, so that the cavalry and the infantry should be
on the same line, and that each should preserve its intervals.
The second, to make the charge only at a walk; the third, to
allow the enemy to fire first.

The prince gave up the Comte de Guiche to his father, but
retained Bragelonne for himself; but the young men asked to
pass the night together, which request was granted. A tent was
pitched for them near the marshal's. Although the day had
been fatiguing, neither of them could sleep.

The eve of a battle is a grave affair, even for veteran troops;
but much more so for young men, now for the first time seeing
this terrible spectacle. At that time one thinks of a thousand
things which had been forgotten till then. The indifferent
become friends, and friends brothers. There is no need to say
that if there is some tender feeling hidden within the heart, it
naturally reaches then the highest degree of exaltation possible
to it. So we must believe that these two felt some like sentiment, for very soon they seated themselves at opposite ends of
the tent, and began to write on their knees.

The letters were long; the four pages were soon closely filled.
From time to time they looked at each other smilingly. They
understood each other without speaking; their highly sym-

pathetic temperaments seemed made to understand without speech.

The letters, when finished, were each put into two envelopes, that the name of the person to whom it was addressed could not be read; then approaching each other, they exchanged letters with a smile.

'If anything should happen to me,' said Bragelonne.

'If I should be killed,' said Guiche.

'Rest easy,' said both of them.

Then they embraced like two brothers, wrapped themselves in their cloaks, and slept that youthful, peaceful sleep which birds, flowers, and children sleep.

XXXVII

A DINNER AS OF YORE

THE second interview of the former musketeers had not been so formal and threatening as the first. Athos had thought, with that prudence in which he so excelled, that the table would be the most speedy and complete centre of reunion; and just when his friends, from regard for his eminence and moderation, did not dare to refer to those dinners of old times at the Pineapple or the Parpaillot,* he was the first to suggest a meeting round some well-covered table, and of each giving himself without reserve to speaking and acting according to his bent—an unconstraint which had kept alive in them that good mutual understanding whence they formerly obtained the name of The Inseparables.

The proposition was acceptable to all, and especially to d'Artagnan, who was eager to resume the piquancy and gaiety of the converse belonging to former days; for during a long time his bright and joyous spirit had met with only insufficient satisfactions—a contemptible sort of food, as he himself called it. Porthos, on the point of being created a baron, was delighted to have the opportunity of studying the tone and manners of people of fashion as seen in Athos and Aramis. Aramis wanted to get the news of the Palais-Royal from d'Artagnan and

Porthos, and to keep in on all occasions with friends so devoted, who formerly upheld his disputes with swords so ready and invincible. As for Athos, he was the only one who had nothing to expect nor receive from the rest, and who was constrained only by a feeling of simple greatness and pure friendship.

It was agreed then that each should give the others an exact address, and that at the desire of any one a meeting should be called at the house of a famous caterer in the Rue de la Monnaie, at the sign of the Hermitage. The first meeting was to take place on Wednesday next,* at 8 p.m. precisely.

On that day the four friends arrived punctually at the hour named, and each from his own quarters. Porthos had had a new horse to try; d'Artagnan came from his guard at the Louvre; Aramis had had to visit one of his penitents in the quarter; and Athos, who had established his domicile at the Rue Guénégaud, found himself close at hand. They were then surprised to meet one another at the door of the Hermitage, Athos coming out by the Pont Neuf, Porthos by the Rue du Roule, d'Artagnan by the Rue des Fossés St Germain l'Auxerrois, Aramis by the Rue de Béthisy.* The first words exchanged, simply from the affected manner which each showed in his welcome to the rest, were somewhat constrained. The repast itself began with a sort of stiffness. It was evident that d'Artagnan forced himself to laugh, Athos to drink, Aramis to tell stories, Porthos to keep silent. Athos noticed this embarrassment, and ordered, as bringing a speedy remedy, four bottles of champagne. On this order being given with Athos's habitual calm, the Gascon's face looked pleased, and Porthos's expanded. Aramis was astonished. He knew not only that Athos no longer drank much, but that he even evinced a distaste for wine. This astonishment was redoubled when Aramis saw Athos pour out a bumper, and drink with his old enthusiasm. D'Artagnan immediately filled and emptied his glass. Porthos and Aramis struck their glasses together. In a short time the four bottles were empty, and this excellent specific had dissipated the slightest cloud which might have remained deep in their hearts. The four friends began to talk loudly without waiting for one to finish before the other began, and to assume their favourite postures at the table. Soon—a most uncommon thing—Aramis undid two aigulets* of his doublet, seeing which, Porthos untied all his.

The battles, the long journeys, the blows given and taken, were the first items of the conversation. Then they passed on to the secret struggles sustained against him who was now called the great cardinal.

'Upon my word,' said Aramis, laughing, 'we have given praise enough to the dead, let us slander the living a little. I should like to have a turn at Mazarin a bit—may I?'

'Go on,' said d'Artagnan, bursting into laughter; 'tell your story, and I will applaud you if it be a good one.'

'A great prince,' said Aramis, 'whose alliance Mazarin desired, was invited by the latter to send a list of the conditions on which he was willing to do him the honour of associating with him. The prince, who had some repugnance against treating with such a vulgar pedant, reluctantly made out the list and sent it to him. In this list were three conditions which displeased Mazarin; he offered the prince ten thousand crowns to give them up.'

'Ah, ah, ah!' exclaimed the three friends, 'that was not dear, and he ran no risk of being taken at his word. What did the prince do?'

'The prince immediately sent fifty thousand livres to Mazarin, begging him never to write to him again, and offering twenty thousand livres in addition if he engaged never to speak to him again.'

'What did Mazarin do?'

'He took offence?' said Athos.

'He beat the messenger?' said Porthos.

'He took the money?' said d'Artagnan.

'You have guessed right, d'Artagnan,' said Aramis.

And they all laughed so boisterously that the host came up to ask if they needed anything. He had thought they were fighting. At last the hilarity died away.

'May we have a laugh at M. de Beaufort?' asked d'Artagnan. 'I feel a strong desire to do so.'

'Go on,' said Aramis, who knew thoroughly that sharp, bold, Gascon spirit which never drew back a step on any ground.

'And you, Athos?' asked d'Artagnan.

'Upon my word, we shall laugh if you say anything funny.'

'Well, then, to begin,' said d'Artagnan. 'M. de Beaufort, talking one day with one of the friends of Monsieur the Prince, told him that in the early disputes between Mazarin and the parliament, he had found himself one day having a difference with M. de Chavigny, and that seeing him attached to the new cardinal, he who held to the older regime in many ways had cudgelled him in good style. This friend, who knew M. de Beaufort as being free with his hands, was not very much astonished at the fact, and went speedily to tell it to Monsieur the Prince. The thing spread about, and everyone began to turn his back on M. de Chavigny. The latter sought for an explanation of this general coolness. No one liked to tell him the reason; at last someone was bold enough to tell him that everyone was surprised that he should allow himself to be beaten by M. de Beaufort, even though he was a prince. "And who said that the prince had cudgelled me?" said Chavigny. "The prince himself," replied the friend. They traced the story to its source, and found the person with whom the prince held the conversation, who, appealed to his honour to tell the truth, repeated it, and confirmed it. Chavigny, filled with desperation at such a calumny, which he could not understand, declared to his friends that he would rather die than support such an affront. He therefore sent two emissaries to the prince to enquire if it was true that he had said he cudgelled M. de Chavigny. "I have said it, and I repeat it," said the prince. "Monseigneur," said one of Chavigny's seconds in reply, "allow me to tell your Highness that blows inflicted on a gentleman degrade the giver as much as the receiver. King Louis XIII was unwilling to have gentlemen for his *valets de chambre*, that he might have the right to beat them." "Well, but," asked M. de Beaufort, astonished, "who has received blows, and who talks of beating?" "Why, you, Monseigneur, who declare you have beaten——" "Whom?" "M. de Chavigny. Have you not *gourmé** M. de Chavigny?" "Yes, bless me! I have so well *gourmé* him that I will give you the exact words," said M. de Beaufort, with all that dignity which you remember he has: "My dear Chavigny, you are to blame for giving help to such a fool as this Mazarin." "Ah, Monseigneur," said the second, "I see now, it is blame [*gourmander*] that you meant." "*Gourmander, gourmer*, what then?" said the prince, "are they not the same thing? In truth, you word-makers are great pedants." '

They laughed a good deal at this mistake in using words by M. de Beaufort, whose blunders of this sort began to be proverbial; and it was agreed that as all party spirit was totally banished from these social reunions, d'Artagnan and Porthos might make their jokes about the princes on condition that Athos and Aramis could *gourmer* Mazarin.

'Upon my word,' said d'Artagnan to his two friends, 'you are right in wishing him ill, for he, on his part, does not wish you well.'

'Bah! really?' said Athos. 'If I thought that this fool knew my name only, I would be unbaptized for fear that people should think that I knew him.'

'He not only knows you by your name, but by your deeds; he knows that there are two gentlemen who have especially contributed to M. de Beaufort's escape, and he is busily on the lookout for them, I can answer for it.'

'Through whom?'

'Through me.'

'How, through you?'

'Yes; he sent for me this morning to learn if I had any information.'

'About these two gentlemen?'

'Yes.'

'And what did you reply?'

'That I had none as yet, but that I was going to dine with two persons who might be able to give me some.'

'You told him that?' said Porthos, with a loud laugh. 'Bravo! And that causes you no fear, Athos?'

'No,' said Athos, 'it is not Mazarin's search that I fear.'

'Tell me,' said Aramis, 'a little of what you fear.'

'Nothing indeed, in the present at least.'

'And in the past?' said Porthos.

'Ah! that's quite a different matter,' said Athos, with a sigh; 'in the past and in the future——'

'Do you feel concerned for your young Raoul?' asked Aramis.

'Nonsense!' said d'Artagnan, 'one is never killed in the first affair.'

'Nor in the second,' said Aramis.

'Nor in the third,' said Porthos. 'Besides, when one is killed one comes back again; and the proof is that we are here.'

'No,' said Athos, 'it is not Raoul that makes me feel at all anxious, for he will, I hope, conduct himself as a gentleman; and if he is killed, well—he will die bravely. Yet, if this should happen, well——' Athos passed his hand across his pale forehead.

'Well,' asked Aramis.

'Well,' he resumed, 'I should regard it as an expiation.'

'Ah!' said d'Artagnan, 'I know what you mean.'

'And I too,' said Aramis; 'but don't let us think of that, Athos. The past is the past.'

'I don't understand,' said Porthos.

'The affair at Armentières,' said d'Artagnan, in a low voice.

'The affair at Armentières?' asked he.

'Milady——' said d'Artagnan.

'Ah, yes,' said Porthos, 'that's true; I had forgotten it.'

Athos looked at him with a grave look.

'You had forgotten that, Porthos?' said he.

'Upon my word, yes; that was a long time ago.'

'The matter does not then weigh at all on your conscience?'

'Indeed, no!' said Porthos.

'And you, Aramis?'

'Well, it sometimes comes into my thoughts,' said Aramis, 'as one of those cases of conscience which give rise to discussion.'

'And you, d'Artagnan?'

'I confess that when my mind dwells on that terrible time, I have recollections only of the icy cold corpse of that unfortunate Madame Bonacieux. Yes, yes,' he muttered, 'I have often regret for the victim, but no remorse for her assassin.'

Athos shook his head with an air of doubt.

'Imagine,' said Aramis, 'if you admit the fact of divine justice, and its participation in mundane affairs, that this woman was punished by God's will. We were the instruments, that's all.'

'What then of free will, Aramis?'

'What does the judge do? He possesses free will, and condemns without fear. What the executioner? He has control over his arms, yet he strikes without remorse.'

'The executioner——' muttered Athos, and it was plain that he was struck by a sudden recollection.

'I know it is dreadful,' said d'Artagnan; 'but when I think we have slain English, people of Rochelle, Spanish, even French, who did us no other harm than meet us in combat and fail to strike, who have never done other wrong than to cross blades with us and not to come to the *parade* quickly enough, I feel excused for the share I took in the death of that woman—word of honour!'

'As for me,' said Porthos, 'now you remind me of it, Athos, I can see it as if it were before me: Milady was there where you are [Athos turned pale]; I was, as it were, where d'Artagnan is; I had at my side a sword which cut like a Damascus blade—you recollect it, Aramis, for you always called it Balisardo.* Well, I swear that if the executioner of Béthune had not been present—was it Béthune?—yes, Béthune, I would have cut off the neck of that wretch without taking breath, or even in taking breath! She was a wicked woman!'

'And then,' said Aramis, with that careless, philosophic air which he had acquired since taking orders in the Church, and in which there was more atheism than trust in God, 'what is the good of thinking about it? What's done is done! We will confess this deed at the last hour, and God knows better than we do whether it is a crime, a fault, or a meritorious action. Do you ask if I repent of it? In faith, no! On my honour and on the cross, I am only sorry that it was a woman.'

'The most satisfactory point in it all,' said d'Artagnan, 'is that no trace remains of it.'

'She had a son,' said Athos.

'Ah, yes, I know that very well,' said d'Artagnan; 'and you have spoken to me of him, but who knows what has become of him? Do you think that Winter, his uncle, would have brought up that young serpent? The serpent dead, the brood dead too! Winter will have condemned the son as he condemned the mother.'

'The child is dead, or may the devil take me!' said Porthos. 'There is so much fog in that frightful country, so d'Artagnan says, at least——'

Just when this conclusion at which Porthos had arrived would perhaps have restored gaiety to these more or less clouded countenances, a noise of feet was heard on the stairs, and a knock came at the door.

'Come in!' said Athos.

'Messieurs,' said the host, 'there is a man in a great hurry who wants to speak to one of you.'

'Which of us?' they all asked.

'The one named the Comte de la Fère.'

'And what is his name?' asked Athos.

'Grimaud.'

'Ah,' said Athos, turning pale, 'back already? What has happened to Bragelonne?'

'Let him come in!' said d'Artagnan.

But Grimaud had already come up, and was waiting at the door. He hurried into the room, and dismissed the host by a sign. The host closed the door; the four friends were in expectation. Grimaud's agitation, his pallor, the perspiration on his face, the dust which soiled his garments, all told that he was the messenger of some important and terrible news.

'Messieurs,' said he, 'that woman had a child; the child has become a man. The tigress had a cub; the tiger is launched. He comes to attack you; take care!'

Athos looked at his friends with a melancholy smile. Porthos sought at his side his sword, which was hanging on the wall; Aramis seized his dagger; d'Artagnan rose to his feet.

'What do you mean, Grimaud!' exclaimed the last.

'That the son of Milady has left England; that he is in France; that he is coming to Paris, if he is not here already.'

'The devil!' said Porthos, 'are you sure?'

'Sure!' said Grimaud.

A long silence followed this statement. Grimaud was so out of breath and fatigued that he fell into a chair.

Athos filled a glass with champagne, and gave it to him.

'Well, after all,' said d'Artagnan, 'though he live and be come to Paris, we have had to do with plenty of others. Let him come!'

'Yes,' said Porthos, throwing a loving look upon his sword hanging upon the wall; 'we await him. Let him come!'

'Besides, he is only a child,' said Aramis.

Grimaud got up.

'A child!' said he. 'Do you know what this child has done? Disguised as a monk, he has found out the whole story while confessing the executioner of Béthune, and after having confessed him and learned all, he for absolution plunged into his heart this poniard which you see here. Observe that it is still red and damp, for it is not more than thirty hours ago that it was drawn from the wound.' And Grimaud threw it on the table.

All but Athos rose and spontaneously took their swords. Athos alone remained seated, calm and reflective.

'And you say he is dressed like a monk, Grimaud?'

'Yes, like an Augustinian monk.'

'What sort of a man is he?'

'Of my height, so the host told me—thin, pale, with bright blue eyes and fair hair!'

'And—he has not seen Raoul?'

'On the contrary, they met; and it was the viscount himself who took him to the bed of the dying man.'

Athos got up without saying a word, and took down his sword also.

'Come now, Messieurs!' said d'Artagnan, trying to laugh, 'we look like so many silly women! How absurd, we four who have without a frown made head against armies are now trembling because of a child!'

'Yes,' said Athos, 'but this child comes in the name of God.'

And they all hurriedly left the hotel.

XXXVIII

THE LETTER FROM CHARLES I

THE reader must now cross the Seine with us, and follow us to the gate of the Carmelite convent in the Rue St Jacques.* It was eleven in the morning, and the pious Sisters had come to say a Mass for the success of Charles I's arms.* On leaving the church, a woman and a young girl dressed in black—the one as a widow and the other as an orphan—had returned to their cell. The woman knelt on a *priedieu* of painted wood; and a few paces from her, the girl, supported by a chair, stood and wept.

The woman would have been beautiful; but sorrow doubtless had made her look old. The girl was charming, and her tears made her seem more so. The woman seemed about forty, the girl fourteen.

'O God,' said the suppliant, 'preserve my husband and my son, and take my life, which is so sad and wretched!'

'O God,' said the girl, 'still preserve my mother!'

'Your mother can do nothing more for you in this world, Henrietta.* She has no longer a throne, husband, son, money, nor friend; your mother, my poor child, is abandoned by all.'

And the woman, falling back into the arms of her daughter, who rushed forward to support her, herself also fell into a fit of weeping.

'Mother, take courage!' said the girl.

'Ah! kings are unfortunate this year,' said the mother, leaning her head on the girl's shoulder; 'no one troubles himself about us in this land, for everyone thinks of his own affairs. So long as your brother* was with us he sustained me; but he has gone. He can send no news of himself to me or to his father. I have pawned my last jewels, sold all my clothes and yours to pay his servants' wages, who would have refused to accompany him if I had not made this sacrifice. Now we are obliged to live at the expense of the Carmelite Sisters. We belong to the poor, who are helped by God.'

'But why do you not apply to the queen, your sister?'* asked the young girl.

'Alas!' said the afflicted mother, 'the queen is no longer queen, my child,—another reigns in her name. One day you will be able to understand all that.'

'Well, then, to the king, your nephew?* Would you like me to speak to him? Mother, you know how he loves me.'

'Alas! the king is not yet king; and he himself, you well know, for Laporte has told us twenty times, is in want of everything.'

'Then let us address ourselves to God,' said the girl. And she knelt down by the side of her mother.

These two females, who were thus praying side by side, were the daughter and granddaughter of Henry IV, the wife and daughter of Charles I. They were ending their prayers when a Sister tapped gently at the cell-door.

'Come in, Sister,' said the elder, wiping away her tears, and rising. The Sister respectfully opened the door.

'Will your Majesty pardon me for disturbing your devotions?' said she; 'but there is in the parlour a foreign lord come from England, who begs the honour of giving your Majesty a letter.'

'Oh, a letter! perhaps from the king! News of your father, without doubt. Do you hear, Henrietta?'

'Yes, Madame, I do, and I hope.'

'And who is this lord? speak!'

'A gentleman about fifty years old.'

'His name? Has he given his name?'

'Lord de Winter.'

'Lord de Winter!' cried the queen—'my husband's friend. Oh, let him come in, let him come in!' And the queen ran to meet the messenger, whose hand she seized with warmth.

Lord de Winter, on entering the cell, knelt down and presented the queen with a letter rolled up in a gold case.

'Ah, my Lord,' said the queen, 'you bring us three things that we have not seen for a long while,—gold, a devoted friend, and a letter from the king.'

Winter again bowed, but he could not reply, he was so greatly moved.

'My Lord,' said the queen, referring to the letter, 'you may suppose that I am very anxious to know its contents.'

'I will withdraw, Madame.'

'No, stay; we will read it before you. Can you not imagine that I have a thousand questions to put to you?'

Winter stepped back a few paces, and remained standing in silence.

The mother and daughter had withdrawn into a recess of the window, and read eagerly the following letter, the girl resting on her mother's arm:

MADAME AND DEAR WIFE—We have reached the end. All the resources that God has left us are gathered together in this camp of Naseby, whence I am writing to you in haste. Here I await the army of my rebellious subjects, and am going to struggle for the last time against them. If conqueror, I continue the struggle; conquered, I am lost utterly. I want, in this latter alternative (alas! when one is where we are, everything should be provided for), to reach the coasts of France. But could they, would they receive an unfortunate king there, who would bring such a sad example to a country already disturbed by civil discord? Your wisdom and affection will serve me for guide. The bearer of this letter will tell you, Madame, what I cannot entrust to the risk of accident. He will explain to you what step I await from you. I give in charge to him also, my blessing for my children, and my heart's best affection for you, Madame and dear wife.

The letter was signed, instead of 'Charles, King', 'Charles, still King'.

This sad perusal, whose impressions on the queen's face Winter followed, yet brought a ray of hope to her mind.

'Though he is no longer king,' she exclaimed, 'though he is conquered, exiled, he yet lives! Alas! the throne is too perilous nowadays for me to wish him to remain on it. But tell me, my Lord, frankly, is his position as desperate as he imagines?'

'Alas, Madame, more desperate than he believes himself. His Majesty has so good a heart that he does not comprehend hatred; so loyal that he does not divine treachery. England is seized with a sort of madness* which I greatly fear will be only removed by blood.'

'But Lord Montrose?'* replied the queen. 'I have heard talk of great and rapid successes—of battles gained at Inverlochy, at Auldearn, at Alfort, and at Kilsyth. I heard that he was marching to the frontier to join his king.'

'Yes, Madame; but there he encountered Leslie. He had wearied victory by force of superhuman enterprises. Victory had abandoned him. Montrose, beaten at Philiphaugh, has been obliged to dismiss the remains of his army, and to flee disguised as a servant. He is at Bergen, in Norway.'

'God preserve him!' said the queen. 'It is at least a consolation to know that those who have so many times risked their lives for us are in safety. And now, my Lord, since the king's situation is so desperate, tell me what my royal husband desired you to say.'

'Well, Madame, the king wishes you to try and ascertain the feelings of the king and queen of France respecting him.'

'Alas, you know that the king is still under age, and the queen is a woman, very weak too; M. de Mazarin is all.'

'Would he desire to play the part in France which Cromwell* does in England?'

'Oh, no! He is a pliable, cunning Italian, who perhaps imagines crime, but will never dare commit it, and quite the opposite to Cromwell, who does as he likes with the two Houses. Mazarin has only the queen's support in his disputes with the Parliament.'

'The more reason, then, why he should protect a king whom the Parliament persecutes.'

The queen shook her head with bitterness.

'My own judgement, my Lord, is that the cardinal will do nothing, or perhaps even will be against us. The presence of myself and daughter in France already lies heavy on him, much more would that of the king. My Lord,' added Henrietta, with a melancholy smile, 'it is sad and almost shameful to have to say it, but we have passed the winter at the Louvre, without money, linen, almost without bread, and often not getting up for want of a fire.'

'Horrible,' exclaimed Winter. 'Henry IV's daughter! King Charles's wife!'

'This is the hospitality which a minister, in answer to a king's request, gives to a queen.'

'But I have heard talk of a marriage between my Lord the Prince of Wales and Mademoiselle d'Orléans.'

'Yes; I did for a while have a hope of it. The children love each other; but the queen, who had at first given her consent, has changed her mind. But M. le Duc d'Orléans, who had encouraged the commencement of their familiarity, has forbidden his daughter to think more of this union. Ah, my Lord,' continued the queen, without even thinking of wiping away her tears, 'it is better to fight as the king has, and to die as he may perhaps, than to live a beggar as I am doing.'

'Courage, Madame,' said Winter, 'courage. Do not despair. It is for the interest of the crown of France, so broken up just now, to oppose rebellion among a people so close to them. Mazarin is a statesman, and sees this necessity.'

'But are you sure,' said the queen, doubtfully, 'that you have not been forestalled?'

'By whom?' asked Winter.

'Why, by the Joyces, the Prides, the Cromwells.'*

'By a tailor, by a carter, by a brewer! Ah, I hope, Madame, that the cardinal will not ally himself with such men.'

'But what is he himself?' asked Henrietta.

'But for the honour of the king and of the queen——'

'Well, let us hope he will do something for that honour. A friend possesses such eloquence, my Lord, that you reassure me. Give me your hand, and let us go to the minister's.'

'Madame,' said Winter, bowing low, 'I am proud of this honour.'

'But what if he refuse,' said Henrietta, stopping, 'and the king should lose the battle?'

'His Majesty might then take refuge in Holland, where I have heard that my Lord the Prince of Wales is.'*

'And would his Majesty be able to count in his flight upon many servants like yourself?'

'Alas, no, Madame; but the thing was foreseen, and I have come to find some allies in France.'

'Allies!' said the queen, shaking her head.

'Madame, if I can find once more some old friends whom I had formerly, I would answer for everything.'

'Go on then, my Lord,' said the queen, with that strong doubt which fills the minds of people who have for a long time been unhappy,—'go on; and may God hear you!'

The queen entered her carriage, and Winter, on horseback, followed by two servants, rode beside her carriage door.

XXXIX

CROMWELL'S LETTER

JUST as Madame Henrietta was leaving the Carmelite convent to go to the Palais-Royal, a cavalier dismounted at the gate of the same royal residence, and told the guards that he had something important to say to Cardinal Mazarin. While the cardinal often felt afraid, yet as he had great need of intelligence, he was tolerably accessible. It was not at the first door that the stranger met any real difficulty, nor at the second, but at the third, for there, beside the guard and ushers, faithful Bernouin watched—a Cerberus whom no words could bend, no branch, even were it gold, could charm. It was, therefore, at the third door that the cavalier had to submit to a formal interrogatory.

The cavalier, having left his horse fastened to the railings, went up the grand staircase, and addressing the guards in the first room, 'M. le Cardinal Mazarin?' said he.

'Pass on,' replied the guards, without raising their heads—some over their cards, others at dice, wishing to show that it was not their business to fill the office of gentleman-usher.

The cavalier entered the second room. This was guarded by musketeers and ushers. He repeated his demand.

'Have you a letter of audience?' asked an usher, coming up to him.

'I have one, but not from Cardinal Mazarin.'

'Go in, and ask for M. Bernouin,' said the usher. And he opened the door of the third room.

Whether by chance or because it was his usual post, Bernouin was standing behind the door, and had heard all. 'It is I whom you want,' said he. 'From whom is the letter which you bring to his Eminence?'

'From General Oliver Cromwell,' said the newcomer. 'Will you announce that name to his Eminence, and let me know whether he will receive me or not?' And he held himself erect in the gloomy and proud attitude peculiar to the Puritans. Bernouin, after giving an inquisitorial look over the whole of the young man's person, entered the cardinal's cabinet, and gave him the message.

'One who brings me a letter from Oliver Cromwell! And what sort of a man is he?'

'A thorough Englishman; hair carroty red, eyes bluish grey, and moreover, proud and cold.'

'Let him give you the letter.'

'Monseigneur wants the letter,' said Bernouin, going back to the antechamber.

'Monseigneur will not see the letter without the bearer,' replied the young man. 'But to convince you that I am really bearer of a letter, look, here it is.'

Bernouin looked at the seal, and seeing that it really came from General Oliver Cromwell, was about to return to Mazarin.

'Add,' said the young man, 'that I am not a mere messenger, but an envoy extraordinary.'

Bernouin re-entered the cabinet, and came out after a few seconds. 'Enter, Monsieur,' said he, holding the door open.

Mazarin required all these ceremonial proceedings to keep down the emotion caused by the announcement of this letter; but however shrewd in mind, he searched in vain to fathom what Cromwell's motive could be for entering into communication with him.

The young man appeared at the threshold of the cabinet. He held his hat in one hand and the letter in the other.

Mazarin rose. 'You have, Monsieur,' said he, 'a letter of introduction to me?'

'This is it, Monseigneur,' said the young man.

Mazarin took the letter, unsealed it, and read:

M. Mordaunt, one of my secretaries, will deliver this letter of introduction to his Eminence the Cardinal Mazarin at Paris. He is also the bearer of a second confidential letter for his Eminence.

OLIVER CROMWELL

'Very well, M. Mordaunt, give me this second letter, and take a seat.'

The young man drew from his pocket a second letter, gave it to the cardinal, and seated himself.

In the mean time, absorbed in his reflections, the cardinal had taken the letter, and without unsealing it, turned it and re-turned it in his hand; but to put the bearer on the wrong scent, he began, as was his wont, to question him, convinced as he was by experience that few men succeeded in concealing anything from him when he interrogated and looked at them at the same time.

'You are very young, M. Mordaunt, for this difficult business of ambassador, in which sometimes the oldest diplomatists are stranded.'

'Monseigneur, I am twenty-three;* but your Eminence is mistaken in saying that I am young. I am older than yourself, although I have not your wisdom.'

'How so, Monsieur? I do not understand you.'

'I mean, Monseigneur, that years of suffering count twice over, and that I have been for twenty years a sufferer.'

'Ah, yes, I see,' said Mazarin; 'want of fortune. You are poor, are you not?' Then he said to himself, 'The English revolutionists are all beggars and rustics.'

'Monseigneur, I ought to have some day a fortune of six millions; but I am deprived of it.'

'You are not then a plebeian?' said the cardinal, astonished.

'If I took my proper title, I should be lord; if I went by my own name, you would hear one of the most illustrious names in England.'

'How do you call yourself, then?' asked Mazarin.

'I call myself M. Mordaunt,' said the young man, bowing.

Mazarin saw that Cromwell's messenger wished to keep his incognito. He was silent a moment; but he looked at him with greater attention than he had done at first. The young man was unmoved.

'To the devil with these Puritans!' said Mazarin to himself. 'They are all cut out of marble.' Then aloud, 'But are none of your relatives living?'

'Yes; one of them.'

'Then he helps you?'

'I have three times been to him to implore his help, and I have been driven away by his servants.'

'Dear me! My dear M. Mordaunt,' said Mazarin, hoping to catch the young man in a snare by his pretended pity, 'how your story interests me! You did not know your high birth?'

'I have known it only a short time.'

'And up to the moment when you knew it——'

'I considered myself an abandoned child.'

'Then you have never seen your mother?'

'Yes, I have, Monseigncur. When I was a mere child, she came three times to my nurse. I remember the last time as if it were today.'

'You have a good memory.'

'Oh, yes, Monseigneur,' said the young man, with such a singular accent that the cardinal felt a chill run through him.

'And who brought you up?'

'A French nurse, who sent me away when I was five years old because she was no longer paid, telling me the name of that relative of whom my mother had often spoken to her.'

'What became of you?'

'As I was crying and begging on the highways, a minister of Kingston took me in, instructed me in the Calvinistic faith, imparted to me all he knew, and helped me in my search after my family. But the search was fruitless; chance did it all.'

'You found out what became of your mother?'

'I learned that she had been assassinated by this relative, aided by four of his friends; but I already had learned that I had been deprived of my title and despoiled of all my property by King Charles.'

'Ah! I see now why you are serving Cromwell. You hate the king.'

'Yes, Monseigneur, I hate him!' said the young man.

Mazarin was astonished at the diabolical expression with which the young man pronounced these words; while ordinary visages have a deep blush, his visage was suffused with gall, and grew livid.

'Yours is a terrible history, M. Mordaunt, and touches me deeply; but happily for you, you serve an all-powerful master.

He ought to help you in your enquiries. We in power procure so much intelligence.'

'Monseigneur, show but the smallest trace of a scent to a high-bred dog, and he will follow it up.'

'But this relative of whom you have spoken, would you wish me to speak to him?' said Mazarin, who attached importance to making a friend near to Cromwell.

'Thanks, Monseigneur, I will speak to him myself.'

'But have you not told me he ill-used you?'

'He will treat me better the next time I see him.'

'You have then a means of softening his heart?'

'I have a means of making him fear me.'

Mazarin looked at the young man, but at the light which flashed from his eyes the cardinal lowered his head, and opened Cromwell's letter. By degrees the eyes of the young man became once more dull and glassy as usual, and he fell into a profound reverie. After having read the first lines, Mazarin ventured to take a sly look to see if Mordaunt were not watching his face; and remarking his indifference, 'Get your affairs done,' said he, imperceptibly shrugging his shoulders, 'by people who are doing their own at the same time! Let us see what the letter contains.'

We produce it verbatim:*

To his Eminence, M. le Cardinal Mazarini

I DESIRE Monseigneur, to know your views respecting the present state of affairs in England. The two kingdoms are too close to keep France from being interested in our condition as we are in that of France. The English are all but unanimous in resisting King Charles's tyranny and that of his partisans. Placed at the head of this movement by the confidence of the nation, I can appreciate better than any one else its nature and consequences. Today I expect to fight a decisive battle with the king. I shall gain it, for the hopes of the nation and the Spirit of the Lord are on my side. This battle gained, the king has no further resources either in England or Scotland, and if not taken or killed, he will try to cross into France to get recruits for his army, and to procure arms and money. France has already received Queen Henrietta, and doubtless without knowing it, has fostered a fire of inextinguishable civil war in my country; but Madame Henrietta is a daughter of France, and the hospitality of France was due to her. As for King Charles, the question differs totally; by receiving and helping him, France would show disapproval of the acts of the English people, and would so sensibly do hurt to England, and especially to the action of the government which she intends setting up, that such a condition would be equivalent to open hostility.

At this point, Mazarin, much annoyed at the turn which the letter took, ceased reading farther and looked slyly at the young man. He was as thoughtful as ever. Mazarin continued:

It is therefore urgent, Monseigneur, for me to know as to what I may rely on in the conduct of France; the interests of that kingdom and of England, although directed in opposite ways, yet approach nearer than one would believe. England has need of internal tranquillity to complete the expulsion of the king. France has need also to strengthen the throne of her young monarch; you need as much as we do that domestic peace which we are approaching, thanks to the energy of our government.

Your disputes with the parliament, your noisy quarrels with the princes, who today fight for you, and will tomorrow fight against you; the popular tenacity directed by the Coadjutor, the President Blanc-mesnil and the Councillor Broussel—all the disorder, in short, which runs through all the different classes of the State, ought to cause you to regard with disquietude the possibility of a foreign war; for then England, aroused by the enthusiasm of new ideas, would become an ally of Spain, which already courts an alliance. I have therefore thought, Monseigneur, knowing your prudence and the thoroughly personal position which events are now making for you, that you would prefer concentrating your strength in the interior of France, and leaving to its own resources the new government of England. This neutrality simply consists in keeping King Charles from French territory, and in not succouring either by arms, money, or troops, this king, entirely a stranger to your country.

My letter is therefore strictly confidential, and for that reason I have sent it by a man who enjoys my intimate confidence; it will precede, by a feeling that your Eminence will appreciate, the measures that I shall take after the events. Oliver Cromwell has thought that he would make an intelligent mind like that of Mazarini better understand reason than a queen, admirable, doubtless, for firmness, but too subject to silly prejudices respecting birth and divine right.

Adieu, Monseigneur. If I do not receive an answer within a fortnight, I shall regard my letter as null and void.

OLIVER CROMWELL

'M. Mordaunt,' said the cardinal, raising his voice as if to arouse the dreamer, 'my reply to this letter will be so much the more satisfactory to General Cromwell because I shall take care that no one shall know that I have made it. Go, therefore, and await it at Boulogne; and promise me to set off tomorrow morning.'

'I promise, Monseigneur; but how many days will your Eminence make me wait for the reply?'

'If you do not get one in ten days, you can set off.'

Mordaunt bowed.

'That is not all, Monsieur,' continued Mazarin. 'Your personal adventures have touched me greatly; besides, M. Cromwell's letter makes you important in my eyes as being his ambassador. Come, I repeat, tell me what I can do for you.'

Mordaunt thought a moment, and after visible hesitation was going to speak, when Bernouin entered hastily, and whispered something in the cardinal's ear. 'Monseigneur,' he said, 'Queen Henrietta, accompanied by an English gentleman, is at this moment entering the Palais-Royal.'

Mazarin started from his chair, a movement which did not escape the young man's notice, and checked the confidence which he was intending to show.

'Monsieur,' said the cardinal, 'you have understood, I hope. I have fixed Boulogne, because to you any French city is the same. If you prefer any other, name it; but you can easily imagine that surrounded as I am by influences from which I escape only by the use of discretion, I do not wish your presence in Paris to be known.'

'I shall set off,' said Mordaunt, making some steps towards the door by which he came in.

'No, not by that door, I beg of you,' the cardinal said quickly. 'Please go by this gallery, whence you will reach the hall. I do not wish any one to see you go out; our interview must be secret.'

Mordaunt followed Bernouin, who took him through an adjoining hall, and placed him in the charge of an usher while pointing out a door for exit. Then he hastily returned to introduce to his master Queen Henrietta, who was already passing along the glass gallery.

XL

MAZARIN AND QUEEN HENRIETTA

THE cardinal rose, and went in haste to receive the Queen of
England. He joined her in the middle of the gallery which led
to his cabinet. He showed all the more respect to this queen
without attendants and jewels, because he himself felt he
deserved reproach for his avarice and want of heart. But
supplicants know how to control their countenances, and Henry
IV's daughter smiled on entering the presence of him whom
she hated and despised.

'Ah!' said Mazarin to himself, 'what a sweet countenance!
Can she be come to borrow some money?'

And he cast an uneasy look upon the panel of his strong
box; he even turned inside the bezel* of the magnificent
diamond whose brilliancy attracted the eyes to his hand, which
was white and handsome. Unfortunately this ring had not the
power of that of Gyges,* which could render its owner invisible
when he did what Mazarin was just doing.

Now, Mazarin would have much liked to be invisible just
then, for he guessed that Madame Henrietta came to ask
something of him. When a queen whom he had so badly treated
appeared with a smile on her lips, instead of a threat on her
tongue, she came as a suppliant.

'Monsieur the Cardinal,' said the august visitor, 'I had had
the idea at first of speaking with the queen, my sister, of the
affair which brings me to you; but I have thought that political
affairs concern men before all.'

'Madame,' said Mazarin, 'believe me, your Majesty quite
confuses me by this flattering distinction.'

'He is very gracious,' thought the queen; 'could he then have
divined my purpose?'

They reached the cardinal's cabinet. He caused the queen
to be seated, and when she was settled in his armchair, 'Give
your commands,' said he, 'to the most respectful of your
servants.'

'Alas, Monsieur! I have lost the habit of giving orders, and have acquired that of making prayers. I come to pray of you, too happy if my prayer be heard by you.'

'I am listening, Madame.'

'Monsieur the Cardinal, it is concerning the war which the king, my husband, wages against his rebellious subjects. You are perhaps not aware that there is fighting in England,' said the queen, with a sad smile, 'and that in a short time they will fight in a manner much more decisive than they have done up to the present.'

'I am quite unaware of it, Madame,' said the cardinal, accompanying the words with a slight shrug. 'Alas! our own wars quite absorb the time and thoughts of a poor weak minister like myself.'

'Well, Monsieur the Cardinal,' said the queen, 'I will tell you then that Charles I, my husband, is on the eve of fighting a decisive battle. In case of defeat'—Mazarin gave a start—'one must provide for every contingency,' continued the queen; 'in case of defeat he desires to withdraw to France, and live there as a private individual. What do you say to this project?'

The cardinal had listened without letting a muscle of his face show his real thoughts; while listening, his smile continued as it always was, insincere and wheedling, and when the queen had finished, 'Do you think, Madame,' said he, in his softest tones, 'that France, as agitated and seething as she is herself, would be a safe harbour for a dethroned king? The crown is already very insecure on Louis XIV's head; how could he support a double weight?'

'That weight has not been very heavy so far as I am concerned,' the queen broke in with a sad smile; 'and I do not ask that more should be done for my husband than for me. You see we are very moderate princes, Monsieur.'

'Oh! for you, Madame,' the cardinal hastened to say, to cut short explanations which he saw coming, 'it is quite a different matter; a daughter of Henry IV—that grand, that sublime king.'

'A thing that does not prevent you from refusing hospitality to his son-in-law, is it not so, Monsieur? You ought, nevertheless, to remember that this grand, this sublime king, proscribed once as my husband is likely to be, had to ask help from

England, and that England gave it to him; it is true, I may add, that Queen Elizabeth was not his niece.*

'*Peccato!*' said Mazarin, struggling against that very simple logic. 'Your Majesty does not understand me; you misjudge my meaning, doubtless because I fail to explain myself clearly in French.'

'Speak Italian, Monsieur; Queen Marie de Médicis, our mother, taught us the language before the cardinal, your predecessor, sent her to die in exile. If anything remains of this grand, this sublime King Henry of whom you were speaking just now, he might indeed be astonished at your deep admiration for him conjoined with such scanty regard for his family.'

The perspiration ran in great drops down Mazarin's forehead.

'My admiration is on the contrary so great and real, Madame,' said Mazarin, not accepting the queen's offer to change the language, 'that if Charles I—whom God preserve from all misfortune!—come to France, I will offer him my own house; but, alas! it would be an insecure retreat. One day the people would set fire to it as they did to that of Marshal d'Ancre.* Poor Concino Concini! yet he wished only the good of France.'

'Yes, Monseigneur, as you do,' said the queen, ironically.

Mazarin pretended not to see the double meaning of the expression which he himself had used, and went on pitying the fate of Concini.

'But in short, Monseigneur,' said the queen, growing impatient, 'what is your reply?'

'Madame,' exclaimed Mazarin, more and more moved, 'would your Majesty allow me to give you some advice? Be it well understood that before being so bold I begin by putting myself at your Majesty's feet as regards anything that will please you.'

'Speak, Monsieur! The advice of a man so far-seeing as you are must assuredly be good.'

'Madame, believe me, the king ought to defend himself to the very last.'

'He has done so, Monsieur; and this final battle that he is about to fight with resources far inferior to those of his enemies proves that he does not count on yielding without fighting. But suppose he be vanquished?'

'Well, Madame, in that case, my advice—I know I am very bold in giving it—but my advice is, the king ought not to leave the kingdom. Absent kings are soon forgotten; if he comes to France, his cause will be lost.'

'But then, if this be your advice, send him succour in men and money, for I can do nothing more; I have sold my last jewel to aid him. If any had been left, I should have bought some fuel to make a fire during this winter to warm myself and my daughter.'

'Ah, Madame! your Majesty does not at all know what you are asking. From the time when help from abroad enters the service of a king to replace him on the throne, an avowal is made that he has aid no longer from his subjects' loyalty.'

'To the point, Monsieur,' said the queen, grown impatient at following this subtle intellect in the labyrinth of words in which he was wandering—'to the point, and reply Yes or No! If the king stays in England, will you send him help? If he comes to France, will you give him hospitality?'

'Madame,' said the cardinal, affecting extreme frankness, 'I am going to show your Majesty how devoted I am, and the desire that I have of ending a matter which you have so much at heart. After which, your Majesty, I think, will no longer doubt my zeal to serve you.'

The queen bit her lips, and moved impatiently in her chair. 'Well! what are you going to do? Let us hear—speak!'

'I am going this very moment to consult the queen, and we will afterwards refer the matter to the parliament.'

'With whom you are at war, are you not? You will perhaps place it in Broussel's hand as advocate. Enough, Monsieur, enough. Go indeed to parliament; for from it, the enemy of kings, has come to the daughter of that great, that sublime Henry IV, whom you admire so much, the only help which has prevented her from dying of cold and hunger this winter.' And at these words the queen got up with a majestic indignation.

The cardinal extended his clasped hands. 'Ah, Madame, Madame, how you misunderstand me!'

But Queen Henrietta, without even turning towards him who was shedding these hypocritical tears, crossed the cabinet, opened the door herself, and through the midst of the numerous guards of his Eminence, and of courtiers anxious to make their court, went and took the hand of Lord de Winter, solitary, isolated, and standing. Poor queen, already fallen, to whom still all bowed for etiquette's sake, but who had in fact only a single arm on which she could lean for support!

'Never mind,' said Mazarin, when alone; 'it has given me some trouble, and it is a hard part to play. But I have said nothing to either the one or the other. H'm! Cromwell is a rough king-hunter; I pity his ministers, if he ever needs any. Bernouin!'

Bernouin entered.

'Find out whether the young man in black doublet and with short hair, whom you just now introduced to me, is still in the palace!' Bernouin went out. The cardinal occupied the time of his absence in turning outside the bezel of his ring, in rubbing the diamond and admiring its water; and as a tear was still in his eye and rendered the sight troubled, he shook his head to cause it to fall. Bernouin returned with Comminges, who was on guard.

'Monseigneur,' said Comminges, 'as I was conducting the young man whom your Eminence enquires for, he approached the glass door of the gallery, and looked at something with astonishment—without doubt Raphael's painting—opposite that door. Then he reflected a moment, and went down the stairs. I believe I saw him mount a grey horse, and leave the palace. But does not Monseigneur go to visit the queen?'

'Why so?'

'M. de Guitaut, my uncle, has just told me that her Majesty has had news from the army.'

'I am glad; I am going, then.'

At this moment, M. de Villequier appeared. He came, in fact, to seek the cardinal on the part of the queen.

Comminges had seen correctly; and Mordaunt had really done as had been related. While crossing the gallery parallel to the grand glass gallery, he saw Winter, who was awaiting the queen. At this sight the young man stopped short, not in admiration of the painting, but as if fascinated by a terrible object. His eyes were dilated; a shudder ran through his body.

He looked as if he wished to break through the rampart of glass which separated him from his enemy. If Comminges had seen the expression of hatred in the eyes of the young man when fixed on Winter, he would not have doubted for an instant that this English lord was his mortal enemy.

But Mordaunt stopped. It was to reflect, without doubt—for instead of yielding to his first intention, which had been to go directly to Lord de Winter, he gently descended the staircase, got on his horse, made him pull up at the corner of the Rue Richelieu, and with eyes fixed on the gate, waited for the queen's coach to leave the court. He had not long to wait, for the queen was scarcely a quarter of an hour with Mazarin; but it seemed an age to him who was waiting.

At length the heavy machine which they then called a coach came, and Winter, still on horseback, leaned over the door to talk with her Majesty. The horses started at a trot, and took the road to the Louvre, which they entered. Before leaving the convent of the Carmelites, Madame Henrietta had told her daughter to come and wait for her at the palace, which she had dwelt in for a long time, and which she had only left because their poverty seemed more heavy in gilded halls. Mordaunt followed the carriage; and when he saw it enter under the gloomy arch of the palace, where the queen's daughter was awaiting her, he placed himself against a wall which lay in shadow, and remained immovable in the midst of Jean Goujon's mouldings like a bas-relief representing an equestrian statue. He waited as he had already done at the Palais-Royal.

XLI

HOW THE UNFORTUNATE SOMETIMES MISTAKE CHANCE FOR PROVIDENCE

'Well, Madame,' said Winter, when the queen had sent away the servants.

'Well, just what I expected has happened, my Lord.'

'He refuses?'

'Have I not already told you in advance?'

'The cardinal refuses to receive the king? France refuses hospitality to an unfortunate prince? Well, it's the first time, Madame.'

'I did not say France, my Lord; I said the cardinal, and he is not even a Frenchman.'

'But have you seen the queen?'

'Useless,' said Madame Henrietta, moving her head sorrowfully. 'The queen will never say Yes when the cardinal has said No. Are you not aware that this Italian directs everything, domestic or foreign? More than that, I should not be astonished if we have been anticipated by Cromwell. The cardinal was embarrassed when speaking to me, and yet firm in his determination to refuse. Then, have you noticed this bustle at the Palais-Royal,—the comings and goings of business people? Have they heard any news, my Lord?'

'It has nothing to do with England, Madame. I have used such diligence that I am sure I have not been forestalled. I set out three days ago, and passed by a miracle through the Puritan army; I came by post with my servant Tony, and the horses we are riding were bought in Paris. Besides, before risking anything, the king, I am sure, will await your Majesty's reply.'

'You will report to him, my Lord,' resumed the queen, in despair, 'that I can do nothing; that I have suffered as much as he—nay, more, I am obliged to eat the bread of exile, and ask hospitality of false friends, who mock at my tears; and that as to his royal person, he must sacrifice himself generously and die like a king. I shall go and die by his side.'

'Madame,' exclaimed Winter, 'your Majesty is giving yourself up to hopelessness, and perhaps some hope still remains.'

'No more friends, no other friend, my Lord, in the whole world but you! O God!' exclaimed Henrietta, lifting her eyes to heaven, 'have you taken away all the noble-hearted who were living on the earth?'

'I hope not, Madame,' replied Winter, fervently. 'I have spoken about four men.'

'What would you do with four men?'

'Four men resolved to die can do much, believe me, Madame; and they did a good deal at one time.'

'And where are these four men?'

'Ah, that I do not know. I have lost sight of them for the last twenty years; and yet, on all occasions where I have seen the king in danger, I have thought of them.'

'And were these men your friends?'

'One of them saved my life. I do not know whether he has continued to be my friend, but since then at least I have been his friend.'

'And these friends are in France, my Lord?'

'I believe so.'

'Tell me their names. Perhaps I have heard of them, and could help you in your enquiry for them.'

'One of them is named Chevalier d'Artagnan.'

'Oh, my Lord, if I am not mistaken, he is lieutenant in the Guards;* but mind, this man, I fear, is quite for the cardinal.'

'In that case, it would be the closing misfortune, and I should begin to think that we are truly under a curse.'

'But the others?' said the queen, who clung to this last hope as a shipwrecked man does to the planks of his ship—'the others, my Lord?'

'The second—I heard his name by chance, for before fighting against us those four told us their names—is the Comte de la Fère. As for the others, the habit I had of calling them by assumed names has made me forget their real ones.'

'Dear me! It would yet be very important to find them, since they might be so useful to the king.'

'Oh, yes, for they are the very ones. Think, Madame. Have you never heard the story that Queen Anne of Austria was formerly saved from the greatest danger that a queen ever encountered?'

'Yes, at the time of her amours with M. de Buckingham; but I do not remember the particulars—something about diamonds,* I believe.'

'Well, that is it, Madame. These men saved her; and if the names of these gentlemen are not known to you, it is because the queen has forgotten them, although she ought to have made them the first lords in the kingdom.'

'Well, my Lord, we must find them; but what could four men do, or rather three?—for we cannot count on M. d'Artagnan.'

'There would be three valiant swords without counting mine. Now, four devoted men around the king, to surround him in battle, to help him with counsel, would be sufficient, not to make the king a conqueror, but to save him if he were vanquished, to help him cross the sea; and whatever Mazarin may say, once on French soil your royal spouse would find here as many retreats as the sea-bird finds in the storms.'

'Seek, my Lord, seek these gentlemen; and if you find them, and if they consent to pass with you into England, I will give each of them a dukedom the day we shall remount the throne, and as much gold beside as would pay for the palace of Whitehall. Seek then, my Lord, seek, I entreat you.'

'I would seek well, Madame,' said Winter, 'and I would find them without doubt, but time fails me. Does your Majesty forget that the king awaits your reply, and awaits it with anguish?'

'Then we are undone!' exclaimed the queen, with the out-burst of a broken heart.

Just then the door opened, and young Henrietta appeared; and the queen, with that sublime control which is the heroism of mothers, checked her tears, and made signs to Winter to change the subject. But this reaction, powerful as it was, did not escape the notice of the young princess.

'Why do you always weep in my absence now, Mother?'

The queen smiled, and in place of answering her, 'Listen, Winter,' she said; 'I have gained at least one thing in being no more than half a queen; and that is that my children call me mother instead of madame.'

Then turning to her daughter, 'What do you want, Henrietta?' she added.

'Mother, a cavalier has just come to the Louvre, and desires to present his respects to your Majesty; he comes from the army, and has a letter to give you from Maréchal de Grammont, I think.'

'Ah!' said the queen to Winter, 'he is one of my faithful friends. But do you not remark, my dear Lord, that we are so poorly served that it is my daughter who undertakes the functions of chamberlain?'

'Madame, have pity upon me,' said Winter, 'you rend my soul.'

'Who is this cavalier, Henrietta?' addressing her daughter.

'I saw him through the window; he is a young man who seems scarcely sixteen, named Vicomte de Bragelonne.'

The queen with a smile made a sign to her daughter, who opened the door; and Raoul appeared at the entrance.

He came towards the queen, and knelt.

'Madame,' said he, 'I bring a letter from my friend the Comte de Guiche, who has enabled me to have the honour of serving you. This letter contains an important piece of news, and the expression of his respects.'

At the name of the Comte de Guiche the young princess blushed; the queen looked at her with some severity.

'But you told me that the letter was from Maréchal de Grammont, Henrietta,' said the queen.

'I thought it was, Madame——' stammered the girl.

'It was my fault, Madame,' said Raoul, 'I actually announced myself as coming from Maréchal de Grammont; but having been wounded in the right arm, he was not able to write, and the Comte de Guiche acted as his secretary.'

'There has been fighting, then?' said the queen, bidding Raoul rise.

'Yes, Madame,' said the young man, handing the letter to Winter, who advanced to take it and hand it to the queen.

On hearing of a battle, the young princess attempted to ask some question, doubtless interesting to herself, but her mouth closed without her having said a word, while her blushes gradually disappeared.

The queen noticed all this confusion, and doubtless her maternal heart translated it; for addressing Raoul afresh, 'And nothing wrong has happened to the young Comte de Guiche?' she asked; 'for not only is he one of our servants, as you have said, Monsieur, but also one of our friends.'

'No, Madame; but on the contrary he has gained great distinction, and had the honour of being embraced by Monsieur the Prince on the field of battle.'

The princess clapped her hands, but ashamed of being drawn into such a demonstration of joy, she turned half round, and bent towards a vase of roses as if to smell them.

'Let us see what the count says.'

'I have had the honour to say to your Majesty that he writes in the name of his father.'

'Yes, Monsieur.'

The queen unsealed the letter and read:

MADAME AND QUEEN—Not being able to write to you myself, on account of a wound which I have received in the right hand, I employ my son, M. le Comte de Guiche, whom you know to be as faithful a servant as his father, to write in my place, and inform you that we have just gained the battle of Lens*—a victory that cannot fail to give great influence to Cardinal Mazarin and the queen upon the affairs of Europe. Your Majesty (if you desire to profit by my advice) will take advantage of this occasion to press on the attention of the king's government the affairs of your august husband. M. le Vicomte de Bragelonne, who will have the honour of handing you this letter, is my son's friend, whose life he saved; he is a gentleman in whom your Majesty can implicitly trust, in case you should have any verbal or written command to send to me.

I have the honour to be with respect, etc.,

MARÉCHAL DE GRAMMONT

Just when there had been a question respecting the service which he had done the count, Raoul could not help turning towards the princess, and had seen in her eyes an expression of infinite gratitude towards himself; he felt no doubt that Charles I's daughter loved his friend.

'The battle of Lens is won! They are fortunate here, they win battles! Yes, the marshal is right, that tends to change the look of their affairs; but I am much afraid that it will do nothing for ours, if indeed it will not do them harm. This news is fresh. Monsieur, I am much obliged to you for having used such diligence in bringing it to me; but for you, I should have been the last in all Paris to learn it.'

'Madame,' said Raoul, 'the Louvre is the second palace which this news has reached. No one knows it yet; and I promised the Comte de Guiche to deliver this letter to your Majesty before even having embraced my guardian.'

'Is your guardian a Bragelonne, like yourself?' asked Lord de Winter. 'I knew a Bragelonne formerly. Is he living?'

'No, Monsieur; but from him my guardian, who was a near relative, inherited the estate of which he bears the name.'

'And your guardian, Monsieur,' asked the queen, who could not help taking an interest in this fine young man, 'what is his name?'

'M. le Comte de la Fère, Madame.'

Winter started with surprise; the queen looked at him with great pleasure.

'Why, that is the name,' she exclaimed, 'which you have told me!'

As for Winter, he could not believe his ears.

'Oh, Monsieur, tell me, I beg of you, is not the Comte de la Fère a brave lord whom I knew, who was a musketeer in Louis XIII's time, and who is perhaps now about forty-seven or forty-eight years old?'

'Yes, Monsieur, you are right on all points.'

'And who served under an assumed name?'

'Under the name of Athos. I lately heard his friend, M. d'Artagnan, call him by that name.'

'That is it, Madame. God be praised. And he is in Paris?' continued Winter, addressing Raoul. Then turning to the queen, 'Hope still; hope,' said he to her. 'Providence declares for us, since it causes me to find this brave gentleman in a manner so miraculous. And where does he stay, Monsieur, I pray you?'

'He is staying at the King Charlemagne Hotel in the Rue Guénégaud.'

'Thanks, Monsieur. Ask this worthy friend to remain at home; I shall go and see him presently.'

'Monsieur, I will obey you with much pleasure if her Majesty will give me leave to go.'

'Go, Monsieur,' said the queen, 'and be assured of our regard.'

Winter and the queen continued to converse for some time in a low voice, so that the young princess might not hear them; but this precaution was needless, as she was absorbed in thought.

Then, as Winter was going to take leave, 'One moment, my Lord,' said the queen. 'I have kept this diamond cross, which belonged to my mother, and this star of St Michael,* which was given me by my husband; they are worth nearly fifty thousand livres. I had determined to die of hunger rather than part with them; but as they might be useful now to him or his defenders, I must sacrifice all to this expectation. Take them; and if there is need, sell them. But if you can keep them, remember, my Lord, that you will have rendered me the greatest service that a gentleman can render a queen, and that in the day of my prosperity he who shall bring back to me this star and this cross will be blessed by me and my children.'

'Madame, your Majesty has in me a devoted servant. I will put these in a safe place—indeed, I would not accept them if we still kept the income of our former estates; but our property is confiscated, our ready money is exhausted, and we are obliged to procure supplies from whatever we possess. In an hour I shall see the Comte de la Fère, and tomorrow your Majesty will have a definite answer.'

The queen extended her hand to Lord de Winter, who kissed it respectfully; and turning towards her daughter, 'My Lord,' said she, 'you are commissioned by this child to take something to her father.'

Winter stood astonished; he did not know what the queen meant. The young Henrietta advanced therefore with a smile and a blush, and lifted her forehead to the gentleman.

'Tell my father that whether he is a king or a fugitive, conqueror or conquered, powerful or poor, he has in me a most obedient and affectionate daughter.'

'I know it, Madame,' replied Winter, touching the forehead of Henrietta with his lips.

Then he went away, passing through, without any attendance, those large, deserted, gloomy apartments, drying up the tears which, though accustomed to court life for fifty years, he could not help shedding at the sight of this royal misfortune, so dignified and so profound.

XLII

WINTER's horse and groom were waiting for him at the gate; he took the road to his rooms, very pensive, and looking behind him from time to time to gaze at the silent, gloomy façade of the Louvre. Then it was he saw a cavalier detach himself, so to speak, from the wall, and follow him at some distance; he remembered, on leaving the Palais-Royal, having seen a somewhat similar shadow. Lord de Winter's groom, who followed him at a few paces, also watched this horseman with an anxious eye.

'Tony,' said the gentleman, making a sign to his servant to approach, 'have you noticed that man who is following us?'

'Yes, my Lord.'

'Who is he?'

'I don't know at all, except that he has followed your Lordship from the Palais-Royal, and stopped at the Louvre to await your coming out, and started from there with you.'

'Some spy of the cardinal,' said Winter to himself, 'trying to prevent us from noticing his surveillance.'

And pushing on, he buried himself in the labyrinth of streets which led to his hotel, situated at the side of the Marais. Having for a long time dwelt in the Place Royale, Lord de Winter had returned quite naturally near his former abode.

The unknown put his horse to a gallop. Winter dismounted at the hotel, determining to have the spy watched; but while putting his gloves and hat on the table, he saw in a glass before him a figure which assumed reality at the entrance of his room.

He turned round; Mordaunt was in front of him.

Winter grew pale, and continued standing and motionless; as for Mordaunt, he kept at the door, cold, threatening, and like the statue of the commander.*

There was a moment of frozen silence between these two men.

'Monsieur,' said Winter, 'I thought I had already made you understand that this pursuit wears me out; withdraw, then, or I shall appeal for help to drive you away as I did in London. I am not your uncle; I don't know you.'

'Uncle,' replied Mordaunt, in a hoarse, jeering voice, 'you mistake. You cannot drive me away as you did in London; you will not dare. As to denying that I am your nephew, you will think twice before doing so, now I know many things of which I was ignorant a year ago.'

'And what does it matter to me what you have learned?'

'Oh! very much indeed, Uncle, I am sure; and you will soon be of my opinion too,' he added with a smile which caused a cold shudder to pass through the veins of the one addressed. 'When I first presented myself before you in London, it was to ask you what had become of my property. When I presented myself the second time, it was to ask you what had sullied my name. This time I come to put to you a question much more terrible—to ask you, as God asked the first murderer, Cain,* Where is thy brother? My Lord, what have you done with your sister who was my mother?'

Winter recoiled under the fire of those blazing eyes.

'Your mother?' said he.

'Yes, my mother, my Lord,' replied the young man, tossing his head.

Winter made a great effort for self-control, and calling up past recollections to seek out a new cause of hatred, he exclaimed, 'Go and enquire what she has become; apply to hell, perhaps that can give you an answer.'

The young man dashed into the room till he faced Lord de Winter, and crossing his arms, 'I have asked the executioner of Béthune,' said Mordaunt, in a hollow voice, and his countenance livid with grief and rage, 'and he has answered me.'

Winter fell into a chair as if struck by lightning, and vainly tried to answer.

'Yes, was it not so?' continued the young man. 'With this all is explained; with this key the abyss opens. My mother inherited the property of her husband, and you have assassinated her. My name secured for me the patrimony, and you have deprived me of my name; and then you despoiled me of my fortune. I am not astonished now that you do not recognize me. When one is a robber, it is unbecoming to style nephew the man whom one has made poor; and when one is a murderer, to so style the one made an orphan.'

These words produced an effect quite contrary to what Mordaunt expected; Winter recalled to his mind what a wretch Milady was. He got up, calm and grave, restraining with his severe look the excited manner of the young man.

'You wish to penetrate that horrible secret, Monsieur? Well, be it so. Learn, then, what sort of a woman that was of whom you ask an account from me today. That woman had, in all probability, poisoned my brother, and in order to inherit my property was going to assassinate me; I have proof of it. What do you say to that?'

'I say she was my mother!'

'She caused the Duke of Buckingham to be stabbed* by a man formerly just, good, and innocent. What do you say to this crime, of which I have proof?'

'She was my mother!'

'On her return to France, she poisoned in the Augustinian convent at Béthune a young woman who loved one of her enemies. Will this crime persuade you that her punishment was just? Of this crime I have the proof.'

'She was my mother!' cried the young man, who had given to his three exclamations an increasing emphasis.

'In short, charged with murders, odious to all, threatening still like a panther thirsty for blood, she succumbed to the blows of men whom she had driven to despair, and who had never caused her the least injury. She found judges whom her hideous attempts had evoked; and this executioner whom you have seen, if he has told you all, ought to have told you that he rejoiced in avenging on her the shame and suicide of his brother. Corrupt girl, adulterous spouse, unnatural sister, murderess, poisoner, execrable to every one who had known her, to all nations who had received her in their boundaries, she died cursed by heaven and by the earth: that is what this woman was.'

A sobbing stronger than Mordaunt's will seized him, and made the blood mount up to his livid face. He clinched his fists; his countenance bathed in perspiration, his hair standing on end, he cried out, devoured with fury—

'Be silent, Monsieur! she was my mother. Her crimes, I know them not! But what I do know is, that five men, leagued against one woman, killed her clandestinely by night like cowards. What I do know is, that you were one of them, and that you said, like the rest, but more emphatically, "*She must die!*" Therefore I forewarn you. Listen to these words, and let them sink into your memory, so that you may never forget them: This murder, which has deprived me of everything, and taken away my name, has made me corrupt, wicked, and implacable; I demand expiation for it, from you first, and then from your accomplices when I know them.'

With hate in his eyes, foaming at his mouth, and fist clinched, Mordaunt had made a step forward towards Winter as if threatening him. The latter put his hand to his sword, and said with the smile of a man who for thirty years had played with death—

'Will you assassinate me, Monsieur? Then I shall recognize you as my nephew, for you are a true son of your mother.'

'No,' replied Mordaunt, exercising strong self-control and forcing all the muscles of his face and of his body to take their habitual place—'no, I shall not kill you now, for without you I should not discover the others. But when I have, you may tremble; I have poniarded the executioner of Béthune without pity, and he was the least guilty of you all.'

Having thus spoken, the young man went out, and down the staircase, calmly enough to avoid remark; then on the lower landing-place he passed Tony, leaning over the baluster, and ready at a mere call to assist his master. But Winter did not call. Crushed, fainting, he stood with attentive ear; then, not till he heard the sound of the horse's feet growing less distinct did he fall into a chair, saying, 'Thank God, he knows me only of them all!'

XLIII

WHILE this terrible scene was taking place at Lord de Winter's, Athos, seated near the window of his room, with his elbow on the table, and his head resting on his hand, listened with open eyes and ears to Raoul, who was telling him the adventures of his journey and the details of the battle. The gentleman's fine noble countenance expressed unspeakable happiness at the recital of these early, fresh and pure emotions; he drank in the sounds of that youthful voice, already attuned to noble feelings, as though he listened to harmonious music. He had forgotten what there was of gloom in the past and of cloudiness in the future. It might be said that the return of this well-beloved youth turned these fears into hopes. Athos was happy; happy as he had never been.

'So you took part in that great battle, Bragelonne?' said the old musketeer.

'Yes, Monsieur.'

'And it was a fierce one, do you say?'

'Monsieur the Prince charged eleven times in person.'

'He is a great warrior, Bragelonne?'

'Yes, a hero, Monsieur. I never lost sight of him for a moment. Oh, it's a fine thing to be called Condé, and to bear thus his name!'

'Calm and brilliant, was he not?'

'Calm as at a parade, brilliant as at a fête. When we met the enemy, it was at a walk; we were ordered not to fire first, and we marched upon the Spaniards, who were on a height, the musketoons at the thigh. Arrived at thirty paces from them the prince turned towards his soldiers: "Children," said he, "you are going to suffer a furious discharge; but afterwards, rest easy, you will have a good price from all those people." There was such silence that friends and enemies heard these words. Then raising his sword, "Sound trumpets!" said he.'

'Well, well! on an occasion you would do thus, Raoul, would you not?'

'I doubt whether I could do it, Monsieur, for I have found it very fine and very grand. When we were arrived at twenty paces, we saw all the musketoons lowered like a brilliant line—for the sun was resplendent on the barrels. "At a walk, children, at a walk," said the prince, "now is the moment." '

'Where you afraid, Raoul?' asked the count.

'Yes, Monsieur,' replied the young man, naïvely; 'I experienced a great chill at my heart, and at the word "Fire!" which resounded in Spanish through the enemy's ranks, I closed my eyes, and I thought of you.'

'Is that true, Raoul?' said Athos, pressing his hand.

'Yes, Monsieur. At the same instant there was such a detonation that one would have said that hell was opening; and those who were not killed felt the heat of the flame. I opened my eyes astonished not to be dead, or at least wounded; a third of the squadron was lying on the ground, mutilated and bleeding. At this moment I met the eye of the prince; I thought then of but one thing; that is, that he was looking at me. I drove in both spurs, and found myself in the midst of the enemy's ranks.'

'And the prince was pleased with you?'

'He told me so at least, Monsieur, when he ordered me to accompany M. de Châtillon* to Paris, who has come to bring the news to the queen, and the captured colours. "Go," said the prince to me, "the enemy will not be rallied in a fortnight. From now till then I have no need of you. Go and embrace those whom you love and who love you, and say to my sister, Madame de Longueville, that I thank her for the gift she has made me in giving you to me." And here I am,' added Raoul, looking at the count with a smile full of love; 'for I thought you would be glad to see me.'

Athos drew the young man to himself and kissed him as he would have kissed a young girl.

'So,' said he, 'you are launched, Raoul; you have dukes for friends, a marshal of France for sponsor, a prince of the blood for captain, and in one day you have been on your return received by two queens; that's not bad for a novice.'

'Ah! Monsieur,' said Raoul, suddenly, 'you remind me of something I was near forgetting. I met a gentleman with her

Majesty the Queen of England, who, when I mentioned your name, uttered a cry of surprise and pleasure, said he was a friend of yours, asked me your address, and is coming to see you.'

'What is his name?'

'I did not dare to ask him, Monsieur; but though he spoke French well, I thought him an Englishman from his accent.'

'Ah!' said Athos; and he lowered his head as if trying to recall him. Then when he lifted his face, his glance was arrested by a man standing at the open door, looking at him with a softened expression.

'Lord de Winter!' exclaimed the count.

'Athos, my friend!' and the two embraced.

Then Athos, taking him by the hands, said to him, while looking at him, 'What is the matter, my Lord? You seem as sad as I am joyful.'

'Yes, dear friend, it is true; and I may say further that the sight of you doubles my fear.'

And Winter looked around him as if he wished to be alone. Raoul saw that they wanted to talk confidentially, and left the room.

'Do you know he is here?' said Winter.

'Who?'

'The son of Milady.'

Athos, struck once more by this name, which seemed to follow him like a fatal echo, hesitated a moment, slightly knitted his brow, then in a calm tone, 'I know it,' he said.

'You know it?' said Winter.

'Yes; Grimaud fell in with him between Béthune and Arras, and returned in great haste to apprise me.'

'Grimaud knew him, then?'

'No; but he attended the death-bed of a man whom Grimaud knew.'

'The executioner of Béthune!' exclaimed Winter.

'You know that?' said Athos, astonished.

'He has this moment left me; he has told all. Ah, my friend, what a terrible scene! pity we did not kill him as well as the mother!'

Athos, like all noble natures, did not reveal to others the sad impressions which he felt; but on the contrary he absorbed them into himself, and in their place returned hopes and consolations. One might say that his personal griefs left his spirit changed into joys for others.

'What do you fear?' said he, bringing his reason to bear on the instinctive horror which he had felt at first. 'Are we not here to defend ourselves? Has this young man become an assassin by profession, a murderer in cold blood? He succeeded in killing the executioner of Béthune in a paroxysm of rage; but now his fury is satiated.'

Winter smiled sadly and shook his head. 'You do not know this race, then?' said he.

'Bah!' said Athos, trying also to smile. 'It will have lost its ferocity in the second generation. Besides, friend, Providence has forewarned us to put us on our guard. We can do nothing but wait. But let us now speak of yourself. What has brought you to Paris?'

'Some affairs of importance that you will learn later on. But what have I heard when with her Majesty the Queen of England—that M. d'Artagnan is of Mazarin's party? Pardon my frankness, my friend, I neither hate nor blame the cardinal, and your opinions will be always sacred to me; are you also for this man?'

'M. d'Artagnan is in the service; as a soldier, he obeys the constituted powers. M. d'Artagnan is not rich, and must live on his pay as lieutenant. Millionaires like you, my Lord, are rare in France.'

'Alas!' said Winter, 'I am today poorer than he is. But let us return to yourself.'

'Well! you wish to know if I am of the Mazarin party. No; a thousand times no! Pardon my frankness also, my Lord.'

Winter arose and pressed Athos in his arms.

'Thanks, Count, for this welcome news. You see me happy and rejuvenated. Ah, you are not for Mazarin, good fortune! Besides, that could not be. But pardon me, are you at liberty?'

'What do you mean by being at liberty?'

'I mean, are you married?'

'No,' said Athos, smiling.

'That young man, so handsome, elegant, gracious?'

'Is a child whom I brought up, and who does not even know who his father was.'

'Very well; you are ever the same, Athos, great and generous.'

'Come, my Lord, what do you wish to ask me?'

'You have still M.M. Porthos and Aramis for your friends?'

'And add d'Artagnan, my Lord. We still continue four devoted friends; but in the matter of serving or opposing the cardinal, of being Mazarins or Frondeurs, we are then only two.'

'M. Aramis is with M. d'Artagnan?'

'No; M. Aramis does me the honour to share my convictions.'

'Could you again introduce me to this charming, clever friend?'

'Certainly; as soon as it will be agreeable to you.'

'Is he changed?'

'He has turned abbé, that's all.'

'You astonish me! His office ought to make him give up all bold enterprises.'

'On the contrary,' said Athos, smiling, 'he has never been so much a musketeer as he is now, and you will find him a real Galaor.* Do you wish me to send Raoul to find him?'

'Thanks, Count, he would not be at home at this hour. But since you think you can answer for him——'

'As for myself.'

'Could you engage to bring him to me tomorrow, at ten in the morning, on the Louvre bridge?'*

'Ah, ah!' said Athos, smiling, 'you have a duel?'

'Yes, Count, a fine duel, to which you will be a party, I hope.'

'Where shall we go, my Lord?'

'To her Majesty the Queen of England, who has charged me to present you to her, Count.'

'Her Majesty is acquainted with me, then?'

'I am acquainted with you.'

'Enigma,' said Athos; 'but no matter; till the moment you have the solution of it I ask nothing further. Will you do me the honour to take supper with me, my Lord?'

'Thanks, Count,' said Winter; 'the visit of this young man, I avow it to you, has deprived me of appetite and will probably cost me my sleep. What enterprise does he come to accomplish at Paris? It is not to meet me that he comes, for he was ignorant of my journey. This young man frightens me, Count. There is for him a future of blood.'

'What does he do in England?'

'He is one of the most ardent followers of Oliver Cromwell.'

'Who won him over to that cause? His mother and father were Catholics, I think.'

'His hatred of the king, who declared him illegitimate, despoiled him of his property, and forbade him to bear the name of Winter.'

'And what name does he bear now?'

'Mordaunt.'

'A Puritan, and disguised as a monk, he is travelling by himself in France.'

'As a monk, do you say?'

'Yes; did you not know it?'

'I only know what he has told me.'

'It is so; and quite by chance—I ask God's pardon if I blaspheme—he heard the confession of the executioner of Béthune.'

'Then I guess all. He comes as envoy from Cromwell.'

'To whom?'

'To Mazarin. And the queen guessed right; we have been forestalled. I can see it all now. Adieu, Count, till tomorrow.'

'But the night is dark,' said Athos, seeing that Lord de Winter suffered from a disquietude greater than he desired to show; 'and you have not, perhaps, any servant?'

'I have Tony—a good but simple fellow.'

'Holloa, Olivain, Grimaud, Blaisois! take your blunderbusses and call Monsieur the Viscount.'

Blaisois was that big fellow, half-servant, half-peasant, whom we met at the Château de Bragelonne, and whom Athos had baptized with the name of the province. Five minutes after the order had been given Raoul entered.

'Viscount,' said Athos, 'go and escort my Lord to his hotel, and don't let any one approach him.'

'Ah, Count,' said Winter, 'for whom now do you take me?'

'For a stranger, who is not acquainted with Paris, and to whom the viscount will show the road.'

Winter clasped his hand.

'Grimaud,' said Athos, 'put yourself at the head of the troop, and beware of the monk.'

Grimaud trembled, and then awaited the departure, caressing with a silent eloquence the butt-end of his blunderbuss.

'Tomorrow, Count,' said Winter.

'Yes, my Lord.'

The little party went off towards the Rue St Louis,* Olivain trembling like Sosia at every doubtful reflection of light; Blaisois tolerably firm because he did not know that they were running any risk; Tony looking right and left, but not able to speak a word because he did not speak French. Winter and Raoul went along side by side, and talked together. Grimaud, who, according to Athos's order, had gone on in front, with a torch in one hand and the blunderbuss in the other, reached Winter's hotel, knocked at the gate, and when it was opened, saluted my Lord without saying a word.

It was the same on the return. The piercing eyes of Grimaud saw nothing suspicious except a kind of shadow ambushed at the corner of the Rue Guénégaud and of the quay; it seemed to him that in going he had before remarked this night watcher who attracted his eyes. He spurred towards him; but before he could reach him the shadow had disappeared into a little street where Grimaud did not think it prudent to follow him.

They gave an account to Athos of their success, and as it was ten o'clock, they all retired to their rooms.

The next day, on opening his eyes, it was the count's turn to see Raoul at his bedside. The young viscount was fully dressed, and was reading a new book by M. Chapelain.

'Already up, Raoul?' said the count.

'Yes, Monsieur; I have not slept well.'

'You, Raoul! not slept well? What has filled your mind?'

'Monsieur, you will say that I am in a great hurry to leave you, when I have scarcely arrived, but——'

'You have, then, only two days' leave, Raoul?'

'On the contrary, Monsieur, I have ten, so it is not to the camp I wish to go.'

Athos smiled.

'Where then?' said he. 'At least, if it is not a secret. You are almost a man, since you have fought your first battle; and you have earned the right of going where you like without asking me.'

'Never, Monsieur,' said Raoul, 'while I retain the happiness of having you as my protector. I should like to go and spend a day at Blois. You look at me, and are going to laugh at me.'

'No; on the contrary,' said Athos, checking a sigh. 'No; I do not laugh, Viscount. It is quite natural that you should desire to see Blois again.'

'So you permit it?' exclaimed Raoul, joyously.

'Assuredly, Raoul.'

'At the bottom of your heart, Monsieur, you are not angry?'

'Not at all. Why should I be angry about what gives you pleasure?'

'Ah, Monsieur, how good you are!' exclaimed the young man, making a movement to throw himself on Athos's neck; but his respect checked him.

Athos opened his arms to him.

'So I can set out immediately?'

'When you please, Raoul.'

Raoul made three steps towards going out.

'Monsieur, I have thought of one thing—of Madame de Chevreuse's kindness to me, to whom I owe my introduction to the prince.'

'And that you owe her thanks for it; is it not so, Raoul?'

'So it seems to me; however, it is for you to decide.'

'Go by the Hôtel de Luynes, and enquire if Madame the Duchess can receive you. I am glad to see you do not forget the duties of etiquette. Take Grimaud and Olivain.'

'Both, Monsieur?' asked Raoul, with astonishment. Then, receiving an affirmative answer, he bowed, and went out. On seeing him close the door, and hearing him call with his joyous voice for Grimaud and Olivain, Athos sighed.

'It is very soon to leave me,' thought he, nodding his head; 'but he is obeying a common law. Nature is so constituted that she looks ahead. He certainly loves that child; but will he love me less for loving others?' And Athos secretly confessed that he did not at all expect this speedy departure; but Raoul was so happy that all else was effaced from Athos's mind by this consideration.

At ten all were ready to set off. As Athos was watching Raoul mount his horse, a groom came from Madame de Chevreuse. He was charged to tell the Comte de la Fère that she had heard of the return of his protégé, and would be happy to see him to present to him her congratulations on his behaviour in battle.

'Tell Madame the Duchess,' replied Athos, 'that Monsieur the Viscount was just going to pay a visit to the Hôtel de Luynes.'

Then, after having given some fresh orders to Grimaud, Athos with a wave of his hand signified to Raoul that he might start off.

After all, on reflection Athos thought that it was perhaps not so bad for Raoul to be absent from Paris just at this time.

XLIV

AGAIN A QUEEN WHO ASKS AID

ATHOS had sent a letter to Aramis early in the morning by Blaisois, his only remaining servant. He found Bazin putting on his beadle's robe, for he was that day on duty at Notre-Dame. Athos had desired Blaisois to try and speak to Aramis himself. Blaisois, a tall, simple fellow, who knew nothing but his orders, had then asked for the Abbé d'Herblay; and in spite of Bazin's assurance that Aramis was not at home, Blaisois had insisted so strongly that Bazin fell into a rage. Blaisois, seeing Bazin in a church dress, was but little disturbed by these denials, and wished to pass beyond, thinking that he with whom he was talking was endowed with all the virtues which his dress would indicate; that is to say, with Christian patience and charity.

But Bazin, always valet of a musketeer when the blood mounted to his great eyes, seized a broomstick and beat

Blaisois, saying, 'You have insulted the Church, my friend; you have insulted the Church!' At this moment and at this unaccustomed noise, Aramis had appeared, opening the door of his bedroom carefully. Then Bazin placed his broom respectfully upon one of its two ends, as he had seen the Swiss at Notre-Dame do with his halberd; and Blaisois, with a look of reproach towards Cerberus, drew his letter from his pocket, and presented it to Aramis.

'From the Comte de la Fère?' said Aramis. 'Very well.'

Blaisois returned dejectedly to the King Charlemagne Hotel. Athos asked how he had succeeded. Blaisois recounted his adventure with Bazin.

'Imbecile!' said Athos, laughing. 'You did not announce to him that you came from me?'

'No, Monsieur.'

'And what did Bazin say when he knew you belonged to me?'

'Ah, Monsieur, he made me all sorts of excuses, and forced me to drink two glasses of a very good Muscat wine, in which he dipped three or four excellent biscuits; but it is all the same, he is devilishly brutal. A beadle! Fie, then!'

'Good,' thought Athos. 'The moment when Aramis receives my letter, however engaged he may be, he will come.'

At ten o'clock Athos, with his habitual punctuality, was on the Louvre bridge. He there met Lord de Winter, who had just arrived. They waited nearly ten minutes. Winter began to fear that Aramis would not come.

'Patience!' said Athos, who kept looking in the direction of the Rue du Bac; 'there is an abbé who is giving a blow to a man and a bow to a woman. That's Aramis.'

It was he indeed. A young fellow who was gaping idly in his path had splashed Aramis, who with a blow of his fist had sent him ten paces. At the same time one of his penitents had passed, and as she was young and pretty, Aramis gave her a most gracious smile. In an instant he had come up to them. There were, as was natural, cordial greetings between him and Lord de Winter.

'Where are we going?' said Aramis. 'Is it for fighting? *Sacrebleu!* I have no sword this morning, and I must return home to fetch one.'

'No,' said Winter. 'We are going to pay a visit to her Majesty the Queen of England.'

'Oh, very well,' said Aramis; 'and what is the purpose of the visit?' he added in Athos's ear.

'In truth, I don't know at all. Some evidence that is needed of us, perhaps.'

'Could it be in that cursed business?' said Aramis. 'In that case I should not be too anxious to go there, for I should not care about pocketing a reprimand; and since I give them to others, I do not like to receive them myself.'

'If that were so, we should not be taken to her Majesty by Lord de Winter, for he would get his share; he was one of our party.'

'Ah, yes, that's true. Come on, then.'

On reaching the Louvre Lord de Winter passed in first; only a single concierge kept the door. By the daylight Athos, Aramis, and the Englishman could remark the frightful destitution of the habitation which a miserly charity granted the unfortunate queen. Some grand apartments quite devoid of furniture; dilapidated walls upon which in places shone the old gilded mouldings, which had resisted neglect; windows which no longer shut, and were without panes of glass; no carpets, no guards, no valets. All this destitution struck at once the eyes of Athos, who made his companion observe it too, by touching him with his elbow and by directing his attention to it.

'Mazarin is better lodged,' said Aramis.

'Mazarin is almost a king,' said Athos; 'and Madame Henrietta is now hardly a queen.'

'If you would condescend to use your wit, Athos,' said Aramis, 'I truly believe you would have more of it than had that poor M. de Voiture.'

Athos smiled.

The queen seemed to be impatiently expecting them—for at the first movement she heard in the hall before her room, she came herself to the door to receive the courtiers of her misfortune.

'Come in and be welcome, Messieurs,' said she.

The gentlemen entered and remained standing, but the queen made a sign to them to be seated. Athos set an example of obedience. He was grave and calm, but Aramis was furious. This royal distress had exasperated him. His eyes studied each new trace of the misery which he observed.

'You are examining my luxury?' said the queen, casting a sad look around her.

'Madame,' said Aramis, 'I ask your Majesty's pardon, but I do not know how to hide my indignation at seeing how the court of France treats the daughter of Henry IV.'

'Monsieur is no longer a soldier?' said the queen to Lord de Winter.

'Monsieur is the Abbé d'Herblay,' replied the latter.

Aramis blushed.

'Madame,' said he, 'I am an abbé, it is true; but it is against my inclination. I am not fitted for the cloth. My cassock only holds by one button, and I am quite ready to become a musketeer again. This morning, not knowing that I should have the honour of seeing your Majesty, I am thus dressed; but I am no less one whom your Majesty will find most devoted to your service, whatever she may wish to order.'

'M. le Chevalier d'Herblay,' replied Winter, 'was one of those valiant musketeers of King Louis XIII of whom I have spoken to you, Madame.' Then turning to Athos, 'As for Monsieur, he is that noble Comte de la Fère, whose great reputation is so well known to your Majesty.'

'Messieurs,' said the queen, 'I had around me, some years ago, gentlemen, treasures, armies; at a mere wave of the hand all those were at my disposal. Now look around me. This sight surprises you, no doubt; but to accomplish a design which ought to save my life I have only Lord de Winter, a friend of twenty years' standing, and you, Messieurs, whom I see for the first time, and whom I know only as my compatriots.'

'That is sufficient, Madame,' said Athos, bowing low, 'if the lives of three men can purchase yours.'

'Thanks, Messieurs. But listen to me: I am not only the most miserable of queens, but the most unhappy of mothers and the most desolate of wives. My children, two at least—the Duke of York* and the Princess Charlotte—are far from me; my husband, the king, drags out in England such a wretched existence that it is true that he seeks for death as being more desirable. Wait, Messieurs; see the letter which he has sent me by Lord de Winter. Read it.'

Athos and Aramis desired to be excused.

'Read it,' said the queen.

Athos read aloud the letter which we already know, in which Charles asked the hospitality of France.

'Well?' asked Athos, when he had finished reading it.

'Well,' said the queen, 'he has been refused.'

The two friends exchanged a look of disgust.

'And now, Madame, what is to be done?' said Athos.

'Have you any pity for so much misfortune?' said the queen, greatly moved.

'I have the honour of asking your Majesty what you wish M. d'Herblay and myself should do to serve you; we are ready.'

'Ah, Monsieur! you have really a noble heart,' exclaimed the queen, with the deepest gratitude shown in the tones of her voice, while Lord de Winter looked at her as much as to say, Did I not answer for them? 'And you, Monsieur?' the queen asked Aramis.

'I, Madame,' he replied, 'wherever the count goes, were it to death, I will follow him without asking why; but when it is a question of serving your Majesty,' looking at the queen with all the grace of his youth, 'then I go before Monsieur the Count.'

'Well, Messieurs,' said the queen, 'since this is the case—since you are willing to devote yourselves to the service of a poor princess whom the whole world abandons—this is what I wish done for me. The king is alone with some gentlemen in the midst of the Scotch, whom he distrusts, although he is a Scotchman himself. Since Lord de Winter has quitted him, I no longer live, Messieurs. Well, I ask a great deal of you, too much perhaps, for I have no claim on you—to cross over to England, join the king, be his friends, be his protectors, march at his side in battle, be near him in the interior of his house, where secret risks are more dangerous than those of war. And for this sacrifice which you make for me, Messieurs, I promise not to recompense you—I think that this word would wound you—but to love you as a sister, and give you a preference over all except my husband and children. I swear this as in

God's presence.' And the queen slowly and solemnly raised her eyes to heaven.

'Madame,' said Athos, 'when shall we set off?'

'You consent, then?' exclaimed the queen, with joy.

'Yes, Madame. Only your Majesty goes too far, it seems to me, in promising to load us with a friendship so far above our merits. We serve God, Madame, in serving a prince so unhappy and a queen so virtuous. Madame, we are yours, body and soul.'

'Ah! Messieurs,' said the queen, moved even to tears, 'this is the first joyful moment which I have felt for five years. God will reward you, who reads in my heart all the gratitude I feel towards him and yourselves. Save my husband, save the king; and although you are insensible to the price which you may receive on earth for this noble action, leave me the hope that I shall see you again to thank you myself. Until then, I wait. Have you anything to ask me? I am from this time your friend; and since you are working for me, I ought to work also for you.'

'Madame,' said Athos, 'I have nothing to ask of your Majesty but your prayers.'

'And I,' said Aramis—'I am alone in the world, and have only your Majesty to serve.'

The queen extended her hand, which they kissed; and she said in a low tone to Winter, 'If you want money, my Lord, don't hesitate a moment; sell the jewels to a Jew. You will get for them from fifty to sixty thousand livres; pay them away, if necessary, but let these gentlemen be treated as they deserve —that is, like kings.'

The queen had ready two letters—one written by herself and one by the princess*—both addressed to the king. She gave one to Athos, and the other to Aramis, so that if perchance they should be separated, they might be able to make themselves known to the king; then they withdrew.

At the foot of the staircase Winter stopped. 'You go your way, and I mine, Messieurs, so as not to arouse any suspicions, and this evening at nine let us meet at the Porte St Denis. We will go with my horses as far as we can, and then we can take post-horses. Once more, thanks, good friends, in my own name and in that of the queen.'

The three gentlemen shook hands; Lord de Winter took the Rue St Honoré, and Athos and Aramis remained together.

'Well,' said Aramis, when they were alone, 'what do you think of this business?'

'Bad, very bad,' replied Athos.

'But you received it with enthusiasm?'

'As I shall always receive the defence of a great principle. Kings can be strong only by means of their nobles; and nobles can only be great through their kings. Let us support the monarchies, for thus we support ourselves.'

'We are going to be assassinated over there,' said Aramis. 'I hate the English; they are coarse, like all people who drink beer.'

'Would it be better to stay here,' said Athos, 'and go and have our turn at the Bastille, or Vincennes prison, for having helped M. de Beaufort to make his escape? Ah! upon my word, Aramis, believe me, there is no need of regret. We escape a prison, and act the part of heroes; the choice is an easy one.'

'That is true; but in every case, my dear fellow, one must come to the leading question—very foolish, I know, but very necessary—have you any money?'

'Something like a hundred pistoles, which my farmer sent me the evening before my departure from Bragelonne; but then I ought to leave half for Raoul. A young gentleman must live decently. I have, therefore, scarcely fifty pistoles. What have you?'

'I? I believe that by turning out all my pockets and opening all my drawers, I should not find ten louis. Fortunately Lord de Winter is rich.'

'He is for the time ruined, for Cromwell has confiscated his property.'

'That is where Porthos would be useful,' said Aramis.

'That is why I regret d'Artagnan,' said Athos.

'What a fat purse!'

'What a trusty sword!'

'Let us entice them to go.'

'The secret is not our own, Aramis; trust me, and don't let us take any one into our confidence. Then, in taking such a step, we should seem to distrust ourselves. Let us regret it privately, but let us not speak.'

'You are right. What are you going to do from now till the evening? I am obliged to put off two things.'

'Are they things which can be put off?'

'*Dame!* they *must* be.'

'What are they?'

'First, a sword-cut to the Coadjutor, whom I met yesterday evening at Madame de Rambouillet's, and whom I found talking in a singular style in regard to me.'

'Fie! a quarrel between priests! A duel between allies!'

'What would you, my dear friend? He is a fighter, and so am I. He runs through the small streets, and so do I. His cassock weighs him down, and I have, I think, enough of my own. I sometimes think that he is Aramis, and I the Coadjutor, so much likeness is there between us. This sort of Sosia wearies me and makes me a shadow; besides, he is a blunderer who will ruin our party. I am convinced that if I gave him a slap as I did this morning to the small boy who splashed me, it would change the face of matters.'

'And I, my dear Aramis,' Athos mildly replied, 'believe it would only change the face of M. de Retz. So take my word for it, these things are best left. You do not belong to yourself any more; you are for the Queen of England, and he for the Fronde. Then, if the second thing that you regret not being able to do is not more important than the first——'

'Oh, the latter was more important.'

'Then set about it at once.'

'Unfortunately, I am not free to do it at any hour I please. It was in the evening—late on in the evening.'

'I see,' said Athos, smiling; 'at midnight.'

'Nearly.'

'Why, my dear fellow, these are things to be put off, and you shall put off this since you would have so good an excuse to give on your return.'

'Yes, if I do return.'

'If you do not, what does it matter to you? Be a little reasonable. Come, Aramis; you are no longer twenty years old, my dear friend.'

'To my great regret, the more's the pity. Ah! if I were that age!'

'Yes,' said Athos, 'I believe you would do some great acts of folly. But we must separate. I have one or two visits to make and a letter to write; come, then, and fetch me at eight, or do you prefer that I should expect you to supper at seven?'

'Very well; I have twenty visits to make, and as many letters to write.'

Upon that they separated. Athos went to pay a visit to Madame de Vendôme, left his name for Madame de Chevreuse, and wrote the following letter to d'Artagnan:

DEAR FRIEND—I am going with Aramis on a matter of importance. I should have liked to make my adieux, but time does not permit. Do not forget that I am writing to repeat to you how much I love you. Raoul has gone to Blois and does not know of my departure. Watch over him in my absence to the best of your ability; and if perchance you receive no news from me in three months, tell him to open a sealed packet addressed to him, which he will find at Blois in my bronze chest, the key of which I send you. Embrace Porthos for Aramis and me. *Au revoir*, and perhaps farewell for ever.'

And he sent the letter by Blaisois.

At the appointed hour Aramis came. He was in cavalier's dress, and had by his side that old sword which he had so often drawn, and which he was more than ever ready to draw.

'Oh, come!' said he, 'I think we are decidedly wrong to part thus without a little word of farewell to Porthos and d'Artagnan.'

'It is done, dear friend; I have seen to it.'

'You are a capital fellow, my dear count. You think of everything.'

'Well, have you made up your mind for the journey?'

'Entirely. And now I have thought about it, I am glad to be leaving Paris just now.'

'So am I; only I regret not having said good-bye to d'Artagnan. But the demon is so cunning that he would have guessed our plans.'

At the end of supper Blaisois returned.

'Monsieur, this is M. d'Artagnan's reply.'

'But I did not tell you to wait for an answer, stupid!'

'I was coming away without waiting for one, but he called me back and gave me this,' and Blaisois presented a small leathern bag quite rounded.

Athos opened it, and first pulled out a small note couched in these terms:

MY DEAR COUNT—When one travels, and especially for three months, one has never too much money. Now, I recall our times of want, and I send you the half of my purse; it is part of the money which I have succeeded in squeezing out of Mazarin. Don't make a very bad use of it on that account, I beg of you. As to not seeing you again, I don't believe a word of it. With your heart and sword one can go anywhere. *Au revoir*, then, and not farewell for ever. There is no need to say that from the first day that I saw Raoul I have loved him as my own son; yet, believe me, I ask God very sincerely that I may not become his father, although I should be proud of a son like him.

Yours,

D'ARTAGNAN

P.S. It is well understood that the fifty louis which I send you are equally for Aramis and yourself.

Athos smiled, and his beautiful eye was clouded by a tear. D'Artagnan, whom he had always tenderly loved, loved him still, though of Mazarin's party.

'Upon my word, here are fifty louis,' said Aramis, turning out the purse on the table, 'all with Louis XIII's effigy. Well, what will you do with it, Count—keep it or send it back?'

'I shall keep it, Aramis, and I shall not need to keep it long. What is offered so nobly ought to be accepted nobly. You take twenty-five, and give me the other half.'

'All in good time; I am glad to see that you are of my opinion. There now, shall we start?'

'When you please. But have you no servant?'

'No; that fool of a Bazin has made himself a beadle, as you know, so that he cannot leave Notre-Dame.'

'That's all right. You shall take Blaisois, with whom I do not know what to do, since I already have Grimaud.'

'Willingly,' said Aramis.

At that moment Grimaud appeared at the door. 'Ready,' said he, in his usually laconic style.

'Let us go, then,' said Athos.

In fact, the horses were waiting saddled. At the corner of the quay they met Bazin running, quite out of breath.

'Ah, Monsieur,' said Bazin, 'thank goodness I am in time.'

'What is the matter?'

'M. Porthos came out of the house, but has left this for you, saying it was very important, and you ought to get it before leaving.'

'Good,' said Aramis, taking a purse which Bazin handed him. 'What is this?'

'Wait, Monsieur the Abbé, there is a letter.'

'You know that I have already told you that if you call me otherwise than chevalier I will break your bones. Let us see the letter.'

'How are you going to read it? It is as dark as pitch.'

'Wait,' said Bazin. He struck a light, and lighted a taper such as he used to light the wax candles. By its light Aramis read:

MY DEAR D'HERBLAY—I learn from d'Artagnan that you are starting on an expedition which will last perhaps two or three months. As I know you do not like to ask aid from your friends, I offer it to you: here are two hundred pistoles which you can make use of, and which you can repay when the occasion offers. Do not fear that you are inconveniencing me. If I have need of money I can get it from one of my châteaux; at Bracieux alone I have twenty thousand livres in gold. That I do not send you more is because I fear that you would not accept a larger sum. I write to you because you know that the Comte de la Fère always overawes me a little in spite of myself, although I love him with all my heart; but it is understood that what I offer you I offer at the same time to him. I am, as you do not doubt I hope,

> Your very devoted,
> DU VALLON DE BRACIEUX DE PIERREFONDS

'Well,' said Aramis, 'what do you say to that?'

'I say, my dear d'Herblay, that it's almost sacrilege to doubt Providence when one has such friends.'

'So then?'

'So then we will divide Porthos's pistoles as we have the louis of d'Artagnan.'

The division was made by the light of Bazin's taper, and the two friends started off. A quarter of an hour after they were at the Porte St Denis, where Winter awaited them.

XLV

IN WHICH IT IS PROVED THAT THE FIRST MOVE IS ALWAYS A GOOD ONE

THE three gentlemen took the route to Picardy,—that route so well known to them and which recalled to Athos and Aramis some of the most picturesque remembrances of their younger days.

'If Mousqueton were with us,' said Athos, on arriving at the place where they had the dispute with the pavers,* 'how he would tremble in passing here! Do you recall it, Aramis? It was here that that famous ball struck him.'

'My faith, I would permit him to do it,' said Aramis, 'for I perceive myself shivering at that recollection; there, just beyond that tree, is a little place where I thought that I was dead.'

They continued their way. Soon it was Grimaud's turn to recall old memories. Arrived in front of the inn where his master and he had formerly had such an enormous feasting, he drew near to Athos, and pointing out the window of the cellar, said to him, 'Sausages!'

Athos began to laugh, and this folly of his youth appeared to him as amusing as if someone had related it as happening to another.

At last, after two days and a night, they reached about evening, in magnificent weather, Boulogne,—a town then almost uninhabited, built entirely on the height. What is called the lower town did not exist. Boulogne was a formidable position.

On reaching the city gates, 'Messieurs,' said Winter, 'let us do here as we did at Paris—separate to avoid suspicion. I know an inn, very little frequented, but whose landlord is thoroughly faithful to me. I am going there, for I expect to find some letters. As for you, go to the best hotel in the town—The Sword of Henry the Great, for example. In two hours be on the jetty; our boat will await us.'

The matter was so arranged.

Lord de Winter kept along the exterior boulevards to enter by another gate, while the two friends entered by the one facing them; at about two hundred yards they found the hotel named.

They baited the horses, but without unsaddling them; the grooms took supper, for it began to grow late, and the two masters, anxious to embark, told them to be on the jetty, with orders not to speak to any one whatsoever. This applied, of course, only to Blaisois; as for Grimaud, it was long since he had needed such orders.

Athos and Aramis went down to the harbour. By the dust upon their clothing, by a certain ease of manner which always shows a man accustomed to travelling, the two friends excited the attention of some promenaders.

They saw one especially on whom their arrival had produced considerable impression. This man whom they had remarked first, for the same reasons which had made them noticed by others, was walking sadly up and down on the jetty. When he saw them he watched them closely, and seemed to burn with the desire to speak to them. He was young and pale; he had eyes of so uncertain a blue that they seemed to grow fierce, like those of a tiger, according to the colours they reflected; his gait, in spite of the slowness and uncertainty of his windings, was stiff and bold; he was dressed in black, and wore a long sword with tolerable ease.

On reaching the jetty, Athos and Aramis stopped to look at a small boat made fast to a pile and all ready to start.

'That is without doubt ours,' said Athos.

'Yes,' replied Aramis, 'and the sloop out there, which is getting under sail, must be the one which should take us to our destination. Now, if only Winter would not make us wait. It is not at all amusing to stop here. There is not a woman about.'

'*Chut!*' said Athos; 'they will hear you.'

In fact, the promenader, who during the examination of the two friends had passed and re-passed several times behind them, had stopped at the name of Winter; but as his face did not express any emotion at the mention of the name, he might have merely stopped by chance.

'Messieurs,' said the young man, bowing with much ease and politeness, 'pardon my curiosity; but I see that you come from Paris, or at least that you are strangers in Boulogne.'

'We come from Paris, Monsieur,' replied Athos, with the same politeness. 'What can we do for you?'

'Monsieur, would you be good enough to tell me if it is true that Cardinal Mazarin is no longer minister?'

'That's a strange question,' said Aramis.

'It is, and it is not,' replied Athos; 'that is to say, that one half of France would drive him away, and that by force of intrigues and promises he maintains his position by the other half. That might continue so for a very long time, as you see.'

'In fact, Monsieur,' said the stranger, 'he is not in flight or in prison?'

'No, Monsieur; not at present, at least.'

'Messieurs, accept my thanks for your kindness,' said the young man, going away.

'What do you think of this questioner?' enquired Aramis.

'I say that he is a provincial who is annoyed, or a spy trying to get information.'

'And you answered him in that manner?'

'Nothing would have authorized me to reply differently. He was polite with me, and I with him.'

'But yet if he is a spy——'

'What do you think a spy could do? We are no longer living in the time of Cardinal Richelieu, who on a mere suspicion had the seaports closed.'*

'No matter; you were wrong to answer him as you did,' said Aramis, watching the young man as he disappeared behind the sand-hills.

'And you forget that you committed a greater imprudence when you mentioned Lord de Winter's name. It was on hearing that that the young man stopped.'

'The greater reason when he did speak to desire him to pass on.'

'A quarrel?' said Athos.

'And how long since a quarrel could make you afraid?'

'A quarrel always causes me fear when one waits for me anywhere, and this quarrel could prevent my arriving. Besides, would you like me to confess something? I was very curious to see this young man quite close.'

'Why so?'

'Aramis, you are going to laugh at me, to call me the most frightened of visionaries.'

'What next?'

'But whom do you think this man is like?'

'In ugliness or in beauty?' asked Aramis, laughing.

'In the former, and as much as a man can be like a woman.'

'Ah!' exclaimed Aramis; 'you set me thinking. No, truly you are not a visionary, my dear friend; and now I reflect—yes, upon my word, you are right—that small receding mouth, those eyes which seem always at the orders of the mind and not of the heart. It is a bastard of Milady.'

'You are laughing, Aramis!'

'By habit, that's all; for I swear to you I should not like any more than you to meet this serpent on my path.'

'Ah, here is Winter coming,' said Athos.

'Good, there will be only one thing wanting,' said Aramis; 'that's our servants who make us wait for them.'

'No,' said Athos, 'I perceive them; they are coming at twenty paces behind my Lord. I recognize Grimaud with his stiff head and his long legs. Tony carries our carbines.'

'Then we are going to embark in the night?' asked Aramis, casting a glance of his eye to the west, where the sun left only a golden cloud which seemed little by little to extinguish itself by dipping into the sea.

'It is probable,' said Athos.

'*Diable!*' replied Aramis; 'I love the sea but little in the daytime, and still less at night; the noise of the waves, the noise of the winds, the terrible movement of the vessel. I confess that I should prefer the convent of Noisy.'

Athos smiled his sad smile, for he was listening to what his friend said while thinking evidently of something else, and walking towards Winter.

Aramis followed him.

'What is the matter with our friend?' said Aramis; 'he resembles the damned of Dante* whose necks Satan had dislocated, and who regarded their heels. What the devil is the matter with him to look thus behind him?'

On seeing them, Winter doubled his pace, and came to them at a surprising speed.

'What is the matter, my Lord?' said Athos. 'What is it that puts you so out of breath?'

'Oh, nothing, nothing. Yet, in passing near the downs I fancied that——' and he turned round again.

Athos looked at Aramis.

'But let us set off,' continued Winter; 'the sloop is waiting for us. You can see it from here. I wish I were aboard;' and he turned round again.

'Have you forgotten anything?' said Aramis.

'No; it is a preoccupation.'

'He has seen him,' said Athos, in a low tone to Aramis.

They had reached the ladder which led to the boat. Winter made the servants go first carrying the arms, then the porters who carried the baggage, and began to descend after them. At that moment Athos saw a man who was following the sea-shore parallel to the jetty, and who hurried his steps as if to be near the other side of the harbour, about twenty yards from where they were embarking. He fancied in the midst of the gloom which was around that he recognized the young man who questioned them.

'Oh, oh!' he said to himself, 'is he really a spy, and would he wish to prevent our embarkation?'

But however, if the stranger had had that intention, he was a little late for putting it into execution. Athos, in his turn, went down the ladder, but without losing sight of the young man. The latter, to make a short cut, had appeared on a flood-gate.

'He sets his mind on us, certainly,' said Athos; 'but let us get on board, and once out at sea, let him come;' and Athos leaped on board the boat, which was at once pushed off, and began to make way under the efforts of four strong rowers.

But the young man began to follow, or rather precede, the boat. It had to pass between the head of the jetty, overlooked by the lighthouse, which was just lighted up, and an overhanging rock. They saw him climb the rock, so as to rise above the boat when it should pass.

'Ah!' said Aramis to Athos, 'that young man is decidedly a spy.'

'Who is that young man?' asked Winter, turning round.

'Why, the one who has followed us, who spoke to us, and who waited for us over there. Look!'

Winter turned round and followed with his glance the direction of Aramis's finger. The light flooded the little passage which they had to clear, and the rock where the young man stood upright, waiting them with bared head and crossed arms.

'That is he!' exclaimed Winter, seizing Athos's arm—'that is he; I thought I had recognized him, and I am not mistaken.'

'Who is *he*?' asked Aramis.

'The son of Milady,' replied Athos.

'The monk!' exclaimed Grimaud.

The young man heard these words. It seemed as if he would throw himself down, so closely did he cling to the edge of the rock, leaning over towards the sea.

'Yes, it is I, uncle; I, the son of Milady; the monk; the secretary and friend of Cromwell, and I know you and your companions.'

There were in that boat three men who were brave, it is true, and whose courage no one would dare to dispute; but at that voice, those gestures, they felt a cold shudder run through their veins.

As for Grimaud, his hair stood up, and the perspiration ran down his forehead.

'Ah!' said Aramis, 'is that the nephew, the monk, the son of Milady, as he himself says?'

'Alas, yes!' murmured Winter.

'Then wait,' said Aramis; and he took up, with that terrible coolness which he showed on all great occasions, one of the two muskets which Tony held, loaded it, and aimed at the man standing upright on the rock like the angel of malediction.

'Fire!' cried Grimaud, quite beside himself.

Athos threw himself on the barrel of the carbine, and stopped the firing of the shot.

'What the devil does it concern you?' exclaimed Aramis. 'I had such a good aim; I should have put a ball into his chest.'

'It is quite enough to have killed his mother,' said Athos, gruffly.

'The mother was a wretch, who had struck us all in our own persons, or in those who were dear to us.'

'Yes; but the son has done nothing to us.'

Grimaud, who had got up to see the effect of the shot, fell back discouraged, striking his hands together.

The young man burst into laughter.

'Ah! It is indeed you, and I know you now.'

His strident laugh and his menacing words passed above the boat, were carried away by the breeze, and then were lost in the depths of the horizon. Aramis shuddered.

'Be calm,' said Athos. 'What the devil! Are we then no longer men?'

'Yes, we are,' said Aramis; 'but that man is a demon. Now, ask the uncle if I did wrong in trying to rid him of his dear nephew.'

Winter only replied by a sigh.

'All would have been finished,' continued Aramis. 'Ah! I fear, Athos, that you have made me commit a folly with your wisdom.'

Athos took Lord de Winter's hand, and tried to turn the conversation. 'When shall we land in England?' he asked the gentleman; but the latter did not hear the words, and did not reply.

'Here, Athos,' said Aramis; 'perhaps there is still time. Look, he remains in the same place.'

Athos turned round with effort; the sight of this young man was evidently painful to him. In fact, he continued erect on his rock, the beacon-light appearing like an aureole of radiance around him.

'But what is he doing at Boulogne?' asked Athos, who, being reason itself, sought in everything the cause, caring little for the effect.

'He was following me, he was following me,' said Winter, who this time had heard the voice of Athos, for it corresponded with his thoughts.

'To follow you, my friend,' said Athos, 'he must have known of our departure; and besides, according to all probability, on the contrary he had preceded us.'

'Then I understand nothing of it!' said the Englishman, shaking his head like a man who thinks it useless to strive against a supernatural force.

'Decidedly, Aramis,' said Athos, 'I think I was wrong not to let you do it.'

'Be silent!' replied Aramis. 'You would make me weep if I could.'

Grimaud uttered a hoarse growl which resembled a roar.

At this moment a voice hailed them from the sloop. The pilot, who was seated at the helm, replied; and the boat came alongside the sloop. In a moment men, servants, and baggage were on board. The captain was only waiting for his passengers before setting out; and scarcely had they set foot on the sloop than he put her head towards Hastings, where they would disembark.

At this moment the three friends, in spite of themselves, threw a last look towards the rock, where the threatening shadow was still visible. Then a voice reached them, which sent them this last menace, 'I shall see you again, Messieurs, in England!'

XLVI

THE TE DEUM FOR THE VICTORY OF LENS

ALL the bustle that Madame Henrietta had remarked, and the reason for which she had vainly sought, was occasioned by the victory of Lens, of the news of which Monsieur the Prince had made the Duc de Châtillon the bearer, who had taken a noble part in it. He was besides charged with the duty of hanging from the arches of Notre-Dame twenty-two flags taken both from Lorrainers and Spaniards.

This news was decisive.* It ended the dispute begun with the parliament in favour of the court. All the imposts summarily enregistered, to which parliament made opposition, were at once passed, from the necessity of sustaining the honour of France, and the hazardous hope of beating the enemy. Since Nordlingen, only reverses had been experienced, and the parliament had had full play to question M. de Mazarin on victories always promised and always postponed; but this time there had been a complete triumph, so everyone felt that this was a double victory for the court—victory abroad, victory at home—so much so that there was no one, even to the young king, who on learning this news had not exclaimed, 'Ah, Messieurs of the parliament, we· are going to see what you will say.'

The queen pressed to her heart the royal child, whose haughty and untamed feelings harmonized so well with her own. A council was held the same evening, to which had been summoned Maréchal de la Meilleraie and M. de Villeroy, because they were partisans of Mazarin; Chavigny and Séguier, because they hated the parliament; and Guitaut and Comminges, because they were devoted to the queen.

Nothing transpired of what had been decided in that council. It was known only that on the Sunday following there would be a Te Deum sung at Notre-Dame in honour of the victory of Lens.

On the next Sunday the Parisians awoke therefore with alacrity. At that period a Te Deum was a grand affair. No abuse of that kind of ceremony had then been made, and it produced its effect. The sun, which seemed to do its part in the fête, had risen radiant, and gilded the sombre towers of the metropolis, already crowded with a multitude of people. The most obscure streets of the city had assumed a holiday look, and along the quays one saw long lines of shopkeepers, artisans, women, and children, going towards Notre-Dame, like a river which was ascending towards its source. The shops were deserted, the houses closed; every one felt a desire to see the young king with his mother and the famous Cardinal Mazarin, whom they hated so much that no one wished to be deprived of his presence.

The greatest liberty, besides, reigned in this immense crowd; all opinions were expressed openly and rang out, so to say, the riot, as the thousand bells of all the churches of Paris rang the Te Deum. The police of the city was furnished by the city itself; nothing threatening came to trouble the concert of the general hatred, and to chill the words in slanderous mouths.

Since eight in the morning the regiment of the queen's Guards, commanded by Guitaut, and by Comminges, his nephew, as second in command, had come, headed by their drums and trumpets, to place itself in echelons from the Palais-Royal to Notre-Dame—a manœuvre which the Parisians witnessed peaceably, always lovers, as they are, of military music and gay uniforms.

Friquet was dressed in his Sunday best, and under the pretext of an inflammation, brought on by introducing an enormous quantity of cherry-stones into one of the sides of his mouth, he had obtained leave from Bazin, his superior, for the whole day.

Bazin had at first refused, for he was in a bad humour—first, at the departure of Aramis, who had gone without telling him where; then at having to serve at a Mass sung in favour of a victory which was not in accord with his own views. Bazin was a Frondeur, as we remember; and if it were possible that in such a solemnity the beadle might absent himself like a simple choir-boy, Bazin would certainly have addressed to the archbishop the same demand as had just been made to him. He at first refused all leave, but in the very presence of Bazin Friquet's inflammation had greatly increased, so that for the honour of the whole choir, who would have been compromised by such a deformity, Bazin had finally yielded with a grumble. At the door of the church Friquet had spit out his inflammation, and sent in the direction of Bazin one of those gestures which assure to the gamin of Paris his superiority over all the other gamins of the universe; and as to his inn, he had naturally got leave by saying that he was to serve at the Mass at Notre-Dame.

Friquet was therefore free, and had dressed in his very best. He had, moreover, as a remarkable ornament of his person, one of those indescribable hats which hold the middle place between the cap of the Middle Ages and the hat of Louis XIII's time. His mother had made this curious head-gear, and whether from caprice or want of enough material, had shown in the making of it little care in blending the colours, so that this *chef-d'œuvre* of the hat manufacture of the seventeenth century was yellow and green on one side, white and red on the other.

But Friquet, who had always a partiality for variety in tints, was only the more proud and triumphant.

On leaving Bazin, Friquet had started off at a run for the Palais-Royal. He reached there just when the Guards regiment was leaving, and as he came for nothing else but to enjoy the sight and music, he took a place at the head of the procession, beating the drum with two slates, and passing from this exercise to that of the trumpet, which he naturally imitated with his mouth in a way which had procured for him more than once the praises of lovers of imitative harmony.

This amusement continued from the Barrière des Sergents to the Place Notre-Dame, and Friquet felt a real pleasure in it; but when the regiment halted, and the companies, in spreading out, extended to the very heart of the city,* being stationed at the end of the Rue St Christophe near the Rue Cocatrix, where Broussel was living, then Friquet, remembering that he had not breakfasted, looked to see in which direction he could turn in order to accomplish this important act of the day, and after having carefully reflected, decided that it should be Councillor Broussel who should bear the expense of his repast. Consequently he took his flight, arrived quite out of breath at the councillor's door, and knocked hard.

His mother, Broussel's old servant, went to open it.

'What are you doing here, scapegrace, and why are you not at Notre-Dame?'

'I was there, Mother; but I saw something going on which M. Broussel ought to know of, and with M. Bazin's permission—you know, Mother, M. Bazin the beadle—I have come to speak to M. Broussel.'

'And what do you want to say to him, you monkey?'

'I wish to speak to him alone.'

'You can't; he is at work.'

'Then I shall wait,' said Friquet, whom that suited so much the better, as he could easily find a way of utilizing the time; and he quickly ran upstairs, while Dame Nanette ascended more slowly behind him.

'Now, for the last time,' said she, 'what do you want with M. Broussel?'

'I want to tell him,' replied Friquet, crying out with all his might, 'that there is a whole regiment of Guards coming from that direction. Now, as I have heard it said everywhere that there is a bad feeling at the court against him, I am come to forewarn him to be on his guard.'

Broussel heard the cry of the young rogue, and pleased with his display of zeal, came down to the first floor, for he did his work in a room on the second.

'Eh!' said he, 'my friend, what is the regiment of Guards to us? And are you not a simpleton to invent such a piece of scandal? Don't you know that it's the custom to do as they are doing, and that this regiment always lines the road when the king passes along?'

Friquet pretended to be astonished, and twisting his new hat between his fingers, 'It is not surprising that you should know this,—you, M. Broussel, who know everything; but I, I swear, did not, and I thought I should be giving you a timely caution. You must not be cross with me for that, M. Broussel.'

'On the contrary, my boy, your zeal pleases me. Dame Nanette, see now if there are any of the apricots which Madame de Longueville sent us yesterday from Noisy, and give half a dozen to your boy, with a crust of new bread.'

'Ah, thank you, M. Broussel,' said Friquet. 'I am very fond of apricots.'

Broussel then went to his wife's room and called for breakfast.

It was half-past nine. The councillor went to the window. The street was quite empty; but there was heard in the distance, like the noise of the tide coming in, the huge roaring of the popular waves which were already increasing around Notre-Dame.

The sound increased greatly when d'Artagnan came with a company of musketeers to stand at the gates of Notre-Dame to allow the church service to be performed. He had advised Porthos to use the occasion for seeing the ceremony; and Porthos, finely dressed, mounted on his best horse, was doing the part of an honorary musketeer, as formerly d'Artagnan so often had done. The sergeant of that company, an old soldier of the Spanish wars, recognized Porthos, his former comrade, and he had soon made known to those under his command the great deeds of this giant—the ornament of the old Musketeers of Tréville. Porthos not only had been well received in the company, but further had been regarded with admiration.

At ten the cannon of the Louvre announced the king's departure. A movement like that among trees when a storm bends and twists their tops ran through the multitude, which was all in motion behind the immovable muskets of the Guards. At last the king appeared with the queen in a gilded coach. Ten other carriages followed, containing the ladies of honour, the royal officers, and all the court.

'*Vive le Roi!*' was cried from all parts.

The young king put his head to the door, looked sufficiently grateful, and bowed slightly, which caused the cries of the multitude to be redoubled.

The *cortège* advanced slowly, and took nearly half an hour in going from the Louvre to Notre-Dame. Arrived there, it passed by degrees under the immense concave of the gloomy cathedral, and divine service began.

Just as the court ceremonial was going on, a coach bearing Comminges's arms quitted the line of court carriages, and came slowly and stopped at the end of the Rue St Christophe, then quite deserted. When there, four guards and an officer mounted the heavy vehicle and closed the canopy in front; then, through an opening skilfully arranged, the officer began to watch the length of the Rue Cocatrix, as if he expected the arrival of some one.

Everyone's attention was occupied with the ceremony, so that neither the coach nor the precautions adopted by those inside it were noticed. Friquet, whose watchful eye alone would have penetrated them, had gone to eat his apricots on the entablature of a house on the open space before Notre-Dame, whence he saw the king, the queen, and M. de Mazarin, and heard Mass as if he had taken part in it. Towards the end of the service the queen, seeing that Comminges, standing close to her, was waiting for a confirmation of an order which she had already given him before leaving the Louvre, said in a low voice, 'Go, Comminges, and may God help you!'

Comminges immediately left the church, and entered the Rue St Christophe. Friquet, who saw this fine officer walking, followed by two guards, amused himself by keeping close behind him, and that with so much the more alacrity as the ceremony finished at the same moment, and the king was re-entering his carriage. The officer had hardly caught sight of Comminges at the end of the Rue Cocatrix than he said a word to the coachman, who immediately brought the coach to Broussel's door. Comminges knocked at the door at the same time that the carriage stopped there. Friquet was waiting behind Comminges till the door should be opened.

'What are you doing there, you monkey?' asked Comminges.

'I am waiting to go into M. Broussel's, Monsieur the officer,' said Friquet, with that wheedling tone which the gamin of Paris so well knows how to assume on occasion.

'He lives here, then?' asked Comminges.

'Yes, Monsieur.'

'And on what floor?'

'The whole house,' said Friquet, 'is his.'

'But where does he generally remain?'

'For work on the second floor, for his meals he comes down to the first; just now he should be dining, for it is noon.'

'Very good,' said Comminges.

Just then the door was opened. The officer questioned the servant, and learned that M. Broussel was at home, and actually at dinner. Comminges went up behind the servant, and Friquet behind Comminges. Broussel was seated at table with his family—his wife, two daughters, and at the end of the table his son, Louvières, whom we have seen already at the time of the accident which befell the councillor. The good man, now restored to full health, was enjoying the fine fruit which Madame de Longueville had sent him.

Comminges, who had prevented the servant from entering first to announce him, opened the door himself, and confronted this family picture.

At the sight of the officer Broussel felt a little agitated, but seeing that he bowed politely, he arose and bowed also. Yet in spite of their mutual politeness, uneasiness was painted on the faces of the women; Louvières became very pale, and waited impatiently for the officer's explanation.

'Monsieur,' said Comminges, 'I am bearer of an order from the king.'

'Very good, Monsieur. What is this order?' and he stretched out his hand.

'I am commissioned to arrest you,* Monsieur,' said Comminges, keeping the same tone of voice, 'and if you will kindly believe me, you will spare yourself the trouble of reading this long letter, and you will follow me.'

If a thunderbolt had fallen among these good people, so peacefully assembled, it could not have produced a more terrible effect. Broussel started back all of a tremble. It was a terrible thing at that time to be imprisoned by order of the king. Louvières made a movement to seize his sword, which was on a chair in a corner of the room, but a look from the good man, Broussel, who in the midst of all this trouble did not lose his head, checked this desperate movement. Madame Broussel, separated from her husband by the width of the table, burst into tears; the two girls clung to their father.

'Come, Monsieur,' said Comminges, 'be quick! You must obey the king.'

'Monsieur,' said Broussel, 'I am in bad health, and I cannot give myself up in this state; I require time.'

'That is impossible; the order is formal, and must be executed at once.'

'Impossible!' said Louvières; 'Monsieur, take care not to drive us to despair.'

'Impossible!' said a screaming voice at the end of the room. Comminges turned round and saw Dame Nanette with a broom in her hand, and eyes sparkling with all the fire of wrath.

'My good Nanette, do keep quiet,' said Broussel, 'I beg of you.'

'I keep quiet when my master is being arrested—he who is the support, the liberator, the father of the poor! Well, yes! you know me—— Will you begone?' said she to Comminges.

Comminges smiled.

'Come, Monsieur,' said he, turning towards Broussel, 'make this woman keep quiet, and follow me.'

'Make me keep quiet! me! me!' said Nanette. 'Ah, indeed! It would take a better man than you to do that, my beautiful king's bird! You will see;' and she dashed to the window, opened it, and with a voice so shrill that it might be heard on the square of Notre-Dame, 'Help!' she cried, 'they are arresting my master, the Councillor Broussel! help!'

'Monsieur,' said Comminges, 'say at once, will you obey, or do you intend rebellion against the king?'

'I obey—I obey, Monsieur,' said Broussel, trying to disengage himself from the embrace of his daughters, and to restrain his son from trying to set him free.

'In that case,' said Comminges, 'impose silence on that old woman.'

'Oh, old woman!' said Nanette, and she began to cry her loudest, while laying hold of the window-bars. 'Help! help! for M. Broussel, who is being arrested because he has defended the people. Help!'

Comminges seized her in his arms, and tried to drag her from her post; but at the same moment another voice, coming from a sort of *entresol*, screamed out in piercing treble, 'Murder! fire! thieves! They are killing M. Broussel!'

It was Friquet's voice. Dame Nanette, feeling herself supported, replied then with greater force, and made the chorus.

Already some curious folk appeared at the windows. The people, drawn to the end of the street, came running up,—first a few men, then groups, then a crowd; cries were heard; the coach was visible, but nothing was understood. Friquet leaped from the *entresol* to the hood of the coach.

'They want to arrest M. Broussel!' cried he; 'there are some guards in the coach, and the officer is up there!'

An angry murmur arose from the crowd, and they began to approach the horses. The two guards who had stopped in the passage went upstairs to help Comminges; those who were in the coach opened the doors and got their pikes ready.

'Do you see them?' cried Friquet. 'There they are.'

The coachman turned round and gave Friquet a stroke of the whip which made him howl with pain.

'Ah, you coachman of the Devil! You are interfering with me! Wait a bit;' and he regained the *entresol*, whence he pelted the coachman with all the missiles he could lay hold of.

In spite of the hostile demonstration of the guards, and perhaps even because of it, the crowd began to growl and approach the horses. The guards made the most mutinous retreat by blows of their pikes. However, the tumult kept growing greater; the street could not hold the spectators, who flowed in from all sides; the press invaded the space which the terrible pikes still kept between the crowd and the coach. The soldiers, pressed back as by living walls, were likely to be crushed between the wheels and panels of the coach. The cries, 'In the king's name!' twenty times repeated by the officer, could do no good against this redoubtable multitude, and seemed, on the contrary, to exasperate it more, when at these cries, 'In the king's name!' a cavalier rode up, and seeing men in uniform being maltreated, dashed into the mêlée sword in hand, and brought unexpected help to the guards.

This cavalier was a young man scarcely sixteen, white with anger. He put himself on foot like the other guards, put his back to the shaft of the coach, made a rampart of his horse, took his pistols from the holsters and put them into his belt, and began to cut and thrust like one to whom the sword was familiar.

For ten minutes the young man by himself stood firm against the whole crowd. Then they saw Comminges appear, pushing Broussel before him.

'Let us smash the coach!' cried the populace.

'Help!' cried the old woman.

'Murder!' cried Friquet, continuing to rain upon the guards all that he could lay hands on.

'In the king's name!' cried Comminges.

'The first who approaches is a dead man!' cried Raoul, who finding himself pressed, pierced with his sword a sort of giant who was ready to crush him, and who, feeling himself wounded, retreated howling; for it was Raoul, who, returning from Blois after five days' absence, had wished to have a view of the ceremony, and had gone by the streets which led him most directly to Notre-Dame. On reaching the neighbourhood of the Rue Cocatrix, he found himself drawn along by the popular wave, and on hearing the cry, 'In the king's name!' he recalled Athos's words, 'Serve the king,' and hastened to fight for the king, whose guards were being ill-used.

Comminges threw, so to speak, Broussel into the coach, and jumped in after him. At that moment a musket-shot was heard, and the ball penetrated Comminges's hat, and broke the arm of a guardsman. Comminges raised his head, and saw in the midst of the smoke Louvières's threatening figure at the second-floor window.

'Very well, Monsieur,' said Comminges, 'you will hear from me about that.'

'And you too, Monsieur,' said Louvières, 'and we shall see which will speak more loudly.'

Friquet and Nanette kept on screaming. Their cries, the shot fired, and the smell of powder, always so maddening, produced their effect.

'Kill the officer! kill him!' yelled the crowd; and a great commotion took place.

'One step more,' cried Comminges, throwing down the coach front that they might see into the vehicle, and putting his sword to Broussel's breast—'one step nearer, and I kill the prisoner. I have orders to take him dead or alive; I will take him dead, that's the whole of it.'

A terrible cry was heard; the wife and daughters of Broussel stretched their hands supplicatingly towards the people. They saw that this officer, so pale, but who seemed so determined, would do as he said. They kept on threatening, but stood aside. Comminges made the wounded guardsman get into the coach, and ordered the others to close the door.

'Stop at the palace,' said he to the coachman, who was more dead than alive.

The latter whipped his horses, and they opened a way through the crowd; but on reaching the quay they had to pull up. The coach was upset; the horses were carried away, choked, pounded by the crowd. Raoul, on foot—for he had not had time to mount his horse—tired of striking with the flat of his sword, as were the guards also, began to use the point. But this terrible and last resource only tended to exasperate the multitude. The glitter of a musket-barrel or the blade of a rapier now began to appear in the midst of the crowd; some shots were heard, fired in the air, no doubt, but whose resound did not the less make hearts beat, and projectiles continued to pour down from the windows. Cries were heard which are heard only in times of revolt; faces were seen which are seen only on days of bloodshed. The cries, 'Kill the guards! Into the Scine with the officer!' arose above the din, great as that was. Raoul, his hat battered, his face all covered with blood, felt that not only his strength, but also his reason began to leave him; his eyes swam in a reddish mist, and across this mist he saw a hundred threatening arms stretched towards him, ready to seize him when he fell. Comminges tore his hair with rage inside the upset coach. The guards could give help to no one, each being fully employed in defending himself. All was over; coach, horses, guards, satellites, and prisoner perhaps, all seemed likely to be torn to ribbons, when all at once a voice well known to Raoul was heard, and suddenly a large sword glittered in the air. At the same moment the crowd opened, gaps were made in it; it was routed, crushed. An officer of Musketeers, striking and cutting right and left, hastened to Raoul, and took him in his arms just when going to fall.

'Good heavens!' cried the officer, 'have they killed him, then? In that case so much the worse for them!' and he turned round, so terrible from strength, anger, and threatening looks, that the maddest of the revolters rushed one upon another to escape, and some even rolled into the Seine.

'M. d'Artagnan,' muttered Raoul.

'Yes, good heavens, myself! and fortunately for you, so it seems, my young friend. Come, this way, you!' cried he, rising in his stirrups and raising his sword, calling by voice and sign to the musketeers, who had not been able to keep up with him. 'Come, sweep away all that! Prepare muskets! Carry arms! Make ready! Pres——'

At this order the crowds gave way so suddenly that d'Artagnan could not keep from a Homeric burst of laughter.

'Thanks, d'Artagnan,' said Comminges, showing half of his body through the window of the upset coach. 'Thanks, young gentleman. Your name, that I may tell it to the queen?'

Raoul was about replying when d'Artagnan whispered to him, 'Be silent,' said he, 'and let me reply.' Then turning towards Comminges, 'Do not lose time,' he said; 'get out of the coach, if you can, and procure another.'

'But what other?'

'Why the first that comes over Pont Neuf. Those who are in it will be too happy, I hope, to lend their coach for the service of the king.'

'But,' said Comminges, 'I don't know.'

'Quick, or in five minutes all the rascals will return with swords and muskets! You will be slain and your prisoner set free. Quick! Stop; there is a coach coming from over there.' Then leaning towards Raoul, 'Above all, do not give your name,' he whispered to him.

The young man looked at him astonished.

'All right, I am off,' said Comminges; 'and if they return, fire.'

'No, no,' replied d'Artagnan, 'let no one stir; on the contrary, a shot fired just now would be paid for too dearly tomorrow.'

Comminges took his four guards and as many musketeers, and ran to the coach. He made the people who were in it get out, and brought them close to the upset coach. But when it became needful to change Broussel from the broken vehicle to the other, the people, on perceiving him whom they called their liberator, sent up unimaginable yells, and rushed a second time towards the coach. 'Be off!' said d'Artagnan. 'Here are ten musketeers to go with you, and I will keep twenty to hold back the people. Be off, and don't lose a moment. Ten men for M. de Comminges!'

Ten men separated from the troop, surrounded the second coach, and set off at a gallop. On this the cries redoubled; more than ten thousand men thronged the quay, blocking the Pont Neuf and the adjacent streets. Some shots were heard. A musketeer was wounded.

'Forward!' cried d'Artagnan, pushed to extremities, and biting his moustache; and he made a charge with his twenty men into the midst of the populace, who, alarmed, were made to fall back. One man alone kept his position with his arquebuse in hand.

'Ah!' said that man, 'it is you who have already wanted to kill him! Wait!' and he aimed his arquebuse at d'Artagnan, who drew near at full gallop.

D'Artagnan leaned forward on the horse's neck. The young man fired; the ball cut the plume of his hat. The fiery horse struck the imprudent man who alone tried to check a tempest, and sent him against the wall. D'Artagnan pulled up his horse short, and while his musketeers continued their charge, he raised his sword over him whom he had upset.

'Ah, Monsieur!' cried Raoul, who recognized the young man as one whom he had seen in the Rue Cocatrix, 'spare his life; it is the councillor's son.'

D'Artagnan checked his arm, then ready to strike.

'Ah, you are his son,' said he; 'that's another matter.'

'Monsieur, I surrender!' said Louvières, handing to the officer the discharged musket.

'No, do not surrender; be off, on the contrary, and quickly too. If I take you, you will be hanged.'

The young man did not need to be told twice; he passed under the horse's neck, and disappeared at the corner of the Rue Guénégaud.

'Upon my word,' said d'Artagnan to Raoul, 'you stopped my hand just in time; he was a dead man, and upon honour, I should have regretted killing him on learning who he was.'

'Ah, Monsieur,' said Raoul, 'after having thanked you for that poor fellow, let me thank you for myself. Monsieur, I was about dying when you came.'

'Stop, stop, young man, and do not fatigue yourself with talking.' Then drawing out from one of his holsters a flagon full of Spanish wine, 'Drink two mouthfuls of this,' said he.

Raoul drank, and wished to renew his thanks.

'My dear fellow,' said d'Artagnan, 'we will talk about that later on.' Then seeing that the musketeers had swept the quay from the Pont Neuf to Quai St Michel, and that they were returning, he raised his sword for them to go at the double-quick.

The musketeers arrived at a trot; at the same time, from the other side of the quay the escort of ten men came, whom d'Artagnan had given to Comminges.

'Holloa!' said he, addressing the latter, 'has anything fresh happened?'

'Eh, Monsieur!' said the sergeant, 'their coach is again broken. There is a curse upon it.'

D'Artagnan shrugged his shoulders.

'They are a set of stupids. When one chooses a coach, it ought to be solid; the one with which to arrest a Broussel ought to carry ten thousand men.'

'What do you command, Lieutenant?'

'Take the detachment and escort it to its destination.'

'But will you retire alone?'

'Certainly. Do you believe that I need the escort?'

'Yet——'

'Go on.'

The musketeers set off, and d'Artagnan remained alone with Raoul.

'Do you feel any pain?'

'Yes; my head feels heavy and burning.'

'What is the matter then with your head?' said d'Artagnan, raising Raoul's hat. 'Ah, ah! a bruise.'

'Yes; I think a flower-pot came down on my head.'

'Rabble!' said d'Artagnan. 'But you have spurs! Were you on horseback?'

'Yes, but I got down to defend M. de Comminges, and my horse was taken; and look, that is it.'

In fact, at that moment Raoul's horse passed, mounted by Friquet, who was going at a gallop, waving his fourcoloured hat and shouting, 'Broussel, Broussel!'

'Holloa! stop, you rogue!' said d'Artagnan; 'bring that horse here.'

Friquet heard well enough, but pretended that he did not, and tried to go on. D'Artagnan felt a desire to give chase to M. Friquet, but did not wish to leave Raoul alone; he contented himself with taking a pistol and loading it. Friquet had a quick eye and a sharp ear; he saw what d'Artagnan meant, and heard the click of the pistol; he stopped the horse abruptly.

'Ah, it is you, Monsieur the officer,' he exclaimed, coming towards d'Artagnan; 'I am really very glad to meet you.'

D'Artagnan looked attentively at Friquet, and recognized the boy of the Rue de la Calandre.

'Oh, it is you, monkey. Come here! You have changed your trade? You are no longer a choir-boy, nor a waiter at a tavern? You are a horse-stealer?'

'Ah, Monsieur the officer, how can you say so? I was looking for the gentleman to whom this horse belongs; a fine cavalier, brave as a Caesar.' He pretended to perceive Raoul for the first time. 'Ah, if I am not mistaken, this is he. Monsieur, you will not forget the boy, will you?'

Raoul put his hand to his pocket.

'What are you going to do?' said d'Artagnan.

'Give ten livres to this fine fellow,' said Raoul, taking a pistole* from his pocket.

'Ten kicks!' said d'Artagnan. 'Be off, you monkey, and don't forget that I have your address.'

Friquet, who did not expect to get off so cheaply, made but one bound from the quay to the Rue Dauphine, where he disappeared. Raoul mounted his horse, and they both at a walk, d'Artagnan guarding the young man as if he were his son, took the road to the Rue Tiquetonne. All along the way there were sullen grumblings and distant threats, but at the sight of this officer, with so military an equipment, and the powerful sword hanging from his wrist supported by its sword-knot, they got out of the way, and no serious attempt was made against the two cavaliers. They reached, therefore, without accident, the Hôtel de la Chevrette.

The fair Madeleine told d'Artagnan that Planchet had returned, and had brought Mousqueton, who had heroically borne the extraction of the ball, and was getting on as well as could be expected.

D'Artagnan ordered Planchet to be called, but he had disappeared.

'Then, some wine!' said d'Artagnan. When the wine had been brought, and they were alone, 'You are satisfied with yourself, are you not?' said d'Artagnan, looking straight at him.

'Well, yes; it seems to me I have done my duty. Have I not defended the king?'

'Who told you to defend the king?'

'Why, the Comte de la Fère himself.'

'Yes, the king; but today you have defended Mazarin, which is not the same thing.'

'But, Monsieur——'

'You have made a great mistake, young man; you have interfered with matters which do not concern you.'

'Yet you yourself——'

'Oh, I! that's another matter; I am bound to obey my captain's orders. Your captain is Monsieur the Prince. Mind that. You have no other. But was there ever such wrong-headedness! In order to win Mazarin's favour, you help to arrest Broussel! Don't breathe a word of that, at least, or the Comte de la Fère would be furious.'

'Do you believe the count would be angry with me?'

'Do I believe it! I am sure of it; but for that, I would thank you, for in fact you have been working for us. So I scold you in his place. Thus,' added d'Artagnan, 'I use the privilege which your guardian has granted me.'

'I do not understand you, Monsieur,' said Raoul.

D'Artagnan rose, went to his secretary, took a letter, and gave it to Raoul. When the young man had read it through, he looked discomposed.

'Oh!' said he, 'Monsieur the Count has then left Paris without seeing me.'

'He has been gone four days.'

'But his letter seems to indicate that he runs the risk of death,' said Raoul.

'Ah, well, yes; he run the risk of death! Be easy. No, he travels on some business and hopes to return soon; but you have no objection, I hope, to accept me in the mean while as your guardian?'

'Oh no; you are so brave a gentleman, and the Comte de la Fère loves you so much!'

'Ah, well! love me also. I shall not trouble you much, but on the condition that you remain a Frondeur, my young friend, and very much a Frondeur, even.'

'But can I continue seeing Madame de Chevreuse?'

'I should think so indeed, and Monsieur the Coadjutor also, and Madame de Longueville; and if the good man Broussel were there whom you have so foolishly helped to get arrested, I should say to you: Make your excuses quickly to him, and kiss him on both cheeks.'

'Well, Monsieur, I will obey you, though I do not understand you.'

'There is no need that you should. Holloa!' continued d'Artagnan, turning towards the door which some one had just opened; 'here is M. du Vallon coming in with his clothes all torn.'

'Yes; but in return,' said Porthos, dripping with perspiration and covered with dust, 'I have well torn their hides. These rascals wanted to take away my sword. Hang it, what a stir!' continued the giant, in his quiet way; 'but I knocked down more than twenty of them with the pommel of Balisardo. A sip of wine, d'Artagnan.'

'Oh, I agree with you,' said the Gascon, filling up Porthos's glass to the brim; 'but when you have finished drinking, give me your opinion.'

Porthos swallowed the glass at a draught. Then when he had placed it on the table, 'On what?' he said.

'Stop!' replied d'Artagnan; 'this is M. de Bragelonne, who assisted with all his might the arrest of Broussel, and whom I had great difficulty to prevent from defending M. de Comminges.'

'Hang it!' said Porthos; 'and what would his guardian say if he knew that?'

'Do you see?' interrupted d'Artagnan. 'Be a Frondeur, my friend, and imagine that I replace the count in everything;' and he made his purse chink. Then turning to his companion, 'Come on, Porthos.'

'Where now?' asked Porthos, pouring out a second glass.

'To present our respects to the cardinal.'

Porthos quietly drank the second glass, took up his hat, which he had placed on a chair, and followed d'Artagnan.

As for Raoul, he still remained quite confused with what he saw, d'Artagnan having desired him not to leave the room till all this disturbance was at an end.

XLVII

THE MENDICANT OF ST EUSTACHE

D'ARTAGNAN had calculated what he was doing in not going at once to the Palais-Royal. He had given Comminges time to be there before him, and consequently to make the valuable services known to the cardinal which he (d'Artagnan) and his friend had rendered that morning for the queen's party. So they were both well received by Mazarin, who paid them many compliments, and told them that each was more than halfway to what he desired; namely, d'Artagnan's captaincy and Porthos's barony.

D'Artagnan would have preferred money to all this, for he knew that Mazarin promised quickly and performed tardily. He therefore valued the cardinal's promises as unsubstantial dishes; but he did not appear at all dissatisfied in Porthos's presence, whom he did not want to discourage.

While the two friends were with the cardinal the queen sent for him. The cardinal thought it would be a means of redoubling the zeal of his defenders to procure them the thanks of the queen herself. He beckoned them to follow him. D'Artagnan and Porthos pointed to their dusty and torn clothes, but the cardinal nodded dissent.

'Those dresses,' said he, 'are worth more than those of the majority of the courtiers, for they have been in the fighting.'

D'Artagnan and Porthos obeyed.

Anne of Austria's court was numerous, and filled with joy, for in fact, after having gained a victory over the Spaniard, they had just gained another over the people. Broussel had been taken out of Paris without resistance, and at that time should be in the prisons of St Germain; and Blancmesnil, who had been arrested at the same time as he, but without noise and difficulty, was entered on the prison-book of Vincennes.*

Comminges was close to the queen, who was asking him the details of his expedition; and all were listening to his story, when he saw at the door behind the cardinal, who was coming in, d'Artagnan and Porthos.

'Ah, Madame,' said he, hastening to d'Artagnan, 'here is one who can tell you better than I, for he saved my life. Without him I should probably be at this moment caught in the nets of St Cloud—* for the proposal was nothing less than to throw me into the river. Speak, d'Artagnan.'

Since d'Artagnan had been lieutenant of the Musketeers he had been a hundred times perhaps in the same apartment as the queen, but the latter had never spoken to him.

'Well, Monsieur, after having done me such a service, are you silent?' said Anne of Austria.

'Madame,' replied he, 'I have nothing to say, except that my life is at your Majesty's service, and that I shall only be happy the day I shall lose it for your Majesty.'

'I know that, Monsieur, and have known it for a long time. I am therefore delighted to be able to give you this public mark of my esteem and gratitude.'

'Permit me, Madame, to share it with my friend,—a former musketeer of the Tréville company, as I was [he paused at these words], who has done wonders.'

'His name?' asked the queen.

'In the Musketeers he was called Porthos [the queen started], but his real name is the Chevalier du Vallon.'

'De Bracieux de Pierrefonds,' added Porthos.

'These names are too numerous for me to recall all of them, and I only wish to remember the first,' said the queen, graciously.

Porthos bowed. D'Artagnan stepped back.

At the moment the Coadjutor was announced. There was an exclamation of surprise in the royal assembly. Although he had preached that same morning,* it was known that he leaned strongly to the side of the Fronde; and Mazarin, in asking the archbishop to get his nephew to preach, had evidently had the intention of making one of those Italian thrusts at M. de Retz which delighted the cardinal so much. In fact, on leaving Notre-Dame the Coadjutor had learned what had happened. Although in close agreement with the principal Frondeurs, he was not so much so that he could not beat a retreat if the court offered him the advantages that he aimed at, and to which the coadjutor-ship opened up a road. M. de Retz wished to become archbishop in the place of his uncle, and a cardinal like Mazarin. Now, the popular party could with difficulty accord these thoroughly royal favours. He went to the palace to compliment the queen on the battle of Lens, determined beforehand to act for or against the court, according as his reception should be good or bad.

He entered, and on seeing him the whole of this rejoicing court felt a double curiosity to listen to his words. The Coadjutor had alone almost as much wit as all those who were united there to deride him. His speech was so perfectly adroit that if the bystanders had any desire to ridicule it, they could find no occasion. He ended by saying that he placed his feeble abilities at the service of her Majesty.

The queen seemed, as long as the speech lasted, to enjoy it greatly, but on its ending by that expression of devotion—the only one which could furnish a handle to the critics—Anne turned round, and a look directed towards her favourites told them that she would deliver the Coadjutor up to them. Immediately the court wits launched into mystification. Nogent Beautin, the court fool, exclaimed that the queen was extremely fortunate in procuring the help of religion in such a moment. Everyone burst out laughing.

The Comte de Villeroy said that he did not see how one could fear for a moment since they had as a defender of the court against the parliament and the citizens of Paris Monsieur the Coadjutor, who by a sign could raise an army of curates, of Swiss, and of beadles.

The Maréchal de la Meilleraie added that in case they came to blows, and Monsieur the Coadjutor should take part in it, it was a pity that the Coadjutor should not be recognized in the mêlée by a red hat, as Henry IV had been by his white plume at the battle of Ivry.

Gondy continued calm and serious before this storm, which he could make fatal for those who bantered him. The queen then asked him if he had anything to add to the fine speech he had just made.

'Yes, Madame,' said he, 'I beg of you to reflect twice before causing civil war in the kingdom.'

The queen turned her back, and the laughter began again.

The Coadjutor bowed, and left the palace, casting on the cardinal, who was looking at him, a look which all saw meant mortal hate. This look was so keen that it reached the bottom of Mazarin's heart, and the latter, feeling it to be a declaration of war, seized d'Artagnan by the arm, and said to him, 'When there is need, Monsieur, you will recognize that man who has just gone out, will you not?'

'Yes, Monseigneur.' Then turning towards Porthos, 'The devil!' said he, 'that's getting bad; I do not like quarrels between churchmen.'

Gondy retired, scattering benedictions on his passage, and giving himself the malicious delight of making everyone, even down to the servants of his enemies, fall on their knees.

'Oh!' he muttered, when clear of the palace, 'the ungrateful court! perfidious! cowardly! I will teach you to laugh tomorrow, but in a different key.'

But while they uttered extravagances of joy at the Palais-Royal to increase the hilarity of the queen, Mazarin—a man of sense, who besides had all the foresight arising from fear—did not lose his time in silly dangerous pleasantries. He left after the Coadjutor, secured his account books, locked up his gold, and contrived, by help of workmen in whom he trusted, hiding-places in his walls.

On returning home the Coadjutor learned that a young man had come after his departure, and was waiting. He asked his name, and was pleased to learn that it was Louvières. He went hastily to his cabinet. Broussel's son, still full of rage and covered with blood from his struggle with the king's officers, was there. The only precaution he had taken before coming was to leave his arquebuse at a friend's house.

The Coadjutor went and shook him by the hand. The young man looked at him as if he wished to read the depth of his heart.

'My dear M. Louvières,' said the Coadjutor, 'believe me, I feel really sorry for the misfortune that has happened to you.'

'Is it true, and do you speak seriously?' asked Louvières.

'From the depths of my heart.'

'In that case, Monseigneur, the time for words is past; the hour of action has come. If you wish it, Monseigneur, my father in three days will be out of prison, and in six months you will be cardinal.'

The Coadjutor started.

'Oh,' said Louvières, 'let us talk frankly, and lay the cards on the table. One does not scatter thirty thousand crowns in alms, as you have done the last six months, out of pure Christian charity; that would be too good. You are ambitious, that's clear. You are a man of talents, and you feel your value. I hate the court, and at this moment have but one wish—vengeance. Give us the clergy and people, of whom you have the disposition. I give you the citizen class and the parliament. With these four elements, in a week Paris is ours; and believe me, the court will give out of fear what it will not give from good-will.'

The Coadjutor regarded Louvières in his turn with his keen eye.

'But do you know, Monsieur, that it is simply civil war that you are now proposing?'

'You have been preparing for it a sufficiently long time, Monseigneur, for it to be welcome to you.'

'Nevertheless, you understand that it requires thought.'

'And how long do you ask for reflection?'

'Twelve hours, Monsieur. Is that too much?'

'It is now noon. At midnight I will be here.'

'If I have not returned, wait for me.'

'Good! At midnight, Monseigneur.'

'At midnight, my dear M. Louvières.'

When alone, Gondy summoned to his house all the priests with whom he was connected. Two hours after, he had assembled thirty parish priests of the most populous and consequently the most turbulent parts of Paris. Gondy told them of the insult he had just received at the Palais-Royal by the jokes of Beautin, of the Comte de Villeroy, and of the Maréchal de la Meilleraie. The curates asked him what was to be done.

'That is simple enough,' said the Coadjutor. 'You control the conscience. Well, cut away that wretched prejudice of fear and reverence for kings; teach your flocks that the queen is a tyrant, and repeat, so often and so strongly that all shall know it, that the misfortunes of France come from Mazarin, her lover and corrupter. Begin this work at once, and in three days I shall hope to hear the result. Moreover, if any one of you has good advice to give me, let him stay; I will listen to him with pleasure.'

Three priests stayed—those of St Merri, St Sulpice, and St Eustache. The others withdrew.

'You think, then, you can help me more effectively than your brother priests. Now, Monsieur the Curate of St Merri, you begin.'

'Monseigneur, I have in my district a man who would be of the greatest use to you.'

'Who is he?'

'A shopkeeper of the Rue des Lombards, who has great influence over the small trade of his neighbourhood.'

'What is his name?'

'His name is Planchet. He got up, scarcely six weeks ago,* a riot; but at the end of it, as he was looked for to be hanged, he disappeared.'

'And can you find him again?'

'I think so. I don't think he has been arrested. And as I am his wife's confessor, if she knows where he is, I shall know it.'

'Well, if you find him, bring him to me.'

'At what time, Monseigneur?'

'At six, if you please.'

'We will be with you at six, Monseigneur.'

'Go, my dear curate, and may God help you!'

The curate left.

'And you, Monsieur?' said Gondy, turning to the Curate of St Sulpice.

'I, Monseigneur, know a man who has done great service to a very popular prince, who would make an excellent leader of a revolt, and whom I can place at your disposal.'

'What is the name of this man?'

'M. le Comte de Rochefort.'

'I know him also; unfortunately he is not in Paris.'

'Monseigneur, he is in the Rue Cassette.'

'When did he arrive there?'

'Three days ago.'

'And why has he not been to see me?'

'He was told—Monseigneur will pardon me?'

'Oh, yes; speak out.'

'That Monseigneur was about coming to terms with the court.'

Gondy bit his lips.

'He has been deceived; bring him to me at eight, Monsieur the Curate, and may God bless you as I do!'

The second curate bowed, and left.

'Now your turn, Monsieur,' said the Coadjutor, turning towards the last who had stayed behind. 'Have you also something to offer me as good as that offered by the two who have just left?'

'Better, Monseigneur.'

'The devil! Mind you are making in that a large promise. One has offered me a shopkeeper; the second a count. You, perhaps, can offer me a prince?'

'I am going to offer you a mendicant, Monseigneur.'

'Ah, ah!' said Gondy, reflecting, 'you are right. Anyone who will stir up all that legion of poor which encumber the public thoroughfares, and who knows how to make them cry loudly enough for all France to hear that it is Mazarin who has brought them to beggary——'

'I have your man exactly.'

'Bravo! and who is he?'

'A simple mendicant who has been asking alms while giving the holy water on the steps of St Eustache Church for nearly six years.'

'And you say that he has great influence over his fellows?'

'Does Monseigneur know that mendicancy is an organization,—an association in which each brings his share, and which is under a chief?'*

'Yes; I have already heard that.'

'Well, this man whom I offer is a syndic-general.'

'And what do you know of him?'

'Nothing, Monseigneur, except that he seems tormented with some feeling of remorse.'

'What makes you believe that?'

'Every twenty-eighth of each month he makes me say a Mass for the repose of the soul of a person who died a violent death. Yesterday I said it again.'

'And you call him?'

'Maillard; but I don't think that that is his real name.'

'And do you think that we should find him at his post at this hour?'

'Decidedly.'

'Let us go and see your mendicant, Monsieur the Curate, and if he is such as you tell me, you are right, it is you who have found the real treasure;' and Gondy dressed himself as a cavalier, put on a large hat with a red feather, girt on a long sword, buckled spurs to his boots, wrapped himself in a wide cloak, and followed the curate.

The Coadjutor and his companion crossed all the streets which separated the archbishop's residence from St Eustache, carefully observing the feelings of the people. They were excited, but like a swarm of frightened bees seemed not to know on what place to settle; and it was evident that if no leaders were forthcoming, all would pass off in mere buzzing. On reaching the Rue Prouvaires, the curate pointed towards the front steps of the church.

'There he is,' said he, 'at his post.'

Gondy looked in that direction, and saw a poor man seated on a chair and leaning against one of the mouldings. He had near him a little pail, and held an *aspergès** brush in his hand.

'Is it by privilege,' said he, 'that he stations himself there?'

'No, Monseigneur. He came to terms with his predecessor for the post.'

'Came to terms!'

'Yes; these places are bought. I think that this man paid a hundred pistoles for his.'

'The fellow is well off, then?'

'Some of these men die leaving sometimes twenty thousand, twenty-five thousand, or thirty thousand livres, and even more.'

'H'm!' said Gondy, laughing; 'I did not believe I was investing my alms so well.'

Meanwhile they advanced towards the steps. As soon as they stepped on the first of them, the mendicant arose and held out the brush. He was a man of about sixty-six, short, tolerably stout, with grey hair and light brown eyes. There was upon his face the look of a struggle between two opposing principles—a bad nature kept under by the will, perhaps by repentance.

On seeing the cavalier who accompanied the curate the mendicant slightly started, and looked at him with an astonished air. They both touched the brush with the tips of their fingers, and made the sign of the cross. The Coadjutor threw a piece of silver into the hat on the ground.

'Maillard,' said the curate, 'we are come, Monsieur and I, to talk a few moments with you.'

'With me?' said the mendicant. 'It is a great honour.'

There was in the voice of the poor man a tone of irony that he could not entirely control, and which astonished the Coadjutor.

'Yes,' continued the curate, who seemed accustomed to the tone—'yes; we wish to know what you think of events now happening, and what you hear persons say who go in and out of the church.'

The mendicant shook his head.

'They are sad events, Monsieur the Curate, which, as is always the case, affect the poor most of all. As for what people say, everyone is discontented and complains; but what everybody says no one says.'

'Explain what you mean, my dear friend,' said the Coadjutor.

'I mean that all these plaints and maledictions produce only a storm and lightnings, that's all; but the thunderbolt will only fall when there is a chief to direct it.'

'My friend,' said Gondy, 'you seem to me a clever man. Should you be disposed to join in a petty civil war in case we should have one, and to place at the disposition of its leader, if we find one, the personal influence which you have acquired over your companions?'

'Yes, Monsieur, provided that this war was approved by the Church, and might consequently conduce to the end I have in view; that is to say, the remission of my sins.'

'This war would not only be approved but directed by the Church. As for the remission of your sins, we have Monsieur the Archbishop of Paris, who has great influence with the court of Rome, and also Monsieur the Coadjutor, who possesses plenary indulgences. We should recommend you to him.'

'Remember, Maillard,' said the curate, 'that I have recommended you to Monsieur, who is a very powerful lord, and in a sort of way I am responsible for you.'

'I know, Monsieur the Curate,' said the mendicant, 'that you have always been kind to me; so for my part, I am disposed to be agreeable to you.'

'And do you think your influence as great over your comrades as Monsieur the Curate recently told me it was?'

'I believe they have a certain regard for me,' said he, with pride, 'and that not only will they do all I ask them, but that they will follow me wherever I go.'

'And could you be responsible for fifty men, thoroughly resolute, good brawlers, able by crying "Down with Mazarin!" to make the walls of the Palais-Royal fall as those of Jericho once fell?'

'I think I can undertake matters more difficult and important than that.'

'Ah, ah!' said Gondy, 'you could undertake, then, in one night to make a dozen or so of barricades?'

'I could manage fifty, and when the day came defend them.'

'Good heavens!' said Gondy, 'you talk with a confidence which delights me; and since Monsieur the Curate is responsible for you——'

'Oh, yes,' said the curate.

'Here is a bag containing five hundred pistoles in gold. Make your arrangements, and tell me where I can find you again this evening at ten.'

'It would be necessary that it should be in an elevated spot, and whence a signal could be seen in all parts of Paris.'

'Would you like me to say a word to the Vicar of St Jacques la Boucherie?* He will admit you into one of the rooms of the tower,' said the curate.

'Capital,' said the mendicant.

'Well, then,' said the Coadjutor, 'this evening, at ten; and if I am satisfied with you, there will be at your disposal another bag of five hundred pistoles.'

The mendicant's eyes glistened greedily, but he checked his emotions.

'This evening, Monsieur,' replied he, 'all will be ready;' and he took his chair into the church, placed near it his pail and brush, took some holy water from the holy-water basin, as if he had no confidence in his own, and left the church.

XLVIII

THE TOWER OF ST JACQUES LA BOUCHERIE

At a quarter of six M. de Gondy had made all his visits, and had returned to his residence. At six the Curate of St Merri was announced. The Coadjutor threw a glance quickly behind him, and saw that he was followed by another man. The curate entered, and Planchet with him.

'Monseigneur,' said the curate, 'this is the person of whom I had the honour of speaking to you.'

Planchet bowed, as a man accustomed to good houses.

'And you are disposed to serve the people's cause?' asked Gondy.

'Most certainly; I am a Frondeur at heart. In my present condition I am condemned to be hanged.'

'And what was the reason?'

'I rescued from Mazarin's police a noble lord whom they were taking back to the Bastille, where he had been five years.'

'What is his name?'

'Oh, Monseigneur knows him very well; I speak of the Comte de Rochefort.'

'Ah, yes, truly,' said the Coadjutor; 'I heard of that affair. You raised the whole district, they tell me.'

'Nearly,' said Planchet, with an air of self-satisfaction.

'And you are of what calling?'

'Confectioner, Rue des Lombards.'

'Explain to me how it happens that with such a peaceful calling you have such warlike inclinations.'

'How is it that Monseigneur, being of the Church, receives me now dressed as a cavalier, with sword and spurs?'

'Not badly answered, upon my word,' said Gondy, laughing. 'But you know I have always had warlike inclinations in spite of my clerical band.'

'Well, Monseigneur, I, before I was a confectioner, was for three years sergeant in the Piedmont regiment, and before that I was eighteen months M. d'Artagnan's servant.'

'The lieutenant of Musketeers?'

'The same, Monseigneur.'

'But he is Mazarin mad.'

'Ay!——'

'What do you say?'

'Nothing, Monseigneur. M. d'Artagnan is in the service, and it is his business to defend Mazarin, who pays him, as it is our duty—we shopkeepers—to attack the cardinal because he robs us.'

'You are an intelligent fellow, my friend. Can we reckon upon you?'

'I believe that Monsieur the Curate has been responsible for me.'

'Yes, truly; but I wish the assurance from your own lips.'

'You can reckon on me, Monseigneur, provided it concerns an overthrow by the city.'

'How many men do you think you could assemble in the night?'

'Two hundred muskets and five hundred halberds.'

'If there were only one man in each district who did as much, we should have tomorrow a tolerably strong force.'

'Yes, indeed.'

'Should you be disposed to serve under the Comte de Rochefort?'

'I would follow him to hell; and that's no small thing to say, for I think him capable of going there.'

'Bravo!'

'By what mark shall we distinguish friends from foes tomorrow?'

'Every Frondeur can carry a bunch of straw in his hat.'

'Very well. Give the order.'

'Do you need money?'

'Money is never a bad thing to have in any matter, Monseigneur. If one hasn't got it, one must make shift without it; if one has it, matters will go more quickly and better.'

Gondy went to a chest and took out a bag.

'Here are five hundred pistoles,' said he; 'if the affair is successful, reckon upon receiving a like sum tomorrow.'

'I will give you a faithful account of it,' said Planchet, putting the bag under his arm.

'That is well; I recommend the cardinal to you.'

'Rest easy; he is in good hands.'

Planchet left; the curate stayed a little behind.

'Are you satisfied, Monseigneur?' said he.

'Yes; the man seems to me to be a resolute fellow.'

'Well, he will do more than he has promised.'

'It is wonderful, then.'

And the curate rejoined Planchet, who was waiting for him on the staircase. Ten minutes after, the Curate of St Sulpice was announced. As soon as the door of Gondy's cabinet was opened, a man hurried in. It was the Comte de Rochefort.

'It is you, then, my dear count!' said Gondy, extending his hand.

'You have then quite made up your mind, Monseigneur?'

'I have done so all along.'

'Don't let us speak further of that. You say so; I believe you. We are going to give a ball to Mazarin.'

'Well, I hope so.'

'And when will the dance begin?'

'The invitations are for tonight, but the violins will not begin playing till tomorrow morning.'

'You can count upon me and fifty soldiers that the Chevalier d'Humières* has promised me when I shall require them.'

'Fifty soldiers?'

'Yes, he is getting recruits, and will lend them to me; when the fête is over I will replace any that may be wanting.'

'Good, my dear Rochefort; but that is not all.'

'What is there besides?' asked Rochefort, smiling.

'What of M. de Beaufort?'

'He is in the Vendômois, where he is staying till I write to him to return to Paris.'

'Write to him that it is time.'

'You are then sure of the matter?'

'Yes, but he must hasten—for the people of Paris will have scarcely begun the revolt before we shall have ten princes for one who will wish to be at its head; if there is delay, the place will be taken.'

'Can I give him this advice as from you?'

'Yes, decidedly.'

'Can I tell him that he may depend on you?'

'Precisely.'

'And you will leave him complete power?'

'As regards warlike matters, yes; but in regard to political——'

'You know that they are not his strong point.'

'He will let me negotiate as I please for the cardinal's hat.'

'Do you stick to that?'

'Since I am obliged to wear a hat of a shape that does not suit me,' said Gondy, 'I desire at least that the hat should be a red one.'

'There is no need to dispute as to tastes and colours,' said Rochefort, laughing; 'I answer for his consent.'

'And you will write to him this evening?'

'I will do better than that; I will send a messenger to him.'

'In how many days can he be here?'

'In five.'

'Let him come, and he will find a great change.'

'I desire it.'

'I am responsible to you for it.'

'Truly?'

'Go and assemble your fifty men, and hold yourself ready.'

'For what?'

'Everything.'

'Is there a rallying sign?'

'A wisp of straw in the hat.'

'Very well. Adieu, Monseigneur. Ah, M. de Mazarin!' said Rochefort, going off with his curate, who had not been able to get in a word throughout the conversation, 'you will see if I am too old to be a man of action!'

It was half-past nine; in half an hour the Coadjutor was to be at the Tower of St Jacques la Boucherie.

The Coadjutor observed a light shining from one of the highest windows of the tower. 'Good,' said he, 'our syndic is at his post.'

He knocked; the door was opened. The vicar himself was waiting, and lighted him to the top of the tower; when there, he showed him a little door, placed the light in a corner of the wall, and went down. Although the key was in the door, the Coadjutor knocked.

'Come in,' said a voice which he recognized as the mendicant's. He was waiting, lying on a sort of pallet. He rose when he saw the Coadjutor. Ten o'clock struck.

'Well,' said Gondy, 'have you kept your word?'

'Not entirely.'

'How so?'

'You asked me for five hundred men, did you not?'

'Yes; well?'

'Well, I shall have two thousand for you.'

'You are not boasting?'

'Would you like a proof?'

'Yes.'

Three candles were lighted, each before a window; one looking towards the city, another towards the Palais-Royal, and the third on the Rue St Denis. The man went silently to each of the three candles, and blew them out one after another. The Coadjutor found himself in the dark; the room was only lighted up by the uncertain rays of the moon, hidden behind some dark clouds, the edges of which were fringed with silver.

'What have you done?' said the Coadjutor.

'I have given the signal for the barricades.'

'Ah, ah!'

'When you leave here you will see my men at work. Only take care not to break your legs in knocking against a chain, or in falling into some hole.'

'Well, here is the money, the same in amount as that you have received. Now remember you are a leader, and do not go and drink.'

'For twenty years I have drunk only water.'

The man took the bag from the Coadjutor, who heard the movement of his hand feeling its contents.

'Ah, ah!' said the Coadjutor; 'you are a miser, you rascal.'

The mendicant sighed, and threw down the bag.

'Shall I then always be the same?' said he; 'and shall I never succeed in destroying the old man? Gold, misery! oh, vanity!'

'You take it, however.'

'Yes, but I make a vow before you to use what remains in pious works.'

His visage was pale and pinched, like that of a man who has just undergone an internal struggle.

'Strange creature!' muttered Gondy, and he took his hat to depart, but on turning round he saw the mendicant between himself and the door. His first thought was that the man wanted to do him some harm; but on the contrary, he saw him join his hands together and fall on his knees.

'Monseigneur,' he said to him, 'before leaving me, your blessing, I pray you!'

'*Monseigneur*,' exclaimed Gondy; 'my friend, you take me for someone else.'

'No, Monseigneur, I take you for what you are; that is to say, Monsieur the Coadjutor. I recognized you at the first glance.'

Gondy smiled. 'And you want my blessing?'

'Yes; I have need of it.'

The mendicant said these words in a tone of so great humility and such deep repentance that Gondy stretched his hand over him, and gave him his blessing with all the unction of which he was capable.

'Now,' said the Coadjutor, 'there is fellowship between us. I have blessed you, and you are sacred to me, as I in my turn am to you. Let us see! Have you committed any crime for which human justice follows you, and from which I can protect you?'

The mendicant shook his head. 'The crime which I have committed, Monseigneur, is not amenable to human justice, and you can deliver me from it only by blessing me often as you have just done.'

'Come now, be frank; you have not all your life followed the calling which you are now pursuing?'

'No, Monseigneur, only the last six years.'

'Before then where were you?'

'In the Bastille.'

'And before being in the Bastille?'

'I will tell you, Monseigneur, when you hear me confess.'

'Very well. At whatever hour of the day or the night you may come, remember I am ready to give you absolution.'

'Thanks, Monseigneur,' said the mendicant, in a hollow voice, 'but I am not yet ready to receive it.'

'That's well; adieu.'

'Adieu, Monseigneur,' said the mendicant, opening the door and bowing before the prelate.

The Coadjutor took the candle, descended, and went out in deep thought.

XLIX

THE RIOT

IT was nearly eleven at night. Gondy had not gone a hundred yards in the streets of Paris before he perceived that a strange change had taken place. The whole city seemed inhabited by fantastic beings; silent shadows were seen removing the street-paving, others drawing and upsetting wagons, others digging trenches to swallow up entire companies of cavaliers. All these people, so actively going, coming, running, seemed like demons accomplishing some unknown work; they were the beggars of the Court of Miracles, the agents of the holy-water giver, preparing the barricades for the next day.

Gondy looked at these midnight workers with a sort of fear. He asked himself if, after having caused these unclean creatures to come forth, he should have the power of making them return to their haunts. When any one of them approached him, he was ready to make the sign of the cross.

He reached the Rue St Honoré, and followed it on his way towards the Rue de la Ferronnerie. There the appearance was changed. There were shopkeepers going from shop to shop. The doors seemed closed as well as the shutters; but they were only pushed to, so that they could be opened or closed immediately to give admittance to men who seemed to fear lest what they carried should be seen. These men were shopkeepers, who, having arms, were lending to those who were without. An individual was going from door to door, bending under the weight of swords, of arquebuses, of musketoons, of all sorts of arms, which he distributed in due proportion. By the light of a lantern the Coadjutor recognized Planchet.

The Coadjutor arrived at the quay by the Rue de la Monnaie; on the quay groups of citizens in black and grey cloaks, according as they belonged to the high or low bourgeoisie, were stationed immovable, while single men passed from one group to another. All these grey or black cloaks were raised behind by the point of a sword, and before by the barrel of an arquebuse or a musketoon.

On reaching the Pont Neuf the Coadjutor found it guarded; a man approached him.

'Who are you?' asked the man; 'I don't recognize you as one of ours.'

'Then you do not recognize your friends, my dear M. Louvières,' said the Coadjutor, raising his hat.

Louvières recognized him and bowed.

Gondy went on as far as the Tower of Nesle.* There he saw a long file of men, who were creeping along the walls. They looked like a procession of ghosts, for they were all enveloped in white cloaks. On reaching a certain spot, all the men seemed to vanish one after another, as if the earth gave way under their feet. Gondy leaned on his elbow in a corner, and saw them disappear, from the first to the last but one. The last raised his eyes, doubtless to make sure that they were not seen, and in spite of the darkness he saw Gondy. He went straight up to him, and put a pistol to his throat.

'Holloa, M. de Rochefort,' said Gondy, laughing; 'do not let us joke with fire-arms.'

Rochefort recognized the voice.

'Oh, it is you, Monseigneur?' said he.

'Myself. What fellows are you thus guiding into the bowels of the earth?'

'My fifty recruits, who are intended for the light horse, and who have received for their sole equipment these white cloaks.'

'And you are going——'

'To a friend of mine—a sculptor; only we descend by the trap by which he takes in the marble.'

'Very well,' said Gondy, and he shook hands with Rochefort, who went down and closed the trap behind him.

The Coadjutor returned home. It was one in the morning. He opened the window, and leaned out to listen. There was through the city a strange, unheard, unknown murmur. It was evident that something unusual and terrible was going on in all the streets, dark as gulfs. From time to time a roaring like that of a storm gathering or of a sea rising made itself heard; but nothing clear, nothing distinct, nothing explainable presented itself to the mind. These sounds seemed like the mysterious and subterranean noises which precede earthquakes.

The preparation for revolt lasted the whole night thus. The next day Paris, on waking, seemed to tremble at her own aspect. The city had the appearance of a siege. Armed men were on the barricades with threatening look, musket at shoulder; words of command, patrols, arrests, even executions—all this the passer-by found at every step. All wearing the plumed hats and gilt swords were stopped and ordered to cry out, 'Long live Broussel! Down with Mazarin!' and whoever refused compliance was hooted, spit upon, and even beaten. No one was killed as yet, but it was felt that the desire was not wanting.

The barricades had been pushed almost up to the Palais-Royal. From the Rue des Bons Enfants to the Rue la Ferronnerie, from the Rue St Thomas du Louvre to the Pont Neuf, from the Rue Richelieu to the gate St Honoré, there were more than ten thousand armed men, the most advanced of whom uttered defiance to the unmoved sentinels of the Guards regiment, placed on the watch all around the Palais-Royal, whose gates were closed behind them, making their situation precarious. In the midst of all, bands of a hundred, hundred and fifty, or two hundred, emaciated, pale, and ragged men were going about carrying a sort of standard, on which were the words, 'See the misery of the people!' Wherever these persons passed wild cries were heard, and there were so many similar bands that cries arose everywhere.

The astonishment of Anne of Austria and Mazarin was great on arising, when they were informed that the city which they had left quiet the evening before was feverish and all in commotion. Neither the one nor the other could believe the reports given them, saying that they would only rely on their eyes and ears. A window was opened; they saw, they heard, and they were convinced.

Mazarin shrugged his shoulders, and pretended to despise the populace; but he became visibly pale, and all of a tremble hurried to his cabinet, enclosing his gold and jewels in their caskets, and putting on his fingers his most beautiful diamonds. As regards the queen, furious and left to her own will, she sent for Maréchal de la Meilleraie, ordered him to take as many men as he pleased, and go and see what this pleasantry meant.

The marshal was usually very overbearing and self-satisfied, having that lofty disdain of the populace which military men professed for it. He took a hundred and fifty men, and attempted to go forth by the Louvre bridge; but there he encountered Rochefort and his fifty light-horse, accompanied by more than fifteen hundred men. He had no means of forcing such a barrier. The marshal did not even attempt it, and went further up the quay.

But on the Pont Neuf he found Louvières and his citizens. This time the marshal attempted a charge, but he was received with a musket fire, while stones fell like hail from all the windows. He left three men dead. He beat a retreat towards the public markets, but there he found Planchet and his halberdiers. These looked threateningly at him. He wished to make head against these grey cloaks, but they held their ground; and the marshal withdrew towards the Rue St Honoré, leaving on the field four of his guards who had been killed with side-arms.

Then he penetrated into the Rue St Honoré, but fell in there with the barricades of the mendicant. They were guarded not only by armed men, but even by women and children. M. Friquet, owner of a pistol and a sword which Louvières had given him, had organized a band of rascals like himself, and at least made a great noise.

The marshal thought this point not so well guarded as the others, and designed forcing it. He dismounted twenty men to do this, while he and the rest of his troop on their horses protected the assailants. The twenty men marched straight upon the obstruction. But behind the timbers, between the wagon-wheels, on top of the stones, a terrible fusillade arose, and at the noise of it Planchet's halberdiers appeared at the corner of the Cimetière des Innocents, and Louvières's citizens at the corner of the Rue de la Monnaie.

The marshal was taken between two fires. He was brave, so he resolved to die where he was. He returned blow for blow, and cries of pain began to arise in the crowd. The guards, better drilled, shot more accurately; but the citizens, more numerous, overpowered them by a veritable storm of fire. They fell about him as they would have fallen at Rocroy or Lerida.* Fontrailles, his aide-de-camp, had his arm broken; his horse was shot in the neck, and he had difficulty in managing it, for the pain almost drove it mad. At last that supreme moment came when the bravest feels a cold shiver and perspiration, when all of a sudden the crowd opened in the direction of the Rue de l'Arbre Sec, crying out, 'Long live the Coadjutor!' and Gondy, in *rochet* and *camail*,* passed quietly in the midst of the fusillade, dispensing blessings to the right and left as calmly as if conducting the procession on Corpus Christi. Everyone fell on his knees. The marshal recognized him, and hastened towards him.

'Help me out of this, in Heaven's name,' said he, 'or I shall leave my own skin and those of my men.'

Such a tumult arose that one could not have heard the thunder of heaven. Gondy raised his hand and called for silence.

'My children,' said he, 'this is M. le Maréchal de la Meilleraie, about whose intentions you are mistaken, and who agrees, on returning to the Louvre, to ask the queen in your name for Broussel's release. Do you agree to do this?' added Gondy, turning towards the marshal.

'Well,' exclaimed he, 'I think, indeed, I do make this promise. I did not expect to get off so cheaply.'

'He gives you his word as a gentleman,' said Gondy.

The marshal raised his hand by way of assent. 'Long live the Coadjutor!' cried the crowd. Some voices even added, 'Long live the marshal!' but all took up in chorus, 'Down with Mazarin!'

The crowd opened; the way by the Rue St Honoré was the shortest. The barricades were opened, and the marshal, with the rest of his troop, retreated, headed by Friquet and his ruffians, some professing to beat the drum, the rest imitating the sound of the trumpet. It was almost a triumphal march, only behind the guards the barricades were closed again. The marshal bit his lips.

During this time, as we have said, Mazarin was in his cabinet, putting his affairs in order. He had summoned d'Artagnan, but in the midst of all this tumult he did not expect to see him, d'Artagnan not being on duty. At the end of ten minutes he appeared, followed by his inseparable Porthos.

'Come, come, M. d'Artagnan,' exclaimed the cardinal, 'and welcome, as well as your friend. But what is going on in this hateful Paris?'

'Nothing good, Monseigneur!' said d'Artagnan, shaking his head. 'The city is in open revolt, and just now, when coming along the Rue Montorgueil with M. du Vallon, in spite of my uniform, and perhaps even because of it, they wanted to make us cry, "Long live Broussel!" and, must I say, Monseigneur, what they wished to make us say besides?'

'Say it, say it!'

'And "Down with Mazarin!" Upon my word, that was the cry they set up.'

Mazarin smiled, but became very pale.

'And you cried it?' said he.

'No, indeed; I was not in voice. M. du Vallon has a cold, and could not cry it either. Then, Monseigneur——'

'Then what?' asked Mazarin.

'Look at my hat and cloak;' and d'Artagnan pointed to four holes made by balls in his cloak, and two in his hat. As for Porthos's dress, a halberd-stroke had cut it on the side, and a pistol-shot had cut his feather.

'*Diavolo!*' said the cardinal, thoughtfully, and looking at the two friends with genuine admiration; 'I should have cried it.'

At that moment the tumult sounded nearer. Mazarin wiped his forehead while looking around him. He had a strong wish to go to the window, but did not dare.

'Just see what is going on, M. d'Artagnan,' said he.

D'Artagnan went to the window with his habitual indifference.

'Oh, oh!' said he, 'what is that? Maréchal de la Meilleraie has returned without his hat; Fontrailles is carrying his arm in a sling; guards and horses wounded. Eh! but what are the sentinels doing? They are presenting arms and going to fire!'

'The order has been given to fire on the populace,' exclaimed Mazarin, 'if they come near the Palais-Royal.'

'But if they fire, all is lost!' exclaimed d'Artagnan.

'We have the railings.'

'The railings! for five minutes. They will be pulled up, twisted, broken to shivers! Don't fire!' cried d'Artagnan, opening the window.

In spite of this request, which in the midst of the tumult was not audible, three or four musket-shots were heard; then a terrible fusillade followed. The balls could be heard rattling on the façade of the Palais-Royal; one of them passed under d'Artagnan's arm, and smashed a glass in which Porthos was complacently looking at himself.

'Oh,' exclaimed the cardinal, 'a Venetian glass!'

'Oh, Monseigneur,' said d'Artagnan, quietly, closing the window, 'do not grieve about that; it's not worth the trouble, for probably in an hour not one will be left in the palace.'

'But what is your advice?' said the cardinal, trembling.

'Eh! why give up Broussel, since they demand him. What the devil would you do with a member of parliament? He is good for nothing.'

'And what is your opinion, M. du Vallon? What would you do?'

'I should give up Broussel.'

'Come, Messieurs, I am going to speak about it to the queen.'

At the end of the corridor he stopped.

'I can depend upon you, can I not, Messieurs?' said he.

'We do not promise faithful service twice,' said d'Artagnan; 'we are pledged to you. Order; we will obey.'

'Eh, well!' said Mazarin, 'go into this room and wait,' and making a detour, he entered the drawing-room by another door.

L

THE RIOT BECOMES A REVOLT

THE room into which d'Artagnan and Porthos had been shown was separated from the drawing-room, where the queen was, only by hangings of tapestry. The slight thickness of this permitted all that was going on to be heard, while the opening between the two curtains, although small, enabled one to see.

The queen was standing, pale from anger; yet her self-control was so great that she showed no signs of emotion. Behind her were Comminges, Villequier, and Guitaut; behind them the ladies. Before her was the Chancellor Séguier, the same who twenty years before had so greatly persecuted her.* He was telling her how his carriage had been broken, he had been pursued, and had taken refuge in the mansion of O——;* that this had been immediately entered and pillaged. Fortunately he had had time to reach a closet hidden in the tapestry, where an old woman had shut him up along with his brother, the Bishop of Meaux. There the danger was so real, the mad crowd had approached this cabinet with such threats, that the chancellor thought his hour had come; and he had confessed to his brother, that he might be ready to die if he was discovered. Happily he had not been; the people, believing that he had escaped through some rear door, retired and left his retreat open. He had then disguised himself in the clothes of the Marquis d'O——, and had come out of the hôtel, stepping over the bodies of his officer and of two guards slain in defending the street-door.

During this narrative Mazarin had come in, and quietly taking a place near the queen, was listening.

'Well,' the queen asked, when the chancellor ended, 'what do you think of that?'

'I think it a very serious matter, Madame.'

'But what advice can you give me?'

'I could give very good advice to your Majesty, but I do not dare.'

'Dare, dare, Monsieur,' said the queen, with a bitter smile; 'you have, indeed, dared other things.'

The chancellor blushed, and stammered out a few words.

'The question is not of the past, but of the present,' said the queen. 'You say you can give me some good advice; what is it?'

'Madame,' said the chancellor, hesitating, 'it is to set Broussel at liberty.'

The queen, although very pale, visibly became paler, and her face contracted.

'Set Broussel at liberty!' said she; 'never!'

Just then some steps were heard in the adjoining room, and without being announced Maréchal de la Meilleraie appeared at the door.

'Ah, it's you, Marshal!' exclaimed Anne of Austria, joyfully. 'I hope you have brought all that rabble to reason.'

'Madame, I have left three men on Pont Neuf, four at the public markets, six at the corner of the Rue de l'Arbre Sec, and two at the gate of your palace—fifteen in all. I have brought back ten or twelve wounded. My hat has gone, I know not where, carried off by a bullet, and most probably I should have been where my hat is, but for Monsieur the Coadjutor, who arrived in time to rescue me.'

'Ah, indeed!' said the queen; 'I should have felt astonished if that bandy-legged turnspit had not been mixed up in it all.'

'Madame,' said La Meilleraie, laughing, 'do not say too much evil about him in my presence, for the service he has done me is still in my mind.'

'It is right that you should be grateful to him as much as you please, but that does not bind me. Here you are safe and sound—that is all I could desire; count yourself not only welcome, but safely returned to us.'

'Yes, Madame; but I am the latter only on one condition—that I transmit to you the will of the people.'

'Their will!' said Anne, knitting her eyebrows. 'Oh, oh, Monsieur the Marshal! you must have been in very great danger to take upon yourself such a strange embassy;' and these words were said with a tone of irony which did not escape the marshal.

'Pardon me, Madame, I am not an advocate, but a soldier; and consequently I perhaps imperfectly understand the significance of words. I should have said the *desire*, not the *will*, of the people. As for the reply with which you have honoured me, I believe you meant that I felt afraid.'

The queen smiled.

'Well, yes, Madame, I did feel afraid; this is the third time in my life that that has been the case, and yet I have been in a dozen pitched battles, and I do not know how many fights and skirmishes. Yes, I did feel afraid; and I prefer being in the presence of your Majesty, however menacing your smile, to that of those demons of hell who accompanied me back here, and who come from I cannot say where.'

'Bravo!' said d'Artagnan in a low voice to Porthos, 'a capital answer.'

'Well,' said the queen, biting her lips, while the courtiers looked at one another with astonishment, 'what is the desire of my people?'

'The release of Broussel, Madame.'

'Never!' said the queen, 'never!'

'Your Majesty is mistress,' said La Meilleraie, bowing and stepping backwards.

'Where are you going, Marshal?' said the queen.

'I am going to take your Majesty's reply to those awaiting it.'

'Stay, Marshal! I do not like to have the appearance of treating with rebels.'

'Madame, I have pledged my word to them,' said the marshal.

'Which means——'

'That if you do not cause me to be arrested, I am compelled to go down to them.'

Anne of Austria's eyes flashed like lightning.

'Oh, don't let that make any difference, Monsieur,' said she; 'I have arrested many of greater importance than you. Guitaut!'

Mazarin stepped forward.

'Madame,' said he, 'may I venture in my turn to give you my opinion?'

'Is it yours also that I should release Broussel, Monsieur? In that case you may spare yourself the trouble.'

'No,' said Mazarin; 'although that may be perhaps as good as any.'

'What then is it?'

'My advice is to summon Monsieur the Coadjutor.'

'The Coadjutor!' exclaimed the queen, 'that frightful mischief-maker! He it is who has caused the whole revolt.'

'The greater reason,' said Mazarin; 'if he caused it, he can quell it.'

'And stay, Madame,' said Comminges, who was keeping close to a window through which he was looking,—'stay, the occasion is favourable, for I see him giving his blessing on the Place Palais-Royal.'

The queen hurried to the window. 'It is true; the arch-hypocrite! Look at him.'

'I see,' said Mazarin, 'that every one kneels before him, although he is only the Coadjutor; yet if I were in his place they would pull me to pieces, although I am a cardinal. I persist, then, in my *desire* [Mazarin emphasized the word] that your Majesty receive the Coadjutor.'

'And why do you not as well say, *in your will* ?' replied the queen, in a low voice.

Mazarin bowed. The queen remained thoughtful a short time. Then raising her head, 'Monsieur the Marshal,' said she, 'go and bring Monsieur the Coadjutor to me.'

'And what shall I say to the populace?'

'To have patience,' said the queen; 'I have had much of it.'

There was in the voice of the haughty Spaniard such imperativeness that the marshal made no observation; he bowed and went out.

D'Artagnan turned towards Porthos.

'How is this going to end?' said he.

'We shall see,' said Porthos, with his usual tranquillity.

During this time Anne of Austria was talking in a low tone to Comminges.

Mazarin, feeling anxious, looked in the direction of d'Artagnan and Porthos. The rest were conversing together in a low tone. The door opened; the marshal appeared, followed by the Coadjutor.

'Madame, here is M. de Gondy, who hastens to receive your Majesty's commands.'

The queen advanced a few paces towards him, then stopped, looking cold, severe, unmoved, with her lower lip scornfully projecting.

Gondy bowed respectfully.

'Well, Monsieur, what do you say about this riot?'

'That it is no longer a riot, Madame, but a revolt.'

'The revolt is on the part of those who think that my people can revolt!' exclaimed Anne, unable to hide her real feelings from the Coadjutor, whom she regarded, with good reason perhaps, as the promoter of this movement. 'A revolt is the name those give it who desire the tumult of which they have been the cause; but wait, wait! the king's authority will put it straight.'

'Is it simply to tell me that, Madame,' coolly replied Gondy, 'that your Majesty has admitted me to the honour of your presence?'

'No, my dear Coadjutor,' said Mazarin, 'it was to ask your advice in the present difficult situation.'

'Is it true,' asked Gondy, putting on an astonished look, 'that her Majesty has summoned me to ask my advice?'

'Yes,' said the queen. 'They have wished it.'

The Coadjutor bowed.

'Her Majesty desires then——'

'That you should tell her what you would do if you were in her place,' Mazarin hastened to reply.

The Coadjutor looked at the queen, who signified her assent.

'If I were in her Majesty's place,' said Gondy, coldly, 'I should not hesitate; I should release Broussel.'

'And if I do not release him, what do you think will happen?'

'I think that by tomorrow there will not be one stone left upon another in Paris,' said the marshal.

'I am not questioning you, but M. de Gondy,' the queen said in a dry tone, and without even turning round.

'Since it is I whom your Majesty questions,' replied the Coadjutor, with the same calmness, 'I say in reply that I am entirely of the marshal's opinion.'

The colour rose to the queen's face; her beautiful blue eyes seemed starting from her head; her carmine lips, compared by all the poets of the time to pomegranates in flower, turned pale, and trembled with rage. She almost frightened Mazarin himself, who was, however, used to the domestic bursts of rage in this disturbed household. 'Release Broussel!' she said at last, with a frightful smile; 'fine advice, upon my word! It is very clear that it comes from a priest.'

Gondy held firm. The insults of the day seemed to glide from him like the sarcasms of the previous evening; but hatred and vengeance were gathering silently and drop by drop at the bottom of his heart. He looked coldly at the queen, who touched Mazarin to get him also to say something.

Mazarin, as was his habit, thought much, but said little. 'Eh, eh!' said he, 'good advice, friendly counsel. I also would release this good man Broussel, dead or alive, and all would be ended.'

'If you were to release him dead, all would be at an end, as you say, Monseigneur, but in a different way from what you mean.'

'Did I say dead or alive?' replied Mazarin. 'It is a form of speech; you know I do not understand French well, and that you speak and write it wonderfully well, Monsieur the Coadjutor.'

'Here's a council of State,' said d'Artagnan to Porthos; 'but we have held better ones at Rochelle with Athos and Aramis.'

'In the Bastion St Gervais,'* said Porthos.

'There and elsewhere.'

The Coadjutor suffered the shower to pass, and continued, always with the same coldness, 'Madame, if your Majesty does not like the advice which I submit to her, it is without doubt because she has better guidance. I know too well the wisdom of the queen and that of her councillors to suppose that they will leave the capital city long in a trouble which may lead to a revolution.'

'So then, in your opinion,' said the Spaniard, with a sneer, and biting her lips with rage, 'this riot of yesterday, which has become today a revolt, may become tomorrow a revolution?'

'Yes, Madame,' the Coadjutor gravely said.

'But if you are right, Monsieur, the nations have then become unmindful of all restraint.'

'The times are unfortunate for kings,' said Gondy, shaking his head; 'look at England, Madame.'

'Yes, but fortunately we have no Oliver Cromwell in France,' replied the queen.

'Who knows?' said Gondy. 'Such men are like thunderbolts; they are known only when they strike.'

Everyone shuddered, and there was a short silence. Meanwhile the queen had rested her hands against her breast; it was clear that she was checking the hurried beatings of her heart.

'Porthos,' whispered d'Artagnan, 'look closely at that priest.'

'Yes, I see him,' said Porthos. 'Well?'

'Well, he is a thorough man.'

Porthos looked at d'Artagnan with some astonishment; it was clear that he did not fully comprehend his friend's meaning.

'Your Majesty,' pitilessly continued the Coadjutor, 'is then going to take measures which please yourself. But I foresee that they will be terrible ones, and such as will irritate the rebels still more.'

'Well then, *you*, Monsieur the Coadjutor, who have such power over them, and who are our friend,' said the queen, ironically, 'will calm them by giving them your blessing.'

'Perhaps it will be too late,' said Gondy, in his freezing manner, 'and perhaps I shall have lost all my influence; while by releasing Broussel your Majesty will cut the root of the sedition, and acquire the right of punishing severely every new growth of revolt.'

'Have I not this right?' exclaimed the queen.

'If you have, use it,' replied Gondy.

'Hang it!' said d'Artagnan to Porthos, 'that is the sort of character I like. Would that he were minister, and I his d'Artagnan, instead of belonging to this rascal Mazarin! Ah, *mordieu!* what splendid strokes we should make together!'

The queen with a sign dismissed the court, except Mazarin. Gondy bowed, and was about retiring like the rest.

'Stay, Monsieur,' said the queen.

'Good,' said Gondy to himself; 'she is going to yield.'

'She is going to have him killed,' said d'Artagnan to Porthos; 'but by no means will I be the doer of it. I take my oath that on the contrary if anything should happen to him I would fall upon those who caused it.'

'So would I,' said Porthos.

'Good!' muttered Mazarin, taking a seat, 'we are going to see something new.'

The queen followed the persons leaving with her eyes. When the last had closed the door, she turned round. It was evident that she was making violent efforts to conquer her anger; she fanned herself, she inhaled a perfume, she walked forward and back. Mazarin remained in his seat as if reflecting. Gondy, who began to feel anxious, scanned all the tapestry, sounded the cuirass which he wore under his long robe, and now and then felt under his *camail* to ascertain if the handle of a good Spanish poniard which he had hidden there was well within reach.

'Now,' said the queen at last, standing still, 'now we are alone, repeat your advice, Monsieur the Coadjutor.'

'This is it, Madame: Profess to have reflected; publicly confess having made a mistake, which is the strength of strong governments; release Broussel from prison, and give him up to the people.'

'Oh!' exclaimed Anne of Austria, 'thus to humiliate me! Am I queen or am I not? Is this howling mob subject to me or not? Have I friends? Have I guards? Ah! by our Lady, as Queen Catherine* used to say, rather than give up this infamous Broussel, I would strangle him with my own hands;' and she stretched her clinched fists towards Gondy, who certainly detested her just then as much as Broussel did.

Gondy did not stir, not a muscle of his face moved; only his icy look crossed blades, as it were, with the furious look of the queen.

'He is a dead man, if there is still a Vitry at court, and he were to enter at this instant,' said the Gascon. 'But I, rather than that should take place, would kill Vitry, and that neatly! Monsieur the Cardinal would be infinitely obliged to me.'

'*Chut!*' said Porthos; 'listen now.'

'Madame!' exclaimed the cardinal, taking hold of Anne of Austria and drawing her back—'Madame, what are you doing?' Then he added in Spanish, 'Anne, are you a fool? You quarrel with the citizens—you, a queen! And do you not see that you have before you in the person of this priest the whole people of Paris, whom it is dangerous to insult, especially now; and that if this priest wishes it, in an hour you would no longer possess a crown? On another occasion, later on, you may keep firm, but today is not the time; today flatter and caress, or you are only a vulgar woman.'

At the beginning of this appeal, d'Artagnan had seized Porthos's arm, and had squeezed it harder and harder; then when Mazarin was silent, 'Porthos,' said he, quite in a whisper, 'never say that I know Spanish in Mazarin's presence, or you and I are lost men.'

'No,' said Porthos.

This severe reprimand, impressed with that eloquence which distinguished Mazarin when he spoke Italian or Spanish, and which he entirely lost in speaking French, was spoken with an emotionless countenance which did not permit Gondy, although a skilful physiognomist, to suppose that it was more than a simple warning to be more moderate.

The queen, thus roughly addressed, grew suddenly milder. She allowed the fire in her eyes, so to speak, to expire; the blood left her cheeks, the strong words of anger her lips. She sat down, and with softened tones, and letting her arms fall by her side, 'Pardon me, Monsieur the Coadjutor,' said she, 'and ascribe this outbreak to my sufferings. As a woman, and consequently subject to the weaknesses of my sex, I have a horror of civil war; as a queen, and accustomed to be obeyed, I am enraged at the first provocation.'

'Madame,' said Gondy, bowing, 'your Majesty deceives herself in qualifying as resistance my sincere advice. Your Majesty has only submissive and respectful subjects. It is not the queen with whom the people feel angry—they call for Broussel, and that's all; too happy to live subject to your Majesty's laws—if your Majesty at once releases Broussel,' added Gondy, with a smile.

Mazarin, who at the words, 'It is not the queen with whom the people are angry,' had at once paid great attention, thinking that the Coadjutor was going to speak of the cries, 'Down with Mazarin!' thought well of Gondy for this omission, and said, in his softest tones and with his most gracious look, 'Madame, trust in the Coadjutor, who is one of the most able politicians that we have; the first vacant cardinal's hat seems fit for his noble head.'

'Ah! so you want me, you tricky rascal!' thought Gondy.

'And what will he promise us,' said d'Artagnan, 'on the day when they want to kill him? Hang it, if he gives away hats so liberally, let us get ready our requests, Porthos, and each of us ask for a regiment after tomorrow. Let the civil war last a year only, and I will have the Constable's sword re-gilt for my own use.'

'And I?' said Porthos.

'You! I will make them give you the *bâton* of Maréchal de la Meilleraie, who does not seem in great favour just at present.'

'So, Monsieur,' said the queen, 'you seriously fear the popular movement?'

'Seriously, Madame,' replied Gondy, astonished at not having made more progress; 'I am afraid that when the torrent has broken its banks it will cause great devastation.'

'I,' said the queen, 'think that in that case new banks must be erected. You can go; I will think it over.'

Gondy looked at Mazarin, quite astonished. Mazarin approached to speak to the queen. At that moment a frightful tumult was heard on the Place du Palais-Royal.

Gondy smiled, the queen looked excited, Mazarin became very pale.

'What more is there?' said the cardinal.

At that moment Comminges came hastily into the room.

'Pardon, Madame,' said he to the queen; 'but the people have crushed the sentinels against the railings, and are now forcing the gates. What orders do you give?'

'Listen, Madame,' said Gondy.

The roar of waves, the roll of thunder, the rumblings of a volcano, are not to be compared to the tempest of cries which then arose.

'What orders do I give?'

'Yes; time presses.'

'About how many men have you at the Palais-Royal?'

'Six hundred.'

'Put a hundred to guard the king, and with the rest sweep away all this mob for me.'

'Madame,' said Mazarin, 'what are you doing?'

'Go!' said the queen.

Comminges went off with a soldier's passive obedience. Just then a terrible crash was heard; one of the gates was giving way.

'Ah, Madame,' said Mazarin, 'you will ruin us all—the king, yourself, and me.'

Anne of Austria, at this cry of distress from the terrified cardinal, herself felt afraid, and recalled Comminges.

'It is too late!' said Mazarin, tearing his hair, 'it is too late!'

The gate gave way, and shouts of joy were heard from the populace. D'Artagnan took his sword in his hand, and made a sign to Porthos to do the same.

'Save the queen!' exclaimed Mazarin, speaking to the Coadjutor.

Gondy sprang to the window and opened it; he recognized Louvières at the head of perhaps three or four thousand men.

'Not a step further!' cried he; 'the queen will sign.'

'What do you say?' exclaimed the queen.

'The truth, Madame,' said Mazarin, handing her paper and pen; 'it must be done.' Then he added, 'Sign, Anne, I pray you; I wish it!'

The queen sank into a chair, took the pen, and signed.

Restrained by Louvières, the populace had not advanced a step; but the terrible murmur indicating the wrath of the multitude continued.

The queen wrote, 'The governor of the prison of St Germain will set Councillor Broussel at liberty,' and she signed it.

The Coadjutor, who devoured with his eyes her slightest movements, seized the paper as soon as the signature was appended, returned to the window, and waving it in his hand, 'This is the order,' said he.

The whole of Paris seemed to send forth a great shout of joy; then the cries were heard, 'Long live Broussel! Long live the Coadjutor!'

'Long live the queen!' said the latter.

Some responses were made to it, but they were few and feeble. Perhaps the Coadjutor raised the cry simply to make Anne of Austria feel her weakness.

'And now that you have gained what you desired,' said she, 'retire, M. de Gondy.'

'When the queen needs me,' said he, bowing, 'her Majesty knows that I am ready to obey her commands.'

The queen made a sign with her head, and Gondy retired.

'Ah, you cursed priest!' exclaimed Anne of Austria, stretching out her hand towards the door, then scarcely closed, 'I will one day make you drink the dregs of the cup which you have today poured out for me.'

Mazarin made a movement to approach her.

'Leave me,' said she; 'you are not a man!' and she went out.

'It is you who are not a woman,' muttered Mazarin.

Then after a little reflection, he remembered that d'Artagnan and Porthos must still be there, and had consequently heard everything. He frowned, and went straight to the tapestry, which he lifted; the cabinet was empty. At the queen's last word d'Artagnan had taken Porthos by the hand, and had led him towards the gallery. Mazarin entered it, and found the two friends walking up and down.

'Why did you leave the cabinet, M. d'Artagnan?'

'Because the queen ordered everyone to leave, and I thought that this order applied to us as well as the rest.'

'So you have been here——'

'Nearly a quarter of an hour,' said d'Artagnan, looking at Porthos as if to wish him not to contradict.

Mazarin caught this look, and felt convinced that d'Artagnan had seen and understood everything, but he was pleased with the falsehood.

'Most decidedly, M. d'Artagnan, you are the very one for whom I was looking, and you may count upon me as your friend.' Then, saluting the two friends with his most charming smile, he returned more at peace to his cabinet, for on Gondy's leaving the tumult had ceased as by enchantment.

LI

MISFORTUNE IS A HELP TO MEMORY

ANNE, furious, had gone into her oratory. 'What!' cried she, wringing her beautiful arms—'what! the people have seen M. de Condé,* the first prince of the blood, arrested by my mother-in-law, Marie de Médicis; they have seen my mother-in-law, their old regent, driven away by the cardinal; they have seen M. de Vendôme, the son of Henry IV, a prisoner at Vincennes; they have said nothing while these great personages were insulted, imprisoned, and threatened. And for a Broussel! Jesus! what then has become of royalty?'

Anne touched unconsciously the heart of the matter. The people had said nothing for the princes. The people had risen for Broussel. It was because it concerned a plebeian; and in defending Broussel the people instinctively felt that they were defending themselves.*

Meanwhile Mazarin was walking to and fro in his cabinet, looking from time to time at his beautiful Venetian glass, all cracked.

'Ah,' said he, 'it is sad, I admit, to be compelled to yield in this way; but bah! we will have our revenge. Who's Broussel? it's a name, it's not a reality.'

Able politician though he was, Mazarin was mistaken this time. Broussel was a reality, not a mere name. So when on the following morning Broussel made his entry into Paris in a fine coach, with his son Louvières by his side and Friquet behind, all the people, still armed, thronged the line of route. The cries, 'Long live Broussel! Long live our father!' resounded from all sides, and carried defiance to Mazarin's ears. From all directions the disagreeable news was brought by the cardinal's and the queen's spies, who found the cardinal very agitated, but the queen very tranquil. The queen seemed to be ripening some great resolve, and this greatly increased Mazarin's disquietude. He knew the haughty princess well, and greatly feared her resolves.

The Coadjutor had returned to the parliament more of a king than Louis XIV, the queen, and the cardinal together; at his proposal, an edict of parliament had invited the citizens to lay down their arms and demolish the barricades. The people knew now that an hour would suffice for resuming their arms, and a night for setting up the barricades.

Planchet had returned to his shop; the victory secured his pardon. He had no further fear of being hanged. He was convinced that if they only threatened to arrest him, the people would rise for him, as they had just done for Broussel. Rochefort had returned his light-horse to Chevalier d'Humières. Two were wanting at the roll-call; but the chevalier, who was at heart a Frondeur, would not hear a word about compensation.

The mendicant had resumed his place under the portico of St Eustache, distributing the holy water with one hand and asking alms with the other; and no one suspected that these two hands had just been helping to pull away from the social edifice the foundation-stone of royalty.

Louvières was boastful and satisfied; he had taken revenge on Mazarin, whom he hated, and he had materially helped in procuring the liberation of his father. His name had been repeated at the Palais-Royal with fear, and he said laughingly to the councillor, restored to his family—

'Do you think, Father, that if I asked the queen for the command of a company she would give it to me?'

D'Artagnan had profited by this moment of calm to send Raoul off, whom he had great difficulty in keeping shut up during the riot, and who wished earnestly to draw his sword for one or the other party. Raoul objected at first, but d'Artagnan had spoken in the name of the Comte de la Fère. Raoul had paid a visit to Madame de Chevreuse, and had set out to rejoin the army.

Rochefort alone found the matter to have turned out badly. He had written to M. le Duc de Beaufort to come; the duke was on the way, and would find Paris quiet. Rochefort went to see the Coadjutor to ask him if he should not send word to the prince to stop where he was; but Gondy after a moment's reflection said, 'Let him continue his journey.'

'But is not the affair all over?'

'Nonsense, my dear count, we are now only at the beginning.'

'What makes you think so?'

'The acquaintance that I have with the queen's disposition. She does not mean to remain beaten.'

'Is she preparing something, then?'

'I hope so.'

'What do you know? Tell me.'

'I know that she has written to Monsieur the Prince to return quickly from the army.'

'Ah, ah!' said Rochefort; 'you are right, we must let M. de Beaufort come.'

On the same evening the rumour spread that Monsieur the Prince had arrived.* It was a very simple and natural piece of news, and yet it made a great impression.

Some indiscretions, it was said, had been committed by Madame de Longueville, to whom Monsieur the Prince, who was accused of having for his sister a tenderness which passed the limits of fraternal friendship,* had made some confidences. These confidences revealed sinister projects on the part of the queen.

On the very evening of Monsieur the Prince's arrival, some citizens of more advanced views than the rest, sheriffs and ward captains, went to their acquaintances, saying, 'Why should we not take the king and place him at the Hôtel de Ville? It is wrong to allow him to be educated by our enemies, who give him bad advice; while if he were controlled by Monsieur the Coadjutor, for example, he would imbibe national principles, and love the people.'

The night was spent in secret agitation; the next day the grey and black cloaks, patrols of shopkeepers in arms, and bands of beggars, were again seen in the streets.

The queen had passed the night in conferring quite alone with Monsieur the Prince; at midnight he had been admitted into her oratory, and he did not leave till five o'clock. Then the queen went to the cardinal's cabinet. Although she had not yet gone to bed, the cardinal was already up. He was drawing up a reply to Cromwell, six days having already passed* out of the ten which he had agreed upon with Mordaunt.

'Bah!' said he; 'I have made him wait a bit, but M. Cromwell knows too well what a revolution is, not to excuse me.'

He therefore re-read with great complacency the first paragraph of the draft, when he heard a gentle rap at the door which led to the queen's apartment. Anne of Austria alone could come by that door. The cardinal rose and opened it.

The queen was in undress, but it became her; for like Diana of Poitiers and Ninon, Anne of Austria retained the advantage of being beautiful at all times; only this morning she was more beautiful than usual, for her eyes had all the brilliancy which a joyful heart imprints on the countenance.

'What is the matter with you, Madame?' said Mazarin, looking disturbed. 'You have such a defiant look.'

'Yes, Giulio, defiant and happy, for I have found a means of suffocating that hydra.'

'You are a great politician, my queen; let me know the means,' and he hid what he was writing by slipping under some white paper the letter which he had begun.

'They want to take the king from me, do you know?'

'Alas, yes; and to hang me.'

'They shall not have the king.'

'And they shall not hang me, *benone*.'*

'Listen: I want to rescue my son and myself, and you with us, from their hands, which in a night will change the face of things without anyone's knowing it except you, myself, and a third person.'

'Who is this last?'

'Monsieur the Prince.'

'Has he then come, as it was reported?'

'Yesterday evening.'

'And you have seen him?'

'I have just left him.'

'Does he lend himself to this project?'

'It comes from him.'

'And Paris?'

'He will force it to surrender by starvation.'

'The project does not lack a certain grandeur; but I see one impediment only.'

'What is that?'

'Its impossibility.'

'A term void of meaning. Nothing is impossible.'

'In idea.'

'In execution. Have we any money?'

'A small amount,' said Mazarin, all of a tremble lest Anne should ask him to open his purse-strings.

'Have we any troops?'

'Five or six thousand men.'

'Have we any courage?'

'Plenty.'

'Then the thing is easy. Oh, do you comprehend, Giulio, that Paris, this odious Paris, will wake up one morning without queen, without king, surrounded, besieged, without food, having no other resource than its stupid parliament and its lean, bandy-legged Coadjutor?'

'Lovely, lovely!' said Mazarin. 'I quite understand the result; but I don't see how it is to be arrived at.'

'*I* will find the means.'

'You know that this means war—civil war, sanguinary, desperate, implacable.'

'Oh, yes; war. I should like to reduce this rebellious city to ashes; I should like to quench the fire in blood; I should like to make a frightful example, that the crime and its punishment might never be forgotten. Paris! I hate it, I abhor it!'*

'Gently, Anne; how sanguinary you are! Take care, we are not in the times of the Malatesta and of the Castruccio Castracani.* You will get yourself beheaded, my fair queen, and that would be a pity.'

'You are laughing at me.'

'I am, but very slightly. War with a whole people is dangerous. Look at your brother, Charles I; he is in a sad plight, very sad.'

'We are in France, and I am a Spaniard.'

'So much the worse, *per Bacco*, so much the worse. I wish you were a Frenchwoman and I a Frenchman; they would hate us both less.'

'However, do you approve of my project?'

'Yes, if I see it to be possible.'

'It is; you have my word for it. Make your preparations for departure.'

'I! I am always ready to set out; only, as you know, I never do set out, and this time probably will be like the rest.'

'Still, if I go, will you go too?'

'I will try.'

'You kill me with your fears, Giulio; and yet, what have you to fear?'

'Many things.'

'What things?'

Mazarin's countenance, from being playful, became dark.

'Anne,' said he, 'you are only a woman, and as such you can insult men as you please, sure of escaping punishment. You accuse me of fear; I have not so much as you, since I do not wish to escape. Against whom do they cry out? Is it against you or against me? Whom do they wish to hang? Is it you or me? Well, I make head against the storm—notwithstanding that you accuse me of being afraid—not as a bully, that is not my way; but I hold firm. Imitate me—not so much noise, more of effect. You cry out very loud, you arrive at nothing. You talk of flight!' Mazarin shrugged his shoulders, took the queen's hand, and led her to the window, 'Look!'

'Well?' said the queen, blinded by her obstinacy.

'Well, what do you see? Those are, if I mistake not, citizens armed with cuirasses, helmets, good muskets, as in the days of the League, and who watch so closely the window from which you look at them that you will be seen if you raise the curtain so high. Now come to this one. What do you see? Men armed with halberds, who guard your gates. At every opening of this palace to which I could take you, you would see the same. Your gates are guarded, so are the air-holes of your cellars; and I will tell you what the good La Ramée told me of M. de Beaufort—unless either a bird or a mouse, you will not get out.'

'*He* got out, however.'

'Do you count on getting out in the same way?'

'Am I then a prisoner?'

'*Parbleu!* I proved it to you an hour ago;' and Mazarin quietly took up his unfinished despatch at the point where he had been interrupted.

Anne, trembling with rage, red from humiliation, left the cabinet, violently shutting the door behind her.

Mazarin did not even turn his head. On reaching her apartments the queen dropped into a chair and began to weep. Then suddenly, struck with a new idea, 'I am saved,' said she, getting up. 'Yes, oh, yes; there is a man who knows how to get me out of Paris whom I have too long forgotten.' Thus musing, though with a feeling of joy, 'How ungrateful I have been!' said she; 'for twenty years I have neglected this man, whom I ought to have made a marshal of France. My mother-in-law wasted gold and honours on Concini, who plotted her ruin; the king made Vitry a marshal of France for an assassination; and I have left in forgetfulness and penury that noble d'Artagnan who saved me,' and she hurried to a table and began to write.

LII

THE INTERVIEW

THIS same morning d'Artagnan was sleeping in Porthos's room. Since the disturbances the two friends had adopted this practice. Under their bolsters were their swords, and on the table, within easy reach, were their pistols. D'Artagnan was sleeping still, and was dreaming that the sky was covered by a great yellow cloud, that from this cloud was falling a rain of gold, and that he held up his hat under a spout. Porthos was dreaming that the panel of his carriage was not large enough to contain the armorial bearings that were being painted on it. They were awakened at seven by a valet, not in livery, who brought d'Artagnan a letter.

'From whom?' asked the Gascon.

'From the queen,' was the reply.

'Holloa!' said Porthos, rising up in bed, 'what did he say?'

D'Artagnan desired the valet to wait in an adjoining room; and when the door was closed he leaped out of bed, and quickly perused the letter, while Porthos looked at him with open eyes, but without venturing to ask any questions.

'Friend Porthos,' said d'Artagnan, handing him the letter, 'this makes your title of baron and my captaincy certain. Take, read, and judge.'

Porthos read these words in a trembling voice:

The queen wishes to speak to M. d'Artagnan. Will he return with the bearer?

'Eh, well! I see nothing in that very extraordinary,' said Porthos.

'*I* see much that is extraordinary. If they want me, things must be in an embroiled state. Just fancy what a disturbance must have taken place in the queen's mind to bring to the surface, after twenty years have passed, a recollection of the service I did her.'

'That is true,' said Porthos.

'Sharpen your sword, Baron, charge your pistols, give food to your horses. I answer for it that there will be something new before tomorrow; and *mum!*'

'But it's not a snare they are laying to get rid of us, is it?' said Porthos, who always seemed preoccupied with the troubles that his future greatness might cause others.

'If it is a snare, I shall detect it; don't disturb yourself. If Mazarin is an Italian, *I* am a Gascon;' and d'Artagnan dressed with surprising quickness.

As Porthos, still in bed, was hooking his friend's cloak, a second knock was heard at the door.

'Come in,' said d'Artagnan.

A second valet entered.

'From his Eminence the Cardinal Mazarin,' said he.

D'Artagnan looked at Porthos.

'This complicates matters,' said Porthos; 'where shall you go first?'

'This happens capitally; his Eminence appoints an interview in half an hour's time. My friend,' said he, turning to the valet, 'tell his Eminence I shall be with him in half an hour.'

The valet bowed, and left.

'It is very fortunate that he did not see the other,' resumed d'Artagnan.

'Do you think, then, that they did not both send for you about the same matter?'

'I don't *think* it; I am sure they did not.'

'Come, come, d'Artagnan, look sharp. Fancy, the queen is waiting for you; after the queen, the cardinal; and after the cardinal, I am.'

D'Artagnan called back the valet of Anne of Austria. 'Here I am, my friend,' said he; 'conduct me.'

The valet took him by the way of the Rue des Petits Champs,* and turning to the left, admitted him by the little garden gate which opens into the Rue Richelieu, then a secret staircase was reached, and d'Artagnan was introduced into the oratory.

A certain emotion for which he could assign no adequate reason made the lieutenant's heart beat. He had no longer the confidence of youth, and experience had taught him the great gravity of recent events.

He knew what was the nobility of princes and the majesty of kings, and he had accustomed himself to class his mediocrity after those illustrious by fortune and by birth. In old times he had approached Anne of Austria as a young man who salutes a woman. Today, it was another thing; he drew near her as a humble soldier draws near an illustrious chief.

A slight sound broke the silence of the oratory. D'Artagnan trembled a little, and saw a white hand lift the tapestry; and from its form, whiteness, and beauty he recognized the royal hand which one day had been given him to kiss.

The queen entered.

'It is you, M. d'Artagnan,' said she, casting on him a look of sweet melancholy—'it is you, and I recollect you well. Look at me now; I am the queen. Do you recognize me?'

'No, Madame,' replied d'Artagnan.

'But do you not remember,' continued Anne of Austria, with that delightful accent which when she liked she knew how to give to her voice, 'that the queen once had need of a young, brave, devoted cavalier; that she found such a one, and that, although he may indeed think she has forgotten him, she has kept a place for him at the bottom of her heart?'

'No, Madame, I don't remember that.'

'So much the worse,' said Anne—'so much the worse, at least, for the queen, for she now needs the same courage and devotion.'

'What!' said d'Artagnan, 'the queen, surrounded as she is by such devoted servants, such wise councillors, men so great from their merits or position, condescends to cast a look upon an obscure soldier!'

Anne understood this veiled reproach; she was moved rather than annoyed by it.

So much of abnegation and of disinterestedness on the part of the Gascon gentleman had a thousand times humiliated her; she had permitted herself to be surpassed in generosity.

'All that you say of those surrounding me, M. d'Artagnan, is true, perhaps; but I have confidence in you only. I know that you are Monsieur the Cardinal's partisan; be mine also, and I will take charge of your future. Come, will you do for me now what that gentleman whom you do not remember did for me in the past?'

'I shall do all that you order me, your Majesty.'

The queen reflected a moment, and seeing the circumspect attitude of the musketeer, 'You love repose, perhaps?' said she.

'I do not know, for I have never reposed, Madame.'

'Have you any friends?' she asked.

'I had three; two have left Paris, and I don't know where they are gone. One only remains; but he is one of those who knew, I believe, the cavalier of whom your Majesty has done me the honour to speak.'

'Very good; you and your friend are worth an army.'

'What do you wish me to do, Madame?'

'Return at five, and I will tell you; but do not speak to a living soul, Monsieur, of the rendezvous I give you.'

'No, Madame.'

'Take your oath that you will not.'

'Madame, I have never belied my word; when I say No, I mean it.'

The queen, although surprised at this language, to which her courtiers had not accustomed her, drew from it a happy omen of the zeal which d'Artagnan would show in the accomplishment of her design. It was one of the Gascon's artifices sometimes to hide a deep subtlety under the appearance of a loyal brusqueness.

'The queen has no other order to give me just now?' said he.

'No, Monsieur; and you can retire till the hour I have fixed.'

D'Artagnan bowed and left.

'The devil!' said he, when he had reached the door; 'it seems that they have much need of me here.'

Then, as the half-hour had elapsed, he went along the gallery and knocked at the cardinal's door. Bernouin showed him in.

'I am come at your orders, Monseigneur,' said he; and according to his custom, d'Artagnan cast a rapid look around him, and noticed that Mazarin had a sealed letter before him, only it was placed on the desk face downwards, so that the address could not be read.

'You have just come from the queen?' said Mazarin, looking straight at d'Artagnan.

'*I*, Monseigneur! Who told you that?'

'No one; but I know it.'

'I am grieved to tell Monseigneur that he is mistaken,' shamelessly replied the Gascon, emboldened by the promise which he had just made to Anne of Austria.

'I myself opened the antechamber door and saw you come from the end of the gallery.'

'I was admitted by the secret staircase.'

'How was that?'

'I don't know; there may have been some mistake.'

Mazarin knew that it was not easy to make d'Artagnan say what he wished to hide, so he gave up for the time any attempt to discover the mystery which the Gascon was making of the matter.

'Let us talk of my affairs,' said the cardinal, 'since you will not say anything of yours.'

D'Artagnan bowed.

'Do you like travelling?'

'I have passed my life on the great highways.'

'What would retain you in Paris?'

'Nothing except the order of a superior.'

'Well, here is a letter that needs to be delivered to its address.'

'To its address, Monseigneur? But it has none.'

The fact is, the face of the letter was quite blank.

'That means that there are two envelopes.'

'I understand; and I am to tear off the outer one when I have reached the place simply told me.'

'Precisely so. Take it, and set off. You have a friend, M. du Vallon. I have great esteem for him; you will take him with you.'

'The devil!' said d'Artagnan to himself; 'he knows that we heard yesterday's conversation, and he wants to remove us some distance from Paris.'

'Do you hesitate?'

'No, Monseigneur, and I will be off at once. Only I would ask once thing——'

'What is it? Tell me.'

'It is that your Eminence shall go to the queen.'

'When do you mean?'

'At this moment.'

'What to do?'

'To say to the queen simply these words: "I am sending M. d'Artagnan somewhere, and I want him to set off at once."'

'That shows,' said Mazarin, 'that you have been to the queen.'

'I had the honour of telling your Eminence that it was possible there has been some mistake.'

'What does that signify?' asked Mazarin.

'Might I dare to renew my request to your Eminence?'

'It is all right. I am going. Wait for me here.'

Mazarin looked round attentively to see if any key had been left in the drawers, and then went out.

Ten minutes passed, during which d'Artagnan did his best to read through the first envelope what was written on the second; but he quite failed. Mazarin came in again quite pale, and looking very preoccupied; he went and sat down at his desk. D'Artagnan examined him as he had the letter; but the envelope of his countenance was nearly as impenetrable.

'Eh, eh!' said the Gascon, 'he has an angry look. Is it towards me? He is planning something; is it to send me to the Bastille? Gently, Monseigneur, at the first angry word you say to me I will strangle you, and become a Frondeur. I shall have a triumph like Broussel, and Athos would declare me to be the French Brutus. That would be comical.'

The Gascon, who was always giving the reins to his imagination, had already foreseen the benefit that he would derive from the situation. However, Mazarin gave no such order, but on the contrary now began to wheedle d'Artagnan.

'You were right, my dear M. d'Artagnan, and you cannot set out yet.'

'Ah!' said d'Artagnan.

'Return me the despatch, if you please.'

D'Artagnan obeyed. Mazarin assured himself that the seal was unbroken.

'I shall want you this evening,' said he. 'Come back in two hours.'

'In two hours, Monseigneur, I have an appointment which I must not fail to keep.'

'Don't let that distress you at all; it's the same.'

'Good!' thought d'Artagnan; 'I suspected it.'

'Return then at five, and bring me that dear M. du Vallon, only leave him in the anteroom; I want to speak to you alone.'

D'Artagnan bowed, at the same time saying to himself, 'Both the same order, both at the same hour, both at the Palais-Royal. I understand. Ah! here is a secret for which M. de Gondy would have paid a hundred thousand francs.'

'You are reflecting!' said Mazarin, feeling restless.

'Yes; I was asking myself whether we ought to come armed or not.'

'Armed to the teeth.'

'Very well; we shall be.'

D'Artagnan bowed, went away, and hastened to repeat Mazarin's flattering promises to his friend, which gave an inconceivable joy to Porthos.

LIII

THE FLIGHT

THE Palais-Royal, in spite of the signs of agitation seen in the city, presented, when d'Artagnan returned about five o'clock, one of the most pleasing spectacles. Nor was it to be wondered at; the queen had restored Broussel and Blancmesnil to the people. The queen therefore had nothing more to fear because the people had nothing more to ask. Her emotion was the remains of an agitation which required time to calm, as after a storm at sea some days are often needed to cause the swell to subside.

There had been a grand banquet, for which the return of the victor at Lens had been the pretext. The princes and princesses had been invited, and their carriages had blocked up the courtyard since noon. After the banquet there were to be games at cards in the queen's apartments. Anne of Austria was on this day charming with beauty and wit; never had she been seen in a more joyous humour. Vengeance in bloom shone in her eyes and smiled on her lips.

Just as they were rising from table, Mazarin caught sight of d'Artagnan, who was already awaiting him in the anteroom. The cardinal appeared with joyous look, took him by the hand, and led him into his cabinet.

'My dear M. d'Artagnan,' said the minister, seating himself, 'I am going to show you the greatest mark of confidence that a minister can give an officer.'

D'Artagnan bowed. 'I hope that Monseigneur will show it to me without reservation, and with the conviction that I am worthy of it.'

'The worthiest of all, my dear friend, since it is you whom I am addressing.'

'Well,' said d'Artagnan, 'I will confess to you, Monseigneur, that I have been for a long time awaiting such an occasion. So tell me quickly what you have to say.'

'This evening you are going to have the safety of the State in your hands.' He stopped.

'Explain yourself, Monseigneur; I am all attention.'

'The queen has resolved to take a short journey with the king to St Germain.'*

'Ah, ah! that means that the queen intends to leave Paris.'

'You understand feminine caprice.'

'Yes, I understand it very well,' said d'Artagnan.

'It was for that reason that she sent for you this morning, and that she bade you return at five o'clock.'

'It was worth her while to desire me to take a solemn oath that I would not speak of that interview to anyone!' muttered d'Artagnan. 'Oh, woman! though a queen, she is still a woman!'

'Do you disapprove of this little expedition, my dear M. d'Artagnan?' Mazarin asked with some uneasiness.

'I, Monseigneur! and what makes you think so?'

'Because you shrug your shoulders.'

'That is a trick I have when talking to myself, Monseigneur.'

'Then you approve?'

'I neither approve nor disapprove, Monseigneur. I await your orders.'

'Well, it is you whom I have selected to convey the king and the queen to St Germain.'

'A double trick,' said d'Artagnan to himself.

'You see plainly,' resumed Mazarin, noticing d'Artagnan's unconcern, 'that, as I was telling you, the safety of the State will rest in your hands.'

'Yes, Monseigneur, and I feel all the responsibility of such a charge.'

'You accept it, however?'

'Yes, I accept always.'

'You believe the journey possible?'

'Everything is.'

'Will you be attacked on the road?'

'It is probable.'

'But how will you act in that case?'

'I shall cut my way through those who attack me.'

'And if you don't succeed?'

'Then so much the worse for them; I shall pass over them.'

'And you will conduct the king and queen safe and sound to St Germain?'

'Yes.'

'On your life?'

'On my life.'

'You are a hero, my dear fellow!' said Mazarin, looking at the musketeer admiringly.

D'Artagnan smiled.

'And I?' said Mazarin, after a moment of silence, and regarding d'Artagnan fixedly.

'How you, Monseigneur?'

'And I, if I wish to set out?'

'That would be more difficult.'

'How so?'

'Your Eminence can be so easily recognized.'

'Even in this disguise?' and he lifted up a cloak lying upon an armchair on which was a complete cavalier's dress of pearl-grey and garnet with silver lace.

'If your Eminence wears a disguise, it will be easier.'

'Ah!' said Mazarin, drawing a long breath.

'But your Eminence must do what you said you would have done if you had been in our situation.'

'What must I do?'

'Cry out, Down with Mazarin!'

'I will.'

'In French, in good French, Monseigneur; take care of the accent. Six thousand Frenchmen were slain in Sicily because they pronounced Italian badly. Take care that the French do not take their revenge upon you for the Sicilian Vespers.'*

'I will do my best.'

'There are armed men in the streets; are you sure that no one knows the queen's project?'

Mazarin reflected a moment.

'This affair would be a fine thing in the hands of a traitor, Monseigneur. I mean what you are now proposing; the chances of an attack would excuse all.'

Mazarin felt a cold shiver; but then he reflected that no one purposing to be a traitor would forewarn him.

'That's why,' said he, briskly, 'I do not confide in everyone. The proof is that I have selected you to escort me.'

'Do you not go with the queen?'

'No.'

'Then you will set out after the queen?'

'No,' said Mazarin, once more.

'Ah!' said d'Artagnàn, who began to comprehend the design.

'Yes; I have made my plans,' continued the cardinal. 'Going with the queen I double her risk. After the queen's departure I double my own, since when the court is quite safe they might forget me; the great are very ungrateful.'

'That's true,' said d'Artagnan, as he cast, without being able to help it, a look at the queen's diamond which Mazarin was wearing on his finger.

Mazarin noticed the look, and quietly turned the bezel of the ring inwards.

'I want, therefore,' said Mazarin, with his cunning smile, 'to prevent them from being ungrateful to me.'

'It is a mark of Christian charity,' said d'Artagnan, 'not to lead your neighbour into temptation.'

'It is just for that reason that I want to start before them.'

D'Artagnan smiled; he was one who could easily fathom this Italian astuteness.

Mazarin saw him smile, and took advantage of the opportunity.

'You will begin then by helping me to leave Paris first, will you not, my dear M. d'Artagnan?'

'A tough job, Monseigneur,' said d'Artagnan, assuming a serious look.

'But,' said Mazarin, attentively looking at him, so as not to allow a single expression to escape him—'but you have not made these remarks respecting the king and queen.'

'They are my king and my queen, Monseigneur. My life belongs to them; I owe them it.'

'That's quite right,' Mazarin said in a low voice; 'but as your life does not belong to me, I must buy it of you, must I not?' and then, giving a deep sigh, he began to turn the bezel of the ring outwards.

D'Artagnan smiled. These two men touched at one point; namely, at astuteness. If they had also met on the common ground of courage, they together would have done great things.

'But now, you understand, if I ask this service of you, I have the intention of being grateful for it.'

'Has Monseigneur then only the *intention?*' asked d'Artagnan.

'Come,' said Mazarin, taking the ring from his finger, 'my dear M. d'Artagnan, here is a diamond which once belonged to you; it is right that it should be yours again. Take it, I beg of you.'

D'Artagnan did not give Mazarin the trouble of insisting; he took the ring, looked to see if the stone was still the same, and after ascertaining it to be of the finest water, slipped it on his finger with unutterable pleasure.

'I had a great love for it,' said Mazarin, giving it a last look; 'but no matter, I give it to you with great pleasure.'

'And I, Monseigneur, receive it in the spirit in which it is given. But now let us talk of your matters. You wish to set off before the rest?'

'Yes, I hold to that.'

'At what hour?'

'At ten o'clock.'

'And the queen; at what hour does she wish to go?'

'At midnight.'

'Then it is possible; I shall see you off first. I will leave you outside the barrier; I then will return to fetch her.'

'Capital; but how are we to get out of Paris?'

'Oh, as to that, you must leave it for me to do.'

'I give you full power; take as large an escort as you please.'

D'Artagnan shook his head.

'It seems to me to be the safest way,' said Mazarin.

'Yes, for you, Monseigneur, but not for the queen.'

Mazarin bit his lips.

'And you must give me the entire control of the attempt.'

'Still——'

'Or find another,' said d'Artagnan, turning his back to go.

'Eh!' said Mazarin in a low tone, 'I believe he is going off with the diamond;' and he called him back.

'M. d'Artagnan, my dear M. d'Artagnan,' said he, in a most caressing voice, 'will you be responsible for everything?'

'I answer for nothing; I will do my best.'

'Your best?'

'Yes.'

'Well, then, come; I can trust in you.'

'That's fortunate,' said d'Artagnan to himself.

'You will be here then at half-past nine?'

'And I shall find your Eminence ready?'

'Certainly, quite ready.'

'That's settled then. Now will Monseigneur be pleased to allow me to see the queen?'

'What is the good of that?'

'I should prefer receiving her Majesty's orders from her own lips.'

'She charged me to give them to you.'

'She might have forgotten something.'

'You are determined to see her?'

'It is absolutely necessary, Monseigneur.'

Mazarin hesitated a moment; d'Artagnan remained immovable in his determination.

'Come, now, I will take you there; but not a word about our conversation.'

'What has been said between ourselves regards only ourselves, Monseigneur.'

'You swear to be silent about it?'

'I never swear, Monseigneur. I say Yes or No, and as I am a gentleman, I keep my word.'

'Well, I see I must trust in you unconditionally.'

'That is best, believe me, Monseigneur.'

'Come,' said Mazarin.

Mazarin showed d'Artagnan the way to the queen's oratory, and bade him wait. He did not wait long. Five minutes after the queen came to him in full dress. In it she seemed to be scarcely thirty-five, and beautiful as ever.

'M. d'Artagnan,' said she, with a gracious smile, 'I am much obliged for your having insisted on seeing me.'

'I beg your Majesty's pardon; but I wished to receive my orders from your own lips.'

'You know what the matter in question is?'

'Yes, Madame.'

'You accept the mission which I confide to you?'

'Gratefully.'

'Well; be here at midnight.'

'I will.'

'M. d'Artagnan, I know too thoroughly your disinterested-ness to talk just now of my gratitude, but I swear that I will not forget this second service as I did the first.'

'Your Majesty is at liberty to remember and forget, and I do not know what you mean;' and d'Artagnan bowed.

'Go, Monsieur,' said the queen, with her most charming smile, 'and return at midnight.'

She waved her hand by way of saying farewell, and d'Artagnan withdrew; but on retiring he cast his eyes upon the curtain by which the queen had entered, and at the bottom of the tapestry he saw the toe of a velvet slipper.

'Well,' said he to himself, 'there is Mazarin listening to see whether I betray him or not. Really, this Italian puppet does not deserve to be served by an honourable man.'

D'Artagnan was not less punctual at the rendezvous because of this; at half-past nine he entered the anteroom. Bernouin was waiting, and admitted him. He found the cardinal dressed as a cavalier. He looked extremely well in this costume, which he wore in a becoming manner, only he was very pale, and trembling a little.

'All alone?' said Mazarin.

'Yes, Monseigneur.'

'And shall we not have the pleasure of that good M. du Vallon's company?'

'Yes, indeed, Monseigneur; he is waiting in his coach.'

'Where is it?'

'At the gate of the Palais-Royal garden.'

'It is then in his coach that we set out?'

'Yes, Monseigneur.'

'Is there no other escort besides you two?'

'Is not that sufficient? One of us would be enough.'

'Really, my dear M. d'Artagnan, you quite alarm me with your coolness.'

'I should have thought, on the contrary, that it ought to inspire you with confidence.'

'Do I not take Bernouin with me?'

'There is no room for him; he will come to your Eminence afterwards.'

'Let us go,' said Mazarin, 'since I must do just as you wish.'

'Monseigneur, there is still time to withdraw, and your Eminence is perfectly free to do so.'

'No, no; let us start;' and they descended by the secret staircase, Mazarin leaning on d'Artagnan, who felt the cardinal's arm trembling.

They crossed the courts of the Palais-Royal, where some coaches belonging to late stayers at the feast were still standing, reached the garden and the little gate. Mazarin tried to open it by a key which he took from his pocket; but his hand trembled so that he could not find the keyhole.

'Give it to me,' said d'Artagnan.

Mazarin gave him the key. D'Artagnan opened the door and put the key into his pocket; he thought of re-entering that way. The coach-step was lowered; the door opened. Mousqueton stood at the door; Porthos was sitting at the back of the coach.

'Get in, Monseigneur,' said d'Artagnan.

Mazarin did not require to be told twice, but jumped in. D'Artagnan got in after him. Mousqueton closed the door, and with many groans got up behind. He had made some objections to going, under the pretext that his wound still caused him suffering, but d'Artagnan had said to him, 'Remain if you wish, my dear M. Mouston; but I forewarn you that Paris will be burned tonight.'

Upon which Mousqueton had not asked anything more, and had declared that he was ready to follow his master and M. d'Artagnan to the end of the world.

The coach set off at a fair trot, which did not at all indicate that it contained people in any haste. The cardinal wiped his forehead and looked about him. He had Porthos on his left and d'Artagnan on his right, each serving as a protection. Facing them on the front seat were two pairs of pistols, one for each of the two friends, who had besides their swords at their side. A few paces from the Palais-Royal a patrol stopped the coach.

'Who goes there?' said the leader.

'Mazarin!' replied d'Artagnan, bursting out laughing.

The cardinal felt his hair standing on end. The joke seemed much relished by the citizens, who, seeing this coach without arms and escort, would never have believed in the occurrence of such rashness.

'Pleasant journey!' they cried, and they allowed the coach to pass.

'H'm!' said d'Artagnan, 'what does Monseigneur think of that reply?'

'Clever fellow!' exclaimed Mazarin.

'In fact,' said Porthos, 'I understand——'

About the middle of the Rue des Petits Champs a second patrol stopped the coach.

'Who goes there?' cried the leader of the patrol.

'Hide yourself, Monseigneur,' said d'Artagnan; and Mazarin so buried himself between the two friends that he was completely hidden by them.

'Who goes there?' said the same voice, impatiently; and d'Artagnan perceived that they had made a dash at the horses' heads.

He thrust his head out of the window.

'Eh, Planchet!' he said.

The leader came nearer; it was really Planchet. D'Artagnan had recognized his voice.

'What, Monsieur, is it you?'

'Eh! yes, my dear friend. This dear fellow, Porthos, has just received a sword-cut, and I am taking him to his country-house at St Cloud.'

'Oh, really?' said Planchet.

'Porthos,' resumed d'Artagnan, 'if you can speak a word, my dear Porthos, just say something to this good Planchet.'

'Planchet, my friend,' said Porthos, in a doleful voice, 'I am very ill, and if you meet a doctor be good enough to send him to me.'

'Ah my goodness!' said Planchet, 'what a misfortune! And how did it happen?'

'I will tell you that,' said Mousqueton.

Porthos uttered a deep groan.

'Clear the way for us, Planchet,' said d'Artagnan, in a low tone, 'or he will not arrive alive. His lungs are wounded, my friend.'

Planchet shook his head as if he would say, 'In that case he is in a bad state.' Then turning round to his men, 'Let them pass; they are friends.'

The coach moved on again; and Mazarin, who had held his breath, dared again to breathe.

'*Bricconi!*'* he muttered.

A few steps before the gate St Honoré they met a third party. This was composed of ill-looking fellows who looked more like bandits than anything else; they were the men under the mendicant of St Eustache.

'Attention, Porthos,' said d'Artagnan.

Porthos put out his hand towards the pistols.

'What is the matter?' said Mazarin.

'Monseigneur, I believe we are in bad company.'

A man advanced towards the coach-door with a sort of scythe in his hand.

'Who goes there?' this man asked.

'Eh, stupid!' said d'Artagnan, 'don't you recognize the coach of Monsieur the Prince?'

'Prince or not,' said this man, 'open; we have to guard the gate, and no one shall pass without we know who it is.'

'What is to be done?' Porthos asked.

'Why, pass, of course,' said d'Artagnan.

'But how?' said Mazarin.

'Through them or over them. Coachman, go at a gallop.'

The coachman raised his whip.

'Not a step farther,' said the one who seemed to be the leader, 'or I will hough* your horses.'

'Plague you!' said Porthos, 'that would be a pity; beasts that cost me a hundred pistoles apiece.'

'I will pay you two hundred,' said Mazarin.

'Yes, but when these fellows have cut the horses' houghs, they will cut our throats next.'

'There is one coming on my side,' said Porthos; 'ought I to kill him?'

'Yes, a blow with the fist, if you can; fire only at the last extremity.'

'I can do it,' said Porthos.

'Come and open, then,' said d'Artagnan to the man with the scythe, while taking one of the pistols by the barrel, and preparing to strike with the butt-end.

The latter drew near. While he was doing so, d'Artagnan, to be more free in his movements, leaned halfway out of the window; his eyes rested on those of the mendicant, which a lantern shone upon. He doubtless recognized the musketeer, for he became pale; doubtless d'Artagnan recognized him, for his hair stood on end.

'M. d'Artagnan!' he exclaimed, drawing back a step, 'M. d'Artagnan! Let him pass.'

Perhaps d'Artagnan was going to reply, when a blow like that which fells an ox was heard; it was Porthos, who had just knocked down his man. D'Artagnan turned round, and saw the unlucky fellow lying a few paces off.

'Full gallop now!' cried he to the coachman; 'push on.'

The coachman used his whip freely; the noble animals bounded along. Cries were heard like those of men who had been overthrown. Then they felt a double shake; two of the wheels had just passed over some round, flexible body. There was a moment's silence; the coach cleared the gate.

'To the Cours la Reine!'* cried d'Artagnan to the coachman. Then turning towards Mazarin, 'Now, Monseigneur,' he said to him, 'you can say five Paternosters and five Aves to thank God for your deliverance. You are saved; you are free!'

Mazarin could reply only by a sort of groan; he could not credit such a miracle. Five minutes after, the coach stopped; it had reached the Cours la Reine.

'Is Monseigneur satisfied with his escort?' the musketeer asked.

'Delighted, Monsieur,' said Mazarin, venturing to put his head out of the window; 'now do as much for the queen.'

'That will be less difficult,' said d'Artagnan, jumping down. 'M. du Vallon, I commend his Eminence to your care.'

'Very well,' said Porthos, extending his hand.

D'Artagnan took his hand and shook it.

'Oh!' said Porthos, as if in pain.

'What is the matter now?' asked d'Artagnan.

'I believe I have sprained my wrist.'

'Why the devil did you do that? You hit like a deaf man.'

'I was compelled to do it, for my man was going to fire his pistol; but how did you get rid of yours?'

'Oh, mine was not a man.'

'What was it, then?'

'A spectre.'

'And——'

'I conjured him away.'

Without further explanation, d'Artagnan took the pistols from the front seat, belted them on, wrapped himself in his cloak, and not wishing to enter by the same barrier by which he had come out, took his way towards the gate Richelieu.

LIV

MONSIEUR THE COADJUTOR'S COACH

INSTEAD of entering by the gate St Honoré, d'Artagnan, who had some time to spare, made a detour and entered by the gate Richelieu. He was carefully scrutinized, and when the populace saw by his plumed hat and his laced coat that he was an officer of Musketeers, they surrounded him in order to make him cry out, Down with Mazarin! This had at first no other effect than to disquiet him; but he remembered what he was planning to do, and cried out so lustily that the most scrupulous were satisfied.

He went along the Rue Richelieu, thinking of the means by which he could carry off the queen—for he could not think of doing it in one of the royal coaches—when he saw a coach standing at the door of Madame de Guéménée's mansion.* A sudden idea flashed upon him.

'Ah!' said he, 'that would be fair play.'

And he came up to the coach, looked at the coat-of-arms on its panels, and the livery of the coachman on the box. This examination was all the more easy as the coachman was asleep with his hands folded.

'It is indeed Monsieur the Coadjutor's coach,' said he; 'upon my word, I begin to think that Providence is helping us.'

He got softly into the coach, and pulling the check-string,* 'To the Palais-Royal!' he said.

The coachman, starting up from his sleep, drove towards the place named, not supposing that the order came from anyone else than his master. The Swiss was going to close the gates;

but on seeing this magnificent equipage, he did not doubt but that it was a visit of great importance, and allowed the coach to pass in, and it pulled up at the portico. There the coachman first noticed that the footmen were not behind the coach. He thought Monsieur the Coadjutor had disposed of them, got down from his seat without letting go the reins, and came to open the door.

D'Artagnan jumped out, and just when the coachman, frightened at not seeing his master, was stepping back, he seized him by the throat with his left hand, and with the right presented a pistol at him.

'Say but a single word,' said d'Artagnan, 'and you are a dead man.'

The coachman saw by the expression of the speaker that he had been caught in an ambush, and he stood with gaping mouth and widely opened eyes. Two musketeers were patrolling in the courtyard, so d'Artagnan called them by name.

'M. de Bellière,' he said to one of them, 'be good enough to take the reins from the hands of this honest man, take his seat on the coach, drive to the gate of the secret staircase, and wait for me there; this is an important matter connected with the service of the king.'

The musketeer, who knew that his lieutenant could not be playing a joke while on duty, obeyed without saying a word, although the order seemed a curious one.

Then turning towards the second musketeer, 'M. du Verger,' he said, 'help me to take this man to a place of safety.'

The musketeer thought that his lieutenant had just arrested some prince in disguise; he bowed, and drawing his sword, signified that he was ready. D'Artagnan went upstairs, followed by his prisoner, who was himself followed by the musketeer, crossed the vestibule, and entered the anteroom to Mazarin's cabinet. Bernouin was waiting with impatience for some news of his master.

'Well, Monsieur?' said he.

'Everything is going on capitally, my dear M. Bernouin; but here is a man, if you please, for whom you must find a place of security.'

'Where, Monsieur?'

'Where you like, only the place you choose must have shutters which can be padlocked, and a door that can be locked.'

'We have got that, Monsieur;' and they led the poor coachman into a room the windows of which had bars, and which was very like a prison.

'Now, my dear friend,' said d'Artagnan, 'I invite you to let me have your hat and cloak.'

The coachman, as was natural, made no reply; besides, he was so astonished at what had happened that he shook and stammered like a drunken man. D'Artagnan put the hat and cloak under the arm of the *valet de chambre*.

'Now, M. du Verger,' said d'Artagnan, 'remain shut up with this man until M. Bernouin comes and opens the door. This sentry duty will be tolerably long, and not very amusing, I know; but you understand,' he added seriously, 'it is for the king's service.'

'At your orders,' replied the musketeer, who saw that important matters were at stake.

'By the by,' said d'Artagnan, 'if this man tries to escape or cry out, run your sword through his body.'

The musketeer with a motion of the head signified that he would implicitly obey. D'Artagnan went out, taking Bernouin along with him. Midnight struck.

'Take me to the queen's oratory; inform her that I am there, and go and put this parcel with a loaded musket on the box-seat of the coach which is in waiting at the bottom of the private staircase.'

Bernouin conducted d'Artagnan to the oratory, where he sat down in deep thought.

All had gone on at the Palais-Royal as usual. At ten almost all of the guests had retired; those who were to take flight with the court had the watchword, and were asked to be at the Cours la Reine by one in the morning.

At ten Anne of Austria went to the king's apartments. They had just put Monsieur to bed; and young Louis, who remained till the last, was amusing himself by arranging in order of battle his lead soldiers—an amusement which much pleased him. Two children of honour were playing with him.

'Laporte,' said the queen, 'it is time for his Majesty to go to bed.'

The king asked to sit up longer, saying that he did not feel sleepy; but the queen insisted on it.

'Do you not intend to go at six in the morning to bathe at Conflans,* Louis? It was your own suggestion, I believe.'

'You are right, Madame,' said the king, 'and I am ready to go to my room when you have embraced me. Laporte, give the candlestick to M. le Chevalier de Coislin.'

The queen put her lips to the smooth fair brow which the royal child held up to her with a gravity which already smacked of etiquette.

'Go to sleep quickly, Louis,' said the queen, 'for you will be awakened early.'

'I shall do my best to obey you, Madame; but I do not feel any desire to sleep.'

'Laporte,' said Anne of Austria, in a low tone, 'get some wearisome book to read to his Majesty, but do not undress.'

The king went, accompanied by the Chevalier de Coislin, who carried the candlestick. Then the queen returned to her apartments. Her ladies, that is, Madame de Brégy, Mademoiselle de Beaumont, Madame de Motteville and Socratine, her sister, whom they so styled from her wisdom, had just brought into the wardrobe the remains of the dinner, on which she supped, as was customary.

The queen then gave her orders, spoke of a dinner to which she was invited on the day after tomorrow by the Marquis de Villequier, named the persons whom she admitted to the honour of being present there, arranged for a visit the next day to Val de Grâce,* and gave to Béringhen, her first *valet de chambre*, her orders for him to attend her.

The ladies' supper being finished, the queen feigned great fatigue, and went to her bedroom.

Madame de Motteville, whose turn it was to perform the duty that evening, followed her, and helped her to undress. The queen then got into bed, spoke to her affectionately for some minutes, and dismissed her. It was just then that d'Artagnan entered the courtyard of the Palais-Royal with the Coadjutor's coach. A moment after, the coaches of the ladies of honour left, and the gate was closed behind them. The midnight hour struck. Five minutes after, Bernouin knocked at the queen's bedroom, coming by the secret passage from the cardinal's rooms. Anne of Austria went and opened it herself. She was already dressed; that is, she had put on her stockings and a long dressing-gown.

'It is you, Bernouin,' she said; 'is M. d'Artagnan there?'

'Yes, Madame, in your oratory; he is waiting till your Majesty is ready.'

'I am so. Go and tell Laporte to awaken and dress the king; then from there go to Maréchal de Villeroy, and send him to me.'

Bernouin bowed, and went away.

The queen entered the oratory, which was lighted by a single lamp of Venetian glass. She saw d'Artagnan standing and awaiting her.

'It is you?' she said to him.

'Yes, Madame.'

'You are ready?'

'I am.'

'And Monsieur the Cardinal?'

'He has left without accident. He is awaiting your Majesty at Cours la Reine.'

'But in what coach are we going?'

'I have arranged everything; a coach is waiting below.'

'Let us go to the king's rooms.'

D'Artagnan bowed, and followed the queen.

Young Louis was already dressed, except his shoes and doublet. He allowed himself to be dressed with an astonished look, while overwhelming Laporte with questions, who merely said in reply, 'Sire, it is by the queen's order.'

The bed was thrown open; and one could see that the sheets were so old that there were holes in many places. This was one of the results of Mazarin's stinginess.

The queen came in, and d'Artagnan stood at the door. The child, on seeing the queen, slipped out of Laporte's hands and ran to her. The queen made a sign for d'Artagnan to come near. He obeyed.

'My son,' said Anne of Austria, pointing to the musketeer, calm, upright, and uncovered, 'this is M. d'Artagnan, who is as brave as one of those valiant knights whose history you so delight in hearing read to you by my ladies. Carefully remember his name, and look well at him so as not to forget his face, for this evening he will do us a great service.'

The young king looked at the officer with his full, proud eye, and repeated, 'M. d'Artagnan!'

'That's it, my son.'

The young king gently raised his little hand, and held it out to the musketeer, who knelt and kissed it.

'M. d'Artagnan,' Louis repeated; 'it is well, Madame.'

Just then a clamour was heard drawing nearer.

'What is that?' said the queen.

'Oh, oh!' replied d'Artagnan, listening and looking attentively; 'it is the noise of the populace, who are rioting.'

'Must we flee?' said the queen.

'Your Majesty has given the direction of this affair to me. We must stay and know what it means.'

'M. d'Artagnan!'

'I am responsible for everything.'

Nothing is more contagious than confidence. The queen, naturally full of strength and courage, was alive to these two virtues in the highest degree.

'Act,' she said; 'I leave it to you.'

'Will your Majesty allow me in the whole of this affair to give orders in her name?'

'Yes, give your orders.'

'What do these people want, then?' said the king.

'We are going to see, Sire,' said d'Artagnan, and he went quickly out of the room.

The tumult was increasing; it seemed to enclose the Palais-Royal completely. From within, cries were heard whose meaning could not be made out. It was evident that there was clamour and sedition. The king, but half dressed, the queen, and Laporte were all listening and waiting. Comminges, who was on guard that night at the Palais-Royal, hastened up; he had about two hundred men in the courtyards and stables, which he put at the service of the queen.

'Well,' asked Anne of Austria, on seeing D'Artagnan return, 'what is the matter?'

'The matter is, Madame, that a report has spread that the queen has left the Palais-Royal, taking the king away with her, and that the populace demand proof of the contrary, or threaten to pull down the Palais-Royal.'

'Oh, this time they go too far,' said the queen; 'and I will prove to them that I have by no means gone away.'

D'Artagnan saw from the expression of the queen's face that she was going to give some violent command. He approached her, and said to her in a low tone, 'Has your Majesty still confidence in me?'

This voice made her start.

'Yes, Monsieur, full confidence,' said she. 'Speak!'

'Does the queen condescend to follow my advice?'

'Speak!'

'Will your Majesty kindly send away M. de Comminges, and order him to shut up his men and himself in the guard-room and stables?'

Comminges looked at d'Artagnan in that envious way with which every courtier sees the rise of some new aspirant to favour.

'You have understood, Comminges?' then said the queen.

D'Artagnan went to him; he had noticed, with his usual sagacity, that unquiet look.

'M. de Comminges, pardon me; we are both servants of the queen, are we not? It is my turn to be of use to her; do not, therefore, grudge me this happiness.'

Comminges bowed, and went out.

'Now,' said d'Artagnan to himself, 'I have made one enemy more.'

'And now,' said the queen, speaking to d'Artagnan, 'what is to be done? For, as you see, instead of growing less, the noise has much increased.'

'Madame, the populace wish to see the king; they must see him.'

'How do you mean they *must* see him, and where? On the balcony?'

'Not at all, Madame; but here in his bed, while sleeping.'*

'Oh, your Majesty, M. d'Artagnan is quite right,' exclaimed Laporte.

The queen reflected, and then smiled, like a woman to whom duplicity was by no means unknown.

'Do it then,' she murmured.

'M. Laporte,' said d'Artagnan, 'go through the gates and tell the people that they shall be gratified, and that in five minutes not only shall they see the king, but even see him in bed. Add that the king is asleep, and the queen begs that they will be very quiet, so as not to wake him.'

'But not all; a deputation of two or four persons.'

'Everyone, Madame.'

'But it will detain us till daylight; think of that.'

'We shall lose but a quarter of an hour. I will be responsible, Madame. Believe me, I know the people; they are like a big child who needs only to be caressed. In the presence of the king asleep they will be mute, gentle, and timid as lambs.'

'Go, Laporte,' said the queen.

The young king drew near his mother.

'Why are we obliged to do what these people ask?' he said.

'We must, my son,' said Anne.

'But then, if I am obliged to obey, I am no longer king?'

The queen kept silence.

'Sire,' said d'Artagnan, 'will your Majesty allow me to ask you a question?'

Louis XIV turned round, surprised that anyone should dare to speak to him; the queen pressed his hand.

'Yes, Monsieur,' said he.

'Your Majesty will remember having seen, when playing in Fontainebleau Park or in the courtyards of Versailles Palace, the sky suddenly overclouded, and having heard the sound of thunder?'

'Yes, certainly.'

'Well, that thunder-clap, however much your Majesty wished to go on playing, said to you, "Go indoors, Sire; you must."'

'Certainly, Monsieur; but then I have been told that the thunder is the voice of God.'

'Well, Sire,' said d'Artagnan; 'listen to the clamour of the people, and you will see that it is very much like the noise of the thunder.'

In fact just at that moment a terrible shout was heard, brought to them by the night breeze. Suddenly it ceased.

'Listen, Sire,' said d'Artagnan; 'they have just told the people that you are asleep. You see clearly that you are still king.'

The queen looked with astonishment at this remarkable man, whose brilliant courage made him equal to the bravest, and whose subtle intellect made him the equal of all. Laporte came in.

'Well, Laporte?' the queen asked.

'Madame, M. d'Artagnan's prediction is fulfilled; they became calm as by enchantment. The doors are going to be opened for them, and in five minutes they will be here.'

'Laporte,' said the queen, 'if you were to put one of your sons in the place of the king, we could be setting off meanwhile.'

'If her Majesty orders it, my sons, as myself, are at her service.'

'No,' said d'Artagnan, 'for if one of them knew his Majesty, and became aware of the subterfuge, all would be lost.'

'You are right, Monsieur, always right. Laporte, put the king to bed.'

Laporte put the king, dressed as he was, into his bed; then he covered him as far as his shoulders with the sheet. The queen bent over him and kissed him on the forehead.

'Pretend to be asleep, Louis,' said she.

'Yes,' said the king; 'but I don't want one of those men to touch me.'

'Sire, I am here,' said d'Artagnan; 'and I answer for it that if any one has that audacity he shall pay for it with his life.'

'Now what is to be done?' asked the queen; 'for I hear them.'

'M. Laporte, go in front of them, and recommend them once more to keep silence. Madame, wait there at the door. I will be beside the king's bolster, quite ready to die for him.'

Laporte went out; the queen stood up near the tapestry; d'Artagnan slipped behind the curtains. Then they heard the dull and prolonged tread of a great number of men; the queen herself lifted the tapestry, putting her finger to her mouth.

On seeing the queen, these men stopped in an attitude of respect.

'Come in, Messieurs, come in.'

There was then seen in all this multitude a hesitancy almost amounting to shame. They expected resistance—to have to force gates and vanquish guards; but now the gates were open and quite unguarded, and the king, at least to all appearance, had no other guard but his mother. Those who were in front spoke stammeringly, and tried to draw back.

'Come in, pray, Messieurs,' said Laporte, 'since the queen gives you leave.'

Then one man, bolder than the others, ventured to cross the threshold, and advanced on tiptoe. The rest imitated him; and the room was silently filled, as if all these men were the most respectful and devoted courtiers. Right beyond the door could be seen the heads of those who, not having been able to get in, were standing on tiptoe. D'Artagnan saw all that was going on through an opening which he had made in the curtain; he recognized Planchet as the man who had entered first.

'Monsieur,' said the queen to him, observing that he was the leader of this band, 'you have desired to see the king, and I am anxious to show him myself. Come near; look at him, and say if we look like fugitives about to make our escape.'

'No, indeed,' replied Planchet, somewhat astonished at the unexpected honour done to him.

'You will then tell my good and faithful Parisians,' resumed Anne of Austria, with a smile the meaning of which d'Artagnan could not mistake, 'that you have seen the king abed and asleep, and the queen ready also to go to bed.'

'I will tell them, Madame; and all those who are now with me will tell them so too, but——'

'But what?' asked the queen.

'I beg your Majesty's pardon, but is it indeed the king now lying in that bed?'

Anne of Austria started.

'If there is any one of you who knows the king, let him look and say if it is indeed his Majesty who is there.'

A man enveloped in a cloak, which he had so disposed as to hide his face, drew near, leaned over the bed, and looked.

D'Artagnan thought for a moment that this man had some evil design in view, and he put his hand to his sword; but while bending forward the man in the cloak uncovered a part of his face, and d'Artagnan recognized the Coadjutor.

'This is really the king,' said the man, raising himself up. 'May God bless his Majesty!' and all the men, who had come in angry, passing from anger to pity also blessed the royal child.

'Now,' said Planchet, 'let us thank the queen, my friends, and withdraw.'

They all bowed, and left without noise, as they had entered. Planchet, who had entered first, went out last. The queen stopped him.

'What is your name, my friend?' she said.

Planchet turned round, very much astonished at the question.

'Yes,' said the queen; 'I consider myself as much honoured in having received you this evening as if you were a prince, and I desire to know your name.'

'Yes,' thought Planchet, 'to treat me like a prince, thanks!'

D'Artagnan shuddered, fearing that Planchet, seduced like the crow in the fable,* would give his name, and that the queen, on hearing it, would know that Planchet had once belonged to him.

'Madame,' respectfully replied Planchet, 'my name is Dulaurier,* at your service.'

'Thanks, M. Dulaurier; and what is your occupation?'

'Madame, I am a draper in the Rue des Bourdonnais.'

'That's all I wanted to know,' said the queen; 'much obliged, my dear M. Dulaurier. You shall hear from me.'

'Well, well,' muttered d'Artagnan, on coming out from behind the curtain, 'M. Planchet is decidedly no fool, and one can see that he has been brought up in a good school.'

The different actors in this strange scene stood for a moment facing one another without saying a single word—the queen standing near the door; d'Artagnan having half come out from his hiding-place; the king resting on his elbow, and ready to fall back on his bed at the least sound which might indicate the return of this multitude. But instead of drawing nearer, the sound became more and more distant, and soon ceased altogether.

The queen took breath; d'Artagnan wiped his damp brow; the king slipped out of the bed, saying, 'Let us set off.'

At that moment Laporte appeared.

'Well?' the queen asked.

'Well, Madame, I followed them to the gates. They told all their comrades that they had seen the king, and that the queen had spoken to them, so that they went off quite proud and happy.'

'Oh, the wretched creatures!' murmured the queen, 'they shall pay dearly for their audacity, I promise them.'

Then turning towards d'Artagnan, 'Monsieur,' she said, 'you have this evening given me the best advice that I ever received in my life; go on. What shall we do now?'

'M. Laporte,' said d'Artagnan, 'finish dressing his Majesty.'

'We can set off, then?' the queen asked.

'When your Majesty pleases; you have only to go down by the private staircase, and you will find me at the door.'

D'Artagnan went down; the coach was there waiting, the musketeer on the box-seat. D'Artagnan took the packet which he had asked Bernouin to put at the feet of the musketeer. It contained the hat and cloak of M. de Gondy's coachman. He put them on. The musketeer got down.

'Monsieur,' said d'Artagnan, 'you will go and set your comrade at liberty who is guarding the coachman. You will mount your horses, you will go and fetch from the Hôtel de la Chevrette, Rue Tiquetonne, my horse and M. du Vallon's, which you will saddle as for war; then you will leave Paris, leading our horses, and go to the Cours la Reine. If you find no one there, push on to St Germain. On the king's service!'

The musketeer saluted, and went off to execute these orders.

D'Artagnan mounted the box. He had a pair of pistols at his belt, a musket under his feet, his naked sword behind him.

The queen appeared; behind her came the king and M. le Duc d'Anjou, his brother.

'The coach of Monsieur the Coadjutor!' she exclaimed, drawing back a step.

'Yes, Madame,' said d'Artagnan, 'but enter fearlessly; I am the driver.'

The queen gave a cry of surprise, and entered. The king and the duke entered after her, and took their seats at her side.

'Come, Laporte,' said the queen.

'What, Madame! in the same coach as your Majesties?'

'It is not a question tonight of court etiquette, but of the king's safety. Get in, Laporte!'

Laporte obeyed.

'Close the canopy in front,' said d'Artagnan.

'But will not that cause distrust, Monsieur?' the queen asked.

'Your Majesty may be at rest on that point; I have an answer ready.'

The canopies were closed, and they set off at a gallop by the Rue Richelieu. On reaching the gate the chief of the post advanced at the head of a dozen men, holding a lantern in his hand. D'Artagnan made a sign for him to draw near.

'Do you recognize the coach?' said he to the sergeant.

'No.'

'Look at the arms.'

The sergeant held his lantern close to the panel.

'They are Monsieur the Coadjutor's!'

'*Chut*! he is in good favour* with Madame de Guéménée.'

The sergeant began to laugh.

'Open the gate,' he said; 'I know who it is.'

Then, coming close to the lowered canopy, 'Much pleasure, Monseigneur!' said he.

'Indiscreet!' exclaimed d'Artagnan, 'you will get me dismissed.'

The gate creaked on its hinges; and d'Artagnan, seeing the road clear, whipped on his horses, which set off at a good trot. Five minutes after, they had joined the cardinal.

'Mousqueton,' exclaimed d'Artagnan, 'raise the canopy of her Majesty's coach.'

'It is he,' said Porthos.

'Acting as coachman!' exclaimed Mazarin.

'And with the coach of the Coadjutor!' said the queen.

'*Corpo di Dio*, M. d'Artagnan!' said Mazarin; 'you are worth your weight in gold.'

LV

HOW D'ARTAGNAN GAINED TWO HUNDRED AND NINETEEN LOUIS, AND PORTHOS TWO HUNDRED AND FIFTEEN LOUIS, BY SELLING STRAW

MAZARIN wished to set out at once for St Germain; but the queen determined to await those who had been told to meet them there. Only she offered Laporte's place to the cardinal. The latter accepted, and changed coaches.

There was good reason for the report having spread that the king was to leave Paris in the night; ten or twelve persons had been in the secret of this flight since six in the evening, and however careful they might be, they could not give orders for their departure without something transpiring. Besides, each of these had one or two friends for whom they were interested; and as no doubt was felt but that the queen was leaving Paris with terrible projects of revenge, everyone had warned his friends or relatives, so that the report of the departure ran like a train of powder along the streets of the city.

The first coach to arrive after the queen's was that of Monsieur the Prince. It contained M. de Condé, Madame the Princess, and Madame the Princess-dowager. Both had been awakened in the middle of the night, and did not know what was going on.

The second contained M. le Duc d'Orléans, Madame the Duchess, the Great Mademoiselle, and Abbé de la Rivière —the inseparable favourite and intimate counsellor of the prince.

The third contained M. de Longueville and M. le Prince de Conti, brother and brother-in-law of Monsieur the Prince. They got out, drew near the coach of the king and queen, and did homage to her Majesty.

The queen looked into the coach, the door of which remained open, and saw that it was empty.

'But where is Madame de Longueville?' she asked.

'In fact, where then is my sister?' asked Monsieur the Prince.

'Madame de Longueville is indisposed, Madame,' replied the duke; 'and she has asked me to present her excuses to your Majesty.'

Anne glanced quickly at Mazarin, who replied by an almost imperceptible nod of the head.

'What do you think of it?' asked the queen.

'I think she is a hostage for the Parisians,' replied the cardinal.

'Why hasn't she come?' asked Monsieur the Prince of his brother in low tones.

'Silence!' replied he; 'without doubt she has her reasons.'

'She destroys us,' murmured the prince.

'She saves us,' said Conti.

The coaches came up in a crowd. Maréchal de la Meilleraie, Maréchal de Villeroy, Guitaut, Villequier, and Comminges came one after the other, then the two musketeers leading d'Artagnan and Porthos's horses. D'Artagnan and Porthos at once mounted. Porthos's coachman replaced d'Artagnan on the box of the royal coach; Mousqueton replaced the coachman, driving erect for reasons known to him, and like the classical Automedon.*

The queen, though busied about a thousand details, tried to catch d'Artagnan's eye, but the Gascon was already lost in the crowd, with his usual prudence.

'Let us form the advanced guard,' said he to Porthos, 'and secure good lodgings at St Germain, for no one will trouble about us. I feel very tired.'

'I shall fall off my horse from sleepiness,' said Porthos. 'Yet we have not had the least fighting. The Parisians are decidedly great fools.'

'Is it not rather that we have been very adroit?' said d'Artagnan.

'Perhaps.'

'And your wrist, how is it getting on?'

'Better; but do you think we have got them this time?'

'What?'

'You your promotion, and I my title?'

'Faith, yes! I would almost wager it. Besides, if they do not remember it, I will make them.'

'We hear the voice of the queen,' said Porthos; 'I think that she is asking to mount on horseback.'

'Oh, she would like it well; but——'

'But what?'

'But the cardinal does not wish it. Messieurs,' said d'Artagnan, addressing the two musketeers, 'accompany the queen's coach, and do not leave the doors. We are going forward to prepare lodgings;' and d'Artagnan and Porthos pushed forward towards St Germain.

'Let us set off, Messieurs!' said the queen, and the royal coach started off, followed by all the others and more than fifty cavaliers.

St Germain was reached without accident; and on stepping out of the coach, the queen found Monsieur the Prince, standing and uncovered, waiting to offer her his hand.

'What a surprise for the Parisians!' said Anne of Austria, quite radiant with joy.

'It means war,' said the prince.

'Well, war let it be! Have we not with us the conqueror of Rocroy, Nordlingen, and Lens?'

The prince bowed his thanks.

It was three in the morning. The queen was the first to enter the château. All followed her; nearly two hundred persons had accompanied her in her flight.

'Messieurs,' said the queen, laughing, 'you can lodge in the château. There is plenty of room and to spare; but as we were not expected, they tell me that there are in all only three beds,* one for the king, one for me——'

'And one for Mazarin,' said Monsieur the Prince, in a low voice.

'As for me, I shall sleep on the floor, then?' said Gaston d'Orléans, with a very distressed smile.

'No, Monseigneur,' said Mazarin, 'for the third bed is intended for your Highness.'

'But you?' asked the prince.

'I shall not go to bed; I have work to do.'

Gaston ascertained which was the room where the bed was, without disturbing himself about the way in which his wife and daughter could be accommodated.

'Well, I shall go to bed,' said d'Artagnan. 'Come with me, Porthos.'

Porthos followed d'Artagnan with that profound confidence he had in the intellect of his friend.

They were walking side by side in front of the château, Porthos looking with staring eyes at d'Artagnan, who was reckoning on his fingers.

'Four hundred at a louis each make four hundred pistoles.'

'Yes,' said Porthos; 'but what is it which makes four hundred pistoles?'

'One pistole is not enough,' continued d'Artagnan; 'it is worth a louis.'

'What is worth a louis?'

'Four hundred at a louis each make four hundred louis.'

'Four hundred?' said Porthos.

'Yes; there are two hundred of them, and they require at least two for each person. At that rate that makes four hundred.'

'But four hundred what?'

'Listen,' said d'Artagnan; and as there were present all sorts of people who were staring with amazement at the arrival of the court, he finished his sentence quite in a whisper in Porthos's ear.

'I understand,' said the latter; 'thoroughly, upon honour! Two hundred louis each, that's delightful; but what will they say?'

'They may say what they like; besides, how will they know that we are concerned in it?'

'But who will take charge of the distribution?'

'Is not Mousqueton here?'

'What about my livery? They will recognize it as mine.'

'He can turn his coat inside out.'

'You are always right, my dear fellow,' exclaimed Porthos; 'but where the devil do you get all those ideas that you have?'

D'Artagnan smiled.

The two friends took the first street they came to; Porthos knocked at the door of the house on the right, while d'Artagnan took the one on the left.

'Any straw?' they asked.

'Monsieur, we have none,' replied those who answered the door, 'but apply to the forage merchant.'

'And where does he live?'

'At the last big gates in the street.'

'And are there any other places at St Germain where one can buy it?'

'There is the landlord of the Crowned Sheep and Gros Louis the farmer.'

'Where do they live?'

'Rue des Ursulines.'*

'Both?'

'Yes.'

'Very well.'

The two friends made them give the second and third addresses as accurately as they had given the first.

Then d'Artagnan went to the forage merchant, and treated with him for a hundred and fifty trusses of straw for the sum of three pistoles. He went next to the innkeeper, where he found Porthos, who had just arranged to take two hundred trusses for nearly the same sum. Lastly, the farmer Louis supplied eighty. That made a total of four hundred and thirty. St Germain possessed no more.

All this sweeping in took no more than half an hour. Mousqueton, duly instructed, was put in charge of this improvised trade. He was instructed not to allow a single straw to leave his hands at less than a louis the truss; they relied on him for four hundred and thirty louis. Mousqueton nodded assent, but did not understand the speculation of the two friends.

D'Artagnan, carrying three trusses of straw, returned to the château, where every one, shivering with cold, and ready to drop off to sleep, regarded with envy the king, queen, and M. d'Orléans in their camp-beds. D'Artagnan's entrance into the great hall caused a general burst of laughter; but he did not even seem to observe that he was the object of general attention, and began to arrange with much skill and pleasure his couch of straw, which excited the envy of all those wearied ones who were unable to sleep.

'Straw!' they exclaimed; 'where is straw to be got?'

'I will take you to the place,' said Porthos, and he led those who wanted straw to Mousqueton, who generously distributed it at a louis a truss.

They found it a little dear; but when one wants to get rest, who would not pay two or three louis for some hours of good sleep?

D'Artagnan gave up his bed ten times running; and as he was thought to have paid, like the rest, a louis a truss, he in this way pocketed thirty louis in less than half an hour. At five in the morning straw was worth twenty-four francs* a truss, and yet no more could be got.

D'Artagnan had taken care to put aside four trusses for himself. He put into his pocket the key of the room where he had hidden them, and accompanied by Porthos, he returned to settle up with Mousqueton, who shrewdly and like a worthy steward, handed to them four hundred and thirty louis, and still had a hundred louis for himself. Mousqueton, who knew nothing of what was going on at the château, could not understand why the idea of selling straw had not come to him sooner.

D'Artagnan put the gold into his hat, and while returning made up his account with Porthos. Each received two hundred and fifteen louis. Porthos at that moment found he had kept no straw for himself, so he returned to Mousqueton; but the latter had sold all, not keeping any for himself. Porthos then returned to find d'Artagnan, who, thanks to his four trusses of straw, was busy making up his bed, and enjoying the prospect in advance of a bed so soft, so well stuffed at the head, so well covered at the foot, that it would have been envied by the king himself if he had not been so comfortable in his own. D'Artagnan would not at any price disarrange his bed for Porthos, but for four louis which the latter paid, he consented that Porthos should sleep with him. He put his sword by his bolster, his pistols at his side, spread his cloak over his feet, placed his hat on his cloak, and stretched himself voluptuously upon the straw, which rustled under him. He was already cherishing the sweet dreams which the gain of two hundred and nineteen louis in a quarter of an hour had created, when a voice resounded at the hall-door and made him jump.

'M. d'Artagnan!' it exclaimed, 'M. d'Artagnan!'

'Here,' said Porthos, 'here!'

Porthos saw clearly that if d'Artagnan were going away the whole of the bed would be his.

An officer approached. D'Artagnan leaned on his elbow.

'Are you M. d'Artagnan?' said the officer.

'Yes, Monsieur; what do you want of me?'

'I am come to seek you.'

'From whom?'

'From his Eminence.'

'Tell Monseigneur that I am going to sleep, and that I advise him in a friendly way to do the same.'

'His Eminence has not gone to bed, and he wants you at once.'

'Hang him for not knowing enough to sleep at the proper time!' muttered d'Artagnan. 'What does he want? To make me a captain? If so, I will pardon him;' and the musketeer got up, grumbling all the while, took his sword, hat, pistols, and cloak, then followed the officer, while Porthos, left sole possessor of the bed, tried to imitate the luxurious intentions of his friend.

'M. d'Artagnan,' said the cardinal, on perceiving him whom he had sent for so unseasonably, 'I have by no means forgotten with what zeal you have served me, and I am going to give you a proof of it.'

'Good!' thought d'Artagnan, 'that begins well.'

Mazarin looked at the musketeer, and saw his face grow more pleasant.

'Ah, Monseigneur——'

'M. d'Artagnan, do you much wish to be a captain?'

'Yes, Monseigneur.'

'And your friend, does he always desire to be baron?'

'At this moment, Monseigneur, he is dreaming that he is baron.'

'Then,' said Mazarin, taking from a portfolio the letter which he had already shown d'Artagnan, 'carry this despatch to England.'*

D'Artagnan looked at the envelope; there was no address.

'Can I not know to whom I ought to give the letter?'

'On reaching London you will learn; when there you will tear off the outside envelope.'

'And what are my instructions?'

'To obey him in every point to whom this letter is addressed.'

D'Artagnan was going to put some fresh questions, when Mazarin added, 'You will set out for Boulogne; you will find at the Arms of England Hotel a young gentleman named Mordaunt.'

'Yes, Monseigneur, and what must I do with this gentleman?'

'Follow him wherever he may take you.'

D'Artagnan looked at the cardinal with an air of wonderment.

'There, you have received your orders,' said Mazarin. 'Go!'

' "Go" is very easy to say; but in order to go money is needed, and I have none.'

'Ah!' said Mazarin, scratching his ear; 'you say that you have no money? But that diamond which I gave you yesterday evening?'

'I wish to keep that as a souvenir of your Eminence.'

Mazarin sighed.

'Living is dear in England, Monseigneur, and especially as envoy extraordinary.'

'H'm!' said Mazarin, 'it is a very sober country and of simple life since the revolution; but no matter.'

He opened a drawer and took out a purse.

'What do you say to these thousand crowns?'

D'Artagnan considerably protruded his lower lip.

'I say, Monseigneur, that it is little, for I certainly shall not go by myself.'

'I count upon having M. du Vallon, that worthy gentleman, go with you; for after you, my dear M. d'Artagnan, he is certainly the man whom I love and esteem the most.'

'Then, Monseigneur,' said d'Artagnan, pointing to the purse, which Mazarin had not let go—'then, if you love and esteem him so much, you understand——'

'Be it so! in consideration of him I will add two hundred crowns.'

'Niggardly fellow!' muttered d'Artagnan. 'But when we return, at least,' he added aloud, 'shall not M. Porthos be able to count upon having his barony and I my promotion?'

'The word of a Mazarin!'

'I should like some other oath better,' said d'Artagnan to himself; then aloud, 'Can I present my respects to her Majesty the queen?'

'Her Majesty is asleep,' Mazarin replied hastily, 'and you must set out without delay; therefore go, Monsieur.'

'One word more, Monseigneur; if fighting is going on there, shall I fight?'

'You will do what the person orders you to whom I send you.'

'That's enough, Monseigneur,' said d'Artagnan, stretching out his hand to receive the bag; 'and I present you my respects.'

D'Artagnan slowly put the bag into his roomy pocket, and turning towards the officer, 'Monsieur,' he said to him, 'will you please go and wake up M. du Vallon on behalf of his Eminence, and tell him that I am waiting for him at the stables.'

The officer set out immediately with an eagerness which seemed to d'Artagnan to be self-interested.

Porthos had just stretched himself in his bed, and had begun to snore harmoniously, according to his habit, when he felt someone touch him on the shoulder. He thought it was d'Artagnan, and did not stir.

'In the name of the cardinal!' said the officer.

'H'm!' said Porthos, opening his eyes wide; 'what do you say?'

'I say this: his Eminence wishes to send you to England, and M. d'Artagnan awaits you at the stables.'

Porthos heaved a deep sigh, rose, took his hat, pistols, sword, and cloak, and went out, looking regretfully at the bed in which he had promised himself to sleep so soundly.

He had scarcely turned his back before the officer was installed in it. It was very natural; he was the only one in the whole assembly, excepting the king, queen, and M. Gaston d'Orléans, who slept gratis.

LVI

NEWS FROM ARAMIS

D'ARTAGNAN had gone straight to the stables. It was the break of day; he recognized his own horse and that of Porthos tied to the manger, but this was empty. He felt sorry for the poor beasts, and went up to a corner of the stable where he saw a little straw glistening, which had doubtless escaped from the previous night's raid; but in pushing it together with his foot his boot knocked against a round body, which, touched in a sensitive part, uttered a cry and got up on its knees, rubbing its eyes. It was Mousqueton, who, not having any straw for himself, had used that of the horses.

'Mousqueton,' said d'Artagnan, 'look sharp; we are off!'

Mousqueton, on recognizing the speaker, got up hastily, and while doing so let fall some of the louis unlawfully gained during the night.

'Oh, oh!' said d'Artagnan, picking up a louis and smelling it; 'this gold has a strange smell, like straw.'

Mousqueton turned red, and seemed so embarrassed that the Gascon began to laugh, and said to him, 'Porthos would have been in a great rage, my dear M. Mousqueton; but I pardon you. Only recollect that this gold ought to be a balm for your wound, and make you look lively!'

Mousqueton put on a smiling face instantly, saddled his master's horse quickly, and mounted his own without too much of a grimace.

At this time Porthos came with a very sulky face, and was not a little astonished to find d'Artagnan so resigned and Mousqueton almost joyful.

'Ah! come,' said he; 'now you have secured your promotion, and I my barony.'

'We are going to find the warrants, and when we return M. de Mazarin will sign them.'

'And where are we going?'

'First to Paris; I have some business to arrange.'

'Let us go to Paris, then.'

On reaching the gates, they were astonished at seeing the threatening attitude of the capital. Around a coach, broken to pieces, the people were yelling their curses, while the persons who had tried to escape were prisoners. These persons consisted of an old man and two women.

When, on the contrary, d'Artagnan and Porthos demanded entrance, they received nothing but caresses. They were taken to be deserters from the Royalist party, and the populace wished to gain them over.

'What is the king doing?' they were asked.

'He is asleep.'

'And the Spaniard?'

'She is dreaming.'

'And the cursed Italian?'

'He is awake. So keep firm; for if they have gone away, there is certainly some reason for it. But as at the end of the reckoning you are the strongest,' continued d'Artagnan, 'don't go hanging women and old men, but throw the blame on its true causes.'

The people listened with pleasure to all this, and let the ladies go, who thanked d'Artagnan with a grateful look.

So they went on their way, crossing barricades, stepping over chains, pressed, questioned, questioning.

On the Place Palais-Royal d'Artagnan saw a sergeant exercising five or six hundred citizens; it was Planchet, utilizing to the profit of his urban militia his recollections of the Piedmont regiment. While passing in front of d'Artagnan, he recognized him.

'Good-day, M. d'Artagnan,' said Planchet, proudly.

'Good-day, M. Dulaurier,' replied d'Artagnan.

Planchet stopped short, looking at d'Artagnan with widely opened eyes. The first rank, seeing their leader stop, did the same, and so in their turn did the other ranks.

'These citizens make themselves extremely ridiculous,' said d'Artagnan to Porthos, and he went on his way. A few minutes after, they alighted at the Hôtel de la Chevrette. The fair Madeleine hurried out to d'Artagnan.

'My dear Madame Turquaine,'* said he, 'if you have any money or jewels, hide them away quickly; if you have any debtors, make them pay up; or any creditors, don't pay them at all.'

'Why so?' she enquired.

'Because Paris will soon be reduced to ashes, just as Babylon was, of which you may have heard.'

'And you are going to leave me at such a time?'

'This very instant.'

'And where are you going?'

'Ah! if you can tell me you will do me a great service.'

'Oh, dear me! dear me!'

'Have you any letters for me?' asked d'Artagnan, at the same time waving his hand to indicate that all her laments would be unheeded and superfluous.

'There is one which has just come,' and she gave the letter to d'Artagnan.

'From Athos!' exclaimed he, as he recognized the firm, bold handwriting of their friend.

'Ah!' said Porthos, 'let us hear what he has to say.'

D'Artagnan opened the letter and read:

DEAR d'ARTAGNAN, DEAR VALLON—My good friends, you are perhaps receiving news from me for the last time. Aramis and I have been very unfortunate; but God, our own courage, and the remembrance of your friendship, support us. Think of Raoul. I entrust to you the documents at Blois, and in two months and a half, if you get no news from us, examine them. Embrace the viscount with all your heart for your devoted friend,

ATHOS

'I will indeed deliver the message to Raoul, as he is on our route,* and if he have the misfortune to lose our poor Athos, he from that day shall be my son.'

'And I,' said Porthos, 'will make him my sole legatee. Well, what else does Athos say?'

If you meet a M. Mordaunt in your travels, be on your guard against him. I am not able to say more in a letter.

'M. Mordaunt!' said d'Artagnan, with surprise.

'M. Mordaunt, that's right!' said Porthos; 'we shall remember it. But look, there is a postscript from Aramis.'

'So there is,' said d'Artagnan; and he read:

We are keeping our abode a secret, dear friends, knowing your brotherly devotion, and that you would come and die with us.

'*Sacrebleu!*' broke in Porthos, with a burst of anger which made Mousqueton jump to the other end of the room. 'Are they then in danger of death?'

D'Artagnan went on:

Athos bequeaths Raoul to you, and *I* an act of revenge. If you should happily get hold of a certain Mordaunt, tell Porthos to take him into a corner and wring his neck. I dare not say more in a letter.

ARAMIS

'If it is only that,' said Porthos, 'it's soon done.'

'On the contrary,' said d'Artagnan, gravely, 'it is impossible.'

'And why so?'

'This M. Mordaunt is the very man whom we are to rejoin at Boulogne, and with whom we cross to England.'

'Well, suppose instead of going to meet this M. Mordaunt we were to go and join our friends?' said Porthos, with a movement fierce enough to frighten an army.

'I have thought of that too; but the letter has neither date nor stamp.'

'That's true,' said Porthos, and he began walking up and down the room like a wild fellow, gesticulating, and every now and then pulling his sword partly from its scabbard.

As for d'Artagnan, he stood as if struck with consternation; and the deepest distress was imprinted on his face.

'Ah! it is too bad,' he kept saying. 'Athos insults us; he wants to die alone.'

Mousqueton, seeing these two in great despair, burst into tears in his corner.

'Come,' said d'Artagnan, 'all this leads to nothing. Let us set out, Porthos; let us go and embrace Raoul, as you have said, and perhaps he has had news from Athos.'

'Bless me, that's a good idea,' said Porthos; 'in fact, my dear d'Artagnan, I don't know how you do it, but you are never at a loss.'

'Let him beware who looks crossly at my master at this moment,' said Mousqueton; 'I would not give a farthing for his skin.'

They mounted and set off. On reaching the Rue St Denis the friends found a great concourse of people. M. de Beaufort had just arrived* from Vendômois, and the Coadjutor was showing him to the amazed and joyful Parisians. With M. de Beaufort, they regarded themselves as henceforth invincible. The two friends took a side street, so as not to meet the prince, and reached the Barrière St Denis.

'Is it true,' said the guards to the two cavaliers, 'that M. de Beaufort has arrived in Paris?'

'Nothing is more true,' said d'Artagnan; 'and the proof is that he is sending us to meet M. de Vendôme, his father, who will arrive shortly.'

'Long live M. de Beaufort!' cried the guards, and they moved respectfully aside to let the envoys of the great prince pass.

Once outside the barrier, d'Artagnan and Porthos rushed along the road, knowing neither fatigue nor discouragement; their horses flew along, and they did not stop talking of Athos and Aramis.

Mousqueton was suffering all the torments imaginable; but this excellent servitor consoled himself by thinking that his two masters experienced worse sufferings—for he had come to regard d'Artagnan as his second master, and obeyed him even more promptly and exactly than Porthos.

The camp was between St Omer and Lambe. The two friends made a bend to reach the camp, and gave the army full particulars of the flight of the king and queen, a rumour of which only had as yet reached it. They found Raoul near his tent, lying on a truss of hay, of which his horse was stealthily pulling some mouthfuls. The young man's eyes were red, and he seemed dejected. Maréchal de Grammont and Comte de Guiche had returned to Paris, and the poor boy felt lonely.

In a few moments Raoul raised his eyes, saw the two cavaliers, and ran to them with open arms.

'Oh, is it you, dear friends?' he exclaimed. 'Have you come to fetch me? Do you bring me news of my guardian?'

'Haven't you received any news, then?' asked d'Artagnan.

'Alas, no, Monsieur! and in fact I don't know what is become of him, so that I am greatly distressed—even to weeping.' And in fact, two great tears rolled down the bronzed cheeks of the young man.

Porthos turned aside his head to prevent what was passing in his heart from being seen in his face.

'The devil!' said d'Artagnan, more moved than he had been for a long time past; 'don't despair, my friend. If you have not received any letters from the count, we have; we—one——'

'Oh, have you?' exclaimed Raoul.

'And a very reassuring one too,' said d'Artagnan, on seeing the joy this news gave the young man.

'Have you got it?' Raoul asked.

'Yes; that is to say, I had it,' said d'Artagnan, making the pretence of searching for it; 'wait, it ought to be there, in my pocket. He speaks to me of his return, does he not, Porthos?'

Gascon though he was, d'Artagnan was unwilling to take upon himself alone the burden of this falsehood.

'Yes,' said Porthos, coughing.

'Oh, give it to me,' said the young man.

'Eh, I was reading it a second time just now. Could I have lost it! Ah, *pécaire*,* my pocket has a hole in it.'

'Oh, yes, M. Raoul,' said Mousqueton, 'and the letter was even very consoling; these gentlemen read it to me, and I wept with joy.'

'But at least, M. d'Artagnan, you know where he is?' asked Raoul, half satisfied.

'Ah! that,' said d'Artagnan, 'I certainly know; but it is a profound secret.'

'Not for me, I hope.'

'No, not for you, so I am going to tell you.'

Porthos regarded d'Artagnan with astonishment in his great eyes.

'Where the devil am I going to say he is, so that he will not try to go and rejoin him?' murmured d'Artagnan.

'Well! where is he, Monsieur?' asked Raoul, with his soft and caressing voice.

'He is at Constantinople!'

'Among the Turks!' exclaimed Raoul, affrighted. 'Good heavens! what are you telling me?'

'Well, does that make you afraid?' said d'Artagnan. 'Bah! what are the Turks for men like the Comte de la Fère and the Abbé d'Herblay?'

'Ah, his friend is with him,' said Raoul; 'that reassures me a little.'

'What a shrewd fellow is this demon of a d'Artagnan!' said Porthos, quite amazed at his friend's ruse.

'Now,' said d'Artagnan, anxious to change the subject of conversation, 'here are fifty pistoles which Monsieur the Count sent you by the same courier. I suppose you have not too much money, and that they are welcome?'

'I have still twenty pistoles, Monsieur.'

'Eh, well! take them; then you will have seventy.'

'And if you wish for more——' said Porthos, putting his hand to his pocket.

'Thanks,' said Raoul, blushing; 'a thousand thanks, Monsieur.'

At that moment Olivain appeared on the horizon.

'By the bye,' said d'Artagnan, so that the servant should hear him, 'are you satisfied with Olivain?'

'Yes, pretty fairly.'

Olivain pretended to have heard nothing, and entered the tent.

'With what do you reproach that rogue there?'

'He is a glutton,' said Raoul.

'Oh, Monsieur!' said Olivain, re-appearing at this accusation.

'He is light-fingered.'

'Oh, Monsieur, oh!'

'And above all, he is a great coward.'

'Oh, oh, oh! Monsieur, you dishonour me,' said Olivain.

'*Peste!*' said d'Artagnan; 'learn, M. Olivain, that people such as we are don't allow themselves to be served by cowards. Rob your master, eat his sweetmeats, and drink his wine, but *cap de Diou!* don't be a coward, or I will cut off your ears. Look at M. Mouston; tell him to show you the honourable wounds which he has received, and see how much dignity his habitual bravery has stamped upon his face.'

Mousqueton was in the third heaven, and would have embraced d'Artagnan if he had dared; meanwhile he promised himself to be slain for him if the occasion ever presented itself.

'Send away this rascal, Raoul,' said d'Artagnan; 'for if he is a coward, he will dishonour himself some day.'

'Monsieur says that I am a coward,' exclaimed Olivain, 'because he wished to fight the other day with a cornet of the regiment of Grammont, and I refused to accompany him.'

'M. Olivain, a servant should never disobey,' said d'Artagnan, severely.

And drawing him aside, 'You have done well,' said he, 'if your master was wrong, and here is a crown for you; but if he is ever insulted and you do not allow yourself to be cut in quarters with him, I will cut out your tongue and spoil your face. Remember that well.'

Olivain bowed, and put the crown in his pocket.

'And now, friend Raoul,' said d'Artagnan, 'we are setting off, M. du Vallon and I, as ambassadors. I cannot tell you with what object, for I do not know it myself; but if you need anything, write to Madame Madeleine Turquaine, at the Hôtel de la Chevrette, Rue Tiquetonne, and draw on that fund in her hands as on a banker—with carefulness, however, for I presume that it is not quite so well lined as that of M. d'Émery,' and having embraced his ward for the time being, he passed him to the sturdy arms of Porthos, which raised him from the ground, and kept him for a moment hugged to the heart of that redoubtable giant.

'Now, then,' said d'Artagnan, 'we must be off;' and they set off for Boulogne, where towards evening they pulled up their horses, wet with perspiration and white with foam.

A few paces from where they halted before entering the city was a young man dressed in black, who seemed to expect someone, and who, as soon as he saw them, kept his eyes fixed on them.

D'Artagnan approached him, and seeing that the youth was gazing steadily at him, 'Hi, friend!' said he, 'I don't wish to be measured from head to foot.'

'Monsieur,' said the young man, without replying, 'do you not come from Paris?'

D'Artagnan thought him at first to be some inquisitive fellow who wanted news of the capital.

'Yes, Monsieur,' said he, in a milder tone.

'Do you not put up at the Arms of England Hotel?'

'Yes, Monsieur.'

'Are you not charged with a mission from his Eminence, M. le Cardinal Mazarin?'

'Yes, Monsieur.'

'In that case, I am the one whom you want; I am M. Mordaunt.'

'Ah!' said d'Artagnan, in a low voice; 'he against whom Athos told me to be on my guard.'

'Ah!' muttered Porthos, 'the one whom Aramis wishes me to strangle.'

Both regarded the young man attentively. He was deceived in the expression of their looks.

'Do you doubt my word?' said he; 'in that case I am ready to give you every proof.'

'No, Monsieur,' said d'Artagnan; 'and we put ourselves at your disposition.'

'Well, Messieurs, we shall set off without delay, for this is the last day of the time which the cardinal asked me to grant him. The vessel is ready; and if you had not come, I should have gone without you, for General Oliver Cromwell must be impatiently awaiting my return.'

'Ah, ah!' said d'Artagnan, 'then it is to General Oliver Cromwell to whom we are commissioned?'

'Have you not a letter for him?' the young man asked.

'I have a letter, the outside envelope of which I was to open only in London; but since you tell me to whom it is addressed, it is useless to wait till I get there.'

D'Artagnan tore off the outer envelope. It was in fact addressed: 'To M. Oliver Cromwell, General of the troops of the English nation.'

'Ah!' said d'Artagnan, 'strange commission!'

'Who is this Oliver Cromwell?' asked Porthos, in a low voice.

'Formerly a brewer,' replied d'Artagnan.

'Does Mazarin wish to speculate in beer as we did in straw?' asked Porthos.

'Come, come, Messieurs,' said Mordaunt, impatiently, 'let us be off.'

'Oh, oh!' said Porthos, 'without supper? Can't M. Cromwell wait a bit?'

'Yes, but I——' said Mordaunt.

'Well, you,' said Porthos; 'what else?'

'I am in a hurry.'

'Oh, if it is for you,' said Porthos, 'that's nothing to me; and I shall get supper with or without your permission.'

The young man's vague look blazed up, and seemed ready to flash with anger, but he restrained himself.

'Monsieur,' continued d'Artagnan, 'you must excuse hungry travellers. Besides, our supper will not delay you much. We are going to spur our horses to the inn. You go on foot to the port, we will eat a morsel, and we shall be there as soon as you.'

'Whatever you please, Messieurs, provided we set off.'

'What's the name of the vessel?' asked d'Artagnan.

'The *Standard*'.

'Very well. We shall be on board in half an hour,' and giving spurs to their horses, they both hastened to the inn.

'What do you think of that young man?' d'Artagnan asked, while they were going along.

'I say he does not please me at all and I felt a strong desire to follow the advice of Aramis.'

'Don't do it, my dear Porthos; this man is General Cromwell's envoy, and we should secure a bad reception if we told him we had wrung the neck of his confidant.'

'That's all one to me; I have always remarked that Aramis is one who gives good advice.'

'Listen,' said d'Artagnan; 'when our embassy shall be finished——'

'What next?'

'If he reconducts us into France——'

'Well?'

'Well! we will see.'

The two friends had now reached the hotel, where they supped with first-rate appetite; then they immediately went down to the port. A brig was ready to sail, and on the deck they recognized Mordaunt, who was impatiently walking up and down.

'It's incredible,' said d'Artagnan, while the boat was taking them out to the *Standard*, 'it's astonishing how much that young man is like someone whom I know, but I cannot say who.'

They reached the ladder, and an instant after were on board. But the embarkation of the horses was not so easily done, and the brig did not raise her anchor till eight in the evening.

The young man stamped his feet with impatience, and commanded that they should cover the masts with sails.

Porthos, exhausted by three nights without sleep, and by a journey of seventy leagues made on horseback, had retired to his cabin, and was sleeping.

D'Artagnan, surmounting his repugnance for Mordaunt, promenaded with him on the deck, and made up a hundred stories to force him to talk. Mousqueton was sea-sick.

LVII

'L'ECOSSAIS, PARJURE A SA FOI, POUR UN DENIER VENDIT SON ROI'*

AND now our readers must allow the *Standard* to sail tranquilly, not to London, where d'Artagnan and Porthos thought they were going, but towards Durham, where some letters received from England during his stay at Boulogne had ordered Mordaunt to go, and they must follow us to the Royalist camp, situated on this side of the Tyne, near Newcastle.*

There, placed between two rivers, on the Scottish borders but on English soil, the tents of a small army were pitched. It was midnight. Some men, easily recognizable as Highlanders by their naked legs, their short petticoats,* their plaids of mixed colours, and the feathers decorating their bonnets, watched nonchalantly. The moon, gliding between two dark clouds, lighted up every now and then the sentinels' muskets, and showed in clear outline the roofs and towers of the town which Charles I had just yielded to the Parliamentary forces, as well as Oxford and Newark, which held out still for him in the hope of an arrangement.

At one of the extremities of the camp, near a large tent full of Scotch officers holding a sort of council presided over by the aged Earl of Leven, their chief, a man in cavalier's dress, was asleep on the grass, with his right hand resting on his sword. Fifty paces off, another man, also dressed as a cavalier, was talking with a Scotch sentinel, and thanks to his knowledge of English, although a foreigner, he succeeded in understanding the answers made in the Perth dialect.

Just as the Newcastle clocks struck one in the morning the sleeper awoke; and after making all the gestures of a man opening his eyes after a profound sleep, he looked attentively around him. Seeing that he was alone, he rose, and making a detour, drew near the cavalier who was conversing with the sentinel. The latter had doubtless finished his questioning, for he took leave of the man, and followed without any attempt at concealment the same direction which the first cavalier had taken. In the shade of a tent placed by the road the other awaited him.

'Well, my dear friend?' he said to him in the purest French ever spoken from Rouen to Tours.

'Well, my friend, there is no time to lose, and we must inform the king.'

'What is going on there?'

'It would take too long to tell you, besides you will hear it presently. Moreover, the smallest word spoken here might cause us to lose everything. Let us go and find Lord de Winter.'

And they both took their way towards the opposite end of the camp; but as the camp did not cover a surface of more than five hundred paces square, they soon reached the tent of him of whom they were in search.

'Is your master asleep, Tony?' said one of the two cavaliers, in English, to a domestic lying down in the front part of the tent, which served as anteroom.

'No, Count,' replied the servant, 'I think not, for he walked up and down more than two hours after having left the king, and the sound of his footsteps had scarcely ceased ten minutes; however,' he added, lifting up the curtain, 'you can see him.'

In fact Lord de Winter was there, seated before an opening that served as a window, which let the night air enter, and through which he sadly followed with his eyes the moon, lost, as we have said, in the midst of great black clouds.

The two friends approached him; he did not perceive them until he felt a hand on his shoulder. Then he turned round, recognized Athos and Aramis, and stretched out his hand.

'Have you observed,' he said, 'that the moon is tonight of the colour of blood?'

'No,' said Athos; 'it looks to me much as usual.'

'Look, Chevalier,' said Winter.

'I confess that I think as the Comte de la Fère,' said Aramis, 'and that I see nothing in particular.'

'Count,' said Athos, 'in such a precarious situation as ours we should examine the earth and not the sky. Have you watched our Scotch allies, and can you depend on them?'

'The Scotch?' asked Winter, 'what Scotch?'

'Why ours, good heavens!' said Athos; 'those to whom the king is entrusted—the Scotch under the Earl of Leven.'

'No,' said Winter. Then he added, 'So you do not see as I do that reddish tint which covers the sky?'

'Not in the slightest degree,' said Athos and Aramis together.

'Tell me,' continued Winter, still preoccupied with the same idea, 'is it not a tradition in France that on the evening before the day on which Henry IV was assassinated, he was playing at chess with M. de Bassompierre and saw some spots of blood on the board?'

'Yes,' said Athos, 'the marshal has told me the story many times.'

'That is it,' murmured Winter; 'and the next day Henry IV was killed.'

'But what connection has this vision of Henry IV with you, Count?' asked Aramis.

'None, Messieurs; and in truth I am a fool to talk to you of such things when your entrance at this hour into my tent tells me that you bring important news.'

'Yes, my Lord,' said Athos, 'I should like to speak to the king.'

'To the king? but he is asleep.'

'I have some very important things to reveal to him.'

'Can they not be put off till tomorrow?'

'He ought to know them this very instant, and perhaps it is already too late.'

'Let us go then, Messieurs,' said Winter.

Winter's tent was pitched near the royal tent, and a sort of passage united the one to the other. This passage was guarded, not by a sentinel, but by a faithful valet, so that in urgent need the king could at the very instant communicate with his devoted follower.

'These gentlemen are with me,' said Winter.

The lackey bowed, and let them pass.

On a camp-bed, wearing his black doublet, his legs in long boots, his belt loosened, and his hat near him, King Charles, yielding to an irresistible need of rest, was fast asleep. The men advanced, and Athos, who went first, looked for a moment in silence on that pale, noble face, framed by his long black hair, which the perspiration of a troubled sleep had glued to his temples, marbled by large blue veins, which seemed swollen by tears under his wearied eyes.

Athos gave a deep sigh, which awakened the king, whose sleep was very light. He opened his eyes.

'Ah!' said he, rising up and leaning on his elbow, 'it's you, Comte de la Fère?'

'Yes, Sire,' replied Athos.

'You watch while I sleep; and you have come to bring me news?'

'Alas, Sire,' replied Athos; 'your Majesty has rightly guessed.'

'Ah! is the news bad?' said the king, with a melancholy smile.

'Yes, Sire.'

'No matter, the bearer is welcome; and you can never come to me without always giving me pleasure. You, whose devotion knows neither country nor misfortune, were sent to me by

Henrietta. Whatever may be the news you bring, speak with confidence.'

'Sire, M. Cromwell has this night arrived at Newcastle.'

'Ah! to do battle with me?'

'No, Sire; to buy you.'

'What do you say?'

'I say, Sire, that four hundred thousand pounds sterling are due to the Scotch army.'

'For arrears of pay; yes, I know. For nearly a year my faithful Scots have been fighting for honour alone.'

Athos smiled.

'Well, Sire, although honour is a fine thing, they are tired of fighting for it, and tonight they have sold you for two hundred thousand pounds; that is, the half of what is due to them.'

'Impossible!' exclaimed the king. 'The Scots sell their king for two hundred thousand pounds!'

'The Jews sold their Lord for thirty pieces of silver.'

'And who is the Judas who has made this infamous bargain?'

'The Earl of Leven.'*

'Are you sure of it, Monsieur?'

'I heard it with my own ears.'

The king uttered a profound sigh, as if his heart was breaking, and let his head fall into his hands.

'Oh, the Scots!' said he—'the Scots, that I called my faithful ones; the Scots, to whom I confided myself when I could have fled to Oxford; the Scots, my compatriots; the Scots, my brothers! But are you quite sure of it, Monsieur?'

'Lying behind the Earl of Leven's tent, the canvas of which I raised, I saw all, I heard all.'

'And when is this hateful bargain to be completed?'

'Today, in the morning. As your Majesty must see, there is no time to lose.'

'What shall I do—since you say I am sold?'

'You must cross the Tyne, reach Scotland, and join Lord Montrose,* who will not sell you.'

'And what could I do in Scotland? A mere partisan war? Such a war is unworthy of a king.'

'Robert Bruce's* example is there to absolve you, Sire.'

'No, no! I have struggled too long. If they have sold me, let them deliver me up, and may the eternal shame of their treason rest upon them!'

'Sire,' said Athos, 'perhaps a *king* ought to act in this way, but a husband and a father ought not. I have come in the name of your wife and daughter. And in their name and in that of two other children whom you have in London, I say to you, live, Sire; God wills it!'

The king rose, tightened his belt, girt on his sword, and wiping his forehead damp with perspiration, 'Ah, well!' said he, 'what must be done?'

'Sire, have you in the whole army one regiment on which you can rely?'

'Winter,' said the king, 'do you believe that yours is faithful?'

'Sire, they are only men; and men have become very weak, or very wicked. I believe in their fidelity, but I do not answer for it. I would confide my life to them, but I hesitate to entrust to them that of your Majesty.'

'Well,' said Athos, 'if a regiment be wanting, we are three devoted men; we shall be enough. Let his Majesty mount his horse, and put himself in our midst; we will cross the Tyne, reach Scotland, and we shall be saved.'

'Is that your advice, Winter?' the king asked.

'Yes, Sire.'

'Is it yours, M. d'Herblay?'

'Yes, Sire.'

'Let it be done then as you desire. Winter, give the orders.'

Winter went out. During this time the king finished dressing. The first rays of daybreak began to come in through the openings in the tent when Winter entered.

'All is ready, Sire,' said he.

'And we?' asked Athos.

'Grimaud and Blaisois hold your horses all saddled.'

'In that case,' said Athos, 'let us not lose an instant, but set off.'

'Let us set off,' said the king.

'Sire,' said Aramis, 'will not your Majesty inform his friends?'

'My friends?' said Charles, sorrowfully shaking his head; 'I have only you three—a friend of twenty years' standing who has never forgotten me; two friends of a week old whom I shall never forget. Come, Messieurs, come.'

The king left his tent, and found his horse ready. It was a dun-coloured horse which he had ridden for three years, and for which he had a great affection. The horse, on seeing him, neighed with pleasure.

'Ah,' said the king, 'I was unjust; there is one, which, if not a friend, is at least a creature that loves me. You will be faithful, will you not, Arthur?' And as if he had understood these words, the horse put his smoking nostrils to the face of the king, raising his lips and showing his white teeth joyously.

'Yes, yes,' said the king, stroking him with his hand; 'it is well, Arthur, and I am content with you.'

With that alacrity which made the king one of the best horsemen of Europe, Charles mounted into the saddle, and turning towards Athos, Aramis, and Winter, 'Well; Messieurs!' he said, 'I am awaiting you.'

But Athos was standing immovable, with his eyes fixed and his hand stretched towards a black line which followed the bank of the Tyne, and which extended double the length of the camp.

'What is that line?' said Athos, for the last darkness of the night struggling with the first beams of dawn did not yet permit him to see clearly—'what is that line? I did not see it yesterday.'

'It is without doubt the mist which rises from the river,' said the king.

'Sire, it is something more solid than vapour.'

'In fact, I see a sort of reddish barrier,' said Winter.

'It is the enemy, who are coming out of Newcastle to surround us,' exclaimed Athos.

'The enemy!' said the king.

'Yes, the enemy. It is too late. Stop! by the sun's ray, there at the side of the town, do you not see the gleam of the Ironsides?'* (The cuirassiers who formed Cromwell's guard were so called.)

'Ah,' said the king, 'we shall soon know if it be true that my Scots have betrayed me.'

'What are you going to do?' exclaimed Athos.

'To give them the order to charge, and force our way through these miserable rebels.' And the king, spurring his horse, dashed towards the tent of Lord Leven.

'Let us follow him,' said Athos.

'Let us go,' said Aramis.

'Has the king been wounded?' said Winter. 'I see on the ground some spots of blood;' and he dashed off on the track of the two friends.

Athos stopped him.

'Go and muster your regiment,' he said. 'I foresee that we shall need it presently.'

Winter turned round, and the two friends continued their way. In two seconds the king had reached the tent of the General-in-Chief of the Scotch army. He jumped off his horse, and entered. The general was in the midst of the principal chieftains.

'The king?' they exclaimed, rising and looking at him quite stupefied.

In fact, Charles stood before them, frowning, his hat on, and striking his boot with his riding-whip.

'Yes, gentlemen,' said he; 'the king in person! the king, who comes to ask an account of what has passed.'

'What is the matter then, Sire?' asked Lord Leven.

'It is, sir,' said the king, allowing himself to get into a great rage, 'that General Cromwell reached Newcastle last night; that you knew of it, and that I have not been informed of it. The enemy has left the town, and has closed the passage of the Tyne against us; your sentinels ought to have seen the movement. It is that you have, by an infamous treaty, sold me to the Parliament for two hundred thousand pounds; but of this treaty at least I have been informed. This is what is the matter, gentlemen; defend or exculpate yourselves, for I accuse you.'

'Sire,' stammered Lord Leven, 'your Majesty has been deceived by some false report.'

'I have seen with my own eyes the hostile army extending between me and Scotland,' said Charles; 'and I can almost say I have heard with my own ears the clauses of the treaty debated.' The Scottish chieftains looked at one another with a frown.

'Sire,' murmured Lord Leven, bowed down by shame—'Sire, we are ready to give you every proof.'

'I ask only one. Put the army in battle array, and let us march against the enemy.'

'That cannot be done, Sire,' said the earl.

'What! Cannot be done! and what prevents?' exclaimed Charles.

'Your Majesty knows well enough that there is a truce between us and the English army.'

'If there is, the English army has broken it by leaving the town contrary to the articles which contain this provision. Now, I tell you, you must force your way with me through this army, and re-enter Scotland; and if you do not, well! make your choice of the two names which bring men into the contempt or execration of other men—either you are cowards or you are traitors!'

The eyes of the Scots flashed fire, and as often happens on such an occasion, they passed from the extreme of shame to that of impudence, and two chieftains advanced, one on each side of the king. 'Well, yes,' they said; 'we have promised to deliver Scotland and England from him who for twenty-five years has been drinking the blood and gold of England and Scotland. We have promised, and we hold to our promises. Charles Stuart, you are our prisoner.'

And they both raised their hands to seize the king, but before their finger-tips had touched his person, both had fallen—one unconscious, the other dead. Athos had felled one to the earth with the butt of his pistol, and Aramis had run his sword through the body of the other. Then as Lord Leven and the other chiefs drew back, startled at this unexpected succour, coming as it were from heaven to him whom they thought their prisoner, Aramis and Athos led the king out of the perjured tent, and leaping on their horses, took their way at a gallop to the royal tent.

While going, they saw Winter at the head of his regiment. The king made a sign for him to follow them.

LVIII

THE four entered the tent. They had no plan; one must be made. The king sank into a chair.

'I am lost!' he said.

'No, Sire,' replied Athos; 'you are only betrayed.'

The king gave a deep sigh.

'Betrayed, betrayed by the Scots, among whom I was born, whom I have always preferred to the English! Oh, the wretches!'

'Sire,' said Athos, 'this is by no means the time for recriminations, but for showing yourself to be a king and a gentleman. Up, Sire, be stirring!—for you have at least three men here who will not betray you; you can set your mind at ease as to that. Ah, if only we were five!' murmured Athos, thinking of d'Artagnan and Porthos.

'What do you say?' asked Charles, getting up.

'I say, Sire, that there is only one other plan. My Lord de Winter answers for his regiment, or nearly so; don't let us cavil about the words. He will put himself at the head of his men. We will take our places at the side of your Majesty; we will make an opening in Cromwell's army, and reach Scotland.'

'There is another way,' said Aramis; 'let one of us assume the king's dress, and take his horse; while they were hotly pursuing him, the king might perhaps escape.'

'The advice is good,' said Athos; 'and if his Majesty be pleased to do one of us this honour, we shall be very grateful to him for it.'

'What do you think of this counsel, Winter?' said the king, while regarding with admiration these two men whose only thought was to draw on their own heads the dangers which threatened the king's.

'I think, Sire, that if there is a means of saving your Majesty, M. d'Herblay has just suggested it. I therefore very humbly beg your Majesty to make your choice promptly, for we have no time to lose.'

'But if I accept, it is death, or at least prison, for him who takes my place.'

'There is the honour of having saved his king!' exclaimed Winter.

The king looked at his old friend with tears in his eyes, detached the ribbon of the Order of the Holy Ghost,* which he wore in honour of the two Frenchmen who accompanied him, and put it round Winter's neck, who received kneeling this terrible mark of his sovereign's friendship and confidence.

'That is just,' said Athos; 'he has done longer service than we have.'

The king heard these words, and the tears returned to his eyes.

'Messieurs,' said he, 'wait a moment; I have a ribbon also to give each of you.' Then he went to a cupboard, in which his own Orders were locked up, and took out two ribbons of the Garter.

'These Orders cannot be for us,' said Athos.

'And why so, Monsieur?' asked Charles.

'These Orders are almost royal, and we are only simple gentlemen.'

'Pass in review all the thrones of earth, and find me more magnanimous hearts than yours. No, no! you do not render justice to yourselves, Messieurs; but I am here to render it to you. On your knees, Count.'

Athos knelt down. The king passed the ribbon from left to right, as was customary, and raising his sword, instead of the usual formula: 'I make you a knight; be brave, faithful, and loyal,' he said, 'You are brave, faithful, and loyal; I make you a knight, Monsieur the Count.'

Then turning towards Aramis, 'Now, it is your turn, Monsieur the Chevalier,' said he. And the same ceremony was gone over with the same words, while Winter, aided by squires, detached his cuirass, that he might be more easily mistaken for the king. Then, when Charles had finished the ceremony, he embraced them both.

'Sire,' said Winter, who, having before him an act of great devotion, felt all his strength and courage return to him again, 'we are ready.'

The king looked at the three gentlemen.

'So then we must flee?' he said.

'To flee through an army, Sire,' said Athos, 'is in all countries called making a charge.'

'I shall die, then, sword in hand,' said Charles. 'Monsieur the Count, Monsieur the Chevalier, if ever I am king——'

'Sire, you have already honoured us more than is fitting for simple gentlemen, so gratitude comes from us. But do not lose time, for we have already lost too much.'

The king then stretched out his hand to all three, exchanged hats with Winter, and went out. Winter's regiment was drawn up on a platform which overlooked the camp. The king, followed by his three friends, went towards this platform. The Scotch camp seemed at last to be awake; the men had left their tents and formed in line as if for battle.

'Do you see?' said the king; 'perhaps they are repentant, and are ready to march.'

'If so, Sire,' replied Athos, 'they will follow us.'

'Well!' said the king, 'what shall we do?'

'Let us reconnoitre the enemy's forces.'

The eyes of the little group were fixed at the same moment on that line which at daybreak they had taken for mist, but which the sun's early rays showed to be an army in order of battle. The air was soft and fresh, as is usual at early morn. The regiments, the standards, and even the colour of the uniforms and horses could be perfectly distinguished.

Then they saw on a little hill in advance of the enemy's front a short, heavy man, who was surrounded by some officers. He directed a glass at the group, including the king.

'Does this man know your Majesty personally?' asked Aramis.

Charles smiled. 'That man is Cromwell,' said he.

'Then lower your hat, Sire, lest he should perceive the change.'

'Ah!' said Athos, 'we have lost a deal of time.'

'Then,' said the king, 'give the order, and we are off.'

'You give it, Sire?' asked Athos.

'No; I appoint you my lieutenant-general.'

'Listen then, my Lord de Winter,' said Athos. 'Move off a little, Sire, I beg you; what we are going to say does not concern your Majesty.'

The king with a smile moved back a few paces.

'This is what I propose,' continued Athos: "that we divide the regiment into two squadrons. You will head one; his Majesty and ourselves will head the other. If nothing bars our passage, we will charge all together to force the enemy's line, and throw ourselves into the Tyne, which we must cross either by wading or swimming. If on the contrary, they interpose any obstacle on the road, you and your men will fight to the very last, while we and the king continue our route. Once arrived at the bank of the river, should they be three ranks deep, if your squadron does its duty, we shall succeed.'

'To horse!' said Winter and Athos; 'all is decided and arranged.'

'Then, Messieurs,' said the king, 'forward! and let us rally under the old cry of France—Montjoie and St Denis! The cry of England is now uttered by too many traitors.'

They mounted, the king on Winter's horse, and Winter on the king's horse; then Winter placed himself in the first rank of the first squadron, and the king, having Athos on his right and Aramis on his left, in the first rank of the second.

The whole Scotch army regarded these preparations with the impassibility and silence of shame. Several chieftains were now seen leaving the ranks, and breaking their swords.

'Come,' said the king, 'that's some consolation: they are not all traitors.'

At that moment Winter's voice was heard.

'Forward!'

The first squadron moved off; the second followed and descended the platform. A regiment of cuirassiers nearly equal in numbers formed behind the hill, and came at full speed before it. The king pointed out to Aramis and Athos what was passing.

'Sire,' said Athos, 'the case is foreseen; if Winter's men do their duty, that manœuvre will save instead of ruining us.'

Just then was heard, above all the din that the horses made in galloping and neighing, Winter's voice: 'Draw swords!' They came from the scabbards like flashes of lightning.

'Come, Messieurs,' said the king, elated by the din and sight—'come, Messieurs, draw swords!'

But only Athos and Aramis obeyed the order of which the king himself gave the example.

'We are betrayed!' said the king, in a low tone.

'Wait a moment,' said Athos; 'perhaps they did not recognize your Majesty's voice, and await the command from their officer.'

'Have they not heard the voice of their colonel! But see! look!' exclaimed the king, pulling up his horse very short and seizing the bridle of Athos's horse.

'Ah! cowards! ah, traitors!' they heard Winter exclaiming, while his men, quitting the ranks, dispersed over the plain.

Scarcely fifteen men were grouped around him, and awaited the charge of Cromwell's cuirassiers.

'Let us go and die with them!' said the king.

'Let *us* also!' cried Athos and Aramis.

'To me all who are loyal!' cried Winter.

The two friends heard, and set off at a gallop.

'No quarter!' cried out in French, in response to Winter, a voice which made them start.

As for Winter, he turned pale and as if petrified on hearing it. It came from a cavalier mounted on a magnificent black horse, who charged at the head of the English regiment, which in his ardour he had outstripped by ten paces.

'That is he!' murmured Winter, with fixed eye, and letting his sword hang by his side.

'The king! the king!' cried several voices, being deceived by the blue ribbon and dun horse of Winter; 'take him alive!'

'No, it's not the king!' exclaimed the cavalier; 'don't be deceived. You are not the king, Lord de Winter? Are you not my uncle?'

And at the same time, Mordaunt, for it was he, aimed his pistol at Winter. He fired, and the ball entered the old gentleman's breast, who made a bound on his saddle and fell back into Athos's arms, saying, 'The avenger!'

'Remember my mother!' growled Mordaunt, dashing by.

'You wretch!' cried Aramis, firing close at him as he passed by his side, but only the priming* went off.

At that moment the whole regiment fell upon the few who had held their ground, and the two Frenchmen were surrounded and pressed upon. Athos, after being sure that Winter was dead, let go the corpse, and drawing his sword, 'Come on, Aramis, for the honour of France!' said he.

And the two Englishmen who were nearest to the two gentlemen both fell mortally wounded. At the same instant a terrible hurrah arose, and thirty sword-blades glittered above their heads. All at once a man sprang forward from the midst of the English ranks, which he overthrew, rushed on Athos, caught him in his sinewy arms, and snatched away his sword, whispering to him, 'Silence; surrender! To yield to me is not to surrender.'

A giant had also seized Aramis by the wrists, who tried in vain to extricate himself from this formidable grip.

'Surrender!' he said to Aramis, looking hard at him. Aramis looked up; Athos turned.

'D'Art——' exclaimed Athos, whose mouth the Gascon closed with his hand.

'I surrender,' said Aramis, handing his sword to Porthos.

'Fire! fire!' cried Mordaunt, coming up to the group in which the two friends were.

'And why fire?' said the colonel; 'for all have surrendered.'

'It is the son of Milady,' said Athos to d'Artagnan.

'I recognized him.'

'It's the monk,' said Porthos to Aramis.

'I know it.'

At the same time the ranks opened. D'Artagnan held the bridle of Athos's horse and Porthos that of Aramis's. Each of them tried to lead his prisoner far away from the field of battle. This movement exposed the place where the body of Winter lay. With the instinct of hate, Mordaunt had found it and looked at it, leaning over on his horse with a hideous smile. Athos, although quite calm, put his hand to the holsters in which his pistols still were.

'What are you doing?' said d'Artagnan.

'Let me kill him.'

'Not a gesture that can make them believe you know him, or all four of us are lost.' d'Artagnan, then turning towards the young man, exclaimed, 'A fine prize! a fine prize, friend Mordaunt! We have each one; and they are Knights of the Garter—nothing less!'

'But,' exclaimed Mordaunt, looking at Athos and Aramis with bloodthirsty eyes, 'they are French, it seems to me?'

'I know nothing about that, upon my word. Are you French, Monsieur?' d'Artagnan asked Athos.

'I am,' the latter gravely replied.

'Well, my dear Monsieur, you're a prisoner to a compatriot.'

'But the king?' said Athos with anguish—'the king?'

D'Artagnan vigorously squeezed the hand of his prisoner, and said to him, 'Eh! we have him also!'

'Yes,' said Aramis, 'by an infamous act of treachery.'

Porthos tightly squeezed his friend's wrist, and said to him with a smile, 'Eh, Monsieur! War does as much by cleverness as by force. Look!'

In fact, they saw at that moment the squadron which ought to have protected the king going to meet the English regiment and surrounding the king, who was walking alone on foot in a large empty space. He appeared calm; but the perspiration ran down his cheeks, and he wiped his temples and lips with a handkerchief which showed stains of blood.

'There goes Nebuchadnezzar!'* exclaimed one of Cromwell's cuirassiers—an old Puritan whose eyes grew inflamed at the sight of him whom they styled the tyrant.

'Whom do you call Nebuchadnezzar?' said Mordaunt, with a grim smile. 'No, it is the king, Charles I—the good king who despoils his subjects to get their property.'

Charles raised his eyes towards the insolent man who thus spoke, but did not recognize him. However, the calm, devotional majesty of his face made Mordaunt hang down his head.

'Goodbye, Messieurs,' said the king to the two gentlemen, whom he saw, the one in d'Artagnan's hands and the other in those of Porthos. 'The day has been unfortunate; but it is not your fault, God be thanked. Where is my old friend, Winter?'

The two gentlemen turned their heads away, and said nothing.

'Where Strafford is!' said the harsh voice of Mordaunt.

Charles gave a start; the demon had struck home. Strafford was his constant source of remorse—the shadow of his days, the spectre of his nights.

The king looked around, and saw at his feet a corpse; it was the body of Winter. The king uttered no cry, nor did he shed a tear, only a more livid pallor spread over his face. He knelt down, raised Winter's head, kissed it on the forehead, and taking the ribbon of the Order of the Holy Ghost, which he had put round his neck, he put it religiously on his breast.

'Winter is killed, then?' asked d'Artagnan, fixing his eyes on the corpse.

'Yes,' said Athos; 'and by his nephew.'

'Well! this is the first of us who has passed away,' murmured d'Artagnan. 'May he rest in peace! he was a brave man.'

'Charles Stuart,' then said the colonel of the English regiment, advancing towards the king, who had just put on again the marks of royalty, 'will you give yourself up as prisoner?'

'Colonel Tomlinson,' said Charles, 'the king does not surrender; the man yields to force—that's all.'

'Your sword.'

The king took his sword, and broke it on his knee.

At this moment a riderless horse, covered with foam, his eye flaming, his nostrils open, ran up, and recognizing his master, stopped near him, neighing with joy; it was Arthur. The king smiled, caressed him with his hand, and lightly mounted into the saddle.

'Now, gentlemen,' said he, 'lead me where you intend.' Then turning round quickly, 'Wait,' said he; 'I fancy I saw Winter move. If he still lives, by all that you have that is sacred, do not abandon that noble gentleman.'

'Oh, don't distress yourself, King Charles,' said Mordaunt; 'the ball has pierced his heart.'

'Don't breathe a word, don't make a gesture, don't risk a look for me or for Porthos,' said d'Artagnan to his two friends; 'for Milady is not dead, and her soul lives in the body of that demon!' And the detachment took their way towards the town, leading the royal captive; but when halfway an aide-de-camp of General Cromwell brought the order to Colonel Tomlinson to conduct the king to Holdenby Castle.*

At the same time couriers set off in all directions to inform England and all Europe that King Charles Stuart was the prisoner of General Oliver Cromwell.

LIX

OLIVER CROMWELL

'ARE you coming to the general's?' said Mordaunt to d'Artagnan and Porthos; 'you know that he ordered you to do so after the action.'

'We are going first of all to put our prisoners in a safe place,' said d'Artagnan to Mordaunt. 'Do you know, Monsieur, that these are worth fifteen hundred pistoles each?'

'Oh, don't feel alarmed!' said Mordaunt, looking at them with a vain endeavour to repress his ferocity; 'my horse will guard them, and do it well. I can answer for them.'

'I shall guard them better myself,' replied d'Artagnan; 'besides, what is needed is either a strong room with sentinels, or their simple word of honour not to attempt to escape. I am going to give orders to that effect; then we shall have the honour of presenting ourselves to your general, and asking his orders for his Eminence.'

'You count, then, on starting soon?' asked Mordaunt.

'Our mission is finished; and nothing keeps us longer in England but the good pleasure of the great man to whom we have been sent.'

The young man bit his lips, and whispering to the sergeant, 'You will follow these men,' he said to him, 'and not lose them out of your sight; and when you know where they are lodged, return and await me at the town-gate.'

The sergeant signified his obedience. Then, instead of following the mass of the prisoners, who were being marched into the town, Mordaunt went towards the hill whence Cromwell had witnessed the battle, and where his tent had been pitched.

Cromwell had ordered that no one should be allowed to enter his presence; but the sentinel, who knew Mordaunt to be a most intimate friend of the general, thought the prohibition did not apply to the young man. The latter therefore drew aside the tent-canvas, and saw Cromwell seated before a table, his head buried in his hands, his back turned towards him.

Whether or not he heard Mordaunt's entrance, Cromwell did not turn round. Mordaunt remained standing at the entrance. At last, at the end of a second, Cromwell raised his gloomy face, and as if he felt instinctively that some one was there, he slowly turned his head.

'I said that I wanted to be alone!' he exclaimed when he saw the young man.

'They did not think that the order applied to me, sir; however, if you order me I am ready to leave you.'

'Ah, it's you, Mordaunt!' removing, as by force of will, the cloud which covered his eyes; 'as it is you, very well, stay.'

'I bring you my congratulations.'

'For what?'

'The capture of Charles Stuart. You are now the master of England.'

'I was much more so two hours ago.'

'How so, General?'

'England then needed me to capture the tyrant; but now he is captured. Have you seen him?'

'Yes, sir.'

'How did he bear his position?'

Mordaunt hesitated; but the truth seemed to force itself from his lips.

'With dignity and calmness.'

'What did he say?'

'Some words of farewell to his friends.'

'To his friends!' muttered Cromwell; 'he has some friends, then?' Then aloud, 'Did he defend himself?'

'No, sir; he was abandoned by all except three or four men.'

'To whom did he give up his sword?'

'He did not give it up; he broke it.'

'He did well; but instead of breaking it, he would have done better to use it with more effect.'

There was a short silence.

'The colonel of the regiment which served as the escort of the king—I mean Charles—was slain, I believe?' said Cromwell, looking straight at Mordaunt.

'Yes, sir.'

'By whom?'

'By me.'

'What was his name?'

'Lord de Winter.'

'Your uncle?' exclaimed Cromwell.

'My uncle! Traitors to England are no relatives of mine.'

Cromwell continued thoughtful a moment, looking at the young man; then with that deep melancholy which Shakespeare describes so well,* he said, 'Mordaunt, you are a dreadful servant.'

'When the Lord commands, one must not trifle with his orders. Abraham raised the knife over Isaac; and Isaac was his son.'

'Yes,' said Cromwell; 'but the Lord did not allow the sacrifice to be accomplished.'

'I looked around me,' said Mordaunt; 'and I did not see either goat or kid caught in the thickets of the plain.'

Cromwell bowed.

'You are strong among the strong, Mordaunt,' said he; 'and how did the Frenchmen behave?'

'Like brave men, sir.'

'Yes, yes,' murmured Cromwell; 'the French fight well. I think I saw them in the front rank.'

'They were.'

'After you, however.'

'It was not their fault, but that of their horses.'

Again there was a momentary silence.

'And the Scots?' Cromwell asked him.

'They kept their word, and did not stir.'

'The wretches!' murmured Cromwell.

'Their officers asked to see you, sir.'

'I have not the time! Are they paid?'

'Tonight they will be.'

'Let them return to their mountains and hide their shame, if their mountains are high enough for that; I have no further business with them, nor they with me. And now go, Mordaunt.'

'Before going, I have some questions to put you, and a request to make.'

'Of me?'

Mordaunt bowed.

'I come to you, my protector, my father, and ask you, master, are you satisfied with me?'

Cromwell looked at him with astonishment. The young man remained unmoved.

'Yes,' said Cromwell; 'you have done, since I have known you, not only your duty, but even more. You have been a faithful friend, a clever negotiator, and a good soldier.'

'You remember, sir, that I was the first who thought of treating with the Scots for the giving up of their king.'

'Yes, the thought came from you, it is true; I had not then carried my contempt for men so far as that.'

'Have I been a successful ambassador in France?'

'Yes; you have obtained from Mazarin what I asked.'

'Have I always ardently striven for your glory and your interests?'

'Too ardently, perhaps; that was what I was just now reproaching you for. But what are you leading to with all your questions?'

'To tell you, my Lord, that the moment has come when you can, with a word, recompense all my services.'

'Ah!' said Oliver, with a slight expression of contempt, 'that's true; I was forgetting that service merits reward, and that you have served me and are not yet recompensed.'

'Sir, I can be this very instant, and even beyond my wishes.'

'How is that?'

'I have the reward under my hand, and I almost grasp it.'

'And what is this reward?' asked Cromwell. 'Has one offered you gold? Do you ask a rank? Do you desire a government?'

'Sir, will you grant me my demand?'

'Let us see what it is, first.'

'Sir, when you have said to me, "You are to execute an order," have I ever answered you, "Let us see this order"?'

'If, however, your desire was impossible to be realized?'

'When you have had a desire and you have charged me with its accomplishment, have I ever answered, "It is impossible"?'

'But a demand formulated with so much preparation——'

'Ah, rest easy, sir,' said Mordaunt, with a simple expression; 'it will not ruin you.'

'Well,' said Cromwell, 'I promise to grant your demand so far as it lies in my power. Ask!'

'Sir, this morning two prisoners were taken; I ask you for them.'

'They have offered, then, a considerable ransom?'

'On the contrary, I believe they are poor, sir.'

'But perhaps they are your friends?'

'Yes,' exclaimed Mordaunt; 'they are very dear friends of mine, and I would give my life for theirs.'

'Well, Mordaunt,' said Cromwell, forming a better opinion of the young man—'well, I give them to you; I don't want even to know who they are. Do what you please with them.'

'Thanks, sir; my life henceforth belongs to you, and if I were to lose it I should still be your debtor. Thanks; you have just paid me handsomely for my services.'

And he threw himself at Cromwell's knees, and in spite of the efforts of the Puritan general, who did not wish, or at least pretended he did not, to let this almost royal homage be done him, took his hand and kissed it.

'What!' said Cromwell, holding him just as he was rising; 'no other recompense? Not money? not promotion?'

'You have given me all that's in your power, my Lord, and from henceforth I acquit you of the rest.'

And Mordaunt hurried from the general's tent with a joy which overflowed from heart and eyes.

Cromwell followed him with his eyes.

'He has killed his uncle!' he murmured. 'Alas! what men are my servants! Perhaps he who asks nothing, or seems to, has asked more in God's presence than those who retain the gold of the provinces and the bread of the unfortunate; no one serves for nothing. Charles, who is my prisoner, has still friends, perhaps, and I have none.' And he resumed with a sigh the reverie interrupted by Mordaunt.

LX

THE GENTLEMEN

WHILE Mordaunt went to Cromwell's tent, d'Artagnan and Porthos conveyed their prisoners to the house which had been assigned them in Newcastle for lodging. The injunction laid upon the sergeant by Mordaunt had not escaped the Gascon's notice; so with a look he had recommended the greatest caution to Athos and Aramis. They had therefore marched in silence by their vanquishers—a thing by no means difficult to do, each being occupied by his own thoughts.

If ever a man was astonished, it was Mousqueton when from the door-step he saw the four friends approaching, followed by the sergeant and ten men. He rubbed his eyes, not being able to decide whether he really saw Athos and Aramis, but at last was compelled to yield to the evidence. So he was about losing himself in exclamations when Porthos imposed silence on him by a look which allowed no discussion.

Mousqueton remained close to the door, awaiting an explanation of so strange a thing; what puzzled him above all was that the four friends had the air of no longer recognizing one another.

The house to which d'Artagnan and Porthos took Athos and Aramis was that in which they had stayed the night before, and which had been assigned to them by General Oliver Cromwell; it was the corner house, and had a sort of garden and stables at the back. The windows of the ground-floor, as is often the case in small provincial towns, were barred, so that they much resembled those of a prison. The two friends made their prisoners enter first, and remained at the door, after having ordered Mousqueton to take the four horses to the stable.

'Why do you not go in with them?' Porthos enquired.

'Because first,' replied d'Artagnan, 'I must see what this sergeant and his detachment want with us.'

The sergeant and his men took up a position in the little garden. D'Artagnan asked them what they wanted, and why they were there.

'We have had orders to help you guard the prisoners.'

Nothing could be said against that; but on the contrary it was a delicate attention for which it was necessary to show gratitude. D'Artagnan thanked the sergeant, and gave him a crown to drink the health of General Cromwell. The sergeant replied that Puritans did not drink, and put the money into his pocket.

'Ah!' said Porthos, 'what a dreadful day, my dear d'Artagnan!'

'What do you mean by that? Do you call that a dreadful day on which we have again met with our friends?'

'Yes; but under what circumstances?'

'It is true they are embarrassing; but no matter, let us go in, and try to see our position a little more clearly.'

'It is very perplexing,' said Porthos; 'and I see now why Aramis so strongly recommended me to choke that cursed Mordaunt.'

'Be silent, I pray you! and don't utter that name.'

'But,' said Porthos, 'I speak French, and they are English.'

D'Artagnan looked at Porthos with the surprise which a reasonable man cannot refuse to enormities of all sorts. Then as Porthos on his side looked at him without comprehending his astonishment, d'Artagnan pushed him, and said, 'Let us go in.'

Porthos went first; d'Artagnan carefully closed the door, and then heartily embraced his two friends. Athos seemed filled with sorrow. Aramis looked at Porthos and d'Artagnan without speaking; but his look was so expressive that d'Artagnan understood it.

'Do you wish to know how it happens that we are here? Ah, good heavens! it is easy to guess. Mazarin charged us to bring a letter to General Cromwell.'

'But how is it you are with Mordaunt?' said Athos; 'him whom I told you to distrust, d'Artagnan.'

'And whom I had recommended you, Porthos, to strangle?' said Aramis.

'Mazarin again. Cromwell had sent him as envoy to Mazarin; Mazarin sent us to Cromwell. There is a fatality in all this.'*

'Yes, you are right, d'Artagnan—a fatality which divides and destroys us. Therefore, my dear Aramis, let us talk no more about it, but prepare to submit to our fate.'

'Hang it, no!' said d'Artagnan. 'Let us, on the contrary, talk about it; for it was agreed, once for all, that we are a brotherhood, although of opposite parties.'

'Oh, yes, very opposite,' said Athos, smiling; 'for here I ask you what cause are you serving? Ah, d'Artagnan, see how the wretched Mazarin employs you! Do you know of what crime you have become guilty today? Of the king's capture, his ignominy, and death.'

'Oh, oh!' said Porthos; 'do you believe that?'

'You exaggerate, Athos,' said d'Artagnan; 'we do not believe it.'

'Ah, good heavens! we state the truth. For what do they arrest a king? When they wish to respect him as a master, they do not purchase him as a slave. Do you think Cromwell has paid two hundred thousand pounds to set the king on his throne again? My friends, they will kill him; be sure of that, and it is the least crime they can commit. It is better to behead than beat a king.'

'I do not say this is not possible,' said d'Artagnan; 'but what have we to do with it? I am here because I am a soldier, because I serve my superiors; that is, those who give me my pay. I have sworn to obey, and I obey; but you who have taken no oath, what cause do you serve?'

'The most sacred cause in the world,' said Athos—'that of misfortune, royalty, and religion. A friend, a wife, a daughter, honoured us by calling us to their aid. We have done our best for them, and God will take account of the will though the power was lacking. You look at things from another point of view, my friend. I do not turn you from it, but I blame you.'

'Oh, oh!' said d'Artagnan; 'and how, after all, does it concern me that M. Cromwell, who is an Englishman, should rebel against his king, who is Scotch? *I* am a Frenchman; these things do not concern me. Why, then, should you make me responsible for them?'

'Yes, indeed,' said Porthos.

'Because all gentlemen are brothers. You are a gentleman, and kings of all countries are the first among gentlemen. Because the blind and ungrateful populace always delight in bringing down what is higher; and it is you—you, d'Artagnan, the man of high birth, good name, and of great bravery, who have helped to hand over a king to sellers of beer, tailors, and wagoners! Ah, d'Artagnan, as a soldier you have perhaps done your duty, but as a gentleman you are culpable. I tell you so.'

D'Artagnan was chewing a flower-stalk, and did not reply, feeling ill at ease—for when he turned his eyes from Athos, he met the eyes of Aramis.

'And you, Porthos,' continued the count, as if he had pity on d'Artagnan's embarrassment—'you, the kindest-hearted man, the best friend, the best soldier that I know; you whose soul made you worthy of being born on the steps of a throne, and who sooner or later will be recompensed by an intelligent king—you, my dear Porthos, you, a gentleman by manners, tastes, and courage, are as culpable as d'Artagnan.'

Porthos blushed, but from pleasure more than confusion; and lowering his head as if he felt humiliated, 'Yes, yes,' he said; 'I think you are right, my dear count.'

Athos rose. 'Come,' said he, going to d'Artagnan and extending his hand to him—'come, do not sulk, my dear son, for all that I have said to you I have told you, if not with the voice, at least with the heart of a father. It would have been easier for me, believe me, to thank you for having saved my life, and not to have uttered a single word of my sentiments.'

'Without doubt, without doubt, Athos,' replied d'Artagnan, pressing his hand in his turn; 'but it is also a fact that you have devilish sentiments which everyone cannot have. Who could imagine that a reasonable man would leave his home, France, his ward, a charming young man—for we have seen him in camp—to run where? To the aid of a rotten and worm-eaten royalty,* which will crumble one of these days like an old barrack? The sentiments that you express are fine, so fine that they are superhuman.'

'Whatever they may be, d'Artagnan,' replied Athos, without falling into the snare that with his Gascon address his friend had spread for his paternal affection for Raoul—'whatever they may be, you know well at the bottom of your heart that they are just; but I am wrong to discuss with my master. D'Artagnan, I am your prisoner; treat me then as such.'

'Ah, *pardieu!*' said d'Artagnan, 'you know well enough you will not be long *my* prisoner.'

'No,' said Aramis; 'we shall be treated, doubtless, like those who were made prisoners at Philiphaugh.'*

'And how were they treated?' asked d'Artagnan.

'Why,' said Aramis, 'one half was hanged, and the other half shot.'

'Well, *I* will answer for it that as long as a drop of blood flows in my veins you will be neither hanged nor shot. *Sangdiou!** let them try it. Do you see that door, Athos?'

'Well?'

'Well! you shall go out by that door when you like, for from this very moment, you and Aramis are as free as the air.'

'I recognize you well in this, my brave d'Artagnan,' replied Athos; 'but you are no longer our master. That door is guarded, you know well enough.'

'Well, you will force it open,' said Porthos. 'What is there to prevent it? Ten men at the outside.'

'That would be nothing for us four, but too much for us two. No; divided as we now are, we must perish. See the fatal example: on the road to the Vendômois, Porthos so valiant and strong, and d'Artagnan so brave, you were both beaten; this time, Aramis and I must take our turn. Now, that never happened when we four were united. Let us die, like Winter; for my part, I declare I will not consent to flee unless we four do so together.'

'Impossible,' said d'Artagnan; 'we are under Mazarin's orders.'

'I know it, and will not press it further; since my reasoning has had no effect, doubtless it was unsound, since it has not won over minds as reasonable as our own.'

'And besides, should it have succeeded,' said Aramis, 'we could not have compromised two excellent friends like d'Artagnan and Porthos. Don't be disturbed, Messieurs, we will die honourably; as for me, I feel quite proud of meeting the balls, or even the rope, with you, Athos, for you have never appeared so great as today.'

D'Artagnan said nothing; but after having chewed the flower-stalk, he bit his fingers.

'You imagine,' he replied at last, 'that you are going to be slain? Why should they kill you? What would they gain by your death? Besides, you are our prisoners.'

'Fool, triple fool!' said Aramis; 'don't you know Mordaunt? Well; I have exchanged one look with him, and I saw in that that we were condemned.'

'The fact is, I am sorry that I did not strangle him as you advised me, Aramis,' replied Porthos.

'Ah! I don't care for that Mordaunt!' exclaimed d'Artagnan. 'Hang it all! if he come buzzing too near me, I will crush him—the insect! Don't escape, then; it is useless—for I take my oath you are as safe here as you were twenty years ago—you, Athos, in the Rue Férou, and you, Aramis, in the Rue de Vaugirard.'*

'Stop,' said Athos, pointing towards one of the two barred windows which gave light to the room, 'you will know presently what you have to expect, for there he is coming this way.'

'Who?'

'Mordaunt.'

In fact, d'Artagnan saw Mordaunt coming at a gallop. D'Artagnan hurried out of the room. Porthos was going to follow him.

'Stop,' said d'Artagnan, 'don't come till you hear me play with my fingers on the door.'

LXI

THE LORD OUR SAVIOUR

WHEN Mordaunt reached the front of the house, he saw d'Artagnan at the door, and the soldiers lying here and there, with their arms on the grass-plot in the garden.

'Holloa!' he cried, with a voice hoarse from the haste with which he came, 'the prisoners are all safe there?'

'Yes, sir,' said the sergeant, rising up quickly, as well as the men, who all saluted him.

'Well. Four men to take them at once to my lodging!'

Four men got ready.

'What is your pleasure?' said d'Artagnan, with that bantering air which our readers must have seen many times in him; 'what is it, if you please?'

'It is, Monsieur,' said Mordaunt, 'that I have ordered four men to take to my lodging the prisoners captured this morning.'

'And why so?' d'Artagnan asked. 'Pardon the curiosity; but you comprehend that I desire to be enlightened on this subject.'

'Because the prisoners are mine now,' replied Mordaunt, haughtily; 'I can dispose of them as I please.'

'Excuse me, my young Monsieur,' said d'Artagnan; 'you are wrong, it seems to me. Prisoners generally belong to those who have captured them. You might have taken my Lord de Winter, who was your uncle, so they say; but you have preferred to kill him. We, M. du Vallon and myself, could have killed these two gentlemen; but we preferred capturing them. Everyone to his taste.'

Mordaunt's lips became white. D'Artagnan saw that matters would soon be in a worse state, and began to tap the march of the Guards on the door. Porthos came out and placed himself at the other side of the door, of which his feet touched the step and his head the top. The manœuvre did not escape Mordaunt's notice.

'Monsieur,' said he, with an anger which began to appear, 'you would make a useless resistance; these prisoners have just been given me by the General-in-Chief, M. Oliver Cromwell.'

D'Artagnan was struck by these words as by a clap of thunder. The blood mounted to his temples; a cloud passed before his eyes. He comprehended the bloodthirsty hope of the young man, and his hand went instinctively to his sword-hilt. As for Porthos, he looked at d'Artagnan to know what he ought to do, and to rule his movements by his friend's. This look of Porthos disquieted more than reassured d'Artagnan; and he reproached himself for having invited Porthos's brute force in a matter which it seemed to him should be carried on by cunning.

'Violence,' said he to himself, 'would ruin us all. D'Artagnan, my friend, prove to this young serpent that you are not only stronger, but also more cunning, than he.'

'Ah!' said he, making a profound bow, 'what a pity you did not begin by saying so, M. Mordaunt! So you come in the name of M. Oliver Cromwell, the most illustrious general of these days?'

'I left him this very instant,' said Mordaunt, dismounting, and giving his horse to a soldier to hold.

'Why did not you tell me that at once, my dear Monsieur?' continued d'Artagnan. 'All England belongs to M. Cromwell; and since you have just demanded these prisoners in his name, I yield, Monsieur. They are yours; take them.'

Mordaunt gladly stepped forward, and Porthos, thunderstruck, and looking at d'Artagnan with a profound stupor, was about to speak. D'Artagnan trod on his comrade's boot; and Porthos then saw that his friend was playing a deep game. Mordaunt put his foot on the first step, and with hat in hand was ready to pass between the two friends, making a sign for the four men to follow him.

'But, I beg pardon,' said d'Artagnan, with a charming smile, and putting his hand on the young man's shoulder, 'if the illustrious general, Oliver Cromwell, has given you these prisoners, he has attested this deed of gift by some writing.'

Mordaunt stopped short.

'He has given you some little letter for me, the least scrap of paper, indeed, which attests that you come in his name. Kindly entrust me with this scrap that it may serve at least as a pretext for deserting my compatriots. Otherwise, you comprehend, although I am sure that General Cromwell does not wish them any harm, it would have a very bad effect.'

Mordaunt drew back, and feeling the blow, sent a terrible look at d'Artagnan; but the latter replied by a most amiable and friendly smile.

'Do you doubt me?' said Mordaunt, angrily.

'I!' exclaimed d'Artagnan—'*I* doubt what you say? On the contrary, I regard you as a worthy and accomplished gentleman, judging by appearances. And then, Monsieur, do you wish me to speak frankly?' he added with an open smile.

'Speak, Monsieur.'

'M. du Vallon is a rich man. He has an income of forty thousand francs, and consequently does not need money; I therefore speak not for him, but only for myself.'

'What then, Monsieur?'

'Well, I am not rich. This is no dishonour in Gascony; everyone there is poor, and Henry IV of glorious memory, who was king of the Gascons, had never a sou in his pocket.'

'Finish, Monsieur—I see what you are driving at; and if it is what I think it is, the difficulty can easily be removed.'

'Ah, I knew very well that you were a clever fellow. Well, here's the fact. Here's where the shoe pinches, as we Frenchmen say: I am an officer who has risen by merit—nothing else; I have what my sword brings me, that is to say, more blows than bank-notes. Now, when this morning I took two Frenchmen who seemed of high birth—two Knights of the Garter, in short—I said to myself, my fortune is made. I say two, because in such circumstances M. du Vallon, who is rich, would give his prisoner up to me.'

Mordaunt, completely deceived by d'Artagnan's wordy frankness, smiled as one who wonderfully comprehends the reasons given him, and replied mildly, 'I shall have the order signed presently, Monsieur, and with it I shall have two thousand pistoles; but meanwhile, Monsieur, let me take these men away.'

'No,' said d'Artagnan; 'what does a quarter of an hour's delay matter to you? Let us do these things according to rule.'

'Yet,' replied Mordaunt, 'I could force you, Monsieur. I command here.'

'Ah, Monsieur,' said d'Artagnan, smiling pleasantly, 'I can see well enough that though M. du Vallon and I have had the honour of travelling in your company, you do not know us. We are able to kill you and your eight men. For God's sake, M. Mordaunt, do not play the obstinate man—for when anyone is obstinate, I am obstinate also, and then I become of a ferocious stubbornness; and here is Monsieur,' continued d'Artagnan, 'who in that case is more stubborn still and much more ferocious than I; not to add that we were sent by M. le Cardinal Mazarin, who represents the King of France, so that we in our character as ambassadors are inviolable—a thing which M. Oliver Cromwell is quite able to understand. Ask him therefore for the written order. What will that cost you, my dear M. Mordaunt?'

'Yes, a written order,' said Porthos, who began to understand d'Artagnan's meaning; 'we ask only that.'

Whatever desire Mordaunt might have had to use force, he regarded the reasons given him by d'Artagnan as good ones. Besides, d'Artagnan's reputation made an impression upon him, and what he had seen him do that morning coming to the aid of his reputation, he reflected. Being completely ignorant of the deep friendship which existed between these four French-men, all his anxiety had disappeared in face of the very plausible motive of getting the ransom.

He resolved then to go not only to get the order, but also the two thousand pistoles at which he had himself estimated the value of the two prisoners.

Mordaunt therefore remounted his horse, and having charged the sergeant to keep a strict guard, he turned round and was off.

'Good!' said d'Artagnan; 'a quarter of an hour to go to the tent, another to return, is more than we need.' Then returning to Porthos, without allowing his face to show the least change, 'Friend Porthos,' he said, 'listen well to this—first, not a single word to our friends of what you have just heard; it is useless that they should know the service we are doing them.'

'Well,' said Porthos, 'I understand.'

'Go to the stable; you will find Mousqueton there. You will saddle the horses, put the pistols into the holsters, and bring the horses into the street round the corner, in order that there may be nothing else to do but to mount. The rest concerns myself.'

Porthos did not make the least observation, but obeyed with that truly sublime confidence which he had in his friend.

'I am going,' said he; 'only do me the favour of getting my purse, which I have left on the chimney.'

'Very well.'

Porthos went calmly towards the stable, and passed through the soldiers, who could not help admiring his great height and

sinewy limbs, Frenchman though he was. At the corner of the
street he met Mousqueton, whom he took with him.

Then d'Artagnan went in, whistling an air that he had begun
when Porthos left him.

'My dear Athos, I have been reflecting on your arguments,
and am convinced. I decidedly regret being mixed up in this
whole affair. You have said that Mazarin is a vulgar pedant. I
have therefore resolved to fly with you. Now, no observations.
Be ready. Your two swords are in the corner; don't forget them,
for they are tools which in our circumstances may be very
useful—that reminds me of Porthos's purse. Good! here it is.'

And d'Artagnan put the purse in his pocket.

The two friends looked at him with astonishment.

'Well, what is there, I ask, astonishing in this? I was blind;
Athos has made me see clearly, that's all. Come here.'

The two friends drew near.

'Do you see that street? There you will find the horses. Go
out and turn to the left; mount your horses, and all is said.
Don't be disquieted about anything except listening for the signal.
This will be when I cry out, "The Lord our Saviour!" '

'But your word of honour that you will come, d'Artagnan,'
said Athos.

'I take my oath that I will.'

'It is agreed,' exclaimed Aramis; 'at the cry of "The Lord
our Saviour!" we go out, we overthrow everything that bars
our passage, we run to our horses, we leap into the saddle and
put the spur to the horses. Is that it?'

'Exactly.'

'You see, Aramis,' said Athos; 'I always told you d'Artagnan
was the best of us all.'

'Good!' said d'Artagnan; 'you are paying compliments. I run
away. Adieu!'

'And you will fly with us, will you not?'

'I think so, indeed. Don't forget the signal: "The Lord our
Saviour".' And he went out at the same pace as he had entered,
resuming the air that he was whistling when he went in.

The soldiers were playing or sleeping; two were singing out
of tune in a corner the psalm, 'By the waters of Babylon',* etc.

D'Artagnan called the sergeant.

'My dear Monsieur,' he said to him, 'General Cromwell has sent for me by M. Mordaunt; kindly guard the prisoners.'

The sergeant signified that he did not understand French. Then d'Artagnan tried to make him comprehend by signs what he had not understood by words. D'Artagnan went down to the stable; he found the five horses saddled, his own among the rest.

'Each of you lead a horse,' said he to Porthos and Mousqueton; 'turn to the left so that Athos and Aramis may see you clearly from their window.'

'They intend to come, then?' said Porthos.

'In an instant.'

'You have not forgotten my purse?'

'No; it's all right.'

'Good.'

And Porthos and Mousqueton, each holding a horse, went to their posts. Then d'Artagnan, now alone, struck a light, lighted a piece of touchwood no bigger than a pea, got on his horse, and pulled up in the midst of the soldiers before the door. Then, while stroking the animal he introduced the little piece of burning touchwood into the horse's ear. There was need to be a first-rate horseman, as d'Artagnan was, to risk such a means, for scarcely had the animal felt the burning stuff than he gave a cry of distress, and kicked and pranced as if mad. The soldiers, whom he nearly ran over, quickly got out of the way.

'Here, here!' cried d'Artagnan. 'Stop, stop! my horse has the staggers.'* In fact, in an instant the blood appeared to come out of the animal's eyes, and he became white with foam. 'Help!' d'Artagnan continued calling, without the soldiers venturing to his aid. 'Help! will you let me be killed? The Lord our Saviour!'

Scarcely had d'Artagnan uttered this cry than the door opened, and Athos and Aramis dashed out sword in hand. But thanks to d'Artagnan's trick, the road was clear.

'The prisoners are escaping! the prisoners are escaping!' cried the sergeant.

'Stop, stop!' cried d'Artagnan, giving the furious horse his head, who sprang forward, upsetting two or three men.

'Stop, stop!' cried the soldiers, running for their arms.

But the prisoners were already in saddle, and lost no time in dashing towards the nearest gate. In the street they saw Grimaud and Blaisois, who were returning in search of their masters. By a sign Athos explained matters to Grimaud, who followed the small troop, which flew like a whirlwind, while d'Artagnan, who was in the rear, urged them on with his voice. They passed through the gate like shadows, without the guards thinking even of stopping them, and were soon in the open country.

During this time the soldiers kept calling out, 'Stop! stop!' and the sergeant, who began to see that he had been duped, tore his hair. While all this was going on, they saw a cavalier coming at a gallop, holding a paper in his hand. It was Mordaunt returning with the order.

'The prisoners?' he cried, leaping off his horse.

The sergeant had not the strength to reply; he pointed to the open door and the empty room. Mordaunt dashed up the steps, understood all, uttered a piercing cry, and fell fainting on the stone.

LXII

IN WHICH IS PROVED THAT IN THE MOST TRYING CIRCUMSTANCES BRAVE MEN NEVER LOSE THEIR COURAGE, NOR HUNGRY ONES THEIR APPETITE

THE little troop, without exchanging a word or looking behind, went along at a fast gallop, fording a little river whose name none of them knew, and leaving at their left a city which Athos claimed was Durham. At last they saw a wood, and gave a last stroke of the spur while going in the direction of it.

When they had disappeared behind a curtain of verdure sufficiently thick to hide them from the view of any who might be pursuing, they stopped to hold council. They gave their horses to the two servants, that they might take breath without being unsaddled, and they stationed Grimaud as sentinel.

'First, let me embrace you, my friend,' said Athos to d'Artagnan; 'you have saved us. You are the true hero among us.'

'Athos is right, and I admire you,' said Aramis, in his turn pressing him in his arms; 'to what should you not lay claim, with an intelligent master, an infallible eye, arm of steel, conquering spirit?'

'Now, that's all very well,' said the Gascon. 'I accept for myself and Porthos your embraces and thanks; but we have no time to lose—come! come!'

The two friends, reminded by d'Artagnan of what they also owed to Porthos, pressed in turn his hand.

'Now,' said Athos, 'we must not trust to chance like fools, but we must decide on a plan. What are we going to do?'

'What are we going to do, *mordioux!* It is not difficult to say.'

'Say it, then, d'Artagnan.'

'We must gain the nearest seaport,' said d'Artagnan, 'unite all our small resources, charter a ship, and cross over to France. As for me, I shall spend even to my last sou. The first treasure is life; and ours, we must admit, only holds by a thread.'

'What do you say, Vallon?' Athos asked.

'I?' said Porthos; 'I am quite of the same opinion as d'Artagnan. This England is a villainous country.'

'You are quite decided on leaving it, then?' asked Athos.

'Good heavens!' said d'Artagnan; 'I don't see what should keep me here.'

Athos exchanged looks with Aramis.

'Go then, my friends,' said he, with a sigh.

'What! go?' said d'Artagnan. 'Let us all go, it seems to me.'

'No, my friend,' said Athos; 'you must leave us.'

'Leave you!' said d'Artagnan, quite stunned by this piece of unexpected news.

'Bah!' said Porthos; 'why leave you, then, since we are again together?'

'Because *your* mission is done, and you can and ought to return to France, but *ours* is not.'

'Your mission is not accomplished?' said d'Artagnan, looking at Athos with surprise.

'No, my friend,' said Athos, in a mild yet firm voice. 'We came to defend King Charles. We have badly defended him; it remains for us to save him.'

'Save the king!' exclaimed d'Artagnan, looking at Aramis as he had at Athos.

Aramis simply nodded his head. d'Artagnan's face assumed an air of deep compassion; he began to think he had to do with two men out of their senses.

'You cannot be speaking seriously, Athos. The king is in the midst of an army, which is taking him to London. This army is commanded by a butcher, or the son of one, no matter which—Colonel Harrison. His Majesty will be put on trial on reaching London, I answer for it. I have heard sufficient from M. Cromwell's mouth to know what to rely upon.'

Athos and Aramis exchanged a second look.

'And the trial finished, judgment will not delay being put into execution.'

'And to what punishment do you think the king will be condemned?' asked Athos.

'I am afraid that it will be death; they have done too much against him for him to pardon them. They have but one resource left; that is, to kill him. Don't you know the saying of M. Oliver Cromwell when he came to Paris, and they showed him the prison of Vincennes where M. de Vendôme was confined.'

'What is this saying?' asked Porthos.

'One should strike princes only at the head.'*

'I know it,' said Athos.

'And do you think that he will not put his maxim into execution, now that he holds the king?'

'That is the greater reason for not abandoning the august head thus threatened.'

'Athos, you are becoming a fool.'

'No, my friend,' he mildly replied; 'but Winter came to France to seek us. He introduced us to Madame Henrietta; her Majesty honoured M. d'Herblay and myself by asking our aid for her husband. We gave our word of honour that we would give it. That included everything—our strength, intelligence, our life, in short. We must keep our word. Is this your opinion, d'Herblay?'

'Yes,' said Aramis, 'we gave our promise.'

'Then,' continued Athos, 'we have another reason, and here it is; listen well: Everything is poor and mean in France at this time. We have a king of ten years of age who does not know yet what he wishes; we have a queen whom a belated passion renders blind; we have a minister who rules France as he would a vast farm—that is to say, preoccupying himself only with what will bring in gold, and working for it with Italian intrigue and cunning; we have princes who make a personal and ego- tistic opposition, who will accomplish nothing except to draw from the hands of Mazarin some ingots of gold, some bribes of power. I have served them, not from enthusiasm—God knows that I estimate them for what they are worth, and that they are not very high in my esteem—but from principle. Today it is another affair. Today I meet on my route a great misfortune, a royal misfortune, an European misfortune; I attach myself to its cause. Thus,' continued Athos, 'if we succeed in saving the king, it will be a fine thing; if we die for him, it will be grand!'

'So you know beforehand that you will perish?' said d'Ar- tagnan.

'We fear it; and our only grief is to die far from you.'

'What can you do in a foreign, hostile land?'

'When young I travelled in England. I speak English like an Englishman, and Aramis has some acquaintance with the lan- guage. Ah, if we had you, my friends! We four, reunited for the first time after twenty years, would be able to bear up against not only England, but the three kingdoms.'*

'And have you promised this queen,' replied d'Artagnan, crossly, 'to capture the Tower of London; to kill a hundred thousand soldiers; to struggle victoriously against the will of a nation and the ambition of a man, when that man is called Oliver Cromwell? Athos and Aramis, you have neither of you seen this man. Well, he is a man of genius, who has much reminded me of our cardinal—the other, the great one!* you remember. Do not exaggerate your duties, then. In Heaven's name, my dear Athos, do not perform a useless act of self- devotion! When I look at you, in truth, it seems to me that I see a reasonable man; when you reply it seems as if I had to do with a fool. Come, Porthos, what do you think of this affair? Speak frankly.'

'Nothing good,' said Porthos.

'See,' continued d'Artagnan, impatient because Athos, instead of listening to him, seemed to listen to a voice speaking within himself; 'you have never come out badly after following my counsels. Well; believe me, Athos, your mission is terminated, nobly terminated. Return with us into France.'

'Friend,' said Athos, 'our resolution is not to be shaken.'

'But you have some other motive that we do not know.'

Athos smiled.

D'Artagnan struck his thigh with anger, and murmured the most convincing reasons he could find; but to them all Athos contented himself with answering by a calm, sweet smile, and Aramis by signs of his head.

'Ah, well,' exclaimed d'Artagnan, furious at last, 'since you wish it, let us leave our bones in this blackguard country, where it is always cold, where fine weather is mist, mist is rain, the rain a deluge; where the sun resembles the moon, and the moon cheese *à la crème*. In fact, to die here or die elsewhere, since we must die, concerns us little.'

'Only think of it,' said Athos, 'dear friend; it is to die sooner.'

'Bah! a little sooner or a little later, that is not worth the trouble of cavilling about.'

'If I am surprised at anything,' said Porthos, sententiously, 'it is that that has not already happened.'

'Oh! that will happen, rest assured, Porthos,' said d'Artagnan. 'Thus it is agreed,' continued the Gascon; 'and if Porthos does not oppose——'

'I?' said Porthos, 'I will do what you wish. Besides, I very much admire what the Comte de la Fère said just now.'

'But your future, d'Artagnan? Your ambitions, Porthos?'

'Our future, our ambitious desires!' said d'Artagnan, with a feverish volubility; 'have we any need to bother about that, since we are saving the king? The king saved, we will collect his friends, will beat the Puritans, reconquer England, re-enter London with him, fix him firmly on his throne——'

'And he will make us dukes and peers,' said Porthos, whose eyes sparkled with joy, even in seeing this future through a fable.

'Or he will forget us,' said d'Artagnan.

'Oh! said Porthos.

'Oh, yes; that has happened, friend Porthos. We formerly rendered a good service to Queen Anne which was not much less than that we wish to do for Charles I, yet the queen has forgotten us for nearly twenty years.'

'Well, in spite of that,' said Athos, 'are you sorry for having done her that service?'

'No, in faith,' said d'Artagnan; 'and I confess also that even in my worst humours I have found comfort in the recollection.'

'You see clearly, d'Artagnan, that princes are often ungrateful, but that God is never so.'

'Hold, Athos,' said d'Artagnan; 'I believe if you should meet the Devil on earth, you would manage him so well that you would bring him back with you to heaven.'

'So then?' said Athos, giving his hand to d'Artagnan.

'So then, it is agreed upon. I find England a charming country, and I will remain here, but on one condition.'

'What is it?'

'That I am not forced to learn English.'

'Well, now,' said Athos triumphantly, 'I swear to you, my friend, by the God who hears us, by my name, that I believe is without stain, I believe there is a Power who watches over us, and I have the hope that we four shall see France again.'

'So be it,' said d'Artagnan; 'but I confess that I have an entirely contrary conviction.'

'This dear d'Artagnan,' said Aramis, 'he represents among us the opposition of the parliaments, which always says No, and always acts Yes.'

'Yes; but which, meanwhile, saves the country,' said Athos.

'Ah, well! now all is decided,' said Porthos, rubbing his hands, 'suppose we think about dinner. It seems to me that in the most critical situations in our life we have always dined.'

'Oh, yes; talk now of dinner in a country where they eat boiled mutton at every feast, and where at every entertainment they drink beer! How the devil did you come into such a country, Athos? Ah, pardon!' added he, smiling, 'I was forgetting that you are no longer Athos. But no matter, let us now see your plan for dinner, Porthos.'

'My plan!'

'Yes; have you a plan?'

'No; I have an appetite, that's all.'

'*Pardieu!* if it is only that, I also have an appetite; but that is not all, we must find something to eat, and at least browse the grass like our horses——'

'Ah!' said Aramis, who was not so entirely detached from earthly things as Athos, 'when we were at Parpaillot, do you recollect the fine oysters we ate?'

'And those legs of mutton of the salt-pits!' said Porthos, drawing his tongue across his lips.

'But,' said d'Artagnan, 'have we not our friend Mousqueton, who made you live so well at Chantilly,* Porthos?'

'In fact,' said Porthos, 'we have Mousqueton; but since he is steward he has grown very heavy. No matter, let us call him.'

And to be sure that he answered agreeably, 'Hi, Mouston!' cried Porthos.

Mousqueton appeared, but with a very piteous face.

'What's the matter now, my dear M. Mouston?' said d'Artagnan. 'Are you ill?'

'Monsieur, I am very hungry.'

'Ah, well, that's the very reason why we called you. Could you not catch with a snare some of those nice rabbits and some of those tender partridges with which you made the *ragoûts* and *salmis* at the Hotel of—faith, I've forgotten its name—and with a string some of those bottles of old Burgundy which healed your master so quickly of his sprain?'

'Alas, Monsieur, I am afraid all you ask for is very scarce in this frightful country, and we should do better to ask hospitality from the master of a small house on the edge of the wood.'

'What! is there a house hereabouts?' enquired d'Artagnan.

'Yes, Monsieur,' replied Mousqueton.

'Well, my friend, let us go and ask the master of the house to let us dine there. Messieurs, what do you say of it?'

'Eh!' said Aramis; 'suppose the master is a Puritan?'

'So much the better!' said d'Artagnan; 'we will give him news of the king's capture, and in honour of that event he will give us his white fowls.'

'But if he is a Cavalier?' said Porthos.

'In that case we will assume an air of mourning, and we will pick his black fowls.'

'You are a happy fellow,' said Athos, smiling in spite of himself at the sally of the uncontrollable Gascon, 'for you see everything in a droll light.'

'What would you have? I was born where there is not a cloud in the sky.'

'It is not as in this country,' said Porthos, stretching out his hand to assure himself that a feeling of freshness which he had just felt upon his cheek was really caused by a drop of rain.

'Come on, then; the greater reason for our moving on. Holloa, Grimaud!'

Grimaud appeared.

'Have you seen anything, my friend?' asked d'Artagnan.

'Nothing,' replied Grimaud.

'Those imbeciles,' said Porthos, 'they have not even pursued us. Oh, if we had been in their places!'

'Eh! they were wrong,' said d'Artagnan; 'I would willingly have said two words to Mordaunt in this little Thebais.* See what a nice place to lay a man neatly on the ground.'

'Decidedly,' said Aramis, 'I think, Messieurs, that the son has not the energy of the mother.'

'Eh, dear friend!' replied Athos; 'wait then—we have left him scarcely two hours; he does not know yet in what direction we are going, he is ignorant of where we are. We will say that he is less strong than his mother when we set our feet on the soil of France, if from now till then we are neither killed nor poisoned.'

'Then let us get dinner,' said Porthos.

'In faith, yes,' said Athos, 'for I am very hungry.'

'Let the black fowls look out!' said Aramis.

And the four friends, led by Mousqueton, walked towards the house, being already almost restored to their old unconcern—for they were again all reunited and harmonious,* as Athos had said.

LXIII

As they drew nearer the house, our fugitives saw the ground trodden up as if a considerable troop of cavaliers had preceded them. Before the door the marks were still plainer; this troop, whatever it might have been, had made a halt there.

'Ah!' said d'Artagnan, 'the thing is clear; the king and his escort have passed this way.'

'The devil!' said Porthos; 'then everything will have been eaten.'

'Bah!' said d'Artagnan, 'they will have left a fowl, surely,' and he got off his horse and knocked at the door; but no one answered. He pushed open the door, which was not fastened, and saw that the first room was empty.

'Well?' asked Porthos.

'I see no one,' said d'Artagnan. 'Ah, ah!'

'What?'

'Some blood.'

On hearing this the three friends dismounted and entered the first room; but d'Artagnan had already entered the second, and from the expression of his face, it was clear that he saw some extraordinary object. The three friends drew near, and saw a man, still young, stretched on the floor bathed in a pool of blood. They saw that he had tried to get to the bed, but not having strength enough, had fallen before reaching it. Athos was the first to approach the unfortunate man; he thought he saw him move slightly.

'Well?' asked d'Artagnan.

'Well!' said Athos, 'if he is dead, it is quite recently, for the body is still warm. But no, his heart still beats. Ah, my friend!'

The wounded man gave a sigh; d'Artagnan filled his hand with water, and threw it on his face. The man opened his eyes, tried to raise his head, and then fell back. Athos then tried to take him upon his knee, but he perceived that the wound was a little above the cerebellum, and had split the skull; the blood flowed from it freely. Aramis dipped a towel in water, and applied it to the wound, which was a fracture of the skull. The wounded man opened his eyes a second time. He looked with astonishment at these men, who seemed to pity him, and who, as much as they were able, tried to give him help.

'You are with friends,' said Athos, in English, 'don't be uneasy; and if you have strength tell us what has happened.'

'The king is a prisoner,' murmured the wounded man.

'Have you seen him?' Aramis asked him, in English.

The man made no answer.

'Be at your ease; we are faithful servants of his Majesty,' said Athos.

'Is what you say true?' the wounded man asked.

'On the honour of a gentleman.'

'Then I can tell you?'

'Speak.'

'I am the brother of Parry,* the *valet de chambre* of his Majesty.'

Athos and Aramis recollected that that was the name by which Winter had addressed the servant in the corridor of the royal tent.

'We know him,' said Athos; 'he never left the king.'

'Yes,' said the wounded man. 'Well, on seeing the king captured, he thought of me. They had to pass this house; he asked them to stop here in the king's name. The request was granted. The king, they said, was hungry; they let him enter the room in which I now am to take his food, and sentinels were posted at the doors and windows. Parry knew that in this room there was a trap-door which led to the cellar, and that from this cellar the orchard could be reached. He gave me a sign which I understood. But the sign was doubtless observed by the king's guardians, and put them on their guard. Ignorant that they suspected anything, I had only one desire—that of saving his Majesty. I made a pretence of going out to get some wood, thinking that no time was to be lost. I entered the subterranean passage leading to the cellar; I raised the board with my head, and while Parry quietly bolted the door, I made a sign to the king to follow me. Alas! he did not wish to do so, but Parry besought him; so at last he decided on following me. I went along by good fortune in front, the king a few paces behind, when all of a sudden I saw, as it were, a great shadow erect before me. I wanted to warn the king, but had not time; I felt a blow as if the house were falling on my head, and fell down unconscious.'

'Good and loyal Englishman! faithful servant!' said Athos.

'When I came to myself I was lying in the same place. I crawled to the yard; the king and his escort had gone. It took me perhaps an hour to get here; but my strength failed, and I fainted the second time.'

'And now how do you feel?'

'Very badly,' said the wounded man.

'Can we do anything for you?' Athos asked.

'Help me to get on the bed; that will relieve me, I think.'

'Have you any one who can help you?'

'My wife is at Durham, and I expect her back every moment. But do you not need anything?'

'We had come with the intention of asking for something to eat.'

'Alas! they have taken everything; there is not even a crust of bread in the house.'

'Do you hear, d'Artagnan? We must go and seek a dinner elsewhere.'

'That's no matter to me now,' said d'Artagnan; 'I don't feel hungry any longer.'

'Upon honour, neither do I,' said Porthos; and they lifted the man on the bed.

They made Grimaud come and dress the wound. Grimaud had many a time had occasion to make lint and bandages, so that he possessed a little knowledge of surgery.

Meanwhile the fugitives had returned to the front room, and were consulting.

'Now,' said Aramis, 'we know what to rely upon. It is clear that the king and his escort have passed this way; we must take the opposite direction. Is that your opinion, Athos?'

Athos did not reply; he was reflecting.

'Yes,' said Porthos, 'let us take the opposite direction. If we follow the escort, we shall find everything devoured, and shall at length die of hunger. What a cursed country this England is! It is the first time I have lost my dinner. Dinner is my best meal.'

'What do you think, d'Artagnan?' said Athos. 'Are you of Aramis's opinion?'

'Not at all,' said he; 'but quite the contrary.'

'What! do you want to follow the escort?' said Porthos, alarmed.

'No, but to join them.'

Athos's eyes lighted up with joy.

'To join the escort!' exclaimed Aramis.

'Let d'Artagnan speak; you know that he is a man of good counsel,' said Athos.

'Without doubt,' said d'Artagnan, 'we must go where they will not look for us. Now, they will be sure not to think of looking for us among the Puritans; let us therefore go with these.'

'Very well, my friend, very well! excellent advice!' said Athos. 'I was going to give it myself when you forestalled me.'

'It is also your advice?' asked Aramis.

'Yes, they will think we want to leave England, and will seek for us in the ports; meanwhile, we shall reach London with the king. When once in London, we shall not be discoverable; in the midst of a million of inhabitants it will not be difficult to hide ourselves. Without counting,' continued Athos, throwing a look at Aramis, 'the chances which this journey offers us.'

'Yes,' said Aramis, 'I comprehend.'

'But I do not comprehend it,' said Porthos, 'but no matter; since this advice is that of both d'Artagnan and Athos, it must be the best.'

'But,' said Aramis, 'shall we not be looked upon with suspicion by Colonel Harrison?'

'Why, bless my soul!' said d'Artagnan, 'it is exactly upon him that I reckon. He is one of our friends. We have seen him twice at General Cromwell's; he knows that we were sent from France by M. de Mazarin. Besides, is he not the son of a butcher?* Well, Porthos will show him how an ox can be knocked down by a blow of the fist, and I know how to upset a bull by taking him by the horns; that will win his confidence.'

Athos smiled.

'You are the best companion I am acquainted with, d'Artagnan,' said he, giving his hand to the Gascon, 'and I am very happy to have found you again, my dear son.' This was, as we know, the name Athos gave d'Artagnan in his outbursts of tenderness.

At that moment Grimaud came out of the room. The wound was dressed, and the man was better. The four friends took leave of the wounded man, and asked him if he had any message to send by them to his brother.

'Tell him to let the king know that they have not killed me entirely; though I am of little consequence, yet I am sure his Majesty would reproach himself for being the cause of my death.'

'Let your mind be at rest,' said d'Artagnan; 'he shall know it before the evening.'

The little troop resumed their march; they could not mistake the road, because the one they wished to follow was visible right across the plain. At the end of two hours' march in silence, d'Artagnan, who was in front, stopped at a turning of the road.

'Ah, ah!' he said; 'there are the people we want.'

In fact, a considerable troop of horsemen appeared about half a league from them.

'My dear friends,' said d'Artagnan, 'give up your swords to M. Mouston, who will return them at a fitting time and place, and do not forget that you are our prisoners.'

Then they urged on their horses, which were beginning to be tired, and they soon came up to the escort. The king, placed in front, and surrounded by a part of Colonel Harrison's regiment, was going along unmoved, always dignified, and with a sort of resigned readiness.

On perceiving Athos and Aramis, to whom he had not even had time to say good-bye, and on seeing by the looks of these two gentlemen that he still had some friends near him, although he believed them to be prisoners, a blush of pleasure rose to the king's pallid cheeks.

D'Artagnan gained the head of the column, and leaving his friends under the guard of Porthos, went straight to Harrison, who remembered having seen him at Cromwell's, and received him as politely as a man of his condition and character could receive anyone. What d'Artagnan had foreseen was the case; the colonel neither had, nor was likely to have, any suspicion.

A halt was made for the purpose of getting dinner; only this time precautions were taken to prevent any attempt of the king at escape. In the large room of the inn a small table was laid for him, and a large one for the officers.

'Will you dine with me?' Harrison asked d'Artagnan.

'*Diable!* It would give me great pleasure,' said he; 'but I have my companion, M. du Vallon, and my two prisoners, whom I cannot leave, and all these would crowd your table. But let us do better; have a table laid in the corner, and send us what you please from yours, for without that we run a great risk of dying from hunger. That will be dining together, since we shall dine in the same room.'

'Let it be so,' said Harrison.

The thing was arranged as d'Artagnan wished; and when he came back to the colonel, he found the king already seated at the small table, and waited on by Parry. Harrison and his officers were to dine together; and in a corner places were reserved for d'Artagnan and his companions.

The table where the Puritan officers were seated was round; and by chance or gross design Harrison turned his back to the king. The king saw the four gentlemen enter, but did not appear to notice them. They went and seated themselves at the table reserved for them, so as not to turn their backs upon any one. They had in front of them the table of the officers and that of the king.

Harrison, to do honour to his guests, sent them the best dishes from his table; unfortunately for the four friends, wine was wanting. This seemed quite indifferent to Athos; but the other three made a grimace every time they swallowed the beer—that Puritan drink.

'Upon my word, Colonel,' said d'Artagnan, 'we are very grateful to you for your gracious invitation, for without you we ran the risk of losing our dinner, as we lost our breakfast; and there's my friend, M. du Vallon, who also shares my gratitude, for he was very hungry.'

'I am still hungry,' said Porthos, saluting Colonel Harrison.

'And how came this sad event about, then—your. going without breakfast?' asked the colonel, laughing.

'From a very simple cause, Colonel,' said d'Artagnan. 'I was in haste to catch up with you; and to do so I took the same route as you, which such an old quartermaster as I am ought not to have done. For I ought to have known that where a good and brave regiment like yours has passed, nothing remains to be gleaned. So you understand our disappointment, when on arriving at a pretty little house at the edge of a wood, and which from a distance, with its red roof and green shutters,* had a little air of fête which gave us pleasure to see, instead of finding some fowls for roasting and some ham for grilling, we saw only a poor wretch weltering in blood——Ah, Colonel, pay my compliments to the officer of your regiment who gave that blow; it was well given, so well that it drew the admiration of M. du Vallon, who can give blows genteelly.'

'Yes,' said Harrison, laughing, and directing his eyes towards an officer seated at the table; 'when Groslow takes charge of that duty, there is no need to go after him.'

'Ah! it was Monsieur,' said d'Artagnan, saluting the officer; 'I regret that Monsieur does not speak French, that I might make him my compliments.'

'I am ready to receive and return the compliment, Monsieur,' said the officer, in pretty good French, 'for I lived three years in Paris.'

'Well, Monsieur, I hasten to tell you that the blow was so well given that you almost killed your man.'

'I thought I had killed him outright,' said Groslow.

'No; he was very nearly dead, it is true, but not quite.'

And while saying this, d'Artagnan threw a look at Parry, who was standing up before the king, his face as pale as death, to tell him that this news was for him. As for the king, he had listened to the whole of this conversation with his heart full of inexpressible anguish, for he did not know what the French officer was aiming at, and these cruel details, hidden under an appearance of carelessness, were revolting to him. At the last words only did he breathe freely.

'Ah, the devil!' said Groslow, 'I thought I had succeeded better. If it were not so far from here to the house, I would return to finish the wretch.'

'And you would strike hard if you feared that he would recover,' said d'Artagnan, 'for you know when wounds on the head do not kill at once, they get well in a week.'

And d'Artagnan shot another glance at Parry, on whose face such a joyous expression appeared that Charles, smiling, stretched his hand towards him. Parry bent over the hand, and respectfully kissed it.

'Truly, d'Artagnan,' said Athos, 'you are at the same time a man of your word and a man of wit. But what do you say of the king?'

'His countenance pleases me thoroughly,' said d'Artagnan; 'he has an air at once noble and good.'

'Yes, but he allowed himself to be taken prisoner,' said Porthos; 'that was wrong.'

'I have a great desire to drink to the health of the king,' said Athos.

'Then let me give the toast,' said d'Artagnan.

'Do it,' said Aramis.

Porthos regarded d'Artagnan all amazed at the resources which his Gascon wit was constantly furnishing to his comrade.

D'Artagnan then took the pewter cup, filled it, and rose.

'Messieurs,' said he to his companions, 'let us drink, if you please, the health of him who presides at the repast. To our colonel, and let him know we are quite at his service to London and further.'

And as, while saying these words, d'Artagnan looked at Harrison, the latter thought that the toast was for him; so he rose and bowed to the four friends, who with their eyes directed towards King Charles drank together, while Harrison emptied his glass without any distrust.

Charles, in his turn, held out his glass to Parry, who poured a little beer into it—for the king had the same fare as every one else—and raising it to his lips, looking towards the four gentlemen, he drank with a smile full of nobleness and gratitude.

'Now, gentlemen,' exclaimed Harrison, putting down his glass, and without any regard for his illustrious prisoner, 'let us continue our journey.'

'Where shall we put up for the night, Colonel?'

'At Thirsk,'* he replied.

'Parry,' said the king, rising and turning towards his valet, 'my horse; I want to go to Thirsk.'

'In faith,' said d'Artagnan to Athos, 'your king has in truth won me over, and I am entirely at his service.'

'If what you say is sincere,' Athos replied, 'he will never reach London.'

'Why not?'

'Why, before then we shall have carried him off.'

'Ah! this time, Athos,' said d'Artagnan, 'on my word of honour, you are a fool.'

'Have you, then, some plan arranged?' asked Aramis.

'Eh!' said Porthos, 'the thing would not be impossible if we had a good plan.'

'I have none,' said Athos; 'but d'Artagnan will find one.'

D'Artagnan shrugged his shoulders, and they set off.

LXIV

D'ARTAGNAN FINDS A PLAN

ATHOS knew d'Artagnan better perhaps than the latter knew himself. He knew that in an adventurous spirit like that of the Gascon the main thing is to let fall a thought, as letting a seed fall into a rich, vigorous soil is the only thing needed.

He had then quietly left his friend to shrug his shoulders, and continued his way, talking to him of Raoul; a topic which he had under other circumstances allowed to drop, as we remember.

At nightfall they reached Thirsk. The four friends seemed completely indifferent to the precautionary measures for the custody of the king. They withdrew to a private house; and as they had from moment to moment cause to fear for themselves, they established themselves in one room, arranging a means of egress in case of attack. The servants were assigned to different posts. Grimaud slept on a truss of straw before the door.

D'Artagnan was thoughtful, and seemed to have lost for the time his usual loquacity. He did not say a word; he kept incessantly whistling, going from his bed to the window. Porthos, who never saw anything except external things, talked as usual. D'Artagnan replied in monosyllables. Athos and Aramis looked at each other smiling.

The day had been fatiguing; and yet, with the exception of Porthos, whose sleep was as unchangeable as his appetite, the friends slept badly. The next morning d'Artagnan was the first up. He had gone to the stables, had seen to the horses, and had already given the necessary orders before Athos and Aramis were up, and while Porthos was still snoring.

At eight the march began in the same order as the evening before; only d'Artagnan allowed his friends to make the journey together, while he went to renew his acquaintance with Mr Groslow. The latter, whose heart had been won by the praises bestowed on him, received d'Artagnan with a gracious smile.

'In truth, Monsieur,' d'Artagnan said to him, 'I am pleased to find some one with whom to converse in my poor language. M. du Vallon, my friend, is of so melancholy a disposition that one can only draw from him four words a day; as for our two prisoners, you can easily understand that they are not in a mood for much conversation.'

'They are desperate Royalists,' said Groslow.

'The more reason why they should be angry with us for having taken the Stuart, whom, I greatly hope, you are going to bring to trial.'

'Of course,' said Groslow; 'we are taking him to London for that very purpose.'

'And you don't mean to lose him out of your sight, I expect?'

'Hang it! I should think not! You see,' added the officer, laughing, 'he has a truly royal escort.'

'Yes, there is no danger of his escaping you during the day; but at night——'

'The precautions are doubled.'

'And what kind of surveillance do you make use of?'

'Eight men remain constantly in his room.'

'The devil! he is well guarded, then. But besides these men, you doubtless place a guard outside? One cannot use too many precautions with such a prisoner.'

'Oh, no. Just think! what could two men without arms do against eight armed men?'

'How do you mean *two* men?'

'Why, the king and his valet.'

'His valet has permission, then, to be always with him?'

'Yes, Stuart has asked this favour, and Colonel Harrison yielded it. Under the pretext of being king, he cannot dress or undress himself.'

'In truth, Captain,' said d'Artagnan, to continue this system of laudation, which had so far succeeded so well, 'the more I listen the more I am astonished at the easy, elegant manner with which you speak French. You have lived in Paris three years, that's well; but I should live in London all my life, and should not arrive, I am sure, at the point where you are. What did you do then at Paris?'

'My father, who is in trade, placed me with his correspondent, who in return sent his son to my father; it is the custom among merchants to make such exchanges.'

'And did Paris please you, Monsieur?'

'Yes. But you have great need of a revolution like ours; not against your king, who is but a child, but against that stingy Italian, who is your queen's lover.'

'Ah, I am of your opinion, Monsieur; and that this would be soon done, if we only had a dozen officers like you, without prejudices, vigilant, intractable. Ah! we would soon come to the end of Mazarin's reign, and we would bring a fine prosecution against him, like that you are going to bring against your king.'

'But,' said the officer, 'I thought you were in his service, and that it was he who sent you as envoy to General Cromwell?'

'That is to say, I am in the king's service, and knowing that he was going to send someone to England, I asked for the mission, so great was my desire to know the man of genius who at this moment rules the three kingdoms. So when he proposed to M. du Vallon and myself that we should draw our swords in honour of Old England, you have seen how we jumped at the proposal.'

'Yes; I know that you charged by the side of M. Mordaunt.'

'At his right and left, Monsieur. Hang it! what a brave young man he is! How he settled matters with Monsieur his uncle! Did you see that?'

'Do you know him?'

'Well, I can even say that we are very intimate; M. du Vallon and myself came with him from France.'

'It seems that you kept him waiting a long while at Boulogne.'

'How could it be helped? I was like you—I had a king to guard.'

'Ah, ah!' said Groslow; 'what king?'

'Ours, of course! the little king—Louis XIV;' and d'Artagnan took off his hat. The Englishman did so also from politeness.

'And how long did you guard him?'

'Three nights; and upon my word I shall always recall them with pleasure.'

'Is the young king very amiable?'

'The king! he was sleeping soundly.'

'But then what do you mean?'

'I mean that my friends the officers of the Guards and of the Musketeers came to keep me company, and that we passed the nights in drink and play.'

'Ah, yes!' said the Englishman, with a sigh, 'that's true; you Frenchmen are jolly companions.'

'Do not you play in this way when on guard?'

'Never!' said the Englishman.

'In that case you must become very wearied; and I pity you.'

'The fact is that I see my turn come with a certain dread—to watch a whole night is very tedious.'

'Yes, when one watches alone, or with stupid soldiers; but when one watches with a gay partner, and rolls the gold and the dice on a table, the night goes like a dream. Do you like games at cards—*lansquenet*,* for example?'

'I am absurdly fond of it; I used to play at it nearly every evening in France.'

'And since you have been in England?'

'I have not touched a dice-box nor a card.'

'I pity you,' said d'Artagnan, with a look of deep compassion.

'Listen; do this,' said the Englishman.

'What?'

'Tomorrow I am on guard.'

'Over the Stuart?'

'Yes; come and pass the night with me.'

'Impossible.'

'Impossible?'

'Altogether impossible.'

'How is that?'

'Every night I play with M. du Vallon. Sometimes we do not go to bed. This morning, for example, we were still playing at daylight.'

'Well?'

'Well, he would get low-spirited if I did not play with him.'

'Is he a good player?'

'I have seen him lose up to two thousand pistoles, while laughing enough to crack his sides.'

'Bring him, then.'

'How do you mean? How about the prisoners?'

'Ah, the devil! that's true. Make your servants guard them.'

'Yes, for them to escape!' said d'Artagnan. 'I have no guard.'

'These, then, are men of good standing, since you hold them so fast?'

'Rather! One is a rich lord of Touraine; the other is a Knight of Malta* of high family. We have treated for their ransom; each to pay two thousand pounds sterling on reaching France. We do not wish, then, to leave a single moment these men whom our lackeys know to be millionaires. We have stripped them a little on capturing them; and I will even confess to you that it is their purse that M. du Vallon and I are drawing on every night. But they may have concealed from us some precious stone, some diamond of value; so we are like misers who do not leave their treasures. We have constituted ourselves permanent guardians of our men; and when I sleep, M. du Vallon watches.'

'Ah, ah!' said Groslow.

'You see now what compels me to refuse your polite offer, for which I am all the more thankful because nothing is more wearisome than always playing with the same person; chances keep so equal that at the end of a month one finds he has neither gained nor lost.'

'Ah!' said Groslow, with a sigh, 'there is something still more wearisome, and that is not playing at all.'

'I understand that.'

'But come,' resumed the Englishman, 'are these men dangerous?'

'In what respect?'

'Are they likely to attempt making their escape?'

D'Artagnan burst out laughing.

'Good Heavens!' he exclaimed, 'a sort of fever makes one of them tremble, as he is not able to get used to your charming country; the other is a Knight of Malta, as timid as a girl, and for greater security we have taken from them even their knives and pocket scissors.'

'Well,' said Groslow; 'bring them.'

'What! Do you wish it?'

'Yes, I have eight men. Four will guard them, and four the king.'

'In fact, then, the matter can be settled in that way, although I am giving you a good deal of trouble.'

'Bah! come all the same; you shall see how I will arrange.'

'Oh, I am not disturbing myself about it,' said d'Artagnan; to a man like you I would give myself up blindfolded.'

This last bit of flattery drew from the officer one of those chuckling laughs of satisfaction which make friends of those who called them forth, for they are an outcome of tickled vanity.

'But,' said d'Artagnan, 'now I think of it, what prevents us from beginning tonight?'

'What?'

'Our game.'

'Nothing in the world,' said Groslow.

'Well, then, come this evening to us; and tomorrow we will return the visit. If anything in our men disquiets you, they being, as you know, very disconsolate Royalists, well, no harm will have been done, and it will be simply a night well passed.'

'Capital! This evening at your quarters, tomorrow at Stuart's, the day after at mine.'

'And the other days in London. Ah!' said d'Artagnan, 'you see plainly that one can lead a jolly life everywhere.'

'Yes, when one falls in with Frenchmen, and Frenchmen like you.'

'And like M. du Vallon; what a merry soul you will find him!—a desperate Frondeur, a man who nearly killed Mazarin between two gates. He is employed because they fear him.'

'Yes, he has a fine figure; and without knowing him, he pleases me entirely.'

'It will be another thing when you know him. Eh! hold; there he is calling me! Pardon, we are so intimate that he cannot do without me. You excuse me?'

'How, then?'

'Till this evening.'

'At your quarters.'

'At our quarters.'

The two men exchanged salutes, and d'Artagnan returned to his companions.

'What had you to say to that bull-dog?' said Porthos.

'My dear friend, don't speak so ill of M. Groslow; he is one of my most intimate friends.'

'One of your friends!' said Porthos, 'this slayer of peasants!'

'*Chut!* my dear Porthos. Well, yes, M. Groslow is a little passionate, it's true; but at bottom I have discovered in him two good qualities—he is a fool, and proud.'

Porthos opened his great eyes wide with astonishment; Athos and Aramis looked at each other with a smile. They knew that d'Artagnan did nothing without an end in view.

'But,' continued d'Artagnan, 'you will appreciate him for yourself.'

'How so?'

'He is coming this evening to play cards with us.'

'Oh, oh!' said Porthos, whose eyes brightened up at that; 'and is he rich?'

'He is the son of one of the greatest merchants in London.'

'And can he play at *lansquenet*?'

'He adores it.'

'At *basset* and *biribi*?'*

'He is mad over them.'

'Good!' said Porthos; 'we shall pass a pleasant night.'

'The more pleasant because it promises us a better one to come.'

'How so?'

'Yes, he is to play this evening with us; tomorrow we are to play with him.'

'Where will that be?'

'I will tell you by-and-by. Now we must think of one thing only—how to receive worthily the honour which M. Groslow does us. We halt this evening at Derby; let Mousqueton get the start of us, and if there is a bottle of wine to be had there, let him buy it. There will be no great harm if he prepares a little supper, in which you will not take part, because, Athos, you have the fever, and because you, Aramis, are a Knight of Malta, and the wild talk of soldiers like us displeases you and makes you blush. Do you understand this well?'

'Yes,' said Porthos; 'but the devil take me if I can make it out.'

'Porthos, my friend, you know that I am descended from the prophets on my father's side, and from the sibyls* on my mother's, so that I speak in parables and riddles; let those who have ears listen, and let those who have eyes look. I cannot say more at present.'

'Do not,' said Athos; 'I am sure that what you do is well done.'

'And you, Aramis, are you of the same opinion?'

'Entirely, my dear d'Artagnan.'

'Already,' said d'Artagnan, 'I have true believers; and it is a pleasure to work miracles for them. They are not like this unbeliever Porthos, who always wants to see and touch before believing.'

'The fact is,' said Porthos, with a shrewd look, 'I am very incredulous.'

D'Artagnan gave him a slap on the shoulder, and as they reached then the place for breakfast, the conversation stopped.

Towards five in the afternoon, as had been agreed, they sent Mousqueton on in advance. He could not speak English, but he had noticed that Grimaud, by his practice of signs, had quite replaced conversation by means of them. He had therefore set himself to study gestures with Grimaud, and in a few lessons, thanks to the superiority of the master, he had arrived at a certain degree of success. Blaisois went with him.

The four friends, when passing along the High Street of Derby, saw Blaisois standing at the door of a fine-looking house; there the preparations had been made.

During the whole day they had not approached the king for fear of causing suspicion, and instead of dining at Colonel Harrison's table, as they had done the previous evening, they dined by themselves.

At the appointed hour Groslow came. D'Artagnan received him as if he had been a friend of twenty years' standing. Porthos measured him from head to foot, and smiled on observing that notwithstanding the remarkable blow which Groslow had given Parry's brother, he himself was superior to Groslow in strength. Athos and Aramis did what they could to hide the disgust with which this brutal nature inspired them. In short, Groslow seemed satisfied with his reception.

Athos and Aramis played their parts. At midnight they retired into their chamber, the door of which they left open under pretence of good-will. Besides, d'Artagnan accompanied them, leaving Porthos playing with Groslow.

Porthos gained fifty pistoles from Groslow, and found, when the latter had retired, that he was a more agreeable companion than he had at first thought him. As for Groslow, he promised to himself to repair next day the check he had received from Porthos; and he left the Gascon, reminding him of the meeting in the evening. We say the evening, for the players did not leave till four in the morning.

The day passed as usual; d'Artagnan went from Captain Groslow to Colonel Harrison, and from the latter to his friends. To anyone who did not know d'Artagnan, he seemed to be in his ordinary condition, but to his friends, Athos and Aramis, his gaiety was feverish.

'What can he be plotting?' said Aramis.

'Let us wait,' said Athos.

Porthos said nothing; he only counted in his pocket, one after the other, with an air of satisfaction which betrayed itself in his face, the fifty pistoles he had won from Groslow.

On reaching Ryston* in the evening, d'Artagnan assembled his friends. His face had lost that look of careless gaiety which he had worn as a mask the whole day. Athos pressed Aramis's hand.

'The time is drawing near?' he said.

'Yes,' said d'Artagnan, who had overheard the remark—'yes, the time approaches; tonight, Messieurs, we shall save the king.'

Athos trembled; his eyes flamed up.

'D'Artagnan,' said he, doubting after having hoped, 'this is not a mere joke, is it? It would do me much harm.'

'You are a strange fellow, Athos, to doubt me thus. When and where have you seen me jesting with a friend's affection and a king's life? I have told you, and I repeat it, that this night we shall save Charles I. You have relied on me to find a way; the way is found.'

Porthos looked at d'Artagnan with a feeling of deep admiration; Aramis smiled as one who hopes; Athos was pale as death, and trembled all over.

'Speak,' said Athos.

Porthos opened his great eyes. Aramis hung, so to speak, upon the lips of d'Artagnan.

'We are invited to pass the night with M. Groslow, you know.'

'Yes,' replied Porthos, 'he made us promise him to let him have his revenge.'

'Well, he will do so in the king's apartments.'

'Where the king will be?' exclaimed Athos.

'Yes, Messieurs. M. Groslow is the guard of his Majesty this evening; and to amuse him during his duty, he invites us to keep him company.'

'All four?' asked Athos.

'Yes, certainly; all four. Can we leave our prisoners?'

'Ah, ah!' ejaculated Aramis.

'Let us see,' said Athos, panting.

'You are going then to Groslow; we with our swords, you with poniards. We will overmaster those eight fools and their stupid commander. M. Porthos, what do you say about it?'

'I say that it's easily done.'

'We will dress up the king in Groslow's clothes; Mousqueton, Grimaud, and Blaisois will have our horses ready saddled round the first street; we will mount, and before day we shall be twenty leagues from here. Ay! will this plot do, Athos?'

Athos put his hands on d'Artagnan's shoulders, and looked at him with his calm, soft smile.

'I declare, my friend, that you have no equal under heaven for nobleness and courage; while we were thinking you indifferent to our griefs, you alone found what we were vainly seeking. I repeat it, then, d'Artagnan, you are the best of us all; and I bless and love you, my dear son.'

'The idea that I should not find that out!' said Porthos, striking himself on the forehead, 'it is so simple.'

'But,' said Aramis, 'if I understand rightly, we must kill them all; is it not so?'

Athos shuddered, and became very pale.

'Confound it!' said d'Artagnan, 'it really will be necessary. I have tried for a long while to find a way to avoid this, but I confess I have not been able.'

'Come,' said Aramis, 'it is not a question of hesitating about the situation. How are we to proceed?'

'I have a double plan,' replied d'Artagnan.

'Let us hear the first,' said Aramis.

'If we are all four together, at my signal, which shall be the words, *at last*, you two will each stab the man nearest you, while we will do the same on our side. Here, then, will be four dead; we shall be then equal-sided, four against their five. These will surrender and be gagged, or if they resist, we will kill them; but should our entertainer change his opinion and receive only Porthos and me, *dame!* we must resort to grand measures and strike double. It will be longer and hotter work, but you will keep outside with your swords, and hasten in on hearing the din.'

'But what if they hit you?' said Athos.

'Impossible! these beer-drinkers are too heavy and clumsy; besides, you will strike at the throat, Porthos. That kills as quickly, and prevents those we kill from crying out.'

'Very well!' said Porthos, 'it will be a pretty little cutting of throats.'

'Frightful, frightful!' said Athos.

'Bah, Monsieur! you are sensitive; you would strike many more in a battle. Besides, friend, if you think the king's life not worth the cost, we will say no more about it, and I will inform M. Groslow that I am ill.'

'No,' said Athos, 'I am wrong, my friend; pardon me.'

At that moment the door opened, and a soldier appeared.

'M. le Capitaine Groslow,' said he, in bad French, 'begs to send word to M. d'Artagnan and M. du Vallon that he is expecting them.'

'Where?' asked d'Artagnan.

'In the room of the English Nebuchadnezzar,' replied the soldier, a thorough-going Puritan.

'Very well,' said Athos, in excellent English, who coloured deeply at the insult to his royal Majesty; 'tell Captain Groslow that we are coming there.'

Then the Puritan went off. The servants were ordered to saddle eight horses, and go and wait without dismounting or separating at the corner of a street scarcely twenty yards from the house in which the king was staying.

LXV

THE PARTY AT LANSQUENET

IT was nine at night; the posts had been changed at eight, and Captain Groslow's turn of duty had lasted an hour. D'Artagnan and Porthos, armed with swords, Aramis and Athos, each with a poniard hidden in his breast, went towards the house which for that evening served as Charles Stuart's prison. The two latter followed d'Artagnan and Porthos, in appearance humble and disarmed, like captives.

'Upon my word,' said Groslow, when he saw them, 'I had almost given you up.'

D'Artagnan approached him, and said in a whisper, 'In fact, we did hesitate a little, M. du Vallon and myself.'

'And why so?'

D'Artagnan gave a glance towards Athos and Aramis.

'Ah, ah!' said Groslow, 'on account of their opinions? It matters little. On the contrary,' he added, smiling, 'if they want to see their Stuart, they will be able.'

'Do we pass the night in the king's room?' asked d'Artagnan.

'No, but in the room adjoining; and as the door will remain open, it is quite the same as if we were in the room itself. Have you brought a good supply of money? I declare I intend to play a deep game this evening.'

'Do you hear?' said d'Artagnan, chinking the gold in his pockets.

'Very good!' said Groslow, and he opened the door. 'I do it to show you the way, Messieurs,' he said, and went in first.

D'Artagnan turned towards his friends. Porthos was as indifferent as if it were only an ordinary game; Athos was pale but resolute; Aramis wiped with his handkerchief his forehead, which was moistened with a slight perspiration.

The eight guards were at their posts. Four were in the king's chamber, two at the door of communication, two at the door by which the four friends entered. At the sight of their naked swords, Athos smiled; it was then to be not a butchery, but a combat. From this moment all his good-humour appeared to return. Charles, who could be seen through the open door, was on his bed, dressed; only a plaid was thrown over him. At his bolster Parry was seated, reading in a low voice, yet so that Charles could hear, a chapter out of a Catholic Bible.

A coarse tallow candle, placed on a black table, lighted up the resigned face of the king and the far less calm face of his faithful servant.

From time to time Parry stopped, thinking the king to be really asleep; but then the king would open his eyes again, and say to him with a smile, 'Go on, my good Parry, I am listening.'

Groslow went to the entrance of the king's room, purposely putting on his hat again, which he had held in his hand to receive his guests; looked for a moment with contempt at this simple, touching picture of an old servant reading the Bible to his king, a prisoner; ascertained that every man was at the post assigned him, and turning towards d'Artagnan, he looked with triumph at the Frenchman, as if asking for praise for his tactics.

'Wondrous!' said the Gascon; 'you would make a distinguished general.'

'Do you believe,' asked Groslow, 'that the Stuart will escape while I am guarding him?'

'No, truly,' replied d'Artagnan; 'unless at least friends should rain down to him from heaven.'

Groslow's countenance beamed with pleasure.

As Charles Stuart had all this time kept his eyes closed, one could hardly say whether or not he noticed the insolent remark of the Puritan captain. But he could not help, when he heard the accentuated tones of d'Artagnan's voice, re-opening his eyes. Parry started, and broke off the reading.

'What are you considering that makes you leave off?' said the king. 'Go on, my good Parry, unless you are fatigued.'

'No, Sire,' and he resumed his reading.

A table was ready in the first room, covered with a cloth, and on it were two lighted candles, some cards, two dice-boxes, and some dice.

'Messieurs,' said Groslow, 'be seated, I pray you; I, facing the Stuart, whom I like so much to see, especially where he is; you, M. d'Artagnan, in front of me.'

Athos coloured with anger; d'Artagnan looked at him frowning.

'That is it,' said d'Artagnan; 'you, M. le Comte de la Fère, at the right of M. Groslow; you, M. le Chevalier d'Herblay, at his left; you, Vallon, near me. You back me; and these Messieurs back M. Groslow.'

Thus placed, d'Artagnan talked with Porthos by touching his knee; since Aramis and Athos were in front of him, he was able to communicate with them by look.

At the names of the Comte de la Fère and of the Chevalier d'Herblay, Charles opened his eyes, and in spite of himself, raising his head, took in at a glance all the actors of this scene.

At this moment Parry turned over some pages of his Bible and read aloud this verse of Jeremiah:* 'God said, Listen to

the words of my prophets, my servants, whom I have sent you
with great care, and whom I have led towards you.'

The four friends exchanged looks. The words that Parry had
just spoken indicated to them that their presence was attributed
by the king to its true motive. The eyes of d'Artagnan sparkled
with joy.

'You asked me just now if I was in funds?' said d'Artagnan,
putting a number of pistoles on the table.

'Yes,' said Groslow.

'Well,' resumed d'Artagnan, 'it's my turn to say to you, keep
good hold of your treasure, my dear M. Groslow, for we shall
not leave here till we have carried it off.'

'That will not be for want of defence on my part,' said
Groslow.

'So much the better,' said d'Artagnan. 'To the fight! You
know or you do not know that that is what we want.'

'Oh yes, I know well enough,' said Groslow, with a coarse
laugh, 'you seek only wounds and bruises, or all sorts of
mischief, you French.'

Charles had heard and understood all. A slight colour came
into his cheeks. The soldiers on guard saw him little by
little stretch his weary limbs, and under the pretence of the
excessive heat produced by a red-hot stove, throw back the
Scotch plaid by which he was covered. Athos and Aramis
felt pleased at seeing that the king was lying on the bed
dressed.

The play began. This evening fortune was in favour of
Groslow. A hundred pistoles passed from one side of the table
to the other. Groslow seemed to be in the highest glee.

Porthos, who had lost the fifty pistoles he had won the night
before, and besides, thirty pistoles of his own, was very sullen,
and questioned d'Artagnan with his knee, as if to ask him if
it was not soon time to pass to another kind of game; on their
side, Athos and Aramis looked at him from time to time with
scrutinizing eye, but d'Artagnan remained impassive.

Ten o'clock struck. They heard the patrol going its rounds.

'How often do you make the rounds?' asked d'Artagnan,
drawing forth fresh pistoles from his pocket.

'Every two hours,' said Groslow.

'Well,' said d'Artagnan, 'it is prudent.' And in his turn he threw a glance of his eye at Athos and at Aramis.

They heard the patrol's steps receding in the distance. D'Artagnan touched Porthos's knee.

Meanwhile, attracted by the play, so powerful with all men, the soldiers, whose orders were to remain in the king's room, had by degrees come close, and standing on tiptoe, looked over the shoulders of d'Artagnan and Porthos; those at the door drew near also, in this way furthering the desires of the four friends, who preferred to have them near at hand rather than to be forced to run after them to the four corners of the room. The two sentinels at the door had always their naked swords, only they leaned upon their points and looked at the players. Athos seemed to grow calm as the moment approached; his two white and aristocratic hands played with the louis, which he bent and straightened back with the same ease as if the gold had been pewter. Less master of himself, Aramis fumbled continually in his bosom; Porthos, impatient at losing always, kept his knee in constant motion.

D'Artagnan turned round, looked mechanically behind him, and between two soldiers saw Parry standing up and Charles leaning on his elbow, with his hands joined as if in earnest prayer. D'Artagnan felt sure that the moment had come. He cast a preparatory look at Aramis and Athos; they both pushed back their chairs lightly so as to get freedom of movement.

D'Artagnan gave a tap on Porthos's knee; and the latter rose as if for the purpose of stretching his legs, only he took care while rising to feel certain that he could draw his sword readily.

'Hang it all!' said d'Artagnan, 'another twenty pistoles lost! Really, Captain Groslow, you have too much luck; it can't last,' and he took twenty more pistoles from his pocket.

'The last throw, Captain. These twenty pistoles on it.'

And Groslow turned up two cards, as is customary—a king for d'Artagnan, an ace for himself.

'A king!' said d'Artagnan, 'that looks well. M. Groslow,' he added, 'take care of the king!'

And in spite of his self-control there was in d'Artagnan's voice a strange vibration which made his partner start. Groslow began turning up the cards one after another. If he turned up an ace first, he won, but if a king, he lost.

He turned up a king.

'At last,' said d'Artagnan.

At these words Athos and Aramis got up; Porthos drew back a step.

Poniards and swords were going to glitter, when suddenly the door opened and Harrison appeared at the threshold, accompanied by a man wrapped up in a cloak. Behind him they saw the muskets of five or six soldiers glittering.

Groslow rose quickly, ashamed at being surprised in the midst of wine, cards, and dice. But Harrison paid no attention to him, and entering the room of the king, followed by his companion, 'Charles Stuart,' said he, 'the order has come to conduct you to London without stopping day or night. Make ready to start this very moment.'

'And in whose name is this order given?' asked the king; 'by General Oliver Cromwell?'

'Yes,' said Harrison; 'and this is M. Mordaunt who has just brought it, and who is charged with its execution.'

'Mordaunt!' muttered the four friends, exchanging looks.

D'Artagnan swept off the table all the money that he and Porthos had lost, and stuffed it into his capacious pocket. Athos and Aramis placed themselves behind him. At this movement Mordaunt turned round, recognized them, and uttered an exclamation of savage joy.

'I believe we are caught,' said d'Artagnan, in a whisper to his friends.

'Not yet,' said Porthos.

'Colonel, colonel,' said Mordaunt, 'have this room surrounded! You are betrayed! These four Frenchmen escaped from New-castle, and want without doubt to carry off the king. Have them arrested.'

'Oh, young man,' said d'Artagnan, drawing his sword, 'that's an order more easily given than executed.' Then whirling his sword round, 'Retreat, friends,' cried he, 'retreat!'

At the same time he sprang towards the door, and overthrew two of the soldiers who guarded it, before they had time to cock their muskets. Athos and Aramis followed him, Porthos

made the rear-guard; and before soldiers, officers, or colonel
had had time to know where they were, they were all four in
the street.

'Fire on them!' cried Mordaunt.

Two or three musket-shots were actually fired, but had no
other effect than that of showing the four fugitives turning the
corner of the street safe and sound.

The horses were at the appointed place; the servants had
only to throw the bridles to their masters, who sprang into the
saddle with the activity of finished cavaliers.

'Forward!' said d'Artagnan, 'the spur!'

They took the route by which they had come; that is to say,
towards Scotland. They left the town without difficulty, as it
had neither gates nor walls. At fifty paces from the last house,
d'Artagnan stopped.

'Halt!' he said.

'How halt?' exclaimed Porthos, 'at full speed you mean?'

'Not at all,' replied d'Artagnan; 'this time we shall be
pursued. Let us take the route to Scotland, and when we have
seen them pass, let us then go in the opposite direction.'

A few yards off was a stream, over which was a bridge.
D'Artagnan led his horse under the arch; his friends followed
him. They had not been there ten minutes when they heard
the quick gallop of a troop of horsemen. A few minutes after,
these horsemen passed over their heads, far from suspecting
that those they sought were only separated from them by the
thickness of the arch of the bridge.

LXVI

LONDON

WHEN the tramp of the horses was lost in the distance,
d'Artagnan regained the bank of the stream, and began to cross
the plain, directing his course as much as possible in the
direction of London. His three friends followed him in silence,
until by a large semi-circle they had left the city far behind
them.

'This time,' said d'Artagnan, when he thought himself sufficiently far from danger to go at a less rapid pace, 'I think that all is lost, and that the best thing to be done is to get back to France. What do you say about this, Athos? Do you not find it reasonable?'

'Yes, dear friend,' replied Athos; 'but the other day you uttered a saying more than reasonable—a saying noble and generous. You said, "Let us die here!" I would recall your saying.'

'Oh!' said Porthos, 'death is nothing. Death ought not to disquiet us, since we don't know what it is; but it is the idea of a defeat which torments me. In the fashion things are turning out, I see that we shall be obliged to give battle to London, to the Provinces, and to all England; and truly we cannot in the end fail to be beaten.'*

'I think we ought to see the end of this great tragedy,' said Athos. 'Do you think as I do, Aramis?'

'On every point, my dear count, for I confess I should not be sorry to come across Mordaunt again. It seems to me we have an account to reckon with him, and it is not our practice to leave countries without paying debts of this sort.'

'Ah! that's another thing altogether,' said d'Artagnan, 'and seems to me a very plausible reason. In order to come upon Mordaunt again I confess I would wait a year in London if necessary. Only let us lodge with a safe man and one of a kind not to awaken suspicion, for at this moment M. Cromwell will cause us to be sought for; and as well as I can judge, he does not jest. Athos, do you know a decent inn where one can have clean sheets, roast beef properly cooked, and wine not made with hops nor gin?'

'I think I can manage it. Winter took us to a house kept by a Spaniard, who is now a naturalized subject, naturalized through the guineas of his new compatriots. What do you say to this, Aramis?'

'Why, this project of putting up at Señor Pérez's seems to be very reasonable. I adopt it then on my part. We will invoke the memory of that poor Winter, for whom he seemed to have a great veneration; we will tell him that we come as amateurs* to see what is going on; we will expend with him, each of us, a guinea a day, and by means of all these precautions I think we can live there in security.'

'You forget one thing, Aramis,' said d'Artagnan, 'and that a very important precaution.'

'What is that?'

'Changing our dress.'

'Bah!' said Porthos, 'what need is there to do that? We are at ease in this dress.'

'So as not to be recognized,' said d'Artagnan. 'Our clothes have a uniformity of cut and almost of colour, which declares us to be Frenchmen at the first glance. Now, I do not hold enough to the cut of my doublet or to the colour of my breeches to risk, for love of these, being hanged at Tyburn or sent on a voyage to India.* I am going to buy myself a maroon-coloured suit. I have remarked that all those imbeciles of Puritans dote on this colour.'*

'But will you find your man?' said Aramis.

'Oh, certainly,' said Athos, 'he lives in Green Hall Street,* Bedford's Tavern; besides, I could go into the city with my eyes shut.'

'I wish we were already there,' said d'Artagnan; 'and my advice is that we arrive in London before day, even if we kill our horses.'

'Come on,' said Athos, 'for if I am not mistaken in my calculations, we cannot be more than eight or ten leagues from London now.'

The friends pressed on, and actually reached London about five in the morning.

At the gate where they presented themselves, the guard stopped them; but Athos replied in excellent English that they were sent by Colonel Harrison to notify his colleague Pride of the early arrival of the king, and Athos gave such precise and positive details that if the officers had some suspicions they vanished completely. A passage was then opened for the four friends with all kinds of Puritan congratulations.

Athos had been right. He went directly to the Bedford Tavern, and was recognized by the landlord, who was so pleased to see him return with so many companions that he had his best rooms prepared for them at once. Although it was not yet day, our four travellers found the whole city in commotion. The report that the king under Colonel Harrison was on his way to London had spread since the evening; and many had not gone to bed for fear lest the Stuart, as they called him, should arrive in the night, and they should miss seeing him enter.

The project of changing their dress had been unanimously adopted, and the landlord went out to make the purchases. Athos selected a black dress, which made him look like an honest citizen; Aramis, who did not wish to be without his sword, chose a dark dress of military cut; Porthos was attracted by a red doublet and green breeches; d'Artagnan, who had already chosen the colour, was only concerned about the shade, and in the maroon dress which he selected looked exactly like a retired sugar merchant.

Grimaud and Mousqueton, not being in livery, were sufficiently disguised. Grimaud offered the calm, dry, and stiff type of the circumspect Englishman, Mousqueton that of the corpulent, lounging Englishman.

'Now,' said d'Artagnan, 'let us come to the chief thing; let us cut our hair, so as not to be insulted by the populace. Since we can no longer be distinguished as gentlemen by carrying a sword, let us appear to be Puritans by the arrangement of our hair. This is, you know, the important distinction between the Covenanter and Cavalier.'*

On this important point d'Artagnan found Aramis obstinate. He wanted to keep his long hair, on which he bestowed much care; and it was necessary that Athos, to whom all these matters were quite indifferent, should set him the example. Porthos made no objections to giving his head in charge to Mousqueton, who cut off scissors-ful of his thick hair. D'Artagnan cut his into a fanciful form, not much unlike a medal of the time of Francis I or Charles IX.

'We are frightful,' said Athos.

'And it seems to me that we smell enough of the Puritan to make one shudder,' said Aramis.

'I have a cold in the head,' said Porthos.

'And I feel a strong desire to preach a sermon,' said d'Artagnan.

'Now,' said Athos, 'since we do not even know one another, and have consequently no fear of others knowing us, let us go and see the king come into London; if he has marched all night, he cannot be far off.'

The friends had not been in the crowds more than two hours before great shouts and commotion announced Charles's arrival. They had sent a coach on before; and from a distance the gigantic Porthos, who was taller by a head than most other men, announced the approach of the royal coach. D'Artagnan stood on tiptoe, while Athos and Aramis listened for the purpose of satisfying themselves of the public opinion. The coach passed, and d'Artagnan recognized Harrison at one door and Mordaunt at the other. The populace, whose feelings Athos and Aramis were studying, hurled many imprecations at Charles.

Athos returned in despair.

'My dear fellow,' said d'Artagnan to him, 'you persist uselessly, and I protest that the situation is bad. For myself, I only attach myself to it on your account and from a certain artistic interest in politics* *à la mousquetaire*. I think that it would be very pleasant to snatch their prey from all these howlers and laugh at them. I will think of it.'

The next day, on going to the window, which looked out upon the most crowded parts of the city, Athos heard the Act of Parliament* which arraigned the ex-king Charles I publicly cried. D'Artagnan was close to him; Aramis was consulting a map; Porthos was absorbed in the last delicacies of a wholesome breakfast.

'The Parliament!' exclaimed Athos, 'the Parliament cannot possibly have passed such a bill.'

'Listen,' said d'Artagnan, 'I understand English but little, yet as English is only French badly pronounced, here is what I understand: *Parliament's bill*, which means bill of Parliament, or God damn me! as they say here.'

Just then the host entered; Athos called to him.

'Parliament has passed this bill?' Athos asked him in English.

'Yes, my Lord—the purified Parliament.'

'How so? are there then two Parliaments?'

'My friend,' d'Artagnan interposed, 'as I don't understand English, but we all understand Spanish, do me the pleasure of conversing in that language, which is your own, and which consequently you ought to be pleased to speak when you find the occasion.'

'Ah, excellent!' said Aramis.

As to Porthos, as we have said, all his attention was concentrated upon the bone of a cutlet which he was engaged in stripping of its fleshy envelope.

'What do you want to know?' said the host, in Spanish.

'I was asking,' said Athos, 'if there are two Parliaments—one purified and the other not?'

'Oh, how funny it is!' said Porthos, raising his head slowly, and looking at his friends with astonishment; 'I comprehend English now? I understand what you say.'

'It's because we are speaking Spanish, dear friend,' said Athos, with his usual unconcern.

'Ah, *diable!*' said Porthos, 'I am provoked at it; that would have made for me another language.'

'When I call the Parliament purified, Señor,' resumed the host, 'I speak of that which M. le Colonel Pride has purged.'

'Ah!' said d'Artagnan, 'these folks are truly very ingenious. I must, when I return to France, make a present of this method to M. de Mazarin and to Monsieur the Coadjutor. The one will purify in the name of the court, the other in the people's name, so that there will be no longer any Parliament at all.'

'Who is this Colonel Pride?' asked Aramis, 'and what plan did he adopt for purifying the Parliament?'

'Colonel Pride,' said the Spaniard, 'was formerly a carter, a man of much wit, who had noticed that when a stone is met with on the road; it is much easier to lift up the stone than to make the wheel pass over it. Now out of the two hundred and fifty-one members of Parliament, there were one hundred and ninety-one who embarrassed it, and who would have upset his political cart. He took them up as he used to do the stones, and threw them out of the House.'

'Capital!' said d'Artagnan, who, being especially a man of wit, valued mental vigour wherever he fell in with it.

'And all those expelled were for Stuart?' asked Athos.

'Without any doubt, Señor; and you understand that they would have saved the king.'

'*Parbleu!*' said Porthos, majestically, 'they formed the majority.'

'And you think,' said Aramis, 'that he will consent to appear before such a tribunal?'

'He can't help himself; if he tried a refusal, the people would constrain him.'

'Thanks, M. Pérez,' said Athos; 'now I am sufficiently informed.'

'Do you begin at last to believe that it is a lost cause, Athos?' said d'Artagnan; 'and that with the Harrisons, the Joyces, the Prides, and the Cromwells, we shall never be equal to the task?'

'The king will be delivered to the tribunal,' said Athos; 'the silence even of his partisans indicates a conspiracy.'

D'Artagnan shrugged his shoulders.

'But,' said Aramis, 'if they dare to condemn their king, it will be exile or prison, that's all.'

D'Artagnan whistled as if he felt incredulous.

'We shall see,' said Athos, 'for we shall go to the sittings, I expect.'

'You will not have long to wait, for they begin tomorrow,'* said the host.

'Oh, then,' replied Athos, 'the proceedings were all arranged before the king was taken?'

'No doubt,' said d'Artagnan; 'they were begun on the day he was bought.'

'You know,' said Aramis, 'that it was our friend Mordaunt who made, if not the bargain, at least the first overtures in this small matter.'

'You know,' said d'Artagnan, 'that wherever he falls into my hands I will kill that M. Mordaunt.'

'Fie, now!' said Athos; 'such a wretch!'

'But it is just because he is such a wretch that I will kill him. Ah! dear friend, I do your will often enough for you to be indulgent of mine. Besides, this time, whether it pleases you or not, I declare that this Mordaunt shall be killed only by me.'

'And by me,' said Porthos.

'And by me,' said Aramis.

'What touching unanimity!' exclaimed d'Artagnan, 'which so well agrees with our character of good citizens. Let us take a turn about town. Mordaunt himself would not know us four paces off in this fog. Let us go and imbibe a little fog.'

'Yes,' said Porthos, 'that will be a change for us from beer.'

And the four friends actually went out to take, as the common saying is, the air of the place.

LXVII

THE TRIAL

NEXT day a numerous guard conducted Charles I before the High Court instituted to try him. The crowd filled the streets and houses adjoining the palace.

So at the first steps taken by the four friends they were stopped by the almost insurmountable obstacle of this living wall; some of the populace, robust and ill-tempered, even pushed back Aramis so rudely that Porthos raised his formidable fist and let it fall upon the floury face of a baker, which changed at once its colour and became covered with blood, crushed as it was like a bunch of ripe grapes. The affair made a disturbance. Three men wished to attack Porthos; but Athos threw one aside, d'Artagnan another, and Porthos threw the third over his head. Some Englishmen, amateurs of boxing,* appreciated the easy and rapid manner in which this was executed, and clapped their hands. It wanted little, then, that instead of being beaten terribly, as they began to fear, Porthos and his friends were not carried in triumph. But our four travellers, who feared everything that could make them conspicuous, succeeded in declining the ovation. However, they gained one thing from this Herculean demonstration, that the crowd opened before them and they accomplished the result, which seemed a moment before impossible, of reaching the palace.

All London was crowding at the doors of the galleries, so when the four friends succeeded in getting into one, they found the three front rows already filled. That was a small loss for persons not wishing to be recognized; they therefore took their places with satisfaction, except Porthos, who wanted to show

off his red doublet and green breeches, and preferred the front
row.

The seats were arranged as in an amphitheatre, and from
their places the friends overlooked the whole assembly. As
chance would have it, they were in the middle of the gallery
facing the chair set for Charles I.

About eleven o'clock in the morning the king appeared at
the threshold of the hall. He was surrounded by guards, and
kept his hat on,* with a calm, assured look which travelled in
all directions, as if he had come to preside over an assembly
of obedient subjects, rather than to answer the accusations of
a rebel court.

The judges, proud of having a king to humiliate, were
evidently prepared to use the right which they had arro-
gated to themselves. Consequently an usher came to inform
Charles I that it was the usage for the accused to be uncovered.

Charles, without making any reply, pressed his hat more
firmly on his head, which he turned another way; then when
the usher had gone, he sat down on the chair set for him in
front of the president, striking his boot with a small stick which
he held in his hand. Parry, who accompanied him, stood up
behind his chair.

D'Artagnan, instead of paying attention to all this ceremonial, was looking at Athos, whose countenance reflected all the
emotions which the king, by an effort of self-control, succeeded
in checking on his own. This agitation of Athos, who was
usually so cold and calm, frightened d'Artagnan.

'I hope,' said he, whispering in his friend's ear, 'that you
are going to take an example from his Majesty, and not
foolishly get killed in this cage.'

'Set your mind at ease,' said Athos, 'on that point.'

'Ah, ah!' continued d'Artagnan, 'they seem to fear something, for see! they have doubled the posts; there were only
halberds, now see! there are muskets. There is something now
for all; the halberds are for the auditors on the floor, the
muskets are meant for us.'

'Thirty, forty, fifty, seventy men,' said Porthos, counting the
newly arrived soldiers.

'Ah!' said Aramis, 'you are forgetting the officer, Porthos; yet it seems to me he well deserves the trouble of being counted.'

'Holloa!' said d'Artagnan; and he became pale with rage, for he had recognized Mordaunt, who, with drawn sword, conducted the musketeers behind the king; that is to say, facing the galleries.

'Has he recognized us?' continued d'Artagnan, 'because in that case I should promptly beat a retreat. I desire to die in my own way. I don't choose to be shot in a box.'

'No,' said Aramis, 'he has not seen us. He sees only the king. With what eyes he looks at him, the insolent fellow! Does he hate his Majesty as much as he hates us?'

'*We* have deprived him only of his mother; the *king* of his name and property,'* said Athos.

'That's true,' said Aramis. 'But, silence! the president is addressing the king.'

In fact, President Bradshaw was questioning the illustrious accused.

'Stuart,' he said to him, 'listen while the names of your judges are called over, and address to the tribunal any observations you may wish to make.'

The king, as if the words were not at all intended for him, turned his head another way. The president waited; and as no reply came, there was a momentary silence. Out of a hundred and sixty-three members whose names were called, only seventy-three* answered—for the rest, frightened at being accomplices in such an act, had kept away.

'I proceed with the roll-call,' said Bradshaw, without seeming to notice the absence of three-fifths of the court, and he began to name in succession the members present and absent.

Those present answered with a loud or weak voice, according as they had, or did not have, the courage to uphold their opinions. A short silence followed the names of the absent, who were twice called.

The name of Colonel Fairfax came in its turn, and was followed by one of those intervals of short but solemn silence which declared the absence of those members who had not wished personally to take part in the trial.

'Colonel Fairfax,' Bradshaw repeated.

'Fairfax!' responded a mocking voice, which from its silvery quality proved to be that of a woman, 'he has too much good sense to be here.'

A great shout of laughter welcomed these words, spoken with that audacity which women derive from their weakness—a weakness which wards off all thoughts of vengeance.

'That's a woman's voice,' exclaimed Aramis. 'Ah! upon my word I would give much that she should be young and pretty;' and he got up on the seat to try and see whence the voice came.

'Upon my soul,' said Aramis, 'she *is* lovely! Look now, d'Artagnan, everyone is staring at her, and in spite of Bradshaw's look she does not become pale.'

'That is Lady Fairfax* herself,' said d'Artagnan; 'you remember her, Porthos? We have seen her with her husband at General Cromwell's.'

In a short time the quiet which had been interrupted by this episode was re-established, and the roll-call was resumed.

'These simpletons are going to break up the sitting, since they see they are not numerous enough,' said Athos.

'You don't know them, Athos. Notice now the smile of Mordaunt; see how he looks at the king. It is the smile of satisfied hate, of vengeance certain of being satiated. Ah, you cursed basilisk! it will be a happy day for me when I shall cross with you something else besides a look.'

'The king is truly a fine man,' said Porthos; 'then see how carefully he is dressed, though a prisoner. The feather of his hat is worth at least fifty pistoles; look at it, Aramis.'

The roll-call being finished, the president ordered the bill of indictment to be read. Athos turned pale; he was once more deceived in his expectation. Although the number of judges was insufficient, the trial was going to proceed; the king was then condemned in advance.

'I told you so, Athos,' said d'Artagnan, shrugging his shoulders. 'But you are always sceptical. Now pluck up your courage and listen, I pray you, to all the petty horrors that that man in black is about telling his king with licence and privilege.'

In fact, never had more brutal accusations, never more bare insults, never a more bloodthirsty inquisition yet stigmatized royal majesty. Until then they had been content with assassinating kings; and it was only on their dead bodies that they had heaped insults.

Charles I listened to the discourse of the accuser with very close attention, passing by the insults, remembering the wrongs; and when hate went too far and the accuser made himself an executioner in advance, he responded by a smile of contempt. It was after all a capital and terrible instrument, in which this unhappy king found all his imprudences changed into ambushes, his errors transformed into crimes.

D'Artagnan, who allowed this torrent to flow by with all the contempt it deserved, yet brought his judicial mind to bear on some of the counts of the indictment.

'The fact is,' said he, 'that if they punish imprudence and frivolity, this poor king merits punishment; but it seems to me that what he is bearing at this moment is cruel enough.'

'In any case,' replied Aramis, 'punishment ought not to affect the king, but his ministers, since the first principle of the English constitution is: The king can do no wrong.'

'As for me,' thought Porthos, looking at Mordaunt and only occupying himself with him, 'if it was not for troubling the solemnity of the occasion, I would jump down from the gallery; in three bounds I would fall upon M. Mordaunt, whom I would strangle. I would take him by the feet and I would crush all those miserable musketeers who parody the Musketeers of France. During this time, d'Artagnan, who is full of wit and readiness, would find perhaps a means of saving the king. I must speak to him about it.'

As for Athos, with fire in his eyes, his hands nervously twitching, his lips covered with blood from biting them, he sat foaming and furious at this eternal parliamentary insult and this long royal patience; so that his inflexible arm and mighty heart became a trembling hand and a shivering body.

At this moment the prosecutor finished with these words:

'The present indictment is made by us in the name of the English people.'

At these words there was a murmur in the galleries; and another voice, not a woman's, but a man's, loud and furious, thundered behind d'Artagnan—

'You lie!' it said, 'and nine-tenths of the English people are horrified at what you say.'

It was Athos, who, losing control over himself, and standing up with extended arm, had thus addressed the public prosecutor. At this apostrophe, king, judges, spectators, everybody in short, turned their eyes towards the gallery where the four friends were. Mordaunt looked up like the rest, and recognized the gentleman, around whom were standing the other three Frenchmen, pale and threatening. Mordaunt's eyes lighted up with joy; he had found those to whose capture and death he had vowed his life. A furious movement called to him twenty of his musketeers, and pointing to the gallery in which were his enemies, 'Fire into that gallery!'* said he.

But then, quick as thought, d'Artagnan seizing Athos by the middle of his body, and Porthos carrying Aramis, they leaped down the steps, dashed along the passages, descended the staircase, and were lost in the crowd; while inside the hall the levelled muskets threatened three thousand spectators, whose cries for mercy and noisy fears checked the outburst already tending to carnage.

Charles also had recognized the four Frenchmen; he put his hand to his heart to repress its beatings, the other over his eyes so as not to see his faithful friends killed.

Mordaunt, pale and trembling with rage, dashed out of the hall with ten halberdiers, searching the crowd, questioning, panting; but he returned without having found them.

The disturbance was hard to suppress. More than half an hour passed before any one could be heard. The judges believed each gallery ready to thunder. The galleries saw the muskets directed towards them, and divided between fear and curiosity, remained tumultuous and excited. At last quiet was re-established.

'What have you to say in your defence?' asked Bradshaw of the king.

Then, in the tone of a judge, not of one accused, with his head still covered, standing up not at all from humiliation, but as a ruler,* 'Before questioning me,' said Charles, 'answer me. I was free at Newcastle, and there concluded an agreement with the two Houses. Instead of performing your part of this treaty, as I have mine, you have bought me of the Scots; not dearly, I know, and that does honour to the economy of your government. But after having paid for me the price of a slave, do you think that I cease to be your king? No. To reply to you would be to forget it. I will not reply until you have proved your right to question me. To reply to you would be to recognize you as my judges, and I recognize you only as my executioners;' and in the midst of a deathlike silence, Charles, calm, haughty, with covered head, sat down again.

'Why are not my Frenchmen there?' murmured Charles, with pride, turning his eyes towards the gallery, where they had appeared an instant; 'they would see that their friend, living, is worthy of being defended, dead, of being mourned.' But he in vain tried to sound the depth of the crowd, and to ask as it were of God those sweet and consoling presences. He saw only stupefied and fearful faces; he felt that he was battling with hate and ferocity.

'Well,' said the president, on seeing Charles invincibly determined not to speak, 'be it so; we shall try you in spite of your silence. You are accused of treason, abuse of power, and of assassination. The witnesses will prove all this. Go; the next sitting will accomplish what you refuse to do at this.'

Charles rose, and turning towards Parry, whom he saw looking pale, and whose forehead was damp from perspiration, 'Well, my dear Parry, what's the matter with you? and what agitates you so?'

'Oh, Sire,' said Parry, with tears in his eyes, and quivering voice, 'on leaving the hall, do not look to your left.'

'Why not, Parry? What is the matter?' said Charles, trying to see through the hedge of guards who were behind him.

'The matter is—but you will not look, Sire, will you?—it is that on a table they have had the axe placed with which criminals are executed. This sight is hideous; do not look at it, Sire, I beg of you.'

'The fools!' said Charles; 'do they think me a coward then like themselves? You did well to forewarn me; thanks, Parry.'

And as the moment came to withdraw, the king went out, following his guards.

At the left of the door, indeed, the white axe, polished by the executioner's hand, shone with an inauspicious lustre on the red cloth on which it was placed. Charles stopped before it, and turning round, 'Ah,' said he, 'the axe!—an ingenious bugbear, and well worthy of those who do not know how to treat a gentleman. I am not afraid of you,' he added, striking it with the stick in his hand, 'and I strike you, waiting patiently and Christian-like till you return the blow;' and shrugging his shoulders with regal disdain, he moved on, leaving stupefied those who had pressed round the table to watch the king's looks on seeing the axe that was to behead him.

'In truth, Parry,' continued the king, 'all these people take me, God pardon me! for an East Indian cotton merchant, and not for a gentleman accustomed to see the glitter of steel. They think that I have not as much courage as a butcher!'

By that time he had reached the gate; a long line of people had run to it, who, unable to get into the galleries, wished to enjoy at least the end of the spectacle. This countless multitude, whose ranks were thickly sown with menacing faces, drew a slight sigh from the king.

'What a crowd!' he thought, 'and not one devoted friend!' and as he said to himself these words of doubt and discouragement, a voice responding to these thoughts said near him, 'God bless his fallen Majesty!'

The king turned round quickly with tears in his eyes. It was a veteran of the king's Guards, who would not allow his captive king to pass him without paying him this last act of homage. But at the same moment the unfortunate soldier was almost stunned by blows from a sword-hilt. Among the strikers, the king recognized Captain Groslow.

'Alas!' said Charles, 'a harsh chastisement for a small fault.'

Then with wounded heart he went on; but he had not gone a hundred yards before a furious creature, stooping down between two soldiers of the escort, spat in the king's face, as formerly an infamous and accursed Jew spat in the face of Jesus the Nazarene.

Great bursts of laughter and murmurs were heard together; the crowd separated, came together again, undulated like a tempestuous sea, and it seemed to the king that he could see in the midst of the living wave the flashing eyes of Athos. Charles wiped his face and said with a sad smile, 'The wretch! for half-a-crown he would do the same to his father.'

The king was not deceived; he had really seen Athos and his friends, who, again mixed up with the groups, followed the martyr king with a last look. When the soldier saluted Charles, Athos's heart beat with joy; and when the soldier recovered himself, he found in his pocket ten guineas that the French gentleman had slipped into it. But when the cowardly rascal spat in the king's face, Athos put his hand to his poniard. But d'Artagnan stopped the hand, and in a hoarse voice, 'Wait!' said he.

Athos stopped. D'Artagnan leaned upon Athos's arm, made a sign to Porthos and Aramis to keep close to them, and got behind the man with the naked arms, who was still laughing at his dastardly jest, and receiving the congratulations of others as rascally. This man, who seemed a butcher's apprentice, took the road to the city, and with two companions turned down a small, steep, isolated street leading to the river. D'Artagnan had let go Athos's arm, and was walking behind the insulter. On getting near the river, the three men perceived that they were followed, stopped, and looking insolently at the Frenchmen, exchanged some jests with one another.

'I don't know English, Athos,' said d'Artagnan; 'but you know it, and can act as interpreter for me.'

Then, doubling his pace, he passed the three men. But turning round suddenly, d'Artagnan went straight up to the man with bare arms who seemed to be a butcher. The man stopped, and d'Artagnan, touching him on the chest with his forefinger, said to his friend, 'Say this to him, Athos: You have been a coward; you have insulted a defenceless man; you have spat in the face of your king. You shall die!'

Athos, pale as a ghost, translated these strange words to the man, who, seeing these preparations and d'Artagnan's glaring eyes, put himself in an attitude of defence. Aramis at this movement carried his hand to his sword.

'No, not the steel, not the steel!' said d'Artagnan; 'the steel is for gentlemen.' Seizing the butcher by the throat, 'Porthos,' said d'Artagnan, 'crush this wretch with a single blow.'

Porthos raised his terrible arm, made it whiz in the air like a sling, and the weighty mass dropped with a dull thud on the coward's skull, which it broke. The man fell down like an ox under the hammer. His companions tried to cry out and flee; but their voice failed them, and their legs gave under them.

'Tell them also this, Athos,' continued d'Artagnan: 'Thus will die all those who forget that the head of a prisoner is sacred, and that a captive king is doubly the representative of the Lord.'

Athos repeated the words of d'Artagnan. The two men, mute, their hair standing on end, regarded the body of their companion, which was lying in a pool of black blood; then finding at once voice and strength, they took flight with a cry and joining their hands.

'Justice is done!' said Porthos, wiping his forehead.

'And now,' said d'Artagnan to Athos, 'don't at all doubt me, and let your mind be at rest. I take upon myself all that concerns the king.'

LXVIII

WHITEHALL

THE Parliament condemned Charles Stuart to death, as it was easy to foresee. Political trials are always empty formalities, for the same passions which bring the accusation pronounce the judgment also. Such is the terrible logic of revolutions.*

Although our friends expected this result, it yet filled them with grief. D'Artagnan, whose mind was most fruitful of resources in the most critical moments, again swore that he would attempt everything possible to prevent the end of this bloody tragedy. But how? That was what he as yet only saw vaguely. All depended on the nature of the circumstances. Meanwhile, until a complete plan could be arranged, it was necessary at any price to gain time, to prevent the execution from taking place the next day as the judges had decided. The only means was to remove the executioner from London. This done, the sentence could not be carried out. Without doubt one from the town nearest to London would be sent for; but that would cause the gain of a day at least, and a day in such a case might be salvation, perhaps. D'Artagnan undertook this more than difficult task.

A matter not less necessary was to warn Charles Stuart of their attempt to save him, so that he might, as far as possible, second their efforts, or at least do nothing to frustrate them. Aramis undertook this perilous task. Charles had asked permission for Bishop Juxon to visit him in his prison at Whitehall. Mordaunt had that very evening been to the bishop's to acquaint him with the king's desire as well as Cromwell's acquiescence. Aramis resolved to obtain from the bishop, either by terror or persuasion, permission to let him assume his dress and so get admission to Whitehall. Then Athos undertook to have ready, in any case, the means of leaving England in case of failure or success.

Night being come, they fixed upon eleven o'clock for meeting again at the inn; and each started off on his dangerous mission.

Whitehall was guarded by three regiments of cavalry, and still more by the unceasing anxiety of Cromwell, who was going to and fro, and sending his generals or his agents continually.

Alone, and in his accustomed room, which was lighted by two wax candles, the condemned monarch sorrowfully regarded his past grandeur, as on his death-bed one sees the image of life more brilliant and sweet than ever. Parry was still with his master, and since his condemnation had not ceased weeping.

Charles Stuart, leaning on a table, was looking at a medallion, on which were the portraits of his wife and daughter. He was awaiting first Juxon; after Juxon, martyrdom.

Sometimes his thoughts rested upon those brave French gentlemen, who already appeared removed a hundred leagues, fabulous, chimerical, and like those figures one sees in dreams and which disappear on waking. Sometimes Charles asked himself if all that had just happened to him was not a dream, or at least the delirium of a fever.

While thus thinking, he rose, took a few steps as if to shake off his torpor, went to the window, and just below it he saw the muskets of the guards. Then he was compelled to confess that he was indeed awake, and that his bloody dream was very real. He returned silent to his chair, again leaned on the table, and mused.

'Alas!' he said to himself, 'if I only had as confessor one of those luminaries of the Church whose soul has sounded the mysteries of life, and all its littlenesses, his words might perhaps silence the voice which utters its wailing in my soul. But I shall have a priest of common mind, whose career I have cut short by my misfortune. He will talk to me of God and death, as to other dying men, without understanding that I am leaving a throne to a usurper, while my children will be without bread.' Then raising the portrait to his lips, he quietly mentioned by name each of his children.

It was, as we have said, a misty, dark night. The hour was slowly struck by the neighbouring church clock. The pale light of the two candles showed in that large, lofty apartment phantoms lighted up by strange reflections. These phantoms were King Charles's ancestors, who seemed to come forth from their frames of gold; these reflections were the last bluish lights of a coal fire, which was going out.

A deep sadness seized upon Charles. He thought of the world, which seems so beautiful when one is about leaving it; of the caresses of his children, which one feels to be so sweet and gentle when one is separated from them never to see them again; then of his wife, that noble, courageous creature who had sustained him to the very last. He drew from his breast the cross of diamonds and the Star of the Garter which she had sent him by those generous Frenchmen, and kissed them; then remembering that she would never see these objects again until he was laid cold and beheaded in the tomb, he felt one of those cold shivers pass over him which death throws about us as its first cloak.

Then in this room which recalled to him so many royal memories, where had passed so many courtiers and so many flatteries, alone with a despairing servitor whose feeble soul could not support that of royalty, the king suffered his courage to fall to the level of this weakness, of this darkness, and of this winter cold; and—shall we say it?—this king who died so grandly, so sublimely, with the smile of resignation on his lips, wiped away in the shadow a tear which had fallen on the table and trembled on the gold embroidered cloth.

Suddenly steps were heard in the corridors; the door opened, torches filled the chamber with a smoky light, and an ecclesiastic in episcopal dress entered, followed by two guards. The latter retired; the chamber returned to its obscurity.

'Juxon!' exclaimed Charles. 'Thanks, my last friend! you come very opportunely.'

The bishop cast a side-long, suspicious look on the man who was sobbing in the chimney corner.

'Come, Parry,' said the king, 'don't weep any more; God has come to us.'

'If it is Parry,' said the bishop, 'I have nothing further to fear; so, Sire, permit me to salute your Majesty, and to say who I am, and for what I have come.'

On hearing the voice, Charles was going to make an exclamation, but Aramis put his fingers to his lips, and made a low bow to the King of England.

'The chevalier!' murmured Charles.

'Yes, Sire,' said Aramis, raising his voice—'yes, Bishop Juxon, faithful chevalier of Christ, who comes at the desire of your Majesty.'

Charles joined his hands together. He had recognized d'Herblay; he felt stupefied, astounded in the presence of these men, who, foreigners, without any other motive than a sense of duty imposed by conscience, were thus struggling against a people's will and a king's destiny.

'You!' he said—'you! how have you succeeded in reaching here? Good heavens! if they recognize you, you will be lost.'

Parry was standing; his whole figure expressed a naïve and profound admiration.

'Don't think of me, Sire,' said Aramis, enjoining silence on him; 'think only of yourself. Your friends are watching, as you see. What we shall do I know not yet, but four determined men can do much. Meanwhile, do not close your eyes tonight; don't be astonished at anything, and await everything.'

Charles shook his head.

'Friend,' said he, 'do you know that you have no time to lose, and that if you are going to act, you must make haste. At ten tomorrow I must die.'

'Sire, something will happen meanwhile which will render the execution impossible.'

The king looked at Aramis with astonishment. At that moment even a strange sound was heard beneath the window, like that of a load of wood being unloaded.

'Do you hear?' said the king.

This sound was followed by a cry of pain.

'I hear,' said Aramis; 'but I don't understand the noise, and especially that cry.'

'I don't know who uttered the cry,' said the king; 'but the sound I am going to explain to you. Do you know that I am to be executed outside this window?' Charles added, pointing towards the outside, which was guarded by soldiers and sentinels.

'Yes, Sire, I know it.'

'Well, these beams are for my scaffold. Some workman has been wounded in the unloading of them.' Aramis shivered in spite of himself. 'You see it is useless to persevere any longer. I am condemned; leave me to my fate.'

'Sire,' said Aramis, resuming his composure, 'they may erect the scaffold, but they will be unable to find an executioner.'

'What do you mean?' the king asked.

'I mean, Sire, that the executioner is by this time carried away or bribed, and they will have to postpone the execution till the next day.'

'Well?'

'Well, tomorrow night we will carry you off.'

'How can that be done?' exclaimed the king, whose face was lighted up by a flash of joy.

'Oh, Monsieur!' murmured Parry, his hands joined, 'may you be blessed, you and yours!'

'I must know this,' said the king, 'in order to second your efforts if I can.'

'I know not, Sire; but the cleverest, the bravest, the most devoted of us four told me when leaving, "Chevalier, tell the king that tomorrow at ten at night we will rescue him." Since he has said this, he will do it.'

'Tell me the name of this generous friend that I may preserve lasting gratitude for him, whether he succeed or not.'

'D'Artagnan, Sire, the same who failed in saving you when Colonel Harrison entered so inopportunely.'

'You are, in fact, wonderful men; and if I had been told of such deeds, I should not have believed them.'

'Now, Sire, listen to me. Do not forget that we are watching for your safety every moment; the smallest gesture, the slightest song, the least sign from those who approach you, watch, listen to, criticize everything.'

'Oh, Chevalier, what can I say? No words, coming even from the depths of my heart, could express my gratitude. If you succeed, I will not say that you save a king—no, in the sight of the scaffold, royalty is a small thing—but you will preserve a husband to his wife, a father to his children. Chevalier, press my hand; it is that of a friend who will love you to his last sigh.'

Aramis wished to kiss the king's hand, but the king seized his and pressed it against his heart.

Just then a man entered without even knocking at the door; he who entered was one of those Puritan half-priests, half-soldiers, of whom there were swarms about Cromwell.

'What do you want, sir?' said the king.

'I want to know if Charles Stuart's confession is ended.'

'What matters it to you? We are not of the same religion.'

'All men are brethren. One of my brethren is about to die, and I am come to prepare him for death.'

'Enough,' said Parry; 'the king has nothing to do with your exhortations.'

'Sire,' said Aramis, in a low voice, 'treat him gently; he is probably a spy.'

'After the reverend bishop,' said the king, 'I will hear you with pleasure.'

The man retired with a dubious look, not without having observed Juxon with a scrutiny which did not escape the king.

'Chevalier,' said he, when the door was closed, 'I believe that you were right, and that the man came with bad intentions; take care when you withdraw that no harm happen to you.'

'Sire, I thank your Majesty, but don't be uneasy; under this robe I have a coat of mail and a poniard.'

'Go then, Monsieur, and may God keep you in safety, as I used to say when I was king.'

Aramis went out; Charles conducted him to the door. Aramis pronounced his blessing, which made the guards bow, passed majestically through the anterooms, which were filled with soldiers, entered his coach, and returned to the bishop. Juxon awaited him with some anxiety.

'Well?' said he, when he saw Aramis.

'Well,' said the latter, 'all has succeeded according to my wishes; spies, guards, satellites, took me for you, and the king blesses you, waiting for you to bless him.'

'God protect you, my son, for your example has given me both hope and courage.'

Aramis resumed his clothes and cloak, and then left, informing Juxon that he should once more have recourse to him. He had gone scarcely ten yards when he saw that he was followed by a man wrapped up in an ample cloak. The man came straight towards him. It was Porthos.

'My dear friend!' said Aramis, giving him his hand.

'You see, my dear fellow, that each of us has his work; mine was to guard you, and I was doing so. Have you seen the king?'

'Yes; and all goes on well. But where are our friends?'

'We appointed eleven o'clock for meeting at the inn.'

'There is no time to lose, then.'

In fact, half-past ten then struck by the clock of St Paul's. However, as they made haste, they arrived first. After them came Athos.

'All is right,' said he, before his friends had had time to question him.

'What have you done?' said Aramis.

'I have hired a little felucca,* narrow like a *pirogue*, swift as a swallow. It awaits us at Greenwich, opposite the Isle of Dogs; it has a captain and crew of four, who for fifty pounds will be at our disposal for the next three nights. Once on board with the king, we will go down the Thames, and in two hours will be in the open sea. Then like true pirates we will keep to the coast, or if the sea is free, we will make head for Boulogne.

Should I be killed, the captain's name is Rogers, and the felucca's the *Lightning*. A handkerchief knotted at the corners is the sign of recognition.'

A short time after, d'Artagnan came in.

'Empty your pockets,' said he, 'and make up a hundred pounds—for as for mine,' and d'Artagnan turned his inside out, 'they are empty.'

The amount was soon made up. D'Artagnan went out, but returned a moment after.

'There!' said he, 'it is finished. *Ouf!* not without trouble.'

'The executioner has left London?' Athos asked.

'Ah, well! that was not quite sure enough. He could go out by one gate and enter again by another.'

'And where is he?' asked Athos.

'In the cellar of the inn. Mousqueton is seated at the door; and here's the key.'

'Bravo!' said Aramis. 'But how did you get the man to agree to be out of the way?'

'As everything is decided in this world—by money; it has cost me a good deal, but he has agreed to it.'

'And how much did it cost you, friend?' said Athos; 'for you understand that we are no longer poor musketeers without house and home, and that all expenditure must be in common.'

'It has cost me twelve thousand livres,' said d'Artagnan.

'And how did you raise that sum? Did you possess it?'

'From the queen's famous diamond,'* said d'Artagnan, with a sigh.

'Ah, that's true; I have noticed it on your finger.'

'You had repurchased it of M. d'Essarts?' asked Porthos.

'Ah, yes! but it is written that I should not be able to keep it. What would you have? Diamonds, so one is told to believe, have their likes and dislikes, like men; it seems that one detested me.'

'But,' said Athos, 'although matters are all arranged as far as the executioner is concerned, unfortunately they have their assistants, as I know.'

'Yes, that one has his; but we are in luck's way.'

'How so?'

'Just when I thought I was going to have a second bargain to strike, my man was brought home with a fractured thigh. From an excess of zeal he accompanied the wagon which carried the beams and framing timber for the scaffold; one of the beams fell on his leg and fractured it.'

'Ah,' said Aramis, 'it was he, then, who uttered the cry which I heard when in the king's chamber.'

'That's probable,' said d'Artagnan; 'but as he is a very thoughtful man, he promised when leaving to send four skilful men to help those already engaged in the work; and on returning to his master's house, he wrote at once to Mr Tom Low, a journeyman carpenter, who is a friend of his, to be at Whitehall to fulfil his promise. This is the letter, which he sent by a special messenger who was to take it for tenpence, and who has sold it to me for a louis.'

'And what the devil do you mean to do with that letter?' Athos asked.

'You do not guess?' said d'Artagnan, whose eyes brightened up with intelligence.

'No, upon my soul!'

'Well, my dear Athos, who speak English as well as John Bull himself, you are Mr Tom Low, and we are his three companions; now do you understand?'

Athos burst forth into exclamations of joy and gratitude, ran to a closet, and took out some workmen's clothes, in which the four friends dressed themselves; after which they left the inn, Athos carrying a saw, Porthos a crowbar, Aramis an axe, and d'Artagnan a hammer and nails.

The letter of the executioner's assistant proved to the master carpenter that they were the men whom he had been expecting.

LXIX

THE WORKMEN

TOWARDS the middle of the night, Charles heard a great noise under his window; it was caused by hammering, chopping, and sawing. As he had thrown himself on his bed dressed, and was just going to sleep, the disturbance awoke him with a start; and as, besides its material influence, it called up a moral and terrible echo in his soul, the frightful thoughts of the evening began to return afresh. Alone, facing the darkness and isolation, he had not strength to bear this new torture, which formed no part of his punishment, so he sent Parry with word to the sentinel to beg the workmen to make less noise, and have pity for the last sleep of him who had been their king. The sentinel did not wish to leave his post, but allowed Parry to pass. On coming near the window after having made the circuit of the palace, Parry perceived on a level with the balcony, the railing of which had been removed, a large unfinished scaffold, but on which they were beginning to nail a hanging of black cloth.

This scaffold, raised to the height of the window—that is, about twenty feet from the ground—had two lower stages. Parry, though the sight made him shudder, looked among the eight or ten workmen who were erecting the hideous structure to discover those whose blows were most fatiguing to the king, and on the second stage he saw two men who were removing by the aid of a crowbar the last holdfasts of the iron balcony; one of them, a veritable colossus, was doing the work of the ancient battering-ram. At each stroke of his bar the stone flew into shivers. The other on his knees was removing the loosened stones. It was very evident that these were making the noise of which the king so complained. Parry went up the ladder, and came to them.

'My friends,' said he, 'will you work with a little less noise, I beg of you? The king is asleep, and he has need of rest.'

The man who was striking with the crowbar stopped, and turned half round; but as he was standing, Parry could not see his face, lost as it was in the darkness, which was thick near the stage. The man on his knees also turned round; and as he was lower than his comrade, his face was lighted up by the lantern, so that Parry could see it. This man looked hard at him, and put his finger to his mouth. Parry stepped back stupefied.

'Very well, very well,' said the workman, in good English; 'return and tell the king that if he sleeps badly tonight, he will sleep better tomorrow night.'

This coarse speech, which taken literally had a terrible meaning, was received by the workmen with an explosion of tumultuous applause. Parry withdrew, believing himself to be in a dream. Charles awaited him with impatience. Just as he entered the room, the sentinel on guard at the door put in his head to see what the king was doing. The king was on his bed, leaning on his elbow. Parry closed the door, and went to the king, his face radiant with joy.

'Sire,' said he, in a low voice, 'do you know who those workmen are who are making so much noise?'

'No,' said Charles, with a melancholy shake of the head; 'how can I know that? Do I know those men?'

'Sire,' said Parry, leaning over the bed and speaking in a lower tone, 'it is the Comte de la Fère and his companion.'

'Who are making my scaffold?' enquired the king, astonished.

'Yes, and while doing so are making a hole in the wall.'

'*Chut!*' said the king, looking round with terror. 'You saw them?'

'I spoke to them.'

The king joined his hands together, and said a short, fervent prayer. He then went to the window, and drew aside the curtains. The sentinels were still at their posts on the balcony; just beyond it was a sombre platform on which they were moving like shadows. Charles could distinguish nothing more, but he heard beneath his feet the sound of the blows, and each of these found an echo in his heart.

Parry had not been mistaken, and had recognized Athos. He it was indeed who, with the help of Porthos, was making a hole in which one of the transverse beams was to rest. This hole communicated with a sort of cavity existing under the very floor of the royal chamber. Access once gained to this, it was possible by means of a crowbar and good shoulders—and this latter requisite was what Porthos possessed—to loosen one of the floor-boards; the king then could slip through this opening, hide in one of the compartments of the scaffold, which was entirely covered with black cloth, put on a workman's clothes which had been procured, and then without fear descend with his four companions.

The sentinels, without suspicion, seeing workmen who had been engaged on the scaffold, would allow them to pass. As we have said, the felucca was all ready.

The plan of escape was comprehensive, simple, and easy, as are all things which spring from bold resolution.

Therefore Athos was scratching his white, delicate hands to raise the stones torn from their positions by Porthos.

Already he could pass his head under the ornaments decorating the edge of the balcony. Two hours more, and he could pass his whole body. Before daylight the hole would be finished, and would be concealed under the folds of an interior hanging which d'Artagnan would place there. D'Artagnan had passed himself off as a French workman, and placed his nails with the regularity of the most skilful upholsterer. Aramis was cutting off the surplus of the serge which was hanging down to the ground, and behind which arose the frame-work of the scaffold.

The day at last broke. A large fire of peat and coal had helped the workmen to pass this cold night of the 29th of January. At every moment the most determined workers interrupted their work to go and warm themselves. Athos and Porthos alone had not quitted their work; so at the early dawn the hole was finished. Athos entered it, carrying with him the clothes intended for the king wrapped up in a bit of black cloth. Porthos passed him a crowbar, and d'Artagnan nailed up a hanging of cloth which concealed the hole.

Athos had no more than two hours' work to do to enable him to communicate with the king, and the four friends now thought that they had the whole day before them, since as the executioner was not forthcoming, one must be obtained from Bristol.

D'Artagnan went off to resume his maroon dress, and Porthos his red doublet; as for Aramis, he went to the bishop's, in order, if possible, to gain access with him to the king.

The three had arranged to meet at noon before Whitehall, to see what might be going on there. Before leaving the scaffold, Aramis came to the opening where Athos was hidden to tell him that he was going to try and see Charles again.

'Adieu, then, and be of good courage,' said Athos. 'Tell the king how matters stand; tell him that when he is alone he is to knock on the floor, that I may continue my task with certainty. If Parry can help me by removing beforehand the lower slab of the chimney, that would be so much done in advance. You, Aramis, try not to leave the king. Speak loud, very loud, for they will be listening at the door. If there is a sentinel in the room, kill him without hesitating about it; if two, let Parry slay one and you the other; if there are three, let yourself be killed, but at all risk save the king.'

'Don't be disturbed,' said Aramis; 'I will take two poniards, so as to let Parry have one. Is that all?'

'Yes, now go; but urge the king not to be too much influenced by a false generosity. While you are fighting, if it *must* be, let him escape; the hearth-stone once replaced over his head, and you, dead or alive, on it, it will take at least ten minutes to discover the hole by which he has escaped. During these ten minutes we shall have started on our way, and the king will be saved.'

'It shall be done as you say, Athos. Your hand, for perhaps we shall never see each other again.'

Athos passed his arms round the neck of Aramis and embraced him.

'For you,' said he, 'now if I die, say to d'Artagnan that I love him like a child, and embrace him for me. Embrace also our good and brave Porthos. Adieu.'

'Adieu,' said Aramis. 'I am as sure now that the king will effect his escape as I am of pressing the most loyal hand to be found in the world.'

Aramis left, and went back to the inn, whistling an air in praise of Cromwell. He found the two others seated near a good fire, drinking a bottle of port and devouring a cold fowl. Porthos was eating, while uttering many curses against these infamous doings of the Parliamentarians; d'Artagnan was eating in silence, all the time concocting the most daring plans.

Aramis told all that was agreed upon; d'Artagnan nodded assent, Porthos approved audibly.

'Bravo!' he said; 'besides, we shall be there at the time of the flight. There is a good hiding-place under the scaffold, and we can keep in it. Between d'Artagnan, myself, Grimaud, and Mousqueton, we can easily kill eight of them. At two minutes per man, that's four minutes; Mousqueton will lose one, that makes five. During these five minutes you will have gone a quarter of a league.'

Aramis ate a morsel quickly, drank a glass of wine, and changed his clothes.

'Now,' said he, 'I am going to the Right Reverend's. Look well after the arms, Porthos; keep a watch over the executioner, d'Artagnan.'

'All right; Grimaud has relieved Mousqueton, and has his foot on the trap-door.'

'No matter; redouble your watchfulness, and don't remain an instant inactive.'

'Inactive! my dear fellow, ask Porthos. I don't live; I am always on my legs. I have the air of a *danseur*. *Mordioux!* how I love France at this moment, and how good it is to have a country of one's own, when one is so badly off in the country of others!'

Aramis left them, as he had left Athos, after embracing them; then he went to Bishop Juxon's, to whom he sent his request. The bishop consented the more readily to take him, as he had foreseen the need of a priest in case the king should desire to receive the communion.

Aramis, still more disguised by his pallor and sadness than by his deacon's dress, entered the coach with him. It was scarcely nine when the coach reached Whitehall. Nothing seemed changed; the anterooms and passages were filled with guards. Two sentinels kept watch at the door, two others walked up and down on the platform of the scaffold, on which the block was already placed.

The king was full of hope; this, on seeing Aramis, became joy. He embraced Juxon; he pressed the hand of Aramis. The bishop talked in a loud voice of their interview on the preceding evening. The king replied that what had passed on that occasion had borne fruit, and that he desired another conversation. Juxon turned towards those present, and begged them to leave him alone with the king. All retired. When the door was closed, 'Sire,' said Aramis, quickly, 'you are saved! The executioner of London has disappeared; his assistant has broken his thigh. Doubtless they have already noticed the disappearance of the executioner, but there is none nearer than the one at Bristol, and time is needed to send for him. We have then, at least, till tomorrow.'

'But the Comte de la Fère?' asked the king.

'Is two feet from you, Sire. Take the poker and give three knocks; he will make you an answer.'

The king did so, and immediately, replying to the signal, some taps were heard under the floor.

'So,' said the king, 'he who replies there——'

'Is the Comte de la Fère, who is preparing the way by which your Majesty will escape. Parry will lift up this slab of marble, and a passage will be opened.'

'But,' said Parry, 'I have no tools.'

'Take this poniard,' said Aramis; 'only avoid blunting it too much, for you will soon have need of it for digging something else than stone.'

'Oh, Juxon!' said Charles, turning towards the bishop, and taking his two hands— 'Juxon, listen to the prayer of him who was once your king——'

'Who is still, and always will be,' said Juxon, kissing the king's hand.

'Pray all your life for this gentleman whom you see here, for the other whom you hear under our feet, for two others, who, wherever they may be, are, I am sure, watching for my safety.'

'Sire,' replied Juxon, 'you shall be obeyed. Every day, so long as I live, a prayer shall be offered for these faithful friends of your Majesty.'

The underminer continued for some time at his work, and they heard him drawing closer and closer. But all of a sudden and unexpected noise was heard in the gallery. Aramis seized the poker, and gave the signal to stop working.

The noise became louder; it was a tramp of regular steps. The four men remained still, with their eyes fixed on the door, which was quietly opened, and with a sort of solemnity.

Some guards were formed in line in the anteroom to the king's chamber. A parliamentary commissioner, clothed in black, and with a gravity which augured ill, entered, saluted the king, and unrolling a parchment, read to him his sentence, as is the practice in the case of those who are going to die on the scaffold.

'What does that mean?' Aramis asked of Juxon.

Juxon made a sign to intimate that he was as ignorant as Aramis.

'It is, then, settled for today?' the king asked, with an emotion only perceptible to Juxon and Aramis.

'Were you not previously told, Sire, that it was settled for this morning?' replied the man in black.

'And,' said the king, 'must I perish like a common criminal by the hands of the executioner of London?'

'He has disappeared, Sire; but a man has offered to take his place. The execution will be delayed only to give you the time you may request for putting your temporal and spiritual affairs in order.'

A slight perspiration, which came forth like beads from the roots of Charles's hair, was the only mark of the emotion he showed on learning this news.

But Aramis became livid. His heart stopped beating; he closed his eyes, and rested his hand on a table. On observing this deep grief, Charles seemed to forget his own. He went to him, took him by the hand, and embraced him.

'Come, friend,' said he, with a sweet, sad smile, 'keep up your courage.' Then turning towards the commissioner, 'Sir,' he said, 'I am ready. There are only two things I desire, which will not delay you much—to receive the communion, and to embrace and say farewell to my children for the last time. Will these be allowed me?'

'Yes, Sire,' replied the commissioner, and he left.

Aramis recovered his composure, and uttered a loud groan.

'Oh, Monseigneur!' exclaimed he, seizing Juxon by the hands; 'where is God? where is he?'

'My son,' said the bishop, with firmness, 'you do not see him because earthly passions hide him from you.'

'My child,' said the king to Aramis, 'do not grieve so. You ask what God is doing? God sees your devotion and my martyrdom, and believe me, both will be recompensed; then blame men for what happens, and not God. It is men who kill me; it is men who make you mourn.'

'Yes, Sire,' said Aramis; 'you are right. It is men whom I must and will blame.'

'Sit down, Juxon,' said the king, falling on his knees, 'for you must now listen to my confession. Stay, Monsieur,' he said to Aramis, who made a movement to retire; 'stay, Parry, I have nothing to say, even by way of confession, which cannot be said before you all; stay, and I have but one regret, which is that the whole world cannot hear me as you all do.'

Juxon seated himself, and the king, kneeling before him as the humblest of the faithful, began his confession.

LXX

REMEMBER

ON finishing his confession, Charles received the communion; he then asked to see his children. Ten o'clock struck; as the king had said, the delay had not been great.

The populace had already gathered; it was known that ten was the hour fixed for the execution. All the streets adjacent to the palace were crowded; and the king began to distinguish the distant noise which only a crowd and the sea make—the former when agitated by their passions, the latter by storms.

The king's children came—the Princess Charlotte[1]* and the Duke of Gloucester; the one a pretty little fair girl, whose eyes were moist with tears, the other a boy about nine, whose dry eye and lip disdainfully projecting implied a growing haught-

---

[1] Elizabeth.

iness. The boy had wept all night; but before all these spectators he did not weep.

Charles felt his heart breaking at the sight of these children,
whom he had not seen for two years, and whom he saw now
just before his death. A tear came to his eye, and he turned
away to wipe it off, for he wished to appear composed before
those to whom he was leaving such a weighty legacy of
suffering and misfortune.

He first talked to the girl; drawing her towards him, he
recommended her to be pious, and resigned, and to show filial
love. Then he took the young Duke of Gloucester* on his knee
that he might press him to his heart and kiss him.

'My son,' he said to him, 'you have seen many people in the
streets and antechambers; these people are going to cut off your
father's head. Do not forget it. Perhaps one day, having you
in their power, they will want to make you king instead of the
Prince of Wales or the Duke of York, your elder brothers;*
but you are not the king, my son, and you can become so only
by your brother's death. Promise, therefore, not to let the
people put the crown on your head until you have a lawful
right to it. For one day—listen, my son, attentively—if you do
so they will take away all, both head and crown, and then you
will not die as calmly as I am dying. Promise this, my son.'

The child stretched out his little hand, put it into his
father's, and said, 'Sire, I promise your Majesty——'

Charles interrupted him.

'Henry, call me your father.'

'My father, I promise you they shall kill me before they shall
make me king.'

'Right, my son. Now embrace me; and you also, Charlotte,
and don't forget me.'

'Oh, no! never, never!' both the children exclaimed, throwing
their arms round his neck.

'Good-bye, my dear children. Take them away, Juxon; their
tears would deprive me of the courage to die.'

Juxon snatched the poor children from their father's arms,
and gave them to those who had brought them. Behind them
the doors were opened, and everyone could enter. The king,
seeing himself alone in the midst of a crowd of guards and

inquisitive people who invaded the apartment, remembered that the Comte de la Fère was quite near, under the floor, not able to see him, and still hoping. He feared lest the least noise should serve as a signal to Athos, who by resuming his task would betray himself. The king therefore continued motionless, and by his example kept those present quiet.

The king was not mistaken, Athos was actually beneath him. He listened; he despaired of hearing the signal; he sometimes in his impatience began to cut the stone afresh, but fearing to be heard, he immediately stopped. This horrible inaction lasted two hours. The silence of death reigned in the royal chamber.

Then Athos determined to seek the reason for this dumb tranquillity which the din of the crowd alone disturbed. He opened the hanging which hid the hole, and descended to the first stage of the scaffold. Scarcely four inches above his head was the flooring, which was extended at the level of the platform, and which made the scaffold. The noise which he had but indistinctly heard hitherto, but which at this moment met him in full force, made him leap with terror. He went to the edge of the scaffold, opened the black cloth, and saw cavalry ranged against the terrible machine; beyond these, ranks of halberdiers, beyond them musketeers, and still beyond these the first rows of the populace, who, like the gloomy ocean, were bubbling up and groaning.

'What has happened?' said Athos to himself, trembling more than the cloth, the plaits of which he was rumpling. 'The people are pressing forward; the soldiers are under arms; and among the spectators, whose eyes are all fixed on the window, I see d'Artagnan. What is he staring at? Good heavens! have they let the executioner escape?'

All of a sudden the drums rolled discordant and gloomy; a sound of heavy and continuous footsteps was heard above his head. It seemed to him as though an extended procession tramped across the floors of Whitehall; he soon heard the very planks of the scaffold creak. He cast a glance out on the open square, and the attitude of the spectators told what a last hope, still lingering in the depths of his heart, hitherto had prevented him from surmising.

The murmurs of the crowd entirely ceased. All eyes were fixed on the window of Whitehall; half-opened mouths and suspended breaths indicated the expectation of some terrible spectacle. The tramp of steps, which, from his position under the floor of the king's room, Athos had heard above his head, was reproduced on the scaffold, which bent under the weight so that the planks almost touched the head of the unfortunate gentleman. It was evidently two files of soldiers taking position. At the same instant a well-known and noble voice said above his head, 'Colonel, I want to speak to the people.'

Athos shuddered from head to foot; it was really the king who was speaking on the scaffold. In fact, after having drunk some wine and eaten a little bread, Charles, tired of awaiting death, had suddenly determined to take it by the forelock, and had given the signal to march.

Then the window had been opened wide, and the populace saw advancing in silence a man in a mask, whom from the axe in his hand they knew was the executioner. On approaching the block, he placed his axe upon it. This was the first sound that Athos understood.

Then behind the executioner, pale certainly, but calm, and walking with a firm step, came Charles between two clergymen, followed by some superior officers appointed to carry out the sentence, and escorted by two lines of halberdiers, who were drawn up on the two sides of the scaffold.

The sight of the masked man had called forth a prolonged clamour. Everyone was curious to know who this unknown executioner was who had offered himself just in time to enable the terrible spectacle to take place, when the people had thought that it was postponed until the next day. Though closely scanned, all that could be seen was a man of middle height, dressed entirely in black, who seemed to be of mature age—for the end of a beard which was turning grey extended below the mask which covered his face.

But at the sight of the king so calm, noble, and dignified, silence was instantly re-established, so that each one could hear the wish which he expressed of speaking to the people.

To the request of the king to be allowed to speak, the one to whom it had been addressed had evidently assented, for in a firm and sonorous voice which vibrated to the bottom of Athos's heart, the king began to speak. He explained his conduct towards the people, and gave them advice for the welfare of England.

'Oh!' said Athos to himself, 'is it indeed possible that I hear what I hear, and see what I see? Has God abandoned his representative on the earth so far as to let him die so miserably? And I have not seen him! I have not said "Adieu!" to him.'

A noise was heard which sounded as if the instrument of death had been moved on the block.

The king interrupted himself.

'Do not touch the axe,' said he. And he resumed his speech where he had left it.

The speech being ended, an icy silence succeeded above the count's head. He put his hand to his forehead, down which trickled the drops of perspiration, although the air was frosty.

This silence indicated the final preparations. The king had directed a look full of pity upon the crowd; then detaching the Order which he wore, and which was the same diamond star which the queen had sent him, he handed it to the priest who accompanied Juxon. Then he drew from his breast a small diamond cross. This also came from Queen Henrietta.

'Sir,' said he, addressing the priest, 'I shall keep this cross in my hand till the last moment; you will take it from me when I am dead.'

'Yes, Sire,' said a voice which Athos recognized as that of Aramis.

Then Charles, who till then had had his hat on, took it off; then one by one he undid all the buttons of his doublet, and took it off also; then, as it was cold, he asked for his dressing-gown, which was given him. All these preparations were made with an appalling self-possession. One might have thought that the king was going to his bed, and not to his coffin.

Lastly, lifting up his hair, 'Will it inconvenience you?' he said to the executioner. 'In that case it can be tied up with a string.'

Charles accompanied these words with a look which seemed as if it would penetrate under the mask of the unknown. This look, so noble and calm, forced the man to turn away his head, but behind the penetrating look of the king he met the burning look of Aramis.

The king, seeing that he did not answer, repeated his question.

'It will be quite enough,' said the man, in a hollow voice, 'if you remove it from the neck.'

The king separated his hair with his hands, and looking at the block, 'The block seems very low,' he said. 'Would it not be better a little higher?'

'It is as usual,' replied the masked man.

'Do you think you can cut off my head at a stroke?' asked the king.

'I hope so,' answered the executioner.

There was in these three words, *I hope so*, such a strange intonation that everyone shuddered except the king.

'That is right; and now, executioner, listen.'

The masked man took a step towards the king, and leaned on his axe.

'I don't wish you to surprise me. I shall kneel down in prayer. Do not strike then.'

'And when shall I?' asked the man.

'When I place my neck on the block and stretch forth my arms, saying *Remember*,* then strike boldly.'

The masked man slightly bowed.

'The moment has come for leaving the world,' said the king to those who were around him. 'Gentlemen, I leave you in the midst of a storm, and precede you into that land which knows not storms. Farewell.'

He looked at Aramis, and gave him a special sign by a movement of his head.

'Now,' he continued, 'go farther off and let me say my prayers, I beg of you. You also,' he said to the man with a mask; 'it is only for an instant, and I know I belong to you.'

Then Charles knelt, made the sign of the cross, put his mouth close to the planks, as if he wished to kiss the platform, 'Comte de la Fère,' he said, in French, 'are you there, and may I speak?'

This voice struck Athos full in the heart, and pierced him like steel.

'Yes, Majesty,' said he, trembling.

'Faithful friend, generous heart, I cannot be saved; I did not deserve to be. I have spoken to men and to God, to thee I speak last of all. To support a cause which I have thought sacred I have lost the throne of my ancestors and my children's heritage. There remains a million in gold,* which I hid in the cellars of Newcastle when quitting that town. This money employ when you believe it will be most profitable for my eldest son; and now, Comte de la Fère, bid me adieu.'

'Adieu, sacred and martyred Majesty,' stammered Athos, frozen with terror.

There was a momentary silence, then in a full, sonorous voice which was heard not only on the scaffold, but also in the open square before it, the king said, '*Remember!*'

He had scarcely uttered the word before a terrible blow shook the scaffold; the dust was shaken from the drapery, and blinded the unfortunate gentleman beneath. Then suddenly, as if mechanically, Athos raised his head; a warm drop fell on his forehead. He drew back with a shudder, and at the same instant the drops became a black cascade, which gushed on the floor.

Athos had fallen on his knees, and remained for a while as if overcome with madness and loss of strength. Soon, by the decreasing noise, he knew that the crowd was moving away; he remained still for a time, motionless, dumb, and full of dismay. Then returning, he went and dipped the end of his handkerchief in the blood of the martyr-king; and as the crowd was growing less and less, he got down, opened the cloth, slipped between two horses, mixed among the people, whose dress he was wearing, and was the first to reach the inn.

He went to his room, looked at himself in the glass, saw his forehead marked by a large red spot, put up his hand, and drew it back covered with the blood of the king, and then fainted away.

LXXI

THE MAN IN THE MASK

ALTHOUGH it was only four o'clock in the afternoon, it was quite dark; the snow was falling thick and icy. Aramis returned next, and found Athos, if not unconscious, at least crushed. At his friend's first words the count awoke as from a sort of lethargy into which he had fallen.

'Well,' said Aramis, 'conquered by fate!'

'Conquered!' said Athos. 'Noble and unfortunate king!'

'Are you wounded?'

'No; it is his blood.'

The count wiped his forehead.

'Where were you, then?'

'Where you left me—under the scaffold.'

'And you saw everything?'

'No, but I understood all. God preserve me from another such hour as that I have just passed! Is not my hair white?'

'Then you know that I did not leave him?'

'I heard your voice up to the last moment.'

'See here the star and the cross which I took from his hand; he wished them to be restored to the queen.'

'And here is a handkerchief in which to wrap them,' and Athos drew from his pocket the handkerchief that he had dipped in the blood of the king. 'And now,' asked he, 'what have they done with the poor corpse?'

'By Cromwell's order it will receive royal honours.* We have placed the body in a lead coffin; the physicians are employed in embalming the remains, and this work finished, the king will lie in state.'

'Mockery!' sullenly muttered Athos; 'royal honours to him whom they have assassinated!'

'That proves that the king dies, but royalty does not.'

'Alas!' said Athos, 'he is perhaps the last knightly king whom the world will see.'

'Come, do not distress yourself, Count,' said a deep voice on the stairs, on which the heavy steps of Porthos were heard; 'we are all mortal, my poor friends.'

'You arrive late, my dear Porthos,' said the count.

'Yes, there were some fellows on the way who delayed me. They were dancing, the wretches! I took one by the neck, and thought I would choke him a bit. Just at that moment a patrol came up. Happily he with whom I particularly had business was for some minutes without the power of speaking. I profited by this, and turned into a side street, and this led me into another still smaller. Then I lost my way. I don't know London; I don't know English. I thought I should never find my way again; however, here I am.'

'But have you not seen d'Artagnan?' said Aramis; 'and can anything have happened to him?'

'We were separated by the crowd,' said Porthos; 'and in spite of all my efforts I was not able to find him.'

'Oh!' said Athos, with some bitterness, '*I* saw him; he was in the front rank of the crowd, in a good position to see the whole spectacle.'

'Oh, Comte de la Fère,' said a calm voice, though broken by want of breath through his haste, 'is it really you who calumniate the absent?'

This reproach deeply affected Athos. However, as the impression produced by the sight of d'Artagnan in the front ranks of the senseless and ferocious crowd was very strong, he contented himself by replying—

'I do not calumniate you, my friend. We felt disquieted about you, and I told them where you were. You did not know King Charles; he was only a stranger to you, and you were not drawn to love him,' and he extended his hand to his friend. But d'Artagnan pretended not to see Athos's movement, and kept his hand under his cloak.

'*Ouf!* I am tired,' said d'Artagnan, and sat down.

'Drink a glass of port,' said Aramis, taking a bottle and filling a glass; 'drink, that will set you up again.'

'Yes, let us drink,' said Athos, who saw the Gascon's displeasure, and wished to touch glasses with him, 'and then leave this hateful country. The felucca is waiting, as you know. Let us start this evening; we have nothing more to do here.'

'You are in a great hurry, Monsieur the Count,' said d'Artagnan.

'The bloody soil scorches my feet,' said Athos.

'The snow does not produce that effect on me,' the Gascon said quietly.

'But what do you wish us to do, now that the king is dead?'

'So, Monsieur the Count,' said d'Artagnan, carelessly, 'you do not see that something remains to be done by us here?'

'Nothing, nothing,' said Athos, 'except to doubt the divine goodness and to mistrust one's own strength.'

'Ah, well,' said d'Artagnan; 'I, mean wretch, sanguinary loiterer, who placed myself thirty feet from the scaffold to see the head of the king fall, whom I don't know and to whom, as it appears, I was indifferent—I think differently from the count. I shall stay.'

Athos grew very pale; every one of his friend's reproaches penetrated to the depths of his heart.

'So you mean to stay in London?' said Porthos to d'Artagnan.

'Yes, do you?'

'Why, now,' said Porthos, a little embarrassed in the presence of Athos and Aramis, 'if you remain, as I came with you, I shall depart only with you; I shall not leave you by yourself in this hateful country.'

'Thanks, my excellent friend. Then I have a small enterprise to propose, which we will put in execution together so soon as Monsieur the Count has gone; and the idea of it came into my head while I was looking at the spectacle.'

'What is it?' said Porthos.

'It is to know who that man in the mask was who so obligingly offered to cut off the king's head.'

'A man in a mask!' exclaimed Athos; 'you have not let the executioner escape?'

'Oh, no,' said d'Artagnan, 'he is still in the cellar, where he has had, I expect, some acquaintance with our host's wine-bottles. But you make me think——'

He went to the door.

'Mousqueton!' said he.

'Monsieur?' replied a voice which seemed to come up from the depths of the earth.

'Let your prisoner go; all is over.'

'But,' said Athos, 'who then was the wretch who raised his hand against his king?'

'An amateur executioner, who, for all that, wielded the axe with adroitness, for, *as he hoped*,' said Aramis, 'he needed to give but one blow.'

'Did you not see his face?' Athos asked.

'No; he wore a mask,' said d'Artagnan.

'But you who were quite near him, Aramis?'

'I saw only a beard partly grey, which fell below the mask.'

'It was then a man of mature age?' asked Athos.

'Oh,' said d'Artagnan, 'that signifies nothing. When one puts on a mask one can easily put on a beard.'

'I am sorry I did not follow him,' said Porthos.

'Ah, well, my dear Porthos, that is just the idea that occurred to me,' said d'Artagnan.

Athos understood it all now; he got up.

'Pardon me, d'Artagnan,' he said. 'I have doubted God; I was doubting you too. Pardon me, friend.'

'We will see to that by and by,' said d'Artagnan, with a half smile.

'Well?' said Aramis.

'Well,' resumed d'Artagnan, 'while I was looking, not at the king, as the count thinks—for I know what it means when a man is about to die, and although I ought by this time to be used to this kind of thing, I always feel badly—but at the masked man, for I thought I should like to know who he was. Now, as we are in the habit of calling one another to our mutual help as one calls his second hand to the aid of the first, I looked round mechanically to see if Porthos were there—for I had recognized you, Aramis, near the king, and you, Count, I knew would be under the scaffold. This thought makes me pardon you,' he added, giving his hand to Athos, 'for you must have suffered very acutely. I was looking around me, when I saw to my right a head which had been broken, and which, as well as possible, had been patched up with black silk. "Hang it," I said to myself; "I fancy that I had a hand in sewing up that skull." In fact, it was that unfortunate Scot, Parry's brother, you know—the one on whom Groslow was amused to put forth his strength, and who had no more than half a head when we fell in with him.'

'Perfectly,' said Porthos; 'the man with the black fowls.'

'That's right; he was making signs to another man who was to my left. I turned round and recognized honest Grimaud, quite engaged like myself in devouring with his eyes my masked headsman. "Oh," I uttered. Now, as that is an abbreviation which Monsieur the Count uses whenever he speaks to him, Grimaud considered he was the one called, and turned round as if moved by a spring. He at once recognized me; then pointing his finger towards the masked man, "Hi!" said he, as if he meant to say, "Have you observed?" "Yes, indeed," I responded. We had thoroughly understood each other. I then turned towards the Scot, his face, also, had a look of recognition. In short, all ended, you know how, in a very sad fashion. The people went away; by degrees evening drew on. I withdrew into a corner of the space before the palace with Grimaud and the Scot, to whom I had made a sign to stay with us, and I from that point looked at the executioner, who returned into the royal chamber and changed his dress; doubtless it was covered with blood. After this he put on a black hat, covered himself with his cloak, and disappeared. I guessed he was going away, and ran in front of the door. In fact, a few minutes after we saw him come down the staircase.'

'You followed him?' exclaimed Athos.

'Rather! but not without trouble, I can tell you. Every moment he kept turning; then we were obliged to hide or to assume an air of indifference. I should have killed him; but I am not selfish, and it was a feast which I was preparing for you, Aramis and Athos, to console you a little. At length, after half an hour spent in crossing the most crooked streets of the city, he reached a small, isolated house, where not a sound nor a light told of the presence of man.

'Grimaud drew forth a pistol.

' "Hi?" said he, pointing him out.

' "No," I said, and I held his arm. I have told you I had my idea. The masked man stopped before a low door, and took out a key; but before putting it into the lock, he turned round to see if he had been followed. I was hiding behind a tree, Grimaud behind a stone post; the Scot, who had nothing to hide behind, threw himself flat on the street. Without doubt he whom we were pursuing thought himself alone, for I heard the creaking of the key; the door opened, and he disappeared.'

'The wretch!' said Aramis, 'while you have returned he will have escaped, and we shall not discover him.'

'Come now, Aramis, you take me for someone else,' said d'Artagnan.

'Yes,' said Athos, 'in your absence——'

'Well, in my absence had I not Grimaud and the Scot to take my place? Before he had time to take ten steps inside the house, I had made the circuit of it. At the door by which he entered I stationed the Scot, telling him that if the man in the mask went out he must follow him, while Grimaud would himself follow him, and would return to await us where we were. In short, I have placed Grimaud as the second spy, and here I am. The beast is surrounded; now, who wants to see the capture?'

Athos threw himself into the arms of d'Artagnan, who was wiping his forehead.

'Friend,' said he, 'truly, you have been too good to pardon me. I was wrong, a hundred times wrong, for I ought to know you; but there is at the bottom of us something wicked which doubts constantly.'

'H'm!' said Porthos; 'was it perchance Cromwell who was the executioner, to make sure that the task should be well done?'

'How so? M. Cromwell is fat and short; and this man slim, and rather tall than short.'

'Some condemned soldier to whom pardon was offered at that price,' said Athos, 'as was done in the case of the unhappy Chalais.'

'No, no,' continued d'Artagnan; 'it was not the measured step of a foot-soldier, nor was it either the straddling step of a horse-soldier. There was a fine leg and a distinguished bearing. Either I am much deceived, or we have to do with a gentleman in this.'

'A gentleman!' exclaimed Athos, 'impossible! it would be a dishonour to the whole class.'

'A pretty chase,' said Porthos, with a laugh which made the panes of glass shake—'a pretty chase, I declare.'

'Do you mean to go off now, Athos?' asked d'Artagnan.

'No, I shall stay,' replied the gentleman, with a menace which promised no good for him to whom it referred.

'Then our swords,' said Aramis, 'don't let us lose an instant.'

The four friends quickly put on their own clothes, girt on their swords, called up Mousqueton and Blaisois, and ordered them to pay the bill at the inn and to have everything ready for their departure, the probability being that they would leave London the same night.

The gloom had grown deeper; the snow continued falling, and looked like a vast winding-sheet stretched out over the regicide city. It was nearly seven; scarcely a passer-by was to be seen—all were talking over their fires in low voices of the terrible events of that day.

The four friends, wrapped up in their cloaks, went along the streets and squares so frequented by day and so deserted this night. D'Artagnan acted as guide, trying to recognize from time to time the crosses that he had made with his poniard on the walls; but the night was so dark that these indications could scarcely be recognized. However, d'Artagnan had so fixed in his mind the various signs, posts, and fountains, that after half an hour's walk the four came in sight of the lonely house.

D'Artagnan for a moment thought Parry's brother had disappeared. He was mistaken. The sturdy Scot, accustomed to the frosts of his mountains, was leaning against a post, and like a statue thrown from its base, insensible to the inclemency of the weather, was all covered with snow; but at the approach of the four men he stood up.

'Come,' said Athos, 'here is another good servant; thank goodness, brave men are less rare than one thinks—that's encouraging.'

'Don't be in a hurry to weave garlands for our Scot,' said d'Artagnan; 'I believe the fellow is here on his own account. I have heard it said that those who have been born north of the Tweed are very revengeful. Let M. Groslow look out! he would pass an unpleasant quarter of an hour if he fell in with him.'

'Well?' said Athos, in English.

'No one has come out,' said Parry's brother.

'Well, stay with this man, Porthos and Aramis, will you? D'Artagnan will take me to Grimaud.'

Grimaud, not less clever than the Scot, was closely wedged in a hollow willow tree, of which he had made a sentry-box.

For a moment d'Artagnan feared, as in the case of the other sentinel, that the masked man had gone, and that Grimaud had followed him. Presently a head appeared, and gave a slight whistle.

'Oh!' said Athos.

'Yes,' replied Grimaud.

They came up to the willow tree.

'Well,' asked d'Artagnan, 'has anyone gone out?'

'No, but someone has gone in.'

'A man or a woman.'

'A man.'

'Ah! ah!' said d'Artagnan; 'then there are two.'

'I wish there were four,' said Athos; 'the sides at least would be equal.'

'Perhaps there are four.'

'How can that be?'

'Other men might have been in the house before them, and waiting for them.'

'We can see,' said Grimaud, pointing to a window, through the shutters of which filtered some rays of light.

'That's true,' said d'Artagnan; 'let us call the others,' and they went round the house to signal Porthos and Aramis to come. They came in great haste.

'Have you seen anything?' they asked.

'No; but we are going to see,' replied d'Artagnan, pointing to Grimaud, who, by catching on the roughnesses of the wall, had already raised himself five or six feet from the ground.

All four drew closer. Grimaud continued his ascent with the agility of a cat. At last he succeeded in seizing one of the hooks which serve to hold back the shutters when they are open; at the same time his foot found a moulding which furnished him sufficient support, for he made a sign indicating that he had gained his end. Then he applied his eye to the crack in the shutter.

'Well?' asked d'Artagnan.

Grimaud held up his hand closed all but two fingers.

'Speak,' said Athos, 'we cannot see your signs. How many are there?'

'Two,' said he, with a great effort; 'one is facing me, the other has his back towards me.'

'Well, and who is he facing you?'

'The man whom I saw pass.'

'Do you know him?'

'I think I recognize him, and I am not mistaken—fat and short.'

'Who is it?' asked the four, in a low voice.

'General Oliver Cromwell.'

'And the other?'

'Thin and slender.'

'That's the executioner,' said d'Artagnan and Aramis, at once.

'I see only his back,' replied Grimaud; 'but wait—now he is moving; he is turning round; and if he would take off his mask I should be able to see him—ah!'

Grimaud, as if struck to the heart, let go the iron hasp and threw himself back, uttering a low groan. Porthos caught him in his arms.

'Did you see him?' they asked.

'Yes,' said Grimaud, with his hair on end and perspiration on his brow.

'The executioner, in fact?' said Aramis.

'Yes.'

'And who is it?' said Porthos.

'He! he!' stammered Grimaud, pale as death, and seizing with trembling hands the hand of his master.

'What *he*?'

'Mordaunt!' replied Grimaud.

D'Artagnan, Aramis, and Porthos uttered exclamations of joy. Athos took a step backwards, and passed his hand across his forehead.

'Fatality!' he murmured.

LXXII

CROMWELL'S HOUSE

IT was really Mordaunt whom d'Artagnan had followed, but without recognizing him.

On entering the house he had taken off the mask, removed the grey beard which he had worn for a disguise, and then gone upstairs and entered a room hung with dark-coloured hangings, and was in the presence of a man seated at a bureau writing. It was Cromwell.

Cromwell had in London, as is well known, two or three of these retreats unknown even to most of his friends, the secret being only entrusted to those most intimate with him. Mordaunt could be counted in this latter class.

When he entered, Cromwell raised his head.

'Is it you, Mordaunt? You come late.'

'General,' he replied, 'I wanted to see the very last of the ceremony; that has kept me.'

'Ah!' said Cromwell, 'I did not believe that ordinarily you were so inquisitive as that.'

'I am always inquisitive to see the fall of one of your Highness's enemies; and he was not to be reckoned one of the least of them. But were not you, General, at Whitehall?'

'No,' said Cromwell.

There was a momentary silence.

'Have you heard the details?'

'No; I have been here since the morning. I only know that there was a plot for rescuing the king.'

'Ah, you knew that?'

'It was of little consequence. Four men disguised as workmen aimed at getting the king from prison, and taking him to Greenwich, where a ship was waiting.'

'And knowing all that, your Highness remained here, far from the city, calm and inactive?'

'Calm, yes; but who told you I was inactive?'

'But suppose the plot had succeeded?'

'I wish it had.'

'I thought your Highness regarded Charles I's death as a misfortune necessary for England's welfare?'

'Well,' said Cromwell, 'that was always my opinion. But provided he died, that was all that was necessary. It would have been better that it should not have been on a scaffold.'

'Why so, your Highness?'

Cromwell smiled.

'I beg pardon,' said Mordaunt; 'but you know, General, that I am a political apprentice, and wish to profit on all occasions from the lessons which my master may please to give me.'

'Because it would have been said that while I had justly condemned him, I had allowed him to escape from pity.'

'But if he had actually escaped?'

'Impossible; my precautions were taken.'

'And does your Highness know the four men who had undertaken this enterprise of saving the king?'

'They are four Frenchmen, two of whom were sent by Madame Henrietta to her husband, and two by Mazarin to me.'

'And do you believe, sir, that Mazarin commissioned them to do what they have done?'

'It's possible; but he will not acknowledge it.'

'Why not?'

'Because they have been foiled in their object.'

'Your Highness gave me two of those Frenchmen when they were guilty only of having borne arms for Charles's cause. But now they are guilty of plotting against England, is your Highness willing to give me all four of them?'

'Take them,' said Cromwell.

Mordaunt bowed with a smile of triumphant ferocity.

'But,' said Cromwell, seeing that Mordaunt was preparing to thank him, 'let us return, if you please, to the unfortunate Charles. Were there many cries among the people?'

'Very few, except the cry, "Long live Cromwell!"'

'Where were you standing?'

Mordaunt looked at the general for a moment to try and read in his eyes whether the question was from curiosity, or whether he knew all about it. But Mordaunt's keen look could not penetrate the dark depths of Cromwell's face.

'I was so placed that I could see and hear everything.'

It was now Cromwell's turn to look hard at Mordaunt, and for the latter to become impenetrable. After a few seconds spent in examination, he turned away his eyes with indifference.

'It appears,' said Cromwell, 'that the improvised executioner did his duty well. The stroke, at least from what I am told, was applied by the hand of a master.'

Mordaunt recalled what Cromwell had said—that he knew no details; but he was now convinced that the general had been present, hidden behind some curtain or blind.

'In fact,' said Mordaunt, with a calm voice and emotionless countenance, 'one blow sufficed.'

'Perhaps he was a man of that craft.'

'Do you believe it, sir?'

'Why not?'

'The man had not the look of an executioner.'

'And who but an executioner would have wished to practise that frightful occupation?'

'But,' said Mordaunt, 'perhaps it was some personal enemy of King Charles, who had vowed vengeance against him; or perhaps some gentleman who had grave reasons for hating the fallen king, and thus opposed him with axe in hand and masked face, not as the executioner's substitute, but as the minister of fate.'

'It is possible.'

'And if that were so, would your Highness condemn his act?'

'It is not for me to judge,' said Cromwell. 'It lies between him and God.'

'But suppose your Highness knew this gentleman?'

'But I don't know him, sir, and don't wish to. As soon as Charles was condemned, it was not a man who beheaded him, but an axe.'

'And yet, but for this man the king would have been saved.'

Cromwell smiled.

'Without doubt; you have said so yourself—they would have taken him away.'

'They would have taken him away, but only as far as Greenwich. There he would have embarked on the felucca with his four deliverers; but on it were four of my men and five

barrels of powder. At sea the men would enter the boat, and
you are already too clever a politician, Mordaunt, to need the
rest to be told you.'

'Yes, out at sea they would all have been blown up.'

'Exactly. The explosion would have done what the axe had
not. King Charles would have entirely disappeared. It would
have been said that he escaped human justice, and had been
overtaken by divine vengeance. All this your masked gentleman
has caused me to lose, Mordaunt. You see clearly that I had
my reasons for not wishing to know him, for in truth, in spite
of his excellent intentions, I can hardly feel grateful for what
he has done.'

'Sir, as is always the case, I bend in humility before you;
you are a profound thinker, and your idea of the mined felucca
is sublime.'

'Absurd,' said Cromwell, 'since it has become useless. There
is no idea sublime in politics except one which bears its fruits.
Every abortive idea is foolish and barren. You will go then this
evening to Greenwich,' continued Cromwell, getting up; 'ask
for the skipper of the *Lightning*. You will show him a white
handkerchief knotted at the corners; that is the sign agreed
upon. You will tell the men to land, and send back the powder
to the Arsenal, unless——'

'Unless——' replied Mordaunt, whose face was lighted up
by a savage joy while Cromwell was speaking.

'Unless that felucca might be useful for your own private
ends.'

'Ah, my Lord!' exclaimed Mordaunt; 'God, when making
you his elected one, gave you a look which nothing can escape.'

'I think that you call me my Lord!' said Cromwell, laughing.
'That is well enough, as we are alone; but you must pay attention
that no such word escapes you before our imbecile Puritans.'*

'Is it not thus that your Honour will soon be called?'

'I hope so, at least,' said Cromwell; 'but it is not yet time.'
Cromwell rose, and took his cloak.

'You are going, sir?' asked Mordaunt.

'Yes,' said Cromwell. 'I slept here last night and the night
before; and you know it is not my practice to sleep three nights
in the same bed.'

'So then your Highness gives me full liberty for tonight?'

'And even for the day tomorrow, if necessary,' said Cromwell. 'Since last night,' added he, smiling, 'you have done enough for my service; and if you have some personal affairs to arrange, it is just that I should give you your time.'

'Thanks, sir; it will be well employed, I hope.'

Cromwell made an inclination of the head; then turning round, 'Are you armed?' he asked.

'I have my sword.'

'And is anyone waiting for you at the door?'

'No.'

'Then you had better come with me, Mordaunt.'

'Thanks, sir; the windings that you have to make by the subterranean passage would take me too long. I will go out by the other door.'

'Go, then,' said Cromwell.

And putting his hand on a concealed button, he opened a door so well hidden in the tapestry that it was impossible for the most practised eye to notice it. This door, moved by a steel spring, closed behind him. It was one of those secret exists which, as history informs us,* existed in all the mysterious houses in which Cromwell stayed.

The secret way passed under the lonely street, and opened out into a grotto in the garden of another house, situated about a hundred yards from that which the future Protector had just left.

It was during the last part of this scene that Grimaud had perceived, through the aperture of the shutter, two men, and had recognized them successively as Cromwell and Mordaunt. We have seen the effect that this produced. D'Artagnan was the first to recover the full use of his faculties.

'Mordaunt!' said he; 'oh, by heavens! it is God himself who has put him in our way.'

'Yes,' said Porthos, 'let us burst open the door and fall on him.'

'On the contrary,' said d'Artagnan, 'let us burst open nothing. Make no noise—*that* calls people; for if he is, as Grimaud says, with his worthy master, he may have some of his Ironsides lying hidden not far off. Holloa, Grimaud, come here and try to stand on your legs.'

Grimaud came near. Although his rage returned with his consciousness, he was firm on his legs.

'Well,' continued d'Artagnan. 'Now climb up to the balcony again, and tell us if Mordaunt is still in company, if he makes ready to go out or to go to bed. If he is in company we will wait till he shall be alone; if he is going out, we will catch him at the door; if he remains there, we will break open the window. It is much less noisy and difficult than forcing a door.'

Grimaud began making his silent ascent to the window.

'Guard the other way out, Athos and Aramis; we will stay here with Porthos.'

The two friends obeyed.

'Well, Grimaud?'

'He is alone.'

'Are you quite sure of it?'

'Yes.'

'We have not seen his companion go out.'

'Perhaps he went out by the other door.'

'What is he doing?'

'He is putting on his cloak and gloves.'

'Now it's our turn!' muttered d'Artagnan.

Porthos put his hand to his poniard, which he drew forth mechanically from its sheath.

'Put it back, friend Porthos,' said d'Artagnan. 'To strike first is by no means the question. Let us proceed in order. We have some mutual explanations to make, and this is a sequence to the scene at Armentières.* We only hope that this fellow has no offspring; and that if we destroy him, all will be destroyed with him.'

'*Chut!*' said Grimaud; 'he is preparing to go. He approaches the lamp. He puts it out. I see nothing more.'

'Come down, then; come down!'

Grimaud jumped backwards, and alighted on his feet. The snow deadened the sound.

'Go and tell Athos and Aramis to station themselves on each side of the door, as Porthos and I are doing here; let them clap their hands if they get hold of him, and we will do the same.'

Grimaud disappeared.

'Porthos, hide your huge shoulders better, dear friend; he must come out without seeing anything.'

Porthos pressed close against the wall. D'Artagnan did the same. Then Mordaunt's steps were heard on the creaking staircase. An unseen door grated on its hinges. Mordaunt looked out, but saw nothing. Then he introduced the key into the lock; the door opened, and he appeared on the doorstep. At the same moment he found himself facing d'Artagnan. He endeavoured to close the door. Porthos made a dash at the handle and threw it wide open, giving at the same time three claps with his hands. Athos and Aramis ran up.

Mordaunt became livid, but made no cry, nor did he call out for help. D'Artagnan went up to Mordaunt, and pushing him made him go backwards up the staircase, which was lighted by a lamp, enabling the Gascon to see Mordaunt's hands; but Mordaunt felt sure that if he killed d'Artagnan three others would remain to be got rid of. He therefore made no attempt at defence, nor used any threat. On reaching the door, Mordaunt felt himself brought to a stand. He doubtless thought that all would be over with him then; but he was wrong—d'Artagnan put out his hand and opened the door. Porthos entered behind him; he had unhooked the lamp from the ceiling, and by its aid he lit the other. Athos and Aramis appeared, and then locked the door.

'Take the trouble to sit down,' said d'Artagnan, offering a seat to the young man.

The latter took the chair, and seated himself, pale but calm. A little way off the three seated themselves. Athos took his seat in the farthest corner of the room, as if he wished to be a quiet spectator only of what was to go on. Porthos seated himself at the left, and Aramis at the right of d'Artagnan. Athos seemed much depressed. Porthos was rubbing his hands together with a feverish impatience. Aramis, though smiling, bit his lips till they bled. D'Artagnan alone kept calm, at least in appearance.

'M. Mordaunt,' said the last, 'since, after losing so many days in running after one another, chance at last brings us together, let us have some conversation, if you please.'

LXXIII

THE CONVERSATION

MORDAUNT had been surprised so unexpectedly, he had ascended the stairs under the influence of feelings still so confused, that his power of reflection had not been regained.

What was real was that his first feeling had been entirely the surprise and the invincible terror which seizes every man whose mortal enemy, superior in force, grasps his arm at the very moment when he believes that enemy in another place, and occupied with other cares. But once seated, from the moment that he perceived a respite was accorded him, no matter for what purpose, he concentrated all his ideas, and recalled all his powers. The fiery look of d'Artagnan, instead of intimidating, electrified him, so to speak; for this fiercely threatening look which he threw upon him was frank in its hate and its anger. Mordaunt, ready to seize every occasion offered him to extricate himself, either by force or by cunning, gathered himself up as does the bear hemmed in in his den, who follows with an eye apparently motionless every gesture of the hunter who has tracked him. Nevertheless, Mordaunt's eye by a rapid movement glanced at the long and strong sword hanging at his hip; he placed unaffectedly his left hand on its hilt, brought it within reach of his right hand, and seated himself, as d'Artagnan had requested. The latter was waiting doubtless some aggressive word to begin one of those mocking or terrible conversations which he sustained so well. Aramis said to himself, 'We are going to hear some banalities.' Porthos was biting his moustache, muttering, 'Here's a deal of ceremony in crushing this young serpent!' Athos shrunk into the corner of the room, immovable and pale as a marble bas-relief, and feeling, despite his immovability, his forehead grow moist with perspiration. Mordaunt said nothing; only when he was well assured that his sword was ready for use, he coolly crossed his legs, and waited.

The silence could not be prolonged much more without becoming ridiculous. This d'Artagnan felt; and as he had

invited Mordaunt to sit down for a *talk*, he thought he ought
to begin it.

'It seems to me, Monsieur,' said he, with his freezing
politeness, 'that you change your dress almost as rapidly as I
have seen the Italian pantomimists* whom M. le Cardinal
Mazarin brought from Bergamo, and whom he has no doubt
taken you to see during your journey to France.'

Mordaunt said nothing.

'Just now,' continued d'Artagnan, 'you were disguised, I
mean dressed, as an assassin, and now——'

'And now, on the contrary, I have all the appearance of a
man who is going to be assassinated—is it not so?' replied
Mordaunt, in his calm, quick voice.

'Oh, Monsieur!' replied d'Artagnan, 'how can you say such
things when you are in the company of gentlemen, and have
so good a sword by your side?'

'There is no sword so good, Monsieur, as to balance four
swords and four poniards, without counting those of your
acolytes outside.'

'Pardon, sir,' replied d'Artagnan, 'you are mistaken. Those
who await us at the door are not our acolytes, but our servants;
I hold to re-establishing things on their most scrupulous truth.'

Mordaunt only replied by a smile which ironically curled his
lips.

'But this is not the question,' continued d'Artagnan; 'and I
return to my enquiry. I do myself the honour of asking why
you have changed your dress? The mask, it seems to me, fitted
you well enough; the grey beard suited you wonderfully; and
as for the axe with which you gave such an illustrious stroke,
it would not be unbecoming to you at this moment. Why, then,
have you divested yourself of them?'

'Because, when recalling the scene at Armentières, I thought
I should find four axes instead of one, since I was going to
meet four executioners.'

'Monsieur,' replied d'Artagnan, quite calmly, although a
slight knitting of the eyebrows showed that he was beginning
to grow warm— 'Monsieur, although profoundly vicious and
corrupt, you are excessively young, for which reason I will not
dwell on your frivolous remarks. Yes, frivolous, for what you

have just said about Armentières has not the least relation with the present situation. In fact, we were not able to offer a sword to Madame your mother, and beg of her to use it against ourselves; but as for you, a young cavalier who employs the poniard and pistol as we have seen you do, and who wears a sword of the size of yours, there is no one who has not the right to ask the favour of a meeting with you.'

'Ah, ah!' said Mordaunt, 'you wish, then, to fight a duel?' and he got up with flashing eye, as if disposed at once to accept the challenge. Porthos rose also, ready as ever for such adventures.

'Pardon me,' said d'Artagnan, with the same coldness; 'don't let us hurry, for each of us should desire that things should be arranged according to all the rules. Seat yourself, then, dear Porthos, and you, M. Mordaunt, be pleased to remain quiet. We are going to carry on this affair in the best way, and I am going to be frank with you. Confess, now, that you have a great desire to kill one or more of us.'

'One and all of you!'

D'Artagnan turned towards Aramis and said to him—

'It is a great happiness, is it not, dear Aramis, that M. Mordaunt knows so well the intricacies of the French language? We shall thus be sure to have no misunderstanding between us, and can arrange everything marvellously well.'

Then d'Artagnan turned towards Mordaunt and continued, 'Dear M. Mordaunt, these gentlemen reciprocate your good feelings towards them, and would be delighted to kill you also. I will say further that they probably *will* kill you. At any rate it will be as loyal gentlemen; and the best proof I can give you is this.'

Saying this, d'Artagnan threw his hat on the carpet, pushed his chair back against the wall, made a sign to his friends to do the same, and bowing to Mordaunt with a grace quite French, 'At your service, Monsieur,' he continued, 'for if you have nothing to object to the honour which I claim, *I* will begin, if you please. My sword is shorter than yours; but, bah! I hope my arm will make up for it.'

'Halt!' said Porthos, stepping forward; 'I will begin, and without fine speeches.'

'Allow me, Porthos,' said Aramis.

Athos did not move. He seemed like a statue; even his breathing seemed to have stopped.

'Messieurs,' said d'Artagnan, 'be quiet. You shall have your turn. Regard then the eyes of Monsieur, and read there the happy hatred with which we inspire him. See how skilfully he has drawn his sword; admire with what circumspection he looks all around him to find any obstacle which may prevent him from breaking. Well! does not all that prove to you that M. Mordaunt is a fine swordsman, and that you will succeed me in a little while, provided I let him do it? Remain, then, in your places like Athos, whose calm I cannot too much recommend to you, and leave me the initiative, which I have taken. Besides,' continued he, drawing his sword with a terrible gesture, 'I have particularly an affair with Monsieur, and I will begin. I desire it; I wish it.'

It was the first time that d'Artagnan, in this affair, had expressed himself so decidedly to his friends. Up to this time he had contented himself with thinking it. Porthos drew back; Aramis put his sword under his arm; Athos remained immovable in the obscure corner where he was, not calm, as d'Artagnan said, but suffocated and panting.

'Put your sword into its scabbard, Chevalier,' said d'Artagnan to Aramis. 'Monsieur might believe in intentions which you do not have.'

Then turning towards Mordaunt, 'Monsieur,' he said to him, 'I am awaiting you.'

'And I wonder at you, Messieurs. You discuss who shall begin the combat, and do not consult *me* on that point. I hate you all four, it is true, but in different degrees. I hope to kill all four of you; but I have more chance to kill the first than the second, the second than the third, the third than the last. I claim the right therefore of choosing my adversary. If you deny me this right, kill me, I will not fight.'

The four friends looked at one another.

'That's just,' said Porthos and Aramis, who hoped the choice would fall on them. Athos and d'Artagnan said nothing; but their silence gave consent.

'Well!' said Mordaunt in the midst of a profound, solemn silence which reigned in this mysterious house; 'I choose for my first opponent him who, no longer deeming himself worthy to be called the Comte de la Fère, is called Athos.'

Athos rose from his seat as if a spring had brought him to his feet; but to the great astonishment of his friends, after a moment's silence and immobility he said, shaking his head, 'M. Mordaunt, any duel between us is impossible; give to someone else the honour you intend for me.'

And he sat down again.

'Ah!' said Mordaunt, 'there is one already who is afraid.'

'A thousand thunders!' exclaimed d'Artagnan, making a stride towards the young man, 'who dares say that Athos is afraid?'

'Let him say it, d'Artagnan,' replied Athos, with a smile full of sadness and contempt.

'It is your decision, Athos?' replied the Gascon.

'Irrevocable.'

'It is well; we will not speak of it further.'

Then turning towards Mordaunt, 'You have understood it,' said he. 'M. le Comte de la Fère does not wish to do you the honour of fighting with you. Choose one of us to replace him.'

'Now that I cannot fight with him, it matters little to me which it is. Put your names into a hat, and I will draw one.'

'That's a good idea,' said d'Artagnan.

'In fact, that settles all the difficulty,' said Aramis.

'I should never have thought of that,' said Porthos; 'and yet it is very simple.'

'Come, Aramis,' said d'Artagnan, 'write the names for us in that pretty little writing with which you wrote to Marie Michon* to tell her that Monsieur's mother was plotting the assassination of my Lord Buckingham.'

Mordaunt bore this fresh sarcasm without frowning. He was standing, his arms crossed, and seemed as calm as a man can be in such circumstances. If it was not courage, it was at least pride, which resembles it much.

Aramis went to Cromwell's desk, tore three pieces of paper of equal size, wrote the names of the three friends on them, and handed them open to Mordaunt, who, without reading them, made a sign which meant that he left it entirely to him. Then having rolled them up, Aramis put them into a hat, and presented them to the young man.

The latter put his hand into the hat, and took up one of the papers, which he scornfully dropped without reading it on the table.

'Ah, viper!' muttered d'Artagnan. 'I will give all the odds in favour of my captaincy in the Musketeers that that paper bears my name!'

Aramis opened the paper; but however calm and cool he affected to be, one could see that his voice trembled from hate and desire.

'D'Artagnan!' he read in a loud voice.

D'Artagnan uttered a cry of joy.

'Ah,' said he; 'there is then justice in heaven!'

'I hope, Monsieur,' said he, turning towards Mordaunt, 'that you have no objection to make.'

'None, Monsieur,' said Mordaunt, drawing his sword, and resting the point on his boot.

As soon as d'Artagnan was sure that his desire was satisfied, and that his man would not escape him, he resumed all his tranquillity, and even all the slowness which he used when preparing for that serious matter called a duel. He pulled up neatly his ruffles, and rubbed the sole of his boot on the floor, which did not prevent him from noticing that for the second time Mordaunt looked around him with a strange look, which he had once already intercepted.

'Are you ready, Monsieur?' said d'Artagnan, at last.

'It is I who await you, Monsieur,' replied Mordaunt, lifting his head and regarding d'Artagnan with a look whose expression it would be impossible to describe.

'Then take care of yourself, Monsieur,' said the Gascon, 'for I fence tolerably well.'

'And I also,' said Mordaunt.

'So much the better; that quiets my conscience. On guard!'

'One moment,' said the young man. 'Give me your word, Messieurs, that you will only attack me one after the other.'

'Is it for the pleasure of insulting us that you ask that, you little viper!' said Porthos.

'No; but to have, as Monsieur said just now, a clear conscience.'

'It must be for something else,' muttered d'Artagnan, shaking his head, and looking around him with a certain inquietude.

'Upon our honour,' said Aramis and Porthos, together.

'In that case, Messieurs, put yourselves in some corner, as M. le Comte de la Fère has done, who, if he does not wish to fight, appears to me to know the rules of combat; and give us some space. We shall need it soon.'

'Very well,' said Aramis.

'He makes plenty of difficulties,' said Porthos.

'Do as he wishes, Messieurs,' said d'Artagnan; 'we must not give Monsieur the least pretext for behaving badly, of which, it seems to me, saving the respect which I owe him, he has a great desire.'

This fresh raillery made no impression on Mordaunt's impassible face. Porthos and Aramis took the opposite corner to that where Athos was, so that the two champions had the middle of the room; that is, in the full light which the two lamps placed on Cromwell's desk afforded.

'Come,' said d'Artagnan, 'are you at last ready, Monsieur?'

'I am ready,' said Mordaunt.

The two then made a step forward; and thanks to this single and similar movement, their swords were engaged.

D'Artagnan was too distinguished a swordsman to amuse himself by feeling his adversary, as they say in the fencing-school. He made a brilliant, rapid feint, which was parried by Mordaunt.

'Ah, ah!' he exclaimed, with a smile of satisfaction; and without losing any time, thinking he saw an opening, he struck a forward stroke, rapid and blazing like lightning.

Mordaunt parried by a stroke of *quarte* so close that it would not have gone out of a lady's ring.

'I am beginning to think that we are going to amuse ourselves.'

'Yes,' muttered Aramis; 'but while doing so, play close.'

'Hang it, my friend, pay attention!' said Porthos.

Mordaunt smiled in his turn.

'Ah, Monsieur,' said d'Artagnan, 'what a horrid smile you have! It must be the Devil who taught it you, must it not?'

Mordaunt's only reply was by trying to hold down d'Artagnan's sword with a force that the Gascon did not expect to find in a frame apparently so weak; but thanks to a parry not less skilful than that just executed by his adversary, he met Mordaunt's sword in time, which slipped along d'Artagnan's without touching his breast.

Mordaunt rapidly took a step back. 'Ah! you break;' said d'Artagnan, 'you turn! As you please, I even gain something by it; I see no longer your wicked smile. Here I am entirely in the shade; so much the better. You have no idea how false a look you have, Monsieur, especially when you are afraid. Look a little at my eyes, and you will see a thing that your mirror will never show you; that is, a loyal and frank look.'

Mordaunt, to this flow of words, which was not perhaps in very good taste, but which was habitual to d'Artagnan, whose tactics were to preoccupy his adversary, did not reply a single word; but he broke, and turning always, he succeeded thus in changing places with d'Artagnan. He kept smiling more and more. This began to disquiet the Gascon.

'Come, come!' said he, 'this must end. The fool has thighs of iron; to the front with slashing strokes.'

He now pressed Mordaunt hard, who continued to break away, but clearly for tactical purposes, without making a mistake from which d'Artagnan could profit, or letting his sword swerve an instant from the line. Yet, as the combat was going on in a room and the space was scanty, Mordaunt's foot soon touched the wall, on which he rested his left hand.

'Ah!' said d'Artagnan, 'you shall not break away this time, my dear friend! Messieurs,' he added, tightening his lips and frowning, 'have you ever seen a scorpion nailed to a wall? No? Well, you are going to see it.'

And in a second he let fly three terrible blows at Mordaunt. All three touched him, but only to graze him. D'Artagnan did not at all understand this power. The three friends looked on panting and perspiring. At last d'Artagnan, being engaged too closely, took a step back to prepare a fourth stroke, or rather to execute it—for in his case arms were like chess, a vast combination, the parts of which interlaced one another. But just when, after a rapid and close feint, he was attacking swift as lightning, the wall seemed to divide. Mordaunt disappeared by the gaping opening; and d'Artagnan's sword, caught between the two panels, broke like so much glass. D'Artagnan took a step backwards. The wall again closed.

Mordaunt had manœuvred while defending himself so as to have his back against the secret door by which we saw Cromwell pass out. When there, he had with the left hand sought for and pressed the button; he had then disappeared as those evil spirits at the theatre disappear who have the power of passing through walls.

The Gascon uttered a furious imprecation, to which, from the other side of the iron panel, a savage laugh replied—an ominous laugh which sent a shiver into the veins of the sceptical Aramis.

'Help here, Messieurs! let us break open this door.'

'It is the demon in person,' said Aramis, hastening at the call of his friend.

'He has escaped us! he has escaped us!' bawled Porthos, while pressing his huge shoulder against the partition, which, fastened by some secret spring, did not move.

'So much the better,' Athos murmured.

'I was suspicious of it, *mordioux!*' said d'Artagnan, spending himself in vain efforts,— 'I was suspicious of it. When the rascal turned round the room, I expected some infamous manœuvre; but who could have suspected that?'

'It is a frightful misfortune which his friend the Devil sends us!' exclaimed Aramis.

'It's a manifest happiness which God sends us!' said Athos, with evident joy.

'Truly,' replied d'Artagnan, shrugging his shoulders and going away from the door, which could not be opened, 'you deteriorate, Athos! How could you say such things to people like us, *mordioux!* You do not comprehend, then, the situation?'

'What, then? what situation?' asked Porthos.

'At this game here, whoever does not kill is killed,' replied d'Artagnan. 'Come now, my dear fellow, does it enter into your expiatory Jeremiads that M. Mordaunt should sacrifice us to his filial piety? If it is your opinion, say it frankly.'

'Oh, d'Artagnan, my friend!'

'It is truly a pity to see things from this point of view! The wretch is about sending a hundred Ironsides,' said d'Artagnan, 'who will pound us like grain in M. Cromwell's mortar. Come, come, let us be off; if we stay here five minutes only, it is all over with us.'

'Yes, you are right; let us be off!' replied Athos and Aramis.

'And where are we going?' demanded Porthos.

'To the inn, dear friend, to take our things and our horses; then from there, so it please God, to France, where, at least, I know the construction of the houses. Our ship awaits us; upon my word, that's lucky.'

And d'Artagnan, adding example to precept, put the stump of his sword into its sheath, put on his hat, opened the door, and rapidly went downstairs, followed by his companions. At the door the fugitives found their servants, and asked news of Mordaunt, but they had not seen anyone leave the house.

LXXIV

THE *LIGHTNING* FELUCCA

D'ARTAGNAN had guessed rightly; Mordaunt had no time to lose, and had not lost any. He knew how rapidly his enemies decided and acted; he resolved, therefore, to act similarly. This time the musketeers had found an adversary worthy of them.

After having carefully closed the door behind him, Mordaunt slipped into the subterranean passage, and gaining the neighbouring house, he stopped to examine himself and take breath.

'Capital!' said he; 'scarcely anything—a few scratches, that's all; two on the arm, one on the chest. The wounds *I* make are more serious! Let them ask the executioner of Béthune, my uncle Winter, and King Charles! Now there is not a second to lose, for a second lost perhaps saves them; and they all four must die together with a single blow, destroyed by the thunder of man in default of that of God. They must disappear broken, crushed, scattered. Let me run then until my legs can carry me no longer, until my heart swells in my breast; but let me arrive before them;' and Mordaunt started at a rapid pace towards the nearest cavalry barracks, distant about a quarter of a league. He did it in five minutes.

On reaching them, he made known who he was, took the best horse from the stables, and in a quarter of an hour was at Greenwich.

'There's the port, that dark point over there; it's the Isle of Dogs. Good! I am half an hour in advance of them—perhaps an hour. Simpleton that I was! I have just escaped causing asphyxy by my foolish precipitation. Now,' added he, rising in his stirrups to see at a distance among all the ropes and all the masts, 'the *Lightning* where is the *Lightning*?' At the moment when he pronounced mentally these words, as if to answer to his thought, a man lying on a coil of cables rose, and came towards him. Mordaunt took a handkerchief from his pocket, and let it float in the air. The man seemed attentive, but remained in the same place. Mordaunt then knotted the four corners; the man came up to him. It was the pre-arranged signal. The sailor was enveloped in a large woollen wrapper which hid his figure and face.

'Sir,' said the sailor, 'have you perchance come from London to take a turn on the sea?'

'Expressly; from the Isle of Dogs.'

'That is it. And doubtless you have some preference? There is one ship you prefer to the rest? A fast sailer?'

'Like lightning,' replied Mordaunt.

'Well, then, it's my ship you want—I am the skipper.'

'I begin to believe it, especially if you have not forgotten a fixed sign of recognition.'

'Here it is, sir,' said the sailor, taking from his pocket a handkerchief knotted at the four corners.

'Good!' said Mordaunt, dismounting. 'Now, there's no time to lose. Have my horse taken to the first inn, and lead me to your ship.'

'But your companions? I thought there were four of you without counting the servants?'

'Listen,' said Mordaunt; 'I am not the one whom you were expecting, as you are not the one whom they hope to find. You have taken Captain Rogers's place, have you not? By orders from General Cromwell, and I come from him.'

'In fact, I recognize you; you are Captain Mordaunt.'

Mordaunt started.

'Oh, fear nothing,' said the skipper, taking off his hood; 'I am a friend.'

'Captain Groslow!' exclaimed Mordaunt.

'The same. The general remembered that I was formerly in the marines, and gave me this expedition to take charge of. Is anything altered in the plan?'

'No; nothing. On the contrary, all is the same.'

'For a moment I thought that the king's death——'

'That only hastens their flight; in a few minutes they will probably be here.'

'Then what have you come to do?'

'To embark with you.'

'Ah, ah! does the general doubt my zeal?'

'No; but I want myself to help in the work of vengeance. Have you anyone who can take charge of my horse?'

Groslow whistled, and a sailor appeared.

'Patrick,' said Groslow, 'take this horse to the nearest stables. If they ask you whose it is, tell them it belongs to an Irish gentleman.'

'But,' said Mordaunt, 'don't you fear they will recognize you?'

'There is no danger in this dress on such a dark night; besides, *you* did not recognize me—they therefore are less likely to do so.'

'That is true,' said Mordaunt; 'they will besides never dream of seeing you. All is ready, is it not? The cargo has been put on board?'

'Yes.'

'Five barrels full.'

'And fifty empty.'

'That is right.'

'We are taking a cargo of port wine to Antwerp.'

'Capital. Now take me on board and return to your post, for it will not be long before they come.'

'I am ready.'

'It is important that no one of your people should see me come on board.'

'I have only one man on board, and I am as sure of him as of myself. Besides, this man does not know you, and like his companions is ready to obey our orders; but he is ignorant of everything.'

'That is well; let us go.'

They went down to the river-side. A small boat was moored there. They entered it; and Groslow began to row in such a way as to prove to Mordaunt that he had not forgotten his old occupation of mariner.

In about five minutes they got clear of the crowd of ships, which already at that period blocked the approach to London; and Mordaunt could see, like a dark point, the little felucca riding at anchor a few cables' length from the Isle of Dogs.

On approaching the *Lightning*, Groslow gave a sort of whistle, and saw a man's head appear above the bulwarks.

'Is that you, Captain?' the man asked.

'Yes; throw down the ladder;' and Groslow, passing lightly and rapidly as a swallow under the bowsprit, was soon alongside.

'Go up,' said Groslow to his companion.

Mordaunt seized the line, and climbed up the vessel's side with an agility and dexterity unusual in landsmen; but his desire of vengeance took the place of habit, and made him apt at everything.

As Groslow had foreseen, the sailor in charge did not seem to notice that his skipper returned with a companion. Mordaunt and Groslow advanced towards the captain's room. It was a sort of extemporized cabin on deck. The chief cabin had been reserved for Captain Rogers for his passengers.

'And where will *they* be?' asked Mordaunt.

'At the other end of the ship.'

'Then I shall remain hidden here. Return to Greenwich, and bring them back. You have a boat?'

'That in which we came.'

'It seems to me light and well built.'

'A real canoe.'

'Make it fast to the stern. Put some oars into it, that it may follow in the wake, and that there may be only a cord to cut. Supply it with rum and biscuits. If by chance the sea is rough, your men will not be sorry to find something at hand for refreshment.'

'It shall be done as you desire. Do you wish to see the gun-room?'

'Not now, but when you return. I want to put the match myself, to make sure it will not burn too long. Above all, conceal your face, to prevent them from recognizing you.'

'I'll take care of that.'

'Go; ten o'clock has just struck at Greenwich.'

In fact, the vibrations of a bell ten times repeated traversed sadly the air which was heavy with great clouds that moved in the sky like silent waves. Groslow closed the door, which Mordaunt fastened on the inside, and after having given orders to the sailor on duty to watch most attentively, got into the boat, which was soon on the way, tossing up the foam from the oars. The wind was cold and the jetty deserted when Groslow landed at Greenwich; several ships had just sailed at high tide. Just as he landed, he heard a galloping along the pebbly road.

'Oh, oh!' said he, 'Mordaunt was right to hurry me; there was no time to lose. Here they are.'

It was the advanced guard, made up of d'Artagnan and Athos. On reaching the place where Groslow was standing, they stopped, as if they had guessed he was there whom they wanted. Athos alighted, and quietly unrolled a handkerchief with its corners knotted, and let it float in the breeze, while d'Artagnan, always cautious, leaned half over his horse with one hand in the pistol-holsters.

Groslow, who in his doubt if these cavaliers were those he expected had hidden himself behind one of the cannon planted in the ground, which served to coil up the cables, arose then on seeing the signal agreed upon and went right up to the gentlemen. His hooded cloak was wrapped so closely around his head that it was impossible to see his face. Besides, the night was so dark that this precaution was superfluous. However, Athos's quick eye guessed, in spite of the darkness, that it was not Rogers.

'What do *you* want?' said he to Groslow, making a step back.

'I want to tell you, my Lord,' replied Groslow, putting on an Irish accent, 'that you are looking for Skipper Rogers, and sure you will not find him.'

'How's that?' asked Athos.

'Because this morn he fell from the topmast and broke his leg. But I am his cousin; he told me all about it, and charged me to look for the gentleman who should show me a handkerchief knotted at the corners like that you have in your hand, and like the one in my pocket.'

On saying this, Groslow took the handkerchief from his pocket which he had already shown to Mordaunt.

'Is that all?' Athos asked.

'Not at all, your Honour, for there are seventy-five livres promised if I land you safe and sound at Boulogne or some other point in France which you may name.'

'What do you say to that, d'Artagnan?' asked Athos, in French.

'First of all, what does he say?'

Then Athos gave in French the conversation just held with the skipper.

'That seems to me reasonable enough,' said the Gascon.

'So it does to me.'

'Besides,' resumed d'Artagnan, 'if this man deceives us we can at any time blow his brains out.'

'And who will navigate the vessel?'

'You, Athos; I do not doubt you understand something of navigation.'

'Upon my word,' said Athos, smiling; 'though joking you have nearly hit upon the truth. I was intended by my father for the navy, and have some tolerable idea of piloting. Go then, and look for our friends; it's now eleven—we have no time to lose.'

D'Artagnan advanced towards two cavaliers, who, pistol in hand, were stationed *en vedette** at the first houses of the town, waiting on the other side of the road against a sort of shed; three other horsemen were watching and waiting also.

The two watchers who formed the centre were Porthos and Aramis. The three others were Mousqueton, Blaisois, and Grimaud; only this last, on a closer look, was double, for he had Parry's brother on the crupper, who was to take the horses back to London, which had been sold to the innkeeper to pay their bills. Thanks to this stroke of business the four friends were able to carry with them a sum of money, if not very large, yet at least sufficient to meet all contingencies.

D'Artagnan desired them to follow. They dismounted, and unfastened the portmanteaus. Parry felt sorry to separate from his friends; they asked him to go with them to France, but he obstinately refused. 'The reason is plain enough,' Mousqueton had said; 'he has his idea in regard to Groslow.' They recollected that it was Captain Groslow who had broken his head.

The little troop joined Athos; but d'Artagnan had already resumed his natural distrust. He found the quay too deserted, the night too black, the skipper too compliant. He had related to Aramis the incident which we have spoken of, and Aramis, not less distrustful than he, had not a little contributed to increase his suspicions. A little smacking of his tongue against his teeth notified Athos of the Gascon's disquietudes.

'We have no time to be suspicious,' said Athos, 'the boat is waiting; let us get in.'

'Besides,' said Aramis, 'what prevents us from being suspicious, and getting in all the same? We will keep our eye on the skipper.'

'And if he does not act right, I will smash him,' said Porthos; 'that's all.'

'Well said, Porthos,' replied d'Artagnan. 'Get in, Mousqueton.' And d'Artagnan stopped his friends, making the servants first try the plank which led from the jetty to the boat. They passed in, and then their masters without any accident. D'Artagnan went last, still continuing to shake his head.

'What the devil's the matter now, my friend?' said Porthos; 'upon my word, you would make Caesar feel afraid.'

'The matter is that I see on this quay neither superintendent, nor sentinel, nor customs officer.'

'Do you complain, then?' said Porthos; 'everything moves as on a flowery slope.'

'Everything goes too well, Porthos. After all, no matter, we trust in the favour of God.'

As soon as the plank was removed, the skipper took the tiller, and made a sign to one of the sailors, who with a boat-hook endeavoured to get the boat through the labyrinth of ships in the midst of which it was entangled. The other sailor got an oar out to port. When they could use the oars, his companion joined him, and the boat began to make way rapidly.

'At last we are starting,' said Porthos.

'Alas!' replied the count, 'we are going away alone.'

'Yes; but we are all four together, and without a scratch; that's one consolation.'

'We have not yet reached our journey's end,' said d'Artagnan; 'beware of encounters!'

'Why, my dear fellow,' said Porthos, '*you* are like the raven; you always croak of some ill. Who can encounter us on this dark night, when one sees scarcely twenty yards before us?'

'Yes; but tomorrow morning?' said d'Artagnan.

'We shall then be at Boulogne.'

'I hope so heartily, and I confess my weakness,' said the Gascon. 'Stop, Athos, you are going to laugh; but all the time we have been within musket-range of the jetty or the buildings I have been expecting some fusillade which would finish us off.'

'But,' said Porthos, with his large good sense, 'that was impossible, for the skipper and sailors would have been killed too.'

'Bah! how much would that trouble M. Mordaunt? Do you think he makes such fine distinctions?'

'Well,' said Porthos, 'I am very glad that d'Artagnan confesses he feels fearful.'

'Not only confesses it, but boasts of it. I am not a rhinoceros like you. Holloa, what is that?'

'The *Lightning*,' said the skipper.

'We are then arrived?' asked Athos, in English.

'We are arriving,' said the captain.

And after two or three strokes they were alongside the small vessel. The sailor was on watch; the ladder was ready. He had recognized the boat. Athos came on board with all the readiness of a sailor; Aramis, with the dexterity which he had acquired with rope-ladders and other means, more or less ingenious, for reaching forbidden places; d'Artagnan, like a chamois-hunter; Porthos, with that expenditure of force which in his case made up for everything.

With the servants the operation was more difficult—not for Grimaud, a kind of gutter cat, lean and slender, who always found means to raise himself anywhere; but for Mousqueton and Blaisois, whom the sailors had to lift in their arms within reach of Porthos's hand, who grasped them by the collars of their coats, and deposited them upright on the deck of the vessel.

The captain led his passengers to the apartment prepared for them, and which was a cabin for them to use in common; then he tried to get away under the pretext of giving some orders.

'One moment,' said d'Artagnan; 'how many men have you on board, skipper?'

'I don't understand,' replied the latter, in English.

'Athos, ask him in his own language.'

'Three,' replied Groslow, 'without counting me, mind.'

D'Artagnan understood, for in answering the skipper had raised three fingers.

'Oh!' said d'Artagnan; 'three—that reassures me a little. No matter; while you are installing yourselves, *I* will take a turn round the ship.'

'And I,' said Porthos—'I am going to be busy about supper.'

'That project is a good and generous one; put it into execution. Athos, lend me Grimaud, who in company with his friend, Parry's brother, has learned to jabber a little English; he will do for interpreter.'

'Go, Grimaud,' said Athos.

A lantern was on the deck; d'Artagnan took it in one hand and a pistol in the other, and said to the skipper, 'Come.'

This, with 'God damn,' was all he knew of the English language. He descended by the hatchway to the lower deck. This was divided into three compartments—that in which d'Artagnan now was, extending from the mizzen-mast to the end of the poop, and which was consequently under the chamber in which the four friends were preparing to pass the night; the second, amidship, was for the servants; the third under the cabin improvised by the captain, and in which Mordaunt lay hid.

'Oh, oh!' said d'Artagnan, going down the hatchway ladder, holding the lantern at arm's length before him, 'what a lot of casks! It's like Ali Baba's cave.'

*The Thousand and One Nights** had just been translated for the first time, and was very much in vogue at that period.

'What do you say?' asked the captain, in English.

D'Artagnan understood by the intonation of his voice.

'I want to know what there is in these casks?' added d'Artagnan, putting the lantern on the top of one of them.

The skipper moved towards the ladder; but he recollected himself.

'Port,' said he.

'Ah! port wine?' said d'Artagnan; 'that's always satisfactory. Then we shall not die of thirst.'

Then turning towards Groslow, who was wiping the sweat from his brow, 'And are they full?' he asked.

Grimaud translated the question.

'Some are, and some are empty,' said Groslow, in a voice which in spite of his efforts betrayed his disquietude.

D'Artagnan knocked the barrels with his knuckle and discovered that five were full and the rest empty; then he introduced the lantern, to the great fear of the Englishman, between the casks, and observing that the spaces between were unoccupied, 'Well, let us go,' said he, and went towards the door which opened into the second compartment.

'Wait,' said the Englishman, who had stopped behind, still a prey to that feeling of fear—'wait, I have the key;' and passing in front of d'Artagnan and Grimaud, he opened the door with trembling hand into the second compartment, where Mousqueton and Blaisois were getting supper ready. In this compartment there was nothing to find fault with. They looked in all the corners and recesses by the light of the lamp which was used by these worthy companions.

They then visited rapidly the third compartment. This was the forecastle. Three or four hammocks hung from the ceiling; a table kept in position by a stout cord fastened to each of its ends, two forms, very worm-eaten and rickety, completed its furniture. D'Artagnan lifted up two or three old sails hanging against the sides, and not seeing anything which looked suspicious, regained the deck by the hatchway.

'And this cabin?' asked d'Artagnan.

Grimaud translated the musketeer's words.

'This is mine; do you wish to go in?'

'Open the door,' said d'Artagnan.

The Englishman obeyed; d'Artagnan thrust in his arm with the lantern, put his head through the half-opened door, and seeing that the room was really used as a cabin, 'Good,' said he; 'if there is an army on board, it is not hidden in here. Let us go and see if Porthos has found any supper.'

After thanking the skipper by a nod of the head, he returned to his friends.

Porthos had found nothing, as it appeared, or if he had, fatigue had overcome his hunger, for lying on his cloak he was sound asleep.

Athos and Aramis, rocked by the gentle movements of the first waves of the sea, had begun also to close their eyes; they opened them at the noise which the entrance of their companion made.

'Well?' said Aramis.

'All is right,' said d'Artagnan, 'and we can sleep in peace.'

On this assurance, Aramis let his head fall again, Athos gave a friendly nod; and d'Artagnan who, like Porthos, had much more need of sleep than food, dismissed Grimaud, and lay down in his cloak with his drawn sword in such a manner that his body barred the entrance, and it was impossible to enter without striking against him.

LXXV

THE PORT WINE

AT the end of ten minutes the masters were sleeping; but it was not so with the servants, who were hungry, and especially thirsty. Blaisois and Mousqueton were preparing their bed, which consisted of a plank and a portmanteau, while on a table fastened like that in the neighbouring compartment a pot of beer and three glasses were balancing with the rolling of the sea.

'Cursed rolling!' said Blaisois; 'I feel that it is going to make me as sick as I was when I came over.'

'And only to have barley bread and beer to combat sea-sickness,' replied Mousqueton, 'bah!'

'But your straw-covered flask, M. Mouston,' asked Blaisois— 'have you lost it?'

'Parry's brother has kept it. These devils of Scots are always thirsty. And you, Grimaud,' who had just returned after accompanying d'Artagnan, 'are you thirsty too?'

'As a Scotchman,' laconically replied Grimaud; and he took a seat near Blaisois and Mousqueton, took a note-book from his pocket, and began noting down items of expenditure, as he was the steward of the party.

'Oh, la, la!' said Blaisois, 'how out of order my stomach is!'

'If that be so,' said Mousqueton, with the air of a doctor, 'take a little nourishment.'

'You call that nourishment?' said Blaisois, pointing his finger with a piteous look at the barley bread and pot of beer.

'Blaisois,' resumed Mousqueton, 'remember that bread is the proper nourishment of the Frenchman; yet the Frenchman has not always got it. Ask Grimaud.'

'Yes, but the beer,' replied Blaisois, with a promptitude which did honour to his power of repartee; 'is beer his true drink?'

'As for that,' said Mousqueton, caught in a dilemma, and somewhat embarrassed how to reply, 'I must confess it is not, and that beer is as antipathic to him as wine is to the English.'

'What, M. Mouston,' said Blaisois, who doubted for this once Mousqueton's profound knowledge, for which, ordinarily, he had the highest admiration—'what! the English not like wine?'

'They hate it.'

'Yet I have seen them drink it.'

'For penance; and the proof is,' continued Mousqueton, bridling up, 'that an English prince died one day because they put him into a cask of malvoisie.* I have heard M. l'Abbé d'Herblay tell this as a fact.'

'The fool!' said Blaisois. 'I should like to have been in his place!'

'So you can,' said Grimaud, while arranging his figures.

'What do you mean by, *so I can?*' said Blaisois.

'Yes,' continued Grimaud, while remembering four, and carrying it to the next column.

'*So I can?* Explain your meaning, M. Grimaud.'

Mousqueton kept silence during Blaisois's questions, but it was easy to see from the expression of his face that it was not at all from indifference.

Grimaud continued his calculations, and put down the sum total.

'Port,' said he then, stretching out his hand in the direction of the first compartment visited by d'Artagnan and himself.

'What! those casks which I saw through the half-opened door?'

'Port,' Grimaud repeated, beginning a fresh arithmetical operation.

'I have heard say,' replied Blaisois, speaking to Mousqueton, 'that port is an excellent Spanish wine.'

'Excellent,' said Mousqueton, passing the end of his tongue along his lips—'excellent. There is some of it in the cellar of M. le Baron de Bracieux.'

'Suppose we were to ask the English to sell us a bottle?' honest Blaisois asked.

'To sell!' said Mousqueton, carried away by his old marauding instincts. 'It is easily seen, young man, that you have not had much experience of life. Now, why buy when one can take?'

'Take,' said Blaisois; 'covet thy neighbour's goods!—the thing is forbidden, it seems to me.'

'Where?' asked Mousqueton.

'In the commandments of God or of the Church, I am not sure which. But what I know is this: "Thou shalt not covet thy neighbour's house; thou shalt not covet thy neighbour's wife." '*

'That's a child's reason, M. Blaisois,' said Mousqueton, in his most patronizing tone. 'Yes, a child's, I repeat the words. Where have you seen in the Scriptures, I ask you, that the English were your neighbours?'

'Well, nowhere; that's true,' said Blaisois.

'A child's reason, I repeat. If you had been at the wars for ten years, as Grimaud and I have been, my dear Blaisois, you would soon have learned how to distinguish between thy neighbour's goods and thine enemy's. Now, an Englishman is an enemy, I think; and this port wine belongs to the English. Consequently it belongs to us, since we are French. Don't you know the proverb, "It's so much gained of an enemy?" '

This eloquence, supported by all the authority which Mousqueton drew from his long experience, stupefied Blaisois. He lowered his head as if to gather his ideas, and suddenly raising his forehead as a man armed with an irresistible argument: 'And will our masters,' asked Blaisois, 'be of your opinion, M. Mouston?'

Mousqueton smiled contemptuously.

'I should be obliged to go and disturb the sleep of those illustrious lords to tell them: "Messieurs, your servant Mousqueton is thirsty. Will you give him permission to drink?" What matters it, I ask you, to M. de Bracieux whether I am thirsty or not?'

'It is a very expensive wine,' said Blaisois, shaking his head.

'Were it drinkable gold, M. Blaisois,' said Mousqueton, 'our masters would not deprive themselves of it. Learn that M. le Baron de Bracieux is himself rich enough to drink a tun of port, even if obliged to pay a pistole the drop. Now, I don't see why the servants should deprive themselves of it, if the masters would not;' and Mousqueton, getting up, took up the pot of beer which he emptied through a port-hole to the last drop, and then went majestically towards the door leading to the first compartment.

'Ah, locked!' said he. 'These devils of English, how suspicious they are!'

'Locked!' said Blaisois, in a tone no less disappointed than Mousqueton. 'Ah, *peste!* that's unfortunate; especially as I feel my stomach grow more and more disturbed.'

Mousqueton turned towards Blaisois with a face so piteous that it was evident he shared in a high degree the disappointment of the brave fellow.

'Locked!' repeated he.

'But,' ventured Blaisois, 'I have heard you relate, M. Mouston, that once in your youth, at Chantilly I think, you fed your master and yourself by taking some partridges with a snare, some carp with a line, and some bottles of wine with a lasso.'

'Without doubt,' replied Mousqueton, 'it is the exact truth; and here is Grimaud who can vouch for it. But there was a vent-hole to the cellar, and the wine was in bottles. I cannot throw the lasso through this partition, nor draw with a cord a cask of wine which weighs perhaps two quintals.'*

'No, but you could remove two or three planks of the partition,' said Blaisois, and make a hole with a gimlet in one of the casks.'

Mousqueton opened wide his round eyes, and looked at Blaisois like a man astonished at finding in another some unsuspected qualities.

'That's true. It can be done; but we want a chisel to remove the boards, and a gimlet to bore a hole in the cask.'

'The case of tools,' said Grimaud, completing the balance of his accounts.

'Ah, yes! of course, and I did not think of it,' said Mousqueton.

Grimaud was in fact not only the steward, but also the armourer of the company. Besides his account-book, he had his case of tools. It contained a gimlet of tolerable size. Mousqueton took it. To serve as a chisel, Mousqueton took the poniard which he carried in his belt. He then looked where the planks were not closely joined—a thing not difficult to find—and then set to work at once. Blaisois looked at him as he worked, with admiration mixed with impatience, venturing from time to time, on the manner of drawing a nail or making a hole, observations full of intelligence and clearness. In a short time Mousqueton had made three planks yield.

'There,' said Blaisois.

Mousqueton was the opposite to the frog in the fable* who thought himself larger than he was. Unfortunately, if he had succeeded in diminishing his name by a third, it was not the same with his stomach. He tried to get through the opening, but saw with grief that two or three more planks must be removed before the opening suited his bulk. He uttered a sigh. But Grimaud, who had finished his accounts, had seen the fruitless efforts made by Mousqueton to reach the promised land.

'Let me,' said Grimaud.

This expression was worth more from him alone, as is known, than a whole poem.* Mousqueton turned round.

'What, you?' he asked.

'Yes; I shall get through.'

'That's true,' said Mousqueton, casting a look at the slender body of his friend; 'you can easily do so.'

'That's all right; he knows the full casks,' said Blaisois, 'since he has already been in the cellar with M. le Chevalier d'Artagnan. Let M. Grimaud get through, M. Mouston.'

'I should have passed through there as well as Grimaud,' said Mousqueton, a little piqued.

'Yes, but it would take longer and I am very thirsty. I feel my stomach getting more and more upset.'

'Go on, then, Grimaud,' said Mousqueton, giving up to him the beer-pot and the gimlet.

'Rinse the glasses,' said Grimaud. Then he gave Mousqueton a friendly nod that the latter might pardon him for finishing an adventure so brilliantly begun by another, and like a snake glided through the opening and disappeared.

Blaisois seemed in an ecstasy. Of all the exploits performed since their arrival in England by the extraordinary men with whom he had the honour to be connected, this seemed to him, without contradiction, the most miraculous.

'You will see presently,' said Mousqueton, looking at Blaisois with an air of superiority from which the latter did not even attempt to escape—'you will soon see, Blaisois, how we old soldiers can drink when thirsty.'

'The cloak,' said Grimaud, from the bottom of the cellar.

'Quite right,' said Mousqueton.

'What does he want?' asked Blaisois.

'That the opening should be stopped up with a cloak.'

'What's that done for?'

'You innocent! Suppose someone should come in.'

'Ah, that's true!' exclaimed Blaisois, with increasing admiration. 'But he will not see very clearly.'

'Grimaud always sees clearly, by night as well as by day.'

'He is a fortunate fellow; when *I* go without a candle, *I* cannot take two steps without hitting something.'

'That's because you have not been in the service; otherwise you would have learned to pick up a needle in a dark room. But silence! I think someone is coming.'

Mousqueton gave a low whistle of warning which had been familiar to the servants in their younger days, took his place at the table again, and made a sign to Blaisois to do likewise.

Blaisois obeyed. The door opened. Two men enveloped in their cloaks appeared.

'Oh, oh!' said one of them, 'not yet abed at a quarter past eleven? that's against the rules. In a quarter of an hour let all lights be out, and everyone be asleep.'

The two men went to the compartment into which Grimaud had glided, and closed the door behind them.

'Ah!' said Blaisois, trembling; 'he is lost!'

'Grimaud is by far too cunning a fox,' muttered Mousqueton; and they waited, listening closely, and holding their breath. Ten minutes passed, during which they heard no noise leading them to suspect that Grimaud was discovered.

This time passed, Mousqueton and Blaisois saw the door open, and two men in cloaks come out, shut the door with the same precautions they had used in entering it, and then they went out renewing the order to go to bed and put out the lights.

'Shall we obey?' asked Blaisois; 'all this seems to me suspicious.'

'They have said a quarter of an hour; we have still five minutes,' replied Mousqueton.

'If we forewarn the masters?'

'Let us wait for Grimaud.'

'But if they have killed him?'

'Grimaud would have cried out.'

'You know he is almost mute.'

'We should have heard the blow, then.'

'But if he does not come back?'

'Here he is.'

In fact, at that moment Grimaud removed the cloak that covered the opening, and passed his head through the opening, his eyes staring from fright, showing small pupils in large white circles. He held in his hand the beer-pot, full of something or other, which he held near the smoky lamp, and ejaculated the simple monosyllable, 'Oh!' with an expression of such profound terror that Mousqueton stepped back, frightened, and Blaisois felt ready to faint. Nevertheless, they both threw a look of curiosity into the beer-pot; it was full of powder.

Once convinced that the ship was laden with powder instead of wine, Grimaud rushed towards the hatchway, and in a bound reached the cabin where the four friends were asleep. He pushed the door gently open, which awakened d'Artagnan, who lay behind it.

Scarcely had d'Artagnan seen the disturbed look of Grimaud, before he felt sure that something extraordinary was going on; but Grimaud, with a gesture, made more quickly than words could be spoken, put his finger to his lips, and with a good puff extinguished the little lamp three paces off.

D'Artagnan raised himself on his elbow, and Grimaud, kneeling, whispered in his ear an account which was so extremely dramatic as to dispense with gesture or the play of the countenance. During this recital Athos, Porthos, and Aramis were sleeping like men who had not slept for a week; and in the between decks, Mousqueton from precaution was tying up his aigulets, while Blaisois, full of horror, the hair standing erect on his head, was trying to do the same. This is what had happened.

Grimaud had scarcely disappeared through the opening than he began his search, and found a cask. He struck it; it was empty. He went to another; that also was empty. But the third on which he made the trial gave so dull a sound that he could not be deceived. It was full.

He stopped there, felt for a suitable spot for boring a hole, and in the search put his hand on a cock.

'Good!' said Grimaud, 'that will spare me my labour.' And he put the beer-pot to it, turned the cock, and felt the contents passing into the pot. After taking the precaution to close the cock, he was going to put the pot to his lips, being too conscientious to take to his companions a liquor whose quality he could not guarantee, when he heard the signal of alarm given by Mousqueton. He suspected it was the night-watch on their rounds; he slipped between two casks, and hid himself behind one.

A moment after, in fact, two men in cloaks entered, and closed the door behind them. One of them carried a lantern with glass sides, carefully closed, and of such a height that the flame could not reach the top. Besides, the glass itself was covered with a sheet of white paper, which softened, or rather absorbed, the light and heat. This man was Groslow.

The other held in his hand something long, flexible, and twisted like a whitish cord. His face was covered with a broad-brimmed hat. Grimaud, thinking that the same feeling as his own brought them to the cellar, and that, like himself, they came to visit the port wine, shrank more and more behind the cask, saying to himself that if he were discovered the crime was not so very great.

The two men stopped at the cask behind which Grimaud was hiding.

'Have you the match?' asked the one carrying the lantern.

'Here it is,' said the other.

At the voice of the latter, Grimaud shook, and felt a shiver penetrate even to the marrow of his bones. He lifted himself gently, so that his head was just above the cask, and beneath the large hat he recognized Mordaunt's pale face.

'How long will this match burn?' he asked.

'Well, about five minutes.'

This voice also seemed familiar to Grimaud. His glances went from the one to the other, and after Mordaunt he recognized Groslow.

'Then,' said Mordaunt, 'you are going to tell your men to hold themselves in readiness without telling them why. Is the boat in the ship's wake?'

'Just as a dog follows his master at the end of a hempen leash.'

'Then, when the clock chimes the quarter after midnight, collect your men, and get without noise into the boat——'

'After having lighted the match.'

'I will see to that. I wish to make sure of my revenge. Are the oars in the canoe?'

'Everything is ready.'

'Right.'

'All is thoroughly understood, then?'

Mordaunt knelt down, and fastened one end of the match to the cock, so as to have merely to light the other end.

Then when finished, he took out his watch.

'You understand?—a quarter past twelve,' said he, getting up; 'that is to say,'—he looked at his watch—'in twenty minutes.'

'Precisely, Monsieur,' replied Groslow; 'only I think it right to observe, for the last time, that there is some danger in the task you have kept for yourself, and that it would be much better to let one of the men set light to the train.'

'My dear Groslow,' said Mordaunt, 'you know the French proverb, "On n'est bien servi que par soi-même" [If you want a thing done well, do it yourself]. I shall put that in practice.'

Grimaud had heard all, if he had not understood all; but what he saw supplied what he imperfectly comprehended. He had seen and recognized the two mortal enemies of the musketeers. He had seen Mordaunt lay the train; he had understood the proverb, which for its greater pithiness Mordaunt had said in French. Then he felt and felt again the contents of the jug, which he held in his hand, and in place of the liquid which Mousqueton and Blaisois were expecting to find, grains of coarse powder grated and were crushed under his fingers.

Mordaunt and the skipper went off. At the door he stopped, listening.

'Do you hear how soundly they are sleeping?' he said. In fact, one could hear through the boards Porthos snoring.

'It's God who delivers them to us,' said Groslow.

'And this time,' said Mordaunt, 'the Devil could not save them.'

And they both went away.

LXXVI

THE PORT WINE (*concluded*)

GRIMAUD waited till he heard the bolt grate in the lock, and when quite sure that he was alone, he slowly raised himself, and groped for the partition.

'Ah,' he ejaculated, while wiping off with his sleeve the large drops of sweat which beaded his forehead; 'how fortunate it was that Mousqueton was thirsty!'

He hurried back through the opening, thinking it was a dream; but the sight of the powder in the beer-jug proved that this dream was a deadly nightmare.

D'Artagnan, as one may suppose, heard all these details with a growing interest, and without waiting for Grimaud to finish, he got up at once, and putting his mouth close to Aramis's ear, who was sleeping at his left, and touching him on the shoulder to prevent any quick movement, 'Chevalier,' he said to him, 'get up, and don't make the least noise. You have Athos at your left; tell him as I have told you.'

Aramis easily awoke Athos, whose sleep was light, as is the case with all delicately organized natures; but they had greater difficulty in awaking Porthos. He was going to ask the reasons for this interruption of his sleep, which seemed to him very annoying, when d'Artagnan as full explanation put his hand before his mouth.

Then our Gascon, extending his arms, and drawing them towards himself again, enclosed in their circle the three heads of his friends so that they almost touched one another.

'Friends,' said he, 'we must leave this ship at once, or we shall all be dead men.'

'Bah!' said Athos; 'what next?'

'Do you know who the captain is? Why, Captain Groslow.'

A shudder from the three showed d'Artagnan that his words began to make some impression on his friends.

'Groslow!' said Aramis; 'the devil it is!'

'Who is he—Groslow?' asked Porthos; 'I don't remember him.'

'He who broke the head of Parry's brother, and who is now ready to break ours. And his lieutenant? Do you know who he is.'

'His lieutenant? He has none,' said Athos. 'There is no lieutenant to a felucca with a crew of four men.'

'Yes, but M. Groslow is not like other captains; *he* has a lieutenant, and that is M. Mordaunt.'

This time it was more than a shudder—it was almost a cry. These invincible men seemed under a mysterious and fatal influence which this name exercised over them, and felt terror even at hearing the name pronounced.

'What's to be done?' said Athos.

'Seize the felucca,' said Aramis.

'And kill him,' said Porthos.

'The felucca is mined,' said d'Artagnan. 'Those casks that I took for casks of port wine are powder casks. When Mordaunt finds out he is discovered, he will blow all up together, friends and enemies; and upon my word, he is too bad company for me to desire to present myself in his society either in heaven or in hell.'

'Have you formed a plan?' asked Athos.

'Yes.'

'What is it?'

'Have you any confidence in me?'

'Yes. Give your orders,' said all the three friends together.

'Well, come!'

D'Artagnan went to a low window like a port-hole, but big enough to admit a man; he made it turn on its hinge.

'That's the road,' said he.

'The devil!' said Aramis; 'it looks very cold, my friend.'

'Stay here if you like; but I forewarn you that it will become very hot presently.'

'But we cannot reach the land by swimming.'

'The boat is astern; we shall reach it, and then cut the rope. That's all. Come on, Messieurs.'

'One moment,' said Athos; 'the servants?'

'Here we are,' said Mousqueton and Blaisois, whom Grimaud had been to fetch so as to concentrate all their strength in the cabin, and who by the hatchway, which was close to the door, had entered without being seen. Meanwhile the three friends stood motionless before the terrible spectacle which d'Artagnan had exposed to view by raising the shutter. In fact, whoever has once seen this sight knows that nothing is more profoundly startling than a rough sea rolling with the dull sounds of its black waves under the pale light of a wintry moon.

'*Cordieu!*' said d'Artagnan, 'we are hesitating, it seems to me! If *we* hesitate, what will the servants do?'

'*I* don't hesitate,' said Grimaud.

'Monsieur,' said Blaisois, 'I can swim only in rivers, I beg to say.'

'And I can't swim at all,' said Mousqueton.

Meanwhile, d'Artagnan had slipped through the opening.

'You are decided then, friend?' said Athos.

'Yes,' replied the Gascon. 'Come, Athos, you who are a perfect man, command spirit to rule over matter. You, Aramis, give the word to the servants. You, Porthos, kill all who interpose any obstacle.'

And d'Artagnan, after having pressed Athos's hand, chose the moment when by the pitching of the felucca the stern dipped so that he had only to let himself glide into the water, which already reached his waist. Athos followed him before the felucca righted herself. When she did, the rope attached to the boat was seen tightening and rising from the water. D'Artagnan swam towards it, and laid hold of it, where he waited, hanging to this rope by one hand and his head alone at the level of the water. At the end of a second Athos joined him. Then they saw when the felucca dipped two other heads appearing. They were those of Aramis and Grimaud.

'Blaisois troubles me,' said Athos; 'did he not say he knew how to swim in rivers only?'

'When one knows how to swim, you can swim anywhere,' said d'Artagnan; 'to the boat! to the boat!'

'But Porthos? I don't see him.'

'Porthos is coming, rest assured; he swims like leviathan himself.'

Porthos did not appear at all; for a scene half-burlesque, half-dramatic, took place between him, Mousqueton, and Blaisois.

These, frightened by the noise of the water, by the whistling of the wind, scared at the sight of this black water boiling in a gulf, fell back instead of advancing.

'Come, come!' said Porthos, 'jump in!'

'But, Monsieur,' said Mousqueton, 'I don't know how to swim; leave me here.'

'And me also, Monsieur,' said Blaisois.

'I assure you that I shall encumber you in that small boat,' replied Mousqueton.

'And I shall be drowned, I am sure, before reaching it,' continued Blaisois.

'Come now, I will strangle you both if you don't go,' said Porthos, seizing them by the throat. 'Go first, Blaisois.'

A groan stopped by the iron hand of Porthos was all Blaisois's reply, for the giant, holding him by the neck and feet, made him slip through the window like a plank, and sent him head first into the sea.

'Now, Mouston,' said Porthos, 'I hope you will not abandon your master.'

'Ah, Monsieur!' said Mousqueton, with tears in his eyes, 'why did you go back into the service? We were so comfortable at the Château de Pierrefonds!'

And without further word of reproach, now passive and obedient, whether from real devotion, or from the example shown by Blaisois, Mousqueton took a header into the sea—a sublime act in either case, for Mousqueton believed himself drowned.

But Porthos was not a man thus to abandon his faithful companion. The master followed so near his valet that the fall of the two bodies made only one and the same splash; so that when Mousqueton rose to the surface quite blinded, he found himself held up by Porthos's large hand, and could, without the need of any movement, advance towards the rope with the majesty of a sea-god.

At the same instant, Porthos saw something whirling round within reach of his arm. He seized this something by its hair; it was Blaisois, towards whom Athos was already coming.

'Go, go, Count,' said Porthos; 'I have no need of you!'

And in fact, with one stroke of his vigorous leg, Porthos rose up like the giant Adamastor* above the billows, and in three efforts he found himself joined to his companions.

D'Artagnan, Aramis, and Grimaud helped Mousqueton and Blaisois to get in, then came Porthos's turn, who in climbing over the side almost upset the boat.

'And Athos?' asked d'Artagnan.

'Here I am!' said Athos, who like a general conducting a retreat wished to embark last, and remained himself by the boat's edge.

'Are you all here?'

'All,' said d'Artagnan. 'Athos, have you your poniard?'

'Yes.'

'Then cut the rope and come in.'

Athos drew his poniard from his belt, and cut the rope.
The felucca went on ahead; the boat remained stationary,
except what motion the waves gave it. D'Artagnan gave
his hand to the Comte de la Fère, who took his place in the
boat.

'It was time,' said the Gascon; 'and you are going to see
something very curious.'

LXXVII

FATALITY

IN fact, d'Artagnan had hardly finished speaking when a
whistle resounded on the felucca, which began to be hidden in
the mist and darkness. 'That, as you well comprehend,' said
the Gascon, 'means something.' Then a lantern was seen on
deck, and lighted up the shadows in the stern.

Suddenly a terrible cry of despair rang through space, and
as if it had chased away the clouds, the veil which had hidden
the moon moved away, and silvered by her pale light, the grey
canvas and the black rigging of the felucca were outlined on
the sky.

Some shadows were running up and down distracted, and
some lamentable cries accompanied these mad promenades. In
the midst of these cries, Mordaunt was seen on the poop with
a torch in his hand. These shadows which were going up and
down the ship were Groslow and his men, whom he assembled
at the hour named by Mordaunt, while the latter, after listening
at the door of the cabin to know if the musketeers were still
sleeping, had gone down to the hold, reassured by their silence.
Who could indeed have had a suspicion of what had just
happened?

Mordaunt had consequently opened the door, and hastened
to the match; burning with his thirst for revenge, and sure of
it, in his providential ignorance of what had taken place, he
had set fire to the sulphur. Meanwhile Groslow and his sailors
were assembled at the stern.

'Haul in the line,' said Groslow, 'and bring up the boat.'

One of the sailors got over the ship's side, seized the rope and pulled; it came to him without any resistance.

'The rope is cut!' exclaimed the sailor; 'there's no boat there.'

'What do you mean? no boat?' said Groslow; 'it's impossible!'

'That's the case, though,' said the sailor. 'See for yourself; there's nothing in the wake, and besides, here's the end of the rope.'

It was then that Groslow uttered the wild cry which the musketeers had heard.

'What's the matter?' exclaimed Mordaunt, who, coming from the hatchway, hurried aft with the torch in his hand.

'The matter is that our enemies have escaped; they are in the boat.'

Mordaunt made but one bound to the cabin, the door of which he burst open with his foot.

'Empty!' he exclaimed. 'Oh, the demons!'

'We will pursue them,' said Groslow. 'They can't be far off; and we will sink them.'

'Yes; but the fire!' said Mordaunt; 'I have set fire to the match.'

'A thousand thunders!' howled Groslow, tumbling down the hatchway. 'Perhaps there is still time.'

Mordaunt only replied by a terrible laugh; and his features distorted by hate more than fear, were upturned to utter one more blasphemy. He first of all threw the torch into the sea and himself after it.

At the same instant that Groslow put his foot on the hatchway the ship opened like the crater of a volcano. A jet of fire darted upwards with an explosion like that of a hundred pieces of cannon discharged at once. The sky was illuminated by the blazing fragments, then the *Lightning* disappeared; the fragments one after the other fell hissing into the abyss, where they were extinguished, and excepting a vibration in the air it seemed as if nothing had taken place. Only the felucca had disappeared from the face of the ocean, and Groslow and his three men were destroyed.

The four friends had seen all the details of this terrible drama. An instant inundated with this striking light which had illumined the sea for more than a league, each one could have been seen in a different attitude, expressing the consternation which, despite their hearts of bronze, they could not help experiencing. Soon the rain of flames fell all around them; then at last the volcano was extinguished as we have narrated, and everything returned to obscurity—floating bark, and howling ocean. They remained a short time silent and dejected. Porthos and d'Artagnan, each of whom took an oar, kept them mechanically above the waves, leaning their whole weight on them and compressing them with their tight grasp.

'Upon my word,' said Aramis, who was the first to break this deathlike silence, 'this time I really believe all is finished.'

'Help, my Lords! help!' cried someone, in a lamentable voice, the accents of which reached the four friends, and which seemed like that of an ocean spirit.

They looked at one another. Athos himself shook.

'It is he! That's his voice!' said he.

All were silent, for all had recognized that voice. Only their eyes with dilated pupils turned in the direction where the vessel had disappeared, as they eagerly tried to pierce the darkness. Presently they were able to distinguish a man swimming vigorously towards them. Athos pointed him out to his companions.

'Yes, yes,' said d'Artagnan; 'I see him well enough.'

'He again!' said Porthos, breathing like a blacksmith's bellows. 'Ah, come, but he is made of iron?'

Mordaunt made a few strokes, and then raising a hand above the water as a signal of distress, cried, 'Have pity, Messieurs, in Heaven's name! I feel my strength leaving me. I am dying.'

The voice thus imploring was so plaintive that it began to excite the compassion of Athos's heart. 'The wretched being!' he murmured.

'That's all we need,' said d'Artagnan. 'You can't be foolish enough to feel pity for him? In fact, I believe he is swimming towards us. Does he really think we are going to take him in? Row, Porthos, row!'

And setting the example, d'Artagnan plunged his oar into the sea; two pulls carried the boat twenty strokes from the swimmer.

'Oh, you will not abandon me!' exclaimed Mordaunt; 'you will not let me perish! you will not be without pity!'

'Ah, ah!' said Porthos, 'I think we have got you at last, my fine fellow, and that you have no other means of escape than by the gates of hell.'

'Oh, Porthos!' murmured the Comte de la Fère.

'Let me alone, Athos, you really are getting ridiculous with your continual expressions of generosity! Now, I declare that if he comes within ten feet of the boat I will break his head with a blow of the oar.'

'Oh, be pitiful! Don't leave me, Messieurs! have pity on me!' cried the young man, whose pantings for breath caused the icy waters to bubble up when his head disappeared under the wave.

D'Artagnan, who, while following every movement of Mordaunt, had finished his colloquy with Aramis, rose.

'Monsieur,' said he, addressing the swimmer, 'be off, if you please. Your repentance is too recent for us to have much confidence in it. Bear in mind that the ship in which you wanted to grill us still smokes a few feet below the surface, and that the situation in which you are is a bed of roses in comparison with that in which you desired to put us, and in which you have placed M. Groslow and his companions.'

'Messieurs,' replied Mordaunt, with an accent more despairing, 'I swear to you that my repentance is sincere. Messieurs, I am so young—I am scarcely twenty-three. I have been led on by the very natural desire to revenge my mother, and you all would have done what I have done.'

'Ugh!' grunted d'Artagnan, seeing that Athos was much moved, 'that depends on circumstances.'

Mordaunt had no more than three or four strokes to make to reach the boat, for the approach of death seemed to give him supernatural strength.

'Alas! I must die, then; you mean to kill the son as you did his mother! And yet I was not guilty. Besides, if it is a crime, since I repent of it, since I ask pardon, I ought to be pardoned.'

Then, as if his strength failed him, he seemed no longer to have the power of holding himself up, and a wave passed over his head which drowned his voice.

'Oh, how that tortures me!' said Athos.

Mordaunt appeared again.

'And I,' replied d'Artagnan—'I say that we must end this. Monsieur the assassin of your uncle, Monsieur the executioner of King Charles, Monsieur the incendiary, I promise to leave you to sink to the bottom; or, if you approach the boat a single stroke nearer, I will break your head with my oar.'

Mordaunt, as if in despair, made one stroke. D'Artagnan took his oar in both hands. Athos rose.

'D'Artagnan!' he exclaimed; 'D'Artagnan, my son, I beg this of you! The wretch is going to die, and it is terrible to let a man die without giving a hand when a hand can save him. Oh! my heart forbids such an action. He must live!'

'*Mordieu!*' replied d'Artagnan, 'why do you not hand yourself to this wretch at once with your hands and feet tied? It would be sooner finished. Ah, Comte de la Fère! you wish to perish through him; well! I, your son, as you call me, don't wish it.'

This was the first time that d'Artagnan resisted an entreaty made by Athos, addressing him as son. Aramis coolly drew his sword, which he had carried between his teeth when swimming.

'If he puts his hand on the boat's sides, I will cut it off—the regicide that he is,' said the latter.

'And I,' said Porthos, 'wait——'

'What are you going to do?' asked Aramis.

'I am going to throw myself into the water and strangle him.'

'Oh, Messieurs!' exclaimed Athos, with irresistible feeling, 'be men; be Christians!'

D'Artagnan uttered a sigh more like a groan; Aramis lowered his sword; Porthos sat down.

'See,' continued Athos, 'death is painted on his face; one minute more and he sinks to the bottom. Ah! do not give me this horrible remorse, do not force me to die of shame in my turn. My friends, grant me the life of this wretched being, and I will bless you; I will——'

'I am dying!' muttered Mordaunt; 'help!—help!——'

'Let us gain a minute,' said Aramis, leaning to the left while addressing d'Artagnan. 'One pull more,' added he, leaning to the right towards Porthos.

D'Artagnan replied neither by gesture nor word; he began to be moved, partly by Athos's supplications, partly by the spectacle before him. Porthos alone pulled the stroke, and as it had no counterbalance, the boat turned partly round, and thus brought Athos close to the dying man.

'M. le Comte de la Fère!' exclaimed Mordaunt, 'I address you; I implore you to pity me—where are you? I cannot see any more—I am dying! help! help!'

'Here I am, Monsieur,' said Athos, leaning over and extending his arm towards Mordaunt with that nobility and dignity which were habitual to him. 'Take my hand, and come into the boat.'

'I prefer not looking,' said d'Artagnan; 'this weakness is repugnant to me.'

He turned towards the two friends, who, on their part, bent towards the bottom of the boat as if they feared to touch him to whom Athos did not fear to extend his hand. Mordaunt made a last effort, raised himself up and seized tightly the hand outstretched towards him with the vehemence of despair.

'Good,' said Athos; 'put your other hand here,' and he offered him his shoulder as a second support, so that his head almost touched the head of Mordaunt, and the two mortal enemies were embraced like two brothers. Mordaunt clasped with closed fingers Athos's collar.

'Good, Monsieur!' said the count, 'now you are saved; calm yourself.'

'Ah, my mother!' exclaimed Mordaunt, with a fiery look, and in a tone of hate impossible to describe, 'I can offer thee only one victim, but it shall at least be the one whom thou wouldst have chosen.'

And while d'Artagnan uttered a loud cry, Porthos raised the oar, and Aramis sought a point for striking, a terrible toss given to the boat dragged Athos into the water, while Mordaunt, uttering a cry of triumph, clasped the neck of his victim, and for the purpose of paralysing his movements encircled his limbs with his own as a serpent might have done.

For a moment, without cry or call for help, Athos tried to keep above water; but from the weight he gradually sank. Soon no more was seen than his long hair floating. Presently all disappeared; and a vast bubbling, which soon ceased, alone indicated the spot where both had become engulfed.

Dumb with horror, immovable, suffocated by indignation and fear, the three friends sat with open mouth, dilated eyes, extended arms; they looked like statues, but despite their immobility they could hear the beatings of their hearts. Porthos was the first to come to himself, and tearing his hair, 'Oh!' he exclaimed, with a sob, especially terrible in such a man—'oh, Athos, Athos, noble heart! Perdition to us who have let you die!'

'Oh, yes, perdition!' repeated d'Artagnan and Aramis.

At that moment, in the midst of a vast circle lighted up by the moon's rays four or five strokes' length from the boat, the same disturbance of the water which had told of the sinking took place again; and first the hair, then a pale face with open but lifeless eyes appeared, then the body, which, rising as far as the bust above the sea, turned gently on its back, according to the caprice of the waves. In the breast of the corpse a poniard was buried, the gold handle of which glittered.

'Mordaunt! Mordaunt!' the three friends cried out; 'it's Mordaunt!'

'But Athos?' said d'Artagnan.

Suddenly the boat gave a lurch to the left under a new and unexpected weight, and Grimaud uttered a cry of joy. They turned and saw Athos, livid, with dull eye and trembling hand, leaning on the boat's side. Eight strong arms raised him at once into the boat, where in a few seconds Athos felt himself growing warm and re-animated by the attentions and embraces of his friends, who were intoxicated with joy.

'You are not wounded, at least?' asked d'Artagnan.

'No—and he?'

'Oh, he, this time, God be thanked, is really dead! Look!' and d'Artagnan, forcing Athos to turn in the direction which he indicated, pointed to the body of Mordaunt floating on his back, sometimes submerged, sometimes afloat, and which seemed still to pursue the four friends with a look of insult and mortal hate. At last it sank. Athos followed it with an eye full of sorrow and pity.

'Bravo, Athos!' cried Aramis, with an effusiveness very rare from him.

'A fine blow!' exclaimed Porthos.

'I had a son,' said Athos; 'I wished to live.'

'At last,' said d'Artagnan, 'God has spoken!'

'It is not I who killed him,' murmured Athos, 'but destiny.'*

LXXVIII

IN WHICH IS TOLD HOW MOUSQUETON, AFTER HAVING MISSED BEING ROASTED, ESCAPED BEING EATEN

DEEP silence reigned for a long time in the boat after the terrible scene which we have just related. The moon, which had shone for a time, as if God intended* that no details of this event should be hidden from the spectators' eyes, now disappeared behind the clouds. All again fell into that obscurity so terrifying in all solitudes, but especially in that liquid one called the ocean; and nothing was heard but the whistling of the west wind over the crest of the waves.

Porthos was the first to break the silence.

'I have seen a good many things,' said he, 'but nothing has moved me so much as that which I have just witnessed. Yet, disquieted as I am, I declare I feel very happy. I feel as if a hundred pounds were off my breast, and that at last I can breathe freely.'

In fact, Porthos breathed with a noise which did honour to the powerful play of his lungs.

'I shall not say as much as you, Porthos,' said Aramis. 'I am still in a state of fright. I have reached the point of doubting the reality of what I have seen, and I look round the boat expecting every moment to see that wretch, holding in his hand the poniard which was in his heart.'

'Don't be in a hurry to sing a Te Deum, Porthos,' said d'Artagnan. 'We have never encountered a greater danger than the present one—for one man gets the better of another, but it is not so with the elements. Now we are out at sea by night, without pilot, in a frail bark; if a blast of wind should upset us, we should be lost.'

Mousqueton uttered a deep sigh.

'You are ungrateful, d'Artagnan,' said Athos—'yes, ungrateful, to doubt Providence just when it saves us in so miraculous a way. Do you believe that God would have helped us to escape so many perils just to abandon us now? No. We are borne along by a westerly breeze. There's Charles's Wain,* consequently France is over there. Let us keep before the wind, and it will drive us towards Calais or Boulogne. If the boat capsizes, we are strong enough, and good swimmers enough, at least five of us, to right it again, or to hold on if that is beyond our strength. Then we are in the course of ships from Dover to Calais, and from Portsmouth to Boulogne. It is then pretty certain that when day comes we shall fall in with some fishing-boat which will pick us up.'

'But suppose we don't fall in with one, and that the wind should blow from the north?'

'That's another thing,' said Athos; 'we shall then meet no land till we have crossed the Atlantic.'

'Which means that we should die of hunger,' replied Aramis.

'It is more than probable,' said the Comte de la Fère.

Mousqueton breathed a sigh more dolorous than the first.

'Come, Mouston,' asked Porthos, 'what makes you keep on groaning so? It becomes tiresome.'

'The fact is, I am very cold.'

'That's impossible,' said Porthos. 'Your body is covered with a layer of fat, which makes it impenetrable to the air. There is something else; speak out.'

'Well, yes, Monsieur; it is this layer of fat on which you compliment me which frightens me.'

'And why so, Mouston? Speak boldly; these gentlemen allow you.'

'Because, Monsieur, I remember that in the library of the Château de Bracieux there are many books of travels, and among them those of Jean Mocquet, the famous navigator of King Henry IV.'

'What then?'

'Well, he tells a good deal about adventures by sea, and events like that which are now threatening us.'

'Go on, Mouston,' said Porthos; 'this comparison is full of interest to us.'

'Well, Monsieur, in such a case famished voyagers, says Jean Mocquet, have the frightful practice of eating one another, and beginning with——'

'The fattest!' exclaimed d'Artagnan, who was not able to control his laughter in spite of the gravity of the situation.

'Yes, Monsieur,' replied Mousqueton, astonished at this hilarity; 'and permit me to say that I don't see anything laughable in the matter.'

'This brave Mouston is devotion personified,' replied Porthos. 'Let us lay a bet that you see yourself already despatched and eaten by your master.'

'Yes, Monsieur; although this pleasure which you imagine to be mine, is not, I confess, unmixed with sorrow. Yet I should not be very sorry, Monsieur, if by dying I felt sure of still being useful to you.'

'Mouston,' said Porthos, much affected; 'if we ever see again my Château de Pierrefonds, you shall have, in fee simple for yourself and descendants, the vineyard which overlooks the farm.'

'And you shall call it, "Devotion Vineyard", Mouston,' said Aramis, 'to transmit to future ages the recollection of your sacrifice.'

'Chevalier,' said d'Artagnan, laughing again, 'you would have eaten some of Mouston without very much repugnance, would you not, especially after two or three days of abstinence?'

'Upon my word, no,' replied Aramis; 'I should much prefer Blaisois. We have known him much less time.'

It is easily understood that during this interchange of fun, which was especially meant to divert Athos's thoughts from the scenes through which he had just passed, the servants did not feel quite at ease, except Grimaud, who knew that in any case he would be safe from this danger, however great it might be. So Grimaud, without taking part in the conversation, and silent as was his habit, was doing his best at rowing with an oar in each hand.

'Are you rowing, then?' said Athos.

Grimaud signified that he was.

'Why do you row?'

'To keep warm.'

In fact, while the others were shivering with cold, the silent Grimaud was all of a sweat.

Suddenly Mousqueton uttered a cry of joy, as he held a bottle above his head.

'Oh!' said he, passing the bottle to Porthos—'oh, Monsieur, we are saved! the boat is supplied with eatables;' and fumbling quickly under the seat whence he had already drawn the valuable specimen, he took out in succession a dozen similar bottles, some bread, and a piece of salt beef. It is needless to say that this discovery restored liveliness to all except Athos.

'Confound it!' said Porthos, who was already hungry when he embarked on the felucca, 'it is astonishing how hungry the emotions make one!' and he emptied the bottle at a draught, and ate a good third of the bread and salt beef.

'Now,' said Athos, 'sleep, or try to sleep, Messieurs; I will watch.'

For men different from these bold adventurers such a suggestion would have been out of derision. For in fact they were wet to the skin, and an icy wind was blowing; and the feelings which they had so lately experienced seemed to forbid sleep. But for their iron constitutions, with bodies inured to all fatigues, sleep in all circumstances came when called for without ever disobeying the call.

So in a very short time they all, full of confidence in their pilot, reclined as they were able, and tried to profit from the advice of Athos, who, seated at the rudder with eyes fixed on the sky, where doubtless he sought not only the route to France but the face of God, remained, as he had promised, thoughtful and awake, guiding the little boat in the right course.

After they had had some hours of sleep Athos awoke them. The first rays of morning had just lighted up the blue sea, and about ten gunshots off was seen a black mass, above which was spread a triangular sail, fine and long like a swallow's wing.

'A ship!' said the four friends with one voice, while the servants also expressed their joy in various keys.

It was in fact a Dunkirk bark sailing towards Boulogne.

The four masters, with Blaisois and Mousqueton, united their voices into one shout, which vibrated over the elastic surface of the waves, while Grimaud, without saying anything, put his hat on the end of his oar to attract the notice of the ship's crew.

A quarter of an hour after, the ship's boat took them in tow, and they stood on the ship's deck. Grimaud offered twenty guineas to the skipper on his master's behalf, and at nine o'clock, aided by a good wind, our Frenchmen set foot on their native soil.

'I say how strong one is upon this soil!' said Porthos, burying his large feet in the sand. 'Let anyone come to pick a quarrel with me now, and they will soon see whom they have to do with. I could defy a whole kingdom.'

'And I beg of you,' said d'Artagnan, 'not to sound your note of defiance too loud, Porthos, for it seems to me that we are a good deal stared at by those close by.'

'Why, of course,' said Porthos, 'they are admiring us.'

'Ah, well! I am not at all proud of that, I assure you, Porthos; only I see some men dressed in black, and in our position men so dressed make me afraid, I confess.'

'They are the customs clerks,' said Aramis.

'Under the great cardinal,' said Athos, 'they would have paid more attention to us than to the merchandise; but under the present one, rest assured, my friends, they will do the reverse.'

'I don't rely on them,' said d'Artagnan; 'and I shall get off to the sand-hills.'

'Why not the town?' said Porthos. 'I should prefer a good inn to those frightful deserts of sand which God has made only for rabbits. Besides, I am hungry.'

'Do as you please, Porthos,' said d'Artagnan; 'but as for me, I am convinced of this, that nothing is safer for men in our position than the open country;' and d'Artagnan, sure of securing the majority, plunged among the sand-hills without waiting for Porthos's reply. The little troop soon disappeared without having attracted public attention.

'Now,' said Aramis, when they had gone about a quarter of a league, 'let us have a talk.'

'No, no,' said d'Artagnan; 'let us flee. We have escaped Cromwell, Mordaunt, the sea—those abysses which threatened to engulf us; we shall not escape Sieur Mazarin.'

'You are right, d'Artagnan,' said Aramis; 'and my advice is, that for greater security we separate.'

'Yes, yes,' said d'Artagnan; 'let us separate.'

Porthos wished to speak in opposition to this resolution, but D'Artagnan made him understand by pressing his hand that he must be silent. Porthos was very obedient to his companion's signs, whose intellectual superiority he recognized with his usual good-nature. He checked, then, the words which he was on the point of speaking.

'But why should we separate?' said Athos.

'Because,' said d'Artagnan, 'Porthos and I were sent to Cromwell by M. de Mazarin, and instead of serving Cromwell, we have served King Charles I; and that is not at all the same thing. By returning with MM. de la Fère and d'Herblay our crime is proved; by returning alone it remains in doubt, and by means of doubt one can deceive men a good deal. Now, I mean to lead M. de Mazarin a dance—that I do.'

'Come,' said Porthos, 'that's true.'

'You forget,' said Athos, 'that we are your prisoners, that we do not regard ourselves as freed from our parole to you, and that in taking us as prisoners to Paris——'

'Really, Athos,' broke in d'Artagnan, 'I am sorry that a man of sense like you should be always talking of wretched things at which scholars of the third class would blush. Chevalier,' continued d'Artagnan, speaking to Aramis, who, proudly resting on his sword, seemed, although he had at first expressed a contrary opinion, to be at the first word won over to that of his companion—'Chevalier, understand that in this, as is usually the case, my suspicious nature exaggerates. Porthos and I risk nothing, after all. But if by chance, however, they try to arrest us before you, well! they could not arrest seven men as they arrest three; swords would see the light, and the affair, bad for everyone, would become an enormity which would ruin all four of us. Besides, if misfortune happens to two of us, then the other two are at liberty to do what they can to get the others released. And then who knows whether we shall not obtain separately—you from the queen, we from Mazarin—a pardon which they would have refused us unitedly? You, Athos and Aramis, go to the right. You, Porthos, to the left with me;

leave these gentlemen to file off towards Normandy, and we to gain Paris by the shortest route.'

'But if they seize us on the way, how can we mutually be informed of the catastrophe?' asked Aramis.

'Nothing easier,' replied d'Artagnan; 'let us agree on an itinerary from which we will not deviate. You take St Valéry,* then Dieppe, then the direct route from there to Paris. We will go by Abbeville, Amiens, Péronne, Compiègne, and Senlis; and in each house or inn where we stop we will write on the wall with a sharp-pointed knife, or on the window-pane with a diamond, a notice to guide the searches of those who may be free.'

'Ah, my friend,' said Athos, 'how I should admire the resources of your head if I did not stop to adore those of your heart!' and he gave his hand to d'Artagnan.

'Has the fox cleverness, Athos?' said the Gascon, shrugging his shoulders. 'No; he knows how to choke the poultry, track the huntsmen, and find his way back by day as by night—that's all. Well, is it settled?'

'It is settled.'

'Then let us divide the money,' replied d'Artagnan. 'There ought to be a balance of about two hundred pistoles. Grimaud, how much is it?'

'A hundred and eighty half-louis, Monsieur.'

'It's that, is it? Ah, hurrah! there's the sun. Good-day, friend sun! Although you are not the same as that of Gascony, I recognize you. Good-day; it's a long time since I have seen you.'

'Come, come, d'Artagnan,' said Athos, 'don't assume a mock bravery; you have tears in your eyes already. Let us always be frank towards one another.'

'Ah, but could you believe it possible, Athos, to leave without emotion, and at a time not without danger, two friends like you and Aramis?'

'No,' said Athos; 'so come to my arms, my son.'

'Plague on it!' said Porthos, sobbing, 'I believe I am crying. How foolish it is!'

These four men, united by brotherly bonds, were in fact but one soul at that moment.

Blaisois and Grimaud were to go with Athos and Aramis. Mousqueton sufficed for Porthos and D'Artagnan. They divided the money, as they had always done before, with fraternal exactness; then after having individually shaken hands and mutually reiterated the assurance of an eternal friendship, these four gentlemen separated to take the routes arranged, not without turning round and sending after one another loving words which the echoes repeated. At last they were lost to view.

'*Sacrebleu*, d'Artagnan!' said Porthos, 'I must say this immediately, for I cannot keep anything in my heart against you—I have not recognized you in this affair!'

'Why?' asked d'Artagnan, with his cunning smile.

'Because,' said Porthos, 'if, as you say, Athos and Aramis are in danger, this is not the time to leave them. I confess that I was quite ready to follow them, in spite of all the Mazarins on earth.'

'You would be right, Porthos, if this were the case. But remember one small fact, which, small though it be, will quite change your views; it is that it is not those gentlemen who run the gravest danger, but ourselves. It is not to abandon them that we leave them, but so as not to compromise them.'

'Really?' said Porthos, opening his great eyes in astonishment.

'Yes, doubtless; if they are arrested, they will simply get put into the Bastille; but if we are, we shall be hanged in the Place de Grève.'*

'Oh, oh!' said Porthos; 'that's a long way from the baron's coronet that you promised me, d'Artagnan.'

'Bah! not so far as you may think perhaps, Porthos; you know the proverb: "Every road leads to Rome."'

'But how is it we are running greater dangers than Athos and Aramis?'

'Because they have simply executed the mission which they received from Queen Henrietta, and we have betrayed that which we received from Mazarin; instead of helping in the fall of Charles's royal head, condemned by those rascals whom they call MM. Mazarin, Cromwell, Joyce, Pride, Fairfax, etc., we nearly saved him.'

'Upon my word, that's true,' said Porthos; 'but how can you suppose that in the midst of these great affairs, General Cromwell had time to think of——'

'Cromwell thinks of everything, has time for everything; and believe me, my dear friend, we must not lose ours, for it is precious. We shall not be safe until after seeing Mazarin, and yet——'

'The devil!' said Porthos: 'and what shall we say to Mazarin?'

'Leave that to me. I have a plan; they laugh best who laugh last. M. Mazarin is very tricky; M. Cromwell is very strong. But I would rather deal with them than with the late M. Mordaunt.'

'Stop,' said Porthos, 'it is very pleasant to say the "*late* M. Mordaunt."'

'Upon my word, yes; but now let us be off !' And they both, without losing an instant, took the road to Paris, followed by Mousqueton, who, after having been too cold all night, was already too hot at the end of a quarter of an hour.

LXXIX

THE RETURN

ATHOS and Aramis followed the course marked out for them by d'Artagnan, and travelled as fast as they could. They thought it would be more advantageous for them to be stopped near Paris than far from it. Every evening they traced, either on the walls or on the windows, the sign of recognition agreed on; but every morning they awoke free, to their great astonishment.

As they approached Paris, the great events in which they had taken part, and which had revolutionized England, faded away as dreams, while on the other hand those which during their absence had stirred France came before them.

During their six weeks' absence* so many small events had taken place that unitedly they made up a great event.

The Parisians, on awaking in the morning without queen, without king, were much troubled by this abandonment; and the absence of Mazarin, so warmly desired, did not compensate for that of the two illustrious fugitives.

The first feeling which Paris experienced on learning the flight to St Germain—a flight which we have described to our readers—was that sort of fright which seizes hold of children when they wake up in the night or in solitude. The parliament was aroused, and it was decided that a deputation should be sent to the queen to pray her no longer to deprive Paris of her royal presence.

But the queen was still under the twofold influence of the victory of Lens, and the satisfaction from her flight so success-fully executed. The deputies not only were not received by her, but were made to wait on the high-road where the Chancellor Séguier—the same chancellor whom we have seen in the first part of this work pursue so obstinately a letter into the very corset* of the queen—came to bring them the ulti-matum of the court, declaring that if the parliament did not humble themselves before royalty by passing condemnation on all the questions which had led to the quarrel between them, Paris would be besieged the next day;* that even already, in the expectation of that siege, the Duc d'Orléans was holding St Cloud bridge; and that Monsieur the Prince, illustrious from his victory at Lens, held Charenton and St Denis.

Unfortunately for the court, to whom a moderate reply would have restored a good number of partisans, this threatening answer produced an effect contrary to the one expected. It wounded the pride of the parliament, which, feeling itself strongly supported by the citizens, to whom the pardon of Broussel had shown their strength, replied to these letters-patent by declaring that Cardinal Mazarin, being notoriously the author of all these disorders, was the enemy of the king and the State,* ordered him to withdraw from the court the same day, and from France in a week, and should he not obey, enjoined all the king's subjects to attack him.

This energetic response, which the court had by no means anticipated, put both Paris and Mazarin beyond the law. It remained only to be known who would gain the mastery, the parliament or the court.

The court thereupon made preparations for attacking, and Paris for defence. The citizens were engaged in the usual work of citizens in times of riot—that is to say, in stretching chains and unpaving streets—when they saw arriving for their assistance, conducted by the Coadjutor, M. le Prince de Conti, brother of M. le Prince de Condé, and M. le Duc de Longueville, his brother-in-law. This gave them confidence, for besides two princes of the blood, they had the advantage of numbers. It was the 10th of January* when this unhoped-for aid came to the Parisians.

After a stormy discussion, M. le Prince de Conti was named generalissimo of the king's armies out of Paris, with MM. les Ducs d'Elbeuf and de Bouillon, and le Maréchal de la Mothe for lieutenants-general. The Duc de Longueville, without office or title, was satisfied with assisting his brother-in-law.

M. de Beaufort had come from the Vendômois,* bringing, says the chronicle, his haughty look, his fine long hair, and that popularity which was tantamount to the royalty of the markets.

The Parisian army had been organized with that promptitude which the citizens exhibit in making soldiers of themselves when they are driven to it by some impulse or other. On the nineteenth* the improvised army tried a *sortie*, rather for self-assurance and the assurance of others of their real existence than to attempt anything serious, flying above their heads a flag on which was this singular device: 'We seek our king.'

The following days were employed in small operations, which effected nothing else than the capture of some flocks and the burning of two or three houses.

This brings us to the early days of February, and it was on the first that our four companions landed at Boulogne, and took their respective courses towards Paris.

Towards the end of the fourth day of their journey, they carefully avoided Nanterre, so as not to fall into the hands of the queen's party.* It was quite against the grain for Athos to take all these precautions; but Aramis had very judiciously remarked that they had no right to be imprudent, and that the mission received from King Charles at the foot of the scaffold would only terminate at the feet of the queen. Athos therefore agreed.

At the faubourgs our travellers found a strong guard; all Paris was armed. The sentinel refused to let them pass, and called the sergeant. The sergeant came out at once with all the importance which citizens assume when clothed with any military dignity.

'Who are you, Messieurs?' he asked.

'Two gentlemen,' replied Athos.

'Whence do you come?'

'From London.'

'What have you come to do at Paris?'

'To execute a mission to her Majesty the Queen of England.'

'Ah, yes! everybody is going nowadays to the Queen of England. We have already here three gentlemen whose passes we are examining, and they are going to her Majesty. Where are yours?'

'We have none.'

'How so? you have none?'

'No; we are from England, as we have told you. We are completely ignorant of the state of political affairs, having left Paris before the king's departure.'

'Ah!' said the sergeant, with a knowing look, 'you are of Mazarin's party, who want to gain admittance to act as spies.'

'My dear friend,' said Athos, who had hitherto allowed Aramis to make the replies, 'if we were Mazarin's partisans we should, on the contrary, have all the necessary passes. In your present situation, believe me, you should above all be suspicious of those who are perfectly in rule.'

'Go to the guard-room; explain matters to the commanding officer.'

The sergeant made a sign to the sentinel, who put himself in line; the sergeant passed first, the two gentlemen followed him to the guard-room.

This guard-room was quite filled by citizens and men of the lower class; some gambling, others drinking, others again speechifying.

In a corner, almost out of sight, were the three gentlemen who had come first, whose passes the officer was examining.

This officer was in the next room, the importance of his rank conceding to him the honour of a private apartment.

The first act both of the newly arrived and the earlier comers was, to cast a rapid, searching glance at one another from the ends of the guard-room. The first comers were covered with long cloaks in which they were carefully wrapped. One of them, not so tall as his companions, kept in the background in the shade.

When the sergeant, on entering, announced that in all probability he was bringing in two partisans of Mazarin, the three gentlemen listened very attentively. The shortest of these, who had advanced a few paces, retired again into the shade.

On learning that the newcomers had no passes, the unanimous opinion of the guard seemed to be not to give them permission to enter Paris.

'Indeed,' said Athos, 'it is probable, on the contrary, that we shall enter, for we seem to have to do with reasonable people. Now, a very simple thing needs be done; send our names to her Majesty the Queen of England, and if she become answerable for us, I hope you will kindly let us pass freely.'

At these words the attention of the gentleman in the background increased, and was accompanied by such marks of surprise that his hat, pushed back by the cloak which he more carefully drew around him, fell off; he stooped, and picked it up quickly.

'Oh, good heavens!' said Aramis, jogging Athos's elbow; 'did you notice him?'

'Notice what?'

'The shortest of the three gentlemen?'

'No.'

'It seemed to me to be—but it's impossible.'

Just then the sergeant came out of the room of the officer of the guard, and pointing out the three gentlemen, to whom he gave a paper, 'The passes are correct,' said he; 'let these three gentlemen pass.'

The three gentlemen gave a nod, and hastened to make use of the permission to go on their way.

Aramis followed them with his eyes, and just as the shortest passed by him, he pressed Athos's hand.

'What's the matter, my dear fellow?' the latter asked.

'I have—it's a dream, doubtless.'

Then addressing the sergeant, 'Tell me, Monsieur,' he added, 'do you know those three gentlemen who have just left?'

'I know them from their passes; they are MM. de Flamarens, de Châtillon, and de Bruy—three Frondeurs who wish to join M. de Longueville.'

'That's strange,' said Aramis, answering his own thoughts rather than the sergeant; 'I thought I recognized Mazarin himself.'

The sergeant burst out laughing.

'He!' said he, 'to venture thus among us to be hanged!—not such a fool!'

'Ah!' muttered Aramis, 'I may be deceived. I have not d'Artagnan's infallible eye.'

'Who here talks of d'Artagnan?' asked the officer, who at this moment appeared at the door of the room.

'Oh!' muttered Grimaud, opening his eyes.

'What?' Aramis and Athos asked at the same time.

'Planchet!' replied Grimaud; 'Planchet with the high collar.'

'MM. de la Fère and d'Herblay,' exclaimed the officer, 'come back to Paris! How delighted I am, Messieurs! for doubtless you are going to join Messieurs the Princes.'

'As you see, my dear Planchet,' said Aramis, while Athos was smiling, seeing the important grade occupied in the citizen soldiery by the old comrade of Mousqueton, of Bazin, and of Grimaud.

'And M. d'Artagnan, of whom you made mention just now, M. d'Herblay, might I venture to ask if you have any news of him?'

'We left him four days ago, and were led to believe that he had reached Paris before us.'

'No, Monsieur, I am quite certain he is not in Paris, perhaps he has stopped at St Germain.'

'I do not think so; he was to have met us at the Hôtel de la Chevrette.'

'I passed there today.'

'And the fair Madeleine, had she no news of him?' asked Aramis, smiling.

'No, Monsieur; I will not hide from you that she even seemed very much distressed.'

'Indeed,' said Aramis, 'we have lost no time. Allow me, my dear Athos, without further enquiries about our friend, to make my compliments to M. Planchet.'

'Ah, Monsieur the Chevalier!' said Planchet, bowing.

'Lieutenant?' said Aramis.

'Lieutenant, and promise of being captain.'

'That's very fortunate; and how is it these honours have come to you?'

'First of all, you know, Messieurs, that I helped M. de Rochefort to escape.'

'Yes, indeed; he has told us all about that.'

'I nearly got hanged by Mazarin on that occasion, and this has naturally made me more popular than I was.'

'And thanks to this popularity——'

'No, thanks to something better; you know, besides, that I served in the regiment of Piedmont, where I had the honour of being sergeant.'

'Yes.'

'Well, one day no one was able to make a crowd of armed citizens keep rank, some starting with the left foot first, some with the right. I succeeded in making them start with the same foot; and I was made lieutenant at once on the parade ground.'

'There's the explanation,' said Aramis.

'So,' said Athos, 'you have a crowd of nobility with you?'

'Indeed, yes! We have first of all, as you may perhaps know, M. le Prince de Conti, M. le Duc de Longueville, M. le Duc de Beaufort, M. le Duc d'Elbeuf, the Duc de Bouillon, the Duc de Chevreuse, M. de Brissac, the Maréchal de la Mothe, M. de Luynes, the Marquis de Vitry, the Prince de Marcillac, the Marquis de Noirmoutiers, the Comte de Fiesque, the Marquis de Laigues, the Comte de Montrésor, the Marquis de Sévigné—whom do I know besides?'

'And M. Raoul de Bragelonne?' asked Athos, in a voice full of emotion; 'D'Artagnan told me that he recommended him to your care when he left.'

'Yes, Monsieur the Count, as if he were his own son; and I must say that he has not been out of my sight a moment.'

'Then,' replied Athos, in a joyful voice, 'he is quite well? No accident has befallen him?'

'None, Monsieur.'

'And he is staying——'

'At the Charlemagne Hotel, still.'

'He passes his time——'

'Sometimes at the Queen of England's, sometimes with Madame de Chevreuse. He and the Comte de Guiche are inseparables.'

'Thanks, Planchet,' said Athos, giving him his hand.

'Oh, Monsieur the Count!' said Planchet, touching his hand with the tips of his fingers.

'Well, what are you doing, then, Count? to an old lackey!' said Aramis.

'Friend,' said Athos, 'he gives me news of Raoul.'

'And now, Messieurs, what do you intend doing?' asked Planchet, who did not hear the remark.

'Entering Paris, if you can grant us permission, my dear M. Planchet.'

'What! if I will give you permission? You are laughing at me, Monsieur the Count; I am nothing else than your servant,' and he bowed. Then turning to his men, 'Let these gentlemen pass,' said he. 'I know them; they are friends of M. de Beaufort.'

'Long live M. de Beaufort!' cried all the post with one voice, opening the way for Athos and Aramis.

The sergeant alone approached Planchet, 'What! without passport?' he muttered.

'Without passport,' said Planchet.

'Mind, Captain,' he added, giving Planchet in advance his promised rank—'mind; one of the three men who left just now told me in a whisper to be on my guard against these gentlemen.'

'I,' said Planchet, with dignity,—'I know them, and am responsible.'

Having said that, he shook Grimaud by the hand, who seemed honoured by the distinction.

'*Au revoir*, then, Captain,' said Aramis, in his bantering tone; 'if anything happens to us, we shall make use of your name.'

'Monsieur,' said Planchet, 'in that as in everything, I am still your servant.'

'The fellow has much wit,' said Aramis, mounting his horse.

'And why should he not,' said Athos, 'after having for so long a time brushed his master's hats?'

LXXX

THE AMBASSADORS

THE two friends set off at once, descending the rapid slope of the faubourg; but at the bottom of it they saw with astonishment that the streets had become rivers and the squares lakes. In consequence of the heavy rains during January the Seine had overflowed and flooded half the capital.*

Athos and Aramis bravely entered the waters with their horses, but the latter were soon up to their chests. The gentlemen therefore had to dismount and take a boat, which they did, after ordering their servants to go and wait for them at the markets.

They therefore reached the Louvre in a boat. It was quite night, and Paris, thus seen by the light of pale lanterns flickering among these ponds which were being crossed by boats loaded with patrols carrying their glittering arms, with the watchwords exchanged between the posts, presented an appearance which quite bewildered Aramis, a man so easily influenced by warlike emotions.

They reached the queen's apartments, but were obliged to wait, as her Majesty was that very moment giving audience to some gentlemen, who were bearers of news from England.

'And we also,' said Athos to the servant who brought the answer, 'not only bring news from England, but have just come from there.'

'What are your names, Messieurs?' the servant asked.

'M. le Comte de la Fère and M. le Chevalier d'Herblay.'

'Ah! in that case, Messieurs,' said the servant, hearing those names which the queen had so many times pronounced in her hope, 'it is quite another thing; and I believe her Majesty would not pardon me for keeping you waiting a moment. Follow me, I pray you.'

On reaching the queen's apartment he opened the door.

'Madame,' said he, 'I hope your Majesty will pardon me for having disobeyed your orders when you learn that these gentlemen are the Comte de la Fère and the Chevalier d'Herblay.'

At these two names the queen uttered a cry of joy, which the gentlemen heard from the place where they had waited.

'Poor queen!' murmured Athos.

'Oh, let them come in!' exclaimed the princess, hastening to the door.

The poor child did not leave her mother, and tried to make her forget by her filial cares the absence of her two brothers and of her sister.

'Come in, come in, Messieurs,' said she, herself opening the door.

Athos and Aramis entered. The queen was seated in an armchair, and before her, standing, were two of the three gentlemen whom they had met in the guard-room. These were M. de Flamarens and M. Gaspard de Coligny, Duc de Châtillon, brother of the one who was killed in a duel seven or eight years before in a matter respecting Madame de Longueville.

At the announcement of the two friends they withdrew a step, and exchanged some words in a low voice, being evidently ill at ease.

'Well, Messieurs,' exclaimed the queen, on seeing Athos and Aramis, 'you are come at last, my faithful friends; but the messengers of the State are here before you. The court was informed of the state of affairs in London just when you reached the gates of Paris; and these two gentlemen are come from her Majesty, Queen Anne of Austria, to give me the latest news.'

Aramis and Athos looked at each other; this tranquillity, this joy even, which appeared in the queen's looks, quite stupefied them.

'Be pleased to go on,' said she, addressing MM. de Flamarens and de Châtillon; 'you were saying just now that his Majesty, Charles I, had been condemned to death, contrary to the wishes of the majority of his subjects.'

'Yes, Madame,' stammered Châtillon.

Aramis and Athos looked more and more astonished at each other.

'And that led to the scaffold,' continued the queen—'oh, my Lord! he has been saved by the indignant people?'

'Yes, Madame,' replied Châtillon, in so low a voice that the two gentlemen, though very attentive, could scarcely hear this affirmation.

The queen clasped her hands together in abundant gratitude, while her daughter threw her arms round her mother's neck, and embraced her with tears of joy in her eyes.

'Now we have nothing more to do but present to your Majesty our humble respects,' said Châtillon, to whom this role seemed very burdensome, and who blushed when he met the fixed, piercing look of Athos.

'One moment more, Messieurs,' said the queen, detaining them by a gesture. 'One moment, please, for here are MM. de la Fère and d'Herblay, who are come from London, and who will perhaps give us those ocular proofs with which you are unacquainted. You will convey these to the queen, my dear sister. Speak, Messieurs; I am listening. Hide nothing. Since his Majesty is still living, and his royal honour is safe, all else is to me indifferent.'

Athos turned pale, and put his hand to his heart.

'Well,' said the queen, who noticed this movement and paleness; 'speak, Monsieur, I beg of you.'

'I beg pardon, Madame,' said Athos, 'but I do not wish to add anything to the recital of these gentlemen before they have acknowledged that perhaps they are mistaken.'

'Mistaken!' exclaimed the queen, almost suffocated—'mistaken! what has taken place, then? Oh, *mon Dieu!*'

'Monsieur,' said M. de Flamarens to Athos, 'if we are mistaken, the mistake is on the queen's part; and you would not presume, I suppose, to put it right—for that would be to give the lie to her Majesty.'

' "On the queen's part", Monsieur?' replied Athos, with his calm, thrilling voice.

'Yes,' muttered Flamarens, looking down.

Athos sighed sorrowfully.

'Is it not rather on the part of him who accompanied you, and whom we saw along with you in the guard-room at the Barrière du Roule,* that the mistake originates?' said Aramis, with freezing politeness. 'For if we are not deceived, there were three of you who came into Paris.'

Châtillon and Flamarens trembled.

'But explain yourself, Count,' exclaimed the queen, whose distress increased every moment. 'On your face I read despair. Your mouth hesitates to tell some terrible news; your hands tremble. Oh, God! what has happened?'

'Lord,' said the princess, falling on her knees near her mother, 'have pity upon us!'

'Monsieur,' said Châtillon, 'if you are the bearer of sad news, you will act cruelly in telling it to the queen.'

Aramis approached M. de Châtillon so as almost to touch him.

'Monsieur,' said he to him, with pinched lips and flashing eyes, 'you have not, I suppose, the pretention to teach M. le Comte de la Fère and myself what we have to say here?'

During this short altercation Athos, still with hand on his heart and inclined head, drew near the queen, and in a trembling voice, 'Madame,' he said, 'princes, who are by their natures above other men, have been endowed with hearts able to support greater misfortunes than those of common people—for their hearts partake of their superiority. One should not then, as it seems to me, treat a great queen like your Majesty in the same manner as a woman of our condition. O queen, fated to suffer martyrdom on this earth, here is the result of the mission with which you honoured us!'

And Athos, kneeling before the trembling queen, drew from his breast, in the same case, the Order set in diamonds which the queen had entrusted to Lord de Winter, and the wedding-ring which Charles had delivered to Aramis. He opened the box and handed them to the queen with a mute, deep grief.

The queen took the ring, put it convulsively to her lips, and without power to utter a sigh or articulate a sob, she extended her arms, became pale, and fell unconscious into those of her maids and daughter.

Athos kissed the hem of the robe of the unhappy widow, and then rising with a dignity which made a profound impression on those present, 'I, Comte de la Fère,' said he, 'a gentleman who has never told a lie, swear first before God, and then before this poor queen, that all that could be done to save the king, we have done on the soil of England. Now, Chevalier,' added he, turning to d'Herblay, 'let us go; our duty is completed.'

'Not yet,' said Aramis; 'one word must be spoken to these gentlemen.'

And turning towards Châtillon, 'Monsieur,' he said to him, 'will you be good enough not to go before you hear what I wish to say to you out of the queen's presence?'

Châtillon bowed, but did not speak his assent. Athos and Aramis passed out first; the other two followed. They said not a word until they reached a terrace level with a window. Aramis went towards it; at the window he stopped, and turning towards the Duc de Châtillon, 'Monsieur,' he said to him, 'you took the liberty just now, it seems to me, of treating us very cavalierly. That is not pleasant under any circumstances, still less on the part of persons who come to bring the queen the message of a liar.'

'Monsieur!' exclaimed Châtillon.

'What have you done then with M. de Bruy?' Aramis ironically asked. 'Has he not gone to disguise himself because he is too much like M. de Mazarin? We know that there is at the Palais-Royal a good number of spare Italian masks, from Harlequin to Pantaloon.'*

'But you are challenging us, I think?' said Flamarens.

'Ah! you are not certain, Messieurs?'

'Chevalier! Chevalier!' said Athos.

'Eh! let me alone, now,' said Aramis petulantly; 'you know very well I don't like things to be only half done.'

'Finish it, then, Monsieur,' said Châtillon, with a haughtiness which by no means yielded to that of Aramis.

Aramis bowed.

'Messieurs,' said he, 'anyone else would arrest you, for we have some friends in Paris; but we offer you a means of leaving without being disturbed. Come and talk with us for five minutes, sword in hand, upon this secluded terrace.'

'Willingly,' said Châtillon.

'One moment, Messieurs,' exclaimed Flamarens. 'I admit that the proposal is tempting; but it is impossible at this hour to accept it.'

'And why is it?' said Aramis, in his bantering way. 'Is it the nearness of Mazarin which makes you so cautious?'

'Oh! you hear, Flamarens?' said Châtillon; 'not to reply would be a blot on my name and honour.'

'That's my opinion,' said Aramis, coldly.

'You will not answer, however, and these gentlemen very soon will be, I am sure of it, of my opinion.'

Aramis shook his head with an insolent gesture of incredulity.

Châtillon saw this gesture, and carried his hand to his sword.

'Duke,' said Flamarens, 'you forget that tomorrow you command a most important expedition, and one ordered by Monsieur the Prince, approved by the queen; till tomorrow evening you are not at your own disposal.'

'Be it so; on the morning of the day after tomorrow, then,' said Aramis.

'That's a long way off,' said Châtillon.

'It is not I,' said Aramis, 'who ask this delay, and who fix this term; so much the more, as it seems to me, that we might be able to meet in this expedition.'

'Yes, Monsieur, you are right,' exclaimed Châtillon; 'I will meet you with great pleasure tomorrow if you will take the trouble to come as far as the gates of Charenton.'*

'Yes, Monsieur; to have the honour of meeting you I would go to the end of the world; much more will I go one or two leagues.'

'Well, tomorrow, Monsieur!'

'I shall reckon on it. Go away then to join your cardinal. But previously swear on your honour not to inform him of our return.'

'Conditions?'

'Why not?'

'Because it is for the victors to propose them; and you are not so yet, Messieurs.'

'Then let us fight at once. It is quite the same to us who do not command the expedition of tomorrow.'

Châtillon and Flamarens looked at each other. There was so much irony in Aramis's words and gestures that Châtillon especially had great difficulty to restrain his wrath. But on a word from Flamarens he checked himself.

'Well, let it be so,' said he; 'our companion, whoever he is, shall know nothing of what has passed. But you really promise to find me tomorrow at Charenton, do you not?'

'Yes,' said Aramis, 'rest assured about that, Messieurs.'

The four gentlemen bowed, but this time Châtillon and Flamarens left the Louvre first, and the others followed.

'What is the meaning of all this fury, Aramis?' asked Athos.

'Eh! *pardieu!* I have to do with those I blame.'

'What have they done to you?'

'They have done——You haven't seen them?'

'No.'

'They sneered when we swore that we had done our duty in England. Now, they believed it, or they did not. They sneered to insult us. If they did not believe it, the insult was the greater; and it is well to show them that we are good for something. But I am not sorry that they have put off the affair till tomorrow. I think we have something better to do this evening than to draw the sword.'

'What have we to do?'

'Eh! why, we have to effect the capture of Mazarin.'

Athos contemptuously protruded his lips.

'These expeditions don't suit me, you know, Aramis.'

'Why not?'

'Because they resemble surprises.'

'Really, Athos, you would be a strange commander-in-chief! You would fight only in broad daylight. You would inform the enemy of the hour at which you would attack; and you would carefully avoid attempting anything by night, for fear of being accused of having profited by the darkness.'

Athos smiled. 'You know that a man cannot change his nature; besides, do you know where we are, and whether the seizure of Mazarin would not be an evil rather than a good—an embarrassment and not a triumph?'

'Say at once, Athos, that you disapprove of my suggestion.'

'By no means; I think, on the contrary, that it is fair warfare, yet——'

'Yet, what?'

'I think you ought not to have made those gentlemen promise to say nothing to Mazarin, for in doing that, you have already made an engagement to do nothing.'

'Not at all, I swear; I regard myself as perfectly free. Come, come, Athos, let us go.'

'Where?'

'To M. de Beaufort or to M. de Bouillon; we will tell them about it.'

'Yes, but on one condition; that we begin with the Coadjutor. He is a priest; he is learned in casuistry, and we will tell our case to him.'

'Ah!' said Aramis, 'he will spoil everything, will appropriate all to himself; let us take him last instead of first.'

Athos smiled. It was clear there was a thought in his mind which he did not express.

'Well, let it be so; with which shall we begin?'

'With M. de Bouillon, if you don't mind; he is the nearest to where we are now.'

'Now, you will allow me to do one thing, will you not?'

'What is it?'

'Let me go first to the Charlemagne Hotel to embrace Raoul.'

'Why, of course! I will go with you for the same purpose.'

They took the boat which had brought them, and reached the markets. There they found Grimaud and Blaisois in charge of the horses, and all four went off to Rue Guénégaud. But Raoul was not there; he had received a message from Monsieur the Prince, and had set off with Olivain immediately after having received it.

LXXXI

THE THREE LIEUTENANTS OF THE GENERALISSIMO

ACCORDING to arrangement Athos and Aramis, on leaving the Charlemagne Hotel, took their way to the mansion of M. le

Duc de Bouillon.* The night was very dark; and although its silent hours were close at hand, yet still were heard those thousand noises which are especially audible in a city in a state of siege. At every step barricades were encountered; at each winding of the streets chains were outstretched; at the cross-roads were bivouacs of armed men; patrols were passing up and down; messengers sent by the various chiefs were crossing the public squares; and lastly, animated dialogues which indicated the mental agitation were going on between the peaceful inhabitants, who were at the windows, and their more warlike fellow-citizens, who circulated in the streets armed with partisans and arquebuses.

Athos and Aramis had not gone a hundred yards before they were stopped by the sentinels in charge of the barricades, who demanded the watchword; but they replied that they were going to M. de Bouillon to tell him news of importance, and the sentinels were satisfied by furnishing them with a guide, who, with the professed purpose of facilitating their course, was charged to keep a watch over them.

This guide started off preceding them and singing—

> This brave M. de Bouillon
> Is troubled with the gout.

It was one of the newest triolets,* and was composed of I don't know how many couplets, in which everyone was mentioned.

On reaching the neighbourhood of Bouillon's mansion, they passed a small troop of three cavaliers who had all the pass-words, for they marched without guide or escort, and on reaching barricades had only to exchange some words with the guards, and they were at once allowed to pass with all the signs of respect which were doubtless due to their rank.

On seeing them Athos and Aramis stopped.

'Oh, oh!' said Aramis, 'do you see, Count?'

'Yes,' said Athos.

'What do you think of these three cavaliers?'

'And you, Aramis?'

'Why, that they are our men.'

'You are not mistaken. I am sure I recognized M. de Flamarens.'

'So did I M. de Châtillon.'

'As for the cavalier in a brown cloak——'

'That's the cardinal himself. How the devil durst they venture into the neighbourhood of Bouillon's house?' asked Aramis.

Athos smiled, but said nothing. Five minutes after, they knocked at the prince's door.

The door was guarded by a sentinel, as is the custom among people of high rank. There was also a little post in the courtyard, ready to obey the orders of the lieutenant of M. le Prince de Conti. As said the song, M. le Duc de Bouillon had the gout, and was keeping his bed; but in spite of this serious indisposition, which had prevented him for a month* from riding—that is to say, since Paris had been in a state of siege—he was nevertheless ready to receive MM. le Comte de la Fère and le Chevalier d'Herblay.

The two friends were shown into the patient's bedroom, for, though in bed, he was surrounded by the most warlike surroundings possible. There were in all directions hung on the walls swords, pistols, cuirasses, and arquebuses, and it was easy to see that when the gout should leave him, M. de Bouillon would cut out some work for the enemies of parliament. Meanwhile, to his deep regret, he said, he was forced to keep his bed.

'Ah, Messieurs!' he exclaimed, on seeing his visitors, and making an effort to rise up in bed which drew from him a doleful grimace, 'you are very fortunate. You can ride, go, come, and fight for the people's cause. But you see me nailed to my bed. Hang the gout!' said he, making a grimace again.

'Monseigneur,' said Athos, 'we have come from England; and our first care on reaching Paris has been to obtain news of your health.'

'Many thanks, Messieurs, many thanks! My health is bad, as you see——Confound the gout! So you come from England? And King Charles is well, so I have just learned?'

'He is dead,* Monseigneur,' said Aramis.

'Bah!' exclaimed the duke, astonished.

'Died on the scaffold, condemned by Parliament.'

'Impossible!'

'And executed in our presence.'

'What then did M. de Flamarens tell me?'

'M. de Flamarens?' said Aramis.

'Yes; he has just left.'

Athos smiled.

'With two companions?' said he.

'Yes,' replied the duke; then he added with some uneasiness, 'you must have met them.'

'Well, yes, in the street, I believe,' said Athos; and smiling, he looked at Aramis, who in his turn looked at him with some astonishment.

'Confound this gout!' cried Bouillon, evidently ill at ease.

'Monseigneur,' said Athos, 'it needs all your devotedness to the cause of the Parisians to remain in command of troops, suffering as you are; and this perseverance of yours commands the admiration of M. d'Herblay and myself.'

'How can it be helped, Messieurs? One must sacrifice oneself to the public good. You are both examples of this—you, so brave and devoted, to whom my dear colleague, the Duc de Beaufort, owes his liberty, and perhaps his life; but I confess I have got to the end of my strength. Heart and head are good, but this confounded gout is killing me; and I confess that if the court would do justice to my lawful demands, since I simply ask the indemnity promised by the former cardinal himself when I was deprived of my principality of Sedan,*— yes, if they would give me domains of equal value, and indemnify me for the loss of eight years' non-enjoyment of that possession; if, too, the title of prince were granted to my heirs, and if my brother. Turenne* were restored to his command,—I would retire at once to my estates, and leave the court and parliament to arrange matters the best way they could.'

'And you would be quite right, Monseigneur,' said Athos.

'It is your opinion, is it not, M. le Comte de la Fère?'

'Entirely.'

'That's your opinion also, is it not, M. le Chevalier d'Herblay?'

'Decidedly.'

'Well, I assure you, Messieurs, that in all probability I shall adopt this plan. The court has made overtures to me; it rests with me to accept them. I have up to this moment rejected them; but since men of your position tell me I am wrong, since too this dreadful gout makes it impossible for me to render any service to the cause of the Parisians, upon my word I have a good mind to follow your advice, and accept the proposal that M. de Châtillon has just made me.'

'Accept it, Prince,' said Aramis, 'accept it.'

'Upon my word, yes. I am very sorry to have almost rejected it this evening; but there is to be a conference tomorrow, and we shall see.'

The two friends bade the duke good-bye.

'Go, Messieurs,' the latter said to them; 'you must be very fatigued with the journey. Poor King Charles! But the fault was partly his own, and what ought to console us is that France has nothing to reproach herself with in this matter, and that she did all she could to save him.'

'Oh! as to that,' said Aramis, 'we are witnesses of it—M. de Mazarin especially.'

'Ah, well! I am glad to hear you give this testimony; he has some good in him after all—the cardinal; and if he were not a foreigner—well, one ought to do him justice! Ah! confound the gout!'

Athos and Aramis left, but M. de Bouillon's cries reached them even in the anteroom; it was clear he was suffering acutely.

On reaching the door leading into the street, 'Well! Athos,' asked Aramis, 'what do you think about——'

'About whom?'

'Why, M. de Bouillon, of course.'

'My friend, I think of him what the triolet of our guide thinks,' replied Athos—

> This poor M. de Bouillon
> Is troubled with the gout.

'You see,' said Aramis, 'that I did not breathe a word of the object which took us here.'

'And you acted wisely; you would have caused him a fresh attack. Let us go next to M. de Beaufort's;' and the two friends went towards the Hôtel de Vendôme. Ten o'clock struck as they reached it.

The Hôtel de Vendôme was not less well guarded, and presented a not less warlike aspect than the Hôtel de Bouillon. There were sentinels posted in the court, arms piled, horses ready saddled and fastened to rings. Two cavaliers, leaving just as Athos and Aramis entered, were obliged to draw back a little to let the others pass.

'Ah, ah, Messieurs!' said Aramis, 'this is decidedly a night of meetings. I confess that we should be very unfortunate after having met so frequently this evening if we did not succeed in meeting you tomorrow.'

'Oh, as to that, Monsieur,' replied Châtillon (for it was he who with Flamarens had just left the Duc de Beaufort), 'your mind may be at rest; if we have met so often at night without seeking to do so, greater reason is there for our meeting you in the day when looking for you.'

'I hope so, Monsieur,' said Aramis.

'And I am sure of it,' said the duke.

They then went their respective ways. Scarcely had Athos and Aramis given their horses' bridles to their servants, and taken off their cloaks, before a man approached them, who, after having looked at them by the dubious brightness of a lantern hanging in the courtyard, uttered a cry of surprise, and threw himself into their arms.

'Comte de la Fère,' exclaimed this man, 'Chevalier d'Herblay—what, are you here in Paris?'

'Rochefort!' said the two friends together.

'Yes, no doubt. We are come, as you see, from the Vendômois, and are prepared to give Mazarin some work to do. You are still of our party, I suppose?'

'More than ever. And the duke?'

'He is mad against the cardinal. You know his success. He is the real king of Paris; he cannot go out without risk of being squeezed to death by the crowds.'

'Ah, so much the better,' said Aramis; 'but tell me, was it not MM. de Flamarens and de Châtillon who left just now?'

'Yes; they came to have an audience with the duke. They came doubtless from Mazarin; but they have found out with whom they have to talk, I'll answer for it.'

'All in good time!' said Athos. 'And might one be allowed the honour of seeing his Highness?'

'Of course, this very instant. You know he will always see you. Follow me; I desire the honour of presenting you.'

Rochefort went on before. All the doors opened to him and his two friends. They found M. de Beaufort ready to sit down to table. The numerous occupations of the evening had delayed supper till then; but in spite of the importance of this duty to his stomach the prince had no sooner heard the two names pronounced by Rochefort than he rose from the chair on which he had just seated himself, and advancing towards the two friends, 'Oh, you are welcome, Messieurs,' said he. 'You have come to take supper, have you not? Boisjoli, just tell Noirmont* that I have two visitors. You remember Noirmont, don't you, Messieurs? He is my steward, the successor of Father Marteau, who makes those excellent pies which you remember. Boisjoli, let him send one of that make, but not like that which he made for La Ramée. Thank God! we have no further need of rope ladders, poniards, and choke-pears.'

'Monseigneur,' said Athos, 'don't put your steward out for us. We know his numerous and varied talents. This evening, with your Highness's permission, we simply wish to have news of your welfare and to take your commands.'

'Oh, as to my health, you see, Messieurs, it's excellent. A constitution able to resist five years in Vincennes under M. de Chavigny can bear anything. As to commands, I confess that I should find it very difficult to give you any, seeing that everyone gives his own, and the end will be, if this goes on, that I shall give none at all.'

'Really?' said Athos; 'yet I thought that it was on your union that parliament counted.'

'Ah, yes, our union; that's a fine thing! With the Duc de Bouillon it still continues, for he has the gout, and cannot leave his bed. There is a way of putting our heads together; but with M. d'Elbeuf and his elephants of sons——You know the triolet on the Duc d'Elbeuf, Messieurs?'

'No, Monseigneur.'

'Truly.'

The duke began to sing:

> M. d'Elbeuf and his big sons
> Are the rage at the Place Royale;
> There they all four go prancing,
> M. d'Elbeuf and his big sons.
> But as soon as they beat to arms,
> Adieu their martial humour.
> M. d'Elbeuf and his big sons
> Are the rage at the Place Royale.*

'But,' resumed Athos, 'this, I hope, is not the case with the Coadjutor?'

'Ah, well, yes; with the Coadjutor it is still worse. God preserve you from mischief-making bishops, especially when they wear a cuirass under their priest's dress! Instead of keeping himself quiet in his see to chant Te Deums for victories which we do not gain, or for victories in which we are beaten, do you know what he does?'

'No.'

'He raises a regiment to which he gives the name of the regiment of Corinth.* He makes lieutenants and captains neither more nor less than a marshal does, and colonels like the king.'

'Yes,' said Aramis, 'but when there is need of fighting, I hope he keeps in his archbishopric.'

'Oh, no, not at all; there you are mistaken, my dear d'Herblay. When there is need of fighting, he fights; so that as the death of his uncle has given him a seat in parliament, he is now unceasingly on his legs—in parliament, at the council, fighting. The Prince de Conti is general in appearance, and what an appearance! A hunchback prince! Ah, matters are in a bad state, Messieurs; everything is going wrong!'

'So that, Monseigneur, your Highness is discontented?' said Athos, exchanging looks with Aramis.

'Discontented, Count! Say rather my Highness is enraged. It comes to this—mind, I tell *you* what I would not tell to others—it comes to this, that if the queen, acknowledging her wrong-doings to me, should recall my exiled mother, and give me the reversion of the admiralty which belonged to Monsieur my father,* and which was promised me at his death, well, I should not be far from training some dogs whom I would teach to say that there are in France greater thieves than M. de Mazarin.'

It was not only a look, but a look and a smile that Athos and Aramis exchanged; had they not met them they might have guessed that MM. de Châtillon and de Flamarens had been there. So they did not breathe a word concerning Mazarin's presence in Paris.

'Monseigneur,' said Athos, 'we are quite satisfied. We had no other end in view, in coming so late to visit your Highness, than to prove our devotedness, and that we hold ourselves at your disposition as your most faithful servants.'

'My most faithful friends, Messieurs, you have proved to be; and if ever I come to terms with the court, I will prove to you, I hope, that I continue your friend, as also that of your friends—what the devil are their names?'

'D'Artagnan and Porthos.'

'Ah, yes! that is right. I am yours, wholly and always.'

Athos and Aramis bowed, and took their leave.

'My dear Athos,' said Aramis, 'I think that you agreed to accompany me, just to give me a lesson.'

'Wait, my friend,' said Athos; 'it will be time for you to say that when we leave the Coadjutor's.'

And they took the road to the city. They found the streets inundated, and they had to take a boat. It was past eleven; but they knew that there was no fixed hour for visiting the Coadjutor, his incredible activity turning night into day and day into night.

The archiepiscopal palace rose out of the bosom of the water, and one might say from the number of boats moored on all sides around it that one was not in Paris but in Venice. These boats were going, coming, crossing one another in all directions, penetrating the labyrinth of streets in the city, or right away in the direction of the arsenal* or the Quai St Victor, and then floating as on a lake. Some of these boats were silent and dark, others were lighted up and noisy. The two friends glided into the midst of this network of small craft, and landed in their turn.

All the ground-floor of the palace was inundated, but some sort of ladders had been placed against the walls, and all the change caused by the inundation was that in place of entering by the doors one entered by the windows.

Thus it was that Athos and Aramis landed in the prelate's anteroom. It was crowded, for a dozen lords were crammed into a waiting-room.

'Good gracious!' said Aramis, 'just look, Athos! Is this coxcomb of a Coadjutor going to give himself the pleasure of making us wait here?'

Athos smiled.

'My dear friend,' said he, 'you must take people with all the inconveniences of their position; the Coadjutor is just now one of the seven or eight kings reigning in Paris, and has a court.'

'Yes,' said Aramis, 'but *we* are not courtiers.'

'So we are going to send in our names, and if on seeing them he does not give us a favourable reply, well! we will leave him to the affairs of France or to his own. All that needs to be done is to call a servant and put a half-pistole into his hand.'

'Eh! precisely,' exclaimed Aramis. 'I am not mistaken—yes—no—yes, really, Bazin; come here, stupid!'

Bazin, who at that moment was crossing the anteroom, majestically dressed in his ecclesiastical uniform, turned round with a frown to see who the impertinent fellow was that was thus addressing him. But he no sooner recognized Aramis than the tiger was changed into the lamb, and approaching the two gentlemen, 'Why!' said he, 'it is you, Monsieur the Chevalier and Monsieur the Count! You appear just at the time when we were so anxious about you. Oh, how pleased I am to see you again!'

'Much obliged, M. Bazin,' said Aramis; 'a truce to compliments. We are come to see Monsieur the Coadjutor, but are in a hurry, and want to see him at once.'

'Certainly!' said Bazin, 'this very instant, doubtless; it is not for gentlemen of your consideration to be kept waiting. Only just now he is in secret conference with a M. de Bruy.'

'Bruy!' exclaimed Athos and Aramis, together.

'Yes; it was I who announced him, so I am sure that that was the name. Do you know him, Monsieur?' added Bazin, turning towards Aramis.

'I believe I do.'

'I cannot say as much, for he was so closely enveloped in his cloak that however I might have tried, I could not see the smallest part of his face. But I will go and announce you, and this time I may be more fortunate.'

'Useless,' said Aramis; 'we had better give up trying to see the Coadjutor this evening, had we not, Athos?'

'As you please,' said the count.

'Yes, he has most important matters to discuss with this M. de Bruy.'

'And shall I announce to him that you gentlemen came to the palace?'

'No; it is not worth the trouble,' said Aramis. 'Come, Athos.'

And the two friends, pushing through the crowd of men-servants, left the parlour, followed by Bazin, who bore witness to their importance by the profusion of his salutations.

'Well!' asked Athos, when they were in the boat, 'do you begin to believe, my friend, that we should have played a bad game for all these people by the arrest of M. de Mazarin?'

'You are wisdom incarnate, Athos!'

What had above all struck the two friends was the little importance which the court of France attached to the terrible events that had occurred in England, and which, it seemed to them, ought to occupy the attention of all Europe.* In fact, apart from a poor widow and a royal orphan who were weeping in a corner of the Louvre, no one appeared to know that there had existed a King Charles I, and that this king had just died on a scaffold.

The two friends had arranged to meet again the next morning at ten, for although the night was far advanced when they reached the door of the hotel, Aramis had pretended that he had still to make some visits of importance, and had allowed Athos to enter alone.

At ten the next day they again met. Athos had been out since six.

'Well! have you had any news?' asked Athos.

'None. I have seen nothing either of d'Artagnan or of Porthos. Have you?'

'Nothing! and really,' said Athos, 'this delay is inexplicable; they took the shortest route, and ought consequently to have arrived before us.'

'Add to that,' said Aramis, 'we know how rapid d'Artagnan is in his movements, and he is not a man to lose an hour, knowing that we are expecting him——'

'He counted, if you remember, on being here on the fifth day.'

'And now we are at the ninth. It is this evening that the delay expires.'

'What do you think of doing,' Athos asked, 'if we have no news by this evening?'

'Why, beginning a search.'

'Very well.'

'But Raoul?' asked Aramis.

A slight shade passed across the count's face.

'Raoul gives me some uneasiness. He received yesterday a message from the Prince de Condé, and went to join him at St Cloud, and has not come back.'

'Have you been to see Madame de Chevreuse?'

'She was not at home.* I think, Aramis, you ought to call on Madame de Longueville.'

'I have done so. She was not at home either; but at least she had left the address of her new abode.'

'Where was she?'

'Guess. I give you a thousand times to guess it in.'

'How can I guess where she was at midnight?—for I suppose you went to her on leaving me. How can I guess where the most beautiful and active of all the lady Frondeurs is?'

'At the Hôtel de Ville, my dear fellow.'

'What, at the Hôtel de Ville! Is she then nominated provost of the shopkeepers?'

'No; but she has been made provisional queen of Paris, and as she did not dare to take up her residence at first at the Palais-Royal or the Tuileries, she has been installed at the Hôtel de Ville, where she is on the point of giving an heir or heiress* to that dear duke.'

'You had not informed me of this circumstance, Aramis,' said Athos.

'Bah, truly! It was a thing forgotten, then; excuse me.'

'Well,' asked Athos, 'what are we going to do from now till this evening? It seems to me that we are wasting time.'

'You forget, my friend, that we have some work cut out for us.'

'Where is it?'

'In the direction of Charenton, of course. I have the hope of meeting there, according to his promise, a certain M. de Châtillon, whom for a long time I have hated.'

'And why so?'

'Because he is the brother of a certain M. de Coligny.'

'Ah! that's true, I was forgetting—who claimed the honour of being your rival. He was cruelly punished for his audacity, my dear friend; and in truth that ought to satisfy you.'

'Yes; but what could I do? That does not at all satisfy me. I am a rancorous fellow. It is the only point by which I hold to the Church. You understand, Athos, you are by no means obliged to follow me.'

'Come now,' said Athos, 'you are joking.'

'In that case, my dear friend, if you have decided to accompany me, there is no time to lose. The drums have beaten; I have met the cannon, which are setting off. I have seen the citizens who are drawn up in line on the Place de l'Hôtel de Ville; they are certainly going to fight in the direction of Charenton, as the Duc de Châtillon told me yesterday.'

'I should have thought,' said Athos, 'that last night's conferences would have somewhat modified these warlike determinations.'

'Yes, doubtless; but they will fight none the less, were it only to mask these conferences the better.'

'Poor fellows!' said Athos, 'who are going to let themselves be killed in order that Sedan may be handed over to M. de Bouillon, the reversion of the admiralty given to M. de Beaufort, and that the Coadjutor may become cardinal!'

'Come, come, my dear fellow,' said Aramis, 'acknowledge that you would not be so philosophical if your Raoul were not mixed up in the brawl.'

'Perhaps you speak truly.'

'Well! let us go where the fighting is; it's a sure way of finding d'Artagnan, Porthos, and perhaps even Raoul.'

'Alas!' said Athos.

'My good friend,' said Aramis, 'now that we are at Paris, you must, believe me, lose that habit of sighing constantly. In war time, one must do as they do in war time, Athos! Are you no longer a man of the sword, and have you become a churchman? Look! there are some fine-looking citizens going by; it is interesting, indeed! And see that captain! he has almost a military air!'

'They are coming out of the Rue du Mouton.'

'Drums leading, like true soldiers! But do you see that gay fellow? How he swings, how he bends his back!'

'*Heu!*' said Grimaud.

'What?' asked Athos.

'Planchet, Monsieur.'

'Lieutenant yesterday,' said Aramis, 'captain today, colonel, doubtless, tomorrow; in a week the gay fellow will be Marshal of France.'

'Let us ask him for information,' said Athos.

And the two friends drew near Planchet, who, prouder than ever to be seen in command, condescended to explain to the two gentlemen that he had orders to take position on the Place Royale with two hundred men, forming the rear-guard of the Parisian army, and to move from there towards Charenton when there should be need.

As Athos and Aramis were going in the same direction, they escorted Planchet to his assigned position.

Planchet quite skilfully manœuvred his men on the Place Royale and placed them in *échelons* behind a long file of citizens placed in the Rue and Faubourg St Antoine, awaiting the signal for the combat.

'The day will be hot,' said Planchet, in a warlike tone.

'Yes, doubtless,' replied Aramis; 'but it is a long way from here to the enemy.'

'Monsieur, we shall decrease the distance,' replied a citizen.

Aramis saluted, then turning towards Athos, 'I do not care to camp in the Place Royale with all these people,' said he; 'are you willing to go forward? We shall see things better.'

'And then M. de Châtillon will not come to find you in the Place Royale, is not that so? Come then, forward, my friend!'

'Shall you not have two words to say on your part to M. de Flamarens?'

'Friend,' said Athos, 'I have formed the resolution no more to draw the sword unless absolutely compelled.'

'Since when was that?'

'Since I drew the poniard.'

'Ah, good! another souvenir of M. Mordaunt; well, my dear fellow, it only remains for you to experience remorse for having killed that fellow!'

'*Chut!*' said Athos, putting his finger to his lips with a sad smile; 'don't let us talk any more of Mordaunt—it would bring us misfortune.'

And Athos pushed on towards Charenton, going along the faubourg, then the Vallée de Fécamp,* now quite dark with armed citizens. It needs hardly be said that Aramis followed him at half his horse's length.

LXXXII

THE COMBAT AT CHARENTON

As Athos and Aramis rode on, they passed the different corps drawn up on the route, they saw polished bright cuirasses follow rusty arms, and glittering muskets follow all kinds of halberds.

'I think that here will be the real battlefield,' said Aramis. 'Do you see this corps of cavalry stationed before the bridge, pistol in hand? Hey! take care, here is some artillery coming!'

'Ah! come, my dear fellow, where have you led us? It seems to me that I see all around us officers of the royal army. Is not that M. de Châtillon himself coming on with his two brigadiers?'

And Athos took his sword, while Aramis, believing that he had really passed the boundaries of the Parisian camp, put his hand to his pistols.

'Good-day, Messieurs,' said the duke; 'I see you do not understand what is going on, but a word or two will explain it all to you. We are for a while keeping a truce; there is a conference going on. Monsieur the Prince, M. de Retz, M. de Beaufort, and M. de Bouillon are talking together on political matters. Now, one of two things will happen: either matters will not be arranged, and we shall meet, Chevalier; or they will be arranged, and as I shall be free from my command, we shall meet still.'

'Monsieur,' said Aramis, 'you talk wonderfully well. Permit me to put you one question. Where are the plenipotentiaries?'

'In Charenton itself; in the second house to the right as you enter from Paris.'

'And this conference was not foreseen?'

'No, Messieurs. It was the result, as it appears, of the fresh proposals which M. de Mazarin caused to be made yesterday evening to the Parisians.'

Athos and Aramis looked at each other, laughing; they knew better than any one what the proposals were, to whom made, and who made them.

'And this house where the parties are,' asked Athos, 'belongs——'

'To M. de Chanleu,* who commands your troops at Charenton. I say *your* troops, because I presume these gentlemen are Frondeurs.'

'Well—almost,' said Aramis.

'How do you mean—almost?'

'Monsieur, you know better than anyone that at present one can hardly say very precisely what one is.'

'We are for the king and Messieurs the Princes,' said Athos.

'It is difficult to understand you,' said Châtillon; 'the king is with us, and he has for his commanders-in-chief, M. d'Orléans and M. de Condé.'

'Yes,' said Athos; 'but his place is in our ranks with MM. de Conti, de Beaufort, d'Elbeuf, and de Bouillon.'

'That may be,' said Châtillon. 'As for myself, I have little sympathy for M. de Mazarin; my interests indeed are in Paris. I have there an important law-suit on which my whole fortune depends, and only just now have I consulted my lawyer——'

'In Paris?'

'No; at Charenton—M. Viole,* whom you know by name, an excellent man, a little obstinate; but he is not in parliament for nothing. I was intending to see him last evening, but our meeting prevented me from occupying myself with my business. Now, as it is necessary that business should be done, I have profited by the truce; and that is how I find myself in the midst of you.'

'M. Viole gives then consultations in the open air?' asked Aramis, laughing.

'Yes, Monsieur, and on horseback even. He commands today five hundred soldiers armed with pistols, and I have made him a visit accompanied, to do him honour, by these two little pieces of cannon, at the head of which you were so astonished to see me. I did not recognize him at first, I must confess; he has a long sword over his robe, and pistols at his waist, which gives him a formidable air, with which you will be amused, if you have the good fortune to meet him.'

'If he is such a curiosity, one might give oneself the trouble to look expressly for him,' said Aramis.

'You must make haste, Monsieur, for the conference cannot last much longer.'

'If the conference breaks up without leading to any result,' said Athos, 'you will try to take Charenton?'

'Those are my orders; I command the attacking troops, and I shall do my best to succeed.'

'Monsieur,' said Athos, 'since you command the cavalry——'

'I beg pardon, I command in chief.'

'Better still. You ought to know all your officers—I mean of course the higher grades.'

'Well, yes; nearly all.'

'Be so good as to tell me then, if you have under your orders, M. le Chevalier d'Artagnan, lieutenant in the Musketeers?'

'No, Monsieur, he is not with us; for more than six weeks he has been away from Paris on a mission, they say, to England.'

'I know that, but I thought he had returned.'

'No, Monsieur, and I don't think anyone has seen him. I am the better able to answer you because the musketeers belong to our troops, and it is M. de Cambon who meanwhile holds M. d'Artagnan's post.'

The two friends looked at each other.

'You see,' said Athos.

'It is strange,' said Aramis.

'Some misfortune must undoubtedly have happened to them on the road.'

'This is now the eighth day, and this evening the delay fixed on expires. If we have no news this evening, we will set out tomorrow morning.'

Athos signified his assent. Then turning round, 'And M. de Bragelonne, a young man of fifteen, an attaché of Monsieur the Prince?' asked Athos, somewhat embarrassed in letting the sceptical Aramis see his paternal solicitude; 'is he known to you, Monsieur the Duke?'

'Yes, certainly,' replied Châtillon. 'He came this morning with Monsieur the Prince. A charming young man! Is he one of your friends, Monsieur the Count?'

'Yes, Monsieur,' replied Athos, somewhat agitated; 'and I greatly desire to see him. Is this practicable?'

'Quite so, Monsieur. Please to go with me, and I will take you to headquarters.'

'Holloa!' said Aramis, turning round; 'there is plenty of noise behind us, it seems to me.'

'It is in fact a number of cavaliers coming to us,' said Châtillon.

'I recognize Monsieur the Coadjutor in his hat of the Fronde style.'

'And I. M. de Beaufort with his white feathers.'

'They are coming on at a gallop. Monsieur the Prince is along with them. Ah! see, he has left them.'

'They are beating the rappel!' exclaimed Châtillon. 'Do you hear? We must inform ourselves.'

In fact, they saw the soldiers running to arms; the cavaliers on foot remounted, the trumpets were sounding, drums beating. M. de Beaufort drew his sword.

In his turn Monsieur the Prince gave a sign of recall, and all the officers of the royal army, for the moment intermingled with the Parisian troops, hastened back to him.

'Messieurs,' said Châtillon, 'the truce is broken, that's evident; they are going to fight. Return then into Charenton, for I shall begin the attack presently. There is the signal that Monsieur the Prince gives me.'

In fact, a cornet elevated three times Monsieur the Prince's colours.

'*Au revoir*, Monsieur the Chevalier!' cried Châtillon; and he set off at a gallop to rejoin his escort.

Athos and Aramis turned their horses' heads, and saluted the Coadjutor and M. de Beaufort. As for M. de Bouillon, he had had, towards the end of the conference, such a terrible attack of gout that he had to be sent back to Paris in a litter. In exchange, M. le Duc d'Elbeuf, surrounded by his four sons as by a staff, passed through the ranks of the Parisian army. Meanwhile, between Charenton and the royal army, a large blank space was left, which seemed meant for the last resting-place of the dead.

'This Mazarin is veritably a disgrace to France!' said the Coadjutor, tightening his sword-belt, which he wore, like the old military prelates, over his archiepiscopal robe. 'He is a stingy fellow, who would like to govern France as he would a small farm. France can never expect peace and happiness until he has left it.'

'It would seem that there has been no agreement about the colour of his hat,' said Aramis.

At the same moment M. de Beaufort raised his sword.

'Messieurs,' said he, 'our negotiations have proved useless. We were desirous of getting rid of this coward Mazarin, but the queen, who is infatuated with him, absolutely intends to keep him as minister; so that only one resource remains—that is, of fighting congruously.'

'Good!' said the Coadjutor; 'spoken with the usual eloquence of M. de Beaufort.'

'Fortunately,' said Aramis, 'he corrects his faults in French with the point of his sword.'

'Pooh!' said the Coadjutor, with contempt. 'I swear that in all this war he has been very pale.'

He then also drew his sword.

'Messieurs,' said he, 'there is the enemy drawing near; we shall well be able, I hope, to spare him half the road.'

And without troubling himself whether he was followed or not, he set off. His regiment, which bore the name of the Corinthian regiment, from the name of his archbishopric, fell into confusion behind him, and began the mêlée.

M. de Beaufort sent forth his cavalry, under the command of M. de Noirmoutiers, towards Etampes, where they expected to meet a convoy of provisions impatiently expected by the Parisians. M. de Beaufort was preparing to support it.

M. de Chanleu, who commanded the place, kept himself with the best of his troops, ready to resist an assault, and even, should the enemy be repulsed, to attempt a sortie.

At the end of half an hour the fighting became general. The Coadjutor, whom the reputation of M. de Beaufort's courage exasperated, threw himself into the front, and did marvellous feats of courage. His real vocation was the sword, and he was happy whenever he could draw it, no matter for whom or for what. But if he understood his vocation as a soldier, he badly performed that of colonel. With seven or eight hundred men he went against three thousand, who marched in one mass and beat the Coadjutor's soldiers, who reached the ramparts in disorder. But Chanleu's artillery fire stopped the royal troops, which for a moment seemed in disorder. But that lasted only a little time, and they retired behind some houses and a little wood, to re-form.

Chanleu thought the moment arrived; he dashed off at the head of two regiments to pursue the king's troops; but, as we have said, they re-formed and returned to the charge, led by M. de Châtillon in person. The charge was so bold and so skilfully executed that Chanleu and his men found themselves almost surrounded. He ordered a retreat, which was conducted foot by foot, and step by step. Unfortunately, a moment after, Chanleu fell mortally wounded.

M. de Châtillon saw him fall, and announced it aloud, which redoubled the courage of the royal troops, and completely demoralized the two regiments with which Chanleu had made the sortie. They fled to the entrenchments, at the foot of which the Coadjutor was trying to re-form his defeated regiment.

Suddenly a squadron of cavalry came to an encounter with the conquerors, who were entering pell-mell with the fugitives into the entrenchments. Athos and Aramis charged at their head, Aramis sword and pistol in hand, Athos sword in scabbard and pistol in holster. Athos was as calm as if on parade, only his face looked sad at seeing so many men cutting one another's throats, and being sacrificed to royal obstinacy and princely rancour. Aramis, on the contrary, was slaying, and growing by degrees more infuriated, as was his habit. His quick eye became burning; his mouth, so finely shaped, smiled a mournful smile; his open nostrils seemed to breathe bloodshed; each of his sword-strokes told, and the butt-end of his pistol finished the wounded who attempted to rise.

On the opposing side, two cavaliers, one covered with a gilt cuirass, the other with one of buff, from which proceeded the sleeves of a close coat of blue velvet, were charging in the front rank. The cavalier in the gilt cuirass came to attack Aramis, and gave him a sword-blow, which Aramis parried with his usual dexterity.

'Ah, it is you, M. de Châtillon!' exclaimed the chevalier; 'I have been awaiting you.'

'I hope I have not kept you waiting too long, Monsieur,' said the duke; 'at any rate, here I am.'

'M. de Châtillon,' said Aramis, drawing a second pistol, which he had reserved for this occasion, 'I think that if your pistol is unloaded you are a dead man.'

'God be thanked, it is not.'

And the duke, taking aim at Aramis, fired. But Aramis bent his head just when he saw the duke's finger on the trigger, and the ball passed over him.

'Oh! you have missed me,' said Aramis. 'But I am not going to miss you, I swear.'

'If I give you the time!' exclaimed Châtillon, spurring his horse and dashing at him with his sword upraised.

Aramis awaited him with that terrible smile, peculiar to him at such a moment; and Athos, who saw M. de Châtillon advancing like lightning on Aramis, was about calling out, 'Fire!' when he fired. M. de Châtillon opened his arms and fell back on his horse. The ball had entered his chest by the notch of the cuirass.*

'I am dead!' murmured the duke; and he slipped off his horse to the ground.

'I told you so, Monsieur, and I am sorry now at having kept my word. Can I be of any service to you?'

Châtillon made a movement with his hand; and Aramis was preparing to dismount, when he suddenly received a violent blow in the side. It was from a sword, but the cuirass parried it. He turned round sharply, seized his new antagonist by the wrist, when two exclamations arose at the same time, one from him, the other from Athos:

'Raoul!'

The young man recognized both the face of Chevalier d'Herblay and the voice of his father, and let his sword drop. Several cavaliers of the Parisian army dashed upon Raoul, but Aramis covered him with his sword.

'My prisoner! Keep off!' he cried.

Athos, meanwhile, took his son's horse by the bridle, and led it out of the mêlée.

At that moment, Monsieur the Prince, who was supporting M. de Châtillon in the second line, appeared in the midst of the mêlée; he was recognized by the blows he dealt, and by the flash of his eagle eye.

At the sight of him, the regiment of the archbishop of Corinth,* whom the Coadjutor in spite of all his efforts could not reorganize, threw itself into the midst of the Parisian troops, and disordered everything while fleeing into Charenton, which it passed through without stopping. The Coadjutor, carried along by it, passed by the group, composed of Athos, Aramis, and Raoul.

'Ah, ah!' said Aramis, who could not help, from jealousy, rejoicing at the check received by the Coadjutor, 'from your position of archbishop you ought to know the Scriptures.'

'And what have the Scriptures in common with what has happened to me?' asked the Coadjutor.

'Why, Monsieur the Prince is treating you today as Saint Paul did the first of the Corinthians.'

'Come, come!' said Athos, 'the joke is not bad, but we must not waste time in compliments here. Forward, or rather rearwards, for it looks as though the combat had been lost by the Frondeurs.'

'That's all the same to me!' said Aramis; 'I came only to meet M. de Châtillon. I have done so, and am satisfied; a duel with a Châtillon—that's flattering!'

'And a prisoner besides,' said Athos, pointing to Raoul.

The three cavaliers went forward at a gallop. The young man had felt a thrill of joy at finding his father. They galloped side by side, the young man's left hand in Athos's right. When they were a good way off the battlefield, 'What were you doing so far forward in the mêlée, my friend?' Athos asked Raoul; 'that was not at all your place, it seems to me, as you are not well armed.'

'In fact I have no business to be fighting at all today, Monsieur; I was sent to the cardinal, and was setting out for Rueil,* when seeing M. de Châtillon charge, I felt a desire to charge along with him. Then he told me that two cavaliers of the Parisian army were enquiring for me, and he mentioned the Comte de la Fère.'

'What! you knew we were here, and yet wished to kill your friend, the Chevalier?'

'I did not recognize Monsieur the Chevalier in his armour,' said Raoul, blushing, 'but I ought to have done so by his coolness and skill.'

'Thanks for the compliment, my young friend,' said Aramis; 'one can easily see who has given you lessons in politeness. But you were going to Rueil, you say?'

'Yes.'

'To the cardinal's?'

'I think so. I have a despatch from Monsieur the Prince for his Eminence.'

'You must take it to him.'

'Oh! as to that, one moment—no false generosity, Count. Why, our fate, and what is of far greater importance, the fate of our friends is perhaps in that despatch.'

'But there is no need that this young man should fail in his duty,' said Athos.

'First of all, Count, this young man is a prisoner; you forget that. What we are doing is by the rules of war. Besides, the vanquished ought not to be too particular as to choice of means. Give me that despatch, Raoul.'

Raoul hesitated, looking at Athos as if for direction.

'Give up the despatch, Raoul,' said Athos, 'you are Chevalier d'Herblay's prisoner.'

Raoul yielded with reluctance, but Aramis, less scrupulous than the count, seized the despatch eagerly, perused it, and giving it to Athos: 'You,' said he, 'who are a believer, read and see in that letter, after reflection, something that Providence judges important for us to know.'

Athos took the letter with a frown, but the thought that in it was something concerning d'Artagnan helped him to overcome the disgust he felt in reading it.

This is what the letter contained:

MONSEIGNEUR—I shall this evening send to your Eminence to strengthen M. de Comminges's troop, the ten men for whom you ask. They are good soldiers, suitable for keeping in hand the two fierce adversaries whose skill and resolution your Eminence fears.

'Oh, oh!' said Athos.

'Well!' asked Aramis, 'what do you think of that? For the safe keeping of two adversaries there are needed, besides Comminges's troop, ten good soldiers. Isn't this description as like d'Artagnan and Porthos as two peas are to each other?'

'We will beat up Paris all day, and if we have no news this evening we will take the route to Picardy; and I answer for it, from d'Artagnan's fertile imagination, that we shall not be long in finding some indication tending to remove our doubts.'

'Let us then beat up Paris, and especially make enquiries of Planchet whether he has heard anything of his old master.'

'Poor Planchet! you speak of him quite coolly, Aramis; he is massacred without doubt. All the warlike citizens will have gone forth and a massacre taken place.'

As this was quite probable, the two friends entered Paris by the Porte du Temple with some feeling of disquietude, and they went towards the Place Royale, where they expected to hear news of these poor citizens. But how great was the astonishment of the two friends to find them drinking and bantering one another; they and their captain still stationed in the Place Royale, and bewailed doubtless by their families, who heard the cannon firing at Charenton and thought them exposed to it.

Athos and Aramis again enquired of Planchet, but he had heard nothing of d'Artagnan. They wished to take him with

them, but he declared he could not leave without orders from
his superiors.

At five o'clock only, they returned to their homes, saying
that they returned from the battle; they had not lost sight of
the bronze horse* of Louis XIII.

'Thousand thunders!' said Planchet, on re-entering his shop
in the Rue des Lombards, 'we have been beaten soundly. I
shall never console myself.'

LXXXIII

JOURNEY TO PICARDY

ATHOS and Aramis, while quite safe in Paris, did not hide
from themselves the fact that directly they put foot outside of
it, they would run great risks; but with such men that was not
an important question. Besides, they felt that the issue of this
second Odyssey was drawing near, and that a new effort was
all that was needed.

In addition to which Paris itself was by no means peaceful;
food was falling short, and as each of M. le Prince de Conti's
generals felt it needful to regain his influence, a small riot took
place which he put down, and which gave him a momentary
superiority over his colleagues.

In one of these riots, M. de Beaufort had caused to be
pillaged the house and library of M. de Mazarin, to give, he
said, something to the poor people to gnaw.*

Athos and Aramis left Paris upon this *coup d'état* which had
taken place on the evening of the same day on which the
Parisians were beaten at Charenton.

The two left Paris in misery, almost arrived at the point of
famine, agitated by fear, and torn by factions. Parisians and
Frondeurs, they expected to find the same misery, the same fears,
the same intrigues in the enemy's camp. Their surprise then was
great when, in passing to St Denis, they learned that at St
Germain they were laughing, singing, and leading a gay life.

The two gentlemen took out-of-the-way roads first, so as not
to fall into the hands of Mazarin's partisans scattered about

the Île-de-France; also to escape the Frondeurs, who held Normandy, and who would certainly have taken them to M. de Longueville, for the latter to recognize them either as friends or enemies. When once these dangers were escaped, they got on to the road from Boulogne to Abbeville, and followed it step by step, trace by trace.

Yet for some time they were in doubt. Two or three inns had been visited, and the innkeepers questioned without a single indication arising to clear up their doubts and guide their search, when at Montreuil* Athos felt something on the table rough to the touch of his delicate fingers. He raised up the cloth and read on the wood these hieroglyphics deeply cut with the blade of a knife: 'Port——d'Artag——2 Feb.'

'Famous,' said Athos, showing the inscription to Aramis; 'we thought of sleeping here, but it is useless. Let us go on further.'

They remounted and reached Abbeville. There they were greatly perplexed on account of the large number of inns. They could not visit them all. How could they guess in which their friends had stayed?

'Believe me, Athos, don't dream of finding out anything at Abbeville. If we are in difficulty, so also were our friends. If it were only Porthos, he would have put up at the finest hotel, and knowing this we should be sure to find traces of his passing through here. But d'Artagnan has none of those weaknesses. Porthos would in vain have observed that he was dying of hunger; the former would have gone on, inexorable as fate.'

They therefore continued their route, but nothing presented itself. This was one of the most distressing and wearisome tasks that Athos and Aramis had ever undertaken; and without the triple motive of honour, friendship, and gratitude in their soul, our two travellers would have, a hundred times, given up searching the soil, questioning passers-by, noticing signs, and scanning countenances.

Thus they came to Peronne. Athos began to despair. His noble, anxious disposition reproached itself for this ignorance in which Aramis and he were. Doubtless he had searched carelessly; they had not been persistent enough in their questionings, nor shown perspicacity in their investigations. They were about re-tracing their steps, when in crossing the faubourg which led to the towngates, on a blank wall forming the angle of a street turning round by the rampart, Athos cast his eyes on a design in black pencil, which represented with the simplicity of a child's first artistic attempts two cavaliers galloping at a mad rate, one of them holding a placard in his hand on which were written in Spanish the words: 'We are being pursued.'

'Oh, oh!' said Athos, 'now all is clear as the day. Pursued as they were, d'Artagnan stopped here five minutes; that proves at any rate that his pursuers were not close; perhaps he may have succeeded in escaping.'

Aramis shook his head.

'If he had escaped we should have seen him again, or at least should have heard of him.'

'You are right, Aramis, let us go on.'

To speak of the distress and impatience of the two friends would be impossible. Athos's tender, loving heart felt the distress; impatience troubled Aramis's nervous mind, so easily disturbed. Thus they both galloped for three or four hours with the frenzy of the two cavaliers of the wall. Suddenly in a narrow gorge, shut in by two declivities, they saw the route half barred by an enormous stone. Its former position was indicated on one of the sides of the declivity by a sort of cavity which had been left there by its removal, proving that it had not rolled down of itself, while its weight showed that to move it the arms of Enceladus or Briareus* were needed.

Aramis stopped.

'Oh!' said he, looking at the stone, 'there is in that something of Ajax,* of Telamon, or of Porthos. Let us get down, Count, and examine this rock.'

The stone had been placed there with the plain purpose of barring the road against some horsemen. It had therefore been placed across at first; but the horsemen had found the obstacle and had removed it.

The two friends examined the stone on the exposed sides, but saw nothing particular. They then called Blaisois and Grimaud. The four together succeeded in turning over the stone. On the side which had touched the earth was written—

'Eight light horse are pursuing us. If we reach Compiègne we shall stop at the Crowned Peacock; the host is a friend of ours.'

'At last here is something definite,' said Athos, 'and in any case we shall know what to be at. Let us go on then to the Crowned Peacock.'

'Yes,' said Aramis; 'but if we mean to get there we must give our horses some rest; they are almost knocked up.'

Aramis spoke the truth. They stopped at the first public-house; they gave each horse a double feed, mixed in some wine, and after a rest of three hours they started again. The men themselves were worn out by fatigue, but hope sustained them.

Six hours later they reached Compiègne, and made enquiries for the Crowned Peacock. They were shown a sign representing the god Pan with a crown on his head. The two friends dismounted without examining the meaning of the sign, which Aramis at any other time would have criticized. They found the landlord an honest fellow, bald and potbellied like a grotesque China figure. When they asked if he had not lodged some time back two gentlemen pursued by some light horse-men, the host without saying a word went to a chest and brought back the half of a rapier-blade.

'Do you know that?' he said.

Athos gave but a mere look at it.

'That's part of d'Artagnan's sword,' said he.

'The large or the small one?' asked the host.

'The small one,' replied Athos.

'I see you are the friends of those gentlemen.'

'Well! what has happened to them?'

'They entered the courtyard with their horses exhausted, and before there was time to close the big gates, eight light horse who were after them entered too.'

'Eight!' said Aramis. 'I am astonished that d'Artagnan and Porthos, two such intrepid men, let themselves be arrested by eight men.'

'Without doubt, Monsieur; and the eight men would not have succeeded had they not been reinforced out of the town by twenty soldiers of the Royal Italian regiment* in garrison here, so that your two friends were literally overwhelmed by numbers.'

'Arrested!' said Athos; 'do you know why?'

'No, Monsieur; they were carried off at once, and had not time to tell me anything. Only when they had gone, I found this fragment of a sword while helping to pick up two dead men and five or six wounded.'

'And did nothing happen to them?' asked Aramis.

'No, Monsieur, I believe not.'

'Come,' said Aramis, 'that's a consolation.'

'And do you know where they are taken?'

'Towards Louvres.'

'Let us leave Blaisois and Grimaud here,' said Athos; 'they can return tomorrow to Paris with the horses, and let us travel post.'

'Let us travel post,' said Aramis.

They sent to seek for horses. Meanwhile the friends took a hasty dinner; they wanted, if they gained any information at Louvres, to be able to continue their journey.

They reached Louvres. There was only one inn. They there drank a liquor,* which has kept its reputation to our own days, and which was manufactured already at that time.

'Let us dismount here,' said Athos; 'd'Artagnan will not have failed on this occasion to leave us some indication.'

They entered and asked for two glasses at the counter as d'Artagnan and Porthos had no doubt done. The drinking-counter was covered with pewter. On this had been scratched with the point of a large pin, 'Rueil, D.'

'They are at Rueil!' said Aramis, who first caught sight of the inscription.

'Let us go then to Rueil,' said Athos.

'That means to throw ourselves into the wolf's throat,' said Aramis.

'If I had been Jonah's friend to the extent I am d'Artagnan's, I would have followed him into the whale's belly, and you would do as much as I, Aramis.'

'My dear Count, I really believe that you make me better than I am. If I were alone, I don't know whether I should thus go to Rueil without great precautions; but where you go, I will go.'

They took horse and set off for Rueil.

Athos, without being aware of it, had given Aramis the best advice possible. The deputies of parliament had just come to Rueil* to take part in those famous conferences which would last three weeks, and lead to that lame peace at the end of which Monsieur the Prince was arrested.* Rueil was crowded, on the part of parliament, with barristers, chief justices, councillors, lawyers of every sort; and on the part of the court with gentlemen, officers, and guards; it was therefore easy to remain as unknown as one desired to be. Besides, the conferences had led to a truce, and to arrest two gentlemen at that moment, even were they leading Frondeurs, was to violate the law of nations.

The two friends believed everybody to be filled with the thought that tormented them. They mixed with the various groups, thinking they would hear something said respecting d'Artagnan and Porthos; but everyone was occupied only with articles and amendments. Athos inclined to the opinion that they ought to go straight to the minister.

'My friend,' objected Aramis, 'what you say on that point is all very well, but take care; our security arises from our obscurity. If we get known, one way or another, we shall go immediately to join our friends at the bottom of some low dungeon, whence the devil will not draw us out. Let us try not to find them by accident, but at our own choice. Arrested at Compiègne, they have been taken to Rueil, as we learned of a certainty at Louvres; at Rueil they have been questioned by the cardinal, who then has either kept them in guard near himself or sent them to St Germain. As for the Bastille, they are not there, since it is in the hands of the Frondeurs, and Broussel's son commands there. They are not dead, for d'Artagnan's death would be notorious. As for Porthos, I believe him eternal as the Deity, though he may be less patient. Don't let us despair, let us stay here, for my conviction is that they are here. But what is the matter?—you look quite pale!'

'I have,' said Athos in a half-trembling voice, 'recollected that at the château of Rueil, M. de Richelieu had made a frightful *oubliette**——'

'Oh! don't be alarmed,' said Aramis. 'M. de Richelieu was a gentleman, our equal in all respects by birth, our superior by position. He was able, like a king, to touch the grandest of us on the head, and make our heads, when he did so, shake on our shoulders. But M. de Mazarin is a pedant who can at the most take us by the collar like a policeman. Be reassured then, my friend; I persist in saying that d'Artagnan and Porthos are at Rueil, not only living, but living comfortably.'

'No matter,' said Athos, 'we must obtain from the Coadjutor the right to belong to the conference, and in that way we might enter Rueil.'

'With all those frightful limbs of the law! Do you believe that the liberty or imprisonment of d'Artagnan and Porthos will be in the least degree discussed? No; my opinion is, we must seek some other means.'

'Well!' replied Athos, 'I return to my first idea. I know no better means than acting frankly and loyally. I shall go, not to Mazarin, but to the queen, and say to her: "Madame, restore our two servants and friends." '

Aramis shook his head.

'It is the last resource, which you will always be free to use, Athos; but, believe me, use it only then; there will always be time to do that. Meanwhile let us go on with our search.'

They continued therefore their search, gathering much information, and making many persons talk under a thousand pretexts, the one more ingenious than the other; finally they found a light horseman who acknowledged that he was one of the escort who had brought d'Artagnan and Porthos from Compiègne to Rueil. Without the light horseman it would not have been known that they had entered the latter town.

Athos kept continually returning to the idea of seeing the queen.

'To see the queen,' said Aramis, 'you must first see the cardinal; and we shall have scarcely seen the cardinal—remember what I am telling you, Athos—before we shall be reunited to our friends, but not in the way you understand it. Now, this fashion of being reunited is very little pleasing to me. Let us act at liberty in order to act well and speedily.'

'I shall see the queen.'

'Well, my friend, if you are determined to do this foolish act, tell me, I pray you, a day in advance.'

'Why so?'

'Because I shall profit from that circumstance to make a visit to Paris.'

'To whom?'

'Hang it! how do I know?—perhaps to Madame de Longueville. She is all powerful there; she will help me. Only let me know by someone if you are arrested; then I will do my best to return.'

'Why not risk the chance of being arrested with me, Aramis?'

'No, thank you.'

'All four arrested and reunited, I believe we should not risk anything further. At the end of twenty-four hours we should be all four at liberty.'

'My dear fellow, since I have killed Châtillon, who was the object of adoration by the ladies of St Germain, I have too much glory around my head not to fear prison doubly. The queen might be ready to follow Mazarin's counsels on this occasion, and Mazarin would advise my trial.'

'But do you think, then, Aramis, that she loves this Italian as much as they say?'

'She once loved an Englishman,* dearly.'

'Ah, my friend, she is a woman!'

'No, you are mistaken, Athos; she is a queen.'

'My dear friend, I am determined on my course; and shall go to seek an audience with Anne of Austria.'

'Adieu, then, Athos, I am going to raise an army.'

'What to do?'

'To come and besiege Rueil.'

'Where shall we meet again?'

'At the foot of the cardinal's gallows.'

And the two friends separated, Aramis to return to Paris, Athos by some preparatory steps to open up a way to the queen.

LXXXIV

ATHOS found much less difficulty than he expected in getting admittance to Anne of Austria's presence. At the first step all was, on the contrary, made smooth, and the audience he desired was granted for the next day at the end of the *levée*, at which his rank gave him the right to be present. A great crowd filled the apartments of St Germain. Never at the Louvre or the Palais-Royal had Anne of Austria had a greater number of courtiers; only it was a movement appertaining to the second rank of the nobility; while all the first gentlemen of France were with M. de Conti, M. de Beaufort, and the Coadjutor.

Great gaiety besides prevailed at this court. The particular feature of this war was that there were more couplets made than cannon fired. The court made ballads about the Parisians, who did the same respecting the court; and the wounds, although not mortal, were not less grievous, inflicted as they were by the arm of ridicule.

But in the midst of this general hilarity, and this apparent want of result, one great preoccupation lay hid in the depths of all minds. Would Mazarin continue minister or favourite, or would he who had come from the South like a cloud, be carried away by the wind which had wafted him hither? Everyone hoped this, and desired it, so that the minister felt that all the homage and courtier-like respect around him only covered up a depth of hate, ill disguised by fear and interest. He felt ill at ease, not knowing on what to reckon nor on whom to rely.

Monsieur the Prince himself, who was fighting for him, never missed an occasion of bantering or humiliating him; and two or three times, Mazarin having in the presence of the conqueror of Rocroy wished to exercise his own will, the latter had made the former clearly comprehend that if he defended him it was neither from conviction nor enthusiasm. Then the cardinal fell back upon the queen, his sole support. But after two or three trials this support seemed to give way under him.

When the hour of audience arrived, the Comte de la Fère was informed that he must wait a short time, as the queen was holding council with the minister. That was true. Paris had just sent a fresh deputation, which sought to give at last some shape to matters, and the queen was consulting with Mazarin on the reception to be given to these deputies.

The minds of the high personages of the State were greatly preoccupied. Athos could not therefore have selected a worse time to speak about his friends—poor atoms lost in this whirlwind let loose. But Athos was of an inflexible nature, which never vacillated when a decision was once taken, when this seemed to emanate from his conscience and to be dictated by duty. He insisted on being introduced, saying that though he had not been deputed either by M. de Conti, or M. de Beaufort, or M. de Bouillon, or M. d'Elbeuf, or the Coadjutor, or Madame de Longueville, or Broussel, or the parliament, and that he came on his own account, he had none the less important matters to speak of to her Majesty.

When the conference was ended the queen desired him to be called into her cabinet. Athos was introduced. His name had too often sounded in her Majesty's ears, and vibrated in her heart, for her not to recognize it; yet she remained impassive, contenting herself with looking at this gentleman with the fixed look only permitted to women, queens by their beauty or rank.

'Do you come to offer to do me a service, Count?' asked Anne of Austria, after a moment's silence.

'Yes, Madame, once more a service,' said Athos, shocked that the queen did not appear to recognize him.

Athos had a great heart, and therefore made a very poor courtier.

Anne frowned. Mazarin, who was seated at a table and was sorting some papers, as if acting as a simple secretary of state, raised his head.

'Speak,' said the queen.

Mazarin again turned over his papers.

'Madame,' said Athos, 'two of our friends, two of the most intrepid servants of your Majesty, M. d'Artagnan and M. du Vallon, sent to England by Monsieur the Cardinal, have suddenly disappeared, just when they set foot on French soil, and we know not what has become of them.'

'Well!' said the queen.

'Well,' said Athos, 'I address myself to your Majesty's good-will to know what has become of these gentlemen, reserving to myself the right, if necessary, hereafter to appeal to her justice.'

'Monsieur,' replied Anne of Austria, with that hauteur which, addressed to certain men, became impertinence, 'is it for this you disturb me in the midst of the great preoccupations which are agitating us? It is a mere police affair! Eh! Monsieur, you know well enough, or ought to if you do not, that we have no longer knowledge of police matters now we are not in Paris?'

'I believe that your Majesty,' said Athos, bowing with cold respect, 'would have no need to enquire of the police to know what has become of MM. d'Artagnan and du Vallon, and that if you would ask Monsieur the Cardinal where these gentlemen are, Monsieur the Cardinal would be able to answer you without questioning anything else than his own recollections.'

'Why, God pardon me!' said Anne of Austria, with that disdainful movement of her lips peculiar to her, 'I think that you are putting the question yourself.'

'Yes, Madame, and I have almost the right, for it concerns M. d'Artagnan—M. d'Artagnan, do you understand thoroughly, Madame?' said he, in a manner to make bend the forehead of the queen under the recollections of the woman.

Mazarin saw clearly that it was time to come to the queen's aid.

'Monsieur the Count, I must tell you something of which her Majesty knows nothing. These gentlemen have disobeyed orders, and they are under arrest.'

'I then supplicate your Majesty,' said Athos, still impassive, and without replying to Mazarin, 'to revoke these arrests.'

'What you ask of me is a question of discipline, and does not concern me at all, Monsieur,' replied the queen.

'M. d'Artagnan never replied so when the service of your Majesty was in question,' said Athos, bowing with dignity; and he took two steps backward to regain the door. Mazarin stopped him.

'You also have come from England, Monsieur?' said he, making a sign to the queen, who was visibly growing pale and preparing to give a severe order.

'Yes, I assisted at the last moments of King Charles I. Poor king! guilty at most of weakness, and whom his subjects have punished very severely; for thrones are much shaken nowadays, and no good comes to devoted souls from serving the interests of princes. This was the second time that M. d'Artagnan went to England; the first occasion was for the honour of a great queen, the second was for the life of a great king.'

'Monsieur,' said Anne of Austria to Mazarin, with a tone of voice the true expression of which her habit of dissimulating could not drive away, 'see if anything can be done for these gentlemen.'

'Madame,' said Mazarin, 'I will do whatever your Majesty pleases.'

'Do what M. le Comte de la Fère asks. Is not that your name, Monsieur?'

'I have another name, Madame, and that is Athos.'

'Madame,' said Mazarin, with a smile which showed how easily he could take a hint, 'your mind may be at rest; your wishes shall be carried out.'

'You have understood, Monsieur?' said the queen.

'Yes, Madame, and I expect nothing less from the justice of your Majesty. So I am to see my friends again—is it not so, Madame?'

'You are going to see them again; yes, Monsieur. But, by the by, you belong to the Fronde, do you not?'

'Madame, I serve the king.'

'Yes, after your manner.'

'My manner is that of all true gentlemen, and I do not know two ways,' replied Athos, with hauteur.

'Go then, Monsieur,' said the queen, dismissing Athos with a sign; 'you have got what you wished to obtain, and we know all we want to know.'

Then addressing Mazarin when the door was closed behind
him, 'Cardinal,' said she, 'have that insolent gentleman arrested
before he leaves the courtyard.'

'I was thinking of that,' said Mazarin, 'and I am happy that
your Majesty has given me an order which I was going to ask
of you. These head-breakers who bring into our times the
traditions of the other reign* trouble us a good deal; and since
two of them are already taken, let us add a third.'

Athos had not been entirely the dupe of the queen. There
was in the tone of her voice something that had struck him,
and which seemed threatening even when promising. But he
was not a man to go away on a mere suspicion, especially when
he had been clearly told that he should see his friends again.
He waited, therefore, in one of the rooms adjoining the cabinet
where the audience took place, expecting that he would be
taken to see them, or they brought to him.

With this expectation he had approached the window, and
was looking mechanically into the courtyard. He there saw a
deputation of Parisians entering, who came to settle the
arrangements for the conference and to salute the queen. There
were some members of parliament, justices, and barristers,
among whom also were a few gentlemen with swords. An
imposing escort awaited them at the gates.

Athos looked with more attention, for in the midst of the
crowd he thought he recognized someone, when he felt himself
lightly touched on the shoulder. He turned round.

'Ah! M. de Comminges!' said he.

'Yes, Monsieur the Count, it is I, and charged with a duty
for which I beg you to accept my excuses.'

'What is that, Monsieur?'

'Be pleased to give me your sword, Count.'

Athos smiled, and opening the window:

'Aramis!' he called out.

A gentleman turned round. It was Aramis. He bowed in a
friendly way to the count.

'Aramis,' said Athos, 'I am arrested.'

'Well,' Aramis phlegmatically answered.

'Monsieur,' said Athos, turning towards Comminges and
giving him politely his sword by the hilt, 'here is my sword;

please to take good care of it, and to restore it when I leave prison. I value it much. It was given by King Francis I to my grandfather.* In his time they armed gentlemen, they did not disarm them. Now, where are you taking me?'

'Why, into my room first. The queen will settle where to put you later on.'

Athos followed Comminges without adding another word.

LXXXV

THE ROYALTY OF M. DE MAZARIN

THE arrest had made no noise, caused no scandal, and was hardly known. It had in no respect impeded the course of events, and the deputation sent by the city of Paris was solemnly informed that it would be received in audience by the queen.

The queen received it, silent and proud as usual. She listened to the grievances and supplications of the deputies; but when they had finished their discourse, no one could have said, from Anne of Austria's looks of unconcern, that she had attended to them. By way of compensation, Mazarin, who was present at the audience, listened attentively to what these deputies asked. It was his own dismissal in clear and precise terms.

The speeches ended, the queen remaining silent, Mazarin said: 'Messieurs, I join with you in supplicating the queen to put an end to her subjects' ills. I have done all I can to alleviate them, and yet the public belief, so you say, is that they proceed from me, a poor foreigner, who has not succeeded in pleasing the French. Alas! I am not understood, and the reason is evident: I succeeded a man of the grandest type, who had till that time upheld the sceptre of the sovereigns of France. The memory of M. de Richelieu crushes me. If I were ambitious I should vainly struggle against it; but I am not so, and I desire to give you a proof of this. I declare myself beaten. I will do what the people ask. If the Parisians have wrongs—and who has not, Messieurs?—Paris has been punished enough, enough blood has been shed, enough misery has fallen on a city deprived both of king and justice. It is not for me, a simple individual, to assume such importance as to divide a queen from her kingdom. Since you demand my retirement, well—I will retire.'

'Then,' said Aramis, in a whisper to his neighbour, 'peace is concluded, and the conference useless. Nothing more is needed than to send M. Mazarin under a good guard to the frontier, and to see that he does not return.'

'Wait a moment, Monsieur,' said the lawyer to whom Aramis spoke. 'Hang it, how you hurry along! It is clear that you are a military man. There is a list of rewards and indemnities to be made clear.'

'Monsieur the Chancellor,' said the queen, turning towards our old acquaintance Séguier, 'you will open the conference; it will take place at Rueil. Monsieur the Cardinal has said things which have greatly moved me. That is why I do not answer you at greater length. As to the question who is to stay or go, I have too much gratitude for Monsieur the Cardinal not to allow him to act freely in all respects. Monsieur the Cardinal will do what he pleases.'

A fleeting pallor clouded the intelligent face of the Premier. He looked at the queen with uneasiness. Her face was so impassive that he, like the rest, could not read what was passing in her heart.

'But,' added the queen, 'while awaiting M. de Mazarin's decision, let there be question only of the king.'

The deputies bowed and went out.

'What!' said the queen, when the last of them had left the room; 'you would give in to these lawyers and barristers?'

'For your Majesty's happiness,' said Mazarin, fixing his piercing eye on the queen, 'there is no sacrifice I am not ready to put upon myself.'

Anne drooped her head, and fell into one of those reveries so habitual to her. The remembrance of Athos came to her mind. His bold mien, his firm, and at the same time, dignified language, the visions which he had called up, reminded her of a past of an intoxicating poetry—youth, beauty, the brightness of the love of twenty; the rough combats of her supporters, and the bloody end of Buckingham, the only man she had really loved; and the heroism of these obscure defenders, who had saved her from the double hatred of Richelieu and the king.

Mazarin looked at her; and now that she believed herself alone, and was no longer watched by a crowd of enemies, he traced her thoughts upon her countenance, as one sees the clouds passing across transparent lakes, reflections of the sky.

'It is necessary,' she murmured, 'to yield to the storm, purchase a peace, and wait patiently for better times.'

Mazarin smiled bitterly at this proposition, which showed that she had taken the minister's proposal quite seriously.

Anne had not seen this smile, but observing that her demand met with no response, she raised her head.

'Well! you do not reply, Cardinal; what are you thinking about?'

'I was thinking, Madame, that that impudent man whose arrest we have just ordered, made allusion to Buckingham, whom you allowed to be assassinated; to Madame de Chevreuse, whom you exiled; to M. de Beaufort, whom you imprisoned. But if he made allusion to me, it is because he does not know what I am to you.'

Anne of Austria trembled as she ever did when wounded in her pride. She blushed, and pressed her sharp nails into her handsome hands instead of replying.

'He is a man of good counsel, honour, and mind, besides being a man of determination. You know something of these qualities, do you not, Madame? I want therefore to tell him—it is a personal favour I am asking—in what he is mistaken respecting me. It is this really—that what is proposed to me is almost an abdication, and this requires reflection.'

'An abdication!' said Anne; 'I believe, Monsieur, that it is only kings who abdicate.'

'Well!' replied Mazarin, 'am I not almost a king, and king of France, even? When thrown on the foot of a royal bed, I assure you, Madame, that my minister's robe resembles at night a royal cloak.'

This was one of the humiliations which Mazarin most frequently subjected her to, and under which she constantly bent her head.

It was only Elizabeth and Catharine II* who remained at once mistresses and queens to their lovers.

Anne of Austria looked with a sort of terror at the menacing countenance of the cardinal, who at these times was not without a certain greatness.*

'Monsieur, have I not said, and have you not understood that I said to these people that you should do what you pleased?'

'In that case I believe I must please myself by remaining. It is not only my own interest, but, I may even dare to say, your safety.'

'Stay, then, Monsieur, I desire nothing else; but then don't let me be insulted.'

'You are speaking of the revolters' pretensions, and of the tone in which they express them. Patience! They have selected a field on which I am a more skilful general than they—the conference. We shall beat them only by temporizing. They are already short of food; it will be worse in a week.'

'Eh! good heavens!—yes, Monsieur, I knew that it will come to that. But it is not of them only that the question is; it is not they who inflict the worst wounds on me.'

'Ah! I understand you. You refer to those remembrances which these three or four gentlemen perpetually call forth. But we hold them prisoners, and they are just guilty enough to allow us to hold them in captivity as long as we like; only one is out of our power and defies us. But, the devil! we shall succeed in sending him to join his companions. We have done many things more difficult than that, I think. I have shut up at Rueil, under my own eyes, within the reach of my hand, the two most intractable. This very day the third shall join them.'

'So long as they are prisoners it will be all right, but they will go forth one day or other.'

'Yes, if your Majesty gives them their liberty.'

'Ah,' continued Anne, replying to her own thoughts, 'that's why I regret Paris!'

'And why so?'

'For the Bastille, Monsieur, which is so strong and discreet.'

'Madame, with the conference we shall have peace; with peace, Paris; with Paris, the Bastille. Our four Hectors will rot there.'

Anne of Austria slightly frowned while Mazarin kissed her hand to take leave. Mazarin went away after this action, half-humble, half-gallant. Anne of Austria followed him with her eyes, and as he got farther away, a smile of contempt was imprinted on her lips.

'I have despised,' she murmured, 'the love of a cardinal who never said "I will do", but "I have done". He knew safer retreats than Rueil, darker and more silent even than the Bastille. Oh, the degenerate world!'

LXXXVI

PRECAUTIONS

AFTER having left Anne of Austria, Mazarin started for Rueil, where his house was. He took a strong retinue on account of the troublous state of the times, and he often went in disguise. The cardinal, as we have already said, in the dress of a man wearing a sword was a fine-looking gentleman. In the courtyard of the old château he entered a coach and proceeded to the Seine at Chatou.* Monsieur the Prince had furnished an escort of fifty light-horse, not so much for protection as to show the deputies how easily the queen's generals disposed of their troops, and could send them about at their will.

Athos, whom Comminges kept in sight, was on horseback, but without sword. He followed the cardinal without saying a word. Grimaud, who had been left at the gate of the château by his master, had heard the news of Athos's arrest when he called out to Aramis; and on a sign from the count he had gone without a word to take a place near Aramis as if nothing had happened. In fact Grimaud during his twenty-two years in Athos's service had seen the latter escape so many risks that nothing any further troubled him.

The deputies, immediately after their audience, had gone back to Paris; that is, they had preceded the cardinal by about five hundred yards. Athos was therefore able to see before him the back of Aramis, whose gilt sword-belt and proud mien attracted his notice among the crowd quite as much as did the hope of deliverance which he put in him, and the sort of attraction which flows from a close friendship.

Aramis, on the contrary, did not seem in the least anxious whether Athos were behind him or not. Once he turned round, it is true; that was on arriving at the château. He supposed that Mazarin would perhaps leave there his new prisoner in the redoubt of the château, with a sentinel to guard him. But that was not the case. Athos passed Chatou in the cardinal's suite.

At the branching off of the road from Paris to Rueil, Aramis turned round. This time his expectation was not wrong. Mazarin took the right-hand road; and Aramis could see the prisoner disappear at the turn among the trees. Athos, at that very moment struck by a similar thought, looked behind also. The two friends exchanged simple nods, and Aramis put up his finger to his hat as if to salute him. Athos alone understood by this sign that his friend had a project.

Ten minutes after, Mazarin entered the court of the château, which his predecessor, the cardinal, had put at his disposal* at Rueil. As soon as he stepped out of his coach, Comminges drew near.

'Monseigneur,' he asked him, 'where does it please your Eminence to quarter M. de la Fère?'

'Why, in the pavilion of the orangery, facing the pavilion of the guard. I wish every respect paid to M. le Comte de la Fère, so long as he is her Majesty's prisoner.'

'Monseigneur,' Comminges ventured to say, 'he asks the favour of being taken to M. d'Artagnan, who occupies the hunting pavilion facing the orangery.'

Mazarin reflected a moment. Comminges saw he was pondering it.

'It is a very strong post,' he added; 'forty trusty men, nearly all Germans,* and therefore having no interest in the Fronde, or relations with it.'

'If we put these three men together, we must double the post; and we have not men enough to let us do that.'

Comminges smiled; Mazarin saw the smile, and understood it.

'You don't know them, M. de Comminges; but I do, personally and by tradition. I charged them to help King Charles, and they, for this end, did miraculous things; destiny alone has prevented King Charles from being now in safety among us.'

'But if they have served your Eminence so well, why are they kept in prison?'

'In prison! and how long has Rueil been a prison?'

'Since there have been prisoners.'

'These gentlemen are not my prisoners, Comminges,' said Mazarin, with a crafty smile; 'they are my guests, and so prized that I have barred the windows and put bolts to the doors, for fear they should get tired of my company. But prisoners though they seem, I for all that esteem them greatly; and the proof is I want to pay a visit to M. de la Fère for a *tête-à-tête* conversation. So, not to be disturbed, you will take him to the pavilion in the orangery, as I have already told you; and in taking my customary walk there, I will go in and have a talk with him. Much as he seems my enemy, I have great sympathy for him, and if he is amenable to reason, perhaps we shall accomplish something.'

Comminges bowed, and returned to Athos, who with apparent calmness, but really with uneasiness, awaited the result of the conference.

'Well?'

'Monsieur,' replied Comminges, 'it seems quite impossible.'

'M. de Comminges,' said Athos, 'I have been all my life a soldier, and know what orders are; but outside these you might be able to do me a service.'

'I am heartily willing, Monsieur, since I know who you are, and what services you rendered her Majesty, formerly; since also I know how interested you are in that young man who came so bravely to my help on the day when that old fool of a Broussel was arrested; and, saving my orders, I am at your service entirely.'

'Thanks, Monsieur; I ask nothing more, and I am going to ask that which will not compromise you at all.'

'If it compromise me only a little, Monsieur,' said Comminges, smiling, 'keep on asking. I do not care for M. Mazarin much more than you do. I serve the queen, and this naturally leads me to serve the cardinal; but I serve the one joyfully, and the other against my will. Speak, therefore, I beg of you—I will listen.'

'Since no inconvenience arises from my knowing that M. d'Artagnan is here, there can't be more, I presume, in his knowing that I am here?'

'I have received no orders to that effect, Monsieur.'

'Well, do me the pleasure of presenting my respects, and tell him I am his neighbour. You will also tell him that M. de Mazarin has put me in the pavilion of the orangery in order to pay me a visit, and tell him also that I shall use this honour to obtain some amelioration of our captivity.'

'Which cannot last,' added Comminges; 'Monsieur the Cardinal told me so himself. There is no prison here.'

'There are some *oubliettes*,' said Athos, smiling.

'Oh! that's another thing. Yes, I know there are traditions about them; but a man of low birth like the cardinal, an Italian come to seek his fortune in France, would not dare to use such extremes towards men like us; that would be an enormity. That was well enough in the time of the other cardinal, who was a great seigneur; but M. Mazarin, come now!—*oubliettes* are a royal form of vengeance which a rogue like him must not employ. Your arrest is known, and that of your friends will soon be known, Monsieur, and all the nobility of France will demand of him an account of your disappearance. No, no, rest easy; the *oubliettes* of Rueil have become for ten years traditions for the use of children. Rest in this place without any anxiety. I will on my part inform M. d'Artagnan that you are here. Who knows but that in a fortnight you may render me some similar service?'

'I, Monsieur?'

'Eh! without doubt; can I not become the prisoner of Monsieur the Coadjutor?'

'Be sure that in that case, Monsieur,' said Athos, bowing, 'I should endeavour to please you.'

'Will you do me the honour of supping with me, Monsieur the Count?'

'Thanks, Monsieur, I feel out of sorts, and you would pass a dull evening. Thanks.'

Comminges then led the count to a room on the ground-floor
of a pavilion continuous with the orangery, and on a level with
it. The latter was reached by a large court, crowded with
soldiers and courtiers. This court, of a horseshoe shape, had
at its centre the apartments of M. de Mazarin, and at each of
its wings the hunting pavilion, where d'Artagnan was, and the
pavilion of the orangery, where Athos had just been taken.
Behind the extremities of these wings the park extended.

Athos, on entering his room, saw through the window, which
was carefully barred, walls and roofs.

'What building is that?' he said.

'The back of the hunting pavilion, where your friends are
detained. Unfortunately the windows which look this way were
blocked up in the time of the other cardinal, for more than
once the buildings have served as a prison, and M. de Mazarin
in putting you here only restores them to their first destination.
If those windows were not blocked up, you would have had
the consolation of corresponding by signs with your friends.'

'And are you sure, M. de Comminges,' said Athos, 'that the
cardinal will honour me with a visit?'

'He has at least assured me so, Monsieur.'

Athos sighed when he saw the barred windows.

'Yes, it's true,' said Comminges, 'it is almost a prison.
Nothing is wanting, not even the bars. But, really, what a
strange idea must have seized you, who are a flower of nobility,
to go and waste your bravery and loyalty among all those
mushrooms of the Fronde! You, a Frondeur! the Comte de la
Fère of the party of a Broussel, a Blancmesnil, a Viole! Fie
now! That makes me believe that your mother was some little
lawyer's daughter. You a Frondeur!'

'Upon my word, my dear Monsieur, one must be either of
Mazarin's party or a Frondeur. I have often heard these two
names resound in my ears, and I have pronounced in favour
of the latter. At any rate it is a French name. And then I am
a Frondeur with M. de Beaufort, M. de Bouillon, M. d'Elbeuf;
with princes, not with judges, councillors, and lawyers. And
then, what an agreeable result for serving Monsieur the Cardinal! Look at that wall without windows, it will tell you fine
things about Mazarin's gratitude.'

'Yes,' replied Comminges, laughing; 'and especially if it repeat all the maledictions which M. d'Artagnan has let fly at him the last week.'

'Poor d'Artagnan!' said Athos, with that charming melancholy which formed one of the features of his disposition; 'a man so brave, so good, so terrible to those who love not those whom he loves. You have two fierce prisoners, M. de Comminges, and I pity you if these two redoubtable men have been put into your charge.'

'Redoubtable!' said Comminges, smiling; 'eh! Monsieur, you want to frighten me. The first day of his imprisonment, M. d'Artagnan challenged all the soldiers and non-commissioned officers, in order doubtless to have a sword. That lasted to the next day, and even to the day after; but then he became calm and gentle as a lamb. Now he sings Gascon songs which make us die of laughter.'

'And M. du Vallon?'

'Ah! he—that's another matter. I confess he is a terrible gentleman. The first day he forced all the doors with a single push from his shoulder, and I was expecting to see him leave Rueil as Samson came forth from Gaza.* But his humour has followed the same course as that of M. d'Artagnan. Now he is not only used to his captivity, but he even makes a joke of it.'

'So much the better,' said Athos.

'Were you expecting, then, something else?' Comminges asked, who putting together what Mazarin had said of his prisoners with what the count had said, began to feel some anxiety.

Athos for his part was thinking that this amelioration in the conduct of his friends grew certainly out of some plan formed by d'Artagnan. He did not, therefore, wish to harm them by singing their praises too much.

'They?' said he; 'they are of an inflammable disposition. One is a Gascon, the other a Picard; they set one another on fire, but they are quickly put out. You have a proof of that, and what you have just told me proves what I say to be true.'

It was Comminges's opinion; so he withdrew more reassured, and Athos remained alone in that vast room, where, according to the cardinal's orders, he was treated as a gentleman. Besides,

he was awaiting the famous promised visit of Mazarin in order
to form a clear idea of his position.

LXXXVII

STRENGTH OF MIND AND STRENGTH OF ARM

NOW let us cross over to the hunting pavilion. At the end of
the court, where through a portico formed of Ionic columns
some dog-kennels were seen, arose an oblong building, which
seemed to stretch like an arm before this other arm, the
orangery pavilion—a semi-circle enclosing the court of honour.
It was in this pavilion, on the ground-floor, that d'Artagnan
and Porthos were shut up, sharing the long hours of a captivity
hateful to two such temperaments.

D'Artagnan was going up and down like a tiger, his eye fixed,
sometimes growling hoarsely, before the bars of a long window
looking out of a back courtyard. Porthos was digesting in
silence a good dinner, the remains of which had just been
removed. The one seemed deprived of reason, and was thinking; the other seemed meditating profoundly, and was sleeping.
Only his sleep was a nightmare, which could be guessed from
the incoherent and broken manner with which he was snoring.

'See,' said d'Artagnan, 'the day is sinking. It must be about
four o'clock. It will soon be a hundred and eighty-three hours
that we have been in here.'

'H'm!' grunted Porthos, pretending to reply.

'Do you hear, you eternal sleeper?' said d'Artagnan, out of
patience that anyone should sleep by day when he had the
greatest difficulty to sleep at night.

'What?' said Porthos.

'I say that we have been shut up here a hundred and
eighty-three hours.'

'It's your fault,' said Porthos.

'What do you mean?—it's my fault.'

'Yes, I have offered to get us both out.'

'By removing a bar or breaking open a door?'

'Certainly.'

'Porthos, men like us don't get away purely and simply.'

'Upon my word, I would get away with that purity and simplicity which you seem to despise so much.'

D'Artagnan shrugged his shoulders.

'And then, merely escaping from this room is not all.'

'My dear friend, you seem today in a little better humour than you were yesterday. Explain how getting out of this room is not all.'

'It is not all, because having neither arms nor pass-word, we should not take fifty steps in the courtyard without meeting a sentinel.'

'Well,' said Porthos, 'we should knock him down and take his arms.'

'Yes; but before doing that, the Swiss, who has a tough life, would utter a cry or at least a groan which would bring out the guard. We should be tracked and taken like foxes, we who are lions, and thrown into some underground dungeon, where we should not have even the consolation of seeing this frightful grey sky of Rueil, which is no more like the sky of Tarbes* than the moon is like the sun. Hang it all! if we had someone outside who could give us some information on the moral and physical topography of this château, about that which Caesar called *mores locaque*,* as I have been told, at least——Ah! when one thinks that during twenty years when I had nothing to do, the idea never entered my mind of employing one of those idle hours in coming to study Rueil.'

'What does that signify?' said Porthos. 'Let us get away, all the same.'

'My dear fellow,' said d'Artagnan, 'do you know why master cooks never work with their own hands?'

'No; but I should be glad to know.'

'Because they would be afraid of making, before their pupils, tarts too much baked or creams that have turned.'

'Well?'

'Well, they would get laughed, at, and master cooks must not allow themselves to be laughed at.'

'And why are master cooks at all like us?'

'Because we ought, in our adventures, never to suffer any check, nor give occasion for people to laugh at us. In England we were checked and beaten, and that's a blot on our reputation.'

'By whom, now, were we beaten?'

'By Mordaunt.'

'Yes; but we have drowned him.'

'I know that, and that will rehabilitate us a little in the eyes of posterity, if posterity trouble themselves about us. But listen to me, Porthos. Although M. Mordaunt was not to be despised, M. Mazarin is quite a different person, whom we could not so easily drown. Let us be careful then and work cautiously, for,' added d'Artagnan with a sigh, 'while we two are worth eight others, perhaps, we are not equal to the four whom you know.'

'That's true,' said Porthos, answering d'Artagnan's sigh by his own.

'Well, Porthos, do as I do; walk up and down till some news of our friends reach us, or some bright idea strikes us; but don't be sleeping always as you do; there is nothing which stupefies so much as sleep. As for what awaits us, it is perhaps less serious than we thought it at first. I don't think M. de Mazarin thinks of cutting our heads off, because this can only follow a trial, and that makes a stir which would attract our friends' notice, and they would not let M. de Mazarin do it.'

'How well you reason!' said Porthos with genuine admiration.

'Well, yes, not badly. And then, you see, if we are not tried nor our heads cut off, they must guard us here or elsewhere.'

'Yes, that follows of necessity.'

'Well, it is impossible that M. Aramis, that keen-scented hound, and Athos, that wise gentleman, should not discover our retreat; then, my faith, it will be time.'

'Yes; and one is not badly off here, one thing, however, excepted.'

'What is that?'

'Haven't you noticed, d'Artagnan, that they have given us baked mutton three days running?'

'No; but if they give it us a fourth time I will complain of it. Don't be disturbed.'

'And then sometimes I miss my home; it is a long time since I visited my châteaus.'

'Bah! forget them for a time; we shall get back to them, unless at least M. Mazarin should have them razed to the ground.'

'Do you believe he would be allowed to be so tyrannical?' asked Porthos, with some anxiety.

'No; it was all very well for the other cardinal to do such things. Ours is too mean to risk doing them.'

'You set my mind at rest, d'Artagnan.'

'Well, then, put on a good face as I do; joke with the guards, interest the soldiers, since you cannot corrupt them; cajole them more than you do when they come near the bars. Up to the present you have only shown them your fist, and the more it asks respect the less does it attract. Ah! I would give a good deal to have five hundred louis only.'

'And I also,' said Porthos, who did not wish to be behind d'Artagnan in generosity. 'I would give readily a hundred pistoles.'

The two prisoners had come to this point in their conversation when Comminges entered, preceded by a sergeant and two men who brought supper in a hamper filled with basins and plates.

LXXXVIII

STRENGTH OF MIND AND STRENGTH OF ARM
(*concluded*)

'I SAY,' said Porthos, 'here's mutton again!'

'My dear M. de Comminges,' said d'Artagnan, 'you must know that my friend, M. du Vallon, is determined to go to the last extremities if M. de Mazarin persists in feeding him on this sort of meat.'

'I declare even,' said Porthos, 'that I will eat of nothing else unless they take it away.'

'Take away the mutton,' said Comminges; 'I hope M. du Vallon may sup pleasantly, especially as I have a piece of news which will, I am sure, give him a good appetite.'

'Is M. de Mazarin dead?'

'I regret to tell you he is wondrously well.'

'So much the worse,' said Porthos.

'And what is the news?' asked d'Artagnan. 'News is so rare a fruit in prison that you will, I hope, excuse my impatience, will you not, M. de Comminges?—and so much the more as we hear that the news is good.'

'Would you be glad to hear that M. le Comte de la Fère is very well?'

D'Artagnan's small eyes opened their widest.

'Should I be glad?' he exclaimed—'more than glad,—I should be happy.'

'Well, I am desired by himself to present you his best compliments, and to tell you he is in good health.'

D'Artagnan almost leaped with joy. A swift glance translated his thoughts to Porthos. 'If Athos knows where we are,' said this look, if it could speak, 'before long Athos will act.'

Porthos was not very acute in understanding glances; but this time, as he had, at the name of Athos, experienced the same impression as d'Artagnan, he comprehended.

'But,' asked the Gascon, timidly, 'Monsieur the Count, you say, has sent his compliments to M. du Vallon and myself? You have then seen him?'

'Certainly.'

'Where?—if I may ask.'

'Very near here,' replied Comminges, smiling.

'Very near here,' repeated d'Artagnan, whose eyes sparkled.

'So near that if the windows which look on to the orangery were not blocked up, you would see him from where you are.'

'He prowls about the neighbourhood of the château,' thought d'Artagnan. Then aloud: 'You met him while hunting in the park, perhaps?' said he.

'No, no nearer—much nearer. Look, behind this wall,' said Comminges, striking against the wall.

'Behind this wall? What is there behind it? They brought me here at night-time, so may the devil take me if I know where I am.'

'Well,' said Comminges, 'suppose one thing.'

'I will suppose what you like.'

'Suppose there is a window in this wall. Well, from it you would see M. de la Fère at his window.'

'He is then staying at the château?'

'Yes.'

'By what right?'

'The same right as you.'

'Athos a prisoner, then?'

'You know very well,' said Comminges, laughing, 'that there are no prisoners at Rueil, since there is no prison.'

'Don't play on the words, Monsieur; Athos has been arrested?'

'Yesterday at St Germain, on leaving the queen's presence.'

D'Artagnan's arms fell motionless by his side. He looked thunderstruck. A pallor passed like a white cloud across his embrowned face, but disappeared almost immediately.

'Prisoner!' he repeated.

'Prisoner!' Porthos repeated after him, very much depressed.

Suddenly d'Artagnan raised his head, and there was a light in his eyes imperceptible to Porthos himself. Then the same dejection which had preceded it took its place.

'Come, come,' said Comminges, who had a real liking for d'Artagnan since the signal service the latter had rendered him on the day of Broussel's arrest in rescuing him from the Parisians; 'come, don't be cast down. I did not mean to bring you sad news, far from it. In the present war all is uncertainty. Be pleased rather at the chance which brings your friend close to you and M. du Vallon, instead of being cast down.'

But this remark had no influence on d'Artagnan, who kept his melancholy looks.

'And how did he look?' asked Porthos, who seeing that d'Artagnan let the conversation drop, took advantage to interpose his word.

'Oh, very well,' said Comminges. 'At first, like yourselves, he seemed very cast down, but when he knew that Monsieur the Cardinal was going to pay him a visit this very evening——'

'Ah,' uttered d'Artagnan; 'Monsieur the Cardinal means to visit the Comte de la Fère?'

'Yes, he told him beforehand; and Monsieur the Count, on learning this, has desired me to tell you that he would profit by this to plead your cause as well as his own.'

'Ah, the dear Count!' said d'Artagnan.

'A fine affair,' growled Porthos, 'a great favour! Good heavens! Monsieur the Comte de la Fère, whose family is connected with the Montmorencys* and the Rohans, is quite equal to M. de Mazarin.'

'No matter,' said d'Artagnan, in his calmest tones; 'on due reflection, my dear Vallon, it is a great honour for Monsieur the Count. It is a hopeful sign; in my opinion the honour is so great that I think M. de Comminges is mistaken.'

'What! I am mistaken! No, no, no,' said Comminges, who aimed at establishing the facts in all their exactness. 'I perfectly understood what the cardinal told me. He will visit the Comte de la Fère.'

D'Artagnan tried to catch Porthos's eye to see if he understood the importance of this visit, but he failed to do so.

'It is the custom, then, of Monsieur the Cardinal to walk in his orangery?'

'He shuts himself up there every evening. It would appear that there he meditates on state affairs.'

'Then,' said d'Artagnan, 'I begin to think that M. de la Fère will receive a visit from his Eminence; besides, he will be accompanied doubtless.'

'Yes; by two soldiers.'

'And he will talk of matters before two strangers?'

'The soldiers are Swiss, from the small cantons where they speak only German. Besides, in all probability they will wait at the gate.'

D'Artagnan drove the nails into the palms of his hands to prevent his face from expressing anything but what he wished it to express.

'Let M. de Mazarin take care of being alone with M. le Comte de la Fère, for the latter must be furious.'

Comminges began to laugh. 'Oh, come! really, one would think that you were anthropophagi! M. de la Fère is courteous; besides, he has no arms; at the first cry of his Eminence, the two soldiers who always accompany him would run to him.'

'Two soldiers,' said d'Artagnan, appearing to recall his recollection; 'two soldiers—yes; that is why I hear two men called every evening, and why I see them walking sometimes for half an hour under my window.'

'That is it; they wait for the Cardinal, or rather Bernouin, who comes and calls them when the Cardinal goes out.'

'Fine fellows, upon my word!'

'It is the regiment which was at Lens, and which Monsieur the Prince has given to the Cardinal to do him honour.'

'Ah, Monsieur,' said d'Artagnan, as if to sum up the whole of this long conversation, 'perhaps his Eminence will grow mild, and grant our liberty to M. de la Fère.'

'I heartily wish it,' said Comminges.

'Then if he forget this visit, you would not object to remind him of it?'

'No, certainly.'

'Ah! that gives me a little more tranquillity.'

This clever change of the conversation would have seemed a sublime manœuvre to anyone who could have read the Gascon's soul.

'Now,' he continued, 'a last favour, I beg of you, my dear M. de Comminges.'

'Quite at your service, Monsieur.'

'You will see M. le Comte de la Fère again?'

'Tomorrow morning.'

'Will you wish him good-day for us, and ask him to beg for me the same favour he has obtained for himself?'

'You wish, then, that Monsieur the Cardinal should come here?'

'No; I am not so bold, nor exacting. If his Eminence will do me the honour of listening to me, that is all I desire.'

'Oh!' murmured Porthos, shaking his head, 'I should never have thought that of my friend here. How misfortune lowers a man!'

'It shall be done,' said Comminges.

'Also assure the Count that I am quite well, and that you have found me sad, but resigned.'

'You please me, Monsieur, by saying that.'

'You will say the same thing for M. du Vallon?'

'For me—not at all,' exclaimed Porthos. 'I am not resigned at all.'

'He will become so, M. de Comminges. I know him better than he knows himself, and I know a thousand excellent qualities in him which he does not even suspect. Be silent, my dear Vallon, and be resigned.'

'Adieu, Messieurs. Good-night.'

Comminges left. D'Artagnan looked after him with the same humble and resigned look. But scarcely was the door closed than rushing up to Porthos, he embraced him with a joy which could not be mistaken.

'Oh, oh!' said Porthos, 'what is the matter now? Have you gone mad, my poor friend?'

'The matter is—we are saved!'

'I do not at all understand you,' said Porthos, 'I see on the contrary that we are all prisoners, with the exception of Aramis, and that our chances of getting out are diminished since one more of us has entered the mouse-trap of M. de Mazarin.'

'Not at all, Porthos, my friend; this mouse-trap was strong enough for two, but it becomes too weak for three.'

'I do not understand at all,' said Porthos.

'No matter; sit down to table and get some strength; we shall need it tonight.'

'What shall we do then tonight?' asked Porthos, more and more puzzled.

'We shall travel probably.'

'But——'

'Sit down, dear friend; ideas come while eating. After supper, when my ideas have taken shape, I will let you know them.'

Whatever desire Porthos had of being informed of d'Artagnan's plan, as he knew the latter's mode of acting he seated himself at table without insisting further, and ate with an appetite which did honour to his confidence in d'Artagnan's imagination.

LXXXIX

STRENGTH OF ARM AND STRENGTH OF MIND

THE supper was silent, but not sad; for from time to time one of those shrewd smiles which were habitual to him in his moments of good humour, illumined the countenance of d'Artagnan. Porthos did not lose one of those smiles, and at each of them uttered some exclamation which showed his friend that, although he did not understand it, he had not lost sight of the plan which was working in d'Artagnan's brain.

At dessert d'Artagnan sat in his chair with his legs crossed, and with the look of a man thoroughly satisfied with himself. Porthos rested his face on his hands, put his elbows on the table, and looked at d'Artagnan with that air of confidence which gave this Colossus such an admirable appearance of good nature.

'Well?' said d'Artagnan, at the end of an instant.

'Well?' repeated Porthos.

'You said then, dear friend——'

'I! I was saying nothing.'

'Yes, indeed; you were saying that you wanted to go out from here.'

'Ah! as for that, yes; it is not the desire which is wanting.'

'And you added that, to go out from here, it was only necessary to open a door or a wall.'

'It is true I was saying that, and I even say it still.'

'And I answered you, Porthos, that it was a bad way, and that we should not go a hundred paces without being captured and knocked on the head, unless we had dresses to disguise us and arms to defend us.'

'It is true, we need dresses and arms.'

'Well,' said d'Artagnan, getting up, 'we have them, friend Porthos, and even something better.'

'Bah!' said Porthos, looking around him.

'Don't search, it's useless; all those will come to us at the right time. About what hour did we see two Swiss guards walking up and down yesterday?' asked d'Artagnan.

'One hour, I think, after night had fallen.'

'If they come out today at the same time as yesterday, we shall only have a quarter of an hour to await the pleasure of seeing them.'

'Only a quarter of an hour at the most.'

'You always have your arm in fair condition, isn't it so, Porthos?'

Porthos unbuttoned, and pulling up his sleeve regarded with satisfaction his brawny arms, as large as the thighs of ordinary men.

'Yes,' said he, 'pretty good.'

'So that you could make, without much difficulty, a circle out of these tongs, and a corkscrew out of this shovel?'

'Certainly,' said Porthos.

'Let us see,' said d'Artagnan.

The giant took the two objects named, and effected with the greatest ease and without any apparent effort the two metamorphoses desired by his companion.

'There,' said he.

'Magnificent!' said d'Artagnan, 'and truly you are gifted, Porthos.'

'I have heard,' said Porthos, 'of a certain Milo of Crotona* who did some very extraordinary things, as tying a cord around his forehead and breaking it; of killing an ox with a blow of his fist and carrying it home on his shoulders; of stopping a horse by his hind feet, etc. I made them relate to me all his prowesses down there at Pierrefonds, and I have done all that he did, except breaking a cord by swelling my temples.'

'It is because your strength is not in your head, Porthos,' said d'Artagnan.

'No; it is in my arms and in my shoulders,' replied Porthos, naïvely.

'Well, my friend, come near the window and use your strength to unbed a bar. Wait till I extinguish the light.'

STRENGTH OF ARM AND STRENGTH OF MIND (*concluded*)

PORTHOS took hold of one of the window-bars with both hands, threw his strength into them, and pulled it towards him, making it bend like a bow, so that the two ends came from the holes in the stone where for thirty years the cement had held them.

'Well, my friend,' said d'Artagnan, 'that is something which the cardinal never could have done, man of genius as he is.'

'Is there any need to tear away any others?'

'Oh, no, that is sufficient; a man's body can pass through.'

Porthos tried, and his whole body went through. 'Yes,' said he.

'Now, pass your arm——'

'Through where?'

'Through this opening.'

'What to do?'

'You will know presently. Pass it.'

Porthos obeyed, docile as a soldier, and passed his arm through the bars.

'Wonderfully well!' said d'Artagnan.

'It appears that that goes well?'

'On wheels, dear friend.'

'Now what must I do?'

'Nothing.'

'It is then finished?'

'Not yet.'

'I should like, however, to understand better,' said Porthos.

'Listen, and in two words you will be *au fait*. The door of the guard-house opens, as you see.'

'Yes, I see.'

'They are going to send into our courtyard, which M. de Mazarin crosses to get to the orangery, the two guards who accompany him.'

'It is they who are coming out.'

'Provided that they close the door of the post. Good! they close it.'

'What next?'

'Silence! they might hear us.'

'I shall know nothing then.'

'Yes, indeed, for as fast as you execute you will understand.'

'However, I should have preferred——'

'You will have the pleasure of the surprise.'

'That's true,' said Porthos.

'Hush!'

Porthos remained silent and immovable. The two soldiers came near the window, rubbing their hands, for it was the month of February, and it was cold. At that moment the door of the guard-house opened, and one of the soldiers was re-called. The soldier left his comrade and returned to the guard-room.

'Is it working aright?' said Porthos.

'Better than ever,' replied d'Artagnan. 'Now, listen; I am going to call this soldier and talk to him, as I did yesterday with one of his comrades.'

'Yes, only I didn't understand a word of what he said.'

'The fact is that his accent was a little strong, but do not lose a word of what I am going to tell you; all is in the execution, Porthos.'

'Good! execution is my strong point.'

'I know it well, *pardieu!* so I count on you.'

'Speak.'

'I am going to call the soldier and talk with him.'

'You have already said so.'

'I shall turn myself to the left so that he will be on your right as soon as he has got on to the bench.'

'But suppose he does not get up on it.'

'He is sure to do so, don't fear. Directly he does, you stretch out your arm and seize him by the neck. Then lifting him you will draw him into our room, taking care to seize him tight enough to prevent him from crying out.'

'Yes,' said Porthos, 'but suppose I strangle him.'

'Well, it will be only a Swiss the less; but you will not do so, I hope. You will put him down gently, and we will gag

him, and fasten him, no matter where, to something or other.
That will give us a uniform and a sword.'

'Wonderful!' said Porthos, looking at d'Artagnan with the
most profound admiration; 'but one uniform and one sword
are not enough for two.'

'Well, but has he not a comrade?'

'That is true.'

'Then when I cough, put out your arm. It will be time.'

'Good.'

The two friends took their indicated positions. Placed as he
was, Porthos was entirely hidden behind the angle of the
window.

'Good evening, comrade,' said d'Artagnan, with his most
pleasant tones and the most moderate notes of his diapason.

'Goot evening, Monsir,' replied the soldier.

'I believe a glass of wine would not be disagreeable to
you.'

'A glass of fine would be velcome.'

'The fish bites! the fish bites!' murmured d'Artagnan to
Porthos. Then to the soldier, 'I have a bottle here.'

'A bottel full?'

'Quite full, and it is for you if you wish to drink my health.'

'Eheh! much bleasure,' said the soldier, approaching.

'Well, come and take it, my friend,' said the Gascon.

'Ferry villingly. Gut ting, there is a pench!'

'Oh! eh! one might say that it was put there on purpose. Get
up! There, that's it, my friend.'

And d'Artagnan coughed. At the same moment Porthos's arm
fell as swift as lightning, and, with a grip like pincers, his steel
fist seized the soldier's neck, and raised him while choking
him. He drew him to him through the opening, at the risk of
flaying him, and laid him on the ground, where d'Artagnan
gagged him with his scarf, and then began to strip him with
the promptitude and dexterity of one who has learned his trade
on the battlefield.

Then the soldier, garrotted and gagged, was deposited in the
fireplace, the fire of which our friends had previously extinguished.

'Here is at any rate a sword and a uniform,' said Porthos.

'I take these,' said d'Artagnan. 'If you wish another of each, we must make another turn. Attention! I see the other soldier, coming out from the guard-house in this direction.'

'I believe,' said Porthos, 'it would be imprudent to try that manœuvre again. One never succeeds twice, so they say, by the same means. If I fail, all will be lost. I shall get out, seize him just at the moment when he is unsuspecting, and offer him to you already gagged.'

'That's better,' said the Gascon.

'Keep ready,' said Porthos, gliding out by the opening.

The thing was done as Porthos had promised. The giant hid himself, and when the soldier passed before him, he seized him by the throat, gagged him, pushed him like a mummy through the bars, and entered behind him.

They stripped the second prisoner as they had the other. He was laid on the bed and fastened by the straps, and as the bedstead was of massive oak, and the straps were doubled, they were not less sure of him than of the other.

'There,' said d'Artagnan, 'that has succeeded capitally. Now try on the dress of that fine fellow. Porthos, I doubt if it will fit you; but, if it is too tight, don't trouble yourself—the shoulder-belt will be sufficient, and especially the hat with red feathers.'

They found by chance that the second was a gigantic Swiss, so that, with the exception of some stitches that gave way in the seams, all did very well indeed.

For some time nothing was heard but the rustling of cloth, Porthos and d'Artagnan dressing themselves in haste.

'That's done,' said they both at the same time.

'As for you, companions,' they added, turning towards the two soldiers, 'nothing will happen if you are quiet; but if you move, you are dead.'

They kept quiet. They had comprehended from Porthos's fist that the affair was a most serious one, and that there was no question of joking.

'Now,' said d'Artagnan, 'you would not be sorry to under-stand it; isn't that so, Porthos?'

'Yes, indeed.'

'Well, we descend into the courtyard.'

'Yes.'

'We take the place of those jovial fellows.'

'Well?'

'We promenade up and down.'

'And that will be well to do, as it is not hot.'

'And in an instant the *valet de chambre* will call the service, as he did yesterday and the day before.'

'We reply?'

'No, we do not reply, on the contrary.'

'As you wish; I am not set on replying.'

'We do not reply; we only fix our hats firmly on our heads, and we escort his Eminence.'

'Where to?'

'Where he is going—to see Athos; do you think *he* will be sorry to see us?'

'Oh!' exclaimed Porthos, 'I understand.'

'Be careful not to cry out, Porthos, for you are not yet at the end of your tether,' said the Gascon, bantering.

'What is going to happen, then?'

'Follow me. He who lives shall see.'

And passing through the opening, he allowed himself to slip gently into the courtyard. Porthos followed in the same fashion, although with somewhat more difficulty. The two soldiers tied up in the room shivered with fear. D'Artagnan and Porthos had scarcely reached the ground when a door opened and the valet's voice was heard, crying, 'The service!'

At the same time the door of the guard-room opened, and a voice called out:—

'La Bruyère and Barthois—march!'

'It appears that I am called La Bruyère,' said D'Artagnan.

'And I, Barthois,' said Porthos.

'Where are you?' asked the *valet de chambre*, whose eyes, dazzled by the light, could not distinguish our two heroes in the obscurity.

'Here we are,' said d'Artagnan.

Then turning towards Porthos—

'What do you say to that, M. du Vallon?'

'Faith, provided that it lasts, I say that it is nice.'

The two improvised soldiers marched gravely behind the valet. He opened a door in the hall, then another, which seemed to be that of a waiting-room, and pointing out two stools: 'The orders are simple enough,' he said to them; 'only let one person enter here—only one, understand clearly—no more; obey this person in everything. You will wait till I relieve you.'

D'Artagnan was very well known to this valet, who was no other than Bernouin, who, during six or eight months, had introduced him a dozen times to the cardinal. Instead of replying he growled the *Ja* with as little Gascon and as much German accent as possible.

As for Porthos, d'Artagnan had asked and obtained from him the promise that he would in no case utter a word. If he was pushed to an extremity it was permitted to him to offer, as his sole reply, *der Teufel*,* proverbial and solemn.

Bernouin went away on closing the door.

'Oh, oh!' said Porthos, hearing the key in the lock, 'it appears that here it is the fashion to shut up people. We have only, it seems to me, exchanged prisons; instead of being prisoners down there, we are prisoners in the orangery. I don't know if we have gained by it.'

'Porthos, my friend,' said d'Artagnan in a low voice, 'don't doubt Providence, and leave me to meditate and reflect.'

'Meditate and reflect then,' said Porthos, in a bad humour on seeing things turn out thus instead of turning out otherwise.

'We have marched eighty paces,' murmured d'Artagnan; 'we have come up six steps; here then is, as my illustrious friend Vallon has said just now, that other pavilion parallel to ours that they call the pavilion of the orangery. The Comte de la Fère ought not to be far off; only the doors are locked.'

'That's a fine difficulty!' said Porthos, 'and with a blow of the shoulder——'

'For God's sake, Porthos, my friend,' said d'Artagnan, 'husband your feats of strength, or they will no longer have, when the time comes, all the value they merit. Have you not heard that someone is coming here?'

'Yes, indeed.'

'Well, this someone will open the doors for us.'

'But, my dear fellow,' said Porthos, 'if this someone recognizes us, if this someone begins to cry out, we are lost; for in short, it is not part of your plan, I imagine, to make me knock

down or strangle this churchman. These ways are well enough
for the English and the Germans.'

'Oh, God preserve me from it, and you also!' said d'Artagnan. 'The young king would perhaps feel some gratitude to us;
but the queen would not pardon us, and it is she whom we
must manage; then, besides, needless blood! never! never! I
have my plan. Let me carry it out, and we shall have the laugh
on our side.'

'So much the better,' said Porthos; 'I feel the need of it.'

'Hush!' said d'Artagnan, 'here's the someone spoken of.'

There was heard then in the hall the sound of a light step.
The hinges of the door creaked, and a man appeared in
cavalier's dress, enveloped in a brown cloak, a large hat pulled
down over his eyes, and a lantern in his hand.

Porthos kept back against the wall, but he was not able to
prevent himself being seen by the man in the cloak; he handed
him his lantern and said to him, 'Light the lamp in the hall.'
Then addressing d'Artagnan: 'You know the orders,' said he.

'*Ja*,' replied the Gascon, determined to confine himself to
this specimen of the German language.

'*Tedesco*,' said the cavalier, '*va bene*.'*

And going towards the door fronting that by which he had
entered, he opened it and closed it behind him.

'And now,' said Porthos, 'what shall we do?'

'Now we will make use of your shoulder, if this door is
fastened, friend Porthos. Each thing in its time, and everything
comes fittingly to him who knows how to wait. But first let
us barricade the first door in some suitable fashion; then we
will follow this cavalier.'

The two friends began their task at once, and blocked up
the door with all the furniture which they found in the hall.
The door opened inward.

'There,' said d'Artagnan, 'now we are sure of not being
surprised from the rear. Forward!'

M. MAZARIN'S OUBLIETTES

THEY reached the door through which Mazarin had disappeared. It was fastened; d'Artagnan tried in vain to open it.

'Now is the time for using your shoulder. Push, but gently, without noise; don't burst anything; disjoin the woodwork—that's all.'

Porthos pressed his sturdy shoulder against one of the panels, which bent, and d'Artagnan then inserted the point of his sword between the bolt and staple of the lock. The bolt, thus bent, gave way, and the door opened.

'Let us go in,' said d'Artagnan.

They entered. Behind a glazed partition, by the glimmer of the cardinal's lantern, put on the ground in the middle of the gallery, they saw the orange and pomegranate trees of the château, extending in long lines, forming a grand avenue, and two smaller side ones.

'No cardinal,' said d'Artagnan, 'only his lamp; where is he then?'

And as he explored one of the side-wings, after having got Porthos to explore the other, he suddenly observed on the left a flower-box moved from its position, and where the box had stood a gaping hole. Ten men would have found it difficult to move this box, but by some mechanical contrivance it had turned with the flag-stone on which it rested. In this hole was a winding staircase. D'Artagnan called Porthos and pointed out to him the hole and the stairs. The two men looked at each other with a frightened air.

'If we merely wanted gold,' said d'Artagnan, in a low voice, 'we could become rich for ever.'

'How so?'

'Don't you understand, Porthos, that at the bottom of this staircase there is, in all probability, the cardinal's famous treasury about which there is so much talk; and that we should have merely to go down, empty a chest, double-lock the cardinal inside, escape after having put the orange-tree in its place, and no one in the world would think of asking us whence our fortune came—not even the cardinal?'

'That would be a fine stroke of business for peasants,' said Porthos, 'but unworthy, it seems to me, of two gentlemen.'

'That's my opinion. If we wished money merely—but we want something else.'

At the same instant, and as d'Artagnan bent his head towards the cave to listen, a hard, metallic sound, like that of a bag of gold being moved, struck his ear; he started. Immediately a door was closed, and the first rays of a light appeared on the staircase. Mazarin had left his lamp in the orangery to make it appear that he was taking a walk. But he had a wax-taper to explore his mysterious strong room.

'Hey!' said he, in Italian, while coming up the stairs, examining a bag of reals with its rounded paunch; 'here is somewhat with which to pay five councillors of Parliament and two generals of Paris. I also am a great captain; only I make war in my own fashion——'

D'Artagnan and Porthos were crouching in a side alley, each behind an orange-tree tub and waiting. Mazarin came only a few feet from d'Artagnan, and touched a spring hidden in the wall. The stone turned, and the orange-tree supported by it, returned to its position of itself. Then the cardinal extinguished his taper, which he put back into his pocket, and taking up the lamp, 'Let us go and see M. de la Fère,' said he.

'Good, it is our road,' thought d'Artagnan; 'we will go together.'

All three moved off, M. de Mazarin keeping the middle of the avenue, and Porthos and d'Artagnan the parallel alleys. The two latter carefully avoided those long lines of light thrown by the cardinal's lantern between the orange-tree boxes. The latter reached a second glass door without perceiving that he was followed, the soft sand deadening the steps of the two who were following him. Then he turned to the left, took a corridor to which Porthos and d'Artagnan had as yet paid no attention; but just when he was about to open the door, he stopped, thoughtful, and, with a movement of impatience, he turned round to go back.

'Ah, *diavolo!*' said he; 'I was forgetting Comminges's advice. I must take the soldiers and put them at the door that I may not be at the mercy of this raging devil.'

'Do not give yourself the trouble, Monseigneur,' said d'Artagnan, with his foot forward, his hat in hand, and smiling face; 'we have followed your Eminence step by step, and here we are.'

'Yes, here we are,' said Porthos; and he went through the same form of salutation.

Mazarin turned his frightened look from one to the other, recognizing both, and let fall his lantern, uttering a groan of fear.

D'Artagnan picked it up; by good fortune it was not extinguished by the fall.

'Oh, what imprudence, Monseigneur!' said d'Artagnan; 'it is not well to walk here without a light! Your Eminence might hit against some box or fall into some hole.'

'M. d'Artagnan!' murmured Mazarin, not able to recover from his astonishment.

'Yes, Monseigneur, myself; and I have the honour of presenting to you M. du Vallon, my excellent friend, in whom your Eminence formerly had the goodness to interest yourself so warmly.' And d'Artagnan directed the light of the lantern towards Porthos's joyous face, who began to understand how matters stood, and recognized the advantages of the situation.

'You are going to see M. de la Fère,' continued d'Artagnan. 'Pray don't let us disturb you, Monseigneur. Be good enough to show the road, and we will follow you.'

Mazarin recovered his spirits by degrees.

'Have you been a long while in the orangery, Messieurs?' he asked with a trembling voice, thinking of the visit he had just made to his treasure.

Porthos opened his mouth to reply, d'Artagnan made him a sign, and the mouth of Porthos remained mute and closed gradually.

'We came this very moment, Monseigneur.'

Mazarin breathed freely; he feared no longer for his treasure, but only for himself. A sort of smile passed across his face.

'Come,' said he, 'you have taken me in a trap, Messieurs, and I declare myself beaten. You want to ask me for your liberty, do you not? I give it you.'

'Oh, Monseigneur,' said d'Artagnan, 'you are very good; but we have our liberty, and we should like to ask you for something else.'

'You have your liberty?' said Mazarin, frightened.

'Without doubt, and it is you, on the contrary, Monseigneur, who have lost yours; and now what do you expect?—it is the law of war; it is a question of redeeming it.'

Mazarin felt a cold shudder pass through him. His piercing look was in vain fixed upon the mocking face of the Gascon, and the impassive face of Porthos. Both were hidden in the shade, and the Cumaean Sibyl* herself would not have been able to read them.

'Redeem my liberty!' Mazarin repeated.

'Yes, Monseigneur.'

'And how much will that cost me, M. d'Artagnan?'

'Indeed, Monseigneur, I don't know yet. We are going to ask that of the Comte de la Fère, if your Eminence will indeed permit it. Would your Eminence deign then to open the door leading to him, and in ten minutes it will be arranged?'

Mazarin trembled.

'Monseigneur,' said d'Artagnan, 'your Eminence sees how we have hitherto stood upon form, but yet we are obliged to remind you that we have no time to lose. Open then, Monseigneur, if you please, and be good enough to remember, once for all, that at the least movement you make to escape, or the least cry, our position being quite exceptional, you must not blame us if we carry matters to extremities.'

'I shall attempt nothing,' said Mazarin; 'I give you my word of honour.'

D'Artagnan made a sign to Porthos to redouble his vigilance. Then turning to Mazarin: 'Now, Monseigneur, let us go in, if you please.'

XCII

MAZARIN drew back the bolt of a double door, at the threshold of which Athos was quite ready to receive his illustrious visitor, according to the information given him by Comminges.

On perceiving Mazarin he bowed. 'Your Eminence can dispense with any attendance; the honour which I am receiving is too great for me to forget it.'

'So, my dear Count,' said d'Artagnan, 'as his Eminence absolutely did not want us, it is Vallon and myself who have insisted on coming perhaps in an unwelcome manner, so great is our desire to see you.' At this voice, with its bantering tone, Athos made a movement of surprise.

'D'Artagnan, Porthos!' he exclaimed.

'In person, dear friend.'

'In person,' repeated Porthos.

'What does this mean?' asked the count.

'It means,' replied Mazarin, trying to smile, and biting his lips in doing so, 'that the parts are changed, and that instead of these gentlemen being my prisoners, I am theirs; so much so that you see me forced to receive here the law, instead of giving it. But, gentlemen, I give you notice, unless at least you strangle me, that your victory will be of short duration. I shall have my turn; they will come——'

'Ah, Monseigneur,' said d'Artagnan, 'do not threaten; it is a bad example. We are so gentle and so charming with your Eminence. Come, let us put aside all bad humour, let us get rid of all rancour, and let us talk together pleasantly.'

'I ask nothing better, Messieurs,' said Mazarin, 'but at the moment of discussing my ransom, I do not wish that you should think your position better than it is; in taking me in a trap, you are taken in it with me. How will you get out from here? Look at the doors and gates; see or rather imagine the sentinels who keep guard behind them, the soldiers who crowd these courts, and let us come to terms. Come, I want to show you that I am loyal.'

'Good!' thought d'Artagnan; 'let us hold fast, he is going to play us a trick.'

'I was offering you your liberty,' continued the minister. 'I still offer it to you. Do you wish it? Before an hour you will be discovered, arrested, forced to kill me, which would be a horrible crime, and quite unworthy of loyal gentlemen like you.'

'He is right,' thought Athos; and like all that was right, which entered that noble soul, his thought was reflected in his eyes.

'So,' said d'Artagnan, to correct the hope which the silent adhesion of Athos had given Mazarin, 'we resort to that violent act only at the last extremity.'

'If on the contrary,' continued Mazarin, 'you let me go in accepting your liberty——'

'How,' interrupted d'Artagnan, 'do you wish us to accept our liberty, since you could take it from us again, as you have yourself said, five minutes after giving it? And,' added d'Artagnan, 'judging from what I know of you, Monseigneur, you would take it from us.'

'No, on the word of a cardinal! You do not believe me?'

'Monseigneur, I do not believe cardinals who are not priests.'*

'Well, on my word as a minister!'

'You are so no longer, Monseigneur, you are a prisoner.'

'Then, on the word of Mazarin! I am that, and I shall be always, I hope.'

'H'm!' said d'Artagnan, 'I have heard of a Mazarin who had little of religious regard for his oaths, and I am afraid that it might be one of the ancestors of your Eminence.'

'M. d'Artagnan,' said Mazarin, 'you have much wit, and I am thoroughly sorry to be at variance with you.'

'Monseigneur, let us be reconciled, I ask nothing better.'

'Well,' said Mazarin, 'if I set you free securely, in a manner evident, palpable——'

'Ah, that's another matter,' said Porthos.

'Let us see,' said Athos.

'Let us see,' said d'Artagnan.

'First, do you accept?' asked the cardinal.

'Explain to us your plan, Monseigneur, and we will see.'

'Observe well that you are shut up, captured.'

'You know well, Monseigneur,' said d'Artagnan, 'that there remains to us always a last resource.'

'What is it?'

'That of dying together.'

Mazarin shuddered.

'Well,' said he, 'at the end of the corridor is a door of which I have the key; this opens into the park. Take this key and be off. You are alert, strong, and armed. At a hundred yards, on turning to the left, you will reach the wall of the park; climb over it, and you will be in a few steps on the high road, and free. Now I know you well enough to feel sure that if you are attacked that will be no obstacle to your flight.'

'Ah, Monseigneur,' said d'Artagnan, 'that's something like; there is something tangible. Where is that key which you so kindly offer us?'

'Here it is.'

'Ah, Monseigneur,' said d'Artagnan, 'will you yourself conduct us as far as that door?'

'Very willingly,' said the minister, 'if that is necessary to put you at ease.'

Mazarin, who did not expect to be quit of them so cheaply, went quite cheerfully towards the corridor and unlocked the door. It opened on to the park, and the three fugitives felt the night wind which blew hard into the corridor, and made the snow fly into their faces.

'The devil!' said d'Artagnan, 'it's a horrid night, Monseigneur. We don't know our whereabouts, and shall never find our way. Since your Eminence has done so much in coming so far, a few paces more, Monseigneur—conduct us to the wall.'

'So be it,' said the cardinal.

And taking a straight line, he went rapidly towards the wall, the foot of which all four reached in a very short time.

'Are you satisfied, Messieurs?' asked Mazarin.

'I believe so; we should be hard to please. *Peste!* what honour! three poor gentlemen escorted by a prince of the church. Ah, by the by, Monseigneur, you said just now that we were brave, alert, and armed. You are mistaken. Monsieur the Count is not armed, and if we fell in with any patrol, we should have to defend ourselves.'

'But where shall we find a sword?' asked Porthos.

'Monseigneur,' said d'Artagnan, 'will lend the count his own as it is useless to him.'

'Very willingly,' said Mazarin; 'I shall even beg Monsieur the Count to keep it in remembrance of me.'

'That is very gallant, Count,' said d'Artagnan.

'I promise on my part,' replied Athos, 'never to part with it.'

'Very well,' said d'Artagnan; 'exchange of courtesies, how touching it is! Have you not tears in your eyes, Porthos?'

'Yes,' said Porthos, 'but I don't know whether it is this or the wind which makes me weep. I think it is the wind.'

'Now mount, Athos,' said d'Artagnan, 'and be quick.'

Athos, aided by Porthos, who lifted him up like a feather, reached the top.

'Now jump, Athos.'

Athos jumped down and disappeared on the other side of the wall.

'Are you on the ground?' asked d'Artagnan.

'Yes.'

'Without accident?'

'Perfectly safe and sound.'

'Porthos,' said d'Artagnan, 'watch Monsieur the Cardinal while I am mounting; no, I don't need your help, I can mount by myself. Look after the cardinal, that's all.'

'I am doing so,' said Porthos. 'Well?'

'You are right; it is more difficult than I thought. Lend me your back, but without letting go Monsieur the Cardinal.'

'I don't let go of him.'

Porthos gave his back to d'Artagnan, who in a moment, with this support, was astride on the top of the wall. Mazarin pretended to laugh.

'Are you there?' asked Porthos.

'Yes, my friend, and now——'

'Now what?'

'Now pass me up Monsieur the Cardinal, and at the least cry he utters, stifle him.'

Mazarin wished to cry out, but Porthos took him tightly with his hands and lifted him up to d'Artagnan, who seized him by the collar and seated him near him. Then in a menacing tone, 'Monsieur, jump down this very moment near M. de la Fère, or I will kill you, on the word of a gentleman.'

'Monsieur, monsieur!' exclaimed Mazarin, 'you are not keeping your word.'

'I! When did I promise anything, Monseigneur?'

Mazarin gave a groan.

'You are free by my means, Monsieur,' said he. 'Your liberty was to be my ransom.'

'Agreed; but is there not need, Monseigneur, to speak a little about the ransom of that immense treasure hidden in the gallery, which is reached by touching a spring hidden in the wall, which turns one of the orange-tree boxes and thus discovers a winding stair?'

'Good God!' said Mazarin, almost suffocated with emotion, and joining his hands together, 'I am lost!'

But without being stopped by his laments, d'Artagnan took him below the arms and dropped him gently into Athos's hands, who had remained impassive at the foot of the wall. Then turning towards Porthos, 'Take my hand,' said d'Artagnan; 'I am holding on to the wall.'

Porthos made an effort which shook the wall, and so reached the top.

'I did not at all understand matters,' said he, 'but I do now; it's very funny.'

'Do you find it so?—so much the better. But that it may remain so to the end do not lose time;' and he jumped off the wall. Porthos did the same.

'Accompany Monsieur the Cardinal, Messieurs,' said d'Artagnan; 'I will reconnoitre.'

The Gascon drew his sword, and marched forward in front.

'Monseigneur,' said he, 'which way must we go to reach the high road? Think well before speaking; for if your Eminence makes a mistake, it would cause great inconvenience not only to us but to you.'

'Keep along by the wall, Monsieur,' said Mazarin, 'and there is no risk of losing yourselves.'

The three friends doubled their pace, but in a few moments they were obliged to slacken, as the cardinal could not keep up with them. All of a sudden d'Artagnan knocked against something warm, which moved.

'A horse,' said he; 'I have just come upon a horse, Messieurs.'

'So have I!' said Athos.

'And I too!' said Porthos, who, faithful to his orders, kept hold of the cardinal by the arm.

'This is what is called chance, Monseigneur,' said d'Artagnan. 'Just at the moment when your Eminence complained of being obliged to go on foot——'

But just as he was saying this a pistol was aimed at his breast; he heard these words gravely uttered—

'Don't touch.'

'Grimaud!' he cried out, 'what are you doing there? Has Heaven sent you?'

'No, Monsieur,' said the honest domestic; 'it's M. Aramis, who told me to mind the horses.'

'Is Aramis here, then?'

'Yes, Monsieur, since yesterday.'

'And what are you doing?'

'We are on the watch.'

'What! Aramis here?' repeated Athos.

'At the small gate of the château. That was his post.'

'Are there then many of you?'

'Sixty in all.'

'Just let him know.'

'This instant, Monsieur;' and thinking that no one could execute the order better than himself, Grimaud ran off, while the three friends waited in the hope of being reunited. The only ill-humoured one in the whole group was M. de Mazarin.

IN WHICH ONE BEGINS TO BELIEVE THAT PORTHOS WILL
AT LAST BE MADE A BARON, AND D'ARTAGNAN A CAPTAIN

IN about ten minutes Aramis arrived, accompanied by Grimaud and eight or ten gentlemen. He was quite delighted, and threw himself on his friends' necks.

'You are free then, brothers, free without my help! I have then done nothing in your behalf in spite of all my efforts.'

'Do not be distressed, dear friend. What is deferred is not lost. If you have been able to do nothing, you will yet do a good deal.'

'Yet I had taken my measures well. I obtained sixty men from Monsieur the Coadjutor; twenty are guarding the park walls, twenty the route from Rueil to St Germain, and twenty are scattered about in the woods. I have in this way intercepted, thanks to my strategical arrangements, two couriers from Mazarin to the queen.'

Mazarin pricked up his ears.

'But,' said d'Artagnan, 'you have honourably, I hope, sent them back to Monsieur the Cardinal?'

'Ah, yes!' said Aramis, 'in dealing with him one would certainly take pride in such delicacy of conduct. In one of these despatches the cardinal declares to the queen that the money chests are empty, and that her Majesty has no more money; in the other he says that he is going to send his prisoners to Melun, Rueil not seeming to him to be secure enough. You understand, dear friend, that this latter letter gave me much hope. I made an ambuscade with my sixty men, I surrounded the château, and I awaited your coming forth. I scarcely counted on it before tomorrow morning, and I did not expect to set you free without a skirmish. You are free this evening, and without fighting; so much the better. How have you managed to escape from that fellow Mazarin? You must have had much to complain of him?'

'Not to any extent,' said d'Artagnan.

'Truly!'

'I will say even more, we have had reason to praise him.'

'Impossible!'

'Yes, indeed, truly; it is thanks to him that we are free.'

'Thanks to him?'

'Yes, he had us taken into the orangery by M. Bernouin, his *valet de chambre*; thence we followed him to the Comte de la Fère's room. Then he offered to give us our liberty; we accepted it, and he pushed his complaisance so far as to show us the way to the wall of the park, which we had just cleared with the greatest delight, when we fell in with Grimaud.'

'Ah, well!' said Aramis, 'this is something which reconciles me to him; and I wish he were here for me to tell him that I did not think him capable of such a fine action.'

'Monseigneur,' said d'Artagnan, unable any longer to restrain himself, 'permit me to present to you Monsieur le Chevalier d'Herblay, who desires to offer, as you may have understood, his respectful felicitations to your Eminence;' and he drew back, unmasking Mazarin, looking very confused, to the bewildered looks of Aramis.

'Oh, oh!' said the latter, 'the cardinal! A fine prize. Holloa, holloa! friends! the horses!'

Some cavaliers came hastily up.

'Come, now,' said Aramis, 'I shall be useful after all. Monseigneur, will your Eminence deign to receive my homage. I bet that it is that Saint Christopher* of a Porthos who has made this coup. By the by, I was forgetting——' and he gave an order in a low tone to a cavalier.

'I believe it would be prudent to set off now,' said d'Artagnan.

'Yes, but I am expecting someone—a friend of Athos.'

'A friend?' said the count.

'And stop, this is he who is coming at a gallop across the brushwood.'

'Monsieur the Count!' cried out a young voice, which made Athos start.

'Raoul! Raoul!' exclaimed the Comte de la Fère.

In a moment the youth forgot his habitual respect, and threw himself on his father's neck.

'You see, Monsieur the Cardinal, what a pity it would have been to separate persons who love one another as we do. Messieurs,' continued Aramis, speaking to the cavaliers who were flocking in every moment, 'Messieurs, surround his Eminence to do him respect; he intends to accord us the honour of his company, and I hope you will be very grateful to him for it. Porthos, don't lose sight of his Eminence;' and Aramis joined d'Artagnan and Athos in their deliberations.

'Come,' said d'Artagnan, after a short conference, 'let us be off.'

'And where are we going?' Porthos asked.

'To your house, my dear friend, to Pierrefonds; your fine château is worthy of offering its lordly hospitality to his Eminence. And then it is very well situated—neither too near, nor too far from Paris; we can from there establish easy communication with Paris. Come, Monseigneur, you will be treated there like a prince, which you are.'

'A prince fallen,' said Mazarin, piteously.

'War has its chances, Monseigneur,' replied Athos, 'but be assured we will not abuse them.'

'No, but we will use them,' said d'Artagnan.

All the rest of the night the capturers travelled with the rapidity of former time; Mazarin, gloomy and thoughtful, allowed himself to be carried off in the midst of this flight of phantoms. By dawn they had gone a dozen leagues at a stretch; one half of the escort was tired out; some horses fell.

'The horses of today no longer equal those of former times,' said Porthos, 'everything degenerates.'

'I have sent Grimaud to Dammartin,' said Aramis; 'he is to bring us five fresh horses, one for his Eminence, four for us. The chief thing is that we must not leave Monseigneur; the rest of the escort will rejoin us later on; when once St Denis is passed, we have nothing further to fear.'

Grimaud in fact brought back five horses; the lord to whom he had addressed himself, being a friend of Porthos, was desirous not to sell them, as was proposed to him, but to offer their use. Ten minutes afterwards the escort stopped at Ermenonville;* but the four friends hastened on with fresh ardour, escorting M. de Mazarin. At noon they entered the avenue of Porthos's château.

'Ah,' said Mousqueton, who was near d'Artagnan, and who had not spoken a single word during the whole route; 'ah! you may believe me or not, Monsieur, but this is the first time I have drawn a full breath since my departure from Pierrefonds.' And he started at a gallop to announce to the other servants the arrival of M. du Vallon and his friends.

'There are four of us,' said d'Artagnan to his friends; 'we must take turns in guarding Monseigneur, and each will watch three hours. Athos is going to inspect the château, because the point is to make it impregnable in case of siege. Porthos will watch over the provisioning, and Aramis on the admission of a garrison.'

Meanwhile Mazarin was installed in the finest apartment of the château.

'Messieurs,' said he, when the installation was over, 'you do not reckon, I presume, on keeping me long here incognito.'

'No, Monseigneur,' replied d'Artagnan, 'quite the contrary; we reckon on making it known as soon as possible that we are holding you.'

'Then, they will besiege you.'

'We count on that.'

'And what will you do?'

'We will defend ourselves. If the late M. le Cardinal de Richelieu was still living, he would relate to you a certain story of a bastion St Gervais,* which we four held, with our four lackeys and twelve dead bodies, against a whole army.'

. 'Those acts of prowess are done once, Monsieur, but are not repeated.'

'Therefore today we shall have no need of being so heroic; tomorrow the Parisian army will be informed; the day after it will be here. The battle instead of taking place at St Denis or at Charenton, will be towards Compiègne or Villers-Cotterets.'

'Monsieur the Prince will beat you, as he always has.'

'That's possible, Monseigneur; but before the battle we will transfer your Eminence to another château of our friend Vallon; and he has three like this. We don't wish to expose your Eminence to the chances of war.'

'Come,' said Mazarin, 'I see I must capitulate.'

'Before the siege?'

'Yes; conditions will perhaps be more reasonable.'

'Ah, Monseigneur, as regards conditions, you will see how reasonable we are.'

'Come, what are your conditions?'

'Rest yourself first, Monseigneur, and we—we are going to reflect.'

'I have no need of rest, Messieurs, I have need of knowing whether I am in the hands of friends or enemies.'

'Friends, Monseigneur, friends.'

'Tell me at once then what you desire, that I may see if an arrangement is possible between us. Speak, M. le Comte de la Fère.'

'Monseigneur,' said Athos, 'I have nothing to ask for myself, and I should be obliged to ask too much for France. I therefore decline asking, and pass the word to M. le Chevalier d'Herblay,' and Athos, bowing, stepped back, and remained standing as a simple spectator of the conference.

'Speak then, M. le Chevalier d'Herblay,' said the cardinal. 'What do you ask? No ambiguities. Be clear, short, precise.'

'I, Monseigneur, will play with cards on the table.'

'Then lay down your cards.'

'I have in my pocket,' said Aramis, 'the list of the conditions which the deputation, of which I was a member, came the day before yesterday to St Germain to lay before you. Let us first of all respect ancient rights; the demands which were contained therein are to be granted.'

'We were almost agreed upon them,' said Mazarin; 'let us pass on, therefore, to the special conditions.'

'Do you believe that there will be any such?' said Aramis, smiling.

'I don't believe you will all have the same disinterestedness which M. le Comte de la Fère has shown,' said Mazarin, turning towards Athos and bowing.

'Ah, Monseigneur, you are right,' said Aramis, 'and I am glad you are doing justice to the count at last. M. de la Fère has a superior mind, which soars above vulgar desires and human passions; it is a proud soul of older times. Monsieur the Count is a man apart. You are right, Monseigneur, we are not his equals, and we are the first to confess it.'

'Aramis,' said Athos, 'are you jesting?'

'No, my dear count, no; I say what we think, and what all think who know you. But you are right; it is not of you that we are talking, but of Monseigneur and his unworthy servant the Chevalier d'Herblay.'

'Well, what do you ask, Monsieur, besides the general conditions, to which we will return presently?'

'I desire, Monseigneur, that Normandy be given to Madame de Longueville, with full and entire absolution, and five hundred thousand francs. I desire that his Majesty, the king, should deign to be godfather to her newly born son;* then that Monseigneur, after having assisted at the baptism, go to Rome to present his homage to our holy Father the Pope.'

'That is to say, you wish me to resign my office of minister, and to quit France, and exile myself.'

'I wish Monseigneur to become Pope at the first vacancy, reserving to myself the demand of a plenary indulgence for myself and my friends.'

Mazarin made an untranslatable grimace.

'And you, Monsieur?' he asked d'Artagnan.

'I, Monseigneur,' said the Gascon, 'am in accord with M. le Chevalier d'Herblay on all points but the last, and on that I totally differ from him. Far from wishing Monseigneur to leave France, I wish him to remain at Paris; far from wishing him to become Pope, I desire him to remain first minister, for Monseigneur is a great statesman. I will try even, as much as it depends on me, that he shall win the game against the entire Fronde; but on the condition that he bear in mind a little the king's faithful servants, and that he will give the first company of the Musketeers to someone whom I will name. And you, Vallon?'

'Yes, it's your turn, Monsieur,' said Mazarin; 'speak.'

'I,' said Porthos, 'wish Monsieur the Cardinal to do honour to my house, which has afforded him an asylum; and in memory of this adventure, to raise my estate into a barony, with a promise of an order for one of my friends for the first promotion which his Majesty shall make.'

'You know, Monsieur, that to receive an order, proofs of valour must be furnished.'

'This friend will furnish them. Besides, if he absolutely failed in doing this, Monseigneur would tell him how this formality might be avoided.'

Mazarin bit his lips.

'All these views agree very badly, it seems to me, Messieurs,' he said; 'for if I satisfy some, I necessarily dissatisfy the rest. If I stay in Paris I cannot go to Rome and become Pope; if I become Pope I cannot be minister, nor make M. d'Artagnan captain, and M. du Vallon baron.'

'That is true,' said Aramis; 'so, as I am in the minority, I withdraw my proposition respecting the journey to Rome and the resignation of Monseigneur.'

'I remain minister, then?' said Mazarin.

'That is understood, Monseigneur,' said d'Artagnan; 'France has need of you.'

'And I withdraw my proposals,' replied Aramis. 'Your Eminence will continue prime minister, and even the favourite of her Majesty, if she will grant to me and my friends what we ask for France and ourselves.'

'Trouble only about yourselves, Messieurs, and leave France to settle with me as she will be able to,' said Mazarin.

'No, no,' replied Aramis, 'there must be a treaty with the Frondeurs, and your Eminence will be pleased to draw it up and sign it in our presence, at the same time engaging to obtain for it the queen's ratification.'

'I can only answer for myself,' said Mazarin. 'Suppose her Majesty refuse?'

'Oh,' said d'Artagnan, 'Monseigneur knows very well that her Majesty refuses him nothing.'

'Here, Monseigneur,' said Aramis, 'this is the treaty proposed by the deputation from the Frondeurs. Will it please your Eminence to examine it?'

'I know it,' said Mazarin.

'Then sign it.'

'Reflect, Messieurs. A signature given under such circumstances as these would be regarded as obtained by violence.'

'Monseigneur, however, will be there to say it was given voluntarily.'

'But, in short, if I refuse?'

'Then, Monseigneur,' said d'Artagnan, 'your Eminence only is responsible for the consequences of your refusal.'

'Would you dare to raise your hands against me, a cardinal?'

'You have raised yours against the Musketeers of his Majesty.'

'The queen will avenge me, Messieurs!'

'I know nothing about it, though I don't think she would be wanting in the desire to do so; but we will go to Paris with your Eminence, and the Parisians are the people to defend us.'

'How anxious they must be just now at Rueil and St Germain,' said Aramis; 'asking what has become of the cardinal, minister, and favourite! How they must be searching for Monseigneur in all places! and if the Fronde knows of the disappearance of Monseigneur, how it must triumph!'

'It is frightful!' murmured Mazarin.

'Sign the treaty, then, Monseigneur,' said Aramis.

'But if I sign it and the queen refuse to ratify it?'

'I will undertake to go and see her Majesty,' said d'Artagnan, 'and obtain her signature.'

'Take care,' said Mazarin, 'that you get the reception at St Germain which you think you have the right to expect.'

'Ah, bah!' said d'Artagnan, 'I would arrange it so as to be welcomed; I know a means.'

'What?'

'I will take her Majesty the letter in which Monseigneur informs her of the complete exhaustion of the finances.'

'Then?' said Mazarin, getting pale.

'Then, when I see her Majesty at the height of her embarrassment, I will take her to Rueil, get her to enter the orangery, and point out to her a certain spring which makes an orange-box move.'

'That's enough, Monsieur, quite enough! Where is the treaty?'*

'Here it is,' said Aramis, presenting the pen to him.

'You see that we are generous,' said d'Artagnan, 'for we could do many things with such a secret.'

'Sign then,' said Aramis.

Mazarin got up, and walked about for a few seconds, rather in thought than as if beaten. Then stopping suddenly, 'And when I have signed, Messieurs, what will be my security?'

'My word of honour, Monsieur,' said Athos.

Mazarin started, turned towards the Comte de la Fère for a moment, scanned that loyal, noble countenance, and taking the pen, 'That's quite sufficient, Monsieur the Count,' said he, and he signed.

'And now, M. d'Artagnan,' he added, 'get ready to set off for St Germain, and take a letter from me to the queen.'

XCIV

HOW GREATER PROGRESS IS MADE WITH A PEN AND A THREAT THAN BY THE SWORD AND DEVOTEDNESS

D'ARTAGNAN knew his mythology; he knew that Opportunity has only a tuft of hair by which it can be seized, and he was not the man to let it pass without seizing it. He organized a prompt and sure mode of travelling by sending on in advance relays of horses to Chantilly, so that he could be in Paris in five or six hours. But before setting out he reflected that it was a strange intention, in a man of mind and experience, to leave behind him the certain and go towards the uncertain.

'In fact,' he said to himself, when about mounting his horse to fulfil his dangerous mission, 'Athos is a hero of romance for generosity; Porthos an excellent character, but easily influenced; Aramis a complete hieroglyphic, that I can never understand. What will these elements produce when I shall be no longer there to bind them together? Perhaps the deliverance of the cardinal. Now, this would be the ruin of our hopes, and these latter are at present the only recompense for the labours of twenty years, compared with which those of Hercules are but pigmy ones;' and he went to find Aramis.

'You are, my dear Chevalier d'Herblay,' he said to him, 'the Fronde incarnate. Therefore be on your guard against Athos, who does not take the trouble to attend to the affairs of anyone, not even his own. But especially look after Porthos, who to please the count, whom he regards as the Divine Being on earth, will help him to set Mazarin free, if the latter has only the shrewdness to weep or play upon their chivalry.'

Aramis smiled at once shrewdly and resolutely.

'Don't fear,' said he, 'I have my conditions to impose. I am working not for myself, but for others; my small ambition must lead to the advantage of those who have the right to it.'

'Good,' thought d'Artagnan, 'I can be at rest in respect to him.'

He shook Aramis's hand and went to find Porthos.

'Friend,' he said to him, 'you have worked so hard with me to build up our fortune, that just when on the point of reaping the fruit of our labours, it would be a ridiculous proceeding to allow yourself to be overruled by Aramis, with whose shrewdness you are acquainted; or by Athos, a noble, disinterested man, but one tired of the world. What should you say if one or other of our two friends proposed the release of Mazarin?'

'Why, I should say that we have had too much difficulty in taking him to let him go in that way.'

'Bravo, Porthos! and you are right, my friend; for with him you would lose all chance of your barony, which you now hold in your hands; without taking into account the fact that if once Mazarin escaped from here, he would have you hanged.'

'Good! you believe it?'

'I am sure of it.'

'Then I would rather kill him outright than let him escape.

'And you would be right. It is no matter, you understand, that when we have intended to arrange our own affairs, we have also settled those of the Frondeurs, who besides don't understand political questions as we do, being old soldiers.'

'Don't be afraid, dear friend,' said Porthos; 'I shall first see you off, then I shall return to station myself at the glass door of the cardinal's room, whence I shall see everything, and at the least suspicious movement I will put an end to him.'

'Bravo!' thought d'Artagnan, 'the cardinal will, I think, be well guarded from this side,' and he pressed the hand of the Lord of Pierrefonds, and went off to find Athos.

'My dear Athos,' said he, 'I am going. I have only one thing to say to you. You know Anne of Austria. M. de Mazarin's captivity is the sole guarantee of my life. If you let him go, I am a dead man.'

'Nothing less than this consideration, my dear d'Artagnan, makes me decide to do the business of jailer. I give you my word that you will find the cardinal where you leave him.'

'That gives me more reassurance than all royal signatures,' thought d'Artagnan. 'Now that I have Athos's word I can set out.'

D'Artagnan set off quite alone, with no other companion than his sword, and with a simple pass from Mazarin by which to gain admission to the queen.

Six hours after his departure from Pierrefonds, he was at St Germain.

The disappearance of Mazarin was still unknown; Anne of Austria alone knew of it, and concealed her anxiety from her greatest intimates. There had been found in d'Artagnan's and Porthos's room the two soldiers pinioned and gagged. These were at once set free, but they could tell nothing but what they knew, namely, how they had been caught, bound, and stripped. But what Porthos and d'Artagnan had done subsequently they knew no more than others in the château.

Bernouin knew a little more than the rest. He, not finding his master return when midnight struck, had taken upon himself to go into the orangery. The first door, barricaded by the furniture, had already raised some suspicions, but he had not desired to let anyone share them with him, and had patiently worked his way through all this encumbrance. In the corridor he had found all the doors open, as well as that of Athos's room, and the one opening into the park. When there it was easy to follow the footprints in the snow. These he found led up to the wall, on the other side of which he found the same track, then horses' footmarks, then those of a whole troop of cavalry, which went off in the direction of Enghien.* Thereupon he felt not the least doubt that the cardinal had been

carried off by the three prisoners, since they had disappeared
with him, and he had hastened to St Germain to apprise the
queen of his disappearance.

Anne of Austria had enjoined on him silence, and Bernouin
had scrupulously preserved it; only she had informed Monsieur
the Prince, to whom she had told all, and he had immediately
sent forth five or six hundred cavaliers, with orders to search
all the neighbourhood, and to bring to St Germain any suspected troop which might be going from Rueil, no matter in
what direction.

Now, as d'Artagnan was not a troop, being alone, and was
not escaping from Rueil, since he was going to St Germain,
no one troubled about him, and his journey was in no wise
hindered.

On entering the courtyard of the old château, the first
person whom our ambassador saw, was M. Bernouin in person,
who, standing at the door, was awaiting news of his vanished
master.

At the sight of d'Artagnan, who entered on horseback into
the courtyard of honour, Bernouin rubbed his eyes, and thought
he was mistaken. But d'Artagnan gave him a friendly nod,
dismounted, and throwing the bridle of his horse upon the arm
of a passing lackey, he advanced towards the *valet de chambre*,
with a smile upon his lips.

'M. d'Artagnan!' exclaimed the valet, like a man in a nightmare, who speaks in his sleep; 'M. d'Artagnan!'

'Himself, M. Bernouin.'

'And what have you come to do here?'

'To bring some news from M. de Mazarin, and the latest
too.'

'And what has become of him?'

'He is as well as you or I.'

'No harm then has happened to him?'

'Nothing whatsoever. He has simply felt the need of making
a tour in the Île-de-France, and has begged M. le Comte de
la Fère, M. du Vallon, and myself to accompany him. We were
too entirely his servants to refuse such a request. We set out
yesterday evening, and here I am.'

'Here you are?'

'His Eminence had something he wished said to her Majesty, something quite secret and confidential, which could only be entrusted to a reliable person, so that he has sent me to St Germain. So then, my dear M. Bernouin, if you wish to do something very pleasing to your master, inform her Majesty of my arrival, and tell her for what object.'

Whether he spoke seriously, or whether his words were only spoken in a bantering way, Bernouin knew not, yet it was clear that d'Artagnan was, under present circumstances, the only man who could relieve Anne of Austria's anxiety. Bernouin made no difficulty of going to inform her of this singular errand, and the queen gave an order for the instant admittance of M. d'Artagnan. He approached his sovereign with all the marks of the profoundest respect. When three yards off he knelt down, and presented the letter.

It was a simple letter, partly of introduction, partly of confidence. The queen read it thoroughly, recognized the cardinal's handwriting, although it was slightly shaky, and as the letter gave no account of what had happened, she demanded the details. D'Artagnan gave them in that ingenuous, simple manner which he could so well assume under certain circumstances.

The queen's astonishment kept increasing as she looked at him while he was speaking. She could not understand a man daring to form such a project, and still less that he should have the audacity to relate it to her, whose interest, and almost whose duty, it was to punish it.

'What, Monsieur,' exclaimed the queen, red with indignation, when d'Artagnan had finished his recital, 'do you dare to avow your crime, to tell me of your treason?'

'Pardon, Madame, but it seems to me, either I have badly explained myself, or your Majesty has misunderstood me; there is here neither crime nor treason. M. de Mazarin was keeping in prison M. du Vallon and myself, because we could not believe that he had sent us to England quietly to see the execution of King Charles, the brother-in-law of the late king, your husband, the spouse of Madame Henrietta, your sister and your guest; and we had done all we were able to save the life of the royal martyr. We were therefore certain, my friend and myself, that there was some error lying beneath, and that an explanation was needed between us and his Eminence. Now, that an explanation should bear fruit, it was necessary that it should be made tranquilly, far from the noise of importunate persons. Consequently we conveyed Monsieur the Cardinal to the château of my friend, and there we came to an explanation. Well, Madame, what we had foreseen really happened—there was a mistake. M. de Mazarin had thought that we had served General Cromwell in place of King Charles, which would have been a shameful act, reflecting from us to him, and from him on your Majesty; a cowardly act, which would have contaminated, at its source, the royalty of your illustrious son. Now, we have given proof to the contrary, and this proof we are ready to give to your Majesty yourself, by appealing to the august widow who weeps in the Louvre, where your royal munificence has given her an abode. This proof has so well satisfied him, that to mark his satisfaction he has sent me, as your Majesty can see, to talk with you of the amends naturally due to gentlemen so badly appreciated and wrongly persecuted.'

'I listen to you with astonishment, Monsieur,' said Anne of Austria. 'In fact, I have rarely seen a like excess of impudence.'

'Ah!' said d'Artagnan, 'here is your Majesty, who, in her turn, is deceived as to our intentions, as was M. de Mazarin.'

'You are in error, Monsieur,' said the queen, 'and I am deceived so little, that in ten minutes you shall be arrested, and in an hour I shall set out at the head of my army to deliver my minister.'

'I am sure that your Majesty would not do anything so imprudent. Before being delivered Monsieur the Cardinal would be dead, and his Eminence is so well assured of the truth of what I say, that he has, on the contrary, begged me, in case I should see your Majesty inclined to act thus, to do my utmost to get you to change your plans.'

'Well, then, I shall content myself with having you arrested.'

'Madame, my arrest is as well provided against as is the deliverance of the cardinal. If I do not return tomorrow at an hour agreed on, the next morning Monsieur the Cardinal will be taken to Paris.'

'It is evident, Monsieur, that you live far away from men and affairs; for otherwise you would know that Monsieur the Cardinal has been five or six times to Paris, and that he has seen there M. de Beaufort, M. de Bouillon, Monsieur the Coadjutor, M. d'Elbeuf, and not one of them had the idea of arresting him.'

'Pardon, Madame, I know all that. It is not to those he then visited that my friends would conduct Monsieur the Cardinal, seeing that these gentlemen make war on their own account, and that on granting what they ask, Monsieur the Cardinal would have the advantage over them; but to the parliament, whom one can bribe doubtless piecemeal, but whom M. de Mazarin himself is not rich enough to buy *en masse*.'

'I believe,' said Anne of Austria, looking hard at him, a look which was contemptuous in a woman, but which became terrible in a queen; 'I think you are threatening your king's mother.'

'Madame, I threaten because I am compelled. I raise my tone because it is necessary to place myself upon the level of events and of persons. Madame, as true as that my heart beats for you, believe truly that you have been the one idol of our life; that we have, as you know, risked it twenty times for your Majesty. Madame, will not your Majesty have pity on your servants, who have for twenty years languished in the shade, without allowing one breath of the holy solemn secrets which they have had the honour of sharing with you to escape from them? Look at me who am now speaking, Madame, whom you accuse of raising my voice and assuming a menacing tone. What am I?—a poor officer without fortune, without future, unless the regard of my queen, for which I have for so long been looking, be fixed for a moment upon me. Regard M. le Comte de la Fère, a type of nobility, a flower of chivalry; he has enlisted against his queen—or rather he has enlisted against her minister—and he has nothing to ask, as I believe. See M. du Vallon, that faithful friend, that arm of steel; he has for twenty years been waiting for the word from you which will make him, by his coat of arms, what he is in feeling and courage. Then look at your people who love you and yet suffer; whom you love, and who are yet in want of food; who ask nothing better than to bless you, and who yet——No, I am wrong, your people will never curse you, Madame. Well! say but one word, and all is done—peace will follow war; joy, tears; happiness, distress.'

Anne of Austria looked with a certain astonishment at the martial countenance of d'Artagnan, on which could be read a singular expression of tenderness.

'Why did you not say all this before acting?' said she.

'Because, Madame, the point was to prove to your Majesty one thing of which, it seems to me, you were in doubt—that we still have some valour, and that it is right that some value should be set on us.'

'And this valour will not retreat before anything, from what I see.'

'It has not in the past, why should it do less in the future?'

'And this valour in case of a refusal, and still more in case of a struggle, will go to the extent of taking me from the midst of my court to give me up to the Fronde, as you wish to do with my minister?'

'That never entered our minds, Madame,' said d'Artagnan, with that Gascon braggadacio which in him was only frankness; 'but if we had resolved upon it, we four, we should certainly do it.'

'I ought to know that,' muttered Anne of Austria; 'they are men of iron.'

'Alas! Madame, that proves to me that your Majesty has not had a just idea of us until today.'

'Well,' said Anne, 'but this idea, if I have it at last——'

'Your Majesty will do us justice. Doing this, you will no longer treat us as ordinary men. You will see in me an ambassador worthy of the high interests which he is entrusted to discuss with you.'

'Where is the treaty?'*

'Here it is.'

HOW GREATER PROGRESS IS MADE WITH A PEN AND A
THREAT, THAN BY THE SWORD AND DEVOTEDNESS
(*concluded*)

ANNE of Austria cast her eyes over the treaty which d'Artagnan presented to her.

'I see in it,' said she, 'only general conditions. The interests of M. de Conti, M. de Beaufort, M. de Bouillon, M. d'Elbeuf, and Monsieur the Coadjutor, are therein consulted. But yours?'

'We render ourselves justice, Madame, while placing ourselves in our true position. We thought that our names were not worthy to figure among such grand ones.'

'But you have not given up the intention, I presume, of stating your pretensions with the living voice?'

'I consider you to be a great and powerful queen, Madame, and that it would be unworthy of your greatness and power, not to worthily recompense the arms which will bring back his Eminence to St Germain.'

'That is my intention; come now, speak.'

'He who has negotiated the matter (I beg pardon for beginning with myself, but I must grant to myself the importance, not by any means assumed, but which has been given me) of the cardinal's redemption ought to be appointed head of the Guards, something like captain of the Musketeers.'

'That is the post of M. de Tréville.'

'The post is vacant, and has been for a year since M. de Tréville resigned.'

'But it is one of the chief military posts connected with the king's house.'

'M. de Tréville was a simple younger son of a Gascon family, like myself, Madame, and he held the post for twenty years.'

'You have an answer for everything, Monsieur.'

And she took from her desk a commission, which she filled up and signed.

'In truth, Madame,' said d'Artagnan, taking the document with a bow, 'this is a fine and noble reward; but this world's affairs are very unstable, and a man who should fall into disgrace with your Majesty might lose this post tomorrow.'

'What, then, do you want?' said the queen, blushing at being fathomed by this mind as subtle as her own.

'A hundred thousand francs for this poor captain of the Musketeers, payable on the day when his services shall no longer be agreeable to your Majesty.'

Anne hesitated.

'I may say that the Parisians,' resumed d'Artagnan, 'were offering the other day, by decree of parliament, six hundred thousand francs to anyone who would deliver the cardinal dead or alive; living, to hang him; dead, to bury him on the highway.'

'Well, it is reasonable, since you ask the queen for only the sixth part of what the parliament offered.' And she signed a promise for a hundred thousand francs.

'Next?' said she.

'Madame, my friend Vallon is rich, and has no desire for fortune; but I believe there was a question between him and M. de Mazarin, of raising his estate into a barony. It is even, so far as I can remember the matter, a thing promised.'

'A country fellow! They will laugh about it.'

'It may be, but I am sure of one thing, that those who laugh in his presence will not laugh a second time.'

'Let him have the barony,' said Anne of Austria, and she signed.

'Now, there remains the Chevalier, or l'Abbé d'Herblay, as your Majesty may prefer.'

'He wants to be a bishop?'

'Not at all, Madame, he wants something more easily given.'

'What is that?'

'That the king should deign to be godfather to Madame de Longueville's son.'

The queen smiled.

'M. de Longueville is of royal descent, Madame.'

'Yes,' said the queen; 'but her son?'*

'Her son, Madame—ought to be, since the husband of his mother is.'

'And your friend has nothing more to ask for Madame de Longueville?'

'No, Madame; for he presumes, that his Majesty the king, deigning to be the child's godfather, cannot make to the mother for the churching as a present less than five hundred thousand francs, continuing, be it understood, the government of Normandy to the father.'

'As to the latter, I think I can engage myself,' said the queen; 'but as regards the five hundred thousand francs, Monsieur the Cardinal does not cease repeating to me that there is no more money in the State coffers.'

'We will search for it together, Madame, if your Majesty will permit, and we shall find some.'

'Next?'

'That is all.'

'Have you not a fourth companion?'

'Indeed, yes, Madame; M. le Comte de la Fère.'

'What does he ask?'

'He asks for nothing.'

'Is there in the world a man, who, being able to ask, does not ask?'

'There is M. le Comte de la Fère, Madame; he is not a man.'

'What is he then?'

'M. le Comte de la Fère is a demigod.'

'Has he not a son, a young man, a relative or nephew, of whom Comminges has spoken to me as a brave fellow, and who brought the colours from Lens with M. de Châtillon?'

'He has, as your Majesty says, a ward, whose name is the Vicomte de Bragelonne.'

'If a regiment were given this young man, what would his guardian say?'

'Perhaps he would accept it.'

'Perhaps!'

'Yes, if your Majesty herself begged him to accept it.'

'You have truly said, Monsieur, that this is a singular man. Well, we will think it over, and ask him perhaps. Are you satisfied, Monsieur?'

'Yes, your Majesty. But there is one thing the queen has not signed.'

'What?'

'And this thing is the most important.'

'My acquiescence to the treaty?'

'Yes.'

'What is the good? I will sign the treaty tomorrow.'

'There is one thing that I think I can state to your Majesty; namely, that if your Majesty does not sign this document today, you will not find the time to sign it later on. Be pleased, then, I beg of you, to write at the foot of this programme, which is entirely in M. de Mazarin's handwriting, as you see, "I consent to ratify the treaty proposed by the Parisians." '

Anne was caught; she could not retreat; she signed. But she had scarcely done so before her pride broke forth like a tempest, and she began to weep. D'Artagnan started at the sight of these tears. Since that time queens have wept like simple women. The Gascon shook his head. These royal tears seemed to scorch his heart.

'Madame,' said he, kneeling down, 'look at this unfortunate gentleman who is at your feet; he prays of you to believe that at a single gesture from your Majesty everything would be possible to him. He has faith in himself, he has faith in his friends, he wishes also to have faith in his queen; and the proof that he fears nothing, that he speculates on nothing, is that he will bring back Mazarin to your Majesty without any conditions. Here, Madame, are your Majesty's sacred signatures; if you believe you ought to give me them you will do it. But from this moment they do not bind you any longer.'

And d'Artagnan, still on his knees, with a flaming look of pride and manly boldness, returned to Anne of Austria the whole of the papers which he had obtained one by one with so much trouble.

There are moments—for if all is not good, all is not bad in this world—there are moments, when in the driest and coldest hearts there springs up, watered by the tears of extreme emotion, a generous feeling, which calculation and pride smother, if another feeling does not seize it at its birth. Anne was in one of those moments. D'Artagnan, in yielding to his own emotion, in harmony with that of the queen, had accomplished a great diplomatic feat. He was therefore immediately

recompensed for his address, or disinterestedness, according as
one would wish to do honour to his wit or to his heart for the
motive of this action.

'You were right, Monsieur,' said Anne; 'I have not understood you. Here are these signed documents which I voluntarily
return you; go and bring me the cardinal as quickly as possible.'

'Madame,' said d'Artagnan, 'twenty years ago—for I have a
good memory—I had the honour of kissing one of those
beautiful hands behind a tapestry* of the Hôtel de Ville.'

'Here is the other,' said the queen; 'and that the left may
not be less liberal than the right'—she drew from her finger a
diamond ring very much like the former—'take and keep this
in memory of me.'

'Madame,' said d'Artagnan, getting up, 'I have only one
other desire, which is, that the first thing you ask of me may
be my life;' and with that manner which was quite charac-
teristic of him, he rose and went out.

'I have misunderstood those men,' said Anne of Austria,
while looking at d'Artagnan as he withdrew, 'and it is now too
late for me to make use of them; in one year the king will be
of age.'

Fifteen hours after, d'Artagnan and Porthos brought back
Mazarin to the queen, and received, the one his commission
of lieutenant-captain of the Musketeers, the other his title of
baron.

D'Artagnan bowed. Porthos kept turning over his diploma
in his hands, while looking at Mazarin.

'What is there besides?' asked the minister.

'It is, Monseigneur, that there was a promise of the title of
Chevalier of the Order* at the first promotion.'

'But,' said Mazarin, 'you know, Monsieur the Baron, that
one cannot be Chevalier of the Order without proofs of valour.'

'Oh!' said Porthos, 'it is not for myself, Monseigneur, for
whom I ask the blue ribbon.'

'For whom, then?' asked Mazarin.

'For my friend, M. le Comte de la Fère.'

'Oh, for him!' said the queen, 'that alters the case; he has
given sufficient proofs.'

'He shall have it?'

'He has it.'

The same day the treaty of Paris was signed, and it was published abroad that the cardinal had been privately engaged for three days in most carefully elaborating it.

Here is what each gained by this treaty:* M. de Conti had Damvilliers, and having proved his ability as general, he gained the privilege of remaining an officer and of not becoming a cardinal. Further, some words had been dropped of a marriage with a niece of Mazarin; these words had been received with favour by the Prince, to whom it mattered little with whom they should marry him, provided they married him.

The Duc de Beaufort* returned to court, reparation being made for all the injuries done to him. Full pardon was accorded to those who had aided him in his escape, the survival of the admiralship held by the Duc de Vendôme, his father, and an indemnity for his houses and châteaus caused to be burned by the parliament of Brittany.

The Duc de Bouillon* received domains of an equal value to his principality of Sedan, an indemnity for the eight years of non-enjoyment of that principality, and the title of Prince granted to him and his house.

M. le Duc de Longueville, the government of Pont-de-l'Arche,* five hundred thousand francs for his wife, and the honour of seeing his son held at the baptismal font by the young king and the young Henrietta of England.

The Duc d'Elbeuf* obtained the payment of certain sums due to his wife, one hundred thousand francs for the oldest son, and twenty-five thousand for each of the three others.

There was only the Coadjutor* who obtained nothing. It was promised to hold negotiations with the Pope for a cardinal's hat; but he knew what dependence could be placed on such promises, coming from the queen and Mazarin. Quite to the contrary of M. de Conti's case, he was compelled to remain a military man.

So, while all Paris was rejoicing at the approaching king's entry, Gondy alone, in the midst of the general joy, was in such bad humour, that he sent at once for two men, whom he had the practice of sending for, when in this frame of mind.

These two men were the Comte de Rochefort and the mendicant of St Eustache. They came with their usual punctuality, and the Coadjutor passed a part of the night with them.

XCVI

WHERE IT IS SHOWN THAT IT IS SOMETIMES MORE DIFFICULT FOR KINGS TO RETURN TO THEIR CAPITAL THAN TO LEAVE IT

WHILE d'Artagnan and Porthos were gone to conduct the cardinal to St Germain, Athos and Aramis, who had left them at St Denis, had reached Paris. Each of them had a visit to make.

In all haste Aramis went to the Hôtel de Ville, where Madame de Longueville was residing. At the first news of the peace the beautiful duchess uttered indignant cries. War made her queen, peace brought her abdication; she declared she would never sign the treaty, and that she wished eternal war. But when Aramis presented the peace in its true colours—that is, with all its advantages; when he pointed out the gain of the vice-royalty of Pont-de-l'Arche, that is, of the whole of Normandy, in exchange for the precarious government of Paris; when he made the five hundred thousand francs promised by the cardinal to resound in her ears; when he made the honour which would be done her, by the king holding her son at the baptismal font, glitter before her eyes, she no longer contended except from the practice which all beautiful women have of contesting, and only defended for the purpose of surrendering.

Aramis pretended to believe in the reality of her opposition, and did not wish to take away the merit in his own eyes of having won her over.

'Madame,' he said to her, 'you had a strong desire to maintain a good fight against Monsieur the Prince, your brother, who is the greatest general of the time; and when women of genius wish to do so they always succeed. You have succeeded; Monsieur the Prince is beaten, since he can no longer wage war. Now, win him over to your side. Separate him in a gentle manner from the queen, whom he does not like, and from M. de Mazarin, whom he detests. The Fronde is a comedy of which we have played as yet only the first act. Let us leave M. de Mazarin alone until the catastrophe; that is the day when Monsieur the Prince, thanks to you, will be at variance with the court.'

Madame de Longueville was persuaded. She was so fully convinced of the power of her beautiful eyes, this Duchess of the Fronde, that she did not doubt their influence, even over M. de Condé; and the scandalous chronicles of the time say that she did not presume too far.

Athos, on leaving Aramis at the Place Royale, had gone to visit Madame de Chevreuse.* This was another of the Fronde party to be won over, but this was more difficult than in the case of her young rival; no condition had been set down in the treaty in her favour. M. de Chevreuse was not nominated to any government; and if the queen agreed to be godmother it could be only to a grandchild. So, at the first mention of peace, Madame de Chevreuse frowned, and in spite of all Athos's logic to prove to her that a continuation of war was impossible, she insisted on a continuance of hostilities.

'Dear friend,' said Athos, 'permit me to tell you that everybody is tired of war; and with the exception of yourself and Monsieur the Coadjutor, perhaps, everybody desires peace. You will get yourself exiled, as in the time of King Louis XIII. Believe me, we have passed the period of successful intrigue; and your beautiful eyes are not destined to lose their brilliancy in bewailing Paris, where there will always be two queens so long as you are here.'

'Oh!' said the duchess, 'I cannot make war all alone, but I can be avenged on this ungrateful queen and her ambitious favourite, and—on the word of a duchess, I will be avenged.'

'Madame,' said Athos, 'I beg of you not to mar M. de Bragelonne's future; you see him launched forth; Monsieur the Prince desires his advancement—he is young. Let us leave a young king to become established. Alas! excuse my weakness, Madame; there comes a moment when a man lives and grows young again in his children.'

The duchess smiled, half-tenderly, half-ironically.

'Count, you are, I am much afraid, won over to the court. Have you not a blue ribbon in your pocket?'

'Yes, Madame, that of the Garter, which King Charles I gave me a few days before his death.'

The count spoke the truth; he knew nothing of Porthos's request.

'Come! one must become an old woman,' said the duchess, pensively.

Athos took her hand and kissed it. She sighed, looking at him.

'Count,' said she, 'that Bragelonne ought to be a charming residence. You are a man of taste; you must have there water, woods, flowers.'

She sighed again, and rested her charming head upon her hand, coquettishly curved, and always admirable in form and whiteness.

'Madame,' replied the count, 'what were you saying then just now? I have never seen you so young, never more beautiful.'

The duchess shook her head.

'M. de Bragelonne, does he remain in Paris?' said she.

'What do you think of it?' asked Athos.

'Leave him to me,' replied the duchess.

'No, Madame; if you have forgotten the story of Oedipus, I remember it.'*

'Truly, you are charming, Count, and I should like to live a month at Bragelonne.'

'Have you no fear of making many envious of me, Duchess?' replied Athos, gallantly.

'No, I would go incognito, Count, under the name of Marie Michon.'

'You are adorable, Madame.'

'But Raoul, don't keep him with you.'

'Why not?'

'Because he is in love.'

'He, a child!'

'It is also a child whom he loves.'

Athos became thoughtful.

'You are right, Duchess, this singular love for a child of seven years may render him one day very unhappy;* they are going to fight in Flanders, he shall go.'

'Then at his return you will send him to me; I will cuirass him against love.'

'Alas! Madame,' said Athos, 'today love is like war, and the cuirass has become useless in it.'

At that moment Raoul entered. He came to inform them that the Comte de Guiche, his friend, had told him that the ceremonial entry of the king, queen, and minister would take place the next day. Indeed, from early dawn the court was making preparations for leaving St Germain.* The queen had, overnight, sent for d'Artagnan.

'Monsieur,' she had said to him, 'they tell me that Paris is not quiet. I am afraid for the king. Place yourself at the right-hand door of the carriage.'

'Let your Majesty's mind be at rest; I will answer for the king.'

And, bowing to the queen, he went out. As he was leaving, Bernouin came to tell d'Artagnan that the cardinal awaited him on important matters. He went immediately to see the cardinal.

'Monsieur,' Mazarin said to him, 'there is talk of a riot in Paris. I shall be on the king's left, and as I shall be chiefly threatened, place yourself at the left-hand door.'

'Your Eminence may feel quite at your ease,' said d'Artagnan; 'not a hair of your head shall be injured.—The devil!' he ejaculated, when once in the anteroom, 'how am I to get out of this? I cannot at the same time be at both sides of the carriage. Ah, bah! I will guard the king, and Porthos the cardinal.'

This arrangement satisfied everyone—an unusual occurrence. The queen had confidence in d'Artagnan's courage, which she had tried; and the cardinal in Porthos's strength, which he had felt.

The cortège set out for Paris in an order settled beforehand. Guitaut and Comminges at the head of the Guards went first; then came the royal carriage, having d'Artagnan and Porthos at the doors; then the Musketeers, for the last twenty-two years friends of d'Artagnan, who had been their lieutenant for twenty years, their captain since the evening before.

On reaching the barrier, the carriage was welcomed by loud cries of 'Vive le Roi!' and 'Vive la Reine!' A few cries of 'Vive Mazarin!' were interspersed, but they met with no response. They were going to Notre-Dame where a Te Deum was to be chanted.

All Paris was in the streets. The Swiss Guards had been marshalled along the route; but as the distance was considerable, they were stationed from six to eight feet apart, and only one deep. The protection was therefore utterly insufficient, and from time to time, the barrier being broken through by a crush of people, they had the greatest difficulty possible in re-forming.

At each breach of the line, from quite friendly intentions, since it showed the desire the Parisians had to see their king and queen, of whose presence they had been deprived a whole year, Anne of Austria looked at d'Artagnan with anxiety, and the latter reassured her by a smile.

Mazarin, who had expended a thousand louis for the cries of 'Vive Mazarin,' and who had estimated the cries he had heard as not worth twenty pistoles, also looked at Porthos anxiously; but the gigantic bodyguard answered the look in his deep bass, 'All right, Monseigneur!' and Mazarin felt more and more at his ease.

On reaching the Palais-Royal, the crowd was still thicker; it had flowed towards this space from all the adjacent streets, and like a swelling stream, this wave of people came before the carriage, and rolled tumultuously in the Rue St Honoré.

When they came to the place, loud cries were heard of 'Long live their Majesties!' Mazarin leaned towards the door. Two or three cries of 'Vive le Cardinal!' saluted his appearance, but almost immediately hisses and hootings pitilessly drowned them. Mazarin turned pale, and leaned back in the carriage.

'Rabble!' muttered Porthos.

D'Artagnan said nothing, but twisted his moustache with a peculiar gesture, which showed that his fine Gascon good temper was beginning to change. Anne of Austria whispered low into the young king's ear, 'Make a gracious salutation, and address some words to M. d'Artagnan, my son.'

The young king leaned forward at the door. 'I have not yet wished you good day, M. d'Artagnan,' said he, 'and yet I knew you again well enough. You it was who was behind my bed-curtains, on the night when the Parisians wished to see me asleep.'

'And if the king permit me, I shall always be near him when there is any danger to be faced.'

'Monsieur,' said Mazarin to Porthos, 'what would you do if all this crowd fell upon us?'

'I should kill as many as I could of them, Monseigneur.'

'H'm!' said Mazarin; 'although you are brave and strong, you could not kill them all.'

'That is true,' said Porthos, rising up in his stirrups the better to learn the immensity of the crowd; 'that's true; there are many of them.'

'I think I should have preferred the other,' said Mazarin, and he threw himself back in the carriage.

The queen and her minister had reason for feeling some disquietude—especially the latter. The crowd, while preserving the appearance of respect and even of affection for the king and the regent, began to be tumultuously agitated. One heard dull rumours floating about, which, when arising from the waves, indicate a tempest, and which, when they skim along the multitude, presage an outbreak.

D'Artagnan turned towards the Musketeers, and with a look, not observable by the crowd, but readily understood by this brave corps, he gave an order. The rank of horses closed together, and a slight agitation took place among the men. At the barrier of the sergeants a halt had to be made; Comminges left the head of the escort, and came to the queen's carriage. The queen interrogated d'Artagnan with a look; he answered in a similar way.

'Go forward!' said the queen.

·Comminges went back to his post. With an effort the living barrier was violently broken through. Some mutterings arose in the crowd, which were this time addressed to the king as much as to the minister.

'Forward!' cried d'Artagnan aloud.

'Forward!' repeated Porthos.

But, as if the crowd had awaited this demonstration to break out, all the hostile feelings hitherto restrained, broke forth at once. The cries, 'Down with Mazarin! Death to the cardinal!' arose from all sides.

At the same time, by the Rues de Grenelle, St Honoré and Du Coq,* a double wave came pressing in, which broke the feeble line of Swiss Guards, and began to eddy even to the horses' legs. This fresh irruption was more dangerous than the others, as it was composed of armed men, and better armed too than the populace are on such occasions. It was clear that this last movement was the combination of some hostile leader, who had organized an attack.

These two masses were each led by a chief, one of whom seemed to belong to the honourable association of mendicants; the other could be easily recognized as being a gentleman. Both of them were acting as if on a plan previously concerted. There was a sharp shock, which was felt even in the royal carriage; then thousands of cries, making a huge din, arose, interspersed by two or three shots being fired.

'Musketeers, to the rescue!' exclaimed d'Artagnan.

The escort formed in two files; one passed to the right of the coach, the other to the left, thus aiding both d'Artagnan and Porthos.

Then a mêlée took place, all the more terrible because it had no object; all the more fatal because it could not be seen why nor for whom the fighting was going on.

XCVII

WHERE IT IS SHOWN THAT IT IS SOMETIMES MORE DIFFICULT FOR KINGS TO RETURN TO THEIR CAPITAL THAN TO LEAVE IT (*concluded*)

LIKE all the movements of a crowd, the shock was terrific; the Musketeers, few in number, thrown out of line, and unable in the midst of this multitude to make their horses move forward, began to be broken through. D'Artagnan had wished to have the carriage blinds closed, but the young king had stretched out his hand, saying, 'No, M. d'Artagnan, I wish to see.'

'If your Majesty wishes to see, well, let him look!' and turning round with that fury which made him so terrible, d'Artagnan dashed at the chief of the rioters, who, with pistol in one hand and sword in the other, tried to force a passage to the door while struggling with two musketeers.

'Back!' cried d'Artagnan, 'back!'

On hearing this, the man armed with pistol and sword raised his head; but he was already too late—d'Artagnan had given the fatal stroke; his sword had transfixed him.

'Ah, confound it!' cried d'Artagnan, trying too late to recall the stroke, 'what the devil did you come here for, Count?'

'To fulfil my destiny,' said Rochefort, falling on one knee. 'I have already recovered from three of your sword-thrusts, but I shall not from the fourth.'

'Count,' said d'Artagnan, with sincere emotion, 'I struck without knowing who it was. I hope you will not die with any feelings of hatred towards me.'

Rochefort gave d'Artagnan his hand, which he took. The count tried to speak, but an effusion of blood stopped his words; he grew rigid with the last convulsion, and expired.

'Off with you, mob!' cried d'Artagnan. 'Your leader is dead, and you have nothing more to do here.'

In fact, as though the Comte de Rochefort had been the soul of the attack, the crowd, which had followed and obeyed him, took to flight on seeing him fall. D'Artagnan charged with twenty musketeers up the Rue du Coq, and this part of the rioting mob disappeared like smoke, dispersing on the Place de St Germain-l'Auxerrois, and going towards the quays.

D'Artagnan returned to give help to Porthos if he needed it; but Porthos had on his part done his work as conscientiously as the former. The left side of the carriage was also cleared, and the blind of the door which Mazarin, less warlike than the king, had taken the precaution to let down, was now raised.

Porthos had a very melancholy look.

'What a devil of a look you have got, Porthos! What a strange appearance for one victorious.'

'But you yourself,' said Porthos, 'seem to me to be agitated.'

'I have reason to be. I have just killed an old friend.'

'Truly?' said Porthos. 'Who may it be?'

'That poor Comte de Rochefort.'

'Well, that's exactly what I did. I have just killed a man whose face is not unknown to me; unfortunately I struck him on the head, and in an instant he had his face covered with blood.'

'And did he say nothing when he dropped?'

'Oh, yes, he said "Ouf"!'

'I quite see,' said d'Artagnan, unable to keep from laughing, 'that if he said nothing else, that could not enlighten you much.'

'Well, Monsieur?' the queen asked.

'Madame,' said d'Artagnan, 'the route is quite clear, and your Majesty can continue your course.'

In fact the cortège reached Notre-Dame without other accident, under the porch of which all the clergy, the Coadjutor at their head, awaited the king, queen, and minister, for whose happy return a Te Deum was to be sung.

Towards the end of the service a street boy, looking scared, entered the cathedral, ran to the sacristy, put on his dress of choir boy, and making his way, thanks to the respected vestments which he assumed, through the crowd, he approached Bazin, who, clothed in his blue robe, and his staff ornamented with silver in his hand, held his place gravely in front of the Swiss at the entrance of the choir.

Bazin felt himself pulled by the sleeve. He lowered his eyes, previously raised heavenwards, and recognized Friquet.

'Well, stupid, what is the matter that you dare to disturb me in the exercise of my functions?' asked the beadle.

'The matter is, Bazin, that M. Maillard—you know him, the distributor of the holy water at St Eustache——'

'Yes, go on.'

'Well, he has received in the row a sword-cut in the head; it was that great giant who was there who gave it him.'

'In that case,' said Bazin, 'he must be very bad.'

'So bad that he is dying, and he wishes before he dies to confess to Monsieur the Coadjutor, who has power, so they say, to remit great sins.'

'And he supposes that Monsieur the Coadjutor will put himself out of the way for him?'

'Yes, certainly, for it seems that Monsieur the Coadjutor has promised him to do so.'

'And who told you so?'

'M. Maillard himself.'

'You have seen him, then?'

'Certainly; I was there when he fell.'

'And what were you doing there?'

'I kept crying, "Down with Mazarin! Death to the cardinal! To the gallows with the Italian!" Is not that what you have told me to cry out?'

'Hold your tongue, you young fool!' said Bazin, looking anxiously around him.

'So he told me, this poor M. Maillard! "Go and fetch Monsieur the Coadjutor, Friquet; and if you bring him to me I will make you my heir." Fancy now, Father Bazin, the heir of M. Maillard, the holy water giver of St Eustache! Hey, I shall have only to fold my arms! I should like to do him this service. What do you say?'

'I will go and tell Monsieur the Coadjutor,' said Bazin.

In fact, he slowly and respectfully approached the prelate, said something in his ear, to which the latter replied by an affirmative nod, and returning at the same pace he bade Friquet, 'Go and tell the dying man to have patience; Monseigneur will be with him in an hour.'

'Good,' said Friquet; 'now my fortune is made.'

'By the by,' said Bazin, 'where was he carried?'

'To the tower of St Jacques la Boucherie.'

And enchanted with the success of his embassy, Friquet, without taking off his choir dress, which gave him greater liberty of passing to and fro, went from the church, and with all the speed of which he was capable, took the route to St Jacques la Boucherie.

In fact, as soon as the Te Deum was over, the Coadjutor, as he had promised, and without even putting off his sacerdotal dress, took his way towards the old tower which he knew so well. He reached there in time. Although getting fainter and fainter, the wounded man was not yet dead. They opened the door of the room where the mendicant lay in the agonies of death. A moment after, Friquet came out holding in his hand a large leather bag, which he opened as soon as he was out of the room, and which to his great astonishment he found full of gold. The mendicant had kept his word, and had made him his heir.

'Ah, Mother Nanette,' exclaimed Friquet, choking; 'ah, Mother Nanette!'

He could not say more; but the strength which failed him for speaking remained for acting. He took a desperate jump towards the street; and like the Greek from Marathon* falling down in the market-place of Athens with the laurel in his hand, so Friquet reached the doorstep of Councillor Broussel, and fell when he got there, scattering on the floor the louis which were disgorged from his bag.

Mother Nanette began by picking up the louis, and then picked up Friquet.

During this time the cortège returned to the Palais-Royal.

'That M. d'Artagnan is a very valiant man, Mother,' said the young king.

'Yes, my son, and one who did very great services for your father. Treat him with consideration for the future.'

'Monsieur the Captain,' said the king to d'Artagnan, while alighting from his carriage, 'Madame the Queen desires me to invite you to dinner today, you and your friend, the Baron du Vallon.'

It was a great honour for d'Artagnan and Porthos, and accordingly the latter was transported with joy. Nevertheless, during the whole of the repast the worthy gentleman seemed quite preoccupied.

'Why, what was the matter with you, Baron?' said d'Artagnan to him when going down the Palais-Royal staircase; 'you had quite an anxious air during dinner.'

'I was trying,' said Porthos, 'to recall where I had seen that mendicant whom I must have killed.'

'And you could not succeed?'

'No.'

'Well, try and find out, my friend; and when you have, you will tell me, will you not?'

'Yes, of course!' said Porthos.

ON returning to their hotel the two friends found a letter from Athos, appointing a meeting at the Charlemagne Hotel for the morning of the next day.

Both went to bed early, but neither could sleep. They had not gained the object of their wishes without the effect being to drive away sleep at least for the first night.

Accordingly, the next morning at the hour named they called on Athos. They found him and Aramis in travelling dress.

'Well,' said Porthos, 'we are all then about to part. I have also made my preparations this morning.'

'Oh, yes,' said Aramis, 'there is nothing more to be done in Paris now that there is no Fronde.* Madame de Longueville has invited me to go and spend a few days in Normandy, and has commissioned me, while her child's baptism takes place, to go and secure lodgings for her in Rouen. I am going for this purpose; then, if there is nothing new, I shall return and bury myself in my convent at Noisy-le-Sec.'

'I,' said Athos, 'shall return to Bragelonne. You know, my dear d'Artagnan, that I am nothing more than a simple country gentleman. Raoul has no other fortune than mine, poor child, and I must watch over it, since I am in some sort only a life trustee.'

'And what shall you do with Raoul?'

'I shall leave him with you, my friend. There is going to be a campaign in Flanders; you will take him with you; I am afraid that his stay at Blois is only dangerous to him. Take him with you, and teach him to be brave and upright like yourself.'

'And I,' said d'Artagnan, 'though I shall no longer have you, shall at least have him, the dear fair face; and although he is but a youth, as your soul lives entirely again in him, dear Athos, I shall always believe you to be near me, accompanying and sustaining me.'

The four friends embraced with tears in their eyes. Then they separated, without knowing whether they should ever meet again.

D'Artagnan returned to Rue Tiquetonne with Porthos, who was continually pondering and trying to discover who the man was whom he had killed.

On reaching the Hôtel de la Chevrette they found the baron's equipage ready, and Mousqueton in the saddle.

'I say, d'Artagnan,' said Porthos, 'leave the sword and come with me to Pierrefonds, or Bracieux, or Le Vallon; we will grow old together in talking of our companions.'

'No, no,' said d'Artagnan. 'Hang it! the campaign is beginning, and I want to be in it; I hope to win something.'

'And what do you hope to become then?'

'Marshal of France,* by Jove!'

'Ah, ah!' said Porthos, looking at d'Artagnan, whose Gasconnades he had never been able to understand entirely.

'Come with me, Porthos; I will make you a duke.'

'No,' said Porthos. 'Mouston has no longer a liking for war. Besides, they have arranged a triumphal entry at my place, which will make all my neighbours die of envy.'

'To that I have nothing to answer,' said d'Artagnan, who knew the vanity of the new baron. '*Au revoir*, then, my friend.'

'*Au revoir*, dear captain,' said Porthos. 'You know that when you would like to come and see me you will always be welcome in my barony.'

'Yes,' said d'Artagnan, 'on my return from the campaign I will come.'

'The equipage of Monsieur the Baron awaits him,' said Mousqueton, and the two friends separated after shaking hands.

'D'Artagnan stood on the doorstep, following Porthos with melancholy look as he went away. But at the end of a few yards Porthos stopped short, hit his forehead, and returned.

'I recollect,' said he.

'What?' asked d'Artagnan.

'Who that mendicant was that I killed.'

'Ah, really! who is it?'

'Why, that rascal Bonacieux;'* and Porthos, delighted with thus relieving his mind, rejoined Mousqueton, and soon disappeared round the corner of the street.

D'Artagnan remained for a moment immovable and pensive; then turning round, he saw the fair Madeleine, who, perplexed at the new grandeur of d'Artagnan, was standing at the door.

'Madeleine,' said the Gascon, 'give me the apartment on the first floor; I am obliged to keep up my dignity now that I am captain of the Musketeers. But always keep my room on the fifth floor; one never knows what may happen.'

LIST OF HISTORICAL CHARACTERS

D'ALBRET: César-Phébus d'Albret (1614–76) became Marshal of France in 1654.

D'ANJOU: Philippe (1640–1701), Duc d'Anjou, second son of Louis XIII and Anne of Austria, and brother to Louis XIV.

ANNE OF AUSTRIA: Anne of Austria (1601–66), daughter of Philip III of Spain and a member of the Spanish Habsburg family, married Louis XIII in 1615. She remained aloof from the intrigues of Marie de' Medici, the Queen Regent, but actively opposed Richelieu, who set out to destroy Austro-Spanish influence on French policy. She was loyally supported by her 'Spanish entourage', the members of which were steadily eliminated by Richelieu. After Louis's death in 1643, she ruled as Regent during the minority of Louis XIV, working closely with Mazarin, who was almost certainly her lover and possibly her husband. With his help, she defended the interests of the crown during both the 'parliamentary' and 'aristocratic' phases of the Fronde (1648–53). She died of breast cancer in 1666.

ARCHDUKE: 1. Léopold of Austria (d. 1632). 2. Archduke Leopold-William (son of the Emperor Ferdinand II), Governor of the Spanish Netherlands between 1647 and 1656.

D'AUBIGNÉ: Agrippa d'Aubigné (1552–1630), soldier and diplomat in the Protestant cause, historian, and poet. Father of Françoise, the future Madame de Maintenon.

D'AUBIGNÉ: Françoise d'Aubigné (1635–1719) married Scarron in 1652, and subsequently, as Madame de Maintenon, became governess to the royal children and also to the children of Madame de Montespan, the royal mistress. After the death of Queen Henrietta Maria, she married Louis XIV in a secret ceremony in 1684. A woman of austere piety, she thereafter exercised considerable influence over the King.

BACHAUMONT: François Le Coigneux (1624–1702), *sieur* de Bachaumont, a councillor of the Paris Parlement said by some to have first used the words *fronde* and *frondeur*.

BASSOMPIERRE: François de Bassompierre (1579–1646), Marshal of France. For intriguing against Richelieu, he was consigned to the Bastille in 1631, where he remained until the cardinal's death in 1632.

BEAUFORT: François de Vendôme (1616–69), Duc de Beaufort, was the grandson of Henri IV and his royal mistress Gabrielle d'Estrées. He had been gaoled at Vincennes in 1643 for plotting with Madame de Chevreuse against Mazarin. He escaped on Whit Sunday 1648, and for his role in the defence of Paris against the Parlement's forces under Condé he was acknowledged by the people as 'King of Les Halles'. In 1653, he made his peace with the King and later served with honour in the Mediterranean where he died, at the siege of Candia.

BEAUMONT: Mademoiselle de Beaumont (d. 1661) was the daughter of Christophe de Harlay, Comte de Beaumont.

BEAUTIN: see Beautru.

BEAUTRU: Nicolas Beautru (d. 1661), Comte de Nogent-Beautin and Captain of Guards, was famed for his wit.

BEAUVAIS: Catherine-Henriette de Bellier (1608–75), wife of Pierre de Beauvais, first lady-in-waiting to the Queen and, it was said, the first mistress of Louis XIV.

BECK: Jean, Baron de Beck, was a career soldier who died of wounds received at Lens in 1648.

BELLEGARDE: Roger de Saint-Lary et de Termes (1562–1646), Duc de Bellegarde, Governor of Burgundy.

BELLERAY: Jean de Choisy (d. 1660), *seigneur* de Belleray.

BELLIÈVRE: see Plessis-Bellière.

BENSERADE: Isaac de Benserade (1613–91), poet and dramatist. During the Fronde, he was involved in a dispute which centred upon the superiority or otherwise of his sonnet on Job to Voiture's sonnet to Uranie.

BENTIVOGLIO: Guido Bentivoglio (1579–1644) was made cardinal in 1621. He was one of Mazarin's early patrons in the diplomatic service of Rome.

BÉRINGHEN: Henry de Béringhen (1603–92) was first *valet de chambre* to the King before becoming the royal equerry.

BERNOUIN: first *valet de chambre* to Mazarin.

BLANCMESNIL: René Potier de Blancmesnil (d. 1680), senior member of the Grand Chamber of the Paris Parlement.

BLOT: Claude de Chauvigny (*c.*1605–55), Baron de Blot l'Église. Attached to the entourage of Gaston d'Orléans, he was the author of innumerable satirical and often scabrous songs.

BOUILLON: Frédéric-Maurice de la Tour d'Auvergne (1605–52), Duc de Bouillon.

BRADSHAW: John Bradshaw (1602–59), a lawyer, was appointed president of High Court for the trial of Charles I, for which he was richly rewarded with State offices. His 'stiff republicanism' subsequently brought him into conflict with Cromwell. He was buried in Westminster Abbey but, on the Restoration, his body was disinterred and hung beside Cromwell's.

BRÉGIS: Charlotte Saumaize de Chazan (b.1618) was named one of Anne's ladies-in-waiting on her marriage to the Comte de Brégis in 1637.

BRIENNE: Louis-Henri Loménie (1635–98), Comte de Brienne. His *Mémoires*, first published in 1720 and reissued in 1828 and 1838, were one of Dumas's sources of information on the background to the period.

BRISSAC: Louis de Cossé (d.1661), Duc de Brissac.

BROUSSEL: Pierre Broussel (*c*.1576–?1654), led the Paris Parlement's opposition to the Queen's party in 1648. His arrest on 26 August was the spark which ignited the 'Day of the Barricades': see Chapter XLVI.

BUCKINGHAM: George Villiers (1592–1628), first Duke of Buckingham. *The Three Musketeers* chronicles, in exaggeratedly romantic terms, the course of the impossible, requited love he felt for Anne of Austria.

CATHERINE DE' MEDICI: Catherine de' Medici (1519–89), Queen of Henri II.

CHALAIS: Henri de Talleyrand (1599–1626), Comte de Chalais, plotted with Madame de Chevreuse against the life of Richelieu. He failed and in August 1626 was beheaded not by the regular executioner but by an unskilled volunteer who required thirty attempts to complete his task.

CHAPELAIN: Jean Chapelain (1595–1674), poet and champion of classical values, was better known for his conversation than for his writings. When the first twelve cantos of his epic on Joan of Arc appeared in 1656 after twenty years' labour, it was said that the mountain had brought forth a mouse.

CHARLES I: Charles Stuart (1600–49), King of England, was executed at Whitehall on 30 January 1649.

CHÂTILLON: Gaspard de Coligny (1620–49), Duc de Chatillon, died at the battle of Charenton in 1649.

CHAVIGNY: Léon Le Bouthilier (1608–52), Comte de Chavigny, was a Minister of State and member of the Regency Council. He had been appointed Governor of the Château de Vincennes by Richelieu.

CHEVREUSE: Claude de Lorraine (1578–1657), Duc de Chevreuse.

CHEVREUSE: Marie-Aimé de Rohan-Bazon (1600–79), widow of the Duc de Luynes, married the Duc de Chevreuse in 1622. She was one of the Queen's 'frivolous' friends and ran through many lovers most of whom, like Chalais (q.v.), she involved in her plots to unseat Richelieu. Louis XIII exiled her but she regularly returned to court where she continued her intrigues. She abetted Buckingham's plans to invade France in 1628 and was again banished, first to Poitou and later to the château-prison at Loches, 40 km. south of Tours. In 1637, she escaped and fled to Spain and thence to England, where she was caught up in the English Civil War and briefly imprisoned on the Isle of Wight. She lived in Belgium until she was allowed to return to France in 1643 by Mazarin, whom she opposed. She was again exiled for her intrigues, and eventually settled in Brussels, where she continued to side with the enemies of Mazarin. She returned to France after the Amnesty of Reuil on 12 April 1649. She continued to be active throughout the Fronde, but finally withdrew from public life.

CINQ-MARS: Henri Coeffier d'Effiat, Marquis de Cinq-Mars, executed in 1642 for conspiring against Richelieu with Madame de Chevreuse.

COADJUTOR: see Retz.

COISLIN: Armand du Camboust (1635–1702), Duc de Coislin, was brought up by his grandfather, the Chancelier Séguier. He was one of the 'enfants d'honneur' chosen to be companions for the young King.

COLIGNY: Maurice, Comte de Coligny (d. 1644) was fatally wounded in a duel fought on 23 May 1644 in the Place Royale with the Duc de Guise.

COLIGNY: Gaspard, brother of Maurice. See Châtillon.

COMMINGES: Gaston de Comminges (1613–70), nephew of Guitaut (q.v.) whom he succeeded as Captain of the Queen's Guard. He arrested the Duc de Beaufort in 1643. A loyal supporter of Anne of Austria, he later became ambassador to Portugal and London.

CONCINI: Concino Concini, a Florentine adventurer who, abetted by his wife, Laure Galigaï, acquired great power through his influence over Marie de' Medici, wife of Henri IV and Regent of France during the minority of Louis XIII, who made him Maréchal d'Ancre. He died on 24 April 1617 when resisting the King's order for his arrest. He was shot on the Pont du Louvre by the Marquis de Vitry (q.v.), Captain of the King's Guard. After Concini's death, Louis XIII assumed royal power and successfully resisted the Medicis' challenge to his authority.

CONDÉ: Claire-Clémence de Maille-Brézé (*c.* 1620–94), Princesse de Condé, wife of 'Monsieur le Prince'.

CONDÉ: Louis de Bourbon (1621–86), Duc d'Enghien, became Prince de Condé on the death of his father in 1646. Known as 'Monsieur le Prince', he fought with valour at the battles of Rocroy (1643), Nordlingen (1644), and Lens (August 1648). In the autumn of 1648, he threw his military skills behind the royal cause. Believing he had been insufficiently rewarded for his efforts, he reacted with such arrogance that he alienated both the Queen and Mazarin. In 1650, he was jailed at Vincennes. In 1651, the political situation had changed and Mazarin was forced to release him. He thereupon raised an army to rescue the young King from his advisers. He failed, refused to accept the peace of 1653, went over to Spain, and took part in all the campaigns against France. He was reinstated in 1659, and retired to his estate at Chantilly. Recalled to service in 1668, he fought his last battle in 1674.

CONTI: Armand de Bourbon (1629–66), Prince de Conti, brother of Condé and of the Duchesse de Longueville. He led the anti-royalist forces during the first Fronde.

DESPRÉAUX: Gilles Despréaux (1631–69), author of satirical and often slanderous verses and brother of Nicolas Boileau-Despréaux (1636–1711)—poet, arbiter of classical taste, and a founder of French literary criticism—whom he heartily detested.

D'ELBEUF: Charles de Lorraine (1596–1657), Prince d'Harcourt and Duc d'Elbeuf, Beaufort's uncle.

D'ÉMERY: Michel Particelli, *sieur* d'Émery (1595–1660), was appointed Controller General of Finances in 1647. Mazarin made him a scapegoat and ordered his banishment in July 1648. Louis's misgivings about Particelli stem from a misunderstanding: it was not Michel who was financially suspect but his brother Jean, who had been found guilty of embezzlement in 1620.

D'ERLACH: Jean-Louis, Baron d'Erlach (1595–1650), commander of the army of the Duc de Weimar.

DES ESSARTS: François de Guillon, *sieur* des Essarts, Captain of the King's Guards, died at the siege of La Motte in 1645.

DIANE DE POITIERS: Diane de Poitiers (1499–1566) was the mistress of Henri II.

FAIRFAX: Sir Thomas, afterwards Lord Fairfax (1612–71), was appointed supreme commander of the parliamentary forces in 1645, though he was dominated by Cromwell, who in 1648 became the effective military leader of the parliamentary cause. In 1650, Fairfax refused to march against the Scots, and Cromwell replaced him as commander-in-chief. Fairfax withdrew from public life and worked for the restoration of the monarchy.

DE FARGIS: Magdeleine de Silly (d. 1639), Comtesse du Fargis, was close to the Queen in the 1620s. For her loyalty, she was banished from court by Richelieu in 1631.

FELTON: John Felton (1595–1628), the Puritan zealot who murdered the Duke of Buckingham at Portsmouth in 1628. In Dumas's version of events (*The Three Musketeers*, chapter 59), Felton was goaded to his act by Milady.

FIESQUE: Charles-Léon, Comte de Fiesque, celebrated for a duel fought in 1638, and one of the anti-royalist faction in January 1649.

FLAMMARENS: Antoine-Agesilan de Grossolles (d. 1652), Marquis de Flammarens.

FONTRAILLES: Louis d'Astarac (d. 1677), Vicomte de Fontrailles, libertine, atheist, and intriguer.

FUENSALDAGNA: Alphonse Perez de Vivero, Comte de Fuensaldagna (d. 1661), Captain-General of the Spanish Netherlands at the time of the battle of Lens (1648).

GASSION: Jean, Comte de Gassion (1609–47), Marshal of France.

GONDI: see Retz.

GOUJON: Jean Goujon (1510–c.1567), sculptor of the Fontaine des Innocents in Paris. He also worked on the rood-screen of the church of Saint-Germain-l'Auxerrois and executed decorative work in the Louvre palace.

GRAMONT: Antoine de Gramont (1604–78), Comte de Guiche, later Duc de Gramont, was made Marshal of France in 1641. He was the father of Raoul's friend, the Comte de Guiche (q.v.).

GRANDIER: Urbain Grandier (1590–1634), a priest, was sent to the stake at Loudun for witchcraft. Like others since, Dumas was fascinated by Grandier and wrote a play on the subject (1850).

GRASSE: Antoine Godeau (1605–72), Bishop of Grasse.

'GREAT DEMOISELLE': see d'Orléans, Anne-Marie-Louise.

GUÉBRIANT: Jean-Baptiste de Budes (1602–43), Comte de Gué-briant and Marshal of France, died at the battle of Rocroy in 1643.

GUÉMENÉE: Anne de Rohan (1604–85), Princesse de Guémenée, sister-in-law to Madame de Chevreuse.

GUICHE: Armand de Gramont (1637–73), Comte de Guiche. See Gramont.

GUISE: Henri de Lorraine (1614–64), Duc de Guise.

GUITAUT: François de Guitaut, (1581–1663) Comte de Commin-ges, Captain of Anne of Austria's Guards, and uncle of Comminges (q.v.).

D'HARCOURT: Henri de Lorraine (1601–66), Comte d'Harcourt, known as 'le Gros'.

HARRISON: Thomas Harrison (1606–60) was a more uncompromi-sing opponent of royalism than Cromwell. He commanded the guard which escorted Charles to London, sat among his judges, and put his name to the death warrant. When the monarchy was restored in 1660, he refused to flee and was executed for regicide.

HAUTEFORT: Marie de Hautefort (1616–91), a favourite of Louis XIII and an ally of Anne of Austria. She was dismissed, temporarily, from court in 1639.

HENRI IV: Henri IV(1553–1610), grandfather of Louis XIV, had revived French fortunes abroad and at home ended the religious strife of the sixteenth century.

HENRIETTA OF ENGLAND: Henrietta Maria (1609–69), younger sister of Louis XIII, had married Charles of England by proxy in 1625. The marriage had been arranged by Buckingham. After the Rebellion, she parted from Charles in 1644 and escaped to France. By 1648, she was living in the Louvre in reduced circumstances, Mazarin not having paid her allowance for six months.

JOYCE: Cornet George Joyce (*fl.* 1647) was a tailor before becoming a general in Cromwell's new model army. On 3 June 1647 he abducted Charles I from Holmby House in Northamptonshire and escorted him to Newark.

JUXON: William Juxon (1582–1663) had been Bishop of London since 1633. He ministered to the King in his last moments at Whitehall and it was to him that Charles spoke the word: 'Remember!'

LAIGUES: Geoffroy (1614–74), Marquis de Laigues, familiar of Madame de Chevreuse.

LA MOTHE: Philippe de la Mothe-Houdancourt (1605–57), Maréchal de la Mothe.

LAPORTE: Pierre Laporte (1603–80) entered the service of Anne of Austria in 1621. He enabled her to correspond with the Spanish court and for his 'treasons' was imprisoned by Richelieu in 1637. He returned to favour when Anne became Regent in 1643 and was made Louis XIV's *valet de chambre* in 1645, a position which he used to undermine the influence of Mazarin.

LA RAMÉE: according to Guy Joli (*Mémoires* (Geneva, 1779), i. 13), La Ramée, who features in most accounts of the escape of Beaufort, was Governor of the château-prison of Vincennes. The Governor was in fact the largely absentee Chavigny (q.v.) and La Ramée was his deputy. The Christian names given to him on p. 172 are of Dumas's invention.

LA RIVIÉRE: Louis Barbier (1595–1660), known as the Abbé de La Rivière.

LA ROCHEFOUCAULD: see Marcillac.

LAUZUN: Antoine Nompar de Caumont (1632–1723), Duc de Lauzun, Marshal of France.

LA VALLIÈRE: Françoise-Louise de la Baume Le Blanc (1644–1710), known as the Duchesse de La Vallière, was mistress of Louis XIV between 1661 and 1667 and bore him four children. No great beauty and slightly lame, she attracted Louis by the sweetness of her face and manners. After being replaced by Madame de Montespan, she retired from court life in 1670 and took the veil in 1674.

LEVEN: Alexander Leslie, created Earl of Leven in 1640, was commander of the Scots forces which finally deserted Charles's cause in 1646.

LILLEBONNE: François-Marie de Lorraine-Elbeuf, Comte de Lillebonne, younger brother of the Comte d'Harcourt.

LONGUEVILLE: Anne-Geneviève de Bourbon Condé (1619–79), Duchesse de Longueville. She was the sister of Condé ('Monsieur le Prince') and the Prince de Conti, and mistress of La Rochefoucauld. During the first Fronde, she played a crucial role in supporting Retz, to whom she was related, and in persuading Conti to join the cause. Early in 1650, she attempted unsuccessfully to raise Normandy against Mazarin and was forced to flee. Pardoned under the terms of the general amnesty of 1653, she subsequently played a reduced role in public life.

LOUIS XIII: Louis de Bourbon (1601–43), 'Louis the Just'. He was crowned in 1610 on the assassination of his father, Henri IV. After resisting the revolt led by his mother the Regent, Marie de' Medici, Louis appointed Richelieu as his prime minister in 1624.

LOUIS XIV: Louis de Bourbon (1638–1715), the Sun King.

LOUVIÈRES: Jérôme Broussel, *seigneur* de Louvières, son of Pierre Broussel (q.v.). When Le Clerc du Tremblay capitulated to the *frondeurs* in January 1649, he was replaced as Governor of the Bastille by Pierre Broussel, who delegated his functions to Jérôme.

LUYNES: Louis-Charles d'Albert (1620–90), Duc de Luynes, son of Madame de Chevreuse by her first marriage.

MAINTENON, MADAME DE: see d'Aubigné, Françoise.

MARCILLAC: François (1613–80), Prince de Marcillac, later Duc de La Rochefoucauld, author of the cynical *Maximes* (1665) and of *Memoirs* (first published 1662) on which Dumas drew when researching the period. He chivalrously helped Madame de Chevreuse to escape from France in 1637. The Duchesse de Longueville was his mistress between 1646 and 1652.

MARIE DE' MEDICI: Marie de' Medici (1573–1642), mother of Louis XIII. As Regent, she opposed her son's assumption of royal power in 1617 and her supporters attempted to start a civil war: to the disappointment of her followers, she submitted to Louis in 1619 and rejoined the court. When she failed to win Richelieu to her cause, she tried to undermine his influence with the King, was imprisoned at Compiègne, but escaped to Brussels in 1631. In 1641, she was in London but finally settled in Cologne in circumstances so reduced that she died, so it was said, in a hayloft.

MAZARIN: the Italian-born Giulio Mazarini (1602–61), a soldier and diplomat in the service of the Pope who sent him to France to negotiate with Richelieu in 1630. Richelieu retained him to defend French interests in Italy. He was sent to the French court as papal legate in 1634, became Richelieu's protégé and in 1639, on entering the service of the King of France, was naturalized French. In 1641 he was made cardinal through the influence of Richelieu who, shortly before his death, recommended him as his successor. Though personally unpopular, he made himself indispensable to the Queen Regent. Mazarin was her lover and may have been secretly married to her. His power aroused the envy of the nobility, his demands for increased taxes alienated the middle class, and his foreign origins were a focus for popular resentment. He was generally considered to be excessively mean. His diplomatic skills were very great. He secured the alliance of Cromwell and furthered French interests in southern Germany by the Treaty of Westphalia which ended the Thirty Years War in 1648. At home, he survived the Fronde, and so strengthened the French throne that Louis XIV's creation of the modern French nation owed a great deal to him.

MEILLERAIE: Charles de la Porte (1602–64), Duc de la Meilleraie, cousin to Richelieu, was made Marshal of France in 1639.

MÉNAGE: Gilles Ménage (1613–92), scholar, man of letters, and an habitué of the Hôtel de Rambouillet.

MICHON, MARIE: the name by which Madame de Chevreuse is known in *The Three Musketeers*.

MOCQUET: Jean Mocquet (1575–1617), traveller and explorer, published his *Voyages en Afrique, Asie, Indes Orientales et Occidentales* (6 vols.) in 1617. A new edition had appeared in 1831.

MOLÉ: Mathieu Molé (1584–1656), a leading member of the Paris Parlement, and a voice of moderation.

'MONSIEUR': that is, Gaston d'Orléans.

'MONSIEUR LE PRINCE': that is, Condé.

MONTBAZON: Marie d'Avaugour de Bretagne (1612–57), Duchesse de Montbazon, second wife of the Duc de Montbazon, the father of Madame de Chevreuse. Marie de Montbazon was Beaufort's mistress.

MONTBAZON: Hercule de Rohan (1568–1654), Duc de Montbazon, was the father of Madame de Chevreuse.

MONTMORENCY: Henri, Duc de Montmorency, was executed for treason in 1632.

MONTRÉSOR: Claude de Bourdeille (*c*.1608–63), Comte de Montrésor.

MONTROSE: James Graham (1612–50), Marquis of Montrose, at first an opponent of the King but by June 1640 an ardent royalist. In 1644, he rallied the clans and his year-long Scottish campaign was marked by six victories of which Dumas mentions four: Inverlochy (February 1645), Auldearn (May), Alford (July), and Kilsyth (August). He was defeated by Leslie at Philiphaugh in September 1645 and, after failing to raise the Highlands, escaped to Norway in 1646 where he still was when he learned of the execution of the King.

MOTTEVILLE: Françoise Bertaut (1621–89) married Nicolas Langlois, *seigneur* de Motteville in 1639, by which time she was a trusted member of the Queen's 'Spanish' entourage. Her *Memoirs*, first published in 1723 and reprinted in 1824 and 1838, were extensively used by Dumas for the background to the period.

NEUFVILLE: Nicolas de Neufville (1597–1685), Duc de Villeroy, Marshal of France since 1646, was the King's Governor.

NINON DE L'ENCLOS: Ninon de l'Enclos (1620–1705) was one of the most celebrated odalisques of the century.

NOIRMOUTIERS: Louis de la Trémoille (1612–66), Marquis de Noirmoutiers.

ORLÉANS: Anne-Marie-Louise d'Orléans (1627–93), Duchesse de Montpensier, daughter of Gaston d'Orléans, known as 'la Grande Mademoiselle'. In 1681 she was secretly married to the Duc de Lauzun.

ORLÉANS: Gaston-Jean-Baptiste de France, Duc d'Orléans (1608–60), younger brother of Louis XIII, known as 'Monsieur', had regularly participated in the intrigues mounted against Richelieu. On the accession of Louis XIV in 1643, he was appointed Lieutenant-Governor of the Kingdom. He supported Anne of Austria during the first Fronde but after the second was exiled to Blois in 1652. In *The Man in the Iron Mask* (World's Classics edition, p. 190), Aramis judged him to be 'void of courage and honesty', a verdict echoed by contemporaries like Retz, who remarked that Orléans 'had everything a gentleman should have, except courage'.

ORLÉANS: Henri d'Orléans (1595–1663) was the husband of Madame de Longueville, Condé's sister.

ORLÉANS: Marguerite de Lorraine (1613–72), Duchesse d'Orléans, wife of Gaston.

ORNANO: Jean-Baptiste d'Ornano (1583–1626), Comte de Montlaur. For supporting Spanish interests against Richelieu, he was imprisoned at Vincennes, where he died.

PAULET: Angélique Paulet (1591–1650), one-time mistress of Henri IV and star of the salons where she was known as variously as 'the lioness' and 'Parthénie'.

PLESSIS: see Plessis-Bellière.

PLESSIS-BELLIÈRE: Jacques de Rougé, Marquis de Plessis-Bellière, who was killed in action at Naples in 1654. In *The Vicomte de Bragelonne* (Routledge, 1896, iv, chapters 45–6), his wife, Suzanne de Bruc, who died in 1705 aged 'almost a hundred', attempts to ward off Fouquet's ruin with a gift of her silver plate.

PONS: Suzanne de Pons, lady-in-waiting to Anne of Austria.

PRIDE: Thomas Pride (d. 1658), a former drayman, rose through the ranks to command a brigade under Cromwell in Scotland. When the House of Commons seemed inclined to reach a settlement with the King, Colonel Pride was charged by the army to silence its royalist elements who had rejected the army's demand that Charles be brought to trial. On 6-7 December 1648, he arrested sixty uncooperative Members of Parliament. To 'Pride's Purge' were added a further ninety-six exclusions, which left the 'Rump Parliament' of fifty-three members to try the King. Pride was one of his judges and signed his death warrant. He died in 1658, but after the Restoration his body was dug up and hanged with Cromwell's at Tyburn.

PUYLAURENS: Antoine de Laage, Duc de Puylaurens, imprisoned for plotting against Richelieu, died at Vincennes in 1635.

RANDAN: Marie-Catherine de La Rochefoucauld (1588–1677), Marquise de Sennecey, Duchesse de Randan, was disgraced in 1637, but later became governess to Louis XIV and his brother.

RETZ: Jean-François-Paul de Gondi (1613–79) was named Coadjutor to his uncle the Bishop of Paris in 1643 and became a cardinal in 1652. A leading figure in opposing Mazarin in the first Fronde, he rallied to the Queen's party in the second. Dumas drew heavily on his *Memoirs* which had been reprinted in 1837.

RICHELIEU: Armand-Jean du Plessis (1585–1642) was Bishop of Luçon before being appointed cardinal in 1622. He was named Head of the Royal Council in 1624 and became the most powerful man in France during the reign of Louis XIII. An admirer of Machiavelli, he played a crucial role in maintaining France as a great international power and in creating the highly centralized State which Louis XIV was to inherit and further strengthen. It was against the wily and ruthless 'Red Duke' (so called because of his cardinal's robes and his dukedom of Richelieu) that d'Artagnan and his comrades had waged an epic struggle of wits in *The Three Musketeers*.

RIEUX: François-Louis de Lorraine (1623–94), Comte de Rieux and later Duc d'Harcourt.

ROTROU: Jean Rotrou (1609–50), author of tragedies.

SARAZIN: Jean-François Sarazin (1603–54), a poet in the entourage of the Prince de Conti, was briefly banished by Mazarin in 1647 for writing satirical verses.

SCARRON: Paul Scarron (1610–60), burlesque poet, playwright, and author of *Le Roman comique*, a realistic picture of low-life provincial manners deliberately conceived as a reaction against the preciosity and artificiality of fashionable literary taste. He was crippled by tubercular rheumatism by the age of 30, though Dumas prefers to follow the tradition that his disability was the result of an accident. In 1652, he married Françoise d'Aubigné (q. v.), the future Madame de Maintenon. In 1648, he was in receipt of the Queen's patronage.

SCHOMBERG: Charles de Schomberg (1601–56), Duc d'Halluin, second husband of Marie de Hautefort (q. v.).

SCUDÉREY: Georges de Scudéry (1601–67), author, with his sister Madeleine, of two influential novels in the 'precious' style: *Artamène, ou le Grand Cyrus* (1649–53) and *Clélie* (1654–60).

SÉGUIER: Dominique Séguier (1593–1659), brother to the Chancelier Séguier, had been Bishop of Auxerre before becoming Bishop of Meaux in 1637.

SENNECEY: see Randan, Duchesse de.

SÉVIGNÉ: Renaud de Sévigné (*c.*1610–76), commander of Retz's 'Corinthian' regiment in January 1649, and stepfather to the novelist Madame de La Fayette, author of *La Princesse de Clèves* (1678).

'SOCRATINE': 'Socratine' was the 'precious' name given to Madeleine-Eugénie Bertaut, sister of Madame de Motteville.

STRAFFORD: Thomas Wentworth (1593–1641) was made Earl of Strafford in 1640. He was arrested by order of the Parliament and charged with treason. He was executed in 1641.

TALON: Omer Talon (1595–1652) inherited his office of senior magistrate in 1631 from his brother. His *Memoirs*, largely a collection of his speeches and historical documents, were published in 1838 and were used by Dumas.

TOMLINSON: Mathew Tomlinson (or Thomlinson) (1617–81), who was promoted colonel in 1647, guarded the King from December 1648 until the moment of his execution. Appointed one of the King's judges, he declined to sit in court. The King gave him a gold tooth-pick and case as a legacy.

TREMBLAY: Charles Le Clerc du Tremblay, Governor of the Bastille, and brother of François. He surrendered the Bastille to parliamentary forces on 12 January 1649 and was replaced by Pierre Broussel.

TREMBLAY: François Le Clerc du Tremblay (1577–1638) was known as 'le père Joseph' but also as 'l'éminence grise' because of his monkish robes and shadowy power. He became chief adviser and confidant to Richelieu, whom he first met in 1611.

TRÉMOILLE: see Noirmoutiers.

TRÉVILLE: Arnaud-Jean du Peyrer (1598–1672), Comte de Trois-villes (pronounced and usually written Tréville) was a Gascon career soldier like d'Artagnan. His courage and loyalty were admired by Louis XIII who appointed him Captain-Lieutenant of his Musketeers in 1634. In 1642, he was exiled for his opposition to Richelieu, and when Mazarin disbanded the Musketeers in 1646 he retired to Foix as its governor. According to *The Three Musketeers*, which makes the main characters about ten years older than their historical counter-parts, it was in Tréville's office in 1625 that Dumas, following Courtilz de Sandras's pseudo-*Memoirs of d'Artagnan* (i. 13), arranged the first meeting between d'Artagnan, Athos, Porthos, and Aramis.

TURENNE: Henri de la Tour d'Auvergne (1611–75), Vicomte de Turenne, Marshal of France. Drawn into the Fronde by Madame de Longueville, he later rallied to the court party which he served ably. As 'le Grand Turenne', he was one of the greatest military comman-ders of his century.

VALOIS: Louis-Emmanuel de Valois (1596–1650), former Bishop of Agde and Governor of Provence.

VENDÔME: see Beaufort.

VENDÔME: Alexandre de Bourbon (1593–1629), Chevalier de Ven-dôme, appointed Grand Prieur de France in 1618, was arrested by the King in 1626 and died at the Château de Vincennes three years later.

VENDÔME: César de Bourbon (1594–1665), Duc de Vendôme, father of François de Beaufort (q.v.).

VENDÔME: Françoise de Lorraine, Duchesse de Mercoeur, wife of César de Vendôme and mother of François de Beaufort (q.v.).

VILLEQUIER: Antoine d'Aumont de Rochebaron (1601–69), Mar-quis d'Isle et de Villequier, later Marshal of France and Governor of Paris.

VIOLE: Pierre Viole, *seigneur* d'Atis, a President of the Parlement and supporter of Condé.

VITRY: Nicolas de l'Hôpital (1581–1644), Marquis de Vitry. Made Marshal of France on the day he shot Concini (q.v.), Vitry was sent to the Bastille in 1637 for abusing his position as Governor of Provence. He was released on the death of Richelieu in 1642.

VOITURE: Vincent Voiture (1598–1648), an habitué of the Hôtel de Rambouillet, was a poet, letter-writer, and one of the arbiters of grammar and fine language.

EXPLANATORY NOTES

7 *Palais-Cardinal*: Richelieu had acquired land near the Louvre, then the royal palace, on which he built a residence known as the 'Palais-Cardinal', completed in 1636. In 1639, he made a gift of it to Louis XIII, after which it became known as the Palais Royal.

leagued against the minister: Richelieu died in 1642 and Louis XIII in 1643, when Louis XIV was 5. The Queen was named Regent and, as her prime minister, chose Mazarin who, in continuing Richelieu's policy of creating a modern, centralized French State, alienated most sections of society. The nobles resented the appointment of foreigners like Mazarin to high State office; the people and the middle classes resented excessive taxation to finance the German and Spanish wars; and the thirteen *parlements* resisted the erosion of their powers. Mazarin's unpopularity culminated in the 'Fronde', a civil war comprising two quite separate revolts (1648–49 and 1651–3). The first 'Fronde', which is the setting of *Twenty Years After*, began in the summer of 1648, when the Paris Parlement refused to register a new round of tax increases, though Dumas rightly highlights the discontent which had been simmering since 1647 and broke out briefly in January 1648. On 26 August, Mazarin ordered the arrest of the President of the Paris Parlement and of one of its leading councillors, Pierre Broussel. The populace rioted and the court fled from Paris. Discontented nobles—Conti, Longueville, Beaufort, Turenne, led by de Retz—joined the cause of the people and the Parlement and the tide turned in their favour when Condé laid siege to Paris in the autumn. In April 1649, the first, 'parliamentary' phase of the revolt was ended by the 'Pact of Reuil', an agreement which withdrew the new tax proposals and allowed Mazarin and 'the foreigners' to remain in office. *Twenty Years After* does not venture into the second Fronde which broke out in 1651 and ended with the amnesty of 1653. Though Dumas seems to side with the Parlementaires and their royal and noble supporters, he elsewhere acknowledges that the Paris Parlement had been rightly humbled and its political teeth permanently drawn. Likewise, aristocratic power had been broken. The principle of royal absolutism had been challenged and had emerged triumphant. When Louis XIV began his personal rule in 1661, his policy of strengthening the centralizing power of the throne met with little effective opposition. As Dumas makes him say to the older d'Artagnan: 'The Fronde, which threatened to ruin the monarchy, has emancipated it.' (*The Man in the Iron Mask* (World's Classics, 1991) p. 532.)

the Guards, the Swiss, the Musketeers: Richelieu had created his own body of Guards in 1623 which had transferred their loyalties to Mazarin, his successor. Mercenaries of Swiss nationality served in the armies of various continental countries, but especially of France: the last Swiss regiments were disbanded only in 1830. The Musketeers were formed in 1622 as an élite section of the royal bodyguard and served the King, who was their captain. Their commander was known as 'Captain-Lieutenant', and d'Artagnan's quest for promotion to the captaincy therefore has no historical validity. Moreover, the Musketeers were disbanded in 1646 and, consequently, there existed no such company in 1648. They were re-formed in 1657 and were known as 'Grey Musketeers' after the colour of the horses which they rode. In 1660, a second company of 'Black' Musketeers was created—Mazarin's enquiry on p. 14 is therefore anachronistic—and both followed the King to battle and saw service in the siege wars of the period. Charles de Batz, the historical d'Artagnan, was appointed Captain-Lieutenant in 1667.

8 *Earl of Essex*: Robert Devereux (1567–1601), who won the special affections of the elderly Elizabeth I. The story of the ring given to him by the Queen as a royal protection but kept back by the Countess of Nottingham, is an invention of a half-century later. Mazarin could therefore just have heard it.

'*Long live the prince . . . the parliament*': the prince was the Prince de Condé. There were thirteen *Parlements* in France, of which the most important was the Parlement of Paris. They were primarily lawcourts but by tradition enjoyed limited powers to scrutinize and ratify royal edicts. Parisians looked to the Parlement to defend their interests against the increasing absolutism of the throne. The failure of the Fronde curbed its influence severely and an institution which might have exercised limited constitutional control after the manner of the English Parliament turned into an in-bred, conservative body which resisted the new ideas of the *philosophes* of the eighteenth century.

Vincennes: a secure place of detention, six miles east of Paris, which held prisoners of State from the thirteenth century until the French Revolution.

Orléans and Montargis: both *parlements* supported Mazarin.

Princesse Palatine: as Dumas's footnote suggests, though Mazarin was a cardinal, he had never proceeded beyond minor ecclesiastical orders which could have been cancelled. But there is no evidence that he married the Queen. Dumas used La Porte's *Memoirs*, first published in 1755, as a major source of the historical background to the Musketeer saga. The *Mémoires* attributed to Anne de Gonzague de Clèves (1616–84), known as the Princess Palatine, which he also used, are suspect. They first appeared in 1786 and were the work of Sénac de Meilhan (1736–1803): for example, there is no confirmation of the existence of the unlikely underground passage mentioned in another note at the start of Chapter IV.

9 *twelve warrants*: throughout the *ancien régime*, public office was sold by the crown as a means of raising revenue. As Dumas says, the protest was made on 9 January.

seventh of January: 1648. Dumas's account of events between 7 and 12 January is substantially correct, if dramatized and highly simplified.

Madame de Motteville: the remark is correctly attributed to Madame de Motteville (1621–89), a loyal member of the Queen's 'Spanish' entourage. Dumas made extensive use of her *Memoirs* of the life of Anne of Austria (1723) which had been reissued in new editions in 1834 and 1838.

10 *barely escaped assassination*: d'Émery's son, Michel, Président de Thoré, was a member of the Paris Parlement. According to the *Memoirs* of Retz (Geneva, 1779, i. 148) an angry crowd 'shouted insults' at him on 8 January, protesting not against his wife's extravagance, but against the new tax on goods entering Paris; Mazarin's Guards were called out to restore order. Madame d'Émery was the daughter of Nicolas le Camus who had been made Secretary of State by Louis XIII in 1620 and was known as 'Camus le Riche'.

12 *Bed of Justice*: the ceremonial occasion when the kings of France attended session of the Parlement to witness the formal ratification of royal edicts. The king's *lit de justice* was held on 15 January.

more ruinous than the other: 'since the effect would be to ruin the king's interests by forcing into bankruptcy the very men who supported him with loans and credit.' (Retz, *Mémoires*, i. 159.) The first president who spoke out was Molé who, said Retz, was 'to my mind the most intrepid man of his century'.

St Denis and St Martin: popular areas situated in the north and north-east quarters of Paris.

Provost of the merchants: Jérôme le Féron (d. 1669) held the office between 1646 and 1650.

13 *the cross of Du Trahoir*: one of Paris's numerous places of execution. La Croix-du-Trahoir was situated in the rue St Honoré at its junction with the rue de l'Arbre-Sec. A permanent gibbet was maintained there: 'arbre-sec' means 'dry-tree'.

Barrière des Sergents . . . the Quinze-Vingts . . . hill St Roch: the first, situated near where the present rue Saint Honoré crosses the rue Croix-des-Petits-Champs, was one of a ring of customs gates surrounding Paris. The Quinze-Vingts, a hospital for the blind, now located in the 12th *arrondissement*, was then situated in the rue Saint-Honoré. By the 'hill St Roch', Dumas indicated the area further west near the church of Saint-Roch in the angle of the present avenue de l'Opéra and the same rue Saint Honoré.

16 *better soldiers than the Guards*: in *The Three Musketeers*, Dumas had made much of the rivalry, first suggested by Courtilz, between the King's Guards, loyal to Richelieu, and the Musketeers who gave their allegiance to the King.

17 *street of Les Bons Enfants*: runs into the rue Saint Honoré just east of the Palais Royal, the site of the theatre where *Mirame*, supervised rather than written by Richelieu—Desmarets de Saint-Sorlin (1596–1676) is generally reckoned to be its author—was performed in 1641. Mazarin, a music-lover, imported Italian musicians and actors who performed the first Italian opera in Paris, Luigi de Rossi's *Orfeo*, in 1647.

18 *the League*: a mouvement, founded in 1576 by Henri de Lorraine (1550–88), third Duc de Guise, to champion the catholic cause against the Calvinists during the religious wars of the sixteenth century.

stones in the moats of Paris: the word 'fronde' means 'a sling'. The word 'frondeur' had been applied to themselves by the persecuted Calvinists of the Netherlands in the late sixteenth century.

19 *Against Mazarin*: the large number of pamphlets and satires directed against Mazarin were known collectively as 'Mazarinades'. Gilbert Sigaux suggests that Dumas found this example in the new edition (1838) of the *Memoirs* of Mademoiselle de Montpensier.

his uncle's saddle: Comminges had succeeded his uncle Guitaut as Captain of the Queen's Guards. It was he who had arrested Beaufort in 1643.

Diavolo!: 'the Devil!'. Dumas takes care to remind us of Mazarin's Italian origins.

Rue St Thomas du Louvre: in this street were located the townhouse of Madame de Chevreuse and, next door, the Hôtel du Rambouillet.

20 *the Vaudeville*: the Théâtre du Vaudeville was built on the corner of the rue de Chartres and the rue des Orties in 1792; it was destroyed by fire in 1838. The actors moved into another theatre in the rue Vivienne in 1840 which was demolished in 1868: it was there that Dumas *fils*'s *La Dame aux camélias* was first performed in 1852.

Hôtel Rambouillet: built in the rue Saint-Thomas-du-Louvre according to plans drawn by Catherine de Vivonne, Marquise de Rambouillet (1588–1665). Between 1618 and 1650, it was the meeting place of writers, intellectuals, and the best society. The influence of the Marquise's *salon* in refining the language and literature of her time was very considerable.

Benserade: it is not known if Mazarin had written verses in his youth, but it is unlikely that he imitated Benserade, whose work was not known until the mid-1630s.

21 *Pietro Mazarini*: Mazarin's father was Pietro Mazzini (1576–1654), a Sicilian noble, born at Palermo.

22 *Café de Foy*: in the Galeries Montpensier of the Palais Royal. It was founded in 1723 and closed in 1863.

The Three Musketeers: set during the three years leading up to the siege of La Rochelle in 1628.

23 *Rochelle, at Suze, at Perpignan*: Dumas's d'Artagnan had taken part in the siege of La Rochelle in 1628 and, we now learn, in those at Suze (1629) and Perpignan (September 1642). Charles de Batz, the historical d'Artagnan, was present at the latter but was too young to fight the Protestants for Richelieu in the late 1620s.

24 *Comte de Rochefort*: in *The Three Musketeers*, Rochefort, Richelieu's 'evil genius', is the scar-faced man who insults d'Artagnan at Meung. D'Artagnan swears to have his revenge, but by the end of the book they have become firm friends. In Courtilz's pseudo-*Memoirs*, the gentleman who insults d'Artagnan is named

Rosny. Dumas retained the character but renamed him after
another romance by Courtilz entitled *Mémoires de M.L.C.D.R.*
[Monsieur le Comte de Rochefort] (1678), based on the life of
Henri-Louis d'Aloigny (1636–76), Marquis de Rochefort, who was
too young to have had any part in the Fronde.

25 *Bastille*: a fortified gaol built in the fourteenth century in the
east of Paris at the Porte Saint-Antoine. The Bastille held many
notable historical, political, and literary prisoners in its time. It
had room for eighty detainees, but during the reign of Louis XIV
rarely contained half this number. It was much feared and came
to symbolize the repressive nature of the *ancien régime*.

26 *Bassompierre*: Bassompierre's remark was reported in the account
given of the marshal by Tallemant des Réaux (1619–92), on whose
gossipy but usually reliable *Historiettes* (completed by 1659; first
published in 1834) Dumas drew heavily for the background to
the Musketeer saga.

27 *ten thousand livres*: an underestimate. The governorship of the
Bastille was bought and sold, like virtually all public offices, and
incumbents were free to exploit their position. The governor was
paid 50 livres a day for royal prisoners, 30 for aristocrats and
generals, from 5 to 15 for detainees of lesser social standing, and
3 livres for poets and tradesmen. When Baisemaux, who had been
governor for over thirty years, died in 1697, he was worth 2
million livres.

28 *Reinard's*: Renard (*sic*), a former valet of the Bishop of Beauvais,
was the proprietor of an establishment at the western end of the
Tuileries, on a site now part of the Place de la Concorde. It was
a fashionable meeting place for 'persons of the highest quality.
They amused themselves, gambled and there were even frequent
discussions of matters of public moment.' (Guy Joli, *Mémoires*
(Geneva, 1779), i. 82.)

pull cloaks: Dumas borrowed the Pont-Neuf incident from Courtilz's pseudo-*Mémoires . . . de Rochefort* where, however, it ended
with a brief spell in the cells.

the Châtelet: criminal justice was administered from the Châtelet
on the right bank of the Seine near the Pont au Change. It began
as a fortress in 1130 and was demolished in 1802.

29 *when I saw you at Meung*: see *The Three Musketeers*, chapter 1.

still lieutenant of Musketeers: since the Musketeers had been disbanded in 1646, the career hopes of d'Artagnan (admitted to the

company as lieutenant in 1628: *The Three Musketeers*, chapter 67) are Dumas's invention. Little is known of the fortunes of Charles de Batz between his entry into the Musketeers in 1644, with Mazarin's protection, and 1648 when, as Mazarin's correspondence reveals, he was sent on a number of special missions by the cardinal to liaise with military commanders. But the professional loyalty of Dumas's hero, like that of the real d'Artagnan, was certainly to Mazarin.

30 *three cuts of your sword!*: in the epilogue of *The Three Musketeers* (World's Classics edition, p. 607), 'D'Artagnan fought three times with Rochefort; and wounded him three times.'

31 *Planchet*: d'Artagnan's loyal servant in *The Three Musketeers*.

33 *Brussels for the queen?*: Courtliz's pseudo-*Mémoires . . . de Rochefort* sent him to Brussels to spy on Madame de Chevreuse for Richelieu ('the late Cardinal'), an episode Dumas had used in chapter 3 of his historical account of *Louis XIV and his Century* (1844). Here, he uses Rochefort's role as Richelieu's agent to explain his long—and fictitious—detention.

the conspiracy of Chalais: that is, in 1626. Rochefort's attempt to intercept the correspondence of Chalais and Archduke Léopold of Austria was first chronicled in Courtilz's pseudo-*Mémoires de . . . Rochefort*, where Dumas found it.

35 *the seventeen lords*: a group of the highest-ranking aristocrats who, in the previous reign, had formed a companionable 'inner court' to Louis XIII. Bassompierre had been of the number.

36 *judged him good for nothing*: the neglect of d'Artagnan is true only in Dumas's version of history. In reality, during the six years after Mazarin succeeded Richelieu, the services of Charles de Batz had been recognized by the cardinal, who had supported his entry to the Musketeers in 1644.

38 *this deed, my Lord?*: a summary of the 'diamond studs' affair which occupies chapters 10–23 of *The Three Musketeers*.

their true names: as younger sons, Porthos and Aramis had adopted *noms-de-guerre* to avoid confusion with their elders, though this custom was not observed by d'Artagnan, who was a fifth son. Athos's reason for hiding his identity was his unhappy and shameful connection with Milady. D'Artagnan's friends guarded their true identities fiercely: see *The Three Musketeers*, chapter 31.

41 *Alexander*: a *Histoire d'Alexandre le Grand, tirée de Quinte Curce et autres auteurs* had appeared in 1639. Dumas is quite correct in

indicating the tone of Louis's reading. The boy's *valet de chambre*, Laporte, was in the habit of reading out extracts from Mézeray's *Histoire de France* with a view to strengthening his respect for strong kings and his scorn for weak monarchs who relied on ministers like Mazarin.

42 *the smallpox*: Louis caught smallpox in the summer of 1647. Like many of his contemporaries, he bore the scars for the rest of his life.

43 *opera of "Thisbé"*: there was no opera of this name and the line is untraceable.

45 *Monsieur*: i.e. Gaston d'Orléans. 'Monsieur le Prince' is Condé, who was backed by Retz (Coadjutor of the Bishop of Paris since 1644) who enjoyed the confidence of the Princesse de Guéménée, sister-in-law to Madame de Chevreuse.

46 *one of my women*: Constance Bonacieux, wife of d'Artagnan's landlord and the only woman d'Artagnan ever loved, was foully murdered by Milady in *The Three Musketeers*, chapter 63.

water that stagnates: 'there is no water more treacherous than water that stagnates.'

47 *of Chalais, of Montmorency and of Cinq-Mars*: Dumas here expresses his dim view of Gaston d'Orléans, an ambitious conspirator, and lays at his door the deaths of Chalais (1626), Montmorency (1632), and Cinq-Mars (1642).

49 *Felton*: the letters and the dagger play a significant role in Dumas's version of the murder of Buckingham in 1628 (*The Three Musketeers*, chapter 59), where John Felton was goaded to his act by Milady.

50 *M. d'Essart*: read Des Essarts.

51 *while sleeping*: according to the proverb, the same holds true for wealth. Cf. *Cymbeline*, IV. iii: 'Fortune brings in some boats which are not steer'd.'

52 *Mondori or Bellerose*: Guillaume des Gilberts (1594–1653), known as Mondori, retired from the Théâtre du Marais in 1637. Bellerose was the stage name of Pierre Le Messier (d. 1670) of the rival Théâtre de Bourgogne.

53 *Pythagoras*: Pythagoras (582–*c*.500BC), philosopher and mathematician. Obedience, silence, abstinence were observed by his followers, who formed the Pythagorean School.

ball at the Hôtel de Ville: see *The Three Musketeers*, chapter 22.

55 *otherwise called Aramis*: on the original Musketeers, see Introduction, p. xiii.

56 *Rue Tiquetonne*: d'Artagnan's hotel, an invention, was situated at the western end of the present rue Tiquetonne which links the rue Montmartre and the rue Saint-Denis in the 2nd *arrondissement*.

Rue des Fossoyeurs: near the Luxembourg Palace. Dumas borrowed the address from Courtilz's pseudo-*Memoirs of d'Artagnan*. The street became the present rue Servandoni in 1806.

57 *near Blois*: Dumas forgets that in the epilogue of *The Three Musketeers*, Athos 'had inherited a small property in the Roussillon'.

Madame Bonacieux: see note to page 46.

58 *Franche Comté*: there were no actions in this part of France until the European Wars of Louis XIV in the late 1660s.

60 *little more than five*: the French foot (*le pied du roi*) was the equivalent of 12, 8 English inches. In British terms, d'Artagnan was about 5 feet 6 inches tall, which was average for the period. The Swiss (borrowed from the Captain Straatman who marries the innkeeper's widow in Courtilz's pseudo-*Memoirs of d'Artagnan*, i, chapter 4) measured 6 feet 4 inches, which was also the height of Porthos 'the Giant' (p. 108).

61 *William Tell*: hero of the Swiss struggle for independence who freed his native district from the tyranny of Austria in the early fourteenth century.

moats at Montmartre: that is, the fossés Montmartre, a street, opened in 1634.

62 *Playful Cat*: a tavern called the 'Chat-qui-pelote' had opened in 1640—its heyday came during the French Revolution—but not on the site Dumas indicates: it was close by the present Archives Nationales.

63 *my father's château*: in the first chapter of *The Three Musketeers*, Dumas turns d'Artagnan senior into a bluff Polonius. The father of the historical d'Artagnan was a recently ennobled merchant, Bertrand de Batz-Castelmore (d. 1635), who acquired the title (and the small estate near Tarbes which went with it) by marriage to Françoise de Montesquiou, daughter of the *seigneur* d'Artagnan.

Cimetière des Innocents: this cemetery, on the site of the present Square des Innocents, opened in the twelfth century and closed in 1780: during that time, it is reckoned, 2 million dead were interred there.

three sons: Charles de Batz married in 1659 and had two sons who both became soldiers. He separated from his wife in 1665.

64 *the Louvre*: begun in 1204 and completed only during the 1860s, was still the residence of the kings of France. During the reign of Louis XIV, the court removed to Versailles, construction of which began in 1661.

65 *1643*: a number of anachronisms in this and the following paragraph reveal Dumas's carelessness with facts. Richelieu died in 1642. Besançon was not besieged at this time, and the siege of Montmédy occurred in 1657. The father of the real d'Artagnan died in 1635.

66 *M. Coquenard*: the miserly lawyer of *The Three Musketeers* (chapter 32). After his death, Porthos married his widow and thus 'inherited' considerable wealth.

his theses: see *The Three Musketeers*, chapter 26.

67 *Place Royale*: this square was renamed several times during the French Revolution and became the Place des Vosges in 1800. It reverted to its old name twice during the nineteenth century, but has been the Place des Vosges since 1870. The rue Neuve-Sainte-Catherine became part of the rue des Francs-Bourgeois in 1868.

68 *Rue de la Feronnerie*: a narrow street, dating from the thirteenth century, long known for its ironmongers and wheelwrights.

70 *Bazin*: Aramis's trusty servant in *The Three Musketeers*.

72 *clew*: or clue: a ball of wool or twine. Hence anything that guides a seeker through a puzzle. Theseus was guided by a clue of thread through the Cretan labyrinth.

73 *baleine*: that is, his sidesman's wand, inlaid with whalebone. At the battle of Fribourg in 1644, Condé is said to have thrown his marshal's *bâton* into the enemy's lines: his soldiers rushed to retrieve it.

74 *Simara*: a devil of Dumas's invention.

75 *Chut!*: 'Hush!'

77 *Rue des Canettes*: a street of this name now runs north out of the Place Saint-Sulpice. Although it was longer in 1648, it could scarcely have afforded d'Artagnan a useful vantage point. D'Artagnan follows Bazin out of the west door of Notre-Dame through a maze of streets which Dumas names correctly but which have

long since disappeared. The site of Bazin's lodging is now occupied by the Caserne de la Cité.

hippocras: an aromatic medicated wine, much used as a cordial.

78 *Noisy*: Dumas confuses Noisy-le-Sec, 6 km. north-east of Paris 'on the road to Meaux', as we learn at the start of the next chapter, with Noisy-le-Roi, which lies between Versailles and Saint Germain. Aramis has entered a Jesuit monastery at Noisy-le-Sec, but the leading *frondeurs* congregated at Noisy-le-Roi.

80 *Barrière de la Villette*: on Paris's northern edge, one of the ring of customs posts which surrounded the capital. Travellers to Flanders left by this gate.

horrible stuff from Montreuil: wine was made at vineyards at Montreuil, just north of Vincennes, 8 km. east of the centre of Paris. It had a reputation for being thin and acid.

Archbishop of Paris: Jean-François de Gondi (1584–1654), first Archbishop of Paris, was a worldly prelate known less for his piety than for the splendour of his establishments at Saint-Cloud and Noisy-le-Roi. He was uncle to Retz but also to the Duchesse de Longueville.

La Fontaine: Jean de La Fontaine (1621–95). The first collection of his *Fables* appeared in 1668: the reference here is to 'The Hare and the Frogs' (book II, 14, line 2).

81 *de Marcillac*: the incestuous dealings of the Duchesse and her brother were notorious. Her liaison with Marcillac was more than political: she was his mistress between 1646 and 1652.

Chevreuse's lover: in *The Three Musketeers*, Madame de Chevreuse figures off-stage as Marie Michon, Aramis's mistress and secret go-between with the Queen's party. At this point, Dumas seems to have plans to cast Madame de Longueville as a new Chevreuse.

84 *ass of Buridan*: Jean Buridan, a fourteenth-century French scholastic philosopher, is remembered for his sophism which states that a hungry ass, placed exactly between two identical bundles of straw, must starve, since there is nothing to direct the animal's will towards either bundle.

not his voice: d'Artagnan was a Gascon and spoke with a strong southern accent, as Mazarin noticed in Chapter II. Save for a few exclamations, Dumas makes little attempt to reproduce the linguistic mannerisms which are clearly detectable in the surviving letters of Charles de Batz. In *The Three Musketeers* (World's Classics edition, pp. 87 and 471), Athos comments on his 'patois' which was strong enough to enable Richelieu to identify him through a hedge.

86 *prince, or king*: d'Artagnan's opponent, as we shall learn, is the Prince de Marcillac, later Duc de la Rochefoucauld.

88 *and the Archbishop of Bordeaux*: there were several cardinals of Lorraine but the Archbishop of Bordeaux was a nominee of Richelieu, Henri d'Escoubleay de Sourdis (1593–1645), while Cardinal de Lavalette (Louis (1593–1639), Archbishop of Tours) was one of his staunchest supporters.

Alençon: 200 km. west of Paris, renowned for its textiles and in particular its lace.

omelet of Crèvecoeur: see *The Three Musketeers*, chapter 20.

90 *Loches*: for her persistent intrigues, Madame de Chevreuse was exiled at various times by both Louis XIII and Richelieu. Accompanied by a maid, she escaped from the Château de Loches, near Tours, on 6 September 1637, dressed as a man.

Kitty: Milady's maid who abetted d'Artagnan's attempts to foil her mistress in *The Three Musketeers*, chapters 33 and 35. To protect her against the vengeance of Milady, Aramis had arranged for her to enter the service of Madame de Chevreuse.

comme un cadet: Dumas took the text of this song, addressed to Madame de Chevreuse's squire from Tallemant des Réaux's *Historiettes* (ed. A. Adam, (Pléiade, Paris, 1960) i. 163).

91 *permission to come back*: Dumas is in error: Madame de Chevreuse returned to Paris in April 1649, a year after the events described here.

92 *forty-three*: as d'Artagnan points out, he is the youngest of the Musketeers. Athos, at 49 (p. 135) is the oldest. Dumas makes the quartet ten years older than their historical counterparts. Charles de Batz was born in about 1615, as was Armand de Sillègue d'Athos. Isaac de Portau was born in 1617, but the date of birth of Henri d'Aramitz is unknown.

93 *Lafollone*: a detail borrowed from Tallemant des Réaux (*Historiettes*, i. 247) who called the famous La Folène (*sic*) 'the finest eater in the whole court'.

with your poems?: in *The Three Musketeers*, Aramis writes verses, including a poem made up of words of one syllable.

94 *St Louis au Marais*: the church, completed in 1641, was dedicated to Saint Paul and Saint Louis and was situated in the Marais district of Paris.

95 *leaning to the musketeers*: in *The Three Musketeers*, Aramis already showed an interest in theological matters—he intended to join the Lazarists—though his fighting instinct makes him a natural soldier. In *The Vicomte de Bragelonne*, he will become Vicar-General of the Jesuits and have papal ambitions.

96 *Enceladus*: one of the Titans who assailed Olympus. For his ambition, Athena buried him in Mount Etna.

97 *made me lieutenant*: see *The Three Musketeers*, chapter 67.

98 *in four years' time*: Louis XIV came of age in 1652.

100 *humpbacked general!*: it was Conti who was deformed, not Retz, who was not yet a cardinal.

101 *Bishop of Noyon*: Dumas gives conflicting locations of Porthos's scattered estates. D'Artagnan summarizes on p. 245: 'that of Vallon at Corbeil, that of Bracieux in the Soissonnais, and that of Pierrefonds in Valois'. In Chapter XIV, in a passage not translated in this version, it is made clearer still: 'the Château du Vallon, which was near Corbeil; the Château de Bracieux, which was near Meaux, and the Château de Pierrefonds, which was between Compiègne and Villers-Cotterêts'. Yet d'Artagnan will enquire for Bracieux near Compiègne on p. 111.

fugit irreparabile tempus: 'time flees never to return' (Virgil, *Georgics* iii. 284).

105 *family name*: the original Porthos was named Isaac de Portau. Vallon is Dumas's invention.

106 *Pierrefonds*: Dumas knew this road well. Dammartin-en-Goële is about half-way to his birthplace, Villers-Cotterêts, and Nanteuil 10 km. further on. The village of Pierrefonds lies 10 km. north-west of Villers-Cotterêts and here seems to be part of the 'Bracieux estate'.

108 *Duc d'Enghien*: Condé had been Duc d'Enghien until the death of his father in 1646. Charles VII (1403–61) drove the English out of France. Dumas establishes a comparison rather as, on a different level, his Musketeers show the difference between the spirit of the men of 1830 and those of the reign of bourgeois Louis-Philippe.

111 *near Corbeil*: south-east of Paris, near Melun. See note to p. 101.

113 *Pharamond, to Charlemagne . . . to Hugh Capet*: Pharamond, a legendary Frankish leader of the fifth century; Charlemagne (742–814), King of the French and Emperor of the West; Hugues Capet (*c.* 938–96), founder of the Capetian dynasty which replaced the Carolingians.

Coucys . . . Rohans: the Coucys, whose estates were in Picardy, were one of the oldest aristocratic lines. The family motto proclaimed: 'King I am not, nor Prince or Duc, nor Count, but Lord of Coucy.' The Rohans also traced their origins into the mists of the Middle Ages. Porthos is worried because seniority and honour were conferred by lineage: Louis XIV was to develop the tradition further into an elaborate system of court etiquette.

114 *Mouston*: 'Mousqueton' means a small musket, a cumbersome, ungainly weapon. In abbreviating his name, Mouston merely transfers the ridicule: the word suggests a gnat.

quincunx: any arrangement resembling the 5 on a dice.

117 *my ancestors*: Dumas invents a noble past for Porthos. Nothing is known of the forebears of Isaac de Portau.

118 *Bragelonne*: there was no such estate. On Bragelonne, see note to p. 129.

County de la Fère: Dumas makes Athos Comte de La Fère. In the preface to *The Three Musketeers*, Dumas adopts the pleasant fiction that his own role was simply that of editor of the Comte's authentic and hitherto unpublished memoirs.

Scipio: Scipio Aemilianus (185–129 BC), celebrated for his rigorous observance of ancient Roman virtues.

119 *Jussac*: one of the Musketeers' opponents in the dramatic fight between Dumas's quartet and Richelieu's Guards in chapter 5 of *The Three Musketeers*. Claude de Jussac (1620–90) was too young to be a guard in 1625, but he was surely now of an age to be a threat. He later became governor to the Duc de Vendôme.

122 *carrying the letter*: the siege of La Rochelle ended in November 1628. For the incident referred to here, see *The Three Musketeers*, chapter 48. Lord de Winter was Milady's brother-in-law and the letter was intended to warn him against her 'great and terrible designs'. But Dumas's memory is at fault: the sum paid to Planchet was 1,400 livres.

126 *baited*: i.e. fed, in preparation for the journey.

127 *clos Des Carmes*: where the Musketeers fought the four Englishmen in *The Three Musketeers*, chapter 31.

Grimaud: Athos's taciturn servant since the days of *The Three Musketeers*.

128 *Chambord*: 14 km. from Blois.

purity of language: the French spoken in the area between Tours and Anjou is still reckoned to be the purest form of the language.

129 *La Vallière*: a fifteenth-century manor near Reugny, 10 km. north-west of Amboise. There was no estate of Bragelonne.

133 *Mademoiselle de la Vallière*: Dumas based Raoul (born in 1633), whom we shall soon meet, on a stray remark in the *Histoire d'Henriette d'Angleterre* of Madame de La Fayette, who mentioned Louise de La Vallière's early life 'at Blois where a man named Bragelonne had been in love with her'. The romance was terminated when Louis XIV became jealous, though this did not occur until 1661 and looms large in *The Vicomte de Bragelonne*. On this slim base, Dumas built the love of Raoul for Louise, who is made slightly older than her years for fictional purposes.

Madame de Saint-Rémy: Françoise Le Prévôt de la Coutelaye, who became Madame de Rémi on her third marriage which did not occur, however, until 1655.

Duc de Barbé: an invention of Dumas.

137 *a son?*: John Francis de Winter, or Mordaunt (whom we shall soon meet), Milady's son by her second marriage to the brother of Lord de Winter. Her first husband was Athos. See *The Three Musketeers*.

maid of honour: Athos now speaks more openly of his family than he had in *The Three Musketeers*, where his anonymity was part of the plot.

139 *Cellini*: Florentine goldsmith, sculptor, and engraver (1500–71) and author of an *Autobiography* which was first published in 1728.

Marignan: Melegnano, a town south-east of Milan where the French, under François I (1494–1547), scored a famous victory over the Swiss in 1515. Athos's ancestor is an invention, though the Order of Saint Michael, founded in 1469, was real. It became the Ordre du Saint-Esprit in 1578, the *ancien régime*'s primary chivalric order: it was abolished in 1791, revived during the Restoration, and finally disappeared in 1830. Dumas, himself a keen collector of honours, was extremely knowledgeable in such matters.

140 *the Bastion St Gervais*: see *The Three Musketeers*, chapter 46.

fascinating times of chivalry: in the wake of Walter Scott, Romantic writers took a highly coloured view of medieval chivalric values which they readily rediscovered in the *Orlando furioso* of Ariosto (1474–1533) and *Jerusalem Delivered* by Torquato Tasso (1544–95).

141 *He was eighteen*: on the contrary, d'Artagnan was 20 at their first meeting in 1625. However, he was also 20 when the first Musketeer novel closed in 1628. It is not Athos who is forgetful, but Dumas who is careless. The action 'against experienced men' is described in chapter 5 of *The Three Musketeers*.

146 *child of seven years?*: Louise was in fact 4.

Pygmalion: legendary Greek sculptor who persuaded Venus to bring to life his statue of Galatea, whom he promptly married.

149 *lame all her life*: Louise walked with a slight limp, the legacy of a badly set bone broken in a childhood accident.

152 *Coysel*: a lawyer, recorded by Retz as Goisel, who had predicted Beaufort's escape at Whitsun 1648. Guy Joli (*Mémoires*, i. 14) calls him Goiset and mentions an Abbé de Marivaux who also read the future.

154 *made a cardinal*: Dumas embroiders. There is no record that Goisel predicted quite so many things, though he did foretell the escape of Retz from Nantes prison in 1654.

M. de Chavigny: a 'creature of Mazarin', whose son he was reckoned to be, a detail picked up by Dumas on p. 164.

scarcely thirty: Beaufort, born in 1616, had been in prison since his arrest in 1643.

155 *miser in the fable*: La Fontaine, *Fables*, book iv. 20.

156 *mall and tennis*: mall was played in a level alley boarded on both sides, called a 'pall-mall'. Players scored points when, with a mallet, they struck their ball through an iron hoop, called a 'pass', at the far end. Tennis was, of course, real tennis.

160 *facchino Mazarini*: 'Portrait of that eminent scoundrel, Mazarin'. Beaufort's twitting of the cardinal is well attested, though Dumas plays up his boyish high spirits, which make Mazarin seem even more drab than he was.

whose servant he had been: Mazarin was never the servant but rather the protégé of Bentivoglio. The story of Mazarin's role in a tragedy on the subject of Loyola (1491–1556), performed in Rome in 1622, is unverified but often repeated still.

Bayard . . . Trivulce: the name of Pierre du Terrail (1473–1524), *seigneur* de Bayard, is still a by-word in France for courage. The Trivulce were a celebrated Milanese family, distinguished by generations of public and military service.

162 *M. le Camus*: there were several notables, including a bishop, of this name. Dumas seems to have in mind Nicolas Le Camus (see note to p. 10) who, however, was dead in 1648.

163 *[he meant difference]*: Beaufort's malapropisms are well attested.

164 *arsenic*: the cells at Vincennes were notoriously damp and unhealthy, as the Marquis de Sade, detained there between 1778 and 1784, was later to complain, and all three prisoners succumbed to the conditions. As Dumas notes indirectly (p. 179), it was believed that Puylaurens had been poisoned by bad mushrooms. Madame de Rambouillet's remark is reported by Tallemant des Réaux.

asparagus: Dumas was a master cook and took a serious interest in culinary matters. Modern varieties of cultivated asparagus are much quicker growing.

166 *tied to four horses*: that is, of being quartered, then still part of the range of legal punishments.

174 *Astraea*: a vast pastoral novel, completed after his death, by Honoré d'Urfé (1567–1625). The first part appeared in 1607.

178 *Father Marteau*: like the dog Pistache, Marteau is an invention of Dumas's.

181 *Noirmont*: according to Guy Joli (see note to p. 236), the Duc's escape was facilitated by one of his aides named Vaumorin. The story of the pie, however, is a product of Dumas's imagination.

182 *it is Whitsunday*: Beaufort escaped on Whit Sunday 1748. In using history to structure his story, Dumas has mangled the chronology of the tale. When the story opened in January, Mazarin gave d'Artagnan a week to assemble his friends (p. 53). Four months have passed silently.

185 *his gridiron*: Saint Lawrence, the Deacon, was martyred in AD 258. He was condemned to be 'broiled on a gridiron'.

190 *Rue du Faubourg St Marcel*: that is, from the south-east, roughly south of the present Gare d'Austerlitz. Their route takes them through streets which have ceased to exist but which Dumas describes very accurately, though the names of inns are inventions. Athos and Raoul will turn west to the church of Saint-Médard, north along the line of the present rue Mouffetard, then west again past the Panthéon, and hence to the rue de Vaugirard opposite the Sorbonne.

painful years of my life: the rue Férou still exists: it connects the Place Saint-Sulpice to the rue de Vaugirard. There is no indication in *The Three Musketeers* to explain why Athos should treasure its memory so particularly.

Rue du Vieux-Colombier: it was in this quarter of the capital that d'Artagnan and his friends lodged in *The Three Musketeers*, the Musketeers having no regular barracks.

192 *arms of the Luynes*: these streets and the Hôtel de Luynes have disappeared. The house was located on a site where the Boulevard Raspail now leaves the Boulevard St Germain.

the Swiss: the porter.

Duchesse de Chevreuse: Madame de Chevreuse was still living in exile in Belgium, where she plotted from a distance. She did not return to France until 12 April 1649.

193 *1683*: the date is clearly wrong. Dumas refers to a prank which led to the Queen's miscarriage in 1622.

195 *to whom he wrote*: on this correspondence, see *The Three Musketeers*, chapter 48.

196 *Loches*: see note to p. 90.

Marcillac: that is, La Rochefoucauld. In 1637, the King ordered the Chancelier Séguier to search the apartments of Anne of Austria, who was suspected of intelligence with Spain. If damaging letters were found, her 'Spanish' entourage would suffer. Madame de Chevreuse, already imprisoned for her opposition to Richelieu and the King, felt particularly vulnerable and enlisted the help of the impressionable La Rochefoucauld who was forbidden by his father, only recently restored to royal favour and fearful of a new disgrace, to have any dealings with her. The Queen feared for Chevreuse, who had served her well, and arranged with Mademoiselle de Hautefort to send her 'a Book of Hours bound in green, saying it would be a signal that the Queen's affairs would go smoothly towards an accommodation;

but that if she sent her a Book of Hours bound in red, it would be to warn Madame de Chevreuse that she should look to her safety and leave the kingdom as quickly as she could. I do not know which of the two made the mistake, but instead of sending her the Book of Hours intended to reassure her, the copy which she received led her to believe that both the Queen and herself were lost. With the consequence that without further consulting me . . . she resolved to escape to Spain. . . . She disguised herself as a man and set off on horseback, taking none of her women with her, accompanied only by two men.' (La Rochefoucauld, *Mémoires*, pp. 51–2.) La Rochefoucauld adds that her unnecessary journey was attended by 'a thousand perils', and remarks that on one occasion 'she behaved with more modesty and more cruelty to a woman in whose house she lodged on her way than men of her appearance normally show.' According to other accounts, she was more liberal with her favours when forced, because none other was available, to share the bed of a poor country priest. We shall see which version Dumas preferred.

197 *Roche-l'Abeille*: the village exists, but was chosen at random by Dumas.

11th of October: Madame de Chevreuse left Tours on 3 September 1637. As we shall see, Dumas situates the event in 1633, for the purposes of his plot: in 1648, Raoul, as we know, is 15.

198 *Saint Ambrose*: fourth-century Church Father who was rather keen on asceticism.

convent of the old Augustinians: the Couvent des Vieux-Augustins was situated towards the bottom end of what is now the rue Dauphine, on the left bank opposite the Pont Neuf.

202 *Rue des Tournelles*: situated between the Place des Vosges and the Place de la Bastille. Scarron is not associated with this address, which Dumas probably confused with the rue de Turenne, in the 3rd *arrondissement*, which was Scarron's base from 1654 until his death.

205 '*Do gentlemen make verses?*: the social ethos of court-dominated society attributed military and administrative functions to the aristocracy, who could not take part in trade or profession without loss of dignity. Amateur scribbling, however, was tolerated.

206 *Mademoiselle Paulet*: see List of Historical Characters. In the 'precious' style of the times, she was called both 'la lionne' and 'Parthénie'.

207 *crinibus hydri*: Juvenal, *Satires* vii. 69–70. The first line should read: 'Nam si Virgilio puer et tolerabile deesset'. ('Had Virgil not had a slave-boy and an acceptable place to lodge, the Fury would have lost the serpents which it had instead of hair.')

Abbé de Gondy: Paul de Gondi, later Cardinal de Retz, was ugly, extremely short-sighted, and clumsy with his hands, but not the 'hump-back' which Dumas makes him on p. 100.

208 *regime of the community?*: according to French law, formalized by the Napoleonic code at the beginning of the nineteenth century, the property of a married couple, unless a separate marriage contract has been made, is considered to be held in common. Even allowing for the unique position of the Queen, Aramis's question is anachronistic in this context.

209 *deseret orbem*: 'he will [soon] have quitted this globe'. Voiture died on 16 May 1648.

210 *Saintot . . . Renaudot*: Marguerite Vion, the wife of Pierre de Sainctot (*sic*), was the mistress of Voiture, who was also said to have lived 'scandalously' with the daughter of Théophraste Renaudot (1586–1653), founder of *La Gazette de France* (1631), the first French newspaper.

five feet high: which makes him almost as tall as d'Artagnan.

M. de Scudéry: both *Artamène, ou le Grand Cyrus* (1649–53) and *Clélie* (1654–60) had yet to appear in 1648.

211 *St Mandé*: now part of Paris's eastern suburb, Saint-Mandé, in the Bois de Vincennes, was in 1648 a village conveniently near the prison which held Beaufort. Louis XIV's extravagant Superintendant of Finances, Fouquet, built a magnificent palace there in 1658 which became a meeting place for his artistic entourage and political associates.

212 *'Letter from the Carp to the Pike'*: a poem by Voiture, written in 1643 in the precious mode of the fashionable society game which gave its members allegorical names: as we have seen, Mademoiselle Paulet was 'the Lioness'.

Zélide and Alcidalea: *Histoire d'Alcidalis et de Zélide*, a tale, begun by Voiture, completed after his death, and published in 1658.

213 *he repeated*: the story of Voiture's improvisation is found in the memoirs of the times. The poem explicitly evokes Anne's love for Buckingham. For this reason, it was considered too indiscreet to be published and was first printed only in 1833.

215 *the famous Agrippa*: Agrippa d'Aubigné (1552–1630), soldier and diplomat in the Protestant cause, historian and poet.

beautiful Indian: Françoise d'Aubigné earned this description for having lived in Martinique for two years (1645–7)

221 *Pepin's Watering-Place*: the 'Abreuvoir Pépin' was a medieval street which ran across the present Place du Châtelet out of which the rue Saint-Denis leads north.

the Récollets: the Couvent des Recollets, a Franciscan order which received papal approval in 1532, was situated immediately east of what is now the Gare de l'Est.

222 *touch of winter*: Dumas adds to the chronological confusion: it is now Whitsun which, in 1648, fell on 30 May.

St Denis: a large village, Saint-Denis then lay outside the city walls.

223 *to rejoin him*: Saint-Denis is named after the third-century saint of that name who was buried there. An abbey was built over his tomb in 626 by Dagobert I, who was interred in its church. Thereafter, it became the mausoleum of the kings of France. The practice, introduced in the thirteenth century, of erecting monuments over the royal tombs survived until the Renaissance. But Bourbon coffins were placed in the crypt without memorial.

224 *this king*: Louis XIII, who died in 1643. Dumas allows Athos to express his entrenched, almost mystical royalism but also to acknowledge the political achievements of Richelieu, an uncongenial figure in *The Three Musketeers*, who had done so much to strengthen the monarchy.

227 *Antinous*: up to a point. Antinous was a youth of great beauty, a favourite of the Emperor Hadrian whom he accompanied on all his journeys. He drowned in the Nile in AD 122.

236 *Free! free! free!*: Dumas's account of Beaufort's escape from Vincennes on 31 May 1648 is one of his virtuoso orchestrations of plain historical facts. His inventiveness may be gauged by comparing his account with that of Guy Joli (*Mémoires*, 1779, i. 13–14): 'For some time, the Duc had maintained secret dealings with one of the men who guarded him, Vaugrimaut by name, who assembled a good provision of ropes and other articles necessary for his design. On Whit Sunday, at one o'clock in the afternoon, this man entered the yard of the keep where M. de Beaufort strolled each day with the *sieur* de La Ramée, Governor of the Château of Vincennes. He closed and bolted the yard door

on the inside and then attacked the officer with the help of M. de Beaufort. When he had tied him up securely and placed a *poire d'angoisse* in his mouth to prevent his crying out, Vaugrimaut calmly took control of the operation and let himself down by rope into the moat, telling the prince that it was only just that he should be first to reach safety since he was risking his neck, whereas were his Highness to be taken he would merely be confined more closely. And so, after allowing his liberator to go first, M. de Beaufort followed him down into the moat from which both were immediately hauled up with another set of ropes by the men, led by one of the duke's aides named Vaumorin, who were waiting for them. Then mounting a horse, he made good speed to the province of Maine and Anjou where he remained hidden for some time by the priest of La Flèche.'

238 *as at Chantilly*: see *The Three Musketeers*, chapter 25.

240 *cap-a-pie*: 'head to foot'.

Don Quixote: published in Spain in 1605. The first French translation was into its third edition by 1620.

241 *Frederick of Prussia*: Frederick the Great (1712–86) established Prussian power through his political skills and the military might which alienated the eighteenth-century French intellectuals whom he had attracted to his court.

242 *made me lieutenant*: see *The Three Musketeers*, chapter 67.

245 *cemetery of St John*: the cemetery of the church of Saint-Jean-en-Grève was located on the eastern side of the Hôtel de Ville and conveniently near the Place de Grève, which had been in use as a place of execution for State criminals since 1310.

quite two feet: read 'barely two feet'.

St Maur: south-east of Paris, in a bend of the Marne near Créteil.

246 *Vendômois*: read the Vendômois region north of Blois. Beaufort's family name was Vendôme and, as Joli tells, he went into hiding on home ground, at the Château d'Anet, after escaping.

254 *route to Amiens*: see *The Three Musketeers*, chapter 20.

255 *in tierce*: a thrust, with the knuckles upwards, at the opponent's upper breast. A parry *in quarte*, which d'Artagnan executes a few lines on, defends against a stroke aimed at the breast from the ordinary position taken by fencers when they engage.

267 *Rue Pas de la Mule*: in modern terms, they return down the Boulevard Beaumarchais, head west past the Place des Vosges,

and halt in the rue de Sévigné (formerly the rue Sainte-Catherine) which runs alongside the Musée Carnavalet.

Hôtel de Rohan: faces on to the Place des Vosges. It now houses the Musée Victor-Hugo.

271 *a human being*: i.e. Milady. See *The Three Musketeers*, chapter 66.

274 *Louvres*: north-east of Paris, near what is now the Charles de Gaulle airport at Roissy.

Ariadne: the daughter of Minos who gave Theseus the thread which enabled him to find his way out of the labyrinth after he slew the Minotaur.

276 *Senlis*: 51 km. from Paris on the Flanders road. Verberie in the next paragraph is a further 15 km. in the direction of Compiègne and from there it is another 24 km. to Noyon.

281 *Comte de Guiche*: Guiche (see List of Historical Characters), born in 1637, is made older than his years, and introduced as historical leavening in a friendship which is entirely of Dumas's invention.

283 *Great Mademoiselle*: daughter of Gaston d'Orléans, known as 'la Grande Mademoiselle'. The Prince of Wales, son of Charles I of England, had paid court to her in 1646. Dumas knew her *Memoirs*, which had been republished in 1838.

the war: Dumas evokes the culmination of the Thirty Years War which ended in the peace of Westphalia in October 1748. The battle of Lens, one of the greatest achievements of the Prince de Condé, was fought on the Belgian border, and the locations mentioned by Dumas, in the Lille-Béthune area, are historically accurate. However, the battle took place in August, which means that a further two months have passed silently since Beaufort's escape.

288 *cardinal duke*: Cardinal Richelieu, who was also Duc de Richelieu.

290 *Non bis in idem*: a legal maxim meaning that a defendant may not be tried twice on the same charge. Guiche makes it mean: 'lightning does not strike twice in the same place.'

295 *executioner of Béthune*: the man in the red cloak who decapitated Milady. Her death is described in *The Three Musketeers*, chapters 64–6.

302 *Anne de Breuil*: in *The Three Musketeers*, Milady has a variety of names. Her maiden name was de Breuil and she was educated at a convent at Béthune. Subsequently she became the Comtesse de La Fère, wife of Athos, who left her for dead on discovering that

she bore the brand of convict (*The Three Musketeers*, chapter 27).
Her second marriage to the brother of Lord de Winter was
therefore bigamous. But Milady de Winter, Comtesse de Shef-
field, also called herself Charlotte Backson and Lady Clarick. In
Courtilz's pseudo-*Memoirs of d'Artagnan*, where Dumas originally
found her, she is known simply as 'Milédi'.

309 *the enemy was in fact advancing*: Dumas's account of the progress
of the battle, the deployment and location of French and Spanish
forces, is historically accurate.

310 *the Lys*: this river marked the border between France and Belgium.

311 *Rocroy, Fribourg, and Nordlingen*: and of a dozen other lesser
engagements. His greatest victories were his defeat of the Spanish
at Rocroy (1643) and Lens (1648). The battles of Fribourg and
Nordlingen took place in 1644 and 1645 respectively.

'*agl occhi grifani*': Dante, *Inferno*, iv. 123: 'Cesare armato cogli
occhi grifagni' ('Caesar, all armed, with clear and falcon eyes' in
Plumptre's translation). Condé's hawk nose, piercing eyes, and
proud carriage led his contemporaries to compare him with a bird
of prey.

315 *pieces of cannon*: as Gilbert Sigaux notes, these figures are exact.

320 *the Pineapple or the Parpaillot*: the Pomme-de-Pin (literally
'pine-cone') was an ancient tavern, mentioned by Villon and
Rabelais, located in what is now the rue de la Cité near Notre-
Dame: the Musketeers ate there in chapter 7 of *The Three
Musketeers*. The Parpaillot (the word means 'heretic') was a
fictional inn situated in the neighbourhood of La Rochelle. The
gallant quartet had met there in chapter 46 of the first instalment
of their adventures.

321 *Wednesday next*: not the Wednesday after Whitsun, as the pace
of events seems to suggest, but in the third week of August.

... *Rue de Béthisy*: the four friends converge along streets not
all of which existed in 1648: the rue Guénégaud and the Rue du
Roule (which was to replace part of the rue de Béthisy) still lay
in the future. The rue des Fossés-Saint-Germain-l'Auxerrois
skirted the church of that name, west of the Hermitage, Dumas's
fictitious tavern.

322 *aiglets*: or aglets, the tags or metal sheaths at the end of the
laces used to fasten clothes.

323 *gourmé*: 'thrashed'. The translator makes heavy weather of one of Beaufort's celebrated malapropisms: 'gourmander' means 'to reprove'.

326 *Balisardo*: the name of Roland's sword in Ariosto's *Orlando furioso*.

329 *Rue St Jacques*: in what later became the Latin quarter. Louise de la Vallière entered the Carmelite convent there in 1674.

Charles I's arms: for his success in the Battle of Naseby, as is clear from Charles's letter a few pages on. Again, Dumas's chronology is awry, for Cromwell overcame the King's army at Naseby on 14 June 1645.

Henrietta: Henrietta-Maria, Queen of England, had left her husband the King in England in 1644 and had since been resident, in much reduced circumstances, in the Louvre palace. Dumas's reference to 'her son' is puzzling, since she had three sons and three daughters. The daughter who prays with her is Henrietta-Anne (1644–70), later Duchesse d'Orléans, who was 4, not 14.

your brother: i.e. Louis XIII, who had died in 1642.

330 *your sister*: really, sister-in-law, Anne of Austria, widow of Louis XIII.

the king, your nephew?: Louis XIV, then aged 10.

331 *a sort of madness*: this too was Dumas's view of Cromwell's rebellion.

Lord Montrose: de Winter presents as recent events which had occurred two years earlier: again, Dumas's chronology is shaky.

332 *Cromwell*: Oliver Cromwell (1599–1658), Lord Protector of England. Like Athos, who revered the majesty of kings, Dumas had little stomach for wily politicians like Richelieu, Mazarin, Cromwell, and, later, Colbert.

333 *the Joyces, the Prides, the Cromwells*: all three were such 'plain russet-coated captains' as Cromwell loved. George Joyce had been a tailor before becoming a cornet in the new model army, and Colonel Thomas Pride a drayman and brewer. Robert Cromwell (d. 1617), the Lord Protector's father, owned land on which there was a small brewery.

where the Prince of Wales is: Charles (1630–85), Prince of Wales, became Charles II on the Restoration of the monarchy in 1660. He had been in France since 1646, when he had paid court to 'la Grande Demoiselle': see note to p. 283. It was his younger brother James (1633–1701), Duke of York (later James II) who came to France at the start of 1649 after a year spent in Holland.

336 *twenty-three*: Mordaunt was the son of Milady's bigamous marriage to the elder brother of Lord de Winter: see note to p. 137. The biography which Dumas gives him is, like the character, fictitious.

338 *We produce it verbatim*: this, like the letters to and from Charles I, and Cromwell's note which follows, was concocted by Dumas.

341 *bezel*: Mazarin reverses the ring on his finger to hide the gem in its mounting.

Gyges: according to Greek legend, Gyges was a shepherd, who acquired possession of a golden ring which had the power to make him invisible. Using the ring, he murdered King Candaules of Lydia and took his place.

343 *not his niece*: Elizabeth I had supported Henri IV against the League, a catholic association founded in 1576 to defend the catholic cause against the Protestant Reformation. Henrietta notes bitterly that, in international relations, blood is no thicker than water.

Marshal d'Ancre: the title taken by Concini: see List of Historical Characters.

348 *the Guards*: the Queen is mistaken: d'Artagnan was not a lieutenant of Guards, but of the King's own Musketeers: but see note to p. 7.

something about diamonds: the story of how the Musketeers retrieved the diamond studs given to Anne by Buckingham is told in *The Three Musketeers*, chapters 10–23.

351 *the battle of Lens*: news of Condé's victory (at which Gramont was indeed wounded) reached court on 24 August 1648.

353 *star of St Michael*: a military decoration first awarded in 1469.

354 *statue of the commander*: in Molière's *Dom Juan* (1665), the statue of the commander invites the unrepentant libertine to dine but, in the face of Don Juan's obduracy, sends him instead to Hell.

355 *Cain*: a symbolic character for Romantic writers who regarded him as an exemplary incarnation of the theme of revenge. Mordaunt's thirst for vengeance is no less great than that of the Count of Monte Cristo.

356 *to be stabbed*: by John Felton, Milady's pawn, on 23 August 1628: see note to p. 49.

359 *M. de Châtillon*: the news of the victory of Lens was indeed brought to Court by the Duc de Châtillon.

362 *Galaor*: brother of the eponymous hero of the immensely popular *Amadis de Gaule*, a collection of fifteenth-century Spanish romances of chivalry translated into French between 1540 and 1615.

Louvre bridge: Dumas seems to have in mind the Pont Royal, which was not built until 1685.

364 *Rue St Louis*: a street located on the line of what is now the rue de Turenne. Sosia is the valet of Amphitryon in plays by Plautus and Molière. Mercury assumed Sosia's physical appearance the better to execute the wishes of Jupiter.

369 *Duke of York*: the future James II (1633–1701), then in Holland. 'Charlotte' seems to be Elizabeth (1635–50), who had remained in England.

371 *the princess*: Henrietta (1644–70), later Duchesse d'Orléans.

377 *the dispute with the pavers*: see *The Three Musketeers*, chapter 20.

379 *had the seaports closed*: see *The Three Musketeers*, chapter 60.

380 *Dante*: see *Inferno*, xx. 10–15.

384 *news was decisive*: news of the victory of Lens (20 August), the first notable French military triumph since Nordlingen in 1645, was brought by Châtillon to the court on 24 August. A Te Deum was sung four days later. The matter of the 'imposts' (taxes) was not despatched as quickly as Dumas states, but the victory certainly strengthened Mazarin's hand. He ordered troops stationed along the route to arrest troublesome magistrates who, forewarned, dispersed. However, the arrest at his home of Pierre Broussel sparked off a popular riot known as the 'day of the Barricades'.

387 *heart of the city*: Dumas mentions two in the huddle of streets on the Île de la Cité which have long since disappeared.

391 *to arrest you*: Broussel, who was ill, was arrested by Comminges in his house.

399 *a pistole*: the *pistole* was in fact worth 11 livres.

402 *Vincennes*: the two councillors were indeed imprisoned at Saint-Germain and Vincennes respectively.

403 *the nets of St Cloud*: nets were placed across the Seine at the city limits to catch bodies which had been thrown into the river.

that same morning: Retz's sermon was delivered on 25 August, the previous day. Retz was the nephew of the Archbishop of Paris.

407 *scarcely six weeks ago*: Dumas seems to have forgotten that Planchet 'stirred a riot' in January, eight months previously.

408 *under a chief*: Dumas strays on to territory vividly exploited in Hugo's *Notre-Dame de Paris* (1831).

409 *aspergès*: an aspergillum, or holy-water sprinkler.

411 *St Jacques la Boucherie*: the church was demolished in 1797. All that remains is the Tour Saint-Jacques which gives its name to a square near the Châtelet.

414 *Chevalier d'Humières*: Balthazar de Crevant, who served as ensign in Retz's personal guard. His brother Louis was relieved as acting Governor of Lille in 1672 by Charles de Batz Castelmore.

419 *Tower of Nesle*: a thirteenth-century tower situated on the left bank of the Seine on the site of what is now the Institut de France. It was demolished in 1663. Dumas exploited its associations with the crimes of Marguerite de Bourgogne (1290–1315) in his historical drama *La Tour de Nesle* (1832).

422 *Lerida*: like his triumph over the Spanish at Rocroy (1643), Condé's unsuccessful siege of Lerida (1646) in Catalonia had involved great losses.

in rochet and camail: 'in [ecclesiastical] surplice and hood of chain mail': Retz signals his stance as a soldier-priest.

425 *persecuted her*: in August 1637 Pierre Séguier, Keeper of the Seals and Chancellor, had interrogated the Queen for evidence of her 'Spanish' intrigues: see note to p. 196.

Hôtel d'O——: the Hôtel d'O (*sic*) was at the end of the quai des Augustins near the Pont Saint-Michel. Séguier's attempt to seek sanctuary there is vouched for by the *Memoires* of Retz (Pléiade, p. 100).

430 *the Bastion St Gervais*: see *The Three Musketeers*, chapter 46.

432 *Queen Catherine*: Catherine de' Medici.

437 *M. de Condé*: Henri de Bourbon (1588–1646), Prince de Condé, father of 'the Great Condé', was held in the Bastille between 1616 and 1619. Marie de' Medici was the mother of Louis XIII. M. de Vendôme is Beaufort.

defending themselves: Broussel, regarded as the champion of the *Parlement* against the Court, was as popular as Mazarin and Séguier were detested.

439 *the Prince had arrived*: Condé returned to Paris in the middle of September.

fraternal friendship: this rumour, in a year of rumours, was current.

six days having already passed: Mazarin gave Mordaunt his commission on p. 340 some time before the Te Deum was sung on 26 August. Thus Mordaunt has been kicking his heels in Boulogne not for six days, but nearer a month. Again the chronology is faulty.

440 *benone*: 'for sure'.

441 *I abhor it!*': Anne's venom is well authenticated.

Castruccio Castracani: Dumas, who saw all history as conflict, evokes the struggle between the Guelfs (loyal to the Pope and independence) and the Ghibellines (who declared allegiance to the Emperors of Germany) which divided Italy between the twelfth and fifteenth centuries: the dispute ended with the invasion of the French in 1494. The Malatesta, from Rimini, were a leading Guelf family. Castruccio Castracani (1281–1328) attempted to create a Ghibelline state in Tuscany. A parallel with events in France is implied.

445 *Rue des Petits Champs*: still exists: it lies between the Palais-Royal and the Bibliothèque Nationale. The rue de Richelieu, which leads south to the Place du Théâtre Français, was opened in 1638.

451 *journey . . . to St Germain*: the Queen and her party left Paris for Reuil (not Saint-Germain) on 13 September and returned on 30 October.

452 *Sicilian Vespers*: on Easter Monday 1282, as the bell tolled for vespers, the Sicilians, who had been conquered by Charles d'Anjou, rose up and inflicted a massacre on their French invaders.

459 *bricconi*: 'Bandits!'

hough: to cut an animal's 'hough' (or 'hock'): 'to hamstring'.

460 *the Cours la Reine*: on the right bank of the Seine, the usual route to Saint-Germain and Saint-Cloud. It was the site of one of the customs gates which ringed Paris, still a walled city. A barrier for river traffic was established at the western end of the present

Cours la Reine which runs from the Place de la Concorde to the Place du Canada.

461 *Madame de Guémenée's mansion*: in the Place Royale, now Place des Vosges.

the check-string: the silk-thread tied to the driver's finger by which the passenger communicated with the driver over the rattle of wheels and the sound of hooves.

464 *Conflans*: on the Seine, between Charenton and Ivry.

Val de Grâce: a convent in the rue Saint-Jacques, built on the orders of Anne of Austria between 1645 and 1665. There could not have been much to see in 1648.

467 *while sleeping*: the incident took place, but in 1651, when it was masterminded by the Queen.

471 *crow in the fable*: La Fontaine, *Fables*, book 1. 2.

Dulaurier: the leader of the delegation was in fact named Dulaurier.

473 *in good favour*: Madame de Guémenée was Retz's mistress.

475 *Automedon*: the driver of the chariot of Achilles.

476 *only three beds*: the arrival of the royal party in the empty palace at Saint-Germain is well attested, but occurred in January 1649 and not September 1648 as Dumas's chronology requires: see note to p. 451. In fact, time now moves forward silently by almost four months. See note to p. 487.

478 *Rue des Ursulines*: a street of this name existed in Dumas's day (it now leads west from the rue Gay-Lussac to the rue Saint-Jacques) but not in 1648.

479 *twenty-four francs*: the French has '80 francs a truss': one louis was worth 24 livres.

480 *to England*: a suggestion that Charles de Batz paid an official visit to England in 1643 was much expanded in Courtilz's pseudo-*Memoirs of d'Artagnan* which tell (i, ch. 5) how he travelled there with the Comte d'Harcourt 'whom the Queen was sending to that country to bring about some kind of reconciliation between his Britannic Majesty and his Parliament'. According to Courtilz, d'Artagnan fought for Charles against Essex at Newbury (though this battle predates the arrival in France of Henrietta, who said farewell to Charles I in 1644). On his return to France, he was presented to the Queen and attracted the scorn of 'Milédi', who was a member of her entourage (ch. 6). In chapter 13, Courtilz further relates two visits to England made by d'Artagnan on the

orders of Mazarin 'as a result of the pressing entreaties of the Queen of England. The princess, who wanted, as was reasonable, to set everything to work so as not to see the King, her master, perish, after having several times spoken of the matter to the queen-mother, eventually succeeded in again getting someone sent into England to make a last effort there. Many people had already been there without success.' D'Artagnan saw Cromwell with whom he exchanged courtesies and returned to France. Dumas embroiders an episode which itself had already made the most of the fact that Charles de Batz, 'Mazarin's creature', undertook a number of foreign missions for his master before, during, and after the Fronde.

484 *Madame Turquaine*: Madeleine Turquaine, like her tavern, is Dumas's invention.

485 *on our route*: Raoul had returned to Blois after his part in the battle of Lens. Meantime, he has presumably returned to his regiment 'between St Omer and Lambe' (p. 487) (that is, Lambres, near Béthune).

487 *had just arrived*: Beaufort returned to Paris on 13 January 1649 from the Vendômois, where he had withdrawn after his escape. The action of the novel has now shifted from September 1648 to January 1649.

488 *pécaire*: 'confound it!', an exclamation common in various forms to the Languedoc, and a reminder of d'Artagnan's Gascon origins. Cf. 'cap de diou' on p. 489.

493 *vendit son roi*: some versions of this translation render the couplet thus: 'The faithless, perjured Scotsman sold his monarch for a bit of gold'. In May 1646 Charles surrendered himself to the Scots at Newark. The following January, against payment of an indemnity, he was handed over to the English Parliament, and Scottish troops withdrew from England.

near Newcastle: it was at Newcastle, besieged for ten months by the Scots under Leslie in 1644, that Charles resided after surrendering himself at Newark. There, in July 1646, he received Parliament's proposals for ending the Civil War. The pace of the story suggests that only weeks elapse between the capitulation of Charles I in 1646 at Oxford, and his execution two and a half years later. Dumas is a most unreliable guide to the history of the Rebellion.

petticoats: i.e. 'kilts'.

497 *Earl of Leven*: authorization for the final payment of £220,000 to
the Scottish army was made by Charles in August 1642. Dumas
has no doubts about the role played by Alexander Leslie, Earl of
Leven, in the 'infamous bargain', though the opinion of historians
is against him.

Montrose: but Montrose had already fled to Norway: see List of
Historical Characters.

Robert Bruce's: Robert I (1274–1329), the most heroic of the
Scottish kings, routed superior forces at Bannockburn in 1314
and finally achieved recognition of the independence of Scotland
by the Treaty of Northampton in 1328.

499 *the Ironsides*: the name 'ironside' was first applied to Cromwell
by Prince Rupert after the battle of Marston Moor in 1642.
Subsequently, the word was applied to his troops who, however,
did not wear any breastplate other than their iron discipline.

503 *Order of the Holy Ghost*: see note to p. 139. The Order of the
Garter was first awarded in 1348 by Edward III (1312–77).

507 *priming*: the priming which detonated the gunpowder which fired
the shot.

508 *Nebuchadnezzar*: King of Babylon who in 588 BC destroyed Jerusalem and the Temple. Puritans young and old regularly compared Charles with the ogres of the Old Testament.

510 *Holdenby Castle*: Holmby House, near Northampton, where he
remained for four months before being carried off on 3 June 1647
to Newmarket by Cornet Joyce, ostensibly on the order of
Cromwell who then denied charging him with the mission of
abducting the King. Charles was subsequently held at Hampton
Court, fled to the Isle of Wight, and was retaken and detained
at Windsor, where he was guarded by Tomlinson.

512 *describes so well*: presumably Dumas refers to *Hamlet*: his generation revered Shakespeare. And, like his contemporaries, he was
persuaded that great leaders are introspective men who carry the
heavy weight of office as a burden from the gods.

516 *a fatality in all this*: as d'Artagnan remarks, 'Milady is not dead'
(p. 509). A comparable sense of evil and doom informs the climax
of *The Three Musketeers*.

518 *rotten and worm-eaten royalty*: Dumas shared both Athos's contempt for the 'blind and ungrateful populace' of a few paragraphs
earlier and d'Artagnan's judgement of the English monarchy. He

hated vulgarity and despised the bourgeois reign of Louis—
Philippe, which also 'crumbled' and ended in the Revolution of
1848.

519 *Philiphaugh*: where Montrose was defeated on 13 September 1645
by Leslie, who took savage reprisals.

Sangdiou!: a Gascon version of 'Sangdieu!': 'God's Blood!'. Cf.
'mordioux!' ('S'Death', 'God's Death') on p. 528.

520 *Rue de Vaugirard*: their lodgings in *The Three Musketeers*.

525 *Babylon', etc.*: Psalm 137: 'By the rivers of Babylon . . .'.

526 *the staggers*: technically, a functional disturbance of the brain or
spinal cord in horses and cattle.

529 *at the head*: the remark is also attributed to Cromwell by Vigny
in his historical novel *Cinq-Mars* (1826), chapter 23.

530 *the three kingdoms*: England, Scotland, and Ireland.

the great one: Richelieu, now plainly rehabilitated in d'Artagnan's
mind.

533 *at Chantilly*: see note to p. 238.

534 *this little Thebais*: that is, an ideal place for settling accounts.
D'Artagnan, though never much of a books man, refers to the
area of the Upper Nile which was one of the regions of ancient
Egypt. Its capital was Thebes and the reference here is to the
deserts to the west much favoured by hermits.

reunited and harmonious: divided by personal ambition and politics, the four comrades join arms against their old enemy, Milady,
who lives on in her son.

536 *Parry*: the name, like that of Groslow whom we shall soon meet,
is an invention, as are the incidents in which they figure.

538 *son of a butcher?*: Harrison was, according to different accounts
the son of a butcher or a grazier from Newcastle-under-Lyme.

541 *red roof and green shutters*: the description is more French than
English. Dumas's knowledge of England was small.

543 *Thirsk*: about 60 miles from Durham, and more than one day's
ride, as is the next post to Derby (p. 550).

546 *lansquenet*: a card game played with more than one pack of cards
by an unlimited number of players against a banker.

547 *Knight of Malta*: the Ordre de Malte was an ancient religious and
military order developed in the twelfth century, and its Knights

were the equivalent of the Hospitallers of Saint John of Jerusalem. It was also a last, romantic resort for the erring heroes of eighteenth-century novels, an early version of the Foreign Legion.

550 *basset and biribi*: the first is a card game ressembling faro. Biribi was played, with a board divided into seventy squares, by an unlimited number of players.

the sibyls: in Greek mythology, the Sibyls possessed gifts of divination.

552 *Ryston*: perhaps Ryston Hall near Northampton. If the company has maintained its cracking pace, it should indeed be somewhere near Northampton, though Athos will shortly estimate that they are in fact about 30 miles from London.

556 *Jeremiah*: 'hearken to the words of my servants the prophets, whom I sent unto you, both rising up early and sending them, but ye have not hearkened' (Jeremiah, 26: 5).

561 *to be beaten*: quite. For once, history is against Dumas; Charles cannot be saved. His tale begins to slow: we shall see how he rescues the day by gloriously unhistorical means.

amateurs: 'curious lookers-on'.

562 *India*: the British East India Company was just beginning to get under way. It was settled in India by 1653.

dote on this colour: the colour was generally described as 'russet'.

Green Hall Street: the streets and taverns of Dumas's London are pure invention.

563 *Covenanter and Cavalier*: a similar distinction is made by Sellars and Yeatman in *1066 and All That*.

564 *artistic interest in politics*: a clear statement of Dumas's concept of the true Cavalier spirit.

Act of Parliament: on 2 January 1649 Parliament stated the charge against the King who was accused of waging war against the Commons.

566 *tomorrow*: Dumas abridges. Preliminary deliberations were held in the High Court on 8 January. There were never more than Fifty-three members present at the proceedings. On 19 January, Charles was brought from Windsor to Westminster for the start of the trial. The first four days (20–3 January) were taken up by Charles's defence; the next two heard the evidence against him. He was found guilty on 25 January and sentence was passed on

the 26th. The time of execution was fixed for 30 January, a Tuesday.

567 *amateurs of boxing*: an anachronism. The English were better known for their passion for boxing in Dumas's day than in Cromwell's.

568 *kept his hat on*: as a sign of his refusal to recognize the court. Three times he refused to plead, his silence being construed as proof of guilt. Charles's dignified conduct during his trial is well known.

569 *name and property*: Athos, the most principled of the Musketeers, puts the case for Mordaunt. D'Artagnan's view of him is less moral and more practical.

seventy-three: the actual figure varies according to different accounts but is more or less accurate.

570 *Lady Fairfax*: Anne, fourth daughter of Lord Vere, who married Fairfax in 1637.

572 *Fire into that gallery*: the interjection was made by Lady Fairfax during the sitting of 23 January. Colonel Axtell, commander of the guard, shouted 'Down with the whores, shoot them.' Muskets were raised but the 'woman was hustled out'. By putting the order into the mouth of Mordaunt, Dumas not only inserts his characters into historical events but also finds a way of relaunching the simple conflict between good and evil.

573 *as a ruler*: Dumas's picture of the King's dignified bearing is faithful in essentials, though his account of the proceedings and the aftermath is, naturally, abridged.

576 *the terrible logic of revolutions*: Dumas, for once speaking in his own voice, strikes a note of political realism.

582 *felucca*: long, narrow, and light, like a 'pirogue' (or canoe), the felucca had sail and oars but was more at home in the Mediterranean than on the Thames.

583 *the queen's famous diamond*: in *The Three Musketeers* (chapter 47), d'Artagnan had already sold it to finance another rescue operation. He then got 7,000 livres in gold for it. Earlier (p. 56, d'Artagnan estimated that it was worth 'at least 10,000 livres'.

592 *Princess Charlotte*: read: Princess Elizabeth (1635–50).

593 *Duke of Gloucester*: Prince Henry (1639–60).

elder brothers: the Prince of Wales was to be Charles II and the Duke of York James II.

597 *Remember*: we shall see how Dumas will extract maximum drama from Charles's famous last word which he addressed to Bishop Juxon.

598 *a million in gold*: it will remain in Newcastle until *The Vicomte de Bragelonne*, when it becomes an object of quest in the heroic efforts made by the Musketeers, though more divided than ever, to restore the English monarchy in 1660.

599 *royal honours*: Charles I was buried in Saint George's Chapel at Windsor on 7 February.

611 *imbecile Puritans*: Cromwell was a moderate compared with extreme fundamentalist elements. But nothing suggests that he was the cynical manipulator which Dumas here suggests: to Cromwell are attributed the political realism, cunning, and ruthlessness which characterize Mazarin and the Richelieu of *The Three Musketeers*.

612 *as history informs us*: the life of Cromwell is surrounded by legends of this kind, which Dumas the novelist was only too happy to exploit.

613 *scene at Armentières*: where Milady was executed. See *The Three Musketeers*, chapter 66.

616 *Italian pantomimists*: see note to p. 17.

619 *wrote to Marie Michon*: for Aramis's letter to Marie Michon (Madame de Chevreuse), see *The Three Musketeers*, chapter 48.

629 *en vedette*: 'as the advance mounted sentry'.

632 *The Thousand and One Nights*: the first French translation of the *Arabian Nights*, by Antoine Galland, appeared between 1704 and 1717.

635 *cask of malvoisie*: more usually, the butt of Malmsey in which George (1449–78), Duke of Clarence, was famously drowned.

636 *neighbour's wife*: Exodus, 20: 17.

637 *quintals*: the French quintal was the equivalent of 108 pounds avoirdupois.

638 *frog in the fable*: La Fontaine, *Fables*, book I. 3.

a whole poem: an echo of Boileau's dictum (*Art poétique* (1674), ii. 94: 'A sonnet without blemish is the equal of a long poem.')

647 *Adamastor*: in book V of the *The Lusiads*, the Portuguese poet Camoës (1525–80) relates that when Vasco da Gama attempted

to sail round the Cape of Good Hope, Adamastor, the Giant of
the Storm, rose out of the sea to oppose him. Adamastor does
not figure in Greek mythology and was an invention of
Camoës.

655 *but destiny*: Gilbert Sigaux suggests that Dumas developed the
death by drowning of Mordaunt from a brief episode in Courtilz's
pseudo-*Memoirs of d'Artagnan* (i, ch. 13). There Mazarin orders
d'Artagnan, who carried out two unofficial missions to England
for him in 1649, to drown an agent who threatened to destabilize
the Parlement.

as if God intended: the death of Mordaunt is attended by natural
signs, as was that of his mother, Milady, 'that demon escaped
from Hell'; see the start of chapter 65 of *The Three Musketeers*.

656 *Charles's Wain*: i.e. Ursa Major, also known as 'the plough', 'the
wagon', and 'Charles's [Charlemagne's] Wain'.

661 *St Valéry*: 32 km. west of Dieppe on the Normandy coast.

662 *Place de Grève*: the Place de Grève had been a place of public
execution since 1310; the guillotine was used there first in April
1792. Called the Place de l'Hôtel de Ville since 1806, the site is
on the right bank of the Seine, opposite the Pont d'Arcoli.

663 *six weeks' absence*: working back from the death of Charles on 30
January 1649, this means mid-December 1648, a date contradicted
by previous events: the quartet had left for England in September
(see note to p. 476), though—confusingly—not before Beaufort had
returned to Paris on 13 January (note to p. 487). Subsequently,
the compression of events in England since 1646 has scattered
the chronology which, however, now resumes in 'the early days
of February' 1649 (p. 665).

664 *corset*: the Chancelier Séguier had been ordered in 1637 (see note
to p. 182) to search Anne's apartments and, if necessary, her
person (contemporaries mention 'her bosom', but not her stays).
Dumas, bringing it forward by ten years, had used the incident
in *The Three Musketeers* (chapter 16), where Séguier looks for an
incriminating love letter to Buckingham.

the next day: Séguier had negotiated with the Parlement in
October 1648. The blockade of Paris by the Queen's forces under
Condé did not begin 'the next day', but in January 1649.

enemy of the king and the State: the Parlement denounced Mazarin, in the terms Dumas uses, on 8 January. The same day,
measures were set in train for the defence of the city.

665 *10th of January*: on this day, Conti assumed leadership of the Parlement's forces.

had come from the Vendômois: the highly popular Beaufort arrived in Paris on 13 January. He was known by Parisians as 'the King of Les Halles'.

on the nineteenth: the sortie was made on 21 January to bring in a grain convoy, but the convoy could not be located and many of the troops fell ill.

queen's party: Nanterre, half-way along a line from Saint-Germain to Paris, was in territory controlled by Condé who, lacking the forces for a full siege, had occupied Saint-Cloud and Saint-Denis and was master of Lagny, Brie-Comte-Robert, and other towns and hamlets to the north and east of Paris.

671 *flooded half the capital*: contemporaries said that Paris was turned into 'a little Venice'.

674 *Barrière du Roule*: a customs gate situated beyond the western end of the present rue Saint-Honoré.

675 *harlequin to Pantaloon*: Mazarin's origins lend themselves naturally to comparisons with these buffoonish characters from the Commedia dell'Arte.

676 *Charenton*: on the south-eastern edge of Paris. The battle of Charenton, the one major battle of the civil war, took place on 8 February: see Chapter LXXXII.

679 *mansion of M. le Duc de Bouillon*: now part of the École des Beaux-Arts on the quai Malaquais.

one of the newest triolets: numerous collections of such satirical verses helped shape popular opinion during the Fronde.

680 *for a month*: a confirmation that the action takes place on or about 10 February 1649.

He is dead: the news of Charles's death reached Paris on 10 February.

681 *Sedan*: for his part in the plot mounted against Richelieu by Cinq Mars in 1641, the Duc de Bouillon had been deprived of his title to the principality of Sedan. He had demanded its return in the summer of 1648.

Turenne: Bouillon's younger brother was Turenne: see List of Historical Characters.

684 *Noirmont*: see note to p. 181.

685 *Place Royale*: according to Retz, the idea for these verses was his. He quotes the first line (*Mémoires*, Pléiade, p. 150) and notes that their author was Jacques Carpentras de Marigny. They refer to the rivalry between Conti and d'Elbeuf for the command of the anti-royalist forces on 10 January.

regiment of Corinth: in early January, Retz raised a regiment at his own expense which he called the 'régiment de Corinthe' after the special title of Archbishop of Corinth conferred on him by the Pope in 1644. Commanded by Renaud de Sévigné, it first saw action on 28 January, when it was routed.

my father: Beaufort was the son of César (1594–1665), Duc de Vendôme, who married Françoise de Lorraine, Duchesse de Mercœur, in 1609.

686 *arsenal*: on the site of the present Bibliothèque de l'Arsenal. The Quai Saint-Victor is now part of the quai d'Austerlitz.

688 *the attention of all Europe*: the much neglected Henrietta urged Anne to take the events in England as an indication of what might happen in France. It is now accepted that the agreement signed at Reuil, which ended the first Fronde, was at least in part a response to fears that the French monarchy was faced with a situation as grave as that which Charles had failed to resolve.

689 *not at home*: Madame de Chevreuse was not to return from Belgium until 12 April.

an heir or heiress: Madame de Longueville gave birth on 29 January to a son.

692 *Vallée de Fécamp*: long since overtaken by urban development, the site is marked by the rue Fécamp in the 12th *arrondissement*.

693 *M. de Chanleu*: Bertrand d'Ostove, Marquis de Clanleu (*sic*), commander of the Parisian forces. He faced Condé's 7,000 foot soldiers and 4,000 cavalry. He was overwhelmed and died in battle.

M. Viole: Pierre Viole, *seigneur* d'Atis, a President of the Parlement and supporter of Condé.

698 *notch of the cuirass*: Châtillon was killed at Charenton, though this detail seems to be a touch added by Dumas.

699 *Corinth*: Retz's regiment, routed at Antony on 28 January, did not fight at Charenton. The pun a few lines on is found in the memoirs of the times.

700 *Rueil*: now Rueil-Malmaison, 15 km. west of central Paris. It had been built by Richelieu who had given it to de Duchesse

d'Aiguillon, his niece and probably his mistress, who had given it to the Queen. It was used extensively by Mazarin. It was to Rueil that Mazarin and the King had fled in September 1648, an event which Dumas, as we have seen, confused with the Queen's flight to Saint-Germain in January 1649.

702 *bronze horse*: an equestrian statue of Louis XIII had been erected in the Place Royale in 1639. It was overturned in 1792 and melted down.

poor people to gnaw: Mazarin's effects were auctioned in February. Dumas takes the opportunity to embroider history, though it is true that Beaufort, 'father of the people', did everything he could to keep Paris supplied with bread.

703 *Montreuil*: Montreuil-sur-mer, near Calais.

704 *Enceladus or Briareus*: on the first, see note to p. 96. Briareus, sometimes called Aegeon had a hundred hands and fifty heads. He fought for the gods against the Titans.

Ajax: son of Telamon, King of Salamis, Ajax sailed against Troy. Homer ranked him next to Achilles as the most courageous of the Greeks.

705 *Royal Italian regiment*: Mazarin had raised a regiment of Italian soldiers.

706 *a liquor*: Louvres, near Roissy, was known for its ratafia, a sweet cordial flavoured with fruits, usually blackcurrants or the kernels of almonds, peaches, and cherries.

707 *just come to Rueil*: time has again been hurried on. Discussions between Court and Parlement at Rueil began on 4 March and a preliminary agreement was reached on the 11th. The Parlement of Paris finally approved the 'lame peace' (which proved to be a holding measure only) on 1 April.

was arrested: Condé was indeed arrested, along with Conti and Longueville, but not until January 1650.

frightful oubliette: a secret subterranean dungeon with an opening at the top used for persons condemned to perpetual imprisonment. According to tradition, Richelieu despatched many enemies in the quiet of the dungeons of Rueil. There are no grounds for the view expressed here by Aramis (and later by Comminges, p. 722) that *oubliettes* were used exclusively for royal prisoners. Oddly enough, the castle of Pierrefonds, owned by Porthos, was equipped with narrow *oubliettes* located well below moat level.

They are illustrated in Viollet-le-Duc's *Dictionnaire d'architecture* (1853–69).

709 *loved an Englishman*: i.e. Buckingham.

714 *the other reign*: that of Louis XIII, whose reign was marked by frequent revolts against royal authority.

715 *to my grandfather*: a further reminder of Athos's noble lineage which is intended by Dumas to explain something of his high moral values which stem from the old chivalric code.

718 *Elizabeth ... Catharine II*: on Elizabeth I, see note to p. 8. Catherine the Great of Russia (1729–96) maintained a suitable distance from Potemkin (1736–91), who was both her field-marshal and her lover.

a certain greatness: Dumas admired strong leaders and effective manipulators of events—even, at a pinch, Mazarin.

719 *Chatou*: half-way along the road from Saint-Germain to Rueil.

720 *at his disposal*: it was Anne who gave him the use of Rueil: see note to p. 700.

nearly all Germans: mercenary soldiers were a feature of all European armies.

724 *Samson came forth from Gaza*: Judges, 16; 1–3.

726 *Tarbes*: a reminder of d'Artagnan's Gascon origins.

mores locaque: literally, 'manners and places'.

731 *Montmorencys ... Rohans*: the Montmorency family counted amongst the oldest and most venerable aristocracy. See also note to p. 113.

735 *Milo of Crotona*: fabled athlete (and glutton) of the sixth century BC and four times winner of the Olympic and Pythic games. Legend attributes all manner of feats of strength to him.

741 *der Teufel*: 'the devil'.

742 *Tedesco ... va bene*: 'Ah, you're German ... Carry on.'

746 *Cumaean Sibyl*: one of the ten inspired prophetesses of Greek mythology: it is she who conducts the poet into the realm of shades in book vi of Virgil's *Aeneid*.

748 *cardinals who are not priests*: see note to p. 8.

754 *Saint Christopher*: born in Syria and martyred under the Emperor Decius (249–51), he was said to be 12 feet high and colossally

strong. A self-appointed ferryman, he carried Christ across the stream on his shoulders.

755 *Ermenonville*: near Senlis, 47 km. from Paris.

756 *bastion St Gervais*: yet another reference to *The Three Musketeers*, chapter 46.

758 *newly born son*: see note to p. 689.

760 *Where is the treaty?*: the Musketeers, led by d'Artagnan, can thus claim responsibility for ending the first Fronde. Their 'great diplomatic feat' (p. 772) is a good example of the way in which Dumas cheerfully inserts his characters into history.

763 *Enghien*: Enghien-les-bains, 6 km. north-west of Saint-Denis.

768 *the treaty*: the treaty of Rueil, which ended the first phase of the Fronde, was signed on 1 April. It was the result of weeks of intense negotiations and was far less satisfactory than Dumas, now in need of a terminus for his story, suggests.

770 *but her son*: the father of the child was La Rochefoucauld, author of the *Maxims* (1665), but Dumas throws out a strong hint that the child was the result of the amours between Madame de Longueville and Aramis. The King did not stand as its godfather.

773 *behind a tapestry*: see *The Three Musketeers*, chapter 22.

Chevalier of the Order: the Ordre du Saint-Esprit: see note to p. 139.

774 *what each gained by this treaty*: Dumas, amalgamating the two treaties of 11 March and 1 April, hurriedly summarizes the complex distribution of spoils. Conti was made Governor not of Damvilliers in Lorraine, which went instead to La Rochefoucauld, but of Champagne. Conti, who had been intended for the Church, did marry one of Mazarin's nieces, Anne-Marie Martinozzi, in 1654.

Beaufort: Beaufort was rehabilitated and later served under Louis XIV, dying valiantly at the siege of Candia in 1669.

Bouillon: Bouillon was given the governorship of Auvergne in compensation for the loss of the principality of Sedan.

government of Pont-de-l'Arche: the Duc de Longueville was made Governor of Pont de l'Arche in Normandy, but not until September 1649. Charles-Paris, the son born to Madame de Longueville, had no such christening. He died in action in June 1672 when Louis XIV invaded the United Dutch Provinces.

d'Elbeuf: d'Elbeuf was received by the Queen at Compiègne and was given compensation for his loyalty which, however, was to be short-lived.

the Coadjutor: Retz did not allow his name to be placed on the list of those amnestied and was slow to be reconciled with the Queen and Mazarin against whom he acted during the second phase of the Fronde. He was appointed cardinal in 1652.

776 *Madame de Chevreuse*: the duchess returned to France from Belgium on 12 April. Neither she nor her husband gained by the peace.

777 *I remember it*: by this cryptic, pre-Freudian remark, Athos indicates his fear of the subtle powers of Madame de Chevreuse.

very unhappy: in *The Vicomte de Bragelonne*, Raoul's love for Louise is displaced by her love for the King.

778 *leaving St Germain*: the court left Saint-Germain for Compiègne on 18 April 1649 and remained there until August, when it returned to Paris. The Te Deum chanted on p. 779 took place on 5 August and Louis XIV returned in triumph to Paris on the 18th. Once again, time has been telescoped.

781 *... and Du Coq*: that is, near the Barrière des Sergents: see note to p. 13. The crowd subsequently retreats east past the Louvre, across the Place de Saint-Germain l'Auxerrois, and thence down to the Seine. The riot is an invention. In reality the King received a rousing welcome.

785 *Marathon*: Pheidippides, who brought the news of the victory of Marathon.

786 *there is no Fronde*: on the contrary, tension remained high and a second phase began in January 1650, which was to last until 1653.

787 *Marshal of France*: the historical Charles de Batz became Captain-Lieutenant of the Musketeers in 1667. In 1672, he was appointed acting Governor of Lille. Dumas's d'Artagnan, for services rendered in *The Vicomte de Bragelonne*, was finally appointed Marshal of France by Colbert. He was killed at the siege of Maastricht in 1673 while reading the official notification of his promotion. See the final chapter of *The Man in the Iron Mask*.

that rascal Bonacieux: the mendicant of Saint-Eustache is revealed, in an upbeat ending, as the husband of the Constance whom d'Artagnan had loved and lost in *The Three Musketeers*.

A SELECTION OF   **OXFORD WORLD'S CLASSICS**

The Anglo-Saxon World

Beowulf

Lancelot of the Lake

The Paston Letters

Sir Gawain and the Green Knight

Tales of the Elders of Ireland

York Mystery Plays

GEOFFREY CHAUCER **The Canterbury Tales**
Troilus and Criseyde

HENRY OF HUNTINGDON **The History of the English People**
1000–1154

JOCELIN OF BRAKELOND **Chronicle of the Abbey of Bury**
St Edmunds

GUILLAUME DE LORRIS **The Romance of the Rose**
and JEAN DE MEUN

WILLIAM LANGLAND **Piers Plowman**

SIR THOMAS MALORY **Le Morte Darthur**

A SELECTION OF OXFORD WORLD'S CLASSICS

	Eirik the Red and Other Icelandic Sagas
	The German-Jewish Dialogue
	The Kalevala
	The Poetic Edda
LUDOVICO ARIOSTO	**Orlando Furioso**
GIOVANNI BOCCACCIO	**The Decameron**
GEORG BÜCHNER	**Danton's Death, Leonce and Lena,** and **Woyzeck**
LUIS VAZ DE CAMÕES	**The Lusiads**
MIGUEL DE CERVANTES	**Don Quixote** **Exemplary Stories**
CARLO COLLODI	**The Adventures of Pinocchio**
DANTE ALIGHIERI	**The Divine Comedy** **Vita Nuova**
LOPE DE VEGA	**Three Major Plays**
J. W. VON GOETHE	**Elective Affinities** **Erotic Poems** **Faust: Part One and Part Two** **The Flight to Italy**
E. T. A. HOFFMANN	**The Golden Pot and Other Tales**
HENRIK IBSEN	**An Enemy of the People, The Wild Duck, Rosmersholm** **Four Major Plays** **Peer Gynt**
LEONARDO DA VINCI	**Selections from the Notebooks**
FEDERICO GARCIA LORCA	**Four Major Plays**
MICHELANGELO BUONARROTI	**Life, Letters, and Poetry**

A SELECTION OF **OXFORD WORLD'S CLASSICS**

PETRARCH　　　　　　**Selections from the Canzoniere and Other Works**

J. C. F. SCHILLER　　　**Don Carlos** and **Mary Stuart**

JOHANN AUGUST STRINDBERG　　**Miss Julie and Other Plays**

A SELECTION OF   **OXFORD WORLD'S CLASSICS**

LUDOVICO ARIOSTO   **Orlando Furioso**

GIOVANNI BOCCACCIO   **The Decameron**

MATTEO MARIA BOIARDO   **Orlando Innamorato**

LUÍS VAZ DE CAMÕES   **The Lusíads**

MIGUEL DE CERVANTES   **Don Quixote de la Mancha**
                          Exemplary Stories

DANTE ALIGHIERI   **The Divine Comedy**
                          Vita Nuova

BENITO PÉREZ GALDÓS   **Nazarín**

LEONARDO DA VINCI   **Selections from the Notebooks**

NICCOLÒ MACHIAVELLI   **Discourses on Livy**
                          The Prince

MICHELANGELO   **Life, Letters, and Poetry**

PETRARCH   **Selections from the *Canzoniere* and**
                          **   Other Works**

GIORGIO VASARI   **The Lives of the Artists**

The Oxford World's Classics Website

www.worldsclassics.co.uk

- Information about new titles
- Explore the full range of Oxford World's Classics
- Links to other literary sites and the main OUP webpage
- Imaginative competitions, with bookish prizes
- Peruse the Oxford World's Classics Magazine
- Articles by editors
- Extracts from Introductions
- A forum for discussion and feedback on the series
- Special information for teachers and lecturers

www.worldsclassics.co.uk

American Literature

British and Irish Literature

Children's Literature

Classics and Ancient Literature

Colonial Literature

Eastern Literature

European Literature

History

Medieval Literature

Oxford English Drama

Poetry

Philosophy

Politics

Religion

The Oxford Shakespeare

A complete list of Oxford Paperbacks, including Oxford World's Classics, Oxford Shakespeare, Oxford Drama, and Oxford Paperback Reference, is available in the UK from the Academic Division Publicity Department, Oxford University Press, Great Clarendon Street, Oxford OX2 6DP.

In the USA, complete lists are available from the Paperbacks Marketing Manager, Oxford University Press, 198 Madison Avenue, New York, NY 10016.

Oxford Paperbacks are available from all good bookshops. In case of difficulty, customers in the UK can order direct from Oxford University Press Bookshop, Freepost, 116 High Street, Oxford OX1 4BR, enclosing full payment. Please add 10 per cent of published price for postage and packing.